CW00515611

The Raucle Tongue
Hitherto Uncollected Prose
Volume II: 1927–1936

MacDiarmid 2000:
the Collected Works
from Carcanet

Selected Poetry
edited by Michael Grieve & Alan Riach

Selected Prose
edited by Alan Riach

Scottish Eccentrics
edited by Alan Riach

The Complete Poems, I and *II*
edited by Michael Grieve & W.R. Aitken

Lucky Poet
edited by Alan Riach

Contemporary Scottish Studies
edited by Alan Riach

Albyn: Shorter Books and Monographs
edited by Alan Riach

The Raucle Tongue: Hitherto Uncollected Prose I
edited by Angus Calder, Glen Murray & Alan Riach

The Raucle Tongue: Hitherto Uncollected Prose II
edited by Angus Calder, Glen Murray & Alan Riach

Hugh MacDiarmid

THE RAUCLE TONGUE

Hitherto uncollected prose

VOLUME II

Edited by Angus Calder,
Glen Murray and Alan Riach

CARCANET

First published in Great Britain in 1997 by
Carcanet Press Limited
4th Floor, Conavon Court
12–16 Blackfriars Street
Manchester M3 5BQ

A CIP catalogue record for this book
is available from the British Library.
ISBN 1 85754 271 1

The publisher acknowledges financial assistance
from the Arts Council of England.

Set in New Caledonia by XL Publishing Services, Lurley, Tiverton
Printed and bound in England by SRP Ltd, Exeter

Contents

General Editor's Preface and Acknowledgements

The Raucle Tongue gathers in three volumes a comprehensive selection of Hugh MacDiarmid's Hitherto uncollected prose, from 1911, when he was nineteen, to 1978, the year of his death.

We have selected material almost entirely from printed sources, newspapers, literary or political journals, obscure publications (including contributions to books) and some that are better known. When an item has been prepared from manuscript sources, provenance is acknowledged in the text. The location for each item is also acknowledged in the text, as is the author's byline. The author we refer to as Hugh MacDiarmid began publishing using his own name, C.M. Grieve, but adopted a number of pseudonyms over the course of his career, both in journalism and as a poet. The name MacDiarmid became generally accepted in the 1920s, but researchers will be assisted by knowing his other bylines and there is a general interest in them, given their quantity and the compulsion with which they proliferated. Did he feel it necessary to swell the ranks of the literary movement he championed by multiplying his own identity in this way? Was it a tactical move to subvert conservative editors once the name MacDiarmid had become associated with forthright assertion and fearless attack?

Both of these speculations have some truth. Throughout the 1920s and into the 1930s, MacDiarmid's bylines multiplied, initially as a means of legitimating what he described as a distinct literary and cultural 'movement' but eventually, one suspects, to conceal the identity of an author whose name had become associated with merciless criticism of all forms of cultural humbug, political hypocrisy and quisling nationalism. Sometimes it would have been obvious: a Gaelic pronunciation of 'Gillechriosd Moraidh Mac a' Ghreidhir' gives something pretty close to Christopher Murray Grieve, and 'A.K. Laidlaw' was close to a family name. But both 'A.L.' and 'James Maclaren' (which MacDiarmid used repeatedly in the *Scottish Educational Journal*) suggest an attempt to conceal the author's identity rather than clone it, and 'Stentor' and 'Pteleon' would have given no obvious Scottish overtones to readers of the London-based radio magazine *Vox* in the early 1930s. Moreover, the writing styles of articles published under these names are frequently less overbearing and more balanced in tone than those published by 'MacDiarmid', although the subjects and emphases remain recognisable.

In his introduction to MacDiarmid's media in Volume I, Glen Murray discusses these questions in more detail and provides a key to understanding the means and methods of communication open to the writer in the course of his long career. He also discusses the ways in which MacDiarmid turned all the resources that were available to him into the service of his cause, or more precisely, causes.

In his introductions to individual periods of MacDiarmid's career, Angus Calder has provided political and historical contexts in which these causes might best be understood. The broadest understanding of MacDiarmid's work and the fullest appreciation of his achievement would require an international historical context; perhaps this has been held back by the stigma of outrageousness which attaches to his manifest energies. He risked embarrassment and, if polite in private, was not genteel or shy in public. Angus Calder's introductions insist that his political commitments, excessive as they might seem, should be considered in their historical locations. It makes a difference, for example, to understand how much of a Labour man he was before the collapse of Labour support of independence for Scotland. MacDiarmid's quest for a radical solution to personal, poetic and political questions in the 1930s had specific motivations. And MacDiarmid's so-called Fascism is also more explicable by reference to the historical significance of Mussolini in the early 1920s. In his annotation, Angus Calder has provided further details of less familiar figures of the era and engages with some of the questions MacDiarmid was addressing. If some remain unanswered, questions we still ask today, then it is remarkable how many are considered in a light which helps focus their essential matter. Still more remarkable is the fact that MacDiarmid does provide the answers sometimes, and the validity of those answers continues to withstand the opposition.

A full bibliography of all MacDiarmid's contributions to journals or newspapers remains beyond the scope of the present enterprise, but I have provided as full as possible a bibliography as an appendix to Volume Three of *The Raucle Tongue*, so that students wishing to go further than these volumes allow might have some idea where to begin. There are some curious gaps.

There are over forty periodicals and newspapers mentioned in Alan Bold's biography of MacDiarmid as publications to which he contributed. A number of these remain unquarried. There is still an important piece of work to be done on the journalism written in Wales in 1911. I found little enough and nothing I thought worth reprinting from the *Merthyr Pioneer* and his contributions to the *Monmouthshire Labour News* are elusive. Yet to judge from his letters, there is an exciting chapter to be written about this period.

The Montrose Review, for which MacDiarmid worked as a journalist, remains another major source. More fugitive periodicals such as *The Fife Coast Chronicle*, *The Forfar Review*, *The Balkan News*, *The RAMC Magazine*, *The Ironmonger* and the occasional contributions to *The Carlisle Journal* and *The Yorkshire Post*, remain uncollected.

Acknowledgements are due to the Institute for Advanced Studies in the

Humanities at the University of Edinburgh, where I held a Fellowship from February to April 1995 and from December 1996 to February 1997; and to the University of Waikato Research Committee, who have generously supported my work on the 'MacDiarmid 2000' project and whose Academic Visitors Award allowed Angus Calder to visit the University of Waikato in December 1995 to work on the project.

Most grateful thanks are tendered to the staff of the National Library of Scotland, Edinburgh University Library, the Mitchell Library, Glasgow (particularly to Hamish Whyte), the British Library, London, and the British Library (periodicals and newspapers section) at Collingwood (particularly to Richard Price), the National Library of Wales, Aberystwyth, the Marx Memorial Library, London, and the University of Waikato Library, particularly the reference and interloans section.

Thanks for personal kindness, support and generosity towards the project are due to W.R. Aitken, Kenneth Buthlay, David Daiches, George Davie, Duncan Glen, Edwin Morgan; G. Ross Roy and Patrick Scott of the University of South Carolina; my parents Captain J.A. Riach and Mrs J.G. Riach; my wife Rae; and my colleagues at the University of Waikato, Marshall Walker and Jan Pilditch. Particular thanks are due to Joy Hendry and Ian Montgomery. And once again, for faith sustained, I would like to thank the MacDiarmid Estate, Deirdre Grieve, and Carcanet Press, especially Michael Schmidt and Robyn Marsack. Michael Grieve died while *The Raucle Tongue* was in preparation; Angus Calder, Glen Murray and I are agreed that the present volumes, while they carry his father's words, should also be dedicated to Michael's memory.

ALAN RIACH

Volume II: 1927–1936

THE NATIONAL PARTY OF SCOTLAND
THE DEPRESSION

Introduction

The early history of the National Party of Scotland, founded in June 1928, is intricate: so is the process which created, in 1934, the Scottish National Party which flourishes today.

The Party made an early impact on the press. Nationalism was, after all, a potent force in Europe and might become a major influence in Scotland, and for some years the country's bestselling daily newspapers, the *Express* and the *Record*, vied with each other in emphasising their Scottishness. But the remarkable achievement of the writer R.B. Cunninghame Graham in giving Prime Minister Baldwin a close run in the 1928 elections for the Rectorship of Glasgow University – that is, in attracting students – was the most significant poll result achieved by Nationalism until the 1940s, when, at a time when the major parties had a pact not to contest by-elections, the SNP got a couple of good votes, and then Robert McIntyre actually won Motherwell from Labour and sat briefly in the Commons before he was swept away in the 1945 General Election. Only in the 1960s did the SNP at last emerge as a consistently weighty factor in Scottish politics – by which time MacDiarmid himself was a well-established member of the Communist Party.

In 1929, the NPS had 5000 members, as many as the ILP. In 1939, the SNP had only 2000. Nationalism commanded attention only through the personalities who attached themselves to the cause, notably writers. Lewis Spence (1874–1955), who in 1926 adopted MacDiarmid's term 'Scottish Renaissance' in relation to current literature, in an article published in the wierdly named London periodical, *The Nineteenth Century and After*, was one of these, a significant poet. But others are now much more famous: the novelists Neil Gunn, Eric Linklater and Compton Mackenzie, and, of course, Hugh MacDiarmid. Other picturesque personalities included the Duke of Montrose, a moderate, and the Honourable Ruaraidh Stuart Erskine of Marr (1869–1960), an extremist. The wealthy Erskine emphasised ancient cultural roots. He spoke Gaelic after a fashion and his passionate advocacy of the language, backed by cash supporting a series of magazines, chimed with MacDiarmid's own new insistence on the vital importance of that apparently doomed tongue. As C.M. Grieve, and also under the giveaway pseudonym Gillechriosd Mac a' Ghriebhir, the poet published studied and thoughtful articles in Marr's *Pictish Review*, while as Hugh M'Diarmid he also contributed poems.

Since 1886 there had been a cross-party Scottish Home Rule Association. In 1913 it had come to the brink of success. But after the war, the weakness of this

Lib-Lab organisation was exposed when Home Rule bills failed in Parliament in 1926 and 1926. There were other, impatient, groupings. Erskine of Marr led a Scottish National League from which Spence broke away in 1926 to found a Scottish National Movement. It seems to be generally agreed that the main force leading to the fusion of all the groups just mentioned in the National Party of Scotland was the vim and vigour of the Glasgow University Nationalist Association, led by John MacCormick, who would be a dominant and controversial figure in the Home Rule arena for quarter of a century.

The NPS aimed 'to secure self-government for Scotland with independent national status within the British family of nations.' If one recalls that Ireland remained technically a 'dominion' until after the Second World War, the statement might seem quite radical. In 1932 moderates, including Montrose and Linklater, broke away to form the Scottish Party, which fused again with the NPS to create the SNP two years later.

In situations recalling at times the history of Trotskyite sectarianism, such a contumacious person as C.M. Grieve was bound to be involved in squabbles. In any case, he left Montrose in 1929 to work in England, initially for *Vox* magazine. He was finally expelled from the NPS in 1933 for his avowed Communism, and joined the CPGB in 1934. The Communists in turn would expel him in 1938 for Nationalist deviations; it is surprising that the Party had ever tolerated his continued dogmatic assertions in favour of Social Credit. His most active political intervention in this period was to stand as a candidate in the 1935 Edinburgh University Rectorial election. He came bottom of the poll.

Superficially, his shift to overt Marxism by 1931–32, when he published his *First* and *Second Hymns to Lenin*, might seem to align him with those members of the 'Auden Generation' of English intellectuals who became card-carrying or fellow-travelling Communists in the 1930s. But MacDiarmid himself would not have accepted the comparison. He had found his own way to Marxism in a movement of one. The context of his shift, however, is clearly one affecting many other intellectuals: the Great Depression of 1929–33 and, consequent upon this, the rise of Hitler to power in Germany.

In 1929, as the Liberal Party continued its long process of decay, Ramsay MacDonald was able to form a second minority Labour Government. It was not a lucky time to be in power. In October 1929 the New York stock market collapsed – the 'Wall Street Crash'. This had knock-on effects, not least in Germany. American banks were now unwilling to continue loans to that country. The Germans turned self-protectively towards customs union with Austria. The French didn't like this and in May 1931 withdrew funds from the great Kredit Anstallt bank, which collapsed. Other Central European banks followed, and meanwhile American banks were decimated. As banks closed, industrialists could not borrow and had to close their concerns in turn. Governments, too, faced financial crises. In Britain, bankers demanded cuts – lowering the wages of government employees and reducing unemployment benefits. MacDonald and just three members of his Cabinet were prepared to accept these demands. In August 1931 a 'National' government was engineered, with MacDonald still Prime Minister, and the few Labourites who followed him joined with Baldwin's Conservatives and such Liberals as complied in a grand coalition. In the General Election which followed, Labour were slaughtered. The Conservatives got 471 seats, Labour dropped from 289 to 52.

Unemployment in Britain reached 3 million. It was disproportionately heavy in Scotland – 25 per cent in 1932 – but by now Nationalism seemed a side issue. MacCormick had shifted the NPS into a moderate position before its reunion with the breakaway Scottish Party. The choice for many intellectuals appeared to be between Communism and Fascism/Nazism. In Britain, neither the Union of Fascists founded by Oswald Mosley, formerly a Labour Minister, nor the small, if intellectually influential, CPGB, came anywhere near to challenging the established parties. But in Germany, where unemployment reached 6 million and Communism was relatively strong, Hitler won. Industrialists and financiers looked on him as an alternative to Communism. In the presidential election of 1932, Hitler lost to the veteran Hindenburg, but got 13 million votes. He became Chancellor and used the Reichstag fire of February 1933, started by a crazed Dutch Communist, as a pretext for banning civil liberties. When Hindenberg died in August 1934, Hitler declared himself President of the Third Reich.

One has to point out that the journalism of Grieve/MacDiarmid bears on all these events – Slump and Fascism and Nazism – mostly slantwise. In a period of marital breakdown and personal crisis which finally entailed self-exile to the Shetland island of Whalsay in 1933, his poetry certainly hardened into a Marxist position. But one senses in his prose, as in his verse, an individual living apart from mass movements, or attempted mass movement, 'committed' in a profound sense, but usually not 'engaged' except with issues which most intellectuals at the time would have seen as peripheral. To his continued obsession with Scottish culture he added a major interest in Ireland. He showed affinity with T.S. Eliot, who stood aloof from 'struggle' – and admired MacDiarmid's work – and with Edwin Muir, a former ally cast as an enemy because of his deprecation of the Scots language in his *Scott and Scotland* (1936). He and Muir can be seen as two of a kind, men originating in the rural outskirts of Scotland who tracked their own, very different, paths through modern life and thought.

Scottish Home Rule
1927

Sir Walter Scott and Scottish National Finance

At the Annual Convention of Scottish Burghs the other day, attention was drawn to the fact that Scotland's contribution to the national libraries of England and Wales is approximately £40,000, and Scotland is getting back for its own national library less than £2,000. But it is insufficiently realised that this is not an isolated phenomenon, but is characteristic of the whole range of Scottish affairs today. Scotland pays out of all proportion, and receives back for her own affairs only a tithe of what she contributes. It is estimated on a most conservative basis that if the disproportionate payments of Scotland to Imperial purposes were rectified and brought into line with those of England, a sum amounting to several millions per annum, which is now dissipated in the Sahara of Imperialism, would become available for the solution of Scottish national social problems. Such a sum would go a long way to relieve our Slum and Housing problems; to provide better transport facilities in the Highlands and Islands; to restore our agricultural economy; and otherwise to promote such distinctively Scottish projects as afforestation, which are at present being starved simply because they are Scottish, and therefore of comparatively negligible interest to the majority at Westminster.

This is a direct saving that would be promptly effected if Scotland had once again such a Parliament of her own, with fiscal autonomy, as is sought under the new Draft Bill for the Better Government of Scotland promoted by the Scottish National Convention. But the indirect saving that would be effected by such a re-organisation of our affairs as would do away with their progressive Anglification and centralisation in London would be very much greater. How much has Scotland lost, for example, through the wholesale transference of business and railway headquarters to London, through the English control of most of our banks, insurance companies, and other big financial corporations? No one can say: but the sum must be enormous. It is noteworthy at all events that banking and national interests in Scotland are now entirely divorced from each other. The majority of Scottish industries have been passing through difficult times. Not so the banks – whose prime function should surely be to finance and further industry! There is something very far wrong when the banks flourish while all productive labour-employing businesses are in difficulties. There is something still further wrong when English-affiliated banks flourish in a country which is being progressively depopulated and thrown out of cultivation at an alarming rate. That is the position in Scotland today. The banks are positively battening on the accelerated ruination of all the mainstays of our well-being as a nation.

Balance sheets by no means tell the whole tale, but even on the partial evidence of the statements submitted at the annual meeting of the Bank of Scotland the other day, that undertaking is in a position (as it was last year too), to declare a dividend of 16 per cent, less tax, while the amount set to reserve, written off for depreciation, or carried forward, represents as much as would have doubled that figure, 32 per cent! Think of that – and then think of the conditions in our shipyards, in all our big industrial areas, in our depopulated country districts. Think of it in relation to the appalling situation which necessitates that so many of our best men should be taken from our fields and farms and transported to Australia and Canada, to do and to produce exactly what they ought to be doing on and producing from their own land. What is the Bank of Scotland doing in return for its privileges if it prospers when it cannot apply its funds and its financial powers to the development of national prosperity – when, in fact, it prospers all the more the worse our industrial and commercial position becomes. Surely it is time our financial system was revised in such a way as would bring it into harmony with our national economic requirements – or, at least, to discover how and why it has developed so extensive and peculiar a disharmony. A great deal hinges on this. It goes to the very root of our whole national problem.

No wonder Sir Walter Scott, Tory though he was, was up in arms in 1826 when the suggestion was made that Scottish banks should cease to issue bank notes in order to unify paper currency throughout the United Kingdom. He did not hesitate to warn the English in this connection that 'claymores have edges'. Scott's protests were so efficacious that the Government of the day were compelled to drop their proposals in so far as they related to the Scottish pound notes. Would that a Scottish patriot and writer of equal calibre today could do something analogous and expose the tremendous losses to Scotland through the financial assimilation of Scotland to England that has since been consummated. Much has happened in a hundred years – but not for the benefit of Scotland. We have no Scott today – and the changes that he apprehended and warded off then are now fully battening on Scottish interests which are powerless to defend themselves. This is what bank amalgamation or affiliation means; this is why the subordination of Scottish banks, and, following them, other big interests such as the railways, was carried through.

The reason why the demand for the redress of admitted Scottish grievances of all kinds is not acceded to – the reason for the throwing-out of measure after measure for Scottish Home Rule, supported by an overwhelming majority of the Scottish Members of all Parties – is not political; it is in the last analysis financial. If Scottish interests are ever to be re-established, the fight must be waged, less at Westminster than by the development of some effective means of altering the financial system so that banking interests will coincide with national interests – and not be, as at present, independent of them, or antagonistic to them. And the only way that can be done is to drag into the light of day the whole complicated subterranean working at the present time of a business alleged to be equitably administered – which so manipulates its monopolistic powers that it contrives to pay 32 per cent dividends per annum (in addition to undisclosed sums which cannot be ascertained from the ordinary balance sheets) at the very time when the real interests of the nation cannot secure the financial accommodation necessary for their development. The two things are incompatible. One of them must go. Which is it to be? Scotland – or the English-controlled, which in turn is probably American controlled, or international-Jew controlled, financial system? It depends entirely upon the acumen of those who are suffering under the present extra-ordinary and irrational state of affairs. They can end it, if and when they like, simply by realising the cause of it, and taking the means that realisation will bring to them of putting an end to it.

In the meantime, it cannot be too strongly emphasised that the present position of Scotland as compared with its possibilities – *i.e.*, the position it ought to have – will not be properly manifested until a group of competent and disinterested Scotsmen, concerned wholly and solely with the fullest possible development of Scotland's natural resources, to enable it to maintain the largest possible population under the best possible conditions, conduct a thorough enquiry into the relations and policy of existing money interests in regard to our country. If and when they do, the reasons why hundreds of thousands of acres of Scottish land are being turned out of cultivation, and a policy encouraged which causes three times the amount of emigration from Scotland as from England, will become clear – and means will then, and not until then, be found to reverse this suicidal policy.

C.M. Grieve, April 1927

The New Age
1927–1928

Scotland and the Banking System

I

The text has just been issued of a new 'Government of Scotland Bill', to provide for the better Government of Scotland, which is presented by Mr Barr and supported by Messrs Adamson, Kirkwood, Stephen, Buchanan, Wheatley, Johnston, Maxton, and others. The Press is stressing the fact that this is a 'Socialists' Bill' – despite the fact that since 1890 twenty successive Scottish Home Rule Bills and Motions have been supported by an ever-increasing proportion of the Scottish representation *of all parties*, and that the present Draft Bill is supported, not only by MP's and other leading Scots of all parties, but by the Scottish National Convention – by far the biggest Scottish representative body that has come into existence since the Union of the Parliaments. The purpose of these articles is not to argue the case for Scottish Home Rule. The facts stated above speak for themselves and show, at all events, that the present administration of Scotland is being maintained through the systematic vetoing of the majority Scottish vote by the English preponderancy at Westminster. But the new Bill differs from its predecessors in important respects. The antagonistic *Dundee Advertiser* (all the Scottish dailies are antagonistic – for reasons I shall deal with shortly) points out:

> The old Home Rulers, while they aimed at autonomy for the management of the strictly domestic business of Scotland, jealously safeguarded Scotland's position in the United Kingdom and the Empire. Nothing was more repugnant to them than the idea that the country should cease to have its full representation in the Imperial Parliament. In the Socialist Bill this ceases, and Scotland in nearly everything but a joint interest in the armed forces becomes detached and isolated; and provision appears to be made for the severance at some future time of even this link. We should be the last to assert that there are no aspects of the smaller nationalism worth conserving. There are many, but the best of them are alive and effective in Scotland today and they have no necessary connection with the structure of government. But Scotland, without losing her sense of herself as a Scottish nationality, has attained to a full and complete sense of a larger nationality, and she is not going to throw off that sense of partnership in larger nationality under the leadership of archaic and thrown-back minds, all of them belonging to the largely denationalised region of Clydeside.

Apart from the *non sequitur* that assumes that under the provisions of the new Bill any part or parcel that Scotland has in world or Imperial affairs will be foregone (on the contrary, it may be contended that for the first time since the Union they will become realities instead of phrases beggared of content by the power of the 'predominant partner' to outvote any and every Scottish representation[1]), the fact of the matter is that no valuable aspect of 'the smaller nationalism' is now permitted to function except under extraordinary handicaps by the conditions of progressive Anglicisation (in violation of even such safeguarding clauses as the Treaty of Union contained) which have increasingly dominated Scotland during the past hundred years. Scotland has ceased to hold any distinctive place in the political or cultural map of Europe. The centralisation of book-publishing and journalism in London – the London monopoly of the means of publicity – has reduced Scottish arts and letters to shadows of their former selves, qualitatively beneath contempt in comparison with the distinctive arts and letters of any other country in Europe. There is no Scottish writer today of the slightest international standing. There is no Scottish national drama. Scotland is the only country in Europe which has failed to take part in that development of national schools of composers (now in their third and fourth stages of evolution in most other countries) which during the past fifty years has revolutionised the world of music. Scotland connotes to the world 'religious' bigotry, a genius for materialism, 'thrift', and, on the social and cultural side, Harry Lauderism and an exaggerated sentimental nationalism which is obviously a form of compensation for the lack of a realistic nationalism. No race of men protest their love of country so perfervidly as the Scots – no country in its actual conditions justifies any such protestations less. Scottish History and Literature, when they are taught in Scottish schools at all, are only taught subsidiarily to English history and literature. The Scottish national speech (whether Gaelic or Braid Scots) is systematically extirpated – at what violence to the psychology of the children the comparative creative sterility of Scotland attests! Every recent reference book in any department of human activity shows the position to which Scotland has degenerated. Let me mention four. Landormy's *History of Music* has nothing to say about Scotland or any Scotsman in all the thousands of significant names from every other nation it

1. The 'Empire' is a misnomer; the term should be the 'British Association of Free Peoples'. Only by granting each of its units the utmost autonomy can the Association be preserved and the fate of all great centralised empires avoided. From this point of view the demand for Scottish independence is in accordance with the true line of Imperial development for which Scotland in the past has done more than any other contributory element, and in this connection it is well to remember Viscount Dunedin's declaration that 'The autonomy of local law is the rock upon which the Empire is built, the secret of the tie that unites it. And not merely autonomy of local law, but autonomy of local law-making – in other words, legislation.' 'The Privy Council', he further remarked, 'have been more solicitous of the principle of legislative autonomy than the Dominions themselves.'

lists. *Europa, 1926* (although it is presumably designed for British readers) lists contemporary Czech and Bulgarian poets, litterateurs, musicians, etc. (the bare names – which convey nothing!), but it excludes Scotland completely; Ireland, on the contrary, has a section to itself, and a special article on the Boundary Question. Magnus's *Dictionary of European Literature* equally ignores Scotland. Professor Pittard's *Race and History* doing justice to every other people under the sun, deals only very slightly and imperfectly with Scotland, and fails to take account of any of the newer material, e.g., the works of Tocher. In this respect the treatment of Scotland is similar to that accorded to it in most modern surveys of other subjects.

Again, letters from Paris, or 'Our Irish Letter', etc., are familiar features of English newspapers. Whoever saw a 'Scottish Letter'? Concern with Scottish interests of any kind has been so completely excluded from publicity, has been made so completely a case of 'beating the air' – that the usual headlines following a 'Scottish Night' at Westminster are 'Absent Members – Empty Benches – During Discussion on Scottish Estimates', while, from the report, it appears that the debate resolves itself into a pot-pourri of stale jokes. Scotland alone of all European countries that have ever been in anything like its position relatively to any other country, has failed to develop a Nationalist Movement capable of affecting the practical political situation in some measure or other. Why have the Scottish members of all parties who have supported the numerous successive Scottish Home Rule measures acquiesced so tamely in their defeat at the hands of the English majority? There must be more in this acquiescence than meets the eye – it represents an abrogation of themselves, for all effective purposes, of the political leaders of Scotland of which it is inconceivable they should be guilty unless – behind the ostensible position – they were cognisant of a power against which they were incapable of contending – a power so possessed of the monopoly of mass publicity that it could completely stultify them by its all-pervasive *Suppressio veri, suggestion falsi* the instant they went beyond a given line.

Contrasting the pre-Union achievements and promise of Scottish arts and letters with the beggarly results since, it is not too much to assert that Scottish Nationality was sold for 'a mess of pottage' and that Scotland has since been paying the price by submitting to a direction of her entire energies into purely materialistic channels – not, however, as the present condition of Scotland and Scottish industries shows, for its own benefit. For whose then? That it is the purpose of these articles to indicate. But, first of all, it cannot be too strongly stressed that its social, commercial, and industrial conditions today afford strong *prima facie* evidence that if, as is commonly contended, Scotland has owed a great deal materialistically to its Union with England (whatever it may have lost in other directions), it has now wholly ceased to derive any such advantages; the boot, indeed, is on the other foot; and on that, as on other grounds, it is high time to reconsider the relationships between the two countries.

It may also be pointed out in passing that not many months ago this very *Dundee Advertiser*, which is now contending that all the essential characteristics of Scottish nationality have been preserved unimpaired, took exception to that very contention when it was expressed by Mr Baldwin and had no difficulty in showing that the traditional qualities of the Scottish character had practically ceased to exist. Whether those traditional qualities (diligence, love of education, love of country, etc.) ever did exist – at any rate in any special degree in Scotland – is another question into which there is no need to enter; the Scottish Press today is certainly as adept as any other at putting up straw men for the purpose of knocking them down again.

But in another leader, on 'The Uses of the Highlands', the same characteristically inconsistent organ pertinently observed, apropos a Scottish debate in the House of Commons, 'Probably nine people out of ten who know something about the subject would agree that we fail completely to turn these great expanses of mountains and moorland to the best account. But unfortunately agreement generally ends there, and the country has never had the benefit of a policy at once well-informed and positive.'

Alas for the 'power of the Press' this is true, and the reason for it lies in precisely the political relationship of Scotland to England, as an analysis of the actions of Parliament in reference to the matter during the past hundred years abundantly attests.

Not only so; but the depopulation of rural Scotland continues at an accelerating degree. Scotland's population has steadily decreased while England's has increased. Scotland's emigration is 367 per cent greater than England's; yet Scotland's unemployment is 50 per cent worse than England's. And it is the settled policy of successive Governments to maintain emigration policy at this ratio. Over-population is a problem in England, but not in Scotland; why is it then that Government-aided propagandist efforts, properly enough directed perhaps to the relief of English congestion by emigration, should be applied so ardently to Scotland? The result is to place an ever-heavier burden on the rates in Scotland, so that she is falling ever further behind in her appalling housing conditions, and her road and transport facilities.

What prevents the development of well-informed and positive policies in regard to such problems? Col. John Buchan, the Conservative candidate for the Scottish Universities vacancy, expressed the opinion in a letter to the present writer that 'it is impossible to make up one's mind on the Scottish Home Rule question – the necessary facts and figures are not available.' Why are they not available? In certain directions these have been systematically refused by Government Departments – or purposely embodied along with the English in such a way that comparisons between the two countries cannot be instituted. In other directions the refusal of financial facilitation, as Mr William Graham, MP, has pointed out, has resulted in the creation of a tremendous leeway in the economic and social documentation of Scotland, so that in practically every direction laborious independent research is necessary to get at the facts and figures – they are nowhere readily available. Nevertheless they exist, and the movement with which I am connected is busy expiscating and tabulating them, and I propose to present some of the results in the other articles of this series – with special reference to the relation of the policy of the banking interests to the remarkable *absence of policy* in regard to Scottish problems, and to the reasons for the otherwise incredible acquiescence of successive majorities of all parties in the Scottish representation in the systematic abrogation of the Scottish vote in regard to Scottish affairs.

The *Dundee Advertiser* is no worse and no better than any of the other Scottish daily papers in regard to Scottish affairs. Their vested interests are all part and parcel of the sequelae of the Union. They all 'make a show' of Scottishness by dealing in windy and suitably contradictory generalisations on Scottish topics – but they all toe the secret line. Letters sent in by readers on such subjects are carefully censored. Opinions may be expressed (preferably anti-nationalist, or better still, merely 'sentimentally-nationalist'), but facts and figures are not permitted – or, at all events, only isolated ones; nothing can get published that attempts to relate facts and figures in regard to Scottish subjects to each other and, thus, to a national policy of any kind. There is not a single paper that dare publish a series of articles dealing thoroughly and systematically either with the case for Scottish Home Rule or with any of the major social or economic problems of Scotland. Nor dare they relax their vigilance in respect of the utterances of Scottish MP's in Parliament. Only so much is allowed 'through'; the rest must be kept back in the sieve. What does appear must appear so fragmentarily and disjointedly – and be so offset by the facetiousness and belittlement of leaders and tittle-tattle paragraphs – that it cannot conduce to the creation of any 'well-informed and positive policy'. What hidden interests behind the newspapers dictate this corruption of their natural functions and insist upon a journalism to bamboozle rather than educate the public – a journalism to make 'confusion worse confounded' rather than to clarify national issues in a systematic and rational fashion? What is the meaning of the whole position and policy that is, superficially, so determinedly unintelligible?

21 April 1927

II

It is utterly irrational to find all the real practical issues of a nation 'outwith the sphere of practical politics'; and the 'sphere of practical politics' monopolised by professional-politician issues few of which have the most indirect bearing on national realities. It is utterly irrational to find a whole electorate bemused and misled (for all practical purposes) by such an abracadabra. That is the position of Scotland today. All the Scottish papers aver that the demand for Scottish nationalism is made by a 'handful of fanatics', and has no real weight of 'public opinion' behind it – but what is 'public opinion', and how far is it reflected by a

Press which, in a country which has always been overwhelmingly radical and republican, and where today a third of the entire electorate vote Socialist, is solidly anti-Socialist. The *Glasgow Herald*, in a recent leader, observed that there was no need for street-corner oratory in these days of a great free Press whose columns are open for the expression of all manner of opinions, and its editor, Sir Robert Bruce, is frequently to be heard dilating on the high status and professional integrity of the journalist today. Yet it is simple fact to state that there is no free Press; and that journalists hold their jobs by opportunism and cannot afford to 'own their own souls'. A man with 'ideas of his own' is of no use in a modern newspaper office. The vigilance of the Press censorship – the ubiquitous range and insidiousness of the policy behind it – is such that even the *Glasgow Herald* does not, and cannot, permit signed correspondence on such subjects as Scottish music or drama, for example (let alone politics), if these go against the ideas of the vested interests concerned with these departments, not to speak of the veiled interests behind these vested interests which 'hold all their strings in their hands'. Interplay of opinion is confined to opposing views within a certain range; but the essence of the matter all the time, so far as the ultimate interests are concerned, is 'heads I win, tails you lose.' It is this that makes a goblin of our vaunted Scottish hard-headedness and practicality – induces the amazing supineness of the successive protagonists of Scottish Devolution Measures when these are rejected by the English majority at Westminster – prevents any real Scottish issue emerging into the realm of 'practical politics' – makes the systematic neglect of Scottish interests of all kinds a subject for stereotyped jokes in the Scottish Press (professedly favourable to 'legitimate' nationalist aspirations – in China!) – prevents different sections of the Scottish public realising that their diverse grievances and difficulties spring from a common centre and denies them those publicist services which would effectively relate effect to cause – and foists, not least upon Scotsmen themselves, that stock-conception of the 'Canny Scot' which is so belied by the actualities of our national position that it can only be accounted for by saying that if, as M. Delaisi argues, government is impossible unless a myth of some kind is foisted upon the 'people', then, so far as Scotland is concerned, its present disastrous condition is due to the fact that the existing myth is out of touch with economic realities to a degree so abnormal that history presents no parallel to it.

Discussing the possibilities of a Scottish Renaissance,[1] I have suggested that it is probable that the proposals of Major Douglas will be 'discerned in retrospect as having been one of the great contributions of re-oriented Scottish genius to world-affairs', and I went on to say that I wished

> to record my unqualified pride and joy in the fact that of all people in the world a Scotsman – one of the race which has been (and remains) most

1. See my *Contemporary Scottish Studies* (Leonard Parsons, Ltd.), pp. 324–5. [repr. Manchester: Carcanet, 1995 – Eds.]

> hag-ridden by commercial Calvinism, with its hideous doctrines of 'the need to work,' 'the necessity of drudgery,' and its devices of thrift and the whole tortuous paraphernalia of modern capitalism – should have absolutely 'got to the bottom of economics' and shown the way to the Workless State.

The Renaissance spirit will have to develop at a greatly accelerated rate before an effective proportion of the supporters of the new Draft Bill realise the 'true inwardness' of the matter – the real cause of the superficially-incredible stultification of the Scottish Home Rule Movement. Grasps are being made at the shadow-play of politics; and the substance of real affairs behind them is entirely missed every time. The present Bill will undoubtedly go the way of all its predecessors – and its protagonists (or the great majority of them) will accept the result with the amazing supineness which has hitherto prevailed. I say the 'majority of them' advisedly. Happily there are a few readers of *The New Age* and students of the New Economics amongst them – notably Mr Wheatley (to whose special significance in this connection, as to the bearing of the Trade Union Bill on the Scottish political situation, I shall return shortly) – and such articles as that on 'Irish Affairs' (*The New Age*, 6 January 1927) have not been without a certain effect in turning a few of the more alert minds in the movement to the crux of the problem.

It is significant that practically the only, and certainly the only real (if, unfortunately, only very partial and temporary) political triumph Scotland scored over England since the Union of the Parliaments took place just over 100 years ago: and was associated with the name of a great Scotsman and with precisely that type of business which it has since become almost physically impossible to think – let alone speak – about. The Banking System! I refer to Sir Walter Scott's *Letters of Malachi Malagrowther*. Just how much Scott (albeit a Tory of Tories) was roused by the Government's proposal that Scottish Banks should cease to issue notes 'in order to unify paper currency throughout the United Kingdom', can be gauged from his veiled threat that 'claymores have edges'. Scott's agitation was so far successful that the Government dropped their proposals inasmuch as they related to the Scotch pound notes – for the time being. 'Very probably,' says a recent writer, 'they realised that there was real determination behind Scott's reference to claymores – even if it did not mean actually the wielding of these lethal weapons to enforce the protest.' All who are in earnest about Scottish Home Rule should take note of that. Evidences of 'real determination' must be forthcoming if anything is to be achieved. The Parliamentary record of the Scottish Home Rule question would long ago have driven protagonists of any mental and moral calibre to the realisation that an irresistible premium had been put upon recourse to militant methods, and that anything else is a waste of time – 'an expense of spirit in a waste of shame'.

But a great deal has happened since 1826. The existence of a Scotsman of Sir

Walter's calibre was a nasty snag for the Government of the day – but the policy behind them could afford to wait, to pretend to yield; it is not every generation, happily, that throws up such a giant to thwart its purposes. There has appeared no Scotsman since of equal size to do anything analogous and to expose the tremendous losses to Scotland through the financial unification of Scotland with England that has long since been consummated.[1] The dangers that Scott apprehended and warded off a hundred years ago are fully battening on Scottish interests today, and they are powerless to defend themselves. How powerless may be appreciated by two facts. (1) The fact that the Scottish churches, which have lately become alarmed about the 'menace' to 'Scottish National Character' owing to the 'Irish Invasion' (a new-found nationalist concern dictated – like the Union of the churches secured through an English Parliament, hostile to all real Scottish interests – by their emptying Kirks) – are so destitute of all sense of economic reality that the solution they propound is that further immigration into Scotland should be prohibited by law, while an appeal should be made to god-fearing Scottish employers to employ only fellow-countrymen – even if they have to pay higher wages to do so!

(2) By the fact that the Scottish Press (whose columns are shut to all discussion of national realities) gives prominence to such ridiculous statements as that of Mr Ridge-Beedle, prospective Unionist candidate for the Camlachie Division of Glasgow, who says that 'it is owing to the Scottish Home Rule Movement that new industries are not settling in Scotland; industrialists are preferring locations in England where continuity and settled conditions are assured.' Thousands and thousands of Scottish electors are so hopelessly bemused that they swallow an absurdity like that as if it were a self-evident truth. If it were, the difficulties of the Scottish Home Rule movement would be over. Our English competitors would be falling over each other to subsidise it and ensure its success.

28 April 1927

III

With reference to the extent to which an inimical system is battening upon Scotland – and (consummate irony!) appearing a benefactor to its victims – let us glance at the annual report of the Bank of Scotland. Leading Scottish bankers do not discourse like their English brethren on current topics; they confine themselves entirely to the business in hand. Mr McKenna and the like may create a diversion by pretending to let – not the cat but one or two of his miaows – out of the bag occasionally, but in Scotland the public is too docile even to need 'circuses'.

It is noteworthy that banking and national interests in Scotland are far ore conspicuously divorced from each other than in most countries. Every Scottish

1. Although Rosebery confessed that Scotland is 'the milch cow of the Empire'.

industry has been – and is – passing through bad times: Scottish unemployment is 50 per cent worse than English; our slum problem is the worst in Europe; in 1908 there were 119,000 permanent male and 13,000 temporary male workers employed in agriculture, as against 83,300 permanent and 13,000 temporary in 1925; during the decade 1901–11 Scotland's total loss in emigration was 342,241, or one in ten of the population (or 54,689 more than that of Ireland during the same period); hundreds of thousands of acres have been thrown out of cultivation, and yet in Lanarkshire, from 1919–25, only seven out of 414 applications for small holdings were granted, and there are 67,081 unemployed in that area. So the facts could be multiplied. But the English-affiliated (and directly, or indirectly, English-controlled) banks of Scotland nevertheless continue to flourish all right – and apparently all the better the more difficult it becomes (i.e., they make it) for Scottish industrialists and agriculturists alike to get the accommodation they need. The banks are battening on the accelerated ruination of all the mainstays of Scotland's well-being.

Bank balance-sheets by no means tell the whole tale, but even on the partial evidence submitted at the annual meeting of the Bank of Scotland the other day that undertaking is in a position (as it was last year, too) to declare a dividend of 16 per cent less tax, while the amount set to reserve, written off for depreciation, and carried forward, represents as much as would have doubled that figure – 32 per cent! Let Scotsmen think of that – and relate it to the conditions in the Glasgow shipyards, or the Clydeside generally, where, as Mr Ridge-Beedle declares, many of the old big-labour-employing enterprises have closed down permanently and are not being succeeded by any new ones, and in all our rural areas whence continual streams of our best men are being (for some unaccountable reason) drafted to Australia and Canada to do and to produce exactly what they ought to be doing and producing from their own land. What is the Bank of Scotland doing in return for its privileges if it prospers so disproportionately while it cannot apply its funds or its financing powers to the development of national prosperity – and, in fact, prospers in direct proportion the worse our industrial and commercial position becomes.

Wherever the financial aspect is concerned in relation to Scottish affairs it is the same story. What is true of the Bank of Scotland is true of the 'national' Exchequer – it is battening on our national desuetude.

At the annual Convention of Scottish Burghs the other day attention was drawn to the fact that Scotland's annual contribution to the national libraries of England and Wales is approximately £40,000 – and Scotland gets back for its own national library less than £2,000!

But it is insufficiently realised that this is not an isolated phenomenon, but is characteristic of the whole range of Scottish affairs.

Even more characteristic was the case of the Rosyth Naval Dockyard – a bare-faced preference of English to Scottish interests irrespective of the fact that Scotland has to pay its share (and more than its proportionate share) for the upkeep of the Navy and is in equity entitled to a corresponding share of the 'work'. The outcry, and then 'scuttle', of the Scottish Press in this connection was a supreme farce.

The Convention of Scottish Burghs (of which I have been a member) is the oldest municipal institution in Europe – it is also the most effete and powerless. Otherwise its continued existence would not be tolerated for a moment. Let it discuss with any 'real determination' the effect of the amalgamation of Scottish banks, railways, etc., with English – or the relation of the banking system to the policy of neglect and deliberate 'misunderstanding' which is ruining Scotland – and it will speedily see the end of its long history.

Scotland's only hope – a slender one – is through the Scottish Socialist movement, and, in particular its Irish leader, John Wheatley. The closer inter-relationship of the two movements, their increasing identity of personnel, and, happily, their tardy concentration on the financial aspect, is the one promising feature in the situation, unparalleled in history, in which a whole nation reputedly hard-headed and patriotic, have been almost ineradicably persuaded by (mainly alien – or alienated) financial interests that black is white and white black until they wax only the more perfervid in their patriotic protestations, and the more diligent in their Sisyphus task of futile 'thrift', the more their country is denuded of population, status, and prosperity. It is significant that the *Scotsman* and other Scottish papers, dealing with the new Draft Bill, are increasingly conceding the 'advantages' of sentimental nationalism; but simultaneously warning their readers that 'realistic nationalism' will be reactionary and profitless – 'what Scotland wants is not a Parliament of its own, but more employment, new industries', etc., as if the present system was supplying these, and nationalism threatened the supply. Happily, writing some time ago (in the *Irish Statesman*, 16 January, 1926) I was able to claim that

> the Scottish Home Rule Movement is rapidly reorienting itself along realist lines, and has ceased to be mainly sentimental. For the first time it is looking before and after. It is concerning itself less with the past and more and more with the present and the future, and its membership is growing in direct ratio to its increased practicality. It is now generally realised that no form of devolution without fiscal autonomy will meet the case, and that merely constitutional means may not suffice.

This is true – but the degree of realism achieved has not yet reached through to the financial backwork of our affairs, the real manipulation area, without control of which 'self-determination' is only a delusion and a snare. This is not surprising – when that stage has not even been reached in the Irish Free State despite the long history of intense nationalistic activity there, and the relatively great measure of 'political success' achieved. But the Scottish psychology differs from the Irish, and, nationalistically laggard as Scotland has been in comparison with other countries, there are grounds for anticipating that, once it does waken up, it will redeem the leeway at a single stride and be the first to penetrate into that arcanum which still foils even Mr De Valera with its intangible and ubiquitous barriers.

5 May 1927

IV

In the same article I said that

> The majority of the Scottish Labour members returned to the House of Commons went there as 'internationalists.' They were very luke-warm Home Rulers. A short experience of Westminster transformed them completely in this respect... The saltatory emergence of a Socialist preponderance in the Scottish representation is entirely a post-war product, and is to be interpreted from the Scottish Renaissance point of view as a significant assertion of the old Scottish radicalism and republicanism. Prior to the Union, Scotland was always a 'nest of rebels' and 'never noted for loyalty to monarchy', and the old Scots Parliament, though it was far from being a democratic body, placed on its statute-book measures of social reform in many directions in advance of any yet enacted by the Mother of Parliaments. An analysis of the difference in psychology and 'direction' between the English and the Scottish Labour and Socialist Movements shows that this interpretation is by no means far-fetched. The English Movement is constitutional and monarchical; the Scottish revolutionary and republican.

My objection to the Clyde group is that they are not living up to their reputation – they have not yet become adequately Scottish (or revolutionary) in the sense indicated above. They, too, are afflicted with this inexplicable supineness. I know that (unlike their political opponents) they are seriously concerned over their impotence – which they themselves do not understand. Let them cross-examine themselves on their knowledge of, and tactics with regard to, financial control. Till they do that they will remain as impotent as they are now, no matter what else they do. Politics which fail to grapple effectively with 'the Power behind the scenes' play at presenting *The Merchant of Venice* without 'Shylock'. and the best way in which they can begin real business at this juncture is to realise that the menace to their movement in the Government's Trade Union Bill is a purely English thing – that such a measure emanates entirely from the strength of the English Conservative vote, and will be carried through by the English majority – that a Scottish Parliament would be always a radical one – that the unification of the English and Scottish Socialist and Labour Movements is playing into the hands of the common enemy and that the best way the former can pursue its own purposes, and at the same time help the latter (and the International Socialist and Labour Movement) is by immediate and complete disjunction and insistence upon Scottish autonomy in the fullest sense of the term. What a tremendous repercussion that would have! What are the Clyde group afraid of? They have an effective majority of the Scottish electorate behind them as it is. Such a gesture would rally at least two-thirds of the entire Scottish people to their side. England would have to submit to the Scottish demand – and a Scottish Socialist Government could do infinitely more for England than a handful of Scottish members forming part of a minority element at Westminster and subject to nullification by English conservatism.

Were such a step taken, the Scottish Press would immediately find (as the extent of the Socialist vote in Scotland, despite it, already indicates) that it is destitute of power over Scottish public opinion – that it is in the position of the dry bed of a river whose waters have changed their course and are now running underground to find a new outlet. That new outlet will be found as soon as the Scottish Socialist MP's are as good as their words in regard to Scottish nationalism. The rocky wall against which the waters have disappeared from the dry bed of the Scottish Press are seeking to win through is the obdurate inability of the Scottish Socialist MP's to stand out of their own light. Let them cease to be stumbling blocks to their own ideals – and they will be surprised at the power of the current that will flow through the channels they are still inadvertently blocking.

I know most of the Scottish MP's personally and I know that they lack the necessary imaginative power to transform themselves into 'men of destiny'. To them, for the most part, as to their political opponents in Scotland (the same psychology at work on a different plane – 'merely political', but, despite party differences, inspissated with similar reactions to the 'Power behind the scenes') nationalism such as mine is unwelcome and incomprehensible for the same reason (alluded to in *The New Age*, 7 April, 1927) that makes 'many persons who call themselves Labour leaders fear Mr Wheatley as much as they dislike him' – because of his 'uncompromising attitude' to 'official Labour'. *The New Age* said on that occasion: –

> This is precisely what we should expect to be the impression given to outsiders by an otherwise gifted politician who had patiently studied the credit question from the new economic angle. Take Mr Wheatley's so-called revolutionary attitude. When analysed it simply means that he justifies the pressure of the workers for a living wage, and encourages them to ignore the inability of many industries to afford such a wage. To critics who do not hold the key to his philosophy, this appears as evidence of a will-to-revolution. It is nothing of the sort. Mr Wheatley knows that the demands of the workers can be conceded without injury to the employing interests, and with benefit to consumers generally; moreover, he knows how. He also knows that the financial rulers of this country know how. Lastly, he knows that they look like refusing to apply the remedy unless or until forced to do

so by direct action in the industrial field at home, or in the military field abroad. In such circumstances he would be false to his convictions if he preached passive acceptance of things as they are. He rightly leaves that sort of thing to Mr Snowden and others, who seem to conceive that the constitution requires them to put barbed-wire entanglements round the prerogatives of the banking interests, and who fail to realise that in doing so they are assisting in establishing an economic blockade on Capital no less than upon Labour.

It is this blockade upon Capital – even more than upon Labour – and not Mr Ridge-Beedle's ridiculous 'reason', is the explanation of the present position of Scotland in particular. I have already referred to the fact that Scottish bankers do not require to lucubrate like their English confreres – the Scottish people do not even require 'circuses'. This, and a great deal more of stock-conception Scottishness (imposing, in accordance with a well-known psychological law, even more on the Scots themselves than on anyone else), is easily explicable – it is the old story of imitativeness exceeding the model. The Scots have become more English than the English. they have taken their medicine and have got to like it so much that it has become their staple article of diet. I believe this analysis of Mr Wheatley's case is sound – if not we must await a Labour leader it will fit, before there is any promise in the situation. But let me assume that Mr Wheatley answers to it, and transpose what the Editor of *The New Age* wrote from a New Economics angle into the terms of my Scottish nationalist standpoint.

12 May 1927

V

I hope that Mr Wheatley, in particular, will refuse to be supine – because of the devastating light his stand for Scottish nationalism will throw on the absurdity of those pseudo-nationalists (mainly clerical) who imagine that the 'Irish Invasion' is threatening 'Scottish nationality'. My hope is also dictated by a longing to see Mr Wheatley turn the tables in this respect, too, on that 'Moray loon', Mr Ramsay MacDonald, who has all along been such a singularly unhelpful lip-servant of Scottish nationalism. Then one of the principal arguments against such features of Scottish nationalism as the Gaelic and Vernacular interests is that 'the trend of the times', a thing it is impossible to contend against, is too strong for them – 'modern industrial civilisation', we are told, 'demands uniformity.' Yet it is nothing inherent in industrial civilisation that demands anything of the kind – a man who speaks Gaelic can tend a machine as easily and efficiently as a man who speaks English or Esperanto. This uniformity is demanded, not by industrial civilisation, but by the policy of the financial powers which are at present behind industrial civilisation. It is they – not the thing itself – that demands this uniformity, this facilitation of the mass-manipulation of the minds as well as the labour-power of its robots.

Above all, I hope the Wheatley analysis is right because, as a Credit Reformer as well as a Scottish Nationalist, I believe that such a flanking movement as the seizure of Scottish Independence is the best possible tactic that can be employed in the present situation as a whole. I have just referred to the Bourbon psychology of the Scottish banking chiefs – what I have said involves that here is the weakest link in the chain because the least 'prepared'. The *fait accompli* of a Scottish Republic (which I believe Mr Wheatley could carry through at the shortest of notice) would (on the principle that the person of a chain of persons furthest away from a galvanic battery gets the worst shock) have greater effects on Threadneedle Street than any frontal attack on the British banking system. The Old Lady would probably suffer at once from a species of Huntington's chorea. The reason is that the position in Scotland has not been given nearly such an unseizably Protean character as in England. There has been less necessity for 'cover' than at the 'centre'. The facts in regard to Scottish 'National' finance that lie to Mr Wheatley's hands are far more flagrantly indefensible than any similar statistics that can be culled about England. Consider the fact for example that Scotland makes the extraordinary contribution of over £119,000,000 per annum to the Exchequer and receives back only £30,000,000 – a terrific disparity to which no other country in the world offers, or ever has offered, any comparison. And consider, too, the incidence of the distinctive economic interests of Scotland as compared with those of England, and the differences of British policy in regard to the one and the other. Scottish fisheries, for example, are vitally interested in the betterment of relations with Russia. The present Government's attitude to Russia is peculiarly anti-Scottish. The implications of that in itself show the power a Scottish Socialist Government would have, even if England retained a Tory Government, to modify English Foreign Policy in a fashion in accordance with the wishes of the Opposition – a far greater power than Mr Wheatley and his colleagues have just now. Then consider the effect of the present fiscal policy in regard to whisky on the distillery areas of Moray, Banff, Nairn and Inverness – whole towns entirely dependent on an industry that is being taxed out of existence, while cheap foreign wines, and English beers, are being preferentially treated by a Parliament so composed that for all practical purposes Scotland might as well not be represented in it at all. Such points, however, only represent the fringe of the obscure position over which such an action as I suggest Mr Wheatley and his colleagues should take – alike in the interests of Scottish nationalism and of Socialism – would throw a flood of light which is not likely to be released from any other wing on this 'stage of affairs'.

The general policy that is being pursued in regard to all Scottish matters is far better exemplified in the Erribol disclosures. Consider the facts. In 1919 the Scottish Office purchased the estate of Erribol for £12,000 and took over the sheep stock of the late tenant for £45,110. Since that date only one small holding has been created in connection with the scheme, embracing, with previously constituted holdings, an area of 5,500 acres. Twenty-six thousand five hundred acres still remain to be absorbed, and the sheep and other stock have been disposed of for £10,724, after being offered to the crofters for £17,265 cash, an offer they manifestly could not avail themselves of. The loss on the whole transaction is over £33,000. The only possible conclusion is that the scheme has been deliberately neglected by the Scottish Office – devised as a blind behind which the diametrically opposite policy could be pursued to that which it was pretending to follow. It is perfectly obvious that the Government had never any intention of settling the crofters on the land – that it is its real policy to incur such losses, to ship off the crofters to Canada, and to allow the land to degenerate into deer forest. Over the whole field of Scottish affairs the same policy has been ceaselessly pursued by Liberal, Tory, and Labour Governments alike; and the amalgamation of the Scottish banks with the English (which at one stroke withdrew fifteen millions of Scottish money to London headquarters and gave the great London financial corporations a stanglehold over Scottish business) along with such subsidiary developments, or sequelae, of the same policy, as the amalgamation of the railways, and the increasing English control of Scottish newspapers, represents one side of that picture of which the inevitable obverse is the fact that the collective area of deer forests (1,709,892 acres in 1883) is now 3,599,744 acres; seventeen Scottish counties today have a population less than it was fifty years ago, eleven have less than in 1821, and five less than in 1801; and more than 45 per cent (over two million people) live more than two in a room!

These tendencies are continuing at an accelerating rate. This is the price Scotland is paying for its 'sense of participation in a larger nationality' – a sense that even then must be qualified by recognition of the fact that the 'larger nationality' will in turn be subjected to the 'same policy' as the 'smaller' (although, both, no doubt, may continue a while longer to have a 'sense of Empire') _ unless Scotland comes to the rescue of England, via Mr Wheatley in the way I suggest.

C.M. Grieve, J.P., 19 May 1927

Scottish Banking Controversy

The *Glasgow Herald* has recently published a mass of correspondence by Scottish traders protesting against the handicaps and heavier charges 'Scottish' banks are imposing on Scottish trade compared with those imposed by English banks. That paper invited the banks to reply to the first letters that appeared. The banks did so only to evoke a second much bigger and more indignant volume of correspondence. Again the banks replied, 'unofficially', one of their representatives claiming that 'all in all' Scottish terms were more favourable than English terms. Moreover, he added, the English borrower had been 'better trained to give security'. Some Scottish borrowers would 'only give security at the point of the bayonet'. The secretary of one of the banks suggested that the public had not 'the necessary information to come to a proper conclusion' on the subject of banking rates. The correspondence shows that there is a widespread anti-bank feeling in Scottish commercial and industrial circles – a diathesis which it should be the business of men like Mr Wheatley to develop without delay for all they are worth. 'Not only have advances and overdrafts been stringently cut down, but now the business man in Scotland has to compete on an unequal footing with those in England.'

Again,

> A definite distinction is drawn between Scottish and English banks, and the rates fixed by both. But the Scottish banks of today are, as a result of amalgamations and absorptions, really English banks, whose policy and rates are dictated in London. The Scottish directors may take a certain supervision over advances and other matters of administration, but there their powers begin and end. The Scottish railways are controlled in London. Independent shipowners whose head offices used to be in Glasgow have had their businesses absorbed by English combines, again centred in London, probably in search of cheaper banking accommodation than they can get at home.

'Can you wonder that the feeling is growing stronger every day that Scotland is fast becoming the catspaw of England?' The Duke of Montrose has recently suggested that under a re-established Scottish parliament Scottish people might be able to get 4 per cent for their money at home instead of being compelled to send it to London for 3½. Mr Alexander Batchelor, ex–President of the Scottish National Farmers' Union, has just said, with reference to this controversy,

> One saw reported how the banks, by the reduction of the bank rate, were to help all industries. Before the bank rate was reduced, overdraft rates on perfectly secured accounts was 5½ per cent, and on ordinary overdrafts 6 per cent. Since the bank rate was reduced there had been no reduction whatever on these rates. The result was that the banks were charging exactly the same as before the 'reduction'.

All the Scottish daily papers, except the *Glasgow Herald*, have refused to publish any correspondence on this matter. A writer in *The Sunday Post* ridiculed the discussions on finance at the Leicester Conference of the I.L.P. under the caption of 'Half-way to Bedlam'. But the preposition reflects the observer's position. 'From' would have been better.

C.M.G., 26 May 1927

The Truth About Scotland

Probably nothing will ever prevent an ostrich hiding its head in the sand – so long as the sand lasts. There are none so blind as those who will not see, and a technique for preventing this voluntary blindness has yet to be discovered. The way in which publicity is organised – and supervised – will probably ensure not only that a very small percentage of the Scottish people ever hear of Mr Thomson's book [G.M. Thomson, *Caledonia: or the Future of the Scots* (Kegan Paul)] but that most of those who do are immediately re-deceived in the most comforting manner.

The fact of the matter is that the truth about Scotland is incredible. It is infinitely easier to believe the myth that the Scot is a peculiarly religious, patriotic, well-educated, thrifty and enterprising person. Mr Thomson's proofs to the contrary induce a species of mental dislocation. It is repugnant to our natures to allow ourselves to be convinced that the consensus of opinion on any matter is utterly wrong. The demonstration of it, therefore, assumes the aspect of a conjuring trick. Mr Thomson will be dismissed as a clever person – too clever for most of his fellow-countrymen.

Here are the sort of preposterous facts and figures in which he deals. 'It is ludicrous to pretend, as the vast majority of Scots do, that their country is at the same level of prosperity and civilisation as England, and is faced by social problems that do not differ in intensity from England's, so long as 45 per cent of Scotsmen live more than two in a room as compared to 9.6 per cent of Englishmen. Of the inhabitants of Wishaw and Coatbridge, 23 per cent live in one-room houses, the corresponding figure for all England and Wales being 1.7 per cent.' '3,432,385 Scottish acres are devoted to deer forests, and employ a permanent staff of 881 men.'

> As for the Scots, their sublime faith in their own practical clear-headedness has not failed them in this matter any more than in any other. They may be heard positively glorying in the recognition, as they term it, of harsh economic facts. 'Economic' is a word of cabalistic power among them; the sound of its magic syllables gives them the illusion of having finally disposed of a problem without enduring the tedium of having thought about it. It is nothing to them that a Royal Commission, composed mainly of landlords, has pronounced 6,000,000 acres of Scottish soil suitable for afforestation (almost a third of the total area of the country); that another Commission found that over a million and a half acres of the present deer forest area could be put to more profitable use as agricultural holdings; that the annual loss to the national revenue due to replacing even the sheep-run by the deer forest is over £500,000; and that the sheep farms of Scotland support more stock with the labour of fewer men than is known in any other country in Western Europe (this, in fact, they will

probably consider a veritable economic triumph).

Turning to the industrial side, things are in an equally bad way. Concerned over the loss of trade, Glasgow Chamber of Commerce has just set up a special Committee of Inquiry, but the terms of reference are carefully drafted to exclude any consideration of fundamental issues. Anglo-Scottish relationships do not come within purview. The ineptitude of the whole thing may be gauged from the fact that the chairman expressed the opinion that a great deal might be done by means of an advertising campaign to boom Glasgow's facilities. Mr Thomson's book is purely objective – it deals with 'what is', not with 'why it is' or 'how it can be put right'. He has nothing to say about Social Credit, therefore, but he is, of course, fully alive to the anomalies of the existing system. 'Unemployment in Scotland has since the War been more persistent and on a larger scale than in any other industrial country in the world. The proportion of workless in the country has always been greater than in England – from one-third to a half as much again. And the incidence of pauperism is 40 per cent higher than in England and Wales.' Emigration for many years has been 200 times heavier than from England. A great deal is heard about the Irish invasion of Scotland. But Ireland is not the only source 'from which the conquering Scot is being pushed out of his own country. Since the war a strong tide of English immigration has flowed. There are now more Englishmen living in Glasgow than there are Scots in that prostrate Scottish dependency, London. English shops and stores have trebled since 1918.'

Turning to the financial aspect, this is what Mr Thomson has to say:

> Not only is Scottish industry decaying, it is steadily ceasing to be Scottish. Four out of eight banks have been affiliated to English banks on terms which, while leaving them much local freedom, will tend to make them increasingly the slaves of the needs and emergencies of the London money market. Money will be liable to sudden recall from Scotland to meet the wants of the predominant English partners. Already there have been rumours that the local knowledge of branch managers, in which so much trust used to be placed, is no longer being allowed its former liberty to meet local needs. There seems also some danger that the jealously guarded note-issuing power of the trial Scottish banks, which nurtured Scotland's industrial growth, will be lost as a result of these new entanglements. A century ago, when such a proposal was made, Sir Walter Scott talked darkly of claymores, and the Government dropped the idea. Today there are no Scotts, and the Scots will probably congratulate themselves on the removal of an 'anomaly'.

The weakness of Mr Thomson's book is its failure to realise the recent great growth and new tendencies in Scottish Nationalism. Lloyd George may set up a Committee of Inquiry into the Scottish Rural Problem. The Glasgow

Chamber of Commerce may inquire into the possibilities of more effective publicity to stave off the ruin staring them in the face. But the Scottish National Convention is on the right lines in seeking for an inquiry into Anglo-Scottish finances and in its increasing realisation that self-determination means nothing without credit-power.

C.M. Grieve, 10 November 1927

The Poetry of Robert Graves

Poems (1914–1926), by Robert Graves, is a beautifully produced volume (Heinemann, 7s. 6d.) but, in poetry as in life, handsome is as handsome does, and I wish I could say as much for the contents as for the covers. True, Mr Graves is quantitatively one of the most considerable of the English poets of his generation; in this collection he draws on no fewer than nine volumes which he has published since 1914. In that period too, he has written a great deal of prose about poetry. But the whole thing has not got him very much 'forrader'. People who believe – as I saw one writer saying he did the other day – that Edward Garnett's estimate that about a score of Edward Thomas's poems will be absorbed in the corpus of English poetry may well imagine that Mr Graves is a poet of no little consequence. But I question if he has yet written a single poem that will live in this way. That does not detract from – it may even add to – his contemporary interest. It has done so; Mr Graves has been for some years a stimulating figure in the very dull arena of English verse and poetic theory – he has been bearing himself as I would fain see all young aspirants for poetic honours bearing themselves. But the ultimate outcome depends upon their essential quality as poets; the tactics I have been speaking about are only a means whereby they can realise themselves most effectively – if they have really anything to realise. Mr Graves has precious little.

He begins as a writer of nursery rhymes and ends with the 'Marmosite's Miscellany'. In other words he is essentially a false *naïf* who, realising the limitations of that and its special unpopularity at the present juncture, has done his utmost to become a real highbrow. He has accumulated erudition of all kinds, but it has availed him nothing. His intellection remains desperately obvious. His hegira has not served to deepen his intelligence or to give him any psychological interest or, fundamentally, to improve his technique. He has not succeeded by taking thought in adding a cubit to his stature. It is easy to understand why a young fellow with any mettle resented his inability to be more than a very minor poet, specialising in a very inferior kind of poetry, and made herculean efforts to escape from so humiliating a fate. I do not suggest that Mr Graves himself has not a first-rate intelligence. Probably it is just because he has that he has made these pathetic efforts to transcend his insignificant destiny. But *qua* poet he remains a very unrevolutionary simpleton. His mental processes are all too ordinary to answer his purposes. He is like Hindemith, the composer – any amount of technical resource and nothing, or practically nothing, to say. And, as a consequence, he has ceased to count. He has had his chance and failed. The new neo-classical tendencies have come into being just as a long-overdue protest against this particular kind of imposition. He is one of a large number of poets in all countries today who twist themselves into all manner of shapes in a vain endeavour to be clever, and who seek to disguise their essential poverty in a Joseph's coat of miscellaneous information and technical trickery. But the game is up. We are very tired of these little posturing personalities, each with his special little monkey-trick of manipulating the common experience – or want of experience.

Helter-skelter John
Rhymes severely on
As English poets should,

he says in his poem on Skelton. That is the game – put everything in – 'all's grist'. Not like fools like Milton – who exorcised art. It is precisely this interminable casualness and heterogeneity that English poetry is at last reacting against, and not before time.

'Rocky Acres' is one of Mr Graves's poems which has been widely praised. But what a poem! 'A hardy adventure, full of fear and shock!' 'The rocks jut', we are told. Indeed! 'The skies wander overhead, now blue, now slate' – for the sake of the rhyme. He has a horrible lack of subtlety in the use of words. He lets us down with a disgraceful bump at every turn.

This insensitivity and gaucherie in the use of words dogs him fatally when he tries to manipulate ideas.

Yet beyond all this, rest content
  In dumbness to revere
Infinite God without event,
  Causeless, not there, not here.

Certainly not here!

Hugh M'Diarmid, 17 November 1927

Gaelic Poetry

Grace Rhys, *A Celtic Anthology* (Harrap); Humbert Wolfe, *Poems from the Irish* (Augustan Books, Benn); F.R. Higgins, *The Dark Breed* (Macmillan); Saunders Lewis *An Introduction to Contemporary Welsh Literature* (Hughes and Son).

When Dr Petrie addressed a meeting of the Royal Irish Academy upon that celebrated example of early Celtic workmanship, the Tara Brooch, he said: –

> I shall not easily forget that when, in reference to the existence of a similar remain of ancient Irish art, I had first the honour to address myself to a meeting of this high institution, I had to encounter the incredulous astonishment of the illustrious Dr Brinkley (of Trinity College, President of the Academy), which was implied in the following remark, 'Surely, sir, you do not mean to tell us that there exists the slightest evidence to prove that the Irish had any acquaintance with the arts of civilised life anterior to the arrival in Ireland of the English?

The above passage is from the preface to Dr Douglas Hyde's *Literary History of Ireland*. I do not intend to go into the causes of so remarkable and widespread a miscomprehension. The matter is fully analysed in Dr Hyde's book, in Daniel Corkery's *The Hidden Ireland*, and elsewhere. But the same thing prevails in Scotland and Wales, both of which are belatedly seeking to emulate Ireland's literary revival. The ultimate issue may well be a triple entente – amongst Irish, Scots, and Welsh at home and throughout the Empire – to overthrow the Anglo-Saxon hegemony in 'English culture' and establish a paramouncy of neo-Gaelic elements. The thing goes even deeper than that. As Robert Graves points out, dealing with Skelton and Shakespeare, in *Another Future of Poetry* (Hogarth Press):

> The two principles of prosody correspond in a marked way with contrary habits of life, with political principles; the Continental, with the classical principle of pre-ordained structure, law and order, culture spreading downwards from the educated classes – the feudal principle; the native English, with what Mr John Ransom calls the Gothic principle, one of organic and unforeseen growth, warm blood, impulsive generosity, and frightful error – the communal principle, threatening the classic scheme from below… The future of English prosody depends enormously on the outcome of the class antagonism that undoubtedly is now in full swing. A Red victory would bring with it, I believe, a renewal of the native prosody in a fairly pure form, as the white domination of the eighteenth century made for pure classicism, and kept it dominant until the Romantic revival, intimately connected with the French Revolution, re-introduced stress-prosody.

The vast majority of the English-reading public know nothing of Gaelic poetry. The nineteenth century writers in English in Ireland, Wales, and Scotland themselves knew little more, but they made certain translations in forms incapable of transmitting the essential qualities into English, and they evolved a species of poetry of their own out of high-coloured romantic conceptions in little correspondence with the realities in name of which they proferred them. This is the literature of the 'Celtic Twilight'. It makes what English readers and reviewers recognise as the 'Celtic Note'. Just as the Irish school carried this far further than their compeers in Scotland and Wales, and supported it by an ever-increasing recovery of ancient texts, and exploration of technique, so the younger Irish poets have gone beyond this whole 'Celtic twilight' position, and we find F. R. Higgins – the best of them, intimately related in technique to the poets of *The Hidden Ireland* – claiming that –

> Not with dreams but with fire in the mind, the eyes of Gaelic poetry reflect a richness of life and the intensity of a dark people. The younger poets express themselves through idioms taken from Gaelic speech; they impose on English verse the rhythm of a gaffed music, and through their music we hear echoes of secret harmonies and the sweet twists still turning today through many a quaint Connacht song. For, indeed, these poets, in the lineage of the Gaelic, produce in Irish lyric – with its exuberance and wild delicacy – the memories of an ancient and vigorous technique.

This, at least, accurately describes his own very refined and beautiful work.

• • •

I can say nothing of that wonderful technique here. In these days of new and neo-classical tendencies it is well worth the study of every poet – in any language. But how long will it be before its recovery is recognised as the essential objective of all Anglo-Gaelic poetry? Political influences – however unconscious – lead J. C. Squire (like another Dr Brinkley) to wish that Burns had written in English; lead Mr J. G. de Montmorency in the *Contemporary Review* to exclaim naively over Brian Merriman's *Cúirt an Mheadhon Oidhche*, surprised to encounter such a poem in a literature that all English-educated people know 'harps on a single string'; and make even Mrs Rhys omit the later – and, by the same token, far more truly Gaelic – poets in Ireland and prefer instead the work of the earlier revivalists; earlier work and therefore more assimilable to English misconceptions of things Celtic. But she gives Scotland and Wales the same concessions as she gives Ireland, and since they have not gone so far, this means that Mrs Rhys's anthology gives by far the best selection of Scots and Welsh work to be found in any collection to date. But how much of it all is really Celtic? One thing is patent. The technique which prevailed for hundreds of years – imitating no foreign models; so that poets like Keating, 'undoubtedly a man of broad leaning', wrote poetry 'not in the style of Virgil or Dante, nor yet of Ronsard or Spenser, but as the Irish poets who preceded him' – is not represented or indicated; no selections are given of really Irish Irish poets, but only of those who are conveniently English enough.

• • •

As to Mr Humbert Wolfe's seventeen *Poems From the Irish* excellent as they all are, they are far too 'few and far between' to be representative. They remind me of Dr Johnson's definition of a net – 'a bundle of holes tied together with string'.

Hugh M'Diarmid, 2 February 1928

A Goal in View

Mr Gorham B. Munson's latest book [*Destinations: A Canvass of American Literature since 1900* (New York: J.H. Sears & Co.)] is an important document in the new classical movement which is developing in all the arts. It would have been still more important if the movement in question had originated with it, or, at all events, had appeared independently in America instead of being merely the latest American importation from the Old World. But Mr Munson is, at all events, a critic of uncommon penetration, and supports the common thesis with weighty arguments of his own. He has already written an admirable monograph on Waldo Frank (1923), and probably intends to deal elsewhere with T. S. Eliot; but it is perhaps unfortunate that he has, for the purpose of this book, 'taken just a number of specimens, in some cases not the finest available'. Here, with a general foreword and a summarising essay in conclusion, he deals with Paul Elmer More, Irving Babbitt, Theodore Dreiser, Edward Arlington Robinson, Vachel Lindsay, Wallace Stevens, Marianne Moore, William Kenneth Williams [*sic*], Hart Crane, and Jean Toomer.

The 'jacket' points out that a widespread critical attitude in American letters during the past decade has been based on Van Wyck Brooks' *America's Coming of Age* and Waldo Frank's *Our America*, and suggests that *Destinations* may render a similar service during the next decade and prove 'a source-book for critical thinking about the advance of our literature'. It has been expressly designed for that purpose; and the best proof of the upward tendency of American letters lies in comparing it with these two forerunners. For the first time in this book cultural ideas and hopes commensurate to America find expression. He concludes that the dominant generation – that of Dreiser, Sherwood Anderson, Mencken, and Brooks – has failed because it did not aim high enough. On the other hand, he finds himself defending both the older academic generation of More and Babbitt and the younger generation of Kenneth Burke, Hart Crane, and Jean Toomer. He approves More's declaration that literature should be practical – should impel to action as well as stir emotionally and intellectually; and recommends Babbitt's books as a well-developed programme for literary criticism, counter-impressionistic and counter-relativistic in its assumptions and aims. 'Particularly deep', he says, 'is Babbitt's conception of a ripened "literary conscience" as one of the essentials of the ideal critic' (which is on all fours with Saintsbury's dictum that any critic worth his salt must have read *literally everything worth reading*); and he quotes: 'The problem is to find some middle ground between Procrustes and Proteus; and this right mean would seem to lie in a standard that is in the individual and yet is felt by him to transcend his personal self and lay hold of that part of his nature that he possesses in common with other men.'

• • •

Of Mr Munson's own quality I have only space to quote two examples: –

> What is the distinction between major and minor? It appears to me that there exists none in detail or craftsmanship, but that it is to be discovered in the pattern in which details are set and the purpose for which craft is employed. There is a difference in scope. The effect of the major poet is to be comprehensive and precise, whereas the minor poet values precision alone. There is a difference in purpose. The great poet's aim is to see totalities. The minor poet is content with fragments of his experience. Hence the achievement of the minor poet is style and design. The achievement of the great poet is Form – the macrocosmic organism with style, design, precision, and all the other merits of minor poetry manifesting as *characteristics* of an essence than animates them.

and of Jean Toomer he says: –

> He is a dynamic symbol of what all artists of our time should be doing, if they are to command our trust. He has mastered his craft. Now he seeks a purpose that will convince him that his craft is nobly employed.

There Mr Munson touches the core and cause, of the new classical movement – the fact that so many clever writers are content to achieve a certain technical dexterity, but heedless as to how they employ it, or unconscious that they are employing it in ways that the recollection of classical achievements makes insignificant and the conditions of humanity today make positively despicable.

• • •

Mr Munson's conclusion – that, because 'unlike Europe, we (America) were not shattered by the Great War but profited enormously from it', America has left the wilderness to which Europe has reverted and is 'in a position to assume the cultural leadership of the Western world' – suggests that he has not thought out the economic and political pre-requisites for the establishment of a new classical order with anything like the ability he has devoted to discerning the psychological and intellectual requirements. And his taking of the *Mahabharata* as a possible 'new source' and model for the feats in literature to which he conjures young America to address itself is another unfortunate overstepping of his thesis into uncomprehended territory. But, after all, that only shows that Mr Munson has bitten off more than he has yet chewed – which is no bad fault!

C.M. Grieve, 3 May 1928

Lady Chatterley's Lover

I have seen no reference in the English Press – popular or literary – to Mr D. H. Lawrence's latest novel, *Lady Chatterley's Lover*. It has just been published, privately printed in an edition, limited to one thousand copies, signed by the author. The printers are the Tipografia Giuntina, Florence. Mr Lawrence is unquestionably one of the most important of contemporary English writers, and here and there in the 365 pages (rather bigger pages than the normal novel size) of this volume there are passages of divers kinds which exemplify all his special powers at their best, or nearly their best. But these constitute a much smaller percentage of the total than the good things in any of his previous novels. Joseph Collins in *The Doctor Looks at Literature* said: –

> There are two ways of contemplating Mr Lawrence's effort. Has he a fairly clear idea of what he is trying to say, of what he is trying to put over, or is he a poetic mystic groping in abysmal darkness? I am one of those who is convinced that he knows just what he wants to accomplish, and that he could make a statement of it in language that anyone could understand, did the Censor permit him.

That is exactly what Mr Lawrence has at last done, without the Censor's permission. It is the *reductio ad absurdum* of the course he has been pursuing for several years that the result is (apart from the isolated passages of brilliant writing to which I have already referred) indistinguishable from the ruck of pornographic literature that circulates surreptitiously everywhere. Passages of it are duplicates of what may be found on many urinal walls. Mr Lawrence has gone the whole hog; he gives fully particularised descriptions of the sexual act; he refers to the sexual organs and to copulation in terms familiar to most people but seldom used between the sexes at any time, and probably seldom used by men and still less by women talking to others of their own sex. Mr Lawrence is, however, probably right in assuming that most people *think* frequently, if not habitually, of sexual relations in these terms; and I personally have no objection whatever to his open use of them. What I object to – or rather, regret – is not anything that is in the book; it is what the book lacks. Compared with Compton Mackenzie's *Extraordinary Women*, let alone Joyce's *Ulysses* or the *Sodom and Gomorrah* section of Proust's *Recherche du Temps Perdu*, it is negligible. It is painful to realise how small Lawrence has become in relation to such writers – in relation even to his own earlier work.

I agree, of course, with Lawrence's essential thesis: –

> In the short summer night she learnt so much. She would have thought a woman would have died of shame. Instead of which, the shame died. Shame, which is fear; the deep organic shame, the old, old physical fear which crouches in the bodily roots of us, and can only be chased away by the sensual fire, at last was roused up and routed by the phallic hunt of the man, and she came to the very heart of the jungle of herself. She felt now she had come to the real bed-rock of her nature, and was essentially shameless… What liars poets and everybody were! They made one think

> one wanted sentiment, when what one supremely wanted was this piercing, consuming, rather awful sensuality. To find a man who dared do it, without shame or sin or final misgivings!... Ah God, how rare a thing a man is.

And he is right when he says: –

> It's the fate of mankind to go that way. Their spunk is gone dead. Motorcars and cinemas and aeroplanes suck the last bit out of men. I tell you every generation breeds a more rabbity generation, with indiarubber tubing for guts and tin legs and tin faces. Tin people! It's all a steady sort of bolshevism, just killing off the human thing and worshipping the mechanical thing. Money, money, money! All the modern lot get their real kick out of killing the old human feeling out of man, making mincemeat of the old Adam and the old Eve.

And Forbes, the artist, was right when he said:

> Oh you'll see, they'll never rest till they've pulled the man down and done him in. If he has refused to creep up into the middle classes when he had the chance, and if he's a man who stands up for his own sex, then they'll do him in. It's the one thing they won't let you be, straight and open in your sex. You can be as dirty as you like. In fact, the more dirt you do on sex the better they like it. But if you believe in your own sex, and won't have it done dirt to, they'll down you. It's the one insane taboo left: sex as a natural and vital thing. They won't have it and they'll kill you before they'll let you have it... You have to snivel and feel sinful or awful about your sex before you're allowed to have any.

I am at one then, with Lawrence as to the essence of the matter: that does not alter the fact that his preoccupation with this theme has not in this instance led to literature. He has not even beaten the Censor. He has not even stuck to his own case; he gives the woman a private income and so dodges the whole issue. Making her ladyship's lover a gamekeeper, and making him talk mainly in dialect, are also mere evasions. If I had the money and the power I would circulate this book amongst all English-speaking adolescents, but that in no way blinds one to its valuelessness *as literature*. I do not think its author is under any illusion either; the trouble is that he has become more interested in these problems of life than in literature. Mr Lawrence has become like one of his own characters, 'a buck of the King Edward school, who thought life was life, and the scribbling fellows were something else.' The number of people who can copulate properly may be few; the number who can write well is infinitely fewer. I regret that Mr Lawrence should write badly in order to describe a sexual state of affairs which he regards as horrible and hopeless, for the benefit of precisely that worst of all classes, who have sufficient money to buy these expensive limited editions in order to see in print words of virility in sufficient contrast to their own impotence to give them another miserable little *frisson*. What Mr Lawrence should have done was, by hook or crook, to secure a means of publishing at a price accessible to all, and preventing the suppression of, not this silly fiction of his, but an exact specification of the dimensions and weight of his sexual organs – illustrated with appropriate photographs, diagrams, etc., and, in justice to himself, Mr Lawrence ought to have been able to do that *and to make it incontestably great literature too.*

C.M. Grieve, 27 September 1928

The Pictish Review
1927–1928

Towards a 'Scottish Idea'

An effort is at last being made to establish a united front in Scottish arts and affairs, and some account of the ideas at work to that end may be of interest. In Scotland, as in every other country concerned with the maintenance and development or recovery of a national culture, it is becoming realised that sectionised interests are not only incapable of withstanding the great over-ruling tendency towards standardisation inherent in contemporary industrialism, dependent in the last analysis on cosmopolitan finance, but that that sectionising of interests is in itself merely an index of how far disintegration has already gone. Scottish interests have been deplorably 'atomised.' We have a whole series of isolated movements little related, and often antagonistic, to each other and making for nothing that is nationally synthetic. If all these separated organisations could be federated and imbued with a common policy, that would not only in no way depreciate the special activities and purposes of each, but would give them a new force and meaning. The aims and objects of An Comunn Gaidhealach, the Scottish Renaissance Group, the Scots National League, the Scottish Home Rule Association, the Burns Federation and Vernacular Circles, the St Andrews and Caledonian Societies, are ultimately interdependent. They are parts of a potential whole, viz. a reassertion of Scotland as a separate and sovereign entity – just as they all represent parts of the shattered unity of the Scotland that used to be. Parts of that ancient integral Scotland are represented and perpetuated by each. Is reintegration impossible?

Cannot we devise a Scottish policy – an Idea of Scotland – similar to the 'Russian Idea' of Dostoevsky and his fellow-Slavophiles? This has been defined in the following terms:

> Being aware of the materialism by which all modern capitalistic Europe was infected, they considered a passive Europeanisation of the Russian people identical with the materialisation of Russia. Anxious to avoid that, they sought in the true Russian spirit for those elements and values which might counterbalance the menace of a materialistic civilisation, for civilisation's sake. Some of them believed that such elements were to be found in old patriarchal Russian institutions; others sought for them in the orthodoxy of the Russian Church; others again, in the profound religious instinct of the Russian people. Unfortunately, with few exceptions, the seekers were too one-sided, attaching too much importance to external, even

ethnographic or folkloristic attributes.

In the same way Scottish national patriotism has been dispersed into various channels, and trifles have been exaggerated at the expense of essential matters, and the letter preferred to the spirit. The loss of historical perspective has resulted in the identification of attributes as essentially Scottish which are not fundamentally so but which, where they are not later and alien accretions, compensatorily camouflaged antitheses of national attributes, are rather aspects of our national degeneracy which have been thrust into undue prominence in the general breakup of our traditions. National values require to be re-established, and a true perspective secured.

In Scotland far more than in Russia we have cause to complain that external aspects have been seized upon to the exclusion of essential qualities. The Scottish spirit has been largely dissipated in mere antiquarianism. The kilt has become of more importance than the Gaelic language and culture. At the opposite pole of our national tradition Scots Vernacular revivalists are more concerned with making lists of words than with utilising them in the creation of literature, and most of their conceptions of Scots matters spring from the decadent post-Burns period, and take no account of the golden age of Dunbar and the Auld Makars. In the same way the vicious Highland *v.* Lowland antagonism has come into existence, and proved one of the main stumbling-blocks to the reintegration of Scottish nationalism. It is a false antagonism based upon a failure to recognise our racial unity and mutuality of interest on the one hand, and the conditions for the successful continuance and further development of either the Scots or the Gaelic traditions on the other. They depend upon each other. Without a higher synthesis of the two a Scottish cultural unity is impossible, and failing the speedy re-establishment of such a unity now, Scottish nationalism, in any real sense of the term, either in arts or affairs, is doomed to progressive provincialisation and, ultimately, entire supersession.

The future of Scotland politically and culturally will be determined within the next two or three years. Already the promising movements that have manifested themselves during the past five or six years are at a virtual standstill. They can achieve no further development in the absence of a wider and deeper general tendency – a more fundamental policy. The effort to create Scottish art-music, for example, has failed, or is at all events 'hanging fire', for the simple reason that folk-song provides an inadequate basis. We must remain bogged in the pseudo-Celtic 'Hebridean' songs of Mrs Kennedy-Fraser and the like, and unable to advance into major forms unless we can found on a very different basis. Does any such basis exist? It does – in the ancient musical traditions of the Gaels. In the same way, in literature, both in Gaelic and in Scots our efforts are sadly delimited because we are utilising only vernacular instead of classical forms of these languages, and on account of our general lack of tradition. We cannot win on to a major plane until we initiate neo-classical tendencies and acquire, on the one hand, a full canon of Scots, capable of addressing the full range of literary purpose, and, on the other, revive the classical traditions and modes of our ancient Gaelic literature, and reapply both effectively to modern conditions. 'Do you mean that we should try to turn the stream of history uphill,' asks someone, 'and revert to our primitive conditions?' That is again to confuse externals with essences. The very question is a product of the general misconception that is causing the trouble. The stream of ancient Gaelic and Scots culture (this latter really a subsidiary development of the other), has never merged with that of Saxon culture – it has taken a subterranean course in our unconscious, as it were, and it is high time it was reascending into the light of day with all the additional force and new qualities it must have acquired in its hidden progress.

And we should be chary of the word 'primitive'. It implies that we hold a mistaken conception of progress. Any idea that contemporary conditions are the result of a progressive development on the basis of the past – and that folk-art is the primitive foundation upon which we have reared our present 'culture' – is a fallacy. Folk-art, the ballads, etc., are not the primitive beginnings from which we have developed, but the mere debris of a great antecedent culture of which we have little conception today, but which was certainly not inferior to any extant culture, and to which we must return if we are to get out of our present impasse.

As Janko Lavrin says in his book on Dostoevsky:

> The hidden drama of history is an everlasting struggle between the external and the inner values of mankind, between Spirit and Matter, between culture and 'civilisation.' So long as the cultural evolution keeps pace with the speed of materialistic civilisation, culture can make a more or less firm stand. But as soon as the speed of civilisation becomes quicker there arises a menace to culture. And the greater the difference between their rates of speed, the more imminent this menace. The cleavage can be carried even to the point where the values of culture become completely subdued, strangled, and absorbed by the values of civilisation. We then arrive at a striking paradox: the stronger the civilisation, the poorer the culture; the more 'civilised' we are, the less cultured we become. Unfortunately, the whole of so-called modern progress is travelling in this direction… Either we must find a 'superior idea' which can subdue civilisation to cultural values, or culture as such will perish for ever. Is there any such possibility? Are we not too 'poor in spirit,' too 'civilised,' for such a task? More than any one in Europe, Dostoevsky was haunted by this question, as he looked at the inevitable mechanisation and materialisation of mankind.

He came to believe that the chief cause of this evil lies in the elimination of the true religious consciousness – 'the moral idea which created the nation' – from life and culture. As he himself phrased it: 'When nationality begins to lose the desire within itself for a common self-perfection of its individuals in the *Spirit which gave it birth*, then all the civic institutions gradually perish.' The appalling danger – and the only way out – is being more clearly realised throughout Europe now; it accounts for the so-called tendencies towards neo-classicism – the re-concentration of advanced artists in all countries, abandoning so-called ultra-modern experimentalism, on the 'ur-motives' of their respective races. So far as we in Scotland are concerned our 'ur-motives' lie in our ancient Gaelic culture. We must repair the fatal breach in continuity which has cut us off from our own roots. The literary aspect of this is our belated realisation of the dire lack of long-established, adequate, and native moulds in modern literatures and our new scepticism of the honour paid to 'individuality'. This must issue in an increasing endeavour to win back to the tradition and technique of the Bardic Colleges – behind the feminisation of Mary-of-the-Songs. And it must have social and political equivalents. It is along these lines that our 'Scottish Idea' is to be found.

Happily, while there is yet no general recognition of the re-orientation of Scottish tendencies towards a new synthesis, there is every evidence of a changing spirit, and a deepening sense of inter-relationship on the part of the leaders of all Scottish movements. One of them put it very succinctly to me the other day. 'When I listen to a piece of Russian music,' he said, 'I am not concerned whether the composer came from the Ukraine or North Russia or any other part of that huge federation of republics. It is enough for me that it is Russian music. In the same way we want to present to the world not Lowland music or Highland music or "Hebridean music", but, simply, Scottish music. We stultify our whole position as long as we insist upon petty little distinctions amongst ourselves – most of them due to our confusion as to our own racial and cultural history in any case – instead of being content to contribute to a common culture.' And he suggested that it is high time to form a Scottish National Committee to consider our whole position, and devise a programme to effectually interrelate the various elements concerned today with Scottish arts and affairs and engage them in a general synthesis – to give them a new and dynamic relation to their common Gaelic background. The Committee, he contended, should be small but equally representative of arts and affairs, so as to balance the political and cultural aspects of the movement, and he suggested that the following might constitute such a Committee: Messrs Lewis Spence, of the Scottish National Movement; Hon. R. Erskine of Marr, of the Scots National League; R. E. Muirhead, of the Scottish Home Rule Association; Angus Robertson, of An Comunn Gaidhealach; Tom Johnston, MP, author of *The History of the Working Classes in Scotland;* G. M. Thomson, author of *Caledonia: or the Future of the Scots*; R. F. Pollock of the Lennox Players; F. G. Scott, the composer; Alasdair Alpin McGregor, Dr G. P. Insh, Alexander McGill, William Power, editor of *The Scots Observer*, William Gillies, editor of *The Scots Independent*, and myself. Given such a Committee, he said, any joint manifesto they issued, after a comprehensive review of the whole situation, could not fail to have a profound effect and might serve to crystallise the entire issue. I agree with him and would certainly be prepared to act along with those named, and perhaps a few others, on such a Committee.

In a subsequent article under the title of 'Scottish Gaelic Policy', I hope to suggest in greater detail how a 'Scottish Idea', complementary to Dostoevsky's 'Russian Idea' may be reached, and to demonstrate that the future, not only of Scotland, but of Europe, may depend on it. Dostoevsky's mistake was in thinking that Russia alone could save Europe from the menace of the machine age, whereas the way out probably depends upon every nationalism making its distinctive contribution along lines akin to those he endeavoured to establish in Russia.

C.M. Grieve, November 1927

Scottish Nationalism and the Burns Cult

On the eve of the annual Burns celebrations I made certain remarks at a Scottish Nationalist Meeting in Glasgow which received tremendous publicity. The majority of the proposers of 'The Immortal Memory' dealt with them. An analysis of press-cuttings, etc., shows that about 50 per cent of the opinion expressed is with me, at any rate in some respects. Of the remaining 50 per cent a considerable portion of it was irrelevant, based on a misunderstanding and in many cases a constitutional incapacity to understand what I actually said. It is a complicated subject, and my remarks dealt with: (1) the Burns Cult; (2) the question of Braid Scots Revival, (*a*) generally, and (*b*) for literary purposes (two very different and by no means interdependent things); (3) the relations of these to Scottish cultural and political nationalism; and (4) to Scotland's international status; (5) Burns' precise quality and value, (*a*) as a poet, (*b*) as a Scotsman, and (*c*) in relation to world literature and thought.

Despite the furore created in certain quarters by my remarks, and the time-honoured claim that there is a world-wide appreciation of Burns and celebration of his anniversary, I noted with particular interest – as confirmatory of one element in my contentions – that certain Scottish papers (e.g. the Glasgow *Bulletin*), on 26th January, had only one small paragraph relative to the previous night's orgy of eulogy, while the matter was not even so much as mentioned in such papers as *The Manchester Guardian, The Times, The Daily Telegraph,* and *The Daily News*. The majority of English papers which did refer to the matter at all confined themselves to a few paragraphs concerning my 'bombshell'; in certain cases with a few lines stating that, on being interviewed, the Rev. James Barr, MP, or some other prominent Burnsian, agreed that there 'was a good deal in what Mr Grieve said'. Indeed, Sir Robert Bruce, the ex-President of the Burns Federation, speaking at Carlisle, spoke on lines not dissimilar to mine when he denounced 'lip-service' to Burns with no genuine appreciation or exact study behind the annual adulation. If Sir Robert had added 'or progressive development' he would have met my case exactly in this connection.

The most amusing 'reply' to my 'attack' was that of Lord Sands at Stirling Burns Club. He asked us not to make ourselves ridiculous by imagining that any serious contribution could be made to modern literature in the language of Dunbar, and declared that 'no good thing has ever been written in an unfamiliar language'. Burns, himself, had to 'thole' – but persisted and triumphed over – such advisers in his own day, and Lord Sands, a year earlier at Dunfermline United Burns Club, pointed out that it was sometimes imagined that it was an effort for Burns to write in English, whereas the fact of the matter was that it was far more unnatural for him to write in Scots. 'Scots as a literary language was dead in the seventeenth and early eighteenth centuries, and Burns and Fergusson only wrote in it as a deliberate effort to revive it as a literary medium.' Quite. That is exactly what some of us are trying to do in our own day and generation – and Lord Sands is confounded out of his own mouth.

The most ironical suggestion made at any Burns supper this year was made by Sir Iain Colquhoun of Luss, who, declaring that to expect Burns' orators to say anything new at this time of day was out of the question, pleaded that, to relieve them of the effort, a regular ritual should be devised and a stock oration written 'by a master of the *English* language' be used by all proposers of the Immortal Memory. But the sarcasm was too subtle and in many quarters the suggestion has been taken *au sérieux*. If orthodox Burnsianism has descended to this (and Sir Iain's suggestion was received with applause) I need not apologise in any way for that heterodoxy which is above all things anxious to preserve – or rather to create, for it scarcely exists – a vital relationship and reaction between Burns and modern Scottish mentality. I agree that most Burns' orators will follow each other's utterances like so many sheep – but that is not because of the bankruptcy of the subject, but because of the contempt of intellectualism and fear of the progressive and creative mind which leads ninety-nine Burns' Clubs out of every hundred to allocate the principal toast annually to an utterly impossible person. Critical appreciation and comparative studies of Burns have scarcely begun. The cult has eschewed what ought to have been its natural functions in favour of a senseless repetition of stock eulogies of an utterly untenable character.

Two remarks of mine gave particular offence to the devout. The first of these was that Burns had little or no standing in European literature. But surely the contention is easily justified. I did not mean that Burns was not regarded throughout Europe as a great poet in precisely the same way that the reputations of Homer, Vergil, Dante, and Milton are accepted in our own Board Schools – by people who have never read them and have no intention of doing so; people who – if they are honest with themselves – will admit overwhelming preferences for Kipling or Ella Wheeler Wilcox. Burns has certainly a

European – and world – reputation in that sense. What I was concerned with was living influence – with the extent to which Burns bulks in the minds of those who are today vitally concerned with poetry, his place in its continuing evolution. In these respects he is *non est*. He has never been anything else but an eddy divorced from the main stream – whirling in a circle of his own. A fine old Burnsian writes to me, expressing his disagreement with my contentions, on the score of an acquaintanceship with Theocritus, Catullus, Beranger, and Heine (the third name gives a peculiar twist to the quartette) – but that is irrelevant. The significant names with which I am concerned are Baudelaire, Mallarmé, Rimbaud on to Paul Valéry in France and such others in other European countries as Stefan George, Rainer Maria Rilke, Blok, Bely, Ardengo Soffici, T. S. Eliot and the Sitwells. How did (or does) Burns bulk in the minds of any of these? How many of them ever read a line of his works?

So much for the purely literary aspect. But take the broader aspect. What does Burns mean to the world – or to Europe – or to Scotland? A characteristic Burns' Supper claim is that, 'I doubt if there is a father or mother whose love-life has not been deepened' by reading the 'Cottar's Saturday Night'! Well, well! Burns has been translated into many tongues (after a fashion) – but I question very much whether in any country outwith Scotland, England, Ireland, Wales, America, and the Colonies his translated works have had as great a vogue as the translated works of, say, Verlaine in Scotland. And what percentage of people in Sauchiehall Street on a Saturday night could tell us who Verlaine was? Burns means no more to literate Europe than Verhaeran, Foscolo, Ruben D'Ario, Fet, and scores of other poets (I take my names at random) mean to the bulk of Burnsians. What does Burns mean to the teeming millions of India, China, and elsewhere? What does Burns mean even to the bulk of Burnsians? Most of them have little or no use for poetry – and are in no case to institute literary comparisons of any kind. They twist Burns this way and that to suit themselves – acclaiming him as a Forerunner of Socialism, a Reformer of the Church, an anticipator of the League of Nations Union, and what not. I have even heard him claimed as a Temperance Reformer! What drivel all this is! It is, of course, inevitable. My complaint is not that 'pigs is pigs' – but that the Burns Cult has not produced an 'upper hundred', capable of exact study and measured appreciation. The whole of them are bogged in the same morass of self-complacent humbug. The vast mass of Burns' 'literature' scarcely contains a single volume of an intelligent and creditable description. Strindberg – Louis le Cardonnel – the Sitwells have at least been the occasion of far more interesting and intelligent studies than any yet devoted to Scotland's National Bard.

It is not these international and literary considerations that make me denounce the Burns Cult, however. It is the hypocrisy and stupidity of the whole thing in its relation to Scottish life and letters. The very people who acclaim Burns as the supreme embodiment of Scottish nationalism are themselves so indifferent to it that they have allowed the deliberate policy of another and traditionally inimical country to reduce Scotland to such a pass that even Mr Ramsay MacDonald is at long last compelled to cry: 'Scotsmen have to make an effort; if they do not, their children will have nothing to do but to keep anniversaries of the births and deaths of their dead.' Burns repudiated English and reverted to Scots. He can little have imagined that his countrymen would – even while they made a fetish of him – refuse to consolidate what he had regained for them; and only make such efforts to rehabilitate Scots (when the gap between their patriotic protestations and their actual treachery became so obvious as to be embarrassing) as, they were assured, were consistent with their irrational determination to continue the predominancy of English. Even more serious is the fact that the Burns Cult has become a definite endeavour to bog Scotland in static conceptions of nationality, literature, and, even, personality. It is not good for any country to be identified with a single type in this way. Even if Burns had been all that his most fatuous admirers claim for him, it would be vitally necessary to protest against his continuance as an inescapable model and exemplar – as the be-all and end-all – of Scottish song and sentiment for over 130 years. Literatures – and with them the lives of peoples – are built up by continual processes of reaction. Scotland (in so far as it has not escaped into Anglicisation) has been intellectually and spiritually stagnant for over a century – thanks largely to this undue predominance of Burnsianism. To this also are due the egregious accretions of the cult which have prevented the due study and esteem of Burns and his defined and permanent appreciation in his due historical place. The appalling inability of Burnsians to realise the meaning of – and necessity for – the new tendencies which are at long last manifesting themselves in Scots letters is due to their failure to understand what Burns knew so well when he broke away from the old formalisms to spontaneous self-expression and from English to Scots, and what Professor Whitehead so finely expresses when he says:

> The fertilisation of the soul is the reason for the necessity of art. A static value, however serious and important, becomes unendurable by its appalling monotony of endurance. The soul cries aloud for release into change. It suffers the agonies of claustrophobia. The transitions of humour, wit, irreverence, play, sleep, and, above all, art are necessary to it… An epoch gets saturated by the masterpieces of any one style. Something new must be discovered. The human being wanders on. Yet there is a balance in things. Mere change before the attainment of adequacy of achievement, either in quality or output, is destructive of greatness. But the importance of a living art, which moves on and yet leaves its permanent mark, can hardly be exaggerated.

Alas that the name of Burns should be today identified with these 'agonies of claustrophobia', because the cult that has arisen in his name is in effect organised to deny the values for which he stood (and, truly estimated, forever stands), and to subvert his work, so that today he is the fetish of a nation which has 'honoured' him by ceasing to produce other than debasing imitations of his own work in the language to which he so purposefully reverted, and, in particular, of a section of that nation whose insistence upon the world-greatness of Burns is so hopelessly qualified by their declared – or, at all events obvious – ignorance of, and indifference to, literary greatness and spiritual values in general.

Then as to Burns himself and his poetry – but this paper is too long already!

C.M. Grieve, March 1928

The National Idea and the Company it Keeps

The reason why Scottish Nationalism has failed to throw up monuments to itself in arts and affairs – or, in other words, to generate ideas and forces commensurate in significance and power to those generated by the racial consciousness of other peoples – is simply that we entertain it in far too superficial a fashion. Why we entertain it so, what has for centuries prevented us, and is still preventing, getting deep enough to produce results of consequence, is another matter that would call for a detailed analysis of Scottish psychology and the circumstances in which it has been placed over the period in question. Here, however, I am simply concerned with the fact. It is all the more necessary, therefore, that Scots conscious of renascent nationalism today should be as quickly as possible made aware of the true bearings of nationalism as a world-force in the light of contemporary science, culture, and human tendencies generally. Otherwise their renascent nationalism may be delayed in the unprofitable shallows of anachronistic sentimentalities.

I wonder how many Scottish readers follow current literary and philosophical matters closely enough to have encountered and read the two issues so far to hand of Mr Wyndham Lewis's occasional periodical *The Enemy*. It has been well said that his destructive criticism is the best of its kind to be read in English today, and that these two issues constitute the finest and most searching piece of literary criticism we have had for a long time. The whole range of modern literature and thought is brought under examination by a powerful imagination and an analytical mind of altogether exceptional acuity. The intellectual content of *The Enemy* is staggering. Mr Lewis 'thinks all round the wicket' with amazing force and dexterity. But the point here is not only that his work is constructive as well as destructive, that he is seeking that new synthesis which is our prime requirement in these inchoate times, but that his enemies in the world of ideas are, for the most part, also the enemies of Scottish or any other nationalism, that the forces he is attacking are the forces which are making for the abolition of all racial distinctions and the creation of a mere 'economic man', a cultureless machine-minder, and that he not only shows himself an admirable guide as to where the ultimate affiliations and antipathies of any renascent

Scottish nationalism worth talking about must lie, but actually here and there gives us specific Scottish instances.

What Mr Lewis is mainly attacking is the 'flux philosophy' that is so current everywhere and is carrying all standards and values away and reducing mankind to a dreadful melee, a formless mass. What he is seeking is the means of arresting this flux and throwing it into 'significant forms'. He points especially to the general hatred of intellect – the increasing communism which detests all that makes one man or one race distinctive and sets up comparative values. He quotes from Rene Fulöp-Miller's book, *The Mind and Face of Bolshevism*, which he says should really be called 'The Face of Bolshevism', since we learn that 'mind' is of all things what Bolshevism is concerned to deny and prohibit. Fulöp-Miller is relating how the 'higher type of humanity' is to be produced, the super-humanity of which Bolshevism is the religion, and says: –

> It is only by such external functions as the millions have in common, their uniform and simultaneous movements, that the many can be united in a higher unity; marching, keeping in step, shouting 'hurrah' in unison, festal singing in chorus, united attacks on the enemy, these are the manifestations which are to give birth to the new and superior type of humanity. Everything that divides the many from each other, that fosters the illusion of the individual importance of man, especially the 'soul,' hinders this higher evolution and must consequently be destroyed... organisation is to be substituted for the soul.

Mr Lewis goes on to show that this spirit of Bolshevism finds its affinities in many unexpected quarters in contemporary art and affairs. For example, in the works of the English novelist, Mr D. H. Lawrence, who is equally keen on 'soullessness', 'mindlessness', all that is undifferentiated, that escapes from 'individual isolated experience' back to the 'consciousness in the abdomen'.

And he quotes from Mr Lawrence a passage which has special Scottish pertinence. Mr Lawrence has been lauding the primitive 'mindless' Mexican Indians, and goes on to say that there are fishermen in the Outer Hebrides who sing 'mindlessly' in something after their fashion, 'approaching the Indian way', but, of course, being mere Whites, they do not reach or equal it. Still, the Outer Hebrideans do succeed in suggesting to Mr Lawrence a realm inhabited by 'beasts that... stare through... vivid *mindless eyes*.' They do manage to become mindless, though not so mindless as the Indian, therefore inferior. 'This is approaching the Indian fashion', says Mr Lawrence of them, 'but even this is pictorial, conceptual, far beyond the Indian point. The Hebridean still sees himself human, and outside the great naturalistic influences...' The poor white Hebridean still, alas! remains human, he is not totally mindless, though more nearly so than any other white Mr Lawrence off-hand can bring to mind.

Mrs Kennedy-Fraser and her collaborator have done their best to oblige Mr

Lawrence. Their Hebridean songs are as nearly mindless as they can be. This is the register of Celtic decadence; this is the pass to which Scottish culture has been reduced; and the great majority of people in Scotland today have been brought to so admirable a condition from Mr Lawrence's point of view that they regard these inane lucubrations and silly miscognate settings as typical products of Gaelic genius.

This gives the full measure of the ground we have to recover, and it is against enemies of this kind that we must contend if we are to win back to the old traditions, and build anew on true foundations. As I have said elsewhere,

> the growing end of Celtic literature is in the minds of those who understand Eochaidh ó Heoghusa's (in 1603), 'free and easy verses on the open road – since that is what is asked of me, the dunces of the world will not beat me in softness and artlessness. Every poem I composed hitherto used almost to break my heart; this new fashion that has come to us is a great cause of health. A change for the better is to be commended.'

It is unfortunately this change 'for the better' – the relatively short-lived results of the great revolution in technique effected by Mary-of-the-Songs – that is today almost universally regarded as the essence of Celtic culture. The antecedent modes with all their long history are practically forgotten. We must somehow or other recover from this debasement – this effeminisation. Only so can we align ourselves with those other forces in the world today which are standing for the things that are stable and incorruptible.

Mr Lewis himself is significantly sound on the question of nationalism.

> My more abstract interests would naturally make me seek it (i.e. distinction of consciousness) rather in ideas than in races. I admit, however, that the culture of one race, acquiring a political mastery over another, and imposing its ideas upon it, is able and very likely to destroy the soul and so the physical life of another race. There are too many events that testify to it in recent history for that not to be beyond possibility of question.

Anglo-Scottish relationships supply a perfect case in point.

The greatest force that is making for the reduction of humanity to a mindless flux is, of course, international finance. That is its policy – that is what people really mean when they attribute the decline of Gaelic, or the Scots Vernacular to 'economic' causes. It is natural, therefore, that those who are most concerned to expose the machinations of international finance, and the extent to which it is filching humanity's birthright and short-circuiting the higher development of mankind by its base manipulation of mob-psychology, should be equally alive to the virtues of intense raciality. Major C. H. Douglas, the leader of the Credit Reform Movement, in his recent important articles on 'The United States and the British Empire' (articles which should not escape the attention of any Scotsmen concerned to recognise the ultimate implications of a Scottish nationalist attitude) points out that the policy of world hegemony which international finance is pursuing

> carries with it certain fundamental corollaries... It involves the abolition, in everything but name, of the sovereign geographical State... Now it is quite obvious that the scheme of nationality, if it may be so called, can be very easily made to appear to be the cause of many ills which afflict humanity, such as war, and there has been for hundreds of years a steady campaign for the abolition of State barriers in favour of internationalism – a campaign which in recent times has come to be associated with Socialism, which is one reason to suspect Socialism (of that kind). It does not seem to penetrate the minds of the advocates of this sort of internationalism that there is no difference, except in degree, between the abolition of national personality and the abolition of individual personality. There is no reason which can be expressed logically which will justify you making any difference in treatment between Mr James Robinson and Mr John Smith, if you refuse to recognise any difference between Great Britain and, let us say, France. This is, of course, the common cant of internationalism – that there *is* no difference between M. Jacques Bonhomme and Mr John Bull or any of their other national equivalents. Still less is there any difference between Mr Robinson and Mr Smith. It is exactly from there that the whole tremendous fallacy starts. Not only is there a difference between Mr Smith and Mr Robinson, but the whole tendency of human development is the accentuation of this difference, and ultimately to make Mr Smith or Mr Robinson a unique creation, and therefore indispensable, and a law unto himself. It is not, of course, intended for one moment to suggest that humanity has progressed very far along this road; in fact, it is unfortunately true that for practical purposes at the present time most Mr Smiths are largely indistinguishable from their next-door neighbour, Mr Robinson, and every effort is made to keep them that way, but I think that the general trend is plainly towards differentiation. And it is no more reconcilable with the hegemonistic theory of world policy than would be the prescription of a uniform diet for the Australian aborigine and the London clubman.

Hugh McDiarmid, March 1928

Backward *Forward*

Scottish Socialism has contributed nothing of the slightest consequence to Socialist thought. It has taken over its tenets lock, stock, and barrel from Continental thinkers – but the principle of selection has been Scottish – of a sort. The lack of independent thinking of any calibre worth speaking about accounts for the anti-intellectualistic, 'democratic' character of Scottish Socialism – for wholesale borrowing without making any return is a demoralising process; the *morale* – or rather lack of *morale* – of the Scottish Socialist Movement shows this clearly enough. Mr James Maxton, MP, recently told a Glasgow University audience that 'the Scottish Labour Movement owed little or nothing to intellectuals; its progress was due almost entirely to the rank and file.' The former of these statements expresses an obvious enough truth – the condition of the Movement leaves no doubt as to that – although the power of realising that fact, and expressing it in the terms he did, Mr Maxton owes to the intellectuals who have created the Scottish Educational System as it presently exists and endowed the English language with the expressive powers it now possesses. And, despite his statement, Mr Maxton himself did not implore his hearers not to waste their time in acquiring a University education. His remark is just one of these hypocritical utterances dictated by a resolutely plebian pose which characterise his type. But take the second sentence – what 'progress' has Scottish Socialism registered? The present condition of Scotland is an adequate reply. Scottish Socialism has developed *pari passu* with national degeneracy. As to the principle of selection, the application of which has differentiated Scottish Socialism from, say, German or Russian Socialism, this is mainly seen in the adaptation (by no means an improvement) of certain elements of Continental Socialist thought to Scottish Calvinism and Burnsian 'A-Man's-a-manism'. In other words, a manifestation of Nationalism – in however decayed and disreputable a form.

The effect of this on the personnel of the so-called 'Clyde Rebels' and their organ, *Forward*, works out thus: 'We, the workers have been denied spiritual and mental development by the Capitalists. We are more numerous than they are. We have little or no education – let us denounce whatever is beyond us as luxury-art and highbrowism. We have been restricted to a sordid little round of interest – let us pretend that nothing else exists and, if we can, destroy whatever else does.' And so on. The result is that the organ of the Movement claiming to be out for the uplift of the masses jeers at anything intellectual, panders as brazenly to the 'mob' as any 'Capitalist rag', and serves up a hideous mixture of Socialist and Labour politics, Mid-Victorianism, cheap personalia, slang, patent medicine advertisements, and what not, with, like an apparition in the rear, a queer compound of Calvinism, Total Abstinence, and the Musical Festival Movement by way of an adumbration of the Future Culture of Our People.

Surely a saner Socialism would have said: 'Owing to their privileged position the classes have hitherto almost wholly monopolised the Arts and Cultures which should have been the free heritage of all humanity. Belatedly we demand our share. These things are good – they represent the ends to which everything else in life should be merely the means. If we have been brutalised and cut off from these things in the past – it will do us no good now to curse the injustice of the existing social system with one breath and deride all that we allege it has cheated us out of with the next. Either we have been defrauded – or we haven't. If we have been defrauded, there is no sense in minimising our loss by pretending that the culture we were denied wasn't worth having and that in fact we are better without it – healthier, more moral, and so on. If we haven't been defrauded – if there is no heritage to enter into – what are we making all the song about? Let us get on with the business of creating one.' And just there this saner Socialism encounters its principal snag. It can't create anything of the kind. Everything of any value in the world has been – and will remain – the creation of a few; and must be constantly recreated by a few, frequently in the face of the opposition, and nearly always of the apathy and indifference, of the masses who ultimately benefit. This is as true of Socialism as of everything else. It is the product of a few individual thinkers, evolved as the result of processes of thought overpassing national barriers but coloured and determined, none the less, by certain national conditions and qualities.

The Socialist who condemns nationalism exemplifies it. He cannot express his thoughts except by means of a language which is, in itself, as much a determinant as a medium of thought. So that the recent outburst against Scottish Nationalism by John S. Clarke in the *Forward* is typical of the condition in certain directions of contemporary Scottish Nationalism. It is more than that – in its vain effort to deny the existence of Scottish Nationalism it manifests in easily distinguishable forms elements of specifically German Socialism, English propaganda or prejudices, and native stupidity. The practical effect of Mr Clarke's utterances – if utterances so stupid can ever have any practical effect – is simply to prefer English Nationalism (or that variant and projection of it, British Imperialism) to Scottish Nationalism – a preference that is Scottish enough, in all conscience, if only Scottish of the Decadence! I would not be concerned with Clarke here were he not so typical of the whole 'Glasgow School' – but it is seldom the most fatuous of them gives away his preposterous claims for his creed so completely as Clarke does when he declares: 'The people are, as Erskine of Marr deplores, British, not Scottish; they prefer even the "Black Bottom", to the Strathspey, and English fashions to any that can be termed Scottish. I cannot find any impulse towards a "Scottish Renaissance" except in the limited few. As a question of political expediency I am sympathetic to Scottish Home Rule, but I do not want the tin-can of Scottish Nationalism tied on to the Home Rule puppy's tail.'

The difference between Scottish Nationalists and Mr Clarke is that the former while agreeing that most of our people are British rather than Scottish and prefer the 'Black Bottom' to the Strathspey, raise qualitative questions. Is it better to be British than Scottish? Is the Black Bottom preferable to the Strathspey? Wouldn't it be better if there *were* a greater impulse towards a Scottish renaissance, and are those who are endeavouring to create one responsible for the impossibility of making silk purses out of sows' lugs? What has caused our people to have the preferences they have, and can they not be given better ones? Mr Clarke refuses to institute any such inquiries. 'What is, is', so far as he is concerned, and he is prepared to take things as he finds them without making any qualitative comparisons. This is not surprising in one who evidently imagines himself an excellent example of what Leontiev calls the 'aim and object of Western civilisation' – but, to afford any show of consistency, Mr Clarke must agree that other people are as much entitled to hold a diametrically opposite opinion on that score as he is to hold the one implied in his article, and that a mere 'follow-my-nose' opportunism which reduces everything to a question of 'political' expediency represents an attitude which lends itself readily to an attack from the rear as all too obviously the product of shallow thought and inordinate conceit.

The give-away of Mr Clarke's mentality occurs even more amusingly in the latest *Forward* to hand – in which he recommends his readers to make their own anthologies by cutting out poems which appeal to them; and he obligingly supplies half-a-dozen or so 'Poems of Revolt', apparently selected from his own choice collection. Needless to say there is nothing remotely resembling poetry in the lot. Socialist Culture à la Mr Clarke is to be an I.O.G.T. Reciter writ large. The best is Edwin Markham's 'Man with the Muckrake' – but the appalling thing is the way in which a Mr Clarke can reproduce lines such as these about faces full of the 'mindlessness of the ages', brows ruthlessly slanted back, and brains deprived of light, without realising that he, too, is simply full of stupid contempt for the things he does not understand: and that all he has written in his article on 'Scots Nationalism and Socialism' is a glorification of those who cannot, and will not, go down to fundamentals; who have no means and no desire to institute qualitative comparisons, but hate distinction and pride of any kind as intolerable offences to their own immedicable nullity; who are content to acquiesce in the mob-preference for the 'Black Bottom' to the Strathspey, and to something else still worse to the 'Black Bottom' in due course – and yet have the audacity to pretend that they can erect a new social order on the basis of what they themselves simultaneously describe as the brutalised and cultureless condition to which Capitalism has brought the masses. If humanity has been at the mercy in the past of 'blind leaders of the blind', the aim of Socialists like Mr Clarke would seem to be to leave them in the future at the mercy of themselves by extirpating even the quality of leadership that has hitherto mitigated their chaotic condition. Or, if that is not Mr Clarke's aim, it can, at all events, be the only effect of his efforts.

The character of Scottish Socialism is itself an overwhelming proof of the need for a very different Scottish Nationalism.

My friend, Mr J. L. Kinloch, has already replied to Mr Clarke and pointed out that: 'The Russian people, for example, are today more sensitively national as well as international, than they were under the Tsar.' But people like Mr Clarke are impervious to the lessons afforded to anti-nationalist, falsely-international Socialism by Russia on the one hand, and Italy on the other. They do not realise that their thought is as much a product of certain circumstances, and often of the same circumstances, as the 'economic evils' against which they inveigh. They cannot get in behind themselves and see themselves as the result of ascertainable processes capable of impersonal objective evaluation. What a mess and muddle they are in. A Communist with whom I conducted a recent debate – Mr Guy Aldred – asked what would be the place of the artist in such a Worker's Commonwealth as he envisaged, said that the possession of unique facilities would not excuse anyone from doing his full share of the 'dirty work'. All must be manual labourers – and after that anything else they could or cared to be. What a ridiculous attitude at a time when science is manifestly conducing to the Workless State, and when but for an arbitrary and inadequate system – the greater part of all human drudgery could already be eliminated and mankind correspondingly freed for nobler pursuits.

Clarke's mentality is typically Anglo-Scottish, or, if he prefers it, that abominable thing, British; and his Socialism is just the reflection in another sphere of the identical mindlessness and cruelty which lead Rev. J. M. Younie, of Kippen, to cry out that 'the world is too well fed today to have God's presence suggested to them easily. Fatigue heightens suggestibility, but with an eight-hour day for five and a half days a week the world is simply not tired enough to feel its need to rest upon God on Sunday.'

The unfortunate thing is that a considerable part of it is still quite tired enough to swallow Mr Clark's alleged Socialism whole.

C. M. Grieve, May 1928

The Conventional Scot and the Creative Spirit

The muse to whom his hert is given,
    Historia abscondita,
'S already workin' like a leaven
    To manifest her law.

The Gaelic sun swings up again
    And to itsel' doth draw
A' kindlin' things; and a' the lave
    Like rouk are blawn awa'.

– From '*Fier Comme Un Eccosais*'
Hugh M'Diarmid

I am not concerned here with Roman Catholicism or with Calvinism in their religious aspect; but simply and solely in their respective bearings on Scottish arts and secular affairs in general.

In a recent issue of *The Scots Observer*, the Rev. Dr Hector Macpherson quoted a sentence I used in my book, *Albyn: or Scotland and the Future*, with regard to the anti-æsthetic effect of the Reformation; sneered a little at the perfervour of my Nationalism, and at my special brand of Socialism, as judged from some norm he did not specify; went on to admit that what I had said about the anti-cultural character of the Reformation, and the attitude to life, consequent upon it, which has since overwhelmingly characterised Scottish people, is correct; but proceeded, with a hish-hash of trite 'facts' conventionally interpreted, to contend that the Covenanters were concerned about, or effected, something of more consequence than arts and letters – something upon which the possibility or value of these is dependent, but which, if so disposed, can quite well flourish without yielding any such evidences of its existence at all (as – I presume he means – in Scotland's case!). This something he calls Liberty.

But where is this liberty for which, Dr Macpherson tells us, the Covenanters fought? It is as unreal as 'democracy'. Since the function of Art is the preservation of the activity, and extension, of consciousness, how can a superior conception of liberty exist where art is abjured? 'By their fruits ye shall know them.' I am concerned about spiritual values – not about sterile shibboleths. To a 'freedom' which does not issue in vital works of arts and letters, I would prefer any 'tyranny' which does. 'Progress', which eliminates an intelligentsia capable of producing and appreciating a Dunbar, let alone Gaelic culture, in favour of a 'democracy' which, for close on a couple of centuries, has failed to produce arts and letters not immeasurably inferior to those of every other European country seems to me an 'Irishman's rise'. And that nation's tendency to flatter itself that it has gained more than it has lost by such a process is a natural concomitant of its ignorant and degraded condition. It is easy for people to imagine they are free, if they are too stupid to conceive a greater freedom.

In any case, even if the Reformation and its sequelæ had produced in Scotland a people every man-Jack of whom was a Calvin or a Burns in kind and calibre, it would have been instantly imperative to work for a psychological revolution and the creation of different types. As matters stand, a particular type of mentality neither in kind nor calibre of the types mentioned, though largely related to both – as they were to each other – has dominated Scotland for so long that, in Professor A. N. Whitehead's phrase, we are 'stifled with shadows'. 'It is', as he says in his book on *Symbolism*, 'the first step in sociological wisdom to recognise that the major advances in civilisation are processes which all but wreck the societies in which they occur. The art of free society consists first in the maintenance of the symbolic code, and secondly in fearlessness of revision.' Both have been so lacking in post-Reformation Scotland that nothing less than a psychological revolution – throwing upmost types hitherto suppressed – will suffice to produce spiritual goods amongst us.

I do not know where Dr Macpherson gets his information in regard to myself. I profess, as he says, to be a Scottish nationalist and a Socialist – but I have never professed to be a 'democrat' in the usual connotation of that very variable term. I gladly plead guilty to 'strangeness' in my Socialism if that means that, apart from certain specific objections to the existing order, I have nothing whatever in common with the anti-intellectual Calvinistic type of Socialist represented by the majority of our Scottish Socialist MPs – who seem to me amongst the meanest and most hopeless products of the state of affairs against which they are reacting only in one very restricted and comparatively negligible respect. But why should *they* be taken as the 'norm'? This 'strangeness' in my Socialism can only be so to one who has a very inadequate knowledge of the Socialist Movement. Scottish Socialism is destitute of intellectual status: but elsewhere the identification of Socialism and 'Democracy' has been repudiated long ago. Suffice it for me to say here that I have no use whatever for the type of Socialist who has awakened to the fact that the present system has certain material effects upon him or his class or is at variance with certain appetites bred by itself, but who fails to realise that not only all his other ideas and attitudes are equally products of the existing state of affairs, but that his 'class consciousness' or economic awakening is itself a dangerously typical product of the same system, as is the general preoccupation today with social and economic, rather then æsthetic and religious, problems.

So far as the Scottish Renaissance Movement is concerned, I have no concern whatever with the type of 'facts' Mr Macpherson sets forth or with the grubbing, logical, consistent type of mentality that *has* any use for them, any more than I have for Professor R. S. Rait's contention that 'history must be accepted whole', instead of selecting certain elements from it as the basis of a possible new Scotland as I do in my *Albyn*. I depend, instead, upon the truth of Nietzsche's observation that: 'Every great man has a power which operates backward; all history is again placed on the scales on his account, and a thousand secrets of the past crawl out of their lurking-places – into his sunlight. There is absolutely no knowing what history may be some day.' – Even the history of Scotland! I look, in other words, for the emergence of a new spirit in our national life with such a retroactive power as to restore the best elements of the Gaelic Commonwealth and to eliminate all the night-growth that has sprung up since the eclipse of the Gaelic sun – and believe I am finding it.

A laverock in the lift forgets
A'thing except his sang
– A thoosand years o' history I
The Gaelic hills amang.

Feudalism, Calvanism,
Can never be undune?
– Hoots they're as they'd never been
In ony simple tune![1]

1. From Hugh M'Diarmid's *Fier Comme Un Eccosais.*

I hold no brief for any particular creed or school of thought or type of psychology as against those which have – to all intents and purposes – dominated Scotland since the Reformation; but I contend that Scotland needs, above all things, a psychological upheaval which will throw up types of any other kind capable of producing art-products superior to those which have been produced in Scotland since the Reformation subverted our national psychology, and, if not comparable to those of other countries, at least capable of sustaining comparison with our own pre-Reformation products. I do not assert that art-products necessarily consist with any given type of opinion on, or attitude to, politics, religion, etc. But I assert without fear of contradiction that the general type of consciousness which exists in Scotland today – call it Calvinistic or what you will (it has, at any rate, been very largely coloured and determined by the unique and peculiarly unfortunate form the Reformation took in Scotland) – is anti-æsthetic to an appalling degree, and none the less so because it is, *ipso facto*, constitutionally unconscious of its disability, and naïvely disposed to set up its own gross limitations as indispensable criteria. I make no apology for my central position that no amount of theology or morality can compensate for the lack of active creativity and æsthetic perceptiveness in a people. All the Christianity in the world cannot produce a poem; but a poem may, incidentally, produce a great deal of Christianity.

Rosanov, the Russian philosopher, simultaneously wrote conservative articles in the *Novoe Vremya* over his full name, and Radical articles over a pseudonym in the progressive *Russkoe Slovo*. He did not regard this inconsistency as anything outrageous. Politics were to him a very minor business that could not be brought *sub speciem æternitatis*. What interested him in both parties were only the various individualities that went to form them, their 'taste', their 'flavour', their atmosphere. It seems to me that it is high time that an effective minority of Scots were adopting the same attitude to all the things over which Scotland has been so deadly serious since the Reformation. Upon the recognition that these do not matter in and for themselves at least, and generally do not matter at all – that they cannot be brought *sub speciem æternitatis*, and that it is urgently necessary that we should be concentrating on what can the possibility of a Scottish Renaissance depends.

As Professor Whitehead says:

> The type of generality which, above all, is wanted, is the appreciation of variety of value. I mean an æsthetic growth. There is something between the gross specialised values of the mere practical man, and the thin specialised values of the mere scholar. Both types have missed something; and if you add together the two sets of values you do not obtain the missing elements.... What I mean is Art... habits of æsthetic apprehension.

There is no country in the world where these are a greater desideratum than in Scotland today, and none which more urgently requires to realise that 'those societies which cannot combine reverence to their symbols with freedom of revision must ultimately decay either from anarchy, or from the slow atrophy of a life stifled by useless shadows.' The majority of Scotsmen today still exemplify that fact in one form or the other; the former accounting for the 'Clyde Rebel' and the other for the 'Canny Scot'. But happily there is at last an effective leaven at work, and the lump is beginning to be appreciably enlivened.

C.M. Grieve, June 1928

The Evening Times
1928

Is Burns Immortal?
The Lopsidedness of Scots Literature

AN 'ALMOST WORTHLESS' CULT

'A great man does not exist to be followed slavishly, and may be more honoured by divergence than by obedience.' That was the essence of my argument with regard to Burns and the Burns cult in my speech in Glasgow on Saturday, which has evoked such a storm of protest amongst the Bard's enthusiasts. I am writing in advance of the anniversary dinners, at which, I understand, many of the proposers of 'The Immortal Memory' intend to 'lam' me; but various gentlemen have already expressed their opinions. Some of these are wide of the mark, and most of them are at least to some degree irrelevant – owing to the fact that they are replies to a mere fragment of what I said, and not to my full address, which qualified the published extract in many ways. For example, I expressly stated that I was dealing with Burns purely from a literary and nationalistic angle – and was not concerned with what he might be from any other standpoint. But my main implication was that just as it would be a curious country that was 99 per cent bakers and with little or no export trades, so it is a curious literature that is 99 per cent Burns. This lopsidedness is no credit to Scotland. Variety is the spice of life: and all Burns and nothing else has made Scots literature an exceedingly dull affair.

BURNS AS A LITERARY MAN

A well known Burns enthusiast (who significantly prefers to remain anonymous) complains that 'Mr Grieve was talking about Scottish literature as a literary man, but Burns never professed to be a literary man, and earned his living as a ploughman and an exciseman.' I cannot see the point of these sentences. I am, of course, ready to concede that it is unusual for anyone to talk about Scots literature as a literary man. More's the pity! Mr William Power says there are Burns clubs which will listen to a serious discussion and critical comparison of their Bard. But they are few and far between. There is scarcely any modem Scottish poet of the slightest consequence who has not held aloof from the whole cult – and the cult has depended upon speakers of very different type.

Burns, at any rate, made not such a bad show of being a literary man in his spare time, and it is certainly that, and not his ploughmanship or expertise as a 'gauger' that concerns us today, and anywhere else than in Scotland it would be readily conceded that a literary man was therefore at least as capable of dealing with him as an average plumber or butcher. Most of the members of the cult think otherwise. They complain that intellectuals are too coldly analytical to do justice to a genius like Burns, and declare that his great appeal is due to the fact that the common people who love him have, unlike the 'highbrows', a warm humanity which is better than any pedantry. Carried to its logical conclusion, this argument is a defence of illiteracy. What a pity there is any education at all! It makes men so hopelessly unequal. But for that we might all have had a safe, warm humanity – and imagine that a still worse poet than Burns – M'Gonigal, say (or M'Diarmid) – was an unparalleled genius!

A JUSTER ESTIMATE

I agree with Professor Bowman that Burns has had little recognition on the Continent – but I do not believe that this is due to any insensitivity to genius on the part of the great European reading public. I simply believe that Europe has taken a juster estimate of Burns than his infatuated countrymen, and that because great poets are not such infrequent occurrences amongst them as they are with us in Scotland. They are more used to taking the measure of genius. In any case, the fact to which Professor Bowman draws attention enforces my contention that the claims made regarding Burns' world-wide popularity and influence are greatly exaggerated. Only an infinitely small minority of mankind have ever heard of him, or are ever likely to do so. He means as little to literate Europe as Pushkin, Baudelaire, Leopardi, Blok, and scores of other great poets (of whom they have never heard) mean to Burnsians in the mass. That, nevertheless, the best studies of Burns are the work of continental scholars bears out my complaint that the great bulk of Burnsiana is worthless and that little or no real critical analysis has yet been attempted. Burnsians prefer a senseless annual repetition of the stock eulogies to any exact study of their idol.

HAS DEMOCRACY FAILED?

Is Burns immortal? I hope not – for humanity's sake. In reply to Mr Rosslyn Mitchell, MP, who claims that Burns has permeated European thought, I would point out that there is an increasing disposition today to ask whether democracy has not failed, to realise that lip-service to brotherhood does not always promote it, and that, in any case, we have to face the fact that civilisation is being threatened by its hordes of submen. In other words, we are realising that most men are not men for a' that, and that our intellectual and spiritual evolution is not to be suspended in a limbo of fatuous amiability or by the transformation of mankind into an enormous mutual admiration society. We have something better to do than be all 'John Tamson's bairns'. As to 'A man's a man for a' that', from the purely literary point of view I agree with Burns himself (who was an infinitely better literary critic than most of his followers) that it is a precious poor poem, whatever else it may be. Mr Rosslyn Mitchell should not let his particular political prejudices corrupt his literary values.

A STATIC CONCEPTION

My point was that if, at long last, Europe is beginning to repudiate democracy, romantic love, and other basic elements in Burns' creed, that suggests that Burns' work will speedily become more and more old-fashioned and intolerable to modem consciousness. That is as it should be. 'Fixed standards are useless to those who would have men free.' No matter what Burns' work may be in and for itself, if its influence, instead of reviving the medium in which Burns himself wrote, has rendered it impossible to write anything that is not beneath contempt in any form of Scots resembling his – and if the cult that has sprung up in his name is, above all, determined to bog us in a static conception of poetry and nationality, and to prevent any young Scot trying to do in and for Scotland today what Burns tried to do in his day and generation – then both are at least so far from being wholly beneficial as to justify the wildest overstatement that may be made in an effort to restore some measure of cultural balance to a country that in these respects (and all others) needs it infinitely more than any other in Western Europe.

In conclusion, let me say that I do not object to Burns dinners on Temperance grounds. My friend, Mr William Power, has been saying that alcohol is not good for the muses. I do not agree. The drinking at Burns suppers is one of the few elements in the programme which have my invariable and hearty approval. I prefer Burnsians 'speechless'.

C.M. Grieve ('Hugh McDiarmid'), 26 January 1928

The Scots Independent
1927–1929

Wider Aspects of Scottish Nationalism

In the current (first) issue of the Hon R. Erskine of Marr's new paper, *The Pictish Review*, I have the first of a series of articles embodying proposals towards a Scottish National Synthesis. The formation of a representative Committee to this end is suggested, the idea being that the members, by replies to an initial questionnaire (designed to 'scale' their diverse particular interests), subsequent memoranda and cross-criticism, etc., should work out a policy for relating afresh thc various aspects of Scottish arts and affairs with which they are specially concerned in a progressive fashion to each other and to our general Celtic background. There would thus be evolved a 'superior idea' which would not only enhance the tendencious value of each interest by establishing an adequate perspective and affording them those advantages of the consciousness of long-established and native traditions, for lack of which all of them are at present precluded from emerging on to a major plane where they could join issue with the great over-ruling tendencies of the age (which consequently they reflect instead of challenging), but which would make them effectively complementary to the forces in every other country which are resisting the subjugation and supersession of cultural values by those of materialistic civilisation. I instance Dostoevski's 'Russian Idea'. Dostoevski's mistake was in imagining that Russia had a peculiar Messianic mission in this respect and that Russia alone, properly awakened to its special destiny, could prevent the robotisation of Europe or, at all events, preserve itself from sharing that fate. On the contrary, it seems to me that every other people must evolve a like 'fundamental idea' and thus complement the tendencies elsewhere which are opposing the reduction of humanity to a mechanistic sterility. The tremendous forces that are making for standardisation and dehumanisation call for the mobilisation in every possible direction of forces similar to those which Dostoevski recognised as essential and sought to promulgate in Russia.

Three considerations may illustrate this idea: –

MODERN RACIAL TENDENCIES

1. – The widespread volte-face amongst 'advanced' artists in every country today; the change over, particularly in music (e.g., Stravinsky, Bartok, etc.) to tendencies that have been called neo-classical but represent something far more radical than a return to any 'classical' formalism.

On the contrary they are a search for 'fundamental form'; an endeavour, at long last, to get behind the Renaissance, through which the native culture of Greece whitened the native potentialities of all other European peoples and prevented them in turn 'realising themselves' to classic effect as the Greeks themselves did. In other words it is an effort on the part of almost every racial element in Europe in the persons of its most 'advanced' thinkers to resist standardisation and get down to what the Germans call their 'Ur-motives'. Linguistically it accounts for the revival and re-exploitation of all sorts of lapsed, localised and specialised languages and is producing literary phenomena which manifest the extent to which the tendencies towards a world-language have alarmed and repelled the creative imagination of Europe in its most significant contemporary expressions. The lack of such a neo-classicism is responsible for Scotland's failure to develop a national school of composers; and restricts it to mere 'folk song'. Its immediate practical implications are that the continued life and literary development of Gaelic or Scots are dependent upon the recognition of their respective protagonists that they must make common cause with all those who are defending kindred issues through Europe (e.g. the Catalan movement, the Provençal Movement, the Sardinian Movement, etc.). An international organisation to maintain and exploit linguistic and psychological differences must somehow or other be brought into being if the overwhelming tendencies of cosmopolitan finance to cut the masses of mankind off from their racial roots and turn them from distinct peoples into a huge promiscuous rabble destitute of culture and capable of being manipulated at will by the trustified press, *droit administratif*, and similar agencies are to be resisted. The danger is that the entire intellectual development of humanity may be short-circuited if the anti-cultural forces at work can create sufficient mobs of sub-men to submerge all cultural values in a common flux – unstable as water and incapable of excelling. From the scientific standpoint the ideas I am advocating are to be defended on the grounds that evolution proceeds from homogeneity to heterogeneity, and not otherwise – and it is therefore a denial of life itself which is ultimately involved by this 'economic legislation' which is seeking to reverse that process by the obliteration of differences and the promotion of a denationalised 'generality of mankind.'

THE JUNTA AND ITS GRIP

2. – The second point is that the idea I am advocating is in alignment with the increasing recognition of 'democracy as a delusion' and the self-determination of any people as a farce so long as representative assemblies, the will of the people, and so forth, are over-controlled by a junta of financiers whose very names are unknown to the public, but whose decisions are the reality responsible for so-called 'economic laws' and the multitudinous sham fights of 'mere politics'. 'Capital as a factor in evolution' requires to be considered in a very much more fundamental fashion than Sir Arthur Keith imagines: and the attempt to preserve our racial identities must make common cause with the movement which

is at last seeking to remove all those restraints upon the freedom of human development which are due to no fundamental laws, but to an arbitrary financial system. In this connection I shall have something to say in a future paper on the economic ideas De Valera has lately been manifesting, and the reason why he is advocating a high self-sufficiency for Ireland in salient contrast to the efforts of the Federation of British Industries and their Continental associates to abolish tariff barriers of all kinds and give scope to unrestricted international Free Trade. The self-sacrifice that will be involved in De Valera's policy is the moral principle upon which the active continuance of all culture must depend unless and until Credit Reform makes such needless sacrifice unnecessary, and inaugurates the Metaphysical Convention (see Saurat's *The Three Conventions*).

SENTIMENTAL NATIONALISM

3. – Those who have studied Spengler's *Downfall of The Western World*, and the antecedent Russian writings (Danilevsky's *Russia and Europe*, and Leontiev's *Average European as the Means and End of Universal Progress*) which inspired it, should realise the need to mobilise every possible resistance to the Zeitgeist (the tendency of the age, the 'time-stream' philosophy against which Mr Wyndham Lewis is so ably contending in his magazine *The Enemy*). International Finance is bent upon destroying the sub-conscious (the race memory) of all peoples and making them incapable of creative reaction against the Zeitgeist. Everything is to be sacrificed to the illusion of Progress and the sub-conscious elements capable of throwing up any effective cultural challenge to it put permanently out of commission by the destruction of all traditional continuities.

The bearing of these issues on Scottish nationalism, as on any other, can be realised when the folly of hoping, without any fundamental standing-ground, to maintain (let alone recover) any differentiated element or alternative potentiality on the sufferance of the over-ruling tendency already responsible for 'provincialising' it is appreciated, i.e., the advocacy, so common in Scotland, of 'sentimental nationalism' conjoined with the repudiation of all practical political intentions, or the attitude of Scottish Vernacular Revivalists superficially contending against political and economic forces which they sedulously refrain from really engaging, thus obtaining a little longer lease of life for debased dialects on terms so modified as to deprive them of all reconstructive power.

We must not allow ourselves to develop an 'inferiority complex' attitude to the causes we have at heart – to make them an excuse for lapsing back to lower levels of consciousness. Stress must be continually laid on what Mr Erskine calls 'modern applications' of them. They are of value only in so far as we do not seek in them any escape from, rather than a resolution of, the crucial problems of existence, and our constant endeavour should be to resist the all-too-easy compartmenting of our interests, and to act (in the Bolshevik sense) as 'cells' – i.e., to realise practical contemporary bearings and conduce to action; or in other words, to appreciate that the best defensive is always the offensive. The bearing of this on the repudiation of politics by such a body as An Comunn Gaidhealach will be readily apprehended.

A THREE TO ONE COMMITTEE

Another step, then, towards the ends I indicate in the *Pictish Review*, may be taken by the formation, not only of the Scottish Committee suggested there, but of what I may call a 'Three-to-One Committee' – a committee of representative Scots, Irishmen and Welshmen, on lines similar to the Scottish, to advance a far more practical and aggressive policy than that of the Pan-Celtic Congress – subverted as the latter has been by the development (as in the present English Cabinet – to adopt Mr Ramsay Macdonald's criticism) of a 'Y.M.C.A.' element on the one hand, and the 'Forty Thieves', the hangers-on and vulgarisers, on the other. Such a Committee could organise inter-activities along lines similar to the activities which the Scottish Committee would undertake in relation to Scotland itself; and their ultimate object would be to overturn the Anglo-Saxon ascendency in all British and Imperial connections. They could promote this by realising their mutuality of interest – by joint propaganda – by seeking to extend the publics of each to each other; and thus direct against England's hegemony an organised attack on three sides instead of having activities on each of the three sides so unrelated, and occasionally, mutually antagonistic as at present. Such a 'Three-to-One' Committee could do more – and do it far more speedily – than Ireland, Scotland and Wales acting separately, and not realising and taking full advantage of their ultimate identities of interest in this way can do – to falsify the prediction put forward the other day by the egregious Earl of Birkenhead when he claimed that 'The British Empire would endure because its citizens were all one people, the Anglo-Saxon race.'

The policy of the Three-to-One Committee would be to foster all the elements which at home and in the Colonies are endeavouring to destroy the Anglo-Saxon hegemony, and transform the character of the British Empire in all such ways as are calculated to enable it to reflect the traditions and aspirations of the three rather than – as hitherto – of the one.

C.M. Grieve, November 1927

from Neo-Gaelic Economics

As Katherine Mayo points out in her much-discussed book, *Mother India*, the immovable force which holds Indian womanhood in an unspeakable servitude – perpetuating the child-marriage and no-remarriage systems, precluding the victims from any escape from 'Purdah', from any utilisation of modern midwifery methods, and from any form of education – is the influence of the older women continually visiting on their juniors the pains and penalties they themselves had to survive to win to such authority. Similarly such a Socialist as Philip Snowden declares in favour of 'thrift' and against the abolition of struggle from the lives of the masses. Just as Gandhi can inveigh against the fiendish indifference to animal suffering, and even the economic stupidity of it, in cow-venerating India, so in the West the reconciliation of the existing economic system with so-called Christianity; such things as the ridiculing as impracticable of the recent Soviet peace proposals at Geneva, the general repudiation of 'fundamental' thought of any kind, and the cry (in its usual connotation) that 'you cannot put back the clock' – 'regret it as they may, men of commonsense must realise that there can be no return' to this, that, or the other – the force of circumstances is too strong.

All men are ready to admit that the time may come when the multiplication of labour-saving devices will largely, if not wholly, eliminate human drudgery. They are even prepared to admit that, when that time comes, the workless masses will not simply be put painlessly out of existence, but that the economic system, at present based on the principle of work, will be so modified as to permit their continued existence although they no longer work! But 'all this, of course, must be very gradual – frankly, it wouldn't do in the meantime – what would people do with their leisure?' Moralists of all kinds are anxious to postpone such a consummation of the natural tendency of civilisation to as remote a period as possible. And, thanks to the myopic policy of our bankers, politicians, industrialists, and selves in general, it is a tendency that is not developing so rapidly anywhere as to really alarm us. We can continue to distrust ourselves and humanity at large. We can continue to cheat each other out of all but the barest fraction of the real meaning and potentialities of life in the time-honoured fashion, with every possible assistance from the powers-that-be, civil, ecclesiastical, social and personal.

This 'instinctive' sense of the practical impossibility – despite whatever theoretic desirability – of too much 'highbrowism' of any kind, of such a thing as the abolition of usury, of general disarmament on the lines proposed by the Russian delegation at Geneva, or periodic 'national dividends' as proposed by Major Douglas – is the self-same psychological phenomenon that permits of minor divergencies in different directions of people who are otherwise the same – hence the fact that the 'Clyde Rebels' are only Calvinists with a sociological twist instead of a sectarian one (or, in addition to the latter), and, although they may be on the Left Wing in politics, are hopelessly Right Wing in regard to Arts and Letters; or, again, the fact that 'Jix' and Rosslyn Mitchell expressed themselves in practically the same terms apropos the new English Prayer Book. 'Scotland will never unite with people capable of taking such a step Romeward', says Rosslyn Mitchell, at the very same time that such very different, but at least equally good and representative Scots as John Buchan, the Very Rev. Dr Norman Maclean and Dr Garvie are expressing the very opposite views (apart altogether from the fact that this same Scotland has already very large Roman Catholic and English Episcopal elements).

In other words, the danger of our Movement, as of any movement or any man's mind, is not that of being too extreme, but of being not extreme enough. Even Gaelic enthusiasts are not anxious to return to the Gaelic commonwealth, or to embrace the abolition of usury as a principle in Neo-Gaelic Economics. They are willing only to 'think' about a Gaelic movement while remaining for the most part within the circle of the very conditions responsible for the progressive desuetude of the Gaelic language and all that it once connoted. They are so pathetically anxious to impress people as being 'reasonable' – as being, apart from some little detail or other, 'just the same as themselves'. Words like 'Communism', 'Revolution', etc., have become hopeless bogies to them. But it is utter folly to talk about reviving the Gaelic without appreciating that the Gaelic cannot be revived except by restoring social and economic conditions appropriate to it. It cannot be re-introduced and adapted to the existing system, the whole tendency of which has been responsible for its steady attenuation. 'Ideas are known by the company they keep' – and an enthusiasm for the Gaelic, together with a limpet-like clinging to the established order, is the acme of futility.

The extent to which all these things – language and life, politics and psychology – go together is admirably illustrated in Robert Graves's *Another Future of Poetry* (Hogarth Press), where, dealing with Skelton and Shakespeare, he says:

> The two principles of prosody correspond in a marked way with contrary habits of life, with political principles; the Continental, with the classical principle of pre-ordained structure, law and order, culture spreading downwards from the educated classes – the feudal principle; the native English, with what Mr John Ransom calls the Gothic principle, one of organic and unforeseen growth, warm blood, impulsive generosity, and frightful error – the communal principle, threatening the classic scheme from below… The future of English prosody depends enormously on the outcome of the class antagonism that undoubtedly is now in full swing. A Red victory would bring with it, I believe, a renewal of the native prosody in a fairly pure form, as the white domination of the eighteenth century made for pure classicism, and kept it dominant until the Romantic Revival, intimately connected with the French Revolution, re-introduced stress-prosody.

What has happened in Russian post-Revolution literature and language fully substantiates Graves's contention. Now it is 'economic considerations' that are responsible for the preference of English to Gaelic or Scots. If the class-struggle is merely one that will affect English prosody in the way described, what alternative – and greater – issue must we envisage as capable of disposing not merely of one or other of the two warring elements in English, but, so far as we are concerned, disposing of the economic and political pull of English altogether, or at least sufficiently to stimulate bi-lingualism in Scotland to any degree worth considering? If we cannot go the length of embracing a policy that includes abolition of usury, we can only at the very best put ourselves in the position of going backwards at an ever-increasing rate from the goal we have our eyes on. This goal is apt to seem irreconciliably different from what it actually is the further we recede from it in this fashion, although the fixity of our gaze may give us a comforting sensation of consistency no matter what changes are really taking place in our attitude.

An example of this illusion at work is excellently provided by such a leader as that which the *Dundee Courier and Advertiser* devoted to the recent report of the Gaelic Society of London.

> When the London Society declares that 'the soul of a nation is enshrined in its language, and when the language ceases to vibrate the nation is dead,' it merely indulges in a sounding contradiction of history. The Gaelic has been declining as a spoken language since Malcolm Canmore sat in Dunfermline town, and the soul of the nation manages to survive its retreat from by far the larger part of the area in which it once was spoken.

The soul of the nation displays itself, no doubt, to notable effect in this very leader-writer himself, prepared to recognise the virtues of the Gael in whatever contemporary platitudinarians are constrained to admire, just as anything and everything can depend upon its recognition as 'Christian' in the admirable accommodations of religion to the powers-that-be! 'Nine-tenths of the highland people', he goes on to aver, 'today use English in practically all the relations of life, but they are none the less highland on that account.' Nor will they be when the depopulation of the highlands is complete – so far as some other leader-writer of that day is concerned. 'What is of infinitely more importance than the decline of the Gaelic is the remorseless decline of the number of the highland people – a number which is falling heavily in every county, almost every parish, in the highlands'; he concludes, 'what the highlands want desperately is not the teaching of Gaelic in its schools, but a change in the disastrous economic system that is producing this effect.' Precisely.

The decline of the Gaelic is a consequence – not the cause – of the existing economic and political system; an inevitable result of it. Let us change the existing economic system, then, to produce the contrary effect. It may be a matter of indifference to our leader-writer whether, so long as the highlands are repopulated, the people speak English or Cherokee or Double-Dutch. But language goes along with other things – and it is a singular prejudice which would object to Gaelic and prefer English if the economic system which has favoured the latter were reversed. The whole reason for preferring English disappears as soon as it loses its economic advantages. The point therefore is to devise a polity which will not handicap – but, on the contrary, foster – Gaelic. Now, language not only expresses but to a large extent determines thought. Therefore such a policy can only be fully thought and expressed in Gaelic itself – and in a Gaelic that has not been 'standing still', but developing to suit such modern conditions as would be economically feasible were it possible, say, for a Council of Gaels to re-establish a Gaelic Commonwealth in Scotland capable of holding its own in the modern world in competition with nations very differently constituted. The first essential of such a Commonwealth would obviously be that it should be as self-sufficient as possible. To what extent can Gaelic make up that leeway which it has incurred by reason of its progressive decay in comparison with other languages which, during all the changes caused by the growth of modern industrialism, have been in the ascendant, and constantly adding to themselves and adopting themselves to more and more complex conditions of life and international relationships?

The first essential is the elaboration of a Gaelic theory – which is not only a looking-back to what used to be, as something static, but a critical and creative system able to get outside the almost instinctive assumptions they create and challenge all other existing systems and alternative proposals already before the public at all points; based on ancient Gaelic institutions, methods, and rules, but adapted to the infinitely more complex conditions existing today, and capable of devising a new dialectic which will put out of action all opposition based on the 'circumstances are too strong for us: you cannot put the clock back' delusion.

This can only be done by, on the one hand, a thorough reconsideration of Gaelic history and culture in the light of the present and with a view to the future; and, on the other, by an analysis of all the vital thought and tendencies of the world today from a Gaelic standpoint.

In particular, it is obvious that the difference between Russian Bolshevism and neo-Gaelic Communism will lie in the attitude to the arts. Can a Gaelic State in the light of tradition be envisaged in which the keystone of the arch would be the creation, recognition, and use of genius – in which, as a consequence, the synthesis of all the elements would be, not towards the most backward, but towards the most advanced, in which the utmost freedom would be the conscious and co-operative aim of all, and in which the mere means of life would be relegated to as subordinate a place as possible in relation to the ends? Such a state of Society would be in profound harmony with the essentials of the Gaelic genius.

To strive for it is to rally in our distinctive way to 'the defence of the West': to argue for it is again to make a contribution to civilisation in the name of our past; and to 'distinguish and divide' between favouring and antagonistic ideas in every department of human affairs is to exercise our raciality in a fashion which in itself strengthens and develops it.

C.M. Grieve, February 1928

Four Candidates: a study in relative worth

There are four candidates in the field for the Glasgow University Rectorial Election, which takes place in October next, namely, Mr Baldwin, Mr Samuel, Mr Rosslyn Mitchell and Mr R. B. Cunninghame Graham. What are their relative values? It is the fault of the present age to put an altogether disproportionate value on the mere politician. Count Hermann Keyserling is not far wrong, in his scathing indictment of the English character, when he says that mere political ability is probably an attribute of the animal stage – a thing to be outgrown when humanity grows to appreciate higher values; and Mr Compton Mackenzie, the famous novelist, who announced Mr Cunninghame Graham's candidature in independent Scottish Nationalist interests, was certainly right when he said that Mr Graham was one of the very few intelligent men who had occupied a seat in the English Parliament in recent times. The majority of MP's are nonentities, and owe their position to an inversion of all true values, similar to that which leads the false Scot to esteem a mere business man, lawyer, or civil servant above a man of creative genius, saint or sage. It was otherwise in the Gaelic Commonwealth. There is a tradition that literary men do not do well in Parliament. This means that Parliament is an instrument whereby less intelligent men succeed in securing a disproportionate say in affairs. It is not the literary men who are wrong – but the system.

But it is from a somewhat narrower point of view that I want to weigh up the relative values of these four men. How do they stand in relation to Scotland? There is a growing feeling amongst sensible men that Lord Rectors of Universities should not be chosen on merely party-political lines – they should represent something more than the exigencies of current politics. Glasgow has yet, perhaps, to realise the ignominy of having a 'Galloper Smith' for the Lord Rector of its University. St Andrews has set a slightly better example in adjuring party-politics and electing men like Barrie, Kipling, and Nansen – though even here qualitative standards can only have been very negligently applied. However that may be, surely it is not too much to ask that the Lord Rector of any University in Scotland should have a deep and informed regard for Scottish traditions, a genuine knowledge of and concern for, Scotland's condition today, and an inspiring and constructive attitude to its future.

Apart from English party-politics and their money-bags, Messrs Baldwin, Samuel, and Mitchell would never have been selected as candidates for such an election. Their intellectual status is nil; they have no attribute that singles them out above hosts of their fellow-men apart from the accidents of party-politics; they may be remembered to some slight extent in history, but surely a day will yet come when our descendants will marvel at the extraordinary fashion in which we apportioned honour among us when such as these had influence and were esteemed above those obscure elements of genius of which the mobs know nothing, but which are all that in the end remain to characterise any period of history, and to add to the heritage of humanity. Cunninghame Graham is the only one of these four men worth a moment's consideration from such a standpoint.

Baldwin is a half-Scot, but wholly an English Imperialist of the type directly responsible for Scotland's present ignominious position as a nation and its appalling social and economic conditions. The only Scotsman of the slightest intellectual distinction on his side in the House of Commons today – Mr John Buchan – who knows Scotland a million times better than Mr Baldwin knows anything but his bank-book, pigs, and pipe, has put it on record that Mr George Malcolm Thomson's terrible diagnosis and prognostications with regard to Scotland's position and prospects in *Caledonia* are substantially true, and that a great Scottish national awakening is long overdue and urgently necessary.

But Mr Baldwin does not think so. He has the hardihood, in view of the actual facts, to say that in Scotland 'progress has been greater in 1927 than in England, and there has been concurrently a marked decrease in pauperism'! His own Ministers had subsequently to supply facts and figures which gave him the lie direct. He went on to say: – 'In Scotland you are not superficial politicians; you try to get to the bottom of things.' The least superficial Scot would have the utmost difficulty in getting to the bottom of Mr Baldwin's ignorant and presumptuous attitude to Scottish affairs. The very reverse of what he claimed is Scotland's relative position to England. Is a man who comes North and insults the intelligence of every hearer who knows one iota of the truth in regard to Scotland today to be elected Lord Rector of a Scottish University? Mr Baldwin's own Administration has been openly and cynically contemptuous of Scotland's needs; and its policy has led to a very considerable worsening alike of our position and future prospects. Are we to have the anomaly of having the head of a Government which – in violation even of such safeguarding clauses as the corrupt Treaty of Union contained – is deliberately and systematically pursuing a policy which is designed to extinguish Scotland as a nation and reduce it finally to the category of an English country, honoured by our supposedly-intelligent youth? What a Gilbertian situation! If that does occur, it will, on the part of all who vote for him at least, afford substantial grounds for the old gibe that nothing less than a hammer and a twelve-penny nail will drive the point of a joke into the heads of certain types of Scotsmen. 'Honest Mr Baldwin.' How he will laugh up his sleeve – while proliferating in public all over the place about his Macdonald ancestry, Scottish grit, and what-not. He ought to be kidnapped before the election and compelled to spend the intervening period in the foetid atmosphere of one of Glasgow's backland tenements. His pigs are better housed than a substantial proportion of the Scottish population.

Samuel is a Jew. Asquith, in a passage in his *Memoirs* which have been appearing in the *Glasgow Herald*, comments with astonishment on Samuel's intense Jewish nationalism, his hopes for the Zionist movement. Samuel, at all events, cannot fail to realise the ignominy of Scotland preferring such as himself, or Baldwin, to anyone with a genuine love for, and knowledge of, his native country. What interest has Samuel in Scotland? None; but he would not like to see Horatio Bottomley Lord Rector of Jerusalem University. He would not like to see his own people treated as he and his type treat Scotland.

As for Rosslyn Mitchell, he is a Scotsman – of a kind; interested in all that is pseudo-Scottish, sentimental, 'kirky', and a lawyer – in fact, a typical example of the kind of Scot which our unfortunate country has bred in such large quantities since the Union, and advanced to places of 'honour' they could never have had in a country in which any decent values and traditions survived. His Scottish Nationalism – or, rather, his Scottish Home-Ruleism (he is not full-blooded enough to be a Nationalist) – is the typical Socialist blend, i.e., a kind that is resigned to its own indefinite postponement and to the progressive decay of everything that is of the slightest value in our nationality in the interval. Rosslyn Mitchell is the type of Scot who has been far too long dominant in our affairs – the type of Scot who must be wholly transcended before Scotland can once again take a worthy place nationally and internationally. What Scotland needs in nothing short of a psychological revolution which will 'blow the gaff' on its Rosslyn Mitchells and reduce them to their proper insignificance.

It is impossible to take these three candidates seriously. They are grotesque phenomena of a period when all true national values are sadly 'under the weather'. That people can be found to put forward such men for such a post in the present condition of Scotland, and the English parliament's undoubted responsibility for it, is only a further exemplification of our parlous and pitiable condition as a people.

Cunninghame Graham, even apart from his genuine Scottish Nationalism and the veridical spirit of Scotland which expresses itself in so magnificent a fashion in much of his writing, is as different from these three as chalk from cheese. He belongs to an altogether higher category. He is a man of genius. No one with any regard for what is really of significance in human personality; no one who is not prepared to put mere party-politics and miserable little hole-and-corner prejudices before the true values of life can possibly regard the other three as otherwise than utterly negligible in comparison with him. He alone of the four is a man whom the University of Glasgow can not only honour, but whose acceptance of any honour it bestows upon him also honours it in return. The most revealing thing about the other three is that they should have the impudence to set themselves up against him.

C.M. Grieve, June 1928

Nationalism and Socialism: *Forward* burkes the issue

Following upon articles by John S. Clarke, antagonistic to Nationalism in general and Scottish Nationalism in particular, C. M. Grieve wrote to the

Forward. That letter duly appeared together with a rejoinder by Mr Clarke. The discussion aroused considerable interest among *Forward* readers, as was proved by its notices to would-be correspondents that space did not permit of their intervention. Yet, with a further letter from Grieve to which Clarke replied, the controversy was abruptly closed down.

Mr Grieve certainly had not failed once more to attack. Thus, since the *Forward* offered its readers no reason for moving the closure, we can only presume either that things were getting too hot for John S. Clarke, or that the *Forward*, like other Anglo-Scots papers, prefers to attempt to smother discussion of this issue, in the vain hope that by ignoring the rising tide of Scottish Nationalism its progress may be stemmed. King Canute, wet his socks in a somewhat similar attempt. Scottish Nationalism cannot be ignored. Events will speedily prove that the issue is one that profoundly affects Scots Socialists and the constituents of Scots Labour MP's.

Ourselves, we are not moved by any desire to save the face of John S. Clarke. We therefore print the contribution from Mr Grieve which was suppressed by the *Forward*. And, if Mr Clarke has anything to add pertinent to the question, we shall not deny him space in our columns – provided that, in his manner of expression J. S. C. will endeavour to conform to the generally accepted standards of good taste. (Ed.)

WHY NEGLECT OUR HERITAGE?

I feel that Mr Clarke gets down to his true form when he is writing about 'human asses', 'mouldy corpses', and so forth. These phrases ring far more truly than his cant about living in brotherhood.

I am not going to quibble over his definition of Socialism, although the various sections of the international Socialist movement are never done doing so, and I fancy that Mr Clarke is very like Mr Guy Aldred, the anti-Parliamentary communist, with whom I debated this issue some time ago, in the sense that he is the only Socialist in the world who satisfies his own definition of the term once any analysis begins to be made of the latter. Theoretically a Socialist, Mr Clarke, in actual practice, is an English Imperialist.

But, taking Mr Clarke's definition of Socialism for what it is worth, the 'principle' may hold good in Timbuctoo as well as in Scotland, but, as I have already pointed out, there are practical limits to the fields of psychological unity possible even under conditions of World Socialism, and the temper or tone of any one of these fields at any given time would depend very largely upon the characters (and nationalities) of the 'heid bummers'. Mr Clarke has admitted that there are essential differences between peoples of different colours, and he presumably does not look forward to white domination of the Central African Socialist republic. Just as the 'ethos' of the latter would differ from that of his 'Socialist United States of Europe', so would the latter differ if Ramsay Macdonald was its Chief Executive from what it would be with Stalin in that capacity. My point is – as every delegate to International Conferences knows – that there are fundamental national differences, and that anti-national Socialism (which is quite unlike the Socialist movements of France, Germany, Russia, or even England, which have always been thoroughly national) proposes in the last analysis a transference of European power to that nation with the greatest voting strength irrespective of all qualitative distinctions.

I may have a 'lack of contact with life's realities', but I certainly cannot imagine anything more remote from any likelihood of embodiment in practical politics than such a proposal. M. Delaisi has said that no form of human government is possible without a myth of some sort, and I have solid ground for believing that humanity will continue to prefer the myth of nationalism as their 'directive fiction' to the myth of Socialism, which promises a United States of Europe dominated by Germans or Russians, or perhaps Jews, i.e., a form of 'internationalism' as like the present one as Bolshevism is like Fascism.

FREEDOM TO PROGRESS

In any case, as I have already insisted, the different peoples of Europe (even the English) preserve the national characters of their Socialist movements to an extent which reasonably raises the question as to why Scottish Socialists are so fearful of doing likewise. Why must they be 'thirled' to English politics? We should probably have had a Scottish Socialist Government in power long before this if Scotland had broken away from England – and, with that, we could have moderated England's imperial and international policy to a far greater extent than we could do as matters stand, even if our entire Scottish representation at Westminster were Socialist.

Our purblind anti-national Scottish Socialists have, in fact, sacrificed Scottish Socialism to English requirements in the most irrational fashion. Socialism is not incompatible with Nationalism; there is nothing whatever to prevent the growth of Socialism in a Scottish Free State any more than in France or Germany – there is no reason to suppose that that growth would be slower in a Scottish Free State than under the present conditions of affairs – it all depends upon the Scottish people. It is absurd to say that Scottish Nationalism, therefore, is a capitalist dodge – or an anti-capitalist one – although it may well develop a tendency in the former direction for a time if Scottish Socialists persist in violent, vituperative, and insensate anti-Nationalism of the kind served up by Mr Clarke. The sooner they waken up to the fact that a profound development is taking place in Scottish national consciousness, and adjust themselves to it, the better. What of other Scottish Socialists? Do they agree with Mr Clarke? Does the Rev. James Barr do so? Or Mr Tom Johnston? Any more than Keir Hardie would have done!

THE 'INFERIORITY COMPLEX'

There is no question whatever of the appalling anti-intellectualism of Scottish

Socialism, or of the fact that that is part and parcel of the provincialisation and decadence that has overtaken Scotland as a result of the long neglect of Scottish affairs by the English Parliament and the consequent development of an 'inferiority complex' by the great majority of Scots. It is significant in this connection that the only creative artist of the slightest international reputation who has ever been associated with the Scottish Socialist Movement (Mr R. B. Cunninghame Graham) has long since repudiated all connection with it, and now belongs to the Scottish National Party.

I remember a year or two ago sending to *Forward* an article on certain European Socialist poets. It was returned with a note by Mr Emrys Hughes stating that *Forward* was, unfortunately, obliged to 'cater for the mob'. I do not mention this because I bear any grievance over the rejection of my MS; but my feeling at the time was that Scottish Socialists could do with a good deal more acquaintance with international Socialist writings, and more particularly foreign literature inspired by Socialist feeling; but there were very narrow limits to the type of internationalism *Forward* could see its way to promulgate! Nor have these widened since. Mr Clarke knows as well as I do that the proportion of intellectually-convinced Socialists among Socialist voters is exceedingly small, and if, in arguments like this, I seem to be charging the Socialists with defects which they have in common with Liberals and Tories, it is because the former make by far the greater idealistic claims.

It is therefore reasonable to ask now, even while they have not yet attained to political power, for some earnest of these in other directions, say in literature. This the Scottish Socialist Movement (even with Mr Joe Corrie) cannot supply. All they propose to Scotland is its continued and completed submergence in the 'greater whole' of England – an indirect admission that Scots people are, unlike the French, or German, or English, unfit to govern themselves, and therefore obliged to remain in permanent political pupilage to England, while as to any question of continuing or intensifying 'distinctive Scottish culture', the Scottish Socialist leaders are as indifferent to that as the majority of their followers are to anything above the cultural level of *Forward*.

The fact that the latter are so cut off from all that is worth while in arts and letters may be due to the Capitalist system; but it does not help matters for them to say: 'We have been done out of our heritage, therefore we will deny that it exists; we will decry it as a mere Capitalist or bourgeois luxury – something not worth having – and employ our defects in proving that they are superior to what the Classes have gained by victimising us. Instead of endeavouring to undo what the Capitalists have done to our souls, we will make these (lopsided, underdeveloped, and degraded as they are) the basis of our Socialist Commonwealth.'

Scottish Nationalism certainly stands for a very different principle.

C.M. Grieve, September 1928

Scottish Nationalism versus Socialism

Mr Ramsay Macdonald seems to know as little about Scottish Nationalism as he knows about the Scottish Renaissance Movement; and to understand as little what is required for the reconstruction of Scotland as a nation as he understands of the pre-requisites for any national literary and artistic movement worth talking about. This is not surprising. He owes his position to his abilities as a Parliamentary politician and a demagogue. Even his best friends would scarcely claim that he is a thinker of any consequence.

Socialism, like everything else, is a product of a few intellectuals. The Socialist movement, although its popular manifestations mirror them very poorly – although the conceptions of Socialism entertained in the mind of most so-called Socialists are a confused and worthless agglomeration bearing little relation to the real source whence they are derived – owes its power and evolutionary momentum and its significance to the ideas promulgated by these thinkers. Mr Ramsay Macdonald is not of their number.

Scottish Socialism has added little, or nothing, to Socialist thought. It is because of this fact – that they have taken over their ideas ready-made in this way – that Socialism in Scotland has operated so demoralisingly, and is associated in the main with such crude mentalities as that of Davie Kirkwood, and with Calvinistic repressionists whose personalities belie the ideal of freedom their lips invoke. Ex nihilo nihil fit; there is nothing in the personnel of the present Scottish Socialist MP's whence anything of the slightest advantage to Scotland can come.

A CLASH OF INTERESTS

Mr Macdonald himself is aware of this; hence his rebuking of Maxton, Kirkwood, and the like, and his impatience with the 'Socialism in our time' slogan. But although he recognises the deadly evils Scotland is suffering from today, and professes a deep and grave concern for his native country, he cannot see his way to join with the National Party to end the intolerable situation and take part in a great national reconstructive effort. he is too blinded by the party system to be able or willing to co-operate with fellow-Scotsmen of other parties in this great task, although he knows that his own party has no monopoly of wisdom. He says that industrial questions must come first; but wilfully refuses to recognise that it is just because of the grave industrial and commercial problems of Scotland today – and the increasing recognition that the great disparity between English and Scottish conditions in this respect implies that it is not the operation of similar forces that is responsible or the application of the same solution that will suffice – that the new Scottish Nationalism is making such headway.

Scottish interests and English are not a unity; they are increasingly antagonistic – and it is absurd to contend that the former must wait on the latter until the process of Scottish ruin is complete. Mr Macdonald says that many Scotsmen with wide international interests are in favour of Scottish Home Rule, but cannot give it precedence over these 'wider issues'.

The reply to that is two-fold – (1) There is no other country in the world more urgently requiring reconstructive effort today than Scotland, and none that will more amply and promptly repay it; (2) There is nothing whatever to prevent these Scots doing their duty to Scotland, and at the same time maintaining as fully these 'wider issues' as they are at present doing from the platform of Westminster. Mr Macdonald's argument proceeds from a failure to recognise that Scottish Nationalism does not propose to relinquish Scottish interest or influence in Imperial or International affairs, but to regain them. It also involves a blindness to the tendencies of Imperial development and the certainty of the rapid reduction of England's ascendency and the supersession of Westminster as our Imperial Parliament. Mr Macdonald is thinking in terms of mere Home Rule. The sooner he realises that Scottish Nationalism will be content with nothing of the sort the better.

The devolutionary proposals of the Liberal and Socialist parties are hopelessly behind the times; and would, if put into effect, worsen rather than improve Scotland's position – by permanently provincialising us and preventing the emergence of a distinctive Scottish National idea, capable of contributing to the solution of the great problems of modern civilisation along its own lines, which is the aim and object of the National Party. We are not going to be confined within the mentality of English politics at all. We are out for something far bigger – the liberation of the dynamic soul of Scotland once again, without extraneous let or hindrance. Nothing else will regenerate Scotland or enable it to assume once again the place it ought to have in the comity of nations.

Mr Macdonald is afraid of the development of a 'one-idea Nationalism'. Does he really believe that men like R. B. Cunninghame Graham, Compton Mackenzie, Erskine of Marr, C. H. Douglas, and Lewis Spence are less alive to international issues than he is?

It is a false internationalism he stands for, this Welsh MP.

THE NATION AND THE WORLD

True internationalism, and true nationalism go hand in hand. If he had known more about the Scottish Renaissance Movement, Mr Macdonald would have known that it has largely been a refecundation of Scottish culture by the foreign influences most congenial to the Scottish genius, and from which we have been too long cut off by the disastrous predominance of English influences amongst us.

Mr Macdonald professes to be more interested in Scottish arts and letters than in the political side of the Scottish movement. It is precisely because of the necessity of full political autonomy to the redevelopment of distinctive Scottish arts and letters that practically every young Scottish writer and artist of any consequence is a member of the National Party. But while thus stressing the cultural side at the expense of the political, Mr Macdonald does not scruple to cite as contemporary Scottish authors of consequence, Joe Corrie and James Welch, while ignoring writers who have contributed infinitely better work. The latter (although they are thereby the less mercenary and earn less, although, many of them, are just as much working men as Corrie) have concentrated on the more difficult task of the Renaissance – tasks which have little or no popular appeal, and are therefore all the more easily ignored or misrepresented.

But we expect more of an ex-Prime Minister, with Mr Macdonald's professions and pretensions, than this bitter partisan dealing in a matter of this kind. Mr Macdonald is, of course, no literary critic. But let him submit Corrie's work or Welch's to any literary critic of repute – to any one, say, of the brilliant reviewers of the *Daily Herald* – and he will speedily find out that, whatever merit they may have as Socialist propaganda, the writings of Corrie, Welch, and the like, are utterly negligible from the purely literary point of view. There would never be a literary renaissance worth a brass farthing if it depended upon mentalities such as theirs. Splendid work is being done in Scotland today notably by Mr Lewis Spence (whom Mr Macdonald so deliberately refrained from mentioning), but the impulse behind it is Nationalism not Socialism.

A Socialist Government may be returned to power to-morrow; it will not necessarily benefit Scotland one iota – it will not necessarily address itself at all to counter the forces which are making for the aggrandisement (in man and money) of England at the expense of Scotland. It may take over the whole of the means of production, distribution, and exchange, without altering the adverse bias in economic, industrial, and commercial tendency, which is discriminating against Scotland in favour of England.

Something other is wanted – a change of mentality amongst the people of Scotland, a determination not to submit themselves to the abject adjustments involved in these alleged 'economic necessities'. Only the National Party can create that spirit. Under Socialism what is to prevent the Anglicising of Scotland continuing? The great masses of our population to whom the Socialist appeal is addressed are already so Anglicised, and have so little knowledge of Scotland and Scottish history and literature, that to depend upon them to re-Scotticise Scotland, even if they had such a measure of devolution as the Socialists and Liberals propose, is farcical.

IS IT TO BE A LEVELLING DOWN?

A great cry is being made just now about the miners – but the former landowners, the old historic families of Scotland, are as badly off. Are the former of more consequence to Scotland than the latter? Given equal wealth and circumstances (and the necessary number of generations to acquire decent breeding and civilised interests) the former would at best be not dissimilar from the latter. Admittedly the great masses of the workers have been cut off from participation in the great heritage of art and letters, and the art of living; but there is a danger in destroying what has already been achieved in this direction in the hope of achieving for another set of the people or the whole people, in the long run, something not dissimilar.

That is the danger of the Socialist championship of a class – as against the Nationalist espousal of the interests of the whole people. Workers are inveighing against Capitalism; but their employers are also hard put to it. Cannot some economic policy to match the Nationalist concern for the whole people be substituted for the Socialist concern for a section and the spirit of class antagonism it carries with it? Some such economic policy should be part and parcel of the national programme; it should be the master idea which represents the reassertion of our national genius in the sphere of economics – and it is to hand!

The Socialists hate it like poison. It reconciles the interests of Capitalist and wage-earner, rich and poor. It brings the antithesis, upon which party politics are founded, into a new synthesis compatible with a national ideal. Tories, Liberals and Socialists can equally espouse it – although their psychological dispuritives make them Tory or Liberal or Socialist there is no need for them to disregard any longer their common interest in this connection and perpetuate the false antagonisms which are playing into the hands of the bankers – the international financiers – playing one section off against another. This is the Douglas System of Social Credit.

There is bound to be a profound connection in the fact that a Scotsman of Douglas's calibre should emerge in this particular connection at this particular juncture. There is. Douglas feels it. That is why he has joined the National Party. That is why men like Major Galloway, Mr John S. Kirkbride, Mr H. M. Murray, Mr Laurence McEwan, Captain A. G. Pape, Mr William Wilson, Mr James Malcolm, Mr James Murray, and scores of others, have joined us or are attracted to us. We need a principle in economics as in every other sphere of arts and affairs, uniquely in accord with our national genius and capable of being seen in retrospect as the world-mission of the new Scotland – something not only of paramount importance to Scotland itself, but representing a contribution of such moment to world affairs as to constitute a worthy contribution to the solution of international problems to mark the definite re-emergence of Scotland as a distinctive entity among the nations of the world. We have that here. Will Mr Macdonald or any of his henchmen debate it with us?

It will be easy to show that it is in accordance with the principles of the ancient Gaelic Commonwealth; that it supersedes the economic differences of Conservatism and Liberalism on the one hand and Socialism on the other; and that it effectively challenges that standardisation and robotisation of humanity towards which International Capitalism is now tending, and towards which International Socialism would only more quickly hasten us. It affords a means for the retention and revival of individual and national values. Mr Ramsay Macdonald deplores the decadence of old centres like Edinburgh, but is afraid that the attraction of London is too great. But has he ever tried to find a means of overcoming this cursed Metropolitanism, and the soulless Cosmopolitanism to which it in turn is tributary?

The problem is only susceptible of solution on a deeper analysis than the Socialist movement has given it. But the solution is implicit in the new Nationalism which says: 'It matters to us whether we remain Scotsmen – or Englishmen, Canadians, or what not. We are not going to have our distinctive potentialities obliterated by any over-riding power, whether it be English-controlled politics, or the little junta of international financiers, who in turn control *that*. We believe that where there is a will there is a way, and that we have found it.'

C.M. Grieve, February 1929

Towards a Scottish Renaissance: desirable lines of advance

The Editor asks me this month for a 'contribution, limited in extent but wide in its sweep, on the needs, signs, prospects, and tendencies of renaissance of national culture in Scotland.' 'This', he continues, 'is an impossible, outrageous request, but we wish to make our May issue a resumé, catalogue of ideas, as comprehensive as our totally inadequate space allows, of the main aspects of the Scottish National case.'

I would say, in the first place, then, that what Scotsmen today have to remember first of all is that Professor Gregory Smith is right when he points out that Scots is in many respects a superior literary medium to English; and that our abandonment of it is therefore a sacrifice of superior (or, at least, distinctive) values to inferior ones. Such a sacrifice has its consequences in every sphere of our national life. If we thought in Scots instead of English our social, economic and political ideas would be different. We are told that Scots, and, even more, Gaelic, have had to give way owing to over-ruling economic tendencies – but had they? Are these tendencies good in themselves? Is mankind made for economics or economics by mankind? The logical conclusion of the process our opponents defend is the negation of not only nationality, but of personality. In the last analysis this is a reductio ad absurdum of their case.

AN ADEQUATE, DISTINCTIVE MEDIUM

Can Scots be revived as an effective medium for the full range of literary purpose? Yes. Similar feats have been accomplished elsewhere on behalf of less inherently important media of expression. The necessary experimentation to bring Scots out of its present disintegrated condition into full literary effectiveness – and bring it abreast of modern consciousness – is in line with the most significant tendencies in world literature today instead of being the fad our opponents call it.

The task has been begun in Scotland, and is attracting increasing numbers of able young writers. It has a solid basis so far as an adequate potential public is concerned in the extraordinary tenacity of Scots in the lives of a very large proportion of our people, despite their idealogical [*sic*] and practical Anglicisation; and a still more vital justification in the psychological outrage and mental retardation and blunting which the continuing English-ascendancy-tradition of extirpating Scots from our children in our schools is still perpetrating. Most Scottish children have an entirely different linguistic atmosphere at home and in school, and their compulsory adjustment to the latter is indefensible.

But the revival of Scots is only a half-way house. It is time to conceive of Scots not as an intermediate step on the way towards English, but on the way back to Gaelic. Whatever is done in Scots will have its own values, but the best Scots writers to-day all realise that the national potentialities of Scots (as apt from its potentialities for any individual writer) are limited, and that a basis for major forms – for a culture in the real sense of the term, of not only national but international consequence – can only be secured by a return to Gaelic and a resumption and modern application of the classical principles of Gaelic culture.

The mob-mind cannot be expected to appreciate this; and popular journalism lives by pandering to the mob-mind. But no sane citizen of Scotland can deny that it is deplorable that Scotland, alone of European countries, has not even one representative literary organ. Even the *Glasgow Herald*, when its chosen field is invaded by English combines, cries that it is a national organ and protests against the threatened Londonisation of Scottish opinion – thereby conceding the whole case of Scottish nationalism, although, with stupidity, it continues to deny it except in so far as its own private interests are concerned. But if Londonisation is a menace in ordinary journalism (which is little more than backstairs gossip writ large) how infinitely more serious it is that all the literary organs circulating in Scotland are London products. From a cultural standpoint the *Glasgow Herald* and *Scotsman* – the best we have – are infinitely below such periodicals as *The Irish Statesman*, *The New Age*, or *The Criterion*. There is no reason why they should be – except that their editors have a low view of their function. The Man-in-the-Street cannot, if it is put to him, refute this argument; it is the thin end of the wedge to compel him to admit the whole of our cultural case.

THE ACCEPTANCE OF ENGLISH CULTURE

It may be driven in a little further by reminding him that Scotland is the only country which has ever voluntarily given an alien culture precedence in its schools, and eschewed its own. Scottish literature and Scottish history should form the staple of the literature and history lessons in our schools. There is no earthly reason why English literature should be taught to any greater extent than German, French or Italian. The re-Scotisation of Scottish education is a programme no sane Scot can oppose. Any attempt to do so is to put himself in a position no citizen of any other country – above all, no Englishman! – would contemplate for a moment. As well abandon his own personality and merely imitate somebody else! He may say – 'but Scottish literature is relatively poor'! The answer is that if during the past two hundred years it had had the same facilitation, financial and otherwise, it might have been just as much greater – and may even yet make up the difference.

Any other objections are easily met. They are, and can, only be advanced by those who know little or nothing of Scots, and still less of Gaelic, literature and history, and whose views of what is feasible and desirable in cultural tendency are wholly Anglicised but readily susceptible of being reduced to absurdity by those whose knowledge of cultural evolution is not confined to English ideas. The way to make these attitudes preposterous is not to argue with them at all, but to treat them with contempt and appeal right over them and right past England altogether to Europe, and, simultaneously with that propaganda of ideas, create new works in Scots and Gaelic, which by their intrinsic merit will vindicate the new movement in the eyes of all intelligent people, and so come to represent the new Scotland in a fashion to which all the ideas of our own denationalised people are simply negligible. It is in the power of a handful to create or re-create a country in this powerful spiritually dynamic way, and to convict their antipathetic fellow-countrymen of a species of imbecility in the face of the world. The next – or the next – generation will hasten to remove the reproach; and readjust itself to the concepts of these few.

For still deeper reasons aristocratic standards must be re-erected. We in Scotland have been too long grotesquely over-democratised. What is wanted now is a species of Scottish Fascism. The real hope of the Scottish Movement today is that our younger people are everywhere intuitively realising this. Let us completely disassociate ourselves from all the attitudes of mind, from all the modes of activity, which have been and are part and parcel of our denationalised and cultureless condition. Let us take a typical Anglo-Scot, opposed to Nationalism, ignorant of Scots and still more of Gaelic, and carefully catalogue all that he takes for granted as reasonable, natural, and inevitable in any connection – and repudiate the lot, and take up the very opposite positions.

A NEW PSYCHOLOGY

Above all, let us make ourselves psychologically different – let us so react from all these people are and do that it ceases to be a conscious opposition on our part, but becomes the very essence of our nature to be motivated in the very contrary fashion. They are all so 'reasonable', so 'moderate'; let us, then, be utterly irrational and extreme. This new psychology is beginning to manifest itself amongst our young people.

It must be clearly realised that the Scottish National Theatre Movement, the Scottish Musical Festival Movement, the Vernacular Circles, Comunn

Gaidhealach, etc., etc., bear the same relation to our objective as the Scottish Home Rule Association or the measures of devolution offered by the Liberal and Labour parties do to the aims and objects of the National Party. They are all in their various degrees petty inferiority complex manifestations run by negligible people. They have been unable to generate anybody of any consequence in regard to their particular objects, for the simple reason that the spirit animating such movements is trivial. *Ex nihil, nihil fit.*

Fundamental developments inevitably produce big men. That is the main criticism of the National Party so far. There is something wrong with it; it has not produced real leaders – or its organisation is still of such a kind as to frustrate them instead of develop them. What I have said about the need for aristocratic standards, for a species of Fascism, applies equally here. I feel we will never make real headway till we cease to imitate English organisations by running the party on democratic lines – or wanting anything similar either in organisation or programme to the English parties.

Mr Spence in last month's *S.I.* complained of 'youngsters who speak of us as if we were already moss-grown antiquities' – and have taken over the doctrines put forward by us – 'the original Scottish Nationalists' – as if they were their own property. Well, they are. I welcome these youngsters. The more the merrier. I am willing to be superannuated as soon as anybody can do it. The quicker I become out-of-date – the further the new tendencies run beyond my reach – the better pleased I will be; the more my own propaganda will be justified. If there is one thing in Heaven and Earth I do not desire, it is to see the Scottish Movement subjected to the mortmain of Lewis Spence or Hugh McDiarmid. I hope we may both prove Kerenskis who will be speedily superseded by appropriate Lenins. I do not underestimate Mr Spence and all that he has done. Far from it. But it is possible for all of us to outlive our usefulness, and, if we really have a movement at heart, it behoves us to see that we don't. I am not saying this has happened or will happen to Mr Spence; but he is next to saying it, and, if he resents it, he should in justice to himself allow somebody else, rather then himself, to question the value of the tendencies in question from the point of view of the Movement as a whole.

PHENOMENA OF TRANSITION

The Scottish National Academy of Music is a farce. The occupancy of Chairs of History in Scottish Universities by Englishmen – the lack of Chairs of Scottish literature – the relegation of Scottish arts and affairs to a negligible role in our schools – the starving of the Scottish National Library – the scandal of our National Records – these, and a score of other things of like nature, are immediate issues to which we must address ourselves. But a new national consciousness is manifesting itself; the increased interest in so-called Scottish literature of all kinds, and in all manner of quasi-national stunts and societies and developments, is a sign of it.

These things have no significance in and for themselves except as transitional phenomena. They do not yet, alas, constitute anything like the Maelstrom Mr Spence depicts. The sooner they can be brought to that boiling point the better. Mr Spence's phrase about the need to put a strong curb upon the blatant egotism of many of Scotland's protagonists lends itself with fatal readiness to a mere tu quoque. The time for synthesis is far away. Let us not attempt any premature formulation. Except in certain of the concepts of Mr Erskine of Marr there is nothing being expressed in Scotland today that corresponds to anything a Scottish Nationalist should regard as the end of his propaganda. He is our 'point of honour'. Short of that, for one reason or another, we would be simply short-circuiting our own propaganda.

All these hesitations and restraints, and anxieties to keep within bounds and be reasonable, are the by-products of merely partially de-Anglicised minds. Their political issue would be no more than a Scottish equivalent of the Irish Free State, and their cultural issue pastiche at the best. I want a great deal more in both directions. And in every other direction. I may not get it; but at least I can work with others only in so far as they, too, are seeking the same ultimate objectives, and will never have any hesitation in explicitly dissociating myself from them if they reach their 'saturation level' before I do. Any other attitude is only a variant of the *Glasgow Herald's* sneers at 'people who seek Tir-nan-Og'.

Hugh McDiarmid, May 1929

The Stewartry Observer
1927–1930

Scotland and Emigration

The emigration season has begun again, and will soon be in full swing. This is the sort of paragraph which is appearing in the papers: –

> During the week-end several liners are due to leave the Clyde for Quebec, the St. Lawrence River being again free from ice and open to navigation. The Canadian Pacific liners Montrose and Melitia and the Anchor Donaldson Alaunia leave today. The Melitia has on board a number of domestic and farm servants and other 1200 passengers will embark at Glasgow today. The Montrose is taking to Canada the first batch of ex-service men who are going out to the land under the Legion scheme. All the men were trained on the instructional farm of the Ministry of Labour in Suffolk, and the women folk have also been taught to milk cows and rear poultry. The Alaunia, which will be the first to leave, will embark 300 Scottish passengers at the Tail of the Bank today.

And so on. Similar paragraphs will appear weekly all through the summer and autumn. Scottish applicants for admission to America, according to the US Consul in Glasgow, number many times the quota. In all it is anticipated that the drain of emigration during the forthcoming season will deplete Scotland of upwards of 60,000 inhabitants.

The actuating causes in the overwhelming majority of cases are unemployment, the relatively low rates of wages and meagre opportunities for advancement in this country, and the absence of an effective agricultural policy. Recent replies in the House of Commons show that the proportion of Scottish soil thrown out of cultivation is steadily being increased, and that rural depopulation is continuing at a still greater proportion. It cannot be over-emphasised that emigration is not helping to solve our economic ills, but worsening them. To a very large extent those who are emigrating are those we can least afford to lose. If the effect of the emigration was to transfer the surplus unemployed of our city-dwellers to 'fresh fields and pastures new' there might be a great deal to be said for it. But it is doing nothing of the kind. It is taking away the cream of our agricultural labour. This is labour of a kind which is largely irreplacable. The great majority of our urban unemployed cannot take their places. Their emigration represents a loss of inherited ability and temperamental and trained suitability of a kind indispensable to the regeneration of our rural areas. Worst of all is the fact that they are being compelled to go to the Colonies or elsewhere to do and produce precisely what they should and could be doing and producing here. And the majority do not want to go. Let there be no mistake about that. They would infinitely rather stay at home – if there was work for them to do and any chance of getting decent living conditions out of it.

The great congestion and shocking housing conditions of our cities, coupled with acute unemployment is the result of the policies which were set into motion with the Industrial Revolution; but it is generally realised that we have been behind-hand in not at the same time doing what we could do to maintain a sound and progressive agricultural economy as the essential auxiliary of a sound urban development. The latter has developed abnormally at the expense of the former; and now world-conditions have placed us at an acute disadvantage because of our lack of prescience in this connection. We have been so intent upon our manufacturing export trade that we have largely neglected our home market, although that is four times more important than the former. Now we have lost – and, in all likelihood, permanently – many of our foreign markets, and as a consequence the vital importance of our agricultural industry is being realised afresh. The circumstances call for a general re-orientation of our national activities on a 'Back to the Land' basis. These remarks apply both to England and Scotland; but the position in regard to the latter is immensely worse than in regard to the former.

Scotland is under-populated rather than over-populated today. In this respect it differs entirely from England. Yet Scottish emigration is – and has been for many years – almost four times as great as that of England, but the Government persists in applying the same policy to each. The principle is to legislate for England, and then to apply the same policy to Scotland, as if the conditions in both countries were exactly the same. No cognisance is taken by the House of Commons or by governmental departments of the essential differences in the economical conditions and requirements of the two countries. They are treated alike – but the treatment that is good for England is suicidal for Scotland. Scotland requires a different policy altogether, and there is no likelihood of its acquiring anything of the kind until Scottish control over Scottish affairs is re-established through the medium of an independent Scottish Parliament. The record of the House of Commons in regard to Scottish rural problems is a shameful one of progressive dereliction. Nothing constructive has been attempted. Ample land is available for settlement; any number of suitable applications for such settlements are forthcoming; schemes for such settlements are in existence – but nothing is done to correlate these three things. Instead of that, Parliament and Government Departments and all the force of officially-inspired propaganda is brought to bear to induce an increasing flow of emigration from Scotland – and yet with it all unemployment in Scotland remains 50% worse than it is in England. It is time that the actualities of Scottish affairs were being realised and made the basis of a definite Scottish policy, and the continuance of the present policy of national ruination challenged. The Colonies may require development – but is Peter to be robbed to pay Paul? What is gained if Canada is developed at the expense of the dereliction of Scotland? It seemed to be forgotten, when Imperial development is discussed, that Scotland is a part of the Empire, surely as worthy of development as any.

Special Correspondent, 12 May 1927

Scottish Rural Problems: the necessity of co-operative methods

It is being more and more thoroughly recognised that an obstinate conservatism is at the root of Britain's failure to readjust itself successfully to changed conditions of the post-war world – but no means have yet been devised for getting rid of it. While this conservatism is to be found in every department of industry and commerce, it exists in its most intense and obdurate form in relation to agriculture. This is largely due to the comparative neglect of agriculture in Great Britain since the Industrial Revolution. That great movement, which made this country the financial centre and chief export and manufacturing country in the world, seems to have spent itself so far as we are concerned. We can no longer claim primacy in any of these directions. Countries that we formerly supplied with manufactured goods can now supply themselves; some of them are even in a position to compete with us. Our foreign markets have thus been restricted, in many directions permanently, and, as a consequence, we are being driven to a fresh realisation of the actual and potential importance of our agricultural industry. More and more we may have to depend upon it and try to reverse to an effective degree that great movement which has depopulated our countrysides and congested our towns. Efforts are already being made to devise progressive agricultural policies based on the actual conditions and requirements of our country, but little has yet been achieved towards rural regeneration, and this lack of success is largely due to the deep-seated conservatism already mentioned, and, along with it, the vicious uneconomic attitude of those presently administering the industry – an attitude which is due to the false position it has so long occupied and the unrealistic treatment it has received for political and other reasons.

It cannot be too strongly emphasised in this connection that the circumstances and needs of agriculture in Scotland are so different from those in England that an entirely different policy is required for the two countries. There is little hope that any suitable policy will be applied to Scotland so long as the matter depends upon an overwhelmingly English House of Commons, ignorant of, and indifferent to, these differences. If only for this reason, the sooner the control of Scottish affairs passes into the hands of a Scottish Parliament again the better. The psychology and traditions of the people are as intimately bound up with the condition and prospects of agriculture as the actual topographical, climatic, marketing, scientific, and other factors, and although the same essential principle characterised the English policy and the Scottish, the application of it to the existing circumstances would have to be entirely different in the two cases. That intimate and flexible relation between theory and practice cannot be achieved so far as Scotland is concerned by a system of control centralised in London and largely preoccupied with distinctively English interests. Indeed English and Scottish interests are in many directions in agriculture sharply at variance. It is hopeless in such cases to expect fair treatment for Scotland from a legislature where the Scottish representation is hopelessly outnumbered and can be systematically outvoted.

Probably the solution for our agricultural problems lies in an application of co-operative principles to the industry in a fashion adjusted to suit the specific nature and needs of the country. There is, however, no direction in which the basic conservatism of our agriculturists is encountered in a more adamantine form than when this question of co-operation is broached. Despite all the experience of other countries, they will have nothing to do with it. The problem, therefore, is predominantly a psychological one. Somehow or other this irrational antipathy must be overcome. The question is how.

The extent to which this antipathy is carried is admirably illustrated in the remarks made the other day by Sir Archibald Weigall when he announced the death of the Lincolnshire Co-operative Bacon Factory. An English writer commenting on this case very aptly says: – 'No one needs to be told at this time of day what a miracle agricultural co-operation has worked in the state of Denmark. It has converted a poor country into a rich country. It has enabled Denmark to snatch the bacon and butter market of their country from under the very noses of our own obdurate and antiquated farmers. Even now we have not begun to take the lesson seriously to heart. The Lincolnshire incident is a case in point. The Society was formed, but of the 600 members, according to Sir Archibald, only sixty regularly did business with the factory. Some of them even used the factory to enable them to get better prices from the dealers.'

So long as the Lincolnshire farmer 'did the dirty' like that, said Sir Archibald, there was no hope of his ever being able to understand the fundamentals of co-operative marketing.

The fact is that while the foreign farmer is learning to help himself, the English farmer is looking to be spoon-fed from the State with subsidies for this and tariffs for that.

And meantime the foreign farmer, especially the Danish farmer, having learned that union is strength and that co-operative buying, selling, financing, and instruction are the key to success, is snatching the English market out of the hands of the English producer.

What applies to England here applies in equal measure to Scotland. Scottish agriculturists are no whit less obdurate and unenterprising in this connection than their southern confrères. In the adjustment of co-operative schemes to the actual conditions of the various branches of the Scottish agricultural industry, very different methods and forms of organisation would have to be employed than in England – but the essential principle of co-operation must be the ultimate solution in both countries, and, in both, there is the same initial necessity to overcome a deadweight of blind prejudice or a vicious dependence on uneconomic political expedients.

How can this be overcome? Dr Christopher Addison, speaking at a recent Labour Conference, probably hit the nail on the head when he said: – 'I do not believe that you will ever get farmers to volunteer to co-operate on an extensive scale. Therefore we must provide the machinery of co-operation . You have to meet a deep-rooted, age-long prejudice for the purpose of effecting this desired improvement. We must call into being special agricultural committees related to the existing county authorities. If we can, through a media of these, devise good systems of marketing we should get straight to the farmers' hearts.'

Hugh M'Diarmid, 19 May 1929

The 'Irish Invasion' of Scotland

The Scottish Protestant Churches have manifested increasing alarm for several years over what have become known as the 'Irish Invasion' of Scotland. There is no dispute as to the facts. The Irish population is rapidly increasing; the native Scottish population is as rapidly declining. The former is mainly confined to the big industrial centres; the latter is leaving the cities, but to a still greater extent it is leaving the countryside. The position is, that owing to Irish and other alien immigration, our urban congestion is not being relieved by the continual drain of emigration. All that happens is that a certain proportion of Scottish people is being replaced there annually by an equivalent of un-Scottish people. While this is happening in the towns, which, despite all the emigration, continue to show 50 per cent more unemployment than in England, our rural areas are being steadily depopulated by their irreplaceable native peasantry – and nobody is taking their place. The seriousness of the matter on either count cannot be exaggerated. But the vital thing is not the influx of Irish and other aliens; but the exodus of Scots. It is due to our present economic system – to the condition of Scottish industries on the one hand which renders them incapable of paying adequate wages to Scottish employees and ready therefore to supplant them with cheaper Irish labour, and, on the other hand, to the lack of a progressive agricultural policy. The causes are political and economic, and if the consequences have religious and social bearing these should not lead to any misconception as to the causes and any confusion as to how these can, and should be, dealt with. Sectarian trouble, for example, over a purely economic question is not likely to help matters. This is the danger some of the Scottish

Protestant Ministers are running. Their failure to penetrate to the real causes is blinding them to the only solution. That solution is a re-orientation of Scottish affairs on such a basis that Scottish industries and interests would not be systematically sacrificed to English, but developed in accordance with the particular requirements of Scotland, as they could be developed if Scotland were not compelled to pay, as it is under the present system, upwards of £120,000,000 per annum, to the Imperial Exchequer, out of which it only receives back some £30,000,000. If the Scottish contribution was equitably applied many millions a year would become available for Scottish commercial and industrial developments, and not only could the flow of Scottish emigration overseas be arrested, but a stream back to Scotland would speedily set in if Scotland could offer its exiled people anything like the conditions they are obtaining in the Colonies. They did not want to emigrate. Economic conditions forced them. Only economic conditions can bring them back. This will never happen as long as a system is applied which is willing to spend £2000 in settling a Scot overseas, but unwilling to spend £1000 to settle him at home – although the percentage of such home settlements as have been affected (a miserably small percentage of applications) which have been successful has been much greater than amongst overseas settlements, relatively expensive as the latter are. Most important of all is the necessity for devising and financing a thorough-going agricultural policy for Scotland, designed to do for it, in accordance with its specific requirements, something like what Denmark and other small nations have achieved for themselves by co-operative methods. But what hope is there for initiation of any such policy under the present system? Scottish Home Rule is an indispensable preliminary to any attempt to solve Scottish problems in such a fashion as may arrest the deplorable efflux of Scottish people and the progressive dereliction of the Scottish soil.

Dealing with the question of the Irish Immigration, the Committee on Church and Nation of the Established Church of Scotland says:

> There are only two explanations of the great racial problem that has arisen in Scotland – the emigration of the Scots and immigration of the Irish people. There does not seem to be any hope of alleviation of this problem in the future. All available evidence points to its intensification. The outlook for the Scottish race is exceedingly grave. If over there was a call to the Church of Scotland to stand fast for what men rightly counted dearest – their nationality and their traditions – that call is surely sounding now, when our race and our culture are faced with peril which, though silent, and unostentatious, is the gravest with which the Scottish people has ever been confronted.

This is true – but not exactly in the sense the Committee intends. It will not do to identify Scottish nationality and traditions wholly with Protestantism. There has always been a considerable native Catholic population, and many of the finest elements in our traditions, in our literature, in our national history, come down from the days when Scotland was wholly Catholic. Neither, in speaking of a 'silent and unostentatious peril', will it do to overlook the fact that Scotland has been steadily subject to Anglicisation ever since the Union. This, since it does not raise the 'religious bogey' in the way the Irish immigration does, is apt to be overlooked, but it should have at least as much attention as the other from the Scottish Churches if at last they are seriously concerned with Scottish nationalism, and not merely with a sectarian issue. Until they face the whole issue of Scottish Nationalism and define what the mean by it and by a national culture, they will be suspected of merely using the term to cover an interest in special issues by no means synonymous with it, however importantly they may be related to it. But the part is not greater than the whole, and an all-round statesman-like attitude is what is necessary, and should be forthcoming from a Church that is truly Scottish and has the deepest interests of Scotland at heart. Nor will these ministerial protagonists gain anything by suggesting that 'Scottish employers of labour ought to do their utmost to retain their fellow-countrymen at home.' The suggestion takes no cognisance of economic realities. Nor is the suggested restriction of immigration any more feasible under the existing system. It is impossible to discriminate against the Irish in that way as long as we are co-members of the British Empire. If anything is to be done it must be along the lines of re-acquiring Scottish control of Scottish affairs, and more particularly such a measure of financial autonomy as would enable projects like the mid-Scotland ship canal, land settlement on a far greater scale, the creation of co-operative agencies in our agriculture, afforestation and so forth to be developed in a way the House of Commons has not allowed – in short, to undo the present neglect of, and contempt for, Scottish affairs which is largely responsible for the pass to which we have been brought, and which cannot be undone until we have once again a Parliament of our own. Only by so re-orienting and developing Scottish policies in regard to our industries and, above all, our agricultural industry, can more employment be created, higher wages made available, and the flow of emigration stopped.

Special Correspondent, 2 June 1927

Scotland and the Douglas Proposals

Scotland is beginning to take a lively interest in the New Economies, as they are called, or Social Credit proposals associated with the name of Major C. H. Douglas. What is the Douglas theory? It is not easy to explain. Neither is the existing system. How many people have the remotest idea of the methods of finance today? The whole subject is 'wrapt in mystery'. Its critics say that this is deliberately contrived, and that the present system would not be tolerated a moment if a majority of the public understood it. Its own agents claim that it is difficult to understand. Replying to a recent controversy on the disadvantageous position of Scotland as compared with England to the banks today, a banker in *The Glasgow Herald* suggested that the public had not the necessary information to come to a proper conclusion 'on the subject of banking rates'. Whose blame is that? The correspondence in question revealed a wide-spread dissatisfaction with the existing system, which the replies of its apologists did nothing to relieve. If the whole subject is so difficult and complicated, it is unreasonable to expect the means whereby it can be altered to be readily understood by those who do not take the trouble to understand the present system and why it is proposed to alter it. Yet this is the criticism usually brought against Major Douglas's proposals. It is said they are too difficult to be understood by a sufficient number of people to carry them into effect. Their advocates, on the other hand, claim that their apparent difficulty is due to the fact that the whole policy of the existing system has been directed towards making it difficult for people to think about such subjects. Add to this that it is claimed that the existing system controls all the major means of forming public opinion and employs them incessantly to make 'confusion worse confounded', and that, in any case, there is a tremendous apathy and disinclination to serious thinking on the part of the great masses, and a reasonable case has been made out for a very different alternative to the proposals being, in themselves, too difficult. It is a well-known fact that it is the simplest things which are most incomprehensible, and, if it is a great simplification Major Douglas proposes, that would account for the appalling difficulty many people have professed to find in trying to understand his doctrine.

However that may be, the correspondence in the *Glasgow Herald* showed that people are increasingly realising to how great an extent 'incomprehensible finance' dominates and determines their lives, and are manifesting a new anxiety to comprehend just how it works. The banking system and industry are not pulling together. Their interests seem to be becoming more and more divergent. Depression in industry, and widespread unemployment, are not affecting the banks. On the contrary, their dividends are maintained and their accumulated reserves, and their power, are increasing. They have industry and commerce more and more completely at their mercy. Nor are politics any better off. Obviously bank policy dominates treasury policy. The House of Commons is in the last analysis over-ruled by the Bank of England. Is the Bank of England itself a free agent? Is it not over-ruled by America, or by a clique of international multi-millionaires? How closely this effects everybody can be seen in the light of the recent 1/2% reduction in the bank rate. Some of our largest industrialists, welcoming it on the grounds that it would help trade and relieve unemployment, contend that it could have been conceded sooner. Could it? If so, those who withheld it were responsible for a great deal of preventible destitution and difficulty. This is a very serious matter. Surely we should know. Why should it be left to a handful of individuals, whose very names are unknown to the public, to decide in a matter of such moment? Are they infallible? Is the public interest their interest? There can be no more vital question. They are allowed to control that upon which everything else depends. The power of Parliament is negligible in comparison. A further ½% reduction was expected to follow within a week or so of the last. 'So confident was everyone concerned that the lower rate would follow', says the *Glasgow Herald*, 'that the prevailing rate of 4½% was disregarded, and business in the Money Market and on the Stock Exchange was conducted on the assumption of 4 per cent being the standard of money values.' But they were wrong. £2,500,000 in gold was withdrawn by France from the Bank of England, and the prospect of a 4% bank rate immediately vanished. As the *Glasgow Herald* says: 'The whole business is somewhat disturbing in so far as it indicates that this country is not so completely in control of the world's monetary movements as was generally supposed to be the case.' Is she even mistress of her own house?

So far as Scotland is concerned, the position shows that if we had an independent Parliament to-morrow we would still be very far from having control of our own affairs. It is this realisation of the inadequacy of 'mere politics' to rehabilitate Scottish nationalism in any fundamental sense that is exercising some of its ablest protagonists today. In the Irish Free State the same question is afoot. Countess Markiewicz points out that Irish self-determination cannot be other than a snare and a delusion so long as the Bank of Ireland is controlled by the English Banks. But the question is far wider than that. It is not English banks versus Scottish or Irish banks that is being called in question by the gravest problems in trade and industry in all three countries today. It is being increasingly realised that financial reform of such scope and nature as will enable consumption to keep pace with production provides the only escape from the stagnation we are undergoing, and the disaster towards which we are hastening. It is here that Major Douglas comes in, and this is the significance of Mr C. M. Grieve's declaration in his *Contemporary Scottish Studies* that Major Douglas's proposals may well be discerned in retrospect as having been one of the great contributions of re-oriented Scottish genius to world affairs. Douglas believes that the present financial system is a purely arbitary one, bearing no relation to the requirements of the great majority of the people, and that it has the effect of strangulating enterprise, keeping wages down, preventing consumption keeping pace with production and thus causing unemployment and poverty, and preventing the utilisation of new inventions to increase production and cut down hours, or, where these are introduced, preventing the great mas of the people deriving any advantage from their utilisation. What are his proposals?

His constructive proposals, says A. R. Orage,

> concern mainly the only practically important question asked by every consumer – the question of price: and beyond a change in our present price-fixing system there is in his proposals nothing remotely revolutionary. For

> the rest, everything would go on as now. There would be no expropriation of anybody, no new taxes, no change of management in industry, no new political party: no change in fact, in status or privileges of any of the existing factors of industry. Nothing would be changed but prices. But what change would be there! Major Douglas's calm assumption is that from tomorrow morning as the shop opens, the prices of all retail articles could be marked down by at last a half and thereafter progressively reduced, say, every quarter – and not only without bankrupting anybody but at an increasing profit to everybody without exception. Absolutely nobody need suffer that everybody should be gratified. All that would happen to anybody is that the purchasing power of whatever money they have would be doubled tomorrow and thereafter continuously increased. The principle of the proposal is perfectly simple, and it consists in this – that prices ought to fall as our communal powers of production increase.

Let us put it in other words. Douglas contends that under present conditions the purchasing power in the hands of the community is chronically insufficient to buy the whole product of industry. This is because the money required to finance capital production, and created by the banks for that purpose, is regarded as borrowed from them, and therefore, in order that it may be repaid, is charged into the price of the consumers' goods. It is a vital fallacy to treat new money thus created by the banks as a repayable loan, without crediting the community, on the strength of whose resources the money was created, with the value of the resulting new capital resources. This has given rise to a defective system of national loan accountancy, resulting in the reduction of the community to a condition of perpetual scarcity, and bringing them face to face with the alternatives of widespread unemployment of men and machines, as at present, or of international complications arising from the struggle for foreign markets. The Douglas proposals would remedy this defect by increasing the purchasing power in the hands of the community to an amount sufficient to provide effective demand for the whole product of industry. This, of course, cannot be done by the orthodox method of creating new money prevalent during the war, which necessarily gives rise to the 'vicious spiral' of increased currency, higher wages, higher costs, still higher prices and so on. The essentials of the scheme are the simultaneous creation of new money and the regulation of the price of goods at their real cost of production, as distinct from their apparent financial cost under the present system. The adoption of this scheme would result in an unprecedented improvement in the standard of living of the population by the absorption at home of the present unsaleable output and would, therefore, eliminate the dangerous struggle for foreign markets. Unlike other suggested remedies, these proposals do not call for financial sacrifice on the part of any section of the community, while on the other hand, they widen the scope for individual enterprise. Mr Grieve, who is a well-known Scottish poet and critic, contends that they also make real nationalism and real personal individuality possible in a way that the present system, which tends to uniformity and the mechanisation and impoverishment of life and culture, prevents. It is well worth enquiring into. Douglas, too, as Mr Grieve points out, is a Scotsman – an engineer. That, at any rate is strongly in his favour, and should ensure him the attention of his fellow-countrymen.

Special Correspondent, 23 June 1927

Playing Fields or 'Plots' for Scotland?

While the object that has prompted under princely auspices the 'More Playing Fields' Movement, commands universal sympathy, there are other aspects to the matter than those stressed by its promoters, and there may be other ways of securing the ends in view, than by the methods proposed. The object of the movement is to secure the provision of playing fields at a minimum standard of five acres for every 1000 of the population. Its promoters point out that there are thousands of city children in Great Britain who have no playing fields – and not children only, but adults still of an age to play some game or other, to the advantage of their health, who are compelled instead merely to watch a handful of their number engaging in sports without being able to participate in them themselves owing to the lack of facilities. This is undoubtedly true, and is a serious matter from the point of view of public health and national physique, apart altogether from the other problems it creates. But it is also true that hundreds of thousands of these city dwellers are unemployed, and it is being more and more generally realised that the future prosperity of this country depends upon the extent to which we can re-orient our national activities to produce a greater proportion of our own food.

The future of Great Britain depends to an ever-increasing extent upon the better use we can make of our land. We have in the past sacrificed our agriculture to our industries – but we have now reached a stage when it is urgently necessary to reverse that policy. We have lost a large part of our overseas trade, which we are unlikely ever to recover. The countries in question are now for the most part in a position to manufacture for themselves the goods which they formerly imported to us, or to secure them in other markets with which we are not in a position to compete. Our unemployment problem and industrial position and prospects generally, therefore, demand a maximum utilisation of our agricultural resources in the future in a fashion that is incompatible with the provision of great areas for the purpose of playing fields. But that is not to say that the one necessity over-rules the other. They may be harmonised. Recreative and health-giving facilities may be part and parcel of a return to the land rather than of a further withdrawal of great acreages from productive uses.

As another writer on the subject says: –

> There are no available statistics on the subject, but it is well-known to everybody that an enormous amount of land is already devoted in this country to games: and the present movement aims, as a beginning, at adding another quarter of a million acres to the amount. The leading feature of the British economy is that we do not possess enough land capable of cultivation to feed our people. As a matter of fact, we do not produce food enough to supply much more than a quarter of them, and few of the enthusiastic advocates of intensive cultivation are sanguine enough to believe that if we made the utmost use of it we could produce sufficient for half or three-quarters. It will be seen therefore, that any movement which implies a substantial subtraction from the cultivation acreage has a serious economic side to it.

This applies far more forcibly to Scotland than it does to England, for, as Mr R. B. Cunninghame Graham, the famous Scottish author, pointed out at Scotland's Day Demonstration at Stirling, the other week, huge portions of Scotland are 'Millionaires' Playgrounds', devoted to no constructive purpose; and from which the general public are completely debarred. It would surely do far more for the general health and happiness of the people to give them free access to these magnificent regions of mountain, forest, and loch, than to set apart any number of sports grounds. It is by no means certain that the provision of sports grounds will promote better health, since that depends upon a great many other factors than mere facilities for games. It may be that we already devote far too much time and attention to games rather than too little. In any case, as another recent writer has said,

> The old country life has passed away and, in the case of boys at all events, it is much to be regretted. No amount of compulsory and scientifically regulated sports can make up for the free and spontaneous life of the country-bred boy who invents his own games, and creates an ideal world of his own: who catches butterflies in the fields or fishes in the river, and who, in short, lives in the air and the sunshine, among birds and trees and flowers. Above all the old country life brought the boy in contact with older people as well as with all ranks of society and intelligence; the town life of today means herding him with masses of other boys to whose standards, moral, intellectual, and physical, he must conform. The individual is lost in the community and the community is narrowly circumscribed. It may be in harmony with the character and necessities of our modern civilisation, but it is essentially the transference of a mechanical conception of the universe to the so-called spiritual world.

The average height of Scotsmen is 5 feet 8¾ inches; weight 11 stone 11 lbs. while Englishmen have height 5 feet 8 inches; weight 10 stone 12 lbs. But with our increasing urbanisation, our traditional physical superiority is fast disappearing. The population of Scotland has increased enormously during the past few decades, but the number engaged in agriculture has gone down fifteen per cent. Within the last ten years the county of Ross and Cromarty has had its population reduced by 7 per cent; Invernesshire by nearly 9 per cent; Caithness by 11 and Sutherland by 17. That is a very serious matter. As Sir Andrew Caird puts it:

> There is no ready remedy. Englishmen in motor cars and kilts will never make the Highlands what they were. Scottish people do not go touring very much in the Highlands. We know why. There is a remedy. Switzerland and the Pyrenees are the playgrounds of Europe. In the Highlands there should be more freedom, more access, and something should be done to bring the people back and give them a living.

That is the real 'Playing Ground Movement' Scotland needs; but although it is generally admitted, and has been repeatedly urged by eminent Scots of all parties, nothing has been done. The depopulation of our countryside, the emigration of our peasantry continues unchecked – and the congestion of the towns is one of the consequences. Apart from the great national issue involved in these considerations, on the narrower ground of food supply and the best utilisation of available ground near the cities, it is not surprising that, at the annual conference of the National Union of Allotment Holders, our local authorities should have come in for a good deal of criticism for providing playing fields in industrial areas at the expense of dispossessed allotment holders. 'I do not know', observed Mr J. Forbes, 'whether the next war is to be won on the playing fields of Eton, or whether the production of more food at home is of greater importance. It is an insane policy to increase still more the importation of food by depriving small-holders of the very insufficient facilities they already possess, and by compelling housewives to buy Spanish onions, for instance, instead of home grown onions.' The President, Mr John H. Robson of Huddersfield, hit the nail on the head when he said: 'There is urgent need for the colonisation of our country.' There can be no doubt that if a national policy of reversion to the land can be inaugurated it will do infinitely more for the relief of urban congestion and the improvement of national health than can possibly be accomplished by the success of a movement to provide sports grounds which will further increase the already grave insufficiency of cultivated ground in the country. Last year we bought from overseas no less than £4,000,000 worth of food that Scotland could quite well have produced for itself.

Special Correspondent, 7 July 1927

Scotland and the Norman Conquest

The *Glasgow Herald* in a leading article recently conceded that it was possible, if unprofitable, to contend that the Norman Conquest had been unfortunate for

Great Britain but denied that a similar contention could be sustained in respect of the effects of the Union of the Parliaments on Scotland. The vast majority of people are themselves the products of historical happenings which have predetermined to a very large extent the opinions they are capable of forming and it is very difficult, if not impossible, for them to discount their own formative influences and come to any disinterested conclusion on such an issue. Nevertheless what everybody believes or takes for granted is almost invariably undermined by the activity of minority opinions, and subsequent generations come to entertain diametrically opposite views to those of their ancestors and to hold with the same conviction that any point of view other than their own is gratuitously mischievous and nonsensical. It is apparent from a great deal that has been written in connection with the recent 900th anniversary of the birth of King William the First, the so-called Norman Conqueror, that a volte-face has been taking place in educated opinion with regard to what he accomplished and what the effects have been. Mr Arthur Weigall, for example, asserts that 'there was no such thing as the Norman Conquest, but the facts are so often misrepresented that I feel it necessary to put in a word for the honour of England.' He points out that, so far from being French as is generally believed the Normans, as their name implies were Northmen, Danes, still very far from being Frenchified although the Court and upper classes talked French and had assimilated their social usages to those of the French. England at that time was largely inhabited by Danes and

> thus the Norman soldiery who came over to our Islands was closely akin to our own people in blood, speech and habits, and only the chief Officers and nobles were distinct from them, and these only by reason of their veneer of borrowed French culture. Moreover Duke William drew a large part of his army from Brittany, but these men were descendants of the Ancient British who had migrated across to that country some centuries earlier and were still practically the same people as those who formed the bulk of the inhabitants of the West of Britain and who were to be found in smaller numbers throughout the whole of England.

He goes on to show that Duke William's claim to the throne of England was perfectly legal and that the battle of Hastings was simply a dynastic fight, won by William through the accident of Harold's death although for the greater part of the engagement the advantage had been on the other side. 'Thereupon the English who had not died with Harold accepted William as their rightful king. There was no conquest. In short, England quickly absorbed the newcomers, and if two centuries after Hastings an Englishman had been told that his ancestors had been "conquered" he would have stared in blank astonishment. It was only in far more recent times that the erroneous term "the Norman Conquest" came to be used.'

All this represents a tremendous departure from what still passes as the history of the period in the school books. But the important thing is not the fact that racially the effects of the Norman Conquest on England were so small but that the changes in the system of land tenure, in social organisation, and in cultural tendencies they brought in their train represented not a legitimate and natural development of the potentialities of the English people but the super imposition upon them of a foreign system and standards their acceptance of which represented the suspension and subversion of many of their own natural tendencies. The changed attitude of the historians to the 'Conquest' finds its parallel in the increasing realisation of English litterateurs that these potentialities were not thereby killed but have led an underground existence in our national consciousness ever since and that the time has come to bring them to the surface again and enable them to find full and free expression. What the 'Conquest' did culturally was to put the English national spirit in the straight waistcoat of the Renaissance – to induce not self-expression but assimilation to, and imitation of, French models. Modern research has put us in a position to get behind that veneer. English consciousness at the time could not escape the foreign influence and continue to develop as if there had been no 'Conquest'. It is only now, perhaps, that we are in a position to realise the cultural values that were thus denied expression and relegated to the lumber rooms of the national spirit. We can now bring these out and give them their due place and development in the field of British arts and letters. This is not to deny the values of the type and tendencies of the culture which superseded them; but it is to recognise that the superseded disposition had also potential values which it is equally important for us to realise and not allow to remain as 'blind spots' in our national consciousness. This is the true course of progress – to proceed by action and reaction; and it is being increasingly realised that no culture can continue to develop beyond a given point without requiring to give way to the very qualities which it superseded and allow these to develop anew to a further point before it superseded them again.

'Perhaps we do not feel very much interest in William here', writes a Scottish journalist.

> After all it was England, not Scotland, that he 'conquered', and yet our lives in Scotland as well as in England would have been profoundly different if no change such as William introduced had ever taken place. What he did was simply to make England civilised as the South and West of Europe were then civilised. He did his work by armed conquest. Fifty or sixty years later without any fighting on a large scale, it was introduced into Scotland by the Scots kings themselves. But of course England and Scotland were not absolutely barbarous before the Normans came, and there are quite a number of people who feel that William's forcible civilisation on the European plan was a calamity. Would England not have been better if it had gone on in its old ways and with its old language? Did not Scotland lose, by being

> forced into the mould that formed the rest of Western Europe, the chance of developing a unique 'Celtic culture'. Well, of course, we don't know. Ireland had a long experience of 'Celtic culture'. It was not a happy experience, and at the end of it the country was not able to stand up to its neighbours either in arts or in arms. But things might have gone differently with us and the English. It is true that the people who believe that without the Norman Conquest and the feudalism it brought, Scotsmen would be living in a state of communism under which 'the land would belong to the people', forget that the Celts are just as fond of private property as anyone else and that there were great landlords in Scotland before William was born.

In that passage the new attitude, not only to the Norman Conquest but to Celtic Scotland, and to the original native cultures and potentialities of our peoples, is well indicated and it cannot be too clearly realised that historical, literary and political agencies alike today, both in England and in Scotland are joining in the destructive criticism of the tendencies which have dominated our development since 1066 – and more particularly our joint development since the Unions of the Crown and of the Parliaments – and in an attempt to revive the potentialities we had prior to these developments. With these agencies, which have significant counterparts in almost every country in Europe, I believe our cultural future largely lies. There can be little question that we have come to the end of an era and that the Renaissance has spent itself. The future lies in the resumption into contemporary conscience of those pre-Renaissance qualities and aptitudes necessary to reinvigorate us in a fashion of which the exhausted impulses of the Renaissance are incapable. In regard to Scottish nationalism it ought to be realised that this is its underlying issue and, indifferent as the majority of people in Scotland may be to the issue, and unlikely of realisation as it may seem, if, as appears to be the case, it is in essential alignment with such deep and widespread tendencies as have just been indicated it may achieve an unlooked for consummation in a very short space of time.

So far as the comment on Irish culture goes the writer would seem to be relying on the conventional fiction with regard to this propagated in English school books. As a matter of fact the Celtic culture of Ireland, the very existence of which was unsuspected even by English historians and literary critics until recently and the amazing extent and beauty of which is only now being revealed, represents in many respects the goal towards which many of the most significant tendencies in European arts and letters are reorienting themselves today. A great deal more will be heard in this connection within the next quarter of a century; and the idea that Ireland's experience of 'Celtic culture' was an unhappy one, leading to arts inferior to those of Europe, is already as absurd to informed opinion as the notion that there was a 'Norman Conquest'. Nor is the point with regard to the old Scottish land system any more valid. It would be interesting to know the name of any great private owner of land in Scotland in the tenth century. It is more to the point to remember that only a few years ago a Royal Commission suggested that a reversion to the old run-rig system of tenure might be the best solution of the Crofter problem; while the history of the alienation of our common lands and their assumption into private ownership, the subsequent story of the Highland clearances, and the facts in regard to recent increases in the acreage of our deer forests and further decreases in our rural population and cultivated areas will quickly dispose of any tendency to regard what has happened in these connections as 'all for the best', and an ultimate reversion to the original conditions as impossible, let alone undesirable. Finally it may be remarked that if the 'Norman Conquest' was a misnomer, the relation of Scotland to England, although it has never been called a conquest, has exhibited and continues to exhibit, all the elements of subjugation; and that if opinions have changed so remarkably in recent years in regard to the former it is probably only because the latter is still comparatively recent and the vested interests it created still dominate what has not yet been subjected to the same process of revision of opinion – a process which ultimately it cannot escape but which, if too long delayed, may prevent the timeous undoing of some of the unfortunate consequences of a series of events which, if they have had good effects in some directions, have certainly been no more immune than any other concatenation of incidents in human history from 'another side to the story', which calls aloud for a redressing of the balance.

Special Correspondent, 21 July 1927

Canada and Scottish Literature

In a special number of the *Montreal Daily Star* devoted to the Diamond Jubilee of Canadian Federation appears a long article entitled 'Sixty Years of Canadian Literature', by Dr J. D. Logan, Dominion Archivist for the Maritime Provinces. It is, unfortunately, confined to a consideration of the writings in English of authors born or resident in Canada. It takes no cognisance of the Canadian contribution to French literature, although it is assuredly no less Canadian than the English, while its quality is higher. Nor – while it discusses the ideal of 'producing a native and national literature' as a 'spiritual need' of the Dominion – does it deal effectively with the obstacles which stand in the way of the realization of that ideal. Dr Logan, to do him justice, does not over-estimate what has been done; he admits that Canada is still merely 'a literary parish of England', and that the bulk of Canadian literature is imitative, and of pedestrian quality. But he is altogether wrong when he says that

> the distinction between English literature and Canadian literature is no longer relevant or a logical division. English literature can no longer be divided into compartments. It is a family literature, and each literature as

> produced in England, Scotland, Ireland, or Canada, or any other overseas Dominions, and largely in the United States, is the same literature marked by those individual, temperamental, social, and spiritual differences which mark the various individuals of the family.

This is to ignore literary history and current tendencies. All the best American writers today are out to create – not a mere form of English literature, but a native American literature, expressed not so much in English as in a specialised American kind of English which has rhythms and effects peculiarly its own, and little save derivation to relate it to the English used in England. Canada is still pretty much in the position that America occupied in the days of Emerson and Thoreau; it has no equivalents to Whitman, Dreiser, Cabell, Hergesheimer, Willa Cather, Edna Ferber, Vachel Lindsay, Lee Masters, let alone the younger American school, who are manifesting themselves in increasing numbers and to purposes ever more divergent from any compatible with 'English literature' properly so-called, although there are in Canada many inferior signs of Americanism, as is perhaps inevitable.

If Dr Logan's outlook in the way of regarding the literary future of Canada as necessarily bound up with English literature is general, that in itself will account for Canada's failure to produce really distinctive work even in English, while, on the other hand, it will subject it to increasing Americanism. Surely this is not desirable. At least as much attention ought to be paid to the French element as to the English, while it ought to be remembered that Irish and Scottish literatures while partly contributary to English, have also Erse in the one instance and Gaelic and Braid Scots elements in the other, which are separated completely from English literature, and have very different traditions and tendencies of their own. A 'Canadian Literature', properly speaking must comprise the literature produced in and out of Canada in no matter what language, and not confine itself to English in this way; and if there is ever to be a native Canadian literature it must be the synthesis of all the cultural elements which have gone to the making of Canada. Over emphasis on one of these to the exclusion of the others will naturally keep Canadian writers merely 'Colonial'.

Canada has owed a great deal to Scotland. Two of the great fathers of the Confederation were Scots. Sir John A MacDonald, the greatest of them all, and George Brown – the one a native of Glasgow and the other of Alloa. Sir John realised that 'you cannot rule Canada without the French.' Neither can a Canadian, as distinct from a parochial English, literature be created without them. Nor is the French the only other element whose distinctive qualities require to be taken into account. There are large Gaelic-speaking communities in Canada. Are they not applying the distinctive cultural traditions to Canadian purpose? It is a well-known fact that Gaelic publications in Scotland find a large proportion of their readers in Canada. As to Scots Canada, has, of course, its Burns Clubs and its Caledonian and St Andrew Societies. But are Canadian-

Scottish children taught Scots and Scots literature and Scottish history – or are they only taught English and English literature and history? In the latter case they cannot make that distinctive contribution to Canadian culture which they ought to be making. It is a curious and significant fact that with all their reputed patriotism and their enthusiasm for Burns, Canadian Scots have produced no poet or writer using the Scots vernacular to anything like as good an effect as French or English. This is inevitable if they are denied any knowledge of Scots literature at school. Writers of English or French in Canada keep *au fait* with current developments in English and French literature; but do Canadian Scots, who cherish Braid Scots, know anything of the Scottish Renaissance Movement and the new potentialities it is revealing? Are they playing their part with regard to the Movement for the Revival of the Doric? To the 'parochial English' literature Canada has so far produced, many English emigrants or writers of Scottish descent have contributed, and Dr Logan does justice to most of them – Charles Mair, George Murray, and the greatest of them all both in prose and poetry, Duncan Campbell Scott – but if the 'colonial' stage is to be transcended it will not be through a false uniformity in imitative English, but through the sharpest realisation of the fundamental affiliations of each of its creators with their own racial past and their Canadian future. To blur all these essential distinctions in English is a profound mistake. Scots in Canada will not become better Canadians by becoming imitation Englishmen or Americans; and the same thing applies to all the other racial elements in the Dominions.

Special Correspondent, 11 August 1927

The Scottish Industrial Situation

The latest reflection of the lamentable position and prospects of all our major Scottish industries today is the decision of the Glasgow Chamber of Commerce to promote an inquiry into the state of trade and industry in Glasgow and the West. One of the speakers, Mr George A. Mitchell, said that he had felt for a considerable time that Glasgow and the West of Scotland had not been getting their fair share of the new industries that had been established. He thought that this was purely due to the idea that had got abroad that labour in that district was extremist, and that there was great difficulty between employees and employers, which he stigmatized as a false impression, since the extremists were relatively few in number and their utterances were given a publicity out of all proportion to their real influence. This is undoubtedly true. it is also true that there is an unfortunate disposition in certain quarters to treat as extremists the advocacy of views, which, though novel to the majority of people, are far from revolutionary in any proper use of the term. Conservative politicians, and papers such as the *Glasgow Herald*, are largely responsible for creating this bogey of the 'Red Clyde', and it is not surprising to find their panic-stricken utterances reacting on their own interests. There is no ground for believing that the growth of Socialism in Glasgow and the West of Scotland has had any bearing on the desuetude of shipbuilding and the other heavy industries, which is the crux of the problem. Labour troubles have not been more numerous in Glasgow than in other industrial areas where there is no corresponding apprehension of a permanent industrial decline, and it is as absurd to attribute the existing depression and the reasons for fears as to the future to that cause, as it is to attribute them, as one Conservative candidate did recently, to the growth of the Scottish Home Rule Movement and the danger of disjunction with England. As the present writer pointed out at the time, if the growth of Scottish nationalism had been the cause, we would have found our industrial competitors in England falling over each other to subsidise the movement.

The very fact that such obviously inadequate explanations are put forward suggests a reluctance to face the real facts. So far from the undoubted developments of Scottish Nationalism and Scottish Socialism being the cause of these conditions, it is obvious that they are far more likely to be consequences of them, and that it is precisely a lack of an adequate Scottish Nationalism on the one hand, and of a disposition to adopt new political and economic expedients on the other, that is responsible for the failure to find solutions to the problems besetting us.

It is unfortunate that this new inquiry is limited to Glasgow and the West. It ought to have been made a Scottish National inquiry, for precisely the same problems are affecting other areas concerned with ship-building and the heavy industries; and our industrial depression, apparently permanent collapse of old industries, and failure to develop new ones to take their place, is a general phenomenon all over Scotland today. The main causes are not local to Glasgow and the West, but nation-wide, and can probably only be solved by a complete change of national policy in several salient aspects.

The speakers at the Glasgow Chamber of Commerce meeting seemed more concerned with superficial and temporary expedients than with fundamental research into the problems they discussed. The possibilities of more up-to-date publicity methods attracted them rather than the need to examine for example, what bearing the present relations of Scotland to England have upon the matter. Yet the latter lie at the root of the question. The inability of the out-voted Scottish representation at Westminster to secure adequate attention to Scottish affairs; the disproportionate taxation of Scotland for Imperial purposes; the system which robs Scotland of all its best brains owing to the tremendous drain on the best types of Scottish labour through emigration, which is 200 per cent heavier from Scotland than from England – these and a score of similar factors have unquestionably a very great deal to do with the plight in which we find ourselves today. It is noteworthy that, despite the altogether disproportionate drain of emigration from Scotland, Scottish unemployment remains 50 per cent higher than English. But a still clearer light is thrown on the true cause of our position by figures submitted by Mr John Good, the business man's representative for County Dublin, in one of his recent election speeches. He pointed out that from 1923–1926 there was an increase in current accounts in the banks of the Irish Free State of 71.6 per cent. In Great Britain for the same period there was an increase of only 49.5 per cent, and in Scotland an increase of only 27.5 per cent. This amply illustrates the benefits Ireland has derived from a restoration of self-government, and Scotland's position as compared with that of Great Britain as a whole is a convincing example of the fashion in which the present system discriminates against Scottish interests. There can be little doubt that a similar disparity between English and Scottish figures applies to every department of affairs; and Scottish people ought to perpend in the light of this declaration of Major Bryan Cooper, Unionist member for South County Dublin up to 1912, as to his changed opinion in regard to Irish Self-Government. 'My chief reason why I would not go back to the Union', he said, 'is that we can now get things done. When I was in the House of Commons there were all sorts of reforms urgently needed and non-contentious, yet owing to the pressure of business on the House, it was impossible to get time to discuss them. Now we have a situation in which necessary reforms can be made. Moreover, I would not like to return to the position in which Ireland was only a pawn on the chess board of the Imperial politics.'

That is what Scotland remains, and that is what is primarily responsible for its present plight, while the great majority of Scottish industrialists remain in the position Major Bryan Cooper formerly occupied when he was opposed to Irish Home Rule. The Glasgow inquiry will serve no real purpose if those who conduct it are pre-committed to a maintenance of the existing relationships of Scotland and England, on the one hand, and, on the other, to the existing economic system. it is absurd to stigmatise any proposals to alter the latter as, *ipso facto*, revolutionary. Such an inquiry ought to be entered into with an open mind, free of all prejudices, and not conventions. Not only the conditions with regard to shipbuilding and the heavy industries, but such questions as those facing the Greenock sugar-refining industry, Scottish distilling, the Scottish fishing industry, and Scottish shale-mining – all, from a narrow 'business' point of view, unrelated yet all suffering from the foreign or fiscal policy of the British Government – show that the main causes underlying the present situation on Clydeside are not peculiar to that area, but can only be realised and put to rights if the ambit of the enquiry is sufficiently widened to take cognisance of the effects on Scotland of its present unsatisfactory relations with England, and the possibilities latent in a restoration of Scottish independence.

Special Correspondent, 17 November 1927

The Burns Cult Bombshell

Carefully timed for the very eve of the annual Burns celebrations, the bombshell thrown by Mr C. M. Grieve in his address on 'Burns from a Nationalist Standpoint' to the Glasgow Section of the Scottish National Movement has burst with tremendous effect. The majority of the proposers of 'The Immortal Memory' dealt with Mr Grieve's declaration that the best thing Scotland could do with regard to Burns was to set itself deliberately to forget for the next quarter of a century that he ever existed. Those who know Mr Grieve's work know why he said this. It was out of no personal dislike for the Scots Vernacular or the work of Burns. On the contrary Mr Grieve is a specialist in Scots, and 'A.E.' (George Russell) the distinguished Irish Poet and critic declared him to be the 'most vital and original of modern Scots poets and in my opinion the best since Burns'. Mr Grieve, too, has edited a selection of Burns's Poems for Messrs Benn's Augustan Poets' Series with a challenging preface. Why then has he attacked the Burns Cult and the fulsome and untrue claims generally made for our National Bard?

Let us take the cult first. Mr Grieve objects to it because it has done little or nothing to continue Burns's work, to develop Scots letters, and preserve Scots nationality. He points out that the idea that Burns is the be-all and end-all of Scots poetry has resulted in a mass of imitative work beneath criticism. To this is largely attributable the lamentable plight of Scottish literature today. Along with that goes a fixed and inadequate conception of Scottish history and character. It is not good for any nation to confine itself to a given type in this way. The result has been that the great majority of Burnsians have little or no knowledge of, or interest in, Scots literature – let alone any other – and their enthusiasm for the Bard consists with a pitiful ignorance and impotence in regard to the true place and vital problems of Scotland today. This is amply evidenced in the type of mediocre platitudinarian generally chosen to propose the Immortal Memory. Most of these gentlemen have not the slightest shred of literary standing, and their stereotyped tributes – frequently grubbed at the last minute out of the nearest encyclopaedia – are nothing more nor less than an insult to Burns. Mr Grieve rightly contends that at the very least they ought to be men of some literary standing, recognised specialists in Scots language, literature and history, with some first-hand contribution to make to the subject, and a vital interest in the building up, on the basis of Burns's work, of a progressive Scots culture. As matters stand, we find a man like Lord Sands proclaiming (in the name of Burns) that nothing good was ever written in a dead language – the very argument that Burns himself encountered and triumphantly disposed of, when he reverted from writing in English to writing in Scots. Incidentally Mr Grieve was not complaining of the lack of help and support given by the Burns Federation to the Scottish Renaissance Movement. He was merely disposing of the claim made at the Federation's last annual conference that it was in the van of the Renaissance Movement.

But even a keen and intelligent determination to do constructive work for Scottish life and letters is not enough where wider claims are to be made for Burns. If he is to be acclaimed as one of the world's greatest poets, those who so acclaim him must be of the world and able to institute the necessary comparisons. How many Burnsians can do anything of the kind? How many have any knowledge or interest in literature at all, outside Burns? How many have ever made any exact and exhaustive study of Burns himself? Mr Grieve is on safe ground there. For years he himself has acted as foreign literature critic of the *New Age* (London) and written extensively on Russian, French, German, Spanish and other literatures in addition to doing a great deal of translating. He is therefore in an unusually good position to view Burns from the standpoint of world letters, and contends that Burns has no living literary influence whatever. It is not necessary to follow Mr Grieve in his studies of comparative literature; but anyone who knows the average Burnsian (and Burnsians after all form only a very small percentage even of Scots) knows that he is by no means a highly cultivated individual. What does he know about foreign poets? Precious little, if anything. It stands to reason then that the great masses of the people of other countries know as little about Burns as the bulk of Burnsians know about the great continental poets. This reduces those in the civilised world who have ever heard of Burns to a minute proportion of the entire population, and completely pricks the bubble of Burns's world-influence. Burns, as a matter of fact, is little read or appreciated except by Scotsmen themselves – and only by a minority of Scotsmen at that. It is high time the whole matter of the Burns cult was reduced to its proper perspective. Most Burnsians cannot see beyond themselves, and on the occasions of their annual excitement fancy the whole world shares their ecstasy. It does nothing of the kind. Most of the leading London dailies did not even devote one paragraph to the whole of this year's Burns celebrations. Most of those who said anything about it at all confined their mention of it to an account of Mr Grieve's remarks. If the whole thing is not to collapse in ridicule and futility it is high time the Burns Movement were taking steps to convert their enthusiasm into a real national literary and political movement in arts and affairs. Only so can they effectively honour Burns, Scotland, and themselves.

Special Correspondent, 9 February 1928

Scotland and Wales

'I wish I saw a more widespread demand for Scottish Home Rule', wrote Mr J. Ramsay Macdonald the other day. 'Its supporters, however, must have some sense of proportion. No Government, whatever the sympathies of its Ministers may be, can carry such legislation as this except upon a demand which has hardly been more than whispered from Scotland as yet. Scotsmen have to make an effort. If they do not, their children will have nothing to do but keep anniversaries of the births and deaths of their dead.'

Judging by his utterance, Mr Macdonald seems to have come to a new sense of the deadly peril in which Scotland stands today – that of 'gaining the whole world' (in a certain sense) and losing its own soul in every sense. But the rest of his remarks is nonsense. Governments continually pass legislation for which there is no demand, and, indeed, in the teeth of great opposition. They have ways and means, when need be, of transforming popular opposition to a semblance of general approval, which can deceive at least an adequate majority of the electorate. The demand for Scottish Home Rule cannot be more impressively manifested – by constitutional means, through the medium of the Westminster Parliament at all events – than it has been repeatedly manifested during the past century. Time after time, measures designed to give Scotland Home Rule have been thrown out despite the fact that they had the support of four out of every five Scottish MP's of all parties. What more does Mr Macdonald want? The adoption of unconstitutional means, or at any rate, the election of Scottish MP's pledged to abstain from Westminster? That is certainly what is coming. The increasing wave of Scottish nationalism ensures that. The new Scottish National Party will stand for Scottish independence – and until that is secured, nothing else. Will Mr Macdonald join it? No fear! Although decades ago he was an active Scottish Home Ruler he has long ceased to take more than an academic interest in the subject, and has done little or nothing himself to increase the sense of the urgent need for Scottish self-government amongst his countrymen. Nor has he done much, if anything, to forward the movement in his own party. Most Socialists are theoretically Home Rulers – but seventeen English Labour MP's actually voted against the last Scottish Home Rule Bill and now that a definite Scottish National Party is being formed, Socialists who have hitherto been actual Home Rulers are showing a tendency to put party before nation, and to regard it as opposed to their own Parliamentary Labour Party. Despite his words, Mr Macdonald will in actual practice take the same line. Nevertheless, without his assistance, Scotland is at last being rapidly awakened up to a sense of its peril, and there can be no doubt that the new movement will develop at an accelerated rate, irrespective of the difficulties caused by the existing party distinctions.

Other small countries are realising the same need to act – and act rapidly – if they are to preserve their distinctive standing against the tremendous forces which are tending to obliterate all distinctions and reduce humanity to a huge robotised mass. Wales has preceded Scotland in the formation of a National Party, and has already nominated one candidate who is to oppose Mr Lloyd George. The objects of the Welsh Nationalist Party are the securing of a Parliament for Wales: seperate representation for Wales, on the League of

Nations: and recognition of the Welsh tongue as the official language of the country and a sign of its separate nationality.

'Where', asks a leader writer in an Anglo-Scottish daily, 'would Mr Lloyd George have been if Wales had had a Parliament of its own with the Welsh tongue as a sign of its separate nationality? That he is eloquent in Welsh we know, but would he have cut quite the figure he did in world politics during the war if he had been merely representative of Wales on the League of Nations? He is always ready to oblige with orations on the national Celtic tongue, but he would have precious little use for the political opportunities of Welsh National isolationism.'

No doubt; but is Mr Lloyd George so wonderful a personality that Wales ought to regard his existence, and the spectacular satisfaction of his ambitions, as more than adequate compensation for the neglect of its national problems? Would civilisation really have been any the loser if he had never emerged from the obscurity of a Welsh lawyer's office? Is a whole people to be regarded as of no account as weighed against the provision of opportunities for such 'international figures'? The fact of the matter is that the world is more than tired of such super-politicians, who, in the long run, are comparatively negligible figures, of less account than any poet or artist or religious leader, or even a public-spirited local administrator.

If the choice is between the provision of a world stage for a few Scottish politicians with vaulting ambitions on the one hand, and, on the other, such a deplorable eclipse of nationality as Mr Ramsay Macdonald warns Scotland is imminent, few sane men or women will have any difficulty in deciding that it will not matter much how drastically the scope of the former is curtailed, so long as national problems can be effectively tackled and the national spirit preserved and strengthened.

There is an intimate connection – in Scotland as in Wales – between the neglect of national affairs and the emergence of such figures as Mr Lloyd George, and happily an ever-increasing proportion of the electorate in both countries are coming to the conclusion that the latter are luxuries of a kind which cannot be afforded any longer.

Special Correspondent, 16 February 1928

Another Scottish Home Rule Bill

The Rev. James Barr, MP, has introduced another Scottish Home Rule Bill in the House of Commons, and it has had its first reading. The backers of the Bill are Messrs W. Adamson, T. Johnston, G. Buchanan, D. Kirkwood, J. Maxton, Rosslyn Mitchell, T. Westwood, J. Wheatley, T. Wright, and Mr Barr himself. As usual the majority of the daily papers have seized upon it as a 'silly season' topic – akin to the giant gooseberry, the sea-serpent, and other periodical topics of sufficient unimportance to amuse a frivolous public. The comments of the English papers are of no consequence; they are of the stereotyped kind – that is to say, of a kind which would not be used with impunity in regard to the affairs of any other country in the world, and which Scotsmen seem to have little difficulty in tolerating with that peculiar humour they have cultivated – or had insidiously instilled into them – since the Union. It seems extraordinary that the reputedly shrewdest people in the world (next to the Jews) should be prepared to have a joke made in this way of the fact that the affairs of their native country are going to ducks and drakes. It betrays a mental kink unique in history – and which the English themselves, if English affairs were at issue, would be the last to manifest. Indeed the English attitude to Scottish Home Rule shows that – for the perpetuation of the present state of affairs is in English interests. Are the Scots too stupid to appreciate that in thus laughing out of court successive Scottish Home Rule Bills, the English are very subtly and successfully utilising the Scotsman's sense of humour to diddle him out of his rights? But while the humorous comments of the English papers – which can only be properly appreciated if the very substantial considerations which lie behind this way of dealing with Scottish affairs are kept in mind – can be ignored here, the attitude of the Anglo-Scottish dailies calls for comment. Their policy being inspired from London, they naturally take their cue from the English papers and laugh at Scottish affairs in the same way. But they have not the same excuse behind their trickery witticisms: and the stupidest of their readers is beginning at last to say to himself: 'I can understand English papers making a joke of Scottish affairs, but when it come to Scottish papers doing likewise it is beyond a joke. I wonder what the reason for so extraordinary an attitude is.' As soon as any Scotsman reaches that stage and makes a few inquiries, the Scottish Home Rule movement gains a new member. The case for Scottish Home Rule is so overwhelming on all accounts that its opponents have no option but to abuse or ridicule its advocates – they cannot put forward substantial argument against it. No attempt is ever made to do so. Scotsmen as a whole have only to appreciate the true inwardness of that fact for a very complete change in Scottish politics to ensure.

Never in the history of the world in any country has the press treated national affairs in the way the Anglo-Scottish press treats the subject of Scottish nationalism – which, after all, is only a plea that our first duty is to 'mind our own affairs', with the addition that it is mighty high time we did and that if we don't nobody else will. The utter indignity, the readiness of Anglo-Scottish journalism to 'join in the laugh', is unparalleled in journalism. One wonders that readers do not realise *en masse* that the mere fact that Scottish affairs can be written about in this way in Scotland itself, is a damning indictment of the present regime, and shows that under it we have lost our national self-respect to an appalling degree. A typical comment (in a Dundee daily) runs: 'As is usual on these occasions the Sassenach element in the House of Commons prepared to enjoy itself. The festive ones did not fail to remark that the Bill is described as "for the better government of Scotland". I fear that any attempt to secure Scottish Home Rule will always be received with hilarity in the House or with a general desertion of the Chamber by the English MP's in favour of the smoke room.' No doubt – but they will always troop back again when the division bell rings to vote against it if there is the slightest danger of it going through. Trust them! A joke's a joke – but they take precious good care not to carry it too far. The *Glasgow Herald*'s Parliamentary correspondent heads his paragraph: 'A Scottish Hardy Annual'. He goes on to say: 'Naturally there was some amusement', and concludes: 'The member for Motherwell was allowed to bring in his Bill without discussion: he did so to the accompaniment of Socialist cheers and the complacent smiles of the Unionists, who knew that no more would be heard of the matter for at least another year.'

Don't let them be too sure. A great deal more will be heard of it – but not, perhaps at Westminster. There is a growing body of opinion in Scotland in favour – not of asking for Home Rule – but of taking it! The *Glasgow Herald* correspondent, however, did remark that Mr Barr's speech was a pattern of its kind, and that he could not recall any of the Liberals who used to give the subject an annual airing, speaking so persuasively.

The main feature of Mr Barr's Bill is that the proposed Scottish Legislative should be in the form of a single Chamber of 148 members elected by the present constituencies. It would deal with all subjects except those relating to the Army, Navy, and Air Force, questions of foreign policy and the like, which would be jointly administered by England and Scotland. As soon as the Scottish Parliament was constituted, the representation of Scotland in the House of Commons would cease. At present, he pointed out the Secretary for Scotland had control of no fewer than sixteen departments, and it was impossible for any human being to administer so many. There were only two days given for the discussion of Scottish business in the course of the session.

After stressing the fact that the Bill was in the interests of economy, Mr Barr added that when devolution came Scotland would claim a worthy part in the administration of Imperial affairs. How absurd the statement so often made that Scottish Home Rule would be a 'break-up of the Empire' is – and how ignominious as compared with that of the Colonies, is Scotland's position today – can be clearly seen if the arguments against Scottish Home Rule, and the timidities even of many of its advocates, are contrasted with a speech like that which General Hertzog made in the South African Parliament the other day when he declared that nothing could be more fatal to Empire co-operation than the resurrection of the conviction that Empire in any form was inconsistent with Dominion independence, and declared himself in favour of 'our freedom to exercise every function, every power, every privilege of national life, without owing any subordination to any authority outside ourselves.'

If South Africa claims this, can Scotland – one of the great founder nations of the Empire – claim less, or allow its claim to be disregarded when the Colonies are demanding, and securing, their rights in this way?

Special Correspondent, 12 April 1928

Scotland as a Colony

If the effect of the Rev. James Barr's new bill for the better Government of Scotland is to transform Scotland into a colony, surely that is better than having it stealthily transformed into merely the northernmost county of England. It is in accordance with the true lines of Imperial development. Scotland would become a self-governing colony of the Empire, instead of a mere part of the British Isles, with no say in Imperial or International affairs owing to the fact that the Scottish representatives at Westminster can be out-voted all along the line by the permanent majority of English members. The opposition to the Bill of certain Anglo-Scottish dailies is extraordinarily inept. 'Ever since the war', declares a Dundee paper, for example, 'an exaggerated nationalism has been the bane of Europe, and almost the only hope of a good recovery lies in its qualification. Nationalism today stands revealed as a sterilising and crippling form of reactionism. If we may judge by this new Scottish Home Rule Bill, the lessons of the past nine years have all been thrown away upon the Scottish Socialist party. For here we have nationalism in its most violent form.'

This is nonsense. The present condition of Scotland, socially and economically is of the most appalling description. Distinguished Scots of all parties admit that, and express the gravest concern for the future of the country. That pass has not been reached owing to nationalism in Scotland – but owing to its absence. So much is obvious, and it completely disposes of the argument. If Scots had looked after Scottish affairs – instead of those of Mesopotamia, for example – things would have been in a happier case. This is the essence of Nationalism – 'to mind one's own business'. It is difficult to see how this cripples trade or industry, or how leaving one's own affairs to other people is likely to have a better result. The process must end somewhere; everybody cannot look after somebody else's business.

It is absurd, too, to talk of Nationalism as a 'sterilising and crippling form of reactionism'. In music and the arts, for example, all the best products of the past fifty years have been the outcome of re-awakened national consciousness. Scotland alone has been exempt from this process, and it is high time it was profiting by the example of other countries.

Opposition of this kind forgets that all the Colonies are demanding – and securing – self-government along similar lines; and that Scotland cannot afford to be relegated to an inferior position in the Imperial Organisation.

Sooner or later the Colonies – already demanding fuller and fuller autonomy – will reduce England to its proper subordinate place in the economy of the

Empire.

The so-called Imperial Parliament is nothing of the sort, and must ultimately be superseded by a real Imperial Parliament, consisting of representatives of all the free and self-governing colonies, to dispose of joint issues.

Scotland cannot afford to be unrepresented in such a Parliament. Already on the Imperial Economic Council it is denied representation – while Ireland, and South Africa and the other Colonies, are represented. As in Imperial affairs, so in International affairs – Scotland has no effective voice and can make no distinctive contribution.

It is absurd to talk of 'narrow nationalism' in relation to the demand that this extraordinary inequity should be righted and Scotland accorded that share in Imperial and International affairs to which she is entitled as one of the great Founder Nations of the Empire, the youngest colonies of which have already acquired far greater measures of self-government and representative power.

It is absurd to talk of the reactionary effect of Nationalism in view of the existing condition of affairs in Scotland, which could not well be worse, and which is due solely to the lack of Scottish control of Scottish affairs, and the anti-Scottish policy that has been persistently pursued by the Westminster Parliament since the Union.

Special Correspondent, 3 May 1928

Lloyd George and the Highlands

There could be no better illustration of the utter unreality of the English party political system in its relation to Scottish affairs than a politician of Mr Lloyd George's record as the head of a party under whose regime the Highlands steadily degenerated, and developed those grave problems which neither the advent of a Labour Government or the return of a Tory one have prevented from becoming steadily more serious. And the absurdity of the occasion is heightened to the limit when he addresses an audience of people who live in the Highlands, but who are apparently utterly incapable – even if they are at all desirous, which is very questionable – of doing anything at all for the regeneration of the historical areas for which they profess so great an attachment. Characteristically Mr Lloyd George begins his address by expressing his pleasure at being for once in a non-political atmosphere. But he does not condescend to explain how the Celtic spirit can be maintained while the depopulation of the Highlands continues owing to the operation of an adverse political system. English party politicians like to dilate on Scottish topics outwith party political lines, because they know Scottish problems can never be solved on these lines, and have, indeed, been almost wholly created by the English party political system. But neither can problems created by adverse political operations be solved by abstention from political action. What Scottish problems call for is a different kind of political treatment than can possibly be given to them under the English party political system. But it is pure hypocrisy to speak of them as if they were outwith politics, and could safely be left to look after themselves, when the fact of the matter is that a continuous policy in opposition to all real Scottish interests is being pursued, and has been pursued ever since the Union of the Parliaments. Scottish problems have been deliberately excluded by English party politicians from the so-called 'sphere of party politics', in accordance with a policy common to all three existing political parties, and designed to ruin Scotland by taking up the political attention of Scottish people with irrelevant issues, and limiting their attention to what ought to be their real political concerts, to the non-political sphere of empty sentiment and romanticism.

Speaking of Wales, Mr Lloyd George says: 'We are putting up a fight for the language of the Celt, for the traditions of the Celt, and for the mission and message which the Celt has for humanity.' And then, turning to Scotland he continues: 'I do not know what your are doing here in the Highlands. I am sorry your picturesque dress is disappearing. The language is not quite holding its own, I fear, but you are beginning to put up a fight.' And so on. But no one knows better than Mr Lloyd George that that fight is bound to be a losing one unless it can embody itself in effective practical political form, and that, if it could do, any such form would be at the opposite pole from the type of policies of which he is so prominent an exponent. Long ere this, if he had been in earnest, with all his great political power and prestige, he would have found ways and means to give more than lip-service to Gaelic culture and the problems of the Highlands of Scotland. But not he! Not his supporters! Nor the newspapers which give screeds of his flashy rhetoric, while taking particular pains to exclude from their columns anything of real moment to the cause of Scottish Nationalism.

Happily a new spirit is abroad, and the future of the Highlands does not depend upon Mr Lloyd George or those who are prepared to waste time listening to his windy insincerities. 'The Highlander cult is well-known in Scotland, and elsewhere', says a writer in the *Scots Independent*.

> It owes its origin entirely to ancient political knavery: even in these days it derives no mean support and advertisement from some of our modern politicians and self-advertisers who have a political or personal axe to grind. It must be admitted that these associations make a great show of effort to preserve the Gaelic language, but, strange as it may appear, a large number of those who display enthusiasm about this question neither speak nor have any desire to speak or learn Gaelic. At their numerous gatherings, kilts, tartans, and the Oxford accent are much in evidence, while Gaelic is conspicuous by its absence. The rapid decay of the Gaelic language and tradition is an inevitable result of our political subjection. This, of course, is obvious to everyone who can think, but our 'highland' associ-

> ations and their figureheads, almost without exception, are firm believers in the political subordination of Scotland, and enthusiastic supporters of the political eclipse of the Gael, his land, and his language.

An article which effectively pricks the bubble of Lloyd Georgian Celtic oratory, and deserves the careful consideration of every intelligent Scot at home and abroad, ends by saying that

> the whole future of the nation depends entirely on Scots being true to their own race and country. Not as Britishers, not as 'Highlanders' or 'Lowlanders', can we serve Scotland; nor as Scottish sections of the English political parties... The issue is now about to be joined; those who are not for Scotland are against her. All the world knows that the prosperity of a nation, material and spiritual, the preservation of language and traditions, are only possible when the people are in possession of national freedom and independence. The National Party of Scotland has come into being. Its appeal is not to a section but to Scots as a whole. Its battle-cry is 'Scotland a Nation', and its support will come from every section and stratum of society who earnestly believe in the preservation of our Celtic heritage and tradition.

Special Correspondent, 21 June 1928

Scottish People and 'Scotch Comedians'

Mr Ian Bruce in the *Daily Mail* (a paper much more prone to encourage nationalist movements in Europe than in Scotland or our British Colonies) somewhat surprisingly has given space in which to tell the flat truth about Harry Lauder and others of his kind. Mr Bruce, pointing out that there is a world of difference between calling Harry Lauder, Will Fyffe and others of their buffoon species 'Scotch Comedians' and referring to them as 'Scots Comedians', goes on to say: –

> Sir Harry Lauder and Mr Will Fyffe may be perfectly capable artists in their own sphere. I have no doubt that they are, although personally I am in the position of many Scots theatre-goers – I have never seen either Lauder or Fyffe on the stage, and have no wish to see them. English readers of *The Daily Mail* may be interested to know that many Scots, not highbrow Scots, not narrow-minded Scots, consider 'Scotch comedians' to be in very bad taste. It is extremely interesting to note the vacant seats in a Scottish theatre when a 'Scotch' comedian of any description is to appear. It may be that a prophet hath no honour in his own country. But is it not rather the case that in Scotland the worthless show and ridiculous performances of these comedians are clearly recognised for what they are worth,

> while abroad (and by abroad in this instance I include England) they are taken at a little more than face value. Hence the world-wide idea that Scotsmen are red-haired, hairy-kneed, whisky drinkers, and bagpipe players, and that they spend most of their doddering old age in chasing women. We need no more than mention the now exploded myth of a Scotsman's over-love of money.

'Is it not rather hard', concludes Mr Bruce,

> on Scotland that she should have to suffer for the idiocies, sentimentalities, and worse, of a few? Scotland's national conscience is slowly re-awakening and already there are signs of dissatisfaction with the lethargy which has allowed her to become a figure of fun among the nations. These humorists are not Scottish and they pander to an uneducated taste. The man who enjoys them does not understand the real Scotland. The typical 'Scotch' comedian is not a burlesque of the typical Scot. I very much doubt if he knows what a Scotsman is. The 'Scotch' comedian is not even a joke on the typical Scot; he is a buffoon who betrays his country for his own ends. Scotland is handicapped by her so-called comedians.

No Scot of any intelligence will dissent in any particular from these statements. The reason why the Harry Lauder type of thing is so popular in England is because it corresponds to the average Englishman's ignorant notion of what the Scot is – or because it gives him a feeling of superiority which he is glad to indulge on any grounds, justified or otherwise. 'Lauderism' has made thousands of Scotsmen so disgusted with their national characteristics that they have gone to the opposite extreme and become, or tried to become, as English as possible; 'Lauderism' is, of course, only the extreme form of those qualities of canniness, pawkieness and religiosity, which have been foisted upon the Scottish people by insidious English propaganda, as a means of destroying Scottish national pride, and of robbing Scots of their true attributes which are the very opposite of these mentioned. It is high time Scots were becoming alive to the ulterior effect of this propaganda by ridicule.

Another correspondent, replying to Mr Bruce, has pointed out that Sir Harry Lauder earns £1,500 a week; and Sir Harry himself – the cap having evidently fitted only too well – ill-naturedly rejoins that he never fails to receive full houses in Scotland as elsewhere. That may well be. There are plenty of non-Scottish people in Scotland to supply him with the necessary audiences. Besides, what proportion of the population of Scotland – or even of the cities in which he appears – do Sir Harry's audiences constitute? A very small and not necessarily in any way a representative one! The present writer has never met a single intelligent Scot who would be seen at a Lauder performance. The fact that this over-paid clown gets £1,500 a week is a shameful commentary on the low state of public taste. It represents a salary which, divided up into good reasonable sums, would provide for 150 intellectual workers yearly amounts of £500 each. £500 a year is considerably more than the average that has been earned by any of the writers, artists, or musicians of whom Scotland has any right to be proud during the past 200 years. One of the finest of modern Scots, John Davidson, commits suicide because he cannot stand any longer the daily humiliations to which he is exposed through his inability to lower himself successfully to cater for the mass; but Harry Lauder – who has done nothing worth doing and is not fit to blacken Davidson's boots – earns £1,500 a week, a 150th part of which would have kept Davidson in comfort and enabled him to add work of permanent value to the world of letters. Burns, towards the end, is sore depressed for £5. But Harry Lauder earns every week more than double all Burns received for his immortal poems – and has the indecency to take it and think he is worth it.

There are Scots today who will never earn more than a small fraction of Harry Lauder's emoluments, and who wouldn't change places with him supposing these were a million times greater than their present preposterous aggregate. And yet these Scots from any rational standpoint are worth infinitely more than Harry Lauder. And nobody knows it better than Harry himself.

That is the real gravamen of the charge against them – that knowing themselves worthless they are conscienceless enough to pander to the mob and to travesty Scottish national psychology in the crudest and most abominable way for the sake of money with which they do no good.

A tithe of what Sir Harry earns annually would serve to subsidise a Scottish National Theatre in perpetuity – but Sir Harry will never contribute to that or to anything else of the slightest consequence. And yet he has the ingratitude to resent being called the very thing upon which his 'fame' and wealth have been built – i.e., his being 'a perfect fool'. But that resentment only completes the proof, if any were needed. The idea of Sir Harry taking himself seriously is surely the last straw. The fact that Sir Harry possesses great dramatic talent makes it more deplorable that he should use it in the way he does.

The sooner Scotsmen awaken to the need for a realistic concern with their nation's condition and reputation at home and abroad the better. When they do 'Scotch comedians' will disappear with the national decadence of which they are a fungoid manifestation.

Special Correspondent, 23 August 1928

Scottish Nationalism and the Churches

The Scottish churches are at long last bestirring themselves and remembering that they are 'Scottish' as well as churches. Utterances of representative ministers of both the Established and U.F. Churches in different parts of Scotland manifest a determination to maintain the distinctive national values which are threatened by the Government's De-rating and Local Reform proposals, and, in many cases, realisation of the general plight to which Scotland has been reduced and the deplorable extent to which it has lost its fine old traditions and characteristics, and has not only become Anglicised but is rapidly being Americanised. The status of the churches – their comparative intellectual and moral value – is necessarily imperilled by the tendency to completely provincialise Scotland; they can only fully realise their great traditions if they operate as representative factors in a nation in the fullest sense of the term, and this aspect of the Church's relative authority and standing will inevitably be still more sharply raised and realised by the imminent consummation of the Union between the Established and U.F. Churches. If Scotland becomes merely the 'northernmost county of England', then the Scottish Church ceases to be a national church and becomes merely a nonconformist sect. These and other ecclesiastical aspects of the matter are now being widely appreciated alike by clergy and laity, and I am sure that a friend of mine is well within the mark when he writes: – 'Even the ministers are surprised at the Scottish feeling that is manifesting itself throughout the congregations; they feel in their hearts that everything they and their ancestors have lived for is going to pass away unless they bestir themselves.' The feeling is amply justified; there is no time to lose if the great catastrophe is to be avoided – but it is necessary to point out that the elements which have long ago realised that, and been organising to prevent it (with such notable and increasing success during the past few weeks) represent the non-church-going section of Scotland (which is about a third of the entire population) rather than our so-called Scottish Churches. It is also true that the Roman Catholic Church of Scotland has shown a greater concern for national values than the Protestant Churches. So that the phrase 'even the ministers' is all too well warranted; they have been tardy – and, coming late into the movement, they must make good their delay by showing all the greater sense of responsibility, and rising to the truly national stature of the considerations involved. In other words, the responsibility largely lies with them to see that this national movement is not subverted into a mere sectarian squabble, and that they do not merely attempt to use it for ecclesiastical wire-pulling. If they think that by swinging over to the Nationalist side now they can dominate the movement, and make it subserve their particular aims instead of national aims in the widest and deepest sense, they will be guilty of an act of spiritual sabotage which will work incalculable damage to all the higher interests in Scotland.

It is unfortunate that all that concerns as many Protestant ministers and church-members is not the appalling facts in regard to Scotland's political, economic, social and cultural position, but simply and solely the danger that Protestant religious education may not be safeguarded under the contemplated legislation. This is, alas, in keeping with the past record of the Scottish Churches – they have acquiesced in the progressive degradation and subordination of Scotland with scarcely so much as an isolated protest. They have only been alive to their own special interests in the narrowest sense: but to national considerations they have given no consideration whatever. Happily, while sectarian tactics are still all that interest all too many of the ministers, an increasing number do realise that the provincialisation and 'cinematisation' of Scotland is due to the eclipse of true national values, and that the churches are suffering to a very large extent from evils which they could, by a true national policy, have prevented from developing at all, but did not; and that the time has now come to make good that deplorable failure by thinking and acting nationally in the deepest and truest sense of the term. The best of them realise, too, that in the upbuilding of the nation all the elements of the population must contribute, and that a fatal mistake will be made if ultra Protestant elements are permitted to exacerbate religious feeling towards our Roman Catholic fellow-citizens. The true hope of Scotland lies in the comprehensive and statesmanlike co-operation of these elements. The dangers of a species of civil war are latent in most of our industrial centres; and true religious feeling must be alert to prevent these developing by concentrating on a broad Catholic (not Roman Catholic) development. Only so can the churches as corporate bodies take part in the reconstruction of the Scottish nation and make good their remissness in the past.

Special Correspondent, 20 December 1928

The Farce of the Scottish Debate

The farce of the Scottish debate on the Local Government Bill has run its course. The Scottish members practically had the House of Commons to themselves while the measure was under discussion; but the only apparent advantage of this has been to give paragraphists and cartoonists material for facetiae. As few as ten members were at times on the Government benches while Scottish members were speaking and voicing what is undoubtedly the considered opinion of the vast majority of the people of Scotland in regard to the most momentous legislative proposals of recent times affecting their interests. This open contempt for Scottish wishes has no parallel in the treatment of any minority in any other civilised country. It is, in itself, a sufficient answer to those who would attempt to contend that Scottish interests do not suffer under the existing relationship with England. The representatives of Scotland, speaking with the consciousness of having the country almost solidly behind them, are compelled to speak to empty benches; but the great permanent majority of English members, knowing little and caring less about Scottish conditions, requirements, and desire, though they might leave the House to the Scottish members in order to let them discuss a purely Scottish matter, did not fail to troop into the division lobbies and outvote Scottish opinion on matters regarding which they had not even had the elementary courtesy to listen to the arguments. Can anyone attempt to defend such a state of affairs? It is an extremely serious and deliberate abrogation of democratic rights, and a prelude to a still more serious and carefully-planned one in the Bill itself, which is expressly designed to destroy the last vestiges of Scottish control of Scottish affairs, whether, in Mr Churchill's phrase, the country wants it or not. So far as mere talking can do it, the Scottish members put up a gallant protest; but they might as well have saved their breath. One point should be noted in this connection however: the reports that appeared in the Anglo-Scottish papers were mere summaries so selected as to leave out most of the real hits scored by the opposition speakers, and convey the impression that the case against the Government was far weaker than it really was. As a matter of fact – as the verbatim reports in Hansard show – the Scottish opponents of the measure covered the whole field in the most admirable fashion, and did all that could possibly be done under such conditions that, no matter how strong their arguments were, no matter how ungainsayable their facts and figures, they were fore-doomed to be outvoted by a horde of English MPs who did not even listen to the arguments put forward. If the matter had depended upon the strength shown in the debate, no more would ever have been heard of this iniquitous bill. No single valid argument was adduced in favour of the most revolutionary and uncalled for measure ever put forward by a professedly Conservative Government. A strange Conservatism, forsooth, that tears a whole system of administration up by the roots without a shadow of justification.

It ought to be re-emphasised that the Scottish opposition to this Bill transcends all party distinctions – Liberals, Socialists, Conservatives have alike denounced it. They have declared that if it is forced through in the teeth of Scottish opposition it will mean a great access of strength to the Nationalist Party. They are right there. The Nationalist Party is adding rapidly to its numbers; but not so greatly as it should be doing in face of this unconscionable affront to Scottish opinion. Scots of every shade of party politics are sinking their differences and joining the National Party – their eyes open at last to the intolerable and indefensible attitude of England to Scottish affairs. But have the MPs who have foretold that this must be the effect of the Government's conduct, themselves joined the National Party? Have Sir Robert Hamilton and Sir Robert Hutchison had the courage to say they will have no more of what they have condemned as an utter farce, and joined the only party which can put an end to such a shameful state of affairs? Not they! But why not? It requires no elaborate proof to show that men who believe that such a measure is opposed to their country's best interests, who see that it is being foisted on them by men who believe that such a measure is opposed to their country's best interests, who see that it is being foisted on them by men of a different race, and who find themselves reduced to impotence in Parliament in which they are in a hopeless minority, must be singularly supine if they are content to go on working under such conditions. Scottish MPs have far too long been content to protest, and protest, and protest, always in vain, and then acquiesce in the victory of their unscrupulous opponents, no matter how ruinous the effects were on Scotland. Such a process is demoralising in the extreme. The sooner MPs who find themselves helpless to defend their convictions – and the expressed wishes of their constituents – resign and make way for a different type of representative the better. The deplorable condition to which Scotland has been reduced shows only too well the effects of such a system. It is obvious that there will be no betterment until the system is completely changed. If the Scottish MPs at any time during the past fifty years – and certainly at any time during the past three years – had been men of courage and integrity instead of being willing to abjectly adjust themselves after a parade of futile protestation to whatever conditions the English majority imposed, they would have come back to their constituents and said: – 'Look here! We are powerless to protect your interests. We are outvoted by the English every time. The Scottish electorate is to all intents and purposes disenfranchised. We see no use in remaining in Parliament under such humiliating conditions.' Who can doubt that if they had done that the people of Scotland would have risen as one man and insisted upon a change in the relationship of the two countries which would have ensured Scotland fair play? Can anyone imagine the English people – or any other people – submitting to such a state of affairs? Scottish affairs are treated as a joke; Scottish interests are systematically sacrificed to English – and yet Scottish MPs are willing to continue what they themselves can only describe as an utter farce.

The Scottish National Party is out to end that state of affairs. If the present Bill is forced through, the object of the Scottish National Party will be to secure its repeal at the earliest possible moment. English politicians need not imagine that Scottish men and women are always going to be more scrupulous in defense of their rights than their English enemies are in violating them. The methods of the Government are putting an irresistible premium on unconstitutional action in Scotland. Have the Government learned nothing from Irish history? Apparently not. They are treating Scotland as they treated Ireland; but the day of reckoning is at hand. An increasing body of Scottish people is flaming with resentment.

Special Correspondent, 3 January 1929

Scotland 1928–1929

1928 will rank as a historic year so far as Scotland is concerned; it has marked a turning point in our national affairs. The Scottish Renaissance Movement has continued to develop during the past year, but in a subterranean fashion; it is marked by a slow but sure transvaluation of values, a subtle change in the national psychology, and the increasing emergence of an intelligentsia sceptical of all the standards that have hitherto been regarded as essentially Scottish, while all the more determined to recover our old Gaelic and Vernacular heritage and create a new Scottish literature in accordance with these ancient traditions, and obviously and increasingly differentiated from anything English. The standard of literary and artistic endeavour in Scotland is rising. Scotland during the past two centuries has not initiated anything peculiarly its own and yet of international value in any sphere of intellectual activity. It has been content with derivative activities which took their originative genius from other countries. Now all the cleverest of our young Scots are deliberately seeking for ways and means whereby the distinctive genius of Scotland can express itself in unique forms and thus emerge into the forefront of European tendencies. It is precisely in this fashion that other countries have entered upon great periods of intellectual and cultural development. What the subtle factors are that make a nation fertile at one time and sterile at another, or productive of, say, musical genius at one period and of literary or scientific values at another, is difficult to say; but whatever the factors are that so adjust the balance between one nation and another, and one art or activity and another, it is obvious that they are operating in Scotland today, putting an end to a period of comparative mediocrity and imitativeness, and preluding one of dynamic development. Although the past year has not added materially to the intellectual products of the new Scotland which is thus coming into being, the development has gone steadily ahead and become more and more widely diffused. Scotsmen and Scotswomen everywhere and of every class, are conscious of this 'stirring of the dry bones' and are adjusting themselves to it after their fashion. One thing is definite. The tendency towards assimilation to English modes and standards has been completely stopped and to no small extent reversed. Everywhere there is an eagerness to discern and reinforce the essentials of difference between English and Scottish; and a growing intolerance of English superiority and Anglo-Scottish compliance.

But probably the main reason for the lack of any outstanding literary or artistic products of the 'changed consciousness' of contemporary Scotland is the urgency of Scottish political, economic, and social problems, and the growing realisation that before the Scottish Renaissance can make any real headway, the relationships of England and Scotland must be completely altered, Scotland must regain complete control of all Scottish affairs. It is significant that almost all the young writers whom the Scottish Renaissance Movement has brought into being are keen Nationalists. The effective force of the country, therefore is more and more concentrating, for the time being, not in cultural, but in political channels. And the outstanding fact of 1928 is the foundation of the National Party of Scotland and the extraordinary headway it has made since its inception six months ago. The significance of this Party is that it marks a complete reversal of all the tendencies that have been operating in Scotland for the past two hundred years; and that its appeal is firmly based on the lamentable condition of affairs to which Scotland has been reduced by the system which it is at last so comprehensively challenging.

The Scottish Renaissance Movement and the National Party are internal responses to the present state of affairs; but external factors are also operating to bring both into the forefront. The Scottish Movement is aligned with some of the most significant tendencies of modern life – notably the revolt against standardisation, centralisation, and the machinations of international finance. It is precisely the fact that it is so aligned that gives it its high promise – a promise of not only national, but, through national, international consequences. A more immediate, though less important factor is the continued anti-Scottish aggression of the existing system. This contempt for Scottish opinion – this determination to reduce Scotland to the condition of a mere province and destroy the last vestiges of Scottish democratic control of Scottish affairs – is producing a belated but tremendous reaction. Scotland sees what is being attempted; it realises at last the appalling problems that the long-continued deliberate neglect of its needs and indifference to its rights and desires has produced; and there can be little question that the Renaissance Movement and National Party proceeding from the one direction will be met by the great mass of Scottish political opinion revolting from the insult of the Local Government Reform Bill in the other; and that this juncture will, at the forth-coming General Election result in a virtual landslide in favour of the National Party candidates. This will have tremendous national and international repercussions and it is in the prospect of these that I write with confidence that 1929 will mark a great turning point in modern Scottish history and be a red letter year in our calendars. Great events are impending. Let us be prepared and resolute.

Special Correspondent, 10 January 1929

Scottish Nationalism and the Other Parties

The formation of the National Party of Scotland and the candidature of Mr Lewis Spence, its vice-chairman, in the North Midlothian bye-election, has forced the whole question of Scotland's national status into the forefront of practical politics. Spokesmen of the other three parties – Conservative, Liberal, and Labour – have been devoting to the subject of Scottish Home Rule, and to Scottish affairs generally, a measure of attention which, but for this development, would certainly not have been forthcoming, although the admissions of these spokesmen themselves show that the condition of things in Scotland urgently calls for attention of a kind, and on a scale, unlikely to be ever forthcoming from Westminster. It is thought in certain quarters that the professions of all three parties in favour of Scottish Home Rule – and in particular Sir Herbert Samuel's declaration (by kind permission of Mr Lloyd George) on the subject – have disposed of the necessity of a separate Scottish National Party. The Duke of Montrose, for example, a keen Home Ruler, has gone so far as to say that in view of the fact that the Liberal Candidate in North Midlothian is a keen Home Ruler there is not, in his opinion, any need for Mr Spence's candidature. Mr Spence, however, and the National Party as a whole are precisely of the opposite opinion. They point out that the other parties have been making these protestations for half-a-century, without doing anything, even when in power. Even now they are only committing themselves to give a certain measure of devolution to Scotland some time; they refuse to give priority to the issue – despite the appalling facts and figures in regard to Scotland's position today, which go to show that unless a great national reconstructive scheme is engaged upon shortly the Scottish nation will to all intents and purposes be wiped out by emigration and alien immigration. Nor are the measures of devolution proposed adequate to the ends in view or worthy of Scotland's position as one of the mother-nations of the Empire. Other parts of the Empire have received far fuller measures of autonomy than these proposed in these old schemes hastily brought out of the political lumber-rooms of the English controlled parties to meet the new developments of Scottish nationalism. Scotland cannot take less than Southern Ireland or South Africa or Canada. And above all, any measure of Scottish Home Rule that does not carry with it full financial autonomy or that leaves England in the position of being able to outvote Scotland in matters of foreign policy is utterly inacceptable. It would do Scotland more harm than good. It would permanently provincialise Scotland and perpetrate English ascendancy. The Scottish National Party is out to reconstruct Scottish nationhood in the fullest sense of the term, and demands equality of status with England as one of the great mother nations of the Empire.

In party political quarters it is claimed that unemployment and other great economic and industrial and international problems must come first. But in Scottish Nationalist quarters it is claimed that Scottish Independence must come first precisely because of the urgency and magnitude of these problems – in order that Scotland may solve them in her own way. The National Party denies that England and Scotland are an economic unity: on the contrary, it claims that Scottish and English interests have always been antagonistic in certain respects and are becoming increasingly so today, as is evidenced by the 'Southward Trend' which is threatening our basic industries, alarming our Chambers of Commerce, and causing more unemployment in Scotland while emigration from Scotland is 200 per cent greater than from England.

But beyond these considerations the *raison d'etre* of the National Party lies in the fact that everywhere throughout the country today electors are sick of the party system. The National Party puts nation before party. It contends that there is nothing to prevent men and women of very diverse temperaments, traditions and tendencies (very inadequately represented as matters stand by the labels of Conservative, Liberal and Socialist, which only correspond very roughly to these basic psychological, rather than political, differences) joining together for the national weal and each contributing towards that in accordance with his or her particular type. It is this embodiment of a positive principle – the non-

Party principle, adjuring mere partizanship, recognising that each different type in the nation has his or her contribution to make to the common good – that is the real justification of the existence of the National Party. It represents a new ideal in politics – a new angle of approach, which all can share, to the problems of the nation. It has come into existence through the reawakening of the Scottish national consciousness which, as it develops, will take its own forms without regard to the moulds of English party politics. The new wine cannot be poured into the old bottles.

The records of the other parties show that Scotland has little to expect from them. They have promised enough and failed to fulfil in the past – there is no need to trust to their promises now. Their new found zeal for Scottish Nationalism is a bare-faced electioneering dodge. The National Party is on a different footing. It has come into existence with the definite aim and object of resecuring Scottish self-Government, and with a great national reconstructive policy. It is amply justified on the facts and figures in regard to Scottish affairs today in contending that it is high time Scots of all parties were sinking their sectional differences in the national interest. This appeal is not being made in vain. The other parties have 'the wind up' – that is why they are coming forward with their specious pledges now. But their promises are belated and their proposals will by no means fill the bill.

Special Correspondent, 31 January 1929

Scottish Arts and Affairs

BRUCE SEX-CENTENARY

To commemorate the 600th anniversary of the death on 11 March 1329 of Robert the Bruce, a movement has begun among residents of Galloway to erect a monument to Bruce's memory on the scene of his great victory over the English in Glen Trool. High above the glen overlooking some of the most beautiful mountain scenery in Scotland, it is proposed to mount a massive granite boulder, which, it is thought, will be more in keeping with the countryside than a more formal type of memorial. A committee has been formed to decide how the money should be raised, and the full arrangements of the appeal will be made known shortly.

SCOTTISH NATIONALIST AND EDUCATIONAL POLICY

The issue of the preliminary draft memorandum on Educational Policy by Captain A. G. Pape on behalf of the National Party of Scotland marks a significant development in the party. Captain Pape, scientist, educationist and author, was founder of the Scottish Section of the new Education Fellowship and is the author of *Christ of the Aryan Road, The Politics of the Aryan Road*, etc. Captain Pape's memorandum runs to twenty-two pages of print and covers the whole field of the Scottish mission in regard to education. As Captain Pape says: –

> Every progressive university professor of education, director of education, master of method, headmaster, principal, rector, chairman of education authority, and chief inspector of schools in Scotland is in favour 'of preserving and increasing the spiritual power in the child,' which is an essential part of the educational policy of the National Movement in Scotland.

Captain Pape also points out that a condition of the application of this educational policy is the adoption of the National Movement of 'The New Economics', generally known as 'Social Credit', and adds 'Having "the new education" as an educational policy, with "the new economics" as a basic economic policy, the National Movement of Scotland can then lay claim to be in the van of progressive and enlightened national administrations.' In other words, the true strength of the National Movement is that it is embodying a positive development of the Scottish genius.

REORIENTATION OF SCOTTISH SPIRIT

Interviewed with regard to Captain Pape's draft, Mr C. M. Grieve ('Hugh M'Diarmid'), Nationalist candidate for Dundee and a member of the National Council of the National Party, said: –

> I have read Captain Pape's preliminary draft with great pleasure, and believe it to be, in the educational sphere just such a dilineation of the new Scotland as has been manifesting itself in other directions of recent years, and most notably in the new economic movement associated principally with the name of Major C. H. Douglas. I regard all these manifestations as inter-related, and as forming in sum-total that reorientation of Scottish national consciousness which is the real dynamic of the Scottish National Movement. Captain Pape's policy is, as he says, dependent upon the acceptance of Major Douglas's social credit proposals. I believe it is the world mission of a reawakening Scotland to lead the way in translating the latter economic fact, and so on the basis of the economic security of the individual, circumvent the tendencies of the age to the robotisation of humanity, and ensure those further cultural developments for which we are obviously ripe, but which are at present being short-circuited and inhibited owing to the fact that we are pot-bound in an altogether arbitrary, artificial, and inadequate financial system. Witness in respect of this the need that has been found to curtail the number of intending teachers: the continual increase in our midst of 'education trapped' people; the numbers of qualified Scottish doctors who cannot find any professional outlet and have to fall back on poorly-paid clerical jobs and the general lack of genuine creative activity in Scotland which should be the fruit of our relatively advanced educational system.

'OUR GREAT NATIONAL TRADITION'

'From the point of view of Nationalism,' continued Mr Grieve,

> the educational policy here outlined seems to me the fit, natural, and urgently necessary continuance – at present prevented by the interposition of the workings of an inimical system – of our great national tradition in this connection; just as the Douglas economic system seems to me, not only to bring to fruit at long last the peculiar genius of our people in the solution of practical problems, but to represent an evolutionary movement some full circle on a higher turn of the spiral and thus to correspond in a significant fashion to ancient Gaelic economics, with its repudiation of usury. I regard it as vital to the Scottish Movement that it should take advantage of the obvious intention of destiny in throwing up such types of Scotsmen as Major Douglas and Captain Pape at this juncture; and trust the National Party will speedily adopt the policy outlined in Captain Pape's draft and proceed without delay to have the new economic policy upon which it depends similarly drafted and adopted.

'Mountboy', 7 February 1929

The Importance of Arbroath

'Scotland has no national shrine', a friend said to me the other day. 'Shrine is not the right word perhaps. It has no national centre – no place above all others, where one can stand and feel in touch with the profoundest element in our history – not with this or that sectional influence, but with our main-spring as a nation.'

We ran over a few names. Edinburgh was never the Capital of Scotland except in name; it was associated with none of the major events or elements in our history. It looks like a capital, but isn't; a magnificent provision for an unfulfilled function. The time may yet come when Edinburgh will, indeed, become the capital – the living centre – of Scotland, the scene of stirring events. But it is questionable. Scotland, and Edinburgh, will have to change tremendously. So far Edinburgh stands for nothing fundamental and indispensable to which Scots from all parts and of every shade of opinion and section of tradition can, or should, pay equal homage. Stirling is no better. The field of Bannockburn draws tourists certainly – but (although efforts have been made to evoke great national sentiments in connection there-with) it has been a singular failure as a national rallying ground. This is not surprising perhaps. Its appeal, predominantly military – and viewed in relation to Scottish History as a whole, very sectional – is associated with no great vital principle, capable of bringing together in one great unity the scattered elements of our people. 'You can never imagine Bannockburn', continued my friend, 'attracting 20,000 people on an annual day of pilgrimage, as Carfin (with no roots in Scottish history) easily could. That's what I mean. Carfin only appeals to part of our population: its attraction is purely religious. What we want is a centre which will draw them all, despite all the differences of religion and politics and everything else. Iona is like Carfin, except that it has ancient historical traditions – but these, too, are limited in their appeal, and have no real national significance in the sense of which I am speaking. No; in this sense we have no great national rendezvous, no inspiring centre to which our people can make annual pilgrimage to feel themselves in contact with the very core and essence of their nationhood, in touch with a source of perennial pride and inspiration. It must be something very big, very far-reaching, that can endow any place, with such national significance – a religious shrine will not suffice, a battlefield is not enough, merely literary associations are entirely inadequate. We want something greater than Carfin, Iona, Bannockburn, Burns' birthplace, or Edinburgh, even with that National Memorial, which has brought the castle into the life of the people again in so extraordinary a fashion, but which is not yet, by any means, national in the sense of which I am speaking.'

After making a quick mental tour of Scotland I agreed with him; we had no such place. But, immediately he answered: 'Ah, but we have – only we don't know it! Can't you think of it? Even you?' After an effort I had to admit that I couldn't. 'That's the trouble,' he said, 'it is due to the appalling neglect of Scottish history in our schools – the really deep, vital, and significant things are never brought to the notice of our Scottish children at all. We get completely superficial and erroneous ideas – we grasp the shadows and miss the substance. The place I have in mind is – Arbroath!'

Arbroath as a centre of Scottish nationality – a fount of inspiration? I confess it had never occurred to me in that light before. I had associated it with nothing more inspiring than 'smokies' – if with anything at all. It is not a place with any allure – any halo of romance and tradition. And yet at once I saw that my friend had hit upon a great idea, one of those ideas which if it could be realised, might fortify and transform a nation. Can anything good come out of Nazareth? Arbroath counts for little in Scottish life today, but it ought to have that halo of romance and tradition; it is, above all other places in our country, qualified to be our great national centre, our rallying and renewing ground. It is only because we have been 'educated' out of our past – out of all that is noblest in our national tradition – that the significance of Arbroath is forgotten or unused. Arbroath in 1320 witnessed one of the greatest actions in history; it saw the signing of one of the noblest documents to which human signatures were ever appended – a document which, in very truth, as Sir Walter Scott declared, 'ought to be written in letters of gold'. It is high time we rewrote them in letters of living fire on the heart of every Scot.

The significance of the Declaration of Independence, signed at Arbroath in 1320, is not its political or historical significance – it is its permanent human significance as one of the most magnificent gestures ever made in the direction of liberty. For the signatories did not only repudiate the overlordship of the Pope of Rome and the King of England – they told their own beloved king, even as they gave him their homage that he too held his place upon conditions, but that if he or his successors ever surrendered one jot or tittle of Scottish Independence their allegiance would be at an end and instant repudiation would follow.

This tremendous affirmation of Independence – not only against foes without, but against foes within – has no parallel in its uncompromising splendour in the archives of other nations, and to realise its full magnificence, its spiritual magnitude and power, one must take into account the relative condition of Scotland at the time. It turns the politics of today into the veriest shoddy.

How tragic it is that the Anglification of Scottish education should have robbed Scots children of a heritage of history which includes a claim and challenge so stupendous! Surely this, above all else, must be brought back into the proud and perpetual consciousness of our people. Steps must be taken to ensure that no Scots child is allowed to grow up without learning of the stature to which the soul of Scotland sprang six centuries ago; it is in the light of this great declaration that all our present and future achievements and professions must be measured. The Declaration of Independence had military, religious, and political aspects – it is not these with which we are concerned – but the profound significance of the Declaration which includes and underlies all these – the great human courage and determination of it, the uncompromising frankness, the warning to friend and foe alike, the magnificent indifference to odds.

It is good news that the Magistrates and Town Council of Arbroath are to sanction an annual procession of school children to the Regality Room of the ancient Abbey where the Declaration was signed and are, on that day, every year henceforward, to entertain a few distinguished Scotsmen as their guests, It is a small beginning; it may grow. The date should become a great national history; and the site the scene of an annual pilgrimage drawing hundreds of thousands of Scots of every sort and condition to the home of one of the most memorable and inspiring things, not only in Scottish history, but in the history of humanity.

Special Correspondent, 4 April 1929

Major Elliot and Scottish Nationalism

Speaking in Glasgow the other day Major Walter Elliot, MP, Under-Secretary of State for Scotland, referring to the government of Scotland, said that the reforms under the Act for the Reorganisation of Offices were only beginning, but they would become greater and greater as time went on. They all felt that the life of Scotland ought to be extended and developed, and that there were great problems peculiar to Scotland. That Act sought to move, as far as possible, the government of Scotland out of Whitehall to Edinburgh, and it did not involve the setting up of a separate legislature in Edinburgh.

What Major Elliot forgot to add was that it – like the far more revolutionary local Government Bill – was forced upon Scotland against the whole weight of Scottish traditions and desires by dint of English votes. Either may or may not be good in themselves; but the bulk of Scottish representative opinion was against them, and what Major Elliot and his colleagues have to justify is subjecting Scotland to the will of the English majority at Westminster in this way. No matter what motives may be professed by Major Elliot and his colleagues, this is neither more nor less than deliberate treachery to Scottish democracy. Even if the ends justified the means, that would not make the latter less than singularly unscrupulous and indefensible. The mere transference of executive functions from London to Edinburgh means nothing – if the inspiration behind the administration remains English, and the Acts which govern the Departments are English legislation, imposed upon Scotland by a supplementary clause and forced through by English votes against the representations of the majority of the Scottish members of all parties.

The outstanding characteristic of both the Reorganisation of Scottish Offices Act and Local Government is that they are calculated to destroy the last vestiges of Scottish democratic control of Scottish affairs, and give almost dictatorial power to the permanent officials. This is directly contrary to the desires – if not in the interests – of the people of Scotland: and it remains to be seen whether it has any practical advantages to counterbalance its grave and dangerous disadvantages. It certainly cannot be taken for granted that it has; past experience shows conclusively that the imposition of alien legislation on Scotland, unsuited to its particular requirements and foreign to the mentality of its people, has been very largely responsible for the deplorable conditions obtaining in our country today.

It is a sign of grace to find Major Elliot admitting that these problems exist, and that they are peculiarly Scottish in character and consequently require special treatment. But he cannot point to any such treatment being given to them. He carefully avoided going into details concerning these problems. In the opinion of an ever-increasing body of intelligent Scottish opinion, they are directly due to our inequitable treatment by England and the systematic neglect and mishandling of our affairs by the Westminster Parliament. The general realisation today of the existence and nature of these problems is not due to Major Elliot and his friends, but to the persistent propaganda of Scottish nationalists, who have succeeded in breaking down to a certain extent the conspiracy of silence with regard to Scottish affairs so long maintained by English and Anglo-Scottish interests.

Major Elliot said that one of Mr Lloyd George's planks deals with the housing question, and that the Liberal pamphlet gave figures purporting to show the proportion of houses allotted to Scotland. He contended that these figures were not correct. In Scotland, he said, they had had their share, and more than their share, of houses under slum clearances and under the Act of 1924. Taking it all round there was only one Act under which Scotland was allotted a strikingly smaller number of houses than England, and that Act was put on the Statute Book by Mr Lloyd George himself after the War.

The Liberal record in regard to Scotland will certainly not bear inspection, but neither will the Tory record. Major Elliot forgets that not long ago Mr Baldwin came to Scotland and made totally erroneous statements with regard to Scottish housing, which were subsequently exposed in the House of Commons. Even supposing Scotland had had its fair share of houses, that would not matter if the need were greater in Scotland. The fact would remain that Scotland has got infinitely less than its share in many other connections – that that represents a huge aggregate loss to Scotland – and that a fraction of that loss might very well have been applied to the solution of the Scottish housing problem irrespective of what England got. Why should Scottish requirements be measured by English? Scotland built up a splendid educational tradition in the past, simply because the Scottish people were ready to spend far more money on education than the English. Now Scottish educational grants are fixed to a certain proportion of the moneys assessed for by English educational authorities. That is to say the Scottish educational system is financially restricted by the inferior English system, with disastrous results.

Major Elliot has admitted the peculiar and pressing character of Scottish national problems. He cannot escape from the fact that these problems have been allowed to develop under the existing system. It is absurd to expect them to be cured by the very system that has created them. The more Major Elliot and his friends try to avoid the difficulty of recognising the urgent requirements of Scotland today in order to pretend that English control of Scottish affairs is not responsible for the lamentable state of affairs existing in our country today, the more the discrepancies between their claims and the actual facts will lead intelligent Scots to question their basic assumptions. It is, in fact, this process which is so rapidly building up the membership of the Scottish Nationalist Party, whose sound practical programme for the reconstruction of Scotland compares so favourably with the inconsistent pro-English attitude of men like Major Elliot, who are too obviously the servants of the existing order, and only as a very bad second the servants of Scotland.

Special Correspondent, 18 April 1929

The Highland Problem

I

'Oh that my adversary had written a book', was the exclamation of the Patriarch

Job. The Liberal Party has, in this respect, amply gratified the wish of its adversaries, for it has written three books, one yellow, one green, and the last Shepherd Tartan coloured. All these books are full of useful facts, systematically arranged, which, when carefully considered, are a tremendous indictment of the Liberal Party itself. No more damaging condemnation of any political party can be found than the following extract from the Tartan Book, page 345: –

> In short, so serious is the position into which the Highlands have fallen from the past neglect or misuse of its resources that, in effect, the Highland area requires now to be treated as an undeveloped colony. The task is too great and too important to be left to the unregulated and uncoordinated enterprise of private individuals. Success can only be ensured by a national effort such as has been made in the development of our colonies and mandated territories.

And who is responsible for the past neglect and misuse of Highland resources? Why, of course, those parties which have been in power in the House of Commons at Westminster – viz., the Liberals and their present allies the Unionists. The Government of the Highlands has always been in the hands of these two parties, and the confession of failure now recorded in the Tartan Book is proof of the folly of leaving Highland affairs to be further mismanaged and misdirected by them.

Another count in the indictment against the Liberals is recorded at page 320 of their latest book: 'Moreover the procedure of the Board of Agriculture in effecting settlements is costly and dishearteningly dilatory.' Who created the Board of Agriculture and passed the legislation which makes its procedure so costly slow but the great Liberal Party, when it had in the Commons a great majority which it was too supine or too disunited to properly utilize. It is no excuse for the Liberals to say, what is no doubt true, that their legislation was emasculated by the House of Lords. Their own wealthy supporters – the men who provided the funds for the party's election expenses, were accessories to the crimes of the Lords before and after the deed. The simple Highland voters were led to believe that good bills introduced as Government measures would be placed on the statute book unimpaired. They did not know that the Liberal Party would always give way to the House of Lords rather than fight, on a Highland question a general election involving the great constitutional issue of Commons versus Lords, nor that the Highland members of Parliament could always be relied on to submit tamely to whatever their masters in the Cabinet might determine. How differently they dealt with the land question in Ireland. Even a Tory Government passed a great measure of land purchase, but that was because both parties knew that the Irish would stand no nonsense. Where the Highlanders were concerned it was enough 'To promise, pause, prepare, postpone, And end by letting things alone.' In fact the Liberals have been and always will be submissive to the Lords, for Liberal Party funds are mainly secured by selling titles to the wealthy profiteers, the successful 'cornerers' and usurers who pay fabulous sums to get into the peerage.

It may truthfully be said of the Highlands of Scotland that for a period of 100 years ending with the violent evictions of Leckmiln in 1883, their history has been, like that of Ireland, the history of rapine. When the clan or patriarchal system prevailed the lands were held by the cultivators by the law of customary occupation or immemorial right, necessarily embodied in the reciprocal necessities and affections of chief and clansmen – in fact the land in the Highlands was a socialized land. It was not the absolute property of any one individual. But the Whig and Tory oligarchs, into whose hands the malign accident of destiny placed the fortunes of the sylvan tribes who inhabited the mountains, changed all this. They introduced, by legal chicane, the feudal doctrine of property into the Highlands, which threw vast territories into the absolute control of single individuals who had only been the representatives of their tribe.

Under the old system the land was cultivated to its utmost extent, and it maintained a large and vigorous population equal to any other people in Europe. What has to be kept in mind now is that the condition of the Highlands, as we now see it, is wholly the product of the arbitrary action of the landowners. Vast areas were deliberately cleared of their human population in order that the land might be let in form of large sheep farms – an enterprise then highly remunerative from the landlords' point of view. As the rents from sheep-farming declined, the place of sheep was gradually taken by deer, a change which further reduced the population. What population now exists in Sutherland, Ross, and Inverness, and in some places in other shires is comprised in congested crofting townships on the coast. A residue of the evicted people were allowed to settle on the coast on patches of ground that had little or no letting value. Those refugees cleared the ground and built houses for themselves. The townships they built exist today in essentially the same economic state as when founded. They were and are carefully prevented from extending their bounds and increasing. The result is that two-thirds of every family have perforce to seek a living elsewhere, although there is unlimited land available for the expansion of these communities. It is not all good land, but the people are able and anxious to use it – a factor of considerable economic value to the State. They are prevented from using it because their tenancy is supposed to be less profitable to proprietors than occupation by deer or sheep, and everything is done to keep down the population to avoid the disturbance of game and to maintain the high selling price of the land, now rendered more suitable for sporting purposes.

16 May 1929

II

The social economy of the Highlands of Scotland stands in tragic isolation in contrast to the general development of the mountainous districts of Western and Central Europe. In the mountainous districts of France, the Vosges, Jura, Cevennes, Savoy, in the Black Forest and Bavaria in Switzerland and Tyrol, and in Norway, the peasant population has been allowed to work out its own salvation. It was not so in the Highlands of Scotland. The oligarchs who, at Westminster, decided otherwise have made two big errors. Instead of building upon the existing rudimentary civilisation of these regions, to a large extent they extirpated it. Again, in obedience to the current mercantilist doctrines of the day they subordinated everything to hill sheep farming for the production of wool. On the other hand, the peasant communities of the other European districts mentioned relied more on cattle rearing and dairying, and in some parts on the keeping of sheep and goats. These forms of agriculture employ more labour than hill sheep farming, which has implied the least amount of labour on the land and a progressive impoverishment instead of an enrichment of the land. Hence the lower ground is kept up to its best capacity if the valley is inhabited by a peasant community raising cattle. It may not be possible to grow cereals or roots, but the hay crop takes their place, and the cattle are out on the high pastures in the summer and indoors in the winter.

The Highlands might have developed on these lines, and might do so even now. The Crofters' Act of 1886 gave security of tenure, but furnished the landlords with what seemed to them a good reason for opposing an extension of holdings. The result was that the Crofters Acts simply stereotyped conditions and made progress in extending or increasing holdings impossible, and the system now in vogue results in the emigration of the best elements and a tendency to local deterioration. The men with energy, enterprise, and invention go away to enrich our colonies.

If the Highlands were normally populated and had evolved natural economic conditions there would be no transport problem. And if they are to be redeemed and existence made possible for a population such as ought to be usefully employed in them, the State will require to spend large sums in improving communications; but that will prove a first-class investment for the nation, for, as the eminent political economist Professor Marshall says: 'The most valuable of all capital is that invested in human beings.' This expenditure on transport will not be justifiable, unless there is a guarantee of amended land administration. 'Until', as the Scottish Land Court in their annual report for 1916 say, 'that system of law and policy which places the preservation of deer and other game above the production of population of the country for the pleasures of the wealthy of this and foreign nations is completely reversed.' In short, whether by Nationalization or other effective system of government control or taxation, those who are at present preventing the people of the Scottish nation from making full use of the land must have the power to do so taken from them. This would *in effect* be a reversion to the ancient clan-ownership of the land.

The building of the railways that penetrate the Highlands has in no case been attended by an increase of rural population along the route. It is therefore in the interest of the nation, as well as of the Highland people, that land legislation be passed such as will make an increase of population possible not only in the regions served by existing railways, but also along the routes of the 382 miles of new railways recommended by the Rural Transport Committee of 1919.

An increase of population, by adding to the national earnings and by broadening the basis of taxation, represents an indirect return for schemes that in their immediate results may be uneconomic.

That such legislation has not been even proposed by either Liberals or Unionists is damning evidence of their incompetence to govern the country. The leaders of both these parties are dominated by the great landowners and by the sporting interest, and it is hopeless to expect any real land reform from them.

The attempts made by the Liberal Party to remove or to mitigate the clamant evils from which the Highlands suffer have been ineffective. The Crofters Act of 1886, passed to prevent the nobility and landed gentry in the Highlands from stealing their smaller tenants' property, contains a clause to permit a landlord to resume possession of a holding if he requires it for the good of the estate, and by the Act of 1911 he is further empowered to resume possession of a holding for his own occupation. This has led to many crofters being deprived of their holdings – when the landlord sells crofts to individuals who are not crofters but who wish them for their own occupancy. This serious flaw in the Acts is well known to the leaders of both Liberals and Unionists, but neither of these parties has taken any steps to remedy the evil. These acts were in reality mutilated to make them agreeable to the House of Lords.

When the Labour Party was in office, for a few months, their Scottish secretary, Mr Adamson, introduced a bill to amend the Acts, but before it could be passed through Parliament the Liberals, including all the Highland members, voted with the Tories and put the Labour Party out, with the results we know. Crofters may bid farewell to their fancied security of tenure unless Scotland secures self-government. The Act of 1886 applied to only seven counties and covered only tenants whose annual rent did not exceed £30. As was afterwards admitted, when the amending Act of 1911 was passed, the 1886 legislation should have been applied to all Scotland and to all agricultural tenants. Many other instances can be given of the ineptitude of Liberal legislators and even of their total failure to legislate at all when confronted with crying evils.

In the last fifty years the Liberals appointed two Royal Commissions and a Departmental Committee to report, inter alia on the deer forests. These commissions and Committee, composed of mainly landlords and their friends, with absolute unanimity called on the Government to prohibit the extension of deer forests, an extension the Commissions regarded it with '*alarm and reprobation*'. Since the first Commission reported in these strong terms in 1864, the deer forest has been allowed to grow to an almost unbelievable extent; the area under deer has about doubled, and now amounts to about 4 million acres or nearly a fifth of Scotland.

The Departmental Committee (1919) presided over by the greatest living authority on deer forests, a large Highland landlord, who does not conceal his opinion that there is no deer forest however barren and remote which could not serve a better purpose, unanimously recommended that the deer forest lands should be returned to useful purposes. Long before 1884 Hugh Miller wrote in his paper the *Witness*: –

> The cottage and the croft have been *herried* to make way for grouse and deer, and as far as the production of food is concerned – food available for the ordinary purposes of life – hundreds of thousands of acres that once grew and supported soldiers second to none who ever stepped might as well be sunk in the bottom of the sea. Not only are they not cultivated, but in some cases they are not even to be *seen*.

Since Miller's time game preserving has reached alarming proportions in Lowlands as well as in the Highlands.

23 May 1929

III

THE DEER FORESTS

Never within the historical period have there been so many deer in Scotland as there are today. In the winter time they raid farms within a few miles of Glasgow, and never within historical times have so few people been employed on the land. Since 1851 the adult male workers in agriculture in Scotland have diminished by 71,000 or 33⅓ per cent. And since 1869 – the year when complete agricultural statistics were first recorded – half a million acres of good arable ground have gone out of tillage. It is alleged that the rents paid for the deer forests form a compensation to the nation. The assessed annual rental of all the deer forests was in 1921 only 120,000, latest figures available – an absurd yield for about a fifth of the area of Scotland.

And in face of all this the Liberals have the presumption to ask the Highland people to return them again to power. Very competent authorities writing in a judicial capacity (Rural Transport Committee 1919) say:

> Among the possibilities of realising the assets of the Highlands is the development of a tourist industry, such as brings wealth to Switzerland, Tyrol, and the Black Forest. On the whole this is a surer and more stable source of wealth than preserving them for the recreation of the minute minority who are rich enough to afford to rent a deer forest. Moreover, throwing the Highlands open to the tourists is not incompatible with retaining the more modest and less exclusive kind of sport – viz., fishing.

AN ENGLISH CRITIC

In a recent issue of the *Observer*, Mr Garvin writes: –

> There is no prospect of any legislation (even supported by the boldest of forestry programmes) keeping the Highland population upon the land without the aid of what may be called a Holiday Franchise. The great evil caused by a dominant sporting interest is that it obstructs the development of one of the finest natural playgrounds of Europe. To throw the Highlands completely open for holiday purposes would give them a new economic life, whose employments would do more for the small-holder than any amount of State spoon-feeding.

If we had in Scotland an enlightened Government, such as is possessed by the Norwegians or Swiss, the lands now yielding, as deer forests, the above small sum of £120,000 would, when utilized for small holdings, sylviculture, and a tourist industry, yield a rental at least twenty times that amount, or say two and a half million pounds sterling.

The Liberals have permitted a few super-wealthy men to make the most beautiful parts of the Highlands forbidden land to all mankind except the deer stalker and his ghillies. Not one Scotsman in 10,000 has ever seen them, or will be allowed to see them, if Liberal and Tory statesmen are further tolerated by the inhabitants of Scotland.

TRANSPORT AND INDUSTRY

The Liberal failure with land legislation is equalled by its ineptitude, and its omissions by its disastrous neglect of rural transport. The Walpole Commission of 1890 and the Rural Transport Committee (1919) made recommendations equal in importance and in sagacity to those made by the Deer Forest Commissions, and with the same results. Liberals and Unionists treated them all alike by ignoring them, heedless of the interests of Scotland and of the welfare of thousands of families in the rural districts.

The Committee of 1919 made 62 important recommendations: – new railways, new roads, to be provided with public motor services, of a total of 937 miles, much of it in the Lowlands, and nine new steamer services all on the seas north of the Point of Ardnamurchan and round to Wick, covering a similar aggregate distance. These recommendations the Committee think indicate the minimum requirements to arrest the rural depopulation of Scotland, yet not one of the schemes has been commenced, although they have been before our so-called statesmen now for ten years.

FISHING A MINE OF WEALTH

In the Western Highlands and Islands the position is generally that, though in the form of fishing the people have a mine of wealth at their doors, they are unable to exploit it on account of the absence of facilities for transport, and surely there is an obvious obligation on the nation, in its own interest, to remove the isolation in which the people live. The experts who have reported on transport in Scotland take the broad view that there is a national duty to provide every community with reasonably convenient means of communication. The fact that people settle in isolated districts implies no fault on their part; with limited facilities they are endeavouring to utilize the resources of land and sea, and in this way are giving effect to national policy, and are entitled to claim the utmost assistance the State can afford. In considering what assistance is possible, it would be too narrow a view to look merely for a direct pecuniary return on the capital expended. The indirect return is important – the increased production and better diffusion of wealth, and, more than these, the growth of intelligence, efficiency and contentment in the population. They press this view more strongly as it accords with the national aspiration that wherever capacity exists there also should be given opportunity for its fullest development. In fact, the problem of the West Coast is the problem of Scotland as a whole. No systematic attempt has been made to develop agriculture, fishing, and rural industries by the provision of adequate means of transport. That transport facilities exist in other parts of the country is an accident due to industrial conditions. Scotland, compared with other countries in Europe where fair comparison is possible, is at the bottom of the list. Other nations are wiser. If we had such efficient transport as Denmark possesses we would have, in Scotland, 1066 miles of railways alone.

FISH TRANSPORT

For the conveyance of fish to London by express passenger trains the railway companies quote from all stations in Scotland and from Portree and Stornoway the same rate, irrespective of distance. The railways do not provide conveyance from these two ports, but the bringers of fish from them to the rail head at Mallaig or Kyle are allowed a rebate proportionate to the through distance. But the expense of bringing the fish to these seaports or to the rail head from the distant seas round the islands or from the fishing grounds on the west mainland is excessive, and often leaves little or nothing to the fishermen. This applies with great force to the fertile fishing banks west of the Long Island and to that extending from Stoer Point to Rona Island, about 40 miles in length. This bank attracts a large number of fishermen from all parts who, owing to defective transport facilities, lose two days' fishing out of six. It further means that the fish cannot, as a rule, be placed on the market fresh, but must be cured for foreign export. On the mainland coast of Sutherland opposite this bank, agriculture offers few or no possibilities of development, and the fishing alone promises facilities for increase of population, and these facilities, the experts say, are unrivalled in Great Britain.

THE WALPOLE COMMISSION

The Walpole Commission in 1890 realised the true state of affairs, and recommended the Government to adopt for the islands and for the west mainland coast, extending round to Wick, the same solution of the transport difficulty as is adopted in other countries with similar problems – viz., services of small coasting steamers which would give the required facilities and enable the inhabitants of the districts served to compete in the southern markets on more equal terms with their competitors from the continent and from Ireland. The Commission recommended – again following the example of what is done in other countries – an annual grant from the Exchequer of £8000 or £10,000, which the Commission estimated would be sufficient to place these services on a permanent basis. This recommendation, like so many others, our London Government ignored, and our tame Liberal and Conservative MP's in a cowardly manner acquiesced.

30 May 1929

IV

RECOMMENDATIONS OF CARLAW MARTIN COMMITTEE

The next inquiry to report on rural transport in Scotland, the Carlaw-Martin Committee, of 1919, going over the same ground came to the same conclusions, and placed on record their opinion that if the Walpole recommendations had been carried out they would have led to marked development in Lewis, and, of course, in other regions as well. The Carlaw-Martin Committee made essentially the same recommendations as the Walpole Commission, except that in certain places they recommended the construction of narrow gauge light railways, such as are common on the Continent, and of which 2500 miles were constructed in France for the purposes of the Great War. The narrow gauge is only 1 foot 11½ inches while the standard gauge is 4 feet 8 1/2 inches. These narrow gauge railways are economically as superior to the motor as the motor is to the horse drawn cart. They are recommended in Lewis – Stornoway to Ness, with a branch to Carloway. In Skye – from Ardvaser to Dunvegan, with branches in Arran, Blackwaterfoot to Whiting Bay. In Argyllshire – Dunoon to Strachur.

In the fertile Rhinns of Galloway the farmers in the southern end have, through absence of a railway, to convert into cheese the milk which could be sold fresh and with a higher profit in the Clydeside Towns. For the same reason agricultural and fishing industries are not fully developed.

The Glenkens District of Kirkcudbright, which covers an area of 250 square miles, is known to possess agricultural, sylvicultural, and mineral resources which cannot be developed to their full extent without the construction of a light railway from Dalmellington to Parton.

Within twelve miles of Glasgow, as the crow flies, there are 6000 acres of good land let down to permanent grass, which ought to be intensively cultivated for the production of vegetables, fruit, and milk for Glasgow's consumption, but which cannot be so developed for want of a light railway between Balfron and Fintry.

In Ross and Sutherland the construction of two railways is recommended to provide communications between the western seaboard and the existing main line between Wick and Inverness. These railways, the Committee believe, would result in largely increased earnings for the fishermen, cottars, and crofters on the West Coast and in the Outer Hebrides.

These and the other recommendations made by the Committee, who repeat essentially those of the Walpole Commission of 1890, would give all the islands and the mainland coast townships a daily service via Lochinver. This shortening of the passage across the Minch would be a boon to the steerage passengers, and it would bring a great influx of visitors and tourists to Lewis and to the rest of the Outer Hebrides, who directly or indirectly would contribute largely to the wealth of the localities they visit.

The present state of affairs in Scotland – a disappearing peasantry, land going out of cultivation, transport dear and inefficient, bad housing, unemployment, and poverty now colossal in its extent – is more like what we might expect to find in Asiatic Turkey than in a country which prides itself on being one of the most progressive in Europe. Strange results of three generations of compulsory education and of a popular franchise!

The reason, of course, is that we persist in the folly of expecting reforms from a Parliament that is unwilling to grant them.

I find in the Highlands that the continued delay of reforms, and the evasion of their promises by statesmen, have resulted in making the people fatalists without faith in Parliament, and who, whenever possible, leave their country to seek better homes and more remunerative employment elsewhere.

THE MACBRAYNE CONTRACT

Last summer when the MacBrayne contract had to be renewed the Labour Party, led by Mr T. Johnston, succeeded in having it revised so as to bring the new MacBrayne's operations under Government supervision. But the reduction in freights and fares are derisory, the boats will not be speedier nor will they give everywhere a daily service, and they will call only at certain important places. The coasting services recommended by the Walpole Commission and by the Rural Transport Committee are not to be provided, although the expert gentlemen who proposed them assert that they are indispensable for the development and welfare of the Islands and Highlands. Mr Johnston and his friends pressed to have the MacBrayne service taken out of the hands of the capitalists who use it for the pursuit of dividends, and who must, owing to that necessity, charge high rates and stint the service. The Labour men wanted, in the public interest, to make it a nationalized service.

VIEWS OF THE MACLACHLAN

In this endeavour they appear to be in agreement with The MacLachlan of MacLachlan who, in the precis of evidence, which, as Convener of the County Council of Argyle, he submitted to the Select Committee of the House of

Commons, says: –

> In this capacity I have been generally cognisant of the grave dissatisfaction with the transport services on the west coast of this county, and more particularly with the exorbitant rates charged. It is no exaggeration to say that these causes are largely due to the depopulation of the areas affected, and that economic ruin is within a short distance.
>
> I would draw your attention to the fact that the Board of Agriculture have spent large sums of money in the way of housing and other assistance to small-holders, and in the purchase of land for small holdings and installing applicants on them, and these and numerous other crofters and small-holders now find themselves in the position that owing to bad and inefficient steamboat services and exorbitant passenger and freight charges they are for all practical purposes cut off from the main markets, and their means of livelihood is seriously menaced.

He draws attention to the large sums the Government pays for overseas settlement of emigrants. In the five years 1923–27 this amounted to £7,377,913, and in 1927 the amount was £2,038,676, and he continues –

> but if the expenditure of such a large sum in 1927 can be justified for the purpose of taking some of our people out of the country and giving them a chance of success in the colonies, the case is made all the stronger for Government aid to keep the remnant of a sturdy race, who already have some business and employment in their homes with some prospects of making a decent living. The establishment of an adequate transport service would inevitably result in a reduction of emigration, and consequently in the expenditure required for the settlement of the native population of the Highlands in an alien environment overseas.

He then points out that Norway, a poor country, has a similar problem on its thinly peopled coast, which it has solved, since 1857, by strict Government control of its coasting streamers, which fixes the places of call, insists on good accommodation for steerage passengers, fixes fares and rates on the zone principle, and for long distance passengers adopts the principle of quoting rates where the charge per mile falls as the distance increases. Exclusive of subsidies given for conveyance of mails, the Norwegian Government's annual extra grant to meet losses on coasting steamers in 1927 amounted to £354,700. Contrast this with the paltry £50,000 per annum given by the British Government for Scotland's requirements.

Mr Cameron of Lochiel, a recognised authority on Highland affairs, asserts that reductions of at least 50 per cent in the MacBrayne freight charges and passenger fares are necessary if the Highland peasantry is to be preserved, and the figures of the Norwegian subsidy clearly indicate that Lochiel has by no means made an overstatement of what the reduction should be.

One sixth of the sum given by our Government to expatriate crofters, cottars, and farm labourers to the overseas dominions would, if applied as the Chief of the Clan Lachlan suggests, in providing reasonable transport facilities, enable them to remain in useful occupations in their own country and to enrich it with their industry.

The rural population of Scotland, compelled by lack of ordinary commonsense on the part of our masters in London to leave their country, are men who are the back-bone of our native land and deserving our affection and assistance.

Here it should be remarked that the Norwegians are a very democratic people, who, more than a century ago, in 1821, eradicated a caste system of government and abolished all titles of nobility; that their government, free of hereditary taint, is efficient and far-seeing enough to realise that the maintenance of a prosperous peasantry is an essential condition for a stable state.

The Canadian people have recently taken action in this direction, influenced no doubt by the fact that the Constitution of the USA prohibits its citizens from accepting titles of nobility, and no doubt the other Dominions will follow suit. The adoption of this salutary reform – abolition of the privileges of the peerage, now long overdue – would very simply settle the question of the House of Lords, which, without peers or bishops, would remain a court of appellate jurisdiction, with a veto as provided by the Parliament Act, exercised by the judges, men with trained minds with a sense of responsibility.

The existence of the House of Lords, as at present constituted, is a powerful factor in depopulating Scotland.

6 June 1929

V

THE CANALS OF SCOTLAND – HOW THEY MIGHT BE DEVELOPED, WHAT THEY MIGHT DO FOR SCOTTISH TRADE AND INDUSTRY.

Scottish manufacturers and traders are concerned to find that there is a tendency for industries to abandon Scotland for England, where labour and coal are so cheap. The reasons for this drift southward are obvious. The Scottish rural population has diminished, and continues to diminish. Even the southern counties, Galloway especially, are being denuded of their inhabitants. Landlords now appear to be totally oblivious of their duties as custodians of the nation's heritage in the land. Instead of using it for the production of food, they acquire it because of the social prestige which the possession of land alone confers, and use it for the preservation of game and all that that connotes. If Scottish landowners had done their duty, there would be today, at least, a million more inhabitants in rural Scotland, whose needs would employ a corresponding number of industrial workers on the coal belt.

IMPORTANCE OF CANALS

Another reason is that the great English seaports of Liverpool, Manchester, and Hull offer greater facilities for overseas traffic than any of the Scottish ports. Glasgow, owing to its position, cannot compete on level terms with Hull and other east coast English ports connected by canals with the Midlands, the Mersey, and Severn, etc., for the traffic of the North Sea, the Baltic, and the vast hinterlands that extend eastward to the great wall of China. The tendency of shipping is towards the formation of regular lines of vessels of large size for which cargo is obtained by calling at several ports, and it is difficult to fill up steamers of the tonnage now employed with purely local traffic from the Clyde. The cutting of a Forth and Clyde Ship Canal would be of great advantage to Scotland's trade, but it is futile to expect that a Liberal or a Unionist Government would provide the funds for that purpose, both these parties being dominated by the fallacious doctrine that such undertakings are to be embarked on only when there is a certain prospect of a direct yield on the capital expended.

Glasgow's efforts to compete with Hull and other English seaports, and at the same time materially benefit the Highlands, Islands, and the North of Scotland, would be greatly assisted by the reconstruction, on modern lines, of the two canals which are national property, the Crinan and the Caledonian. The former 'is worn out and in need of extensive repairs and alterations if it is to continue in its present form.'

THE HIGHLAND CANALS

The Commissioners in their report for 1917 say, 'that there is a constant and increasing risk of a serious breakdown which will involve the closing of the Crinan Canal.' The Rural Transport Committee, impressed with the great advantages which would accrue by the modernisation of these waterways, recommend that effect should be given to the suggestion made by the Commissioners in 1917 – that the Government should set on foot an inquiry into the questions affecting the future maintenance of the Crinan canal, and that the Caledonian Canal should be in the remit.

In the evidence submitted to the Select Committee on the McBrayne contracts, the Argyll County council wrote as follows re the Crinan Canal: –

> The Council's views regarding the necessity for the development of this important water-way are familiar to the Ministry, and were fully detailed at the inquiry held in 1921. With regard to the ever-recurring objection that it would not pay, my Council desire to express their opinion that it is not necessary that it should. There is no direct return to either the Council or the Ministry for the expenditure on the roads throughout the country and my Council are unable to see why, when the means of communication provided is by water instead of land, the undertaking should necessarily be run

on a profit-and-loss basis. The argument for the canal is the same as the argument for the improvement of the roads – i.e., that it will result in an ultimate profit to the whole community.

The reconstruction of these two canals would reduce the distance between the Clyde and the North Sea for ocean steamers by 335 miles, and save navigating the stormy seas and strong currents met when rounding the Mull of Cantyre [*sic*] and the North of Scotland. The saving to steamers using the canals would be equal to two days' steaming expenses. The cost of reconstruction of the canals, it is estimated, would not exceed a years' interest on the hundred millions the Lloyd-George Coalition Government wasted in a wicked and futile intervention in the political affairs of the Russian people, an intervention which encompassed the death, by violence or by starvation, of millions of men, women, and children in Russia, and which has brought unemployment, reduced wages, and poverty to thousands of Scottish homes.

THE POLITICAL MORAL

He is a very great optimist who believes that the Parliament at Westminster will ever, even in the hands of a Labour Government, pass the legislation and provide the funds required to put Scotland in a position of equality in civilization with other Western Europe countries. The Labour party in its official programme propose to create in Scotland, a legislative assembly 'with autonomous powers in matters of local concern'. The meaning of the word autonomous is – making or having ones own laws – independent. But what are 'matters of local concern'. Can this proposed legislative assembly nationalize the land or disestablish and disendow the Church?

Obviously Scotsmen who believe in self-government will demand and accept nothing less than that Scotland must enjoy all the rights, prerogatives, and immunities of an independent sovereign state.

Special Correspondent, 13 June 1929

Scottish Arts and Affairs

ILLEGAL TRAWLING IN THE FIRTH OF CLYDE – That was a remarkable case reported a short time ago of an English steam trawler trying to set at defiance the law against trawling in the Firths within the prescribed limit.

The master of this trawler when *HMS Spey* signalled him 'by flag, siren, and gunfire' to stop, paid no attention and steamed away at nine knots. When overhauled the trawler was boarded by a party from the Admiralty vessel, but still persisted in attempting to escape, until the boarding party was reinforced. The end of the affair was that the skipper was fined £170 in Campbelltown Sheriff Court. The same offender had been fined £150 a month ago at Rothesay for a similar offence! The fact of the matter is, the fines imposed are not sufficient to stop these depredators from the South, whose proceedings are strongly resented by the local fishers who respect the law. They can pay the fine and make a profit; so the flagrant and impudent poaching goes on. In Iceland the authorities have had similar foreign depredators to deal with, but by imposing fines of £700 or so a time, they have taught these fellows a lesson and caused them to keep outside the limits within which trawling is prohibited. Why are Scottish fisheries not protected by the same means? Iceland has self-government, Scotland has not.

Special Correspondent, 4 July 1929

Politics – a Meditation

'How small of all that human hearts endure,
The part that kings or laws can cause or cure!'

There is truth in this exclamation of the poet, as well as in that famous saying quoted by Fletcher of Saltoun as the opinion of a very wise man of his acquaintance: 'If a man were permitted to make all the ballads, he need not care who should make the laws of a nation.'

Yes, human happiness depends on things more intimate than governments and laws. A good conscience, a congenial occupation, goodwill towards one's neighbours, the habit of letting one's mind dwell on one's opportunities of doing good, rather than one's grievances; such things as these are of more practical importance to the ordinary man than any of the political questions he has to deal with as an elector.

But it is impossible to compress all truth into the compass of a sentence, or even of a treatise, and as the Hindu sage put it: 'To every word there is a word that is equal and opposite!' Politics may deal with matters of secondary importance. It would be as reasonable to despise that importance as it would be to despise science and learning, because these cannot in themselves secure happiness, or even make a man honest or benevolent. In politics, as in engineering, there is a considerable element of the mechanical or material, subject to the laws of mechanic, physics, physiology, and other sciences that deal with matter, and are not directly connected with the higher faculties of man; but it would be folly on that account to ignore the necessary material conditions for the healthy life of the nation or the individual. The use to which the mechanical or political contrivance is put brings in higher considerations. The engine-driver or motorist may be called on to exercise some of man's greatest virtues in governing and controlling his mechanism, and the political leader or partizan ought to be governed by the highest motives in using the political machine. But the mechanical element in engineering and in politics has its own importance, and requires the knowledge and skill of the specialist. Who would think of setting a moral philosopher to design a motor car, however wise he might be, if he had no technical training to fit him for the work? This question, one thinks, reveals the fallacy of those who accuse political reformers of being 'materialists' when the points at issue are of a material or mechanical order.

The question, for example, of whether the laws of a country are to be based on the institution of private property in land, rather than on communal or national ownership, is a material question, and it would be absurd to characterise the one political doctrine rather than the other as being materialistic. The important consideration is whether the one or the other policy would lead to greater welfare of the people: and a sound conclusion on that question is not to be expected unless the problem is studied thoroughly in its 'mechanical' aspect – i.e., by reasoning out in detail the effects of a proposed change in the laws of property (a purely 'materialistic' change) on the life of all the persons affected.

We must assume then, that politics have sufficient importance to warrant the expenditure of time, money, and energy in political affairs. But as things are, there are certain very obvious truths which cannot be denied by any candid observer. Take Scottish politics. London is about 300 miles from the nearest portion of Scottish soil. The government of Scotland is controlled from London. Scottish representatives in Parliament have to make their homes in London for a great part of the year. This means, except in the case of the very rich, that they must either neglect their Parliamentary duties, or make a living out of politics and become – in fact, professional politicians. That the existing conditions should result in Scotland's representatives being chiefly of these two classes is obviously a misfortune for Scotland. But even if Scotland's representatives at Westminster were the best possible, their work for Scotland is rendered futile by the conditions of a United Kingdom Parliament. Only mere fragments of parliamentary time are available for debating Scottish questions, much needed reforms are held up, and when a question in which Scotland is specially interested does get consideration, the preponderance of English members has the decision, and may, and often does, out-vote a majority of Scottish voters. The consequence is that while such questions as housing, coal-mining, agriculture, and education, of vital importance to Scotland could be dealt with effectively in a single session of a Scottish Parliament, they are postponed indefinitely because other affairs monopolise the time and energies of the Parliament at Westminster.

But there are disadvantages for Scotland quite as serious as want of facilities for Scottish legislation, which arise from the fact that Scotland is governed from London. The expense is great. The Corporation of Glasgow alone is computed to have spent a million pounds in twenty years in expenses at London alone. When a drainage scheme was required for Kirkintilloch, estimated to cost £13,000, the ultimate cost amounted to £30,000, of which £10,000 was absorbed by expenses in London. £10,000 in compensation to landlords and the remainder in the actual work. These are two instances, and they could be multiplied indefinitely. But this is not all. London control of Scottish business, and the fact that many of the leaders of Scottish industry and trade have to attend at Westminster, have a continually increasing influence in concentrating the general business of Scotland in London. The Scottish Railways are now controlled from London, as well as half of the chartered banks of Scotland. All this drains away from Scotland much of the best ability that Scotland produces, increasing the unhealthy centralisation in London, and depriving Scotland of what it can ill afford to lose.

The commercial life of Scotland is subordinated to the London market: the public life is reduced to be merely provincial, instead of having a vigorous national character; and the unhealthy attraction of London turns the eyes of young Scotsmen, who might be as a tower of strength to their native land, away from their native country, where there is such need for their best efforts: while the common people of Scotland suffer from a growing deterioration of the conditions of life. In some counties of Scotland, chiefly rural, the population has gone on diminishing for many years. The towns are overcrowded, and the vigour and manhood of the people is being sapped by the conditions under which they have to live and work. There may be the possibility of curing these diseases of the body politic of Scotland by purely non-governmental methods, but surely it is folly to spend the energy which is now spent on the unweildy and inefficient parliamentary machine at Westminster, when it could be spent to so much better purpose in establishing and using a Scottish Parliament on Scottish soil.

Special Correspondent, 25 July 1929

Scotland and the United States of Europe

The renewed discussion of the possibility – or perhaps the urgent need and ultimate inevitability – of a United States of Europe has a special interest for Scottish Nationalists, and the question that arises is whether the natural and most desirable affiliations of Scotland are with Europe or the Empire.

The great majority of Scots today would unhesitatingly prefer the latter, and would point to the undoubted fact that Scotland has contributed enormously, perhaps even more than England, to the upbuilding of the Empire, and is not going to forego her share in that great creation. This, indeed, has been put forward by Sir Robert Horne and others as an argument against Scottish independence, although that is a *non sequitur*. There is nothing whatever to prevent a more elastic Imperial organisation accommodating the fullest measure of Scottish autonomy as against the point of view of typical Imperialists like Sir Robert Horne. It is pointed out in other quarters that Scotland's deplorable position today is mainly due to the fact that (in the Late Lord Rosebery's phrase) 'Scotland is the milch cow of the Empire', and it is cogently contended that, Scotland in the past having done so much for the Empire, it is high time now that the Empire was repaying part of its debt to Scotland. Scotland today needs re-colonisation more urgently than any other part of the Empire, and is more likely to repay it. It may well be asked what reality lies in our Imperial connection if it cannot prevent Scotland – one of the mother nations of the Empire – sinking into progressive depopulation, destitution, and decay. Surely the welfare of the Empire depends upon the welfare of its various parts, and a strong, progressive and prosperous Scotland would be a better Imperial asset – and better able to continue its traditional contribution to Imperial development – than a Scotland in its present parlous plight. The claim that Scotland must specially sacrifice its own welfare to the Empire is one that, to say the least of it, has been very inadequately substantiated. Even if it is true – if the Empire actually needs this continual sacrifice on the part of poor little Scotland – it remains to prove that the Empire is worth it.

One thing is becoming increasingly clear. The Empire is not going to repay any such sacrifice. It will take all it can get and give nothing in return, and other parts of the Empire will not be constrained to similar sacrifices in their turn. They will retain the Imperial connection only so long as it suits their book and then repudiate it. Already in most parts of the Empire the threat of disintegration is becoming increasingly strong. Above all, they resent English domination, and the centralisation of Imperial power in London. Australia, Canada, and South Africa are increasingly anti-English. There can be no doubt that even if some form of Imperial organisation survives England will ere long be reduced to its proper and natural sphere of relative unimportance. Both Scotland and England cannot expect to be treated in the long run by great countries like Canada and Australia otherwise than as relatively small units which have played their parts, and must now be superseded by the giant colonies to which they have given birth and nourishment. The future lies with the latter, the past with the former. Not only so; but the interests of the former and the latter clash, while, in order to maintain the present Imperial organisation, the latter have to pay out of all proportion to the benefits they receive, and are thereby prevented from putting their own houses in order in the fashion their new position and prospects necessitate.

There can be no question that both Scotland and England must increasingly fall back upon their neglected agriculture and strive to become as self-supporting as they can. Their industrial predominance is steadily disappearing, and they have already permanently lost, and must further lose, a great part of their export trade. Not only so, but the natural, and in the long run inevitable, affiliation of various parts of the colonies are not with the British Isles at all, but with other elements. Canada, for example, must sooner or later, join the United States. From the point of view of the world politics it is a false and dangerous imperialism that will seek to preserve an artificial organisation opposed to the true interests of the various discordant parts that compose it. The British Empire is doomed to destruction, like all the great Empires that have preceded it. So far as Scotland is concerned, that need not worry us. Scotland has been reduced to its present sorry pass largely through the Imperial connection, which has battened upon it like an incubus and bled it white. We could not be worse off than we are if we were cut apart from the Empire tomorrow. The condition of other small European countries – Holland, Denmark, Norway and Sweden, for example – is one we have every cause to envy. If the contribution Scotland is presently making to the Empire were to cease there would be nothing to prevent measures of national reconstruction which would speedily make us equally prosperous and self-supporting.

The growth of American competition and financial domination presents us with the alternative of a greater and greater measure of industrial slavery, with an ever-greater burden of unemployment and a steadily declining standard of living. M. Brian is proposing a United States of Europe to counter this great American threat. Incidentally his proposal is anti-British, or, rather, anti-English. He sees the unnatural Imperialism of England as a treachery to European unity. That need not worry us in Scotland. We have suffered sufficiently from English domination in all conscience. Our true affiliations are not with the Empire, but with Europe – and as an independent Scotland in a united Europe we shall be in an immensely better position than as the 'milch-cow of the Empire', and a neglected province of England with no real say either in internal, Imperial, or international affairs.

Scottish Nationalism, therefore, must be anti-English, anti-Imperialist and pro-European.

Special Correspondent, 1 August 1929

'And The House Laughed'

No more cynical exhibition of post-electoral indifference to the promises lavished on the hustings has perhaps ever been seen in British politics than the fashion which the present Government have treated the question of the Scottish Local Government Act. The Socialists when in opposition opposed this Tory measure tooth and nail, and during the election denounced it right and left. The Liberals were equally opposed to it, and many of the Liberal candidates gave pledges to the electors that they would do their very utmost to have it abrogated or, at all events, substantially amended. No measure in recent years has evoked so widespread an opposition throughout Scotland – an opposition not limited to members of any political party, but embracing representative men, and public bodies, of all kinds. There can be no doubt that it was forced through Westminster by dint of the permanent English majority there against the expressed opinion of the great majority of the Scottish Local Authorities and the overwhelming weight of Scottish opinion generally. In this connection it has to be remembered that the Scottish Bill is a far more drastic and revolutionary instrument than its English equivalent. In these circumstances, it is obvious that the general antagonism to the Bill, coupled with the denunciations and promises of repeal made by its opponents, must have been a factor of no little consequence in securing the overthrow of the Tory Government and the establishment of a Socialist administration in its stead. The latter had a clear mandate to repeal the Act or, at all events, to suspend it and appoint a Royal Commission to inquire into the whole matter. There was nothing to prevent them doing so, as in this matter they had the solid support of the Liberals in the House. That being so, it was confidently anticipated that they would have no hesitation in carrying their opposition to its logical conclusion and seizing the first opportunity to undo an iniquitous and utterly uncalled-for piece of legislation.

But they have done nothing of the sort. As soon as they were in the seats of government, they began to shilly-shally in an ominous fashion. They pretended to adhere to their adverse opinion of the Local Government Bill, but explained that the intricacies of parliamentary procedure were such that they could not hope to put through the necessary legislation to repeal or suspend it.

Finally, Mr Ramsay Macdonald announced that all that could be done was to exempt the *ad hoc* Education Authorities from the provisions of the Act. The rest – including the scrapping of many of the major functions of Town Councils, even in the case of Royal Burghs, with whose prerogatives it is a violation of the Act of Union to interfere – must go through. This belated pussilanimity – so completely at variance with the full-blooded denunciations made on the election platforms – was bad enough in all conscience. It deceived nobody with the slightest familiarity with parliamentary procedure. The fact of the matter is that the Labour and Liberal parties had the ball at their feet, and could have made the whole Act a dead letter without the slightest difficulty. Why didn't they? The reason is simply that this is a Scottish issue – of little or no importance to the great majority of the members of the House of Commons. The Scottish Labour members – or some of them – and the Liberal members protested against this scandalous disregard of election promises; but it was no use.

A measure of satisfaction, however, was felt in certain circles that the Education Authorities had been saved from the general wreck of Scottish local administration. It was short-lived. Some of the Scottish Socialist members were in dead earnest about it – notably Mr Adamson, the secretary for Scotland, and Mr Tom Johnston, the under-secretary. They lost no time in preparing and publishing the necessary amending Bill. It was ready two days before it was anticipated. But their effort was of no avail. The other members of the Government had decided to drop it and allow the whole Tory measure to come into operation intact. The means they adopted to go back on their own promises and professions in this way were a pretty exhibition of Parliamentary technique – so pretty that, we are told, 'the House laughed'!

'The House laughed' at the way in which Scottish interests had been so neatly out-manoeuvred and the essential rights and wrongs of this big national question were forgotten in the delight of this predominantly English legislature at a bit of scandalous Parliamentary chicanery almost without parallel in our political history. What an exhibition! The Tory newspapers had anticipated it. They had all along declared that Mr Macdonald's Cabinet would not have the courage to amend the Bill, and that their pretence that they were going to do so was only a mere pretence, trumped up as a 'face saver', so that they could plausibly gull the electors into believing that they had seriously tried to carry out their promises, but had been defeated by the complexity of Parliamentary procedure.

The farce was even carried a stage further, because further discussion of the matter by a few Socialists who were really in earnest about it was deftly blocked by a further manipulation of the accommodating technicalities of Parliamentary debate.

The Liberals were not to blame. They did their very utmost to implement their promises and to secure either suspension or some amendment to the Act. But the treachery of the Government nullified their efforts. The consistency of the handful of Liberals in comparison with the gross betrayal of their own commitments by the great majority of the Socialists provides a salient contrast and, if integrity and honour have any reward in public life, Liberalism should speedily rehabilitate itself in the minds of all Scots who realise the true inwardness of this state of affairs when big Scottish questions cease to be regarded and become a matter for joking and juggling in an English legislature. How long is this intolerable condition of matters to continue? If Scots today were worth their salt, they would speedily put an end to this shameful farce, and the phrase 'And the House laughed' would become the slogan of a general Scottish movement which would – in vulgar parlance – speedily transfer the laugh to the other side of the faces upon which it has appeared. Conditions in Scotland today are so bad that it is high time we ceased to allow our interests to be butchered in this way to make an English holiday. If we have a scrap of National dignity and self-respect left, resentment of such unscrupulous treatment will quickly bring about a national movement which no English MP will be in a position to treat as a joke.

Special Correspondent, 8 August 1929

Wanted: a Scottish Royal Commission

Mr Ramsay Macdonald, the Prime Minister, at the time of his farcical manoeuvres with the Scottish Local Government Bill, which he denounced as a bad, anti-democratic, uncalled-for, and quite unjustifiable measure, but which, nevertheless, he professed to be powerless to suspend or amend, promised that the whole question of Scottish Home Rule should be the subject of an early and exhaustive inquiry. It is difficult to understand why the subject of Scottish independence should call for an inquiry at this time of day from the very people who are most committed to national autonomy everywhere else. They have no hesitation in conceding complete independence to Egypt. Why do they hesitate in regard to Scotland? The subject has had all the inquiring into it needs, and a great deal more. Previous commissions have reported in favour of it. Both the Liberal and Labour parties have been committed to it for many years. Successive Scottish Home Rule Bills introduced into the House of Commons for the past thirty years have had the support of four out of every five Scottish members of all parties. In view of the fact, it is sheer farce to suggest that there is any need for a Royal Commission to inquire into the question of Scottish Home Rule at this juncture. If the Socialists were in earnest on the subject, they could, with the support of the Liberals, give Scotland a full measure of devolution tomorrow. If they do not do this, a Royal Commission ought to be appointed to inquire into their mentalities.

Failing the granting to Scotland at an early date of an ample measure of autonomy (when the whole question would be promptly gone into by a Special Commission of the Scottish Parliament) a Royal Commission ought to be appointed now to consider the financial and other relationships of Scotland and England.

There is no question that Scottish people are being grossly swindled. They are being compelled to pay out of all proportion to England, and are not getting anything like the same return. The case of the miserable pittance granted to the Scottish Library, in comparison with the enormous grants made to the National Library of Wales and the British Museum, is an illustration. In almost every direction a similar disproportion can be found. Most serious of all, however, is the extent to which the industries of Scotland are being undermined by English influence and being transferred to the south of England. It is this so-called southern trend of industry that is the most dead-menace to Scotland today. It is responsible for the fact that Scottish unemployment is almost 50 per cent worse than English, although the drain of emigration from Scotland is nearly 200 per cent greater. It is amazing that facts such as these should not yet have penetrated the Scottish consciousness and stimulated an overwhelming demand for a thorough inquiry into the whole range of Anglo-Scottish relationships. One thing is certain. There may be little organised demand for Scottish independence today, but no such inquiry can be held, and the essential facts and figures disclosed, without leading to an immediate and irresistible demand from the inhabitants of Scotland for the severance of the union of the two countries. Scotland is being bled white. The *Glasgow Herald* has recently published a series of remarkable articles dealing with the plight of the Scottish herring industry. In 25 out of 27 Scottish fishing areas there have been decreases in the number of unemployed, varying from 40 to 80 per cent during the past forty years. But this is only typical of every other department of Scottish life today. Over a fifth of the entire country is reserved for sporting purposes, and is in the hands mainly of Americans. Much of this is agricultural land. No progress is being made with land-settlement or afforestation. Rural depopulation is continuing. There has been a great pother in certain quarters about Irish immigration. Actually, English immigration, of which we hear nothing, is the greater menace. On every hand Scotland is faced with tremendous problems, and the steady expatriation or impoverishment of the native Scottish stock. It is futile to inquire into any of these questions separately – they harry together, and what is needed is a comprehensive inquiry into the whole subject. It will disclose a startling and well-nigh incredible state of affairs.

The inquiry ought to be an independent one – that is to say, the best plan would be to call in distinguished foreign experts with no Anglophile tendencies, and in addition to the Scottish Local Authorities, evidence ought to be taken from the leaders of the Scottish National Party and other organisations which have been conducting research work into Scottish affairs, and have very unorthodox reports and proposals to make. We do not want another Royal Commission on conventional lines, who will simply submit the kind of report which has no other aim or object than to find a resting-place in an official pigeon-hole and accumulate dust. But given a Commission that means business, and which has no restricted views of reference to bind it, the present condition of Scotland, and the extent to which England is directly or indirectly responsible for the shameful state of affairs which has been allowed to develop, should lead to the production of one of the most remarkable documents in modern European history.

Special Correspondent, 22 August 1929

from Christopher M. Grieve: an appreciation

The news that Mr C. M. Grieve, the famous Scots litterateur and poet, has made the decision to leave Scotland permanently, came as a great shock to many, however slightly cognisant of his heroic fight during the last ten years for the auld country.

If ever man had love of country this man had; a love which grew the more intense as he watched day by day the heaping-on of sorrow and distress on Albyn, the beggar-maid among nations.

From 1919 to this year it may be claimed with safety that he was the most formidable champion in the desperate struggle to save Scotland from her enemies – and friends. Not a week passed but articles flowed from his pen in an attempt to re-waken Scots to the plight of their country, to destroy the blight of Anglicisation, to fan nascent nationalism into a steady flame. What if those articles were diverted into subterranean channels or were stopped before they reached the public? Grieve-M'Diarmid knew, or was soon to learn, that the way of the prophet is hard, but such was his courage – a thing far removed from the

Barriesque variety – that he was determined to continue, until Scotland had no use for him.

His decision to accept 'moral banishment' means that he believes Scotland has done with him. For the time being the 'unhidden Scotland' has won, the Scotland for which he had such a vitriolic hatred. The Scotland of britherhoods o' men; of Scots reunions, of critics concerned with the nice conduct of 'tae' and 'to'; of literary bands of Buchan farmers who didn't like their Scots synthetic, of friends who 'admired his courage', of enemies who thought 'the man should be stopped', of poets who derived their inspiration from the special drainpipes fitted to the Infinite.

Perhaps none of us quite realized the struggle Grieve-M'Diarmid had to 'create' a Scottish Renaissance. He and no one else was the genius of this post-war efflorescence, and, despite the array of talent which sprang into view under his standard, he remains its living embodiment. It has cost him ten of the best years of his life to teach the elements of literary geography to his countrymen, who never did like lessons to be pungent in public.

Grieve's first published work, apart from the monumental *Northern Numbers,* by far the best anthology of Scots poetry, was *Annals of the Five Senses,* consisting of marvellous experiments in the cerebral manner. Compared with Joyce at this period he was a more polished craftsman: his work had no blurred edges, but he had no spiritual upheaval similar to Joyce's to liberate a Scottish *Ulysses.*

That period of experimenting in English passed, and, as he once confessed, he could not return to that style, since, from soaking himself in the Scots tongue, he had come to think in Scots. There followed his poems *Sangschaw* and *Penny Wheep,* mercurial flights in lyricism, culminating in *A Drunk Man looks at the Thistle.* Here in one sustained effort was laid bare the soul of Scotland, and M'Diarmid had almost rid himself of the 'unhidden' hand. That the effort was not quite successful is evident from his more recent writings. He seemed to have withdrawn in on himself as one who takes a rest after heavy fighting. That the fight has not been abandoned only time will tell. When Scotland needs Grieve-M'Diarmid it will not call in vain.

Special Correspondent, 12 September 1929

from The Myth of Scottish Educational Supremacy: a frank survey

If it was simply a matter of prestige, if the Scottish Universities offered equal educational facilities with those of Oxford and Cambridge, we could afford to smile at the absence of our young 'maharajas', the nobility, but both in equipment and in numbers and personnel of their staff the Scottish Universities are decidedly inferior to their English counterparts.

THE FINANCIAL HANDICAP

The difficulty of a university like that of Glasgow, in her efforts to maintain the status of Scottish culture, is, on sure evidence, a financial difficulty. Glasgow University has an annual revenue of a little under £250,000; the Oxford colleges which, all told, have many fewer students than Glasgow, together enjoy an income running into several millions. The difference, partly due to the larger fees in the colleges of Oxford University, is to a greater extent accounted for by the larger endowments enjoyed by Oxford University.

It may not be immediately easy to remedy the under-endowment of the Scottish Universities – but it is only right that the Scottish people would understand that in these circumstances only a miracle can preserve the old record of Scottish intellectual attainment. Where the tragedy comes in is that it is not from lack of ability, but from lack of finance, that students in the Scottish universities are not afforded opportunities equal to those provided in England's great National Universities of Oxford and Cambridge.

LOST INTELLECTUAL STANDING

As further proof of the comparative shortcoming of the Scottish universities, the fact may be adduced that the two most distinguished Glasgow arts graduates of last year are now doing undergraduate work at Oxford. It is more than by chance now that scholarships of Glasgow University, for graduates pursuing studies more advanced than those of their student years in Glasgow, are paid to those doing the junior and student-work of Oxford. The late Sir Henry Jones, I believe, made a fight against awards, but there is now no opposition to these payments. The only explanation, as far as can be seen, is that the Senates of the Scottish Universities have finally succumbed and admitted that the institutions, once universities, which they administer, are now in respect of certain faculties little better than glorified public schools (*Anglice*), preparatory for a higher education provided only in England.

Every year there are hundreds of graduates manufactured in Scotland by mass-production; and the prospect which greets the large majority is one of 'displaying the margins of their knowledge to school-children'. Even in Scotland, in most positions, Oxford men and women are preferred, Oxford and Cambridge pass-men appear literally to tumble into interesting and responsible positions. For the Scottish graduate with tastes of the more expensive sorts there is remarkably little employment, unless through the avenue of emigration – the way by which Scotland loses the large part of her best and most enterprising men.

WORK UNACCOMPLISHED

To take an instance of work which Scottish graduates should be tackling, a task of immense value to the Scottish nation on the cultural side, although there are also many practical and scientific tasks for Scottish brains: the shelves of the

Record Office in Edinburgh are lined with hundreds of volumes which contain – nobody knows what – secrets of Scotland's past, simply because their contents have never been investigated. A few research workers would not be enough to tackle the whole of the unread Scottish archives. An army is needed, and it will not be forthcoming until Scotsmen are *able*; there is no doubt of their willingness to extend a little money on the nation's history.

A MISERABLE PLIGHT

Scotland seems to have ceased to regard herself as an individual nation whose story is worth preserving apart from that of England. It looks like the action of Nemesis that the Scottish universities, which in time past so often neglected the preservation of Scottish nationality and culture, should now be reduced, through the loss of national pride and national control, to their present miserable plight.

When one considers their loss of prestige, it is no puzzle to understand why, with 43,192 graduate electors, the Scottish Universities Constituency, though three times more numerous than that of Oxford University, returns only three members, while the comparative handful of Oxford electors have two representatives. It is also the case that the Scottish graduates were represented in proportion to those of Wales, they would elect twelve members instead of three.

It is still the habit of Scotsmen everywhere to boast of Scottish education. In view of the facts and figures, however, it would become us not to indulge in such verbal loyalty till we have done something to try to improve matters, remembering that it would be one of the first tasks of a Scottish Parliament to reinstate Scottish education in its rightful position; for the very highest is no more than the place which it once occupied.

Special Correspondent, 3 October 1929

An Academic Conspiracy

At the last meeting of the General Council of Edinburgh University, a proposal was made which is probably the most revolutionary in the history of Scottish education. Had the real nature and significance of this proposal been understood, it would have been heralded by headlines and leading articles in every Scottish paper, but the report issued by the Council was so obscure and short that no one, who had not been present, could grasp its full meaning, and as a result the scheme has passed almost unheeded.

Briefly stated, this scheme is as follows. Under the present regulations, the degree of Honours in Classics at the University of Edinburgh means that the student must spend four years in studying Latin and Greek, and must take at least two outside classes as well. The new proposal is that these other classes should be eliminated altogether, and that the student should do nothing but Latin and Greek during his whole four years course.

The significance of this step is obvious as soon as it is clearly stated. It means a complete break with all the traditions of Scottish University education and an attempt to bring the Scottish classical degree into line with that of the English Universities of Oxford and Cambridge. As to the reason why it is brought forward just now, we need not seek far. The Professor of Latin and the Professor of Greek at Edinburgh University are both Englishmen; with all their gifts it is hardly possible that they should enter fully into the spirit of Scottish Education, and it is natural that they should attempt to introduce the methods with which they are familiar.

There is, however, a strong element in the General Council, drawn largely from among the representatives of the Education Authorities, which not only favours this proposal regarding Classics, but which actually desires to establish similar regulations regarding all Honours degrees. To all who are familiar with the ancient and honourable traditions of Scottish education, such a proceeding must be regarded as an unmitigated disaster.

It has always been the object of the Scottish Universities to give an education on broad and humane lines, which will prepare the student for later life in the world, and give him a wide and adaptable outlook. This is not to say that there are not opportunities for specialisation at the Scottish Universities, anyone will know that such opportunities are plentiful. It has been considered right, however, that even the specialist should not be allowed to confine himself to one narrow and rigid groove, but have some knowledge outside his own subject. Apart from that, however, the vast majority of University students do not intend to specialise in research work, many of them are destined to be teachers, others to be ministers, social workers, business men; some seek the degree with no definite object but to attain a liberal education which will fit them to cope with life. For those the narrow specialisation involved in the new proposals would mean the loss of much that is most valuable in their college education.

Of what value will be the new degrees instituted under this system? Can the student who has come straight from the high school, and has taken an honours degree in geography, be said to be educated? He may know something of geography, but under the new system he will know nothing else. His mind will be trained only within narrow limits, of real and broad culture he will scarcely have an element. A real understanding of one subject is not possible without some knowledge of others. For the history specialist, a knowledge of English literature, of political economy, of Latin and of some modern languages, is almost indispensible. For English literature, a knowledge of British history and of the classics is called for; this is shown by the fact that the Professor of English literature at Edinburgh – where Latin is no longer a compulsory subject – has thought it necessary to institute within his own department a special course in the Classical Origins of English Literature.

What do our reformers offer us in exchange for the broad cultural training which we have striven to give in the past? Only a feeble imitation of Oxford and Cambridge. The two great universities are the typical products of the English educational system, embodying all its best and its worst. But we may be sure that in any attempt that is made to introduce their methods in Scotland it will be the worst and not the best that is obtained. It is not easy to naturalise a thoroughly national educational system in another country which, though one with England in blood and interest, is wholly distinct in spirit and tradition. The Scottish Universities, even though many alterations have been made, still offer to the world something that is unique, something valuable, because it represents the finest product of Scottish intellect, all that a nation has gathered from the wisdom and experience of centuries. From all over the world students come to study in our universities, but if we throw aside the old tradition to snatch at something new and alien, we shall be able to offer the world only an inferior copy of what is found in England, and the world – and rightly – will turn from it with contempt.

'Mountboy', 19 December 1929

Starving the Records: why we have no Scottish histories

The Under-Secretary for Scotland has recently made some useful and telling criticisms upon the teaching of History in Scottish schools, and the text-books employed there. These criticisms were fully justified, for as a matter of fact the great majority of the text-books employed in the teaching of Scottish history are such as no conscientious historian could recommend. They are usually badly written, and often inaccurate and out of date. Mr Tom Johnston, however, has got hold of the stick at the wrong end. For this state of affairs it is not the teachers who are to blame, nor even the writers of the text-books. It is the Government. So long as the Scottish Register House continues to be starved and neglected by the Government, so long will Scottish history be badly written and probably badly taught.

The Scottish Register House stands in the same position to Scotland as the Public Record Office does to England, each is the depository of the official records of the national history. Each depends upon an annual grant made by the Government. The figures may vary slightly from year to year, but roughly speaking the historical department of the Scottish Register House receives about £630 a year, while the Public Record Office in London receives about £50,000.

Now, it may be fairly argued that the English records deserve a larger grant, but surely no one will have the audacity to maintain that they ought to receive more than seventy times as much.

The result of this differentiation is that, while the English Record Office can maintain a continual series of valuable and important publications, the Scottish Register House can afford to do very little of the same sort. The monumental edition of the Register of the Privy Council is almost the limit of their work. The Register House is full of documents of first-rate importance to the historical writer, which have never been published, and many of which have never been fully examined. As long as these documents remain inaccessible, it is impossible that Scottish history should be adequately written.

In every respect the Register House is starved and neglected. Clerks employed on historical work there receive smaller salary and fewer privileges than clerks employed on similar work in the public record office in London. The whole place is understaffed and underpaid. The accommodation is limited. Until a few years ago there was no cloak-room of any sort provided for female employees. There is even now no cloak-room whatever for the use of visitors. Students who are working there are obliged to hang their coats and hats over the back of their chairs. In the case of the Public Record Office or the British Museum such a state of affairs would not be tolerated for a moment.

For this neglect the staff of the Register House are not responsible. In spite of all the trying disadvantages under which they labour, their courtesy and good-will is above all praise, and their expert assistance is always at the service of the historical or other student. So far as personal relations are concerned, there is no public library so pleasant to work in as the Scottish Register House. It is the London Government and not the Scottish Authorities who are responsible for bad conditions.

This studied neglect has gone on for years in spite of the continued protests of persons interested in the study of Scottish history and the preservation of Scottish interests; and there is one consideration which makes it all the more disgraceful. Certain fees are by statutory authority charged to these who come to the Register House to consult certain legal documents – for example, to obtain a copy of a will. These fees must all be sent up to the central government in London.

As a general rule, the amount thus obtained in fees, and sent from Scotland to London, is actually *more* than the total annual grant given by the Government to the Register House. The central government, therefore, not merely starves the Register House, but actually makes a profit out of it. Where does this surplus go? Presumably to swell the already immense resources of the Public Record Office in London.

If, therefore, Mr Tom Johnston really desires to encourage the production of better text-books, and raise the standard of history in the Scottish schools, he must first remove this injustice, see that the Scottish research student obtains equal encouragement and help, and ensure that the study of Scottish history occupies a position as honourable as that of English history.

Special Correspondent, 23 January 1930

The Land and the People

Not long since Cameron of Lochiel, in an address on the Highlands, which was broadcast, made the statement that it was misconception 'that the land belonged originally to the people', and added that there was 'no historical foundation for such a statement'. Lochiel, himself the representative of a race of landlords most deservedly popular and respected, was perfectly sincere in making such a statement, but he was singularly mistaken.

That the land belonged originally to the people, throughout the whole part of the British Isles inhabited by those races which for convenience's sake we may call 'Celtic', is an indisputable fact. Both in Wales and in Ireland the popular ownership of the land continued down to comparatively recent times. Here is what Sir John Davies, an Englishman, writing in the seventeenth century says of Ireland: –

> The chieftains of every country and the chief of every sept had no longer estate than for life in their chieferies, the inheritance whereof did rest in no man… and when their chieftains were dead their sons or next heirs succeed them, but their *tanists*, who were elective, and purchased their election by show of hands… By the Irish custom… the inferior tenancies were partible among all the males of the sept, and after partition made if any one of the sept had died his portion was not divided among his sons, but the chief of the sept made a new partition of all the lands belonging to that sept, and gave every one his part according to his antiquity.

This clearly shows that the land was considered to belong to the whole clan. Ancient Welsh laws which have been preserved show that the same ideas and customs prevailed in Wales, where the land was equally divided among all the free tribesmen.

The evidence for the Highlands is not so full, because as yet no scholar of equal reputation and equipment to Seebohm, Maitland, and Maine, has devoted his attention to the history of land tenure there, but it is clear enough that the same customs ruled. Traces of the communal ownership and working of land remained in some districts even to the present day, in spite of the effects of centuries of feudal law in effacing them.

The superior intelligence and advantages of the chiefs, and the blind loyalty of their clansmen, enabled them to supersede these old customs by obtaining charters from the Crown giving them personal ownership of the lands. But these charters, which were obtained without the knowledge or consent of the clansmen, cannot be considered to over-ride the *moral* rights of the people, whatever *legal* right they confer. The chiefs themselves only acknowledged the chartered right when it suited them to do so. The King conferred some of the lands (it is interesting to note) of the Camerons, and the lands of MacDonald of Keppoch, upon MacIntosh by charter. But Keppoch maintained that the charter could not supersede the moral rights of his clan, and he actually maintained his ownership against the law, the King, and MacIntosh for several hundred years.

As soon as it became to the interest of the chiefs to sever the old bonds between them and the people, they took advantage of the chartered rights, and they began to evict their tenantry. As a modern poet puts it:

> Comes the red deer softly stepping down the corrie,
> Where of old the sheilings clustered; did some foray
> From Breadalbane sweep the glen.
> No! the chief, who should have been the clansmen's father,
> Razed the houses, that more guineas he might gather
> From the grouse than from the men.

Special Correspondent, 20 March 1930

The Nineteenth Century
1929

Contemporary Scottish Poetry: another view

Mr Lewis Spence, in his article on 'Scots Poetry Today' in the August issue of *The Nineteenth Century*, performs the old trick of setting up a straw man for the purpose of knocking it down again when he suggests that the term 'Scottish Renaissance' implies a claim instead of merely advocating an effort, and writes as though the movement was wholly or mainly concerned with the resuscitation of Scots and must stand or fall by its success or failure in that connexion. He considers that it has failed, but comes to that conclusion mainly, it would seem, on the ground that it has not succeeded in doing precisely what it never attempted to do. In order to condemn it in this way he has to write as if there were no instances in literary history of 'arrogance and exclusiveness' producing results quite as good as, or at all events scarcely less important than, their opposites; he has to accuse its protagonists of lack of scholarship, of consistency and decency in controversy, and even of personal integrity, without producing any evidence to justify his charges; he condemns work which has been widely praised and quoted as 'unquotable', and finally he strings together a few names, mainly of very young poets, with little or no work to their credit, and asserts on that basis that Scots poetry is today making great strides. The quality – or lack of quality – of the poems he quotes is the *reductio ad absurdum* of his article.

The Scottish Renaissance movement (a title not arrogated to it by any of its protagonists, but bestowed on it by a French critic, Professor Denis Saurat) is a complex movement, affecting every aspect of Scottish arts and affairs, and its relation to Scots poetry – that is to say, poetry in the Scots vernacular, and not the work of Scottish poets in other languages – cannot be properly appreciated unless this is clearly understood. It is essential to know the governing ideas, or spirit, of the movement as a whole before its special application in any particular direction can be followed.

> The Anglicising of all our artistic experience is fatal to us [said Mr Ramsay MacDonald recently]. Here, again, one comes back upon the educational system. There is too much English influence in it for me. We have the Celtic tradition, the Lowland Scottish tradition, and what I might call the tradition of a philosophic theology, mingled with the spirit of robust democracy, and from these sources a characteristic and copious Scottish spiritual life can be brought forth.

Without agreeing that Mr MacDonald has catalogued the essential elements of

Scottish culture, or any of them, in these remarks, it was, roughly, that point of view which led to the beginning in 1920 of this so-called Scottish Renaissance movement, under the influence, no doubt, of the general post-war intensification of nationalism all over the world. Young Scots came home and began a national stock-taking. Space does not permit of any reference here to Scottish national affairs, into which, as into Scottish arts, a searching investigation was instituted. It will serve to say that all those who have concerned themselves with this process of revaluation have been, in greater or less measure, driven back upon the political and economic situation of Scotland and the nature of its relationships with England and the Empire on the one hand and Europe on the other. Mr Robert Boothby, MP, and many other defenders of the Union of the two kingdoms have stressed the value of 'spiritual nationalism', but deprecated any separatist, or even devolutionary, tendencies in practical affairs. On the other hand, almost without exception those who, as poets, artists, composers, novelists, and so forth, can perhaps claim more concern with 'spiritual nationalism' than Anglo-Scottish politicians are members of, or sympathetic to, the National Party of Scotland, whose aim and object is the achievement of Scottish independence in the fullest sense of the term. They are unable to see how Scotland can acquire a 'spiritual nationalism' so long as its connexion with England cuts it off from the ways and means of encouraging, financially and otherwise, those distinctively Scottish traditions, tendencies, and potentialities which naturally run counter to the increasing assimilation of Scotland to England, inevitable under the present system. It is important to point out that the great majority of these younger Scottish intellectuals, who have come, with such unanimity, to precisely the opposite conclusions on Anglo-Scottish relationships to those held by their elders, and by the overwhelming majority of representative Scots right back to shortly after the Union of Parliaments, did not begin as political nationalists. All manner of considerations, such as the stinting of the Scottish National Library in respect of grants as compared with the English and Welsh copyright libraries; the paucity of attention given in Scottish schools to Scottish history, literature, and other national subjects; the centralisation of literary journalism and book publishing in London, and the like, drove them into the camps of the Home Rulers or the Separatists. Most of them could say, as Mr William Power, one of the ablest of contemporary Scottish essayists and journalists, has said: 'My interest in Scots literature does not arise from my desire to see Scotland a nation once again. It is the other way about. I wish all Scots to recognise the fact of nationality, which is vitally implicit in Scots literature.'

Confining ourselves to the purely cultural aspect, the indictment framed by these younger Scots as a result of their stock-taking was roughly as follows:

(1) Scottish education has been almost wholly Anglicised. Scottish history and literature and the Gaelic and Scots languages are completely neglected.

(2) What is regarded as distinctively Scottish literature is mainly 'kailyaird'

stuff (psychologically a mere 'compensation' for what should be our proper pre-occupation), qualitatively not better than dialect products in Dorsetshire or Northumberland and in no sense truly national, or worthy of the ancient traditions of the great Gaelic poets, or, in Scots, the 'auld makars'.

(3) The rest of Scottish literary effort is tributary to English literature, but practically irrelevant to it. It is impossible to contend that if the entire Scottish contribution were excised, English literature would be materially affected.

(4) We are the only European nation which has wholly failed to develop a distinctive national drama.

(5) Although we possess one of the finest folk-song heritages in the world, we are the only country in Europe which has failed, on that basis, to evolve any art-music – any school of composers working in a distinctively national idiom.

(6) In regard to art, our position is little, if any, better than in regard to music or drama.

(7) English influences are everywhere amongst us far too prominent. We ought to select appropriate influences from all over Europe – not mainly from or through England.

(8) No Scots writer or artist as such (and few, if any, even of those generally regarded as English rather than Scottish) is to be found mentioned in any modern survey – e.g., Landormy's *History of Music*, where, amongst hundreds of names, not one Scot is deemed worthy of mention.

(9) Every other country in Europe has essays constantly being written about its intellectual and artistic tendencies – the multitude of schools and groups it is exhibiting – but Scotland is never mentioned: nothing is happening there; it is a blank.

(10) None of the spiritual and intellectual movements of modern times are originating in Scotland. Our composers, our artists, can study on the Continent and acquire various techniques there; but they never seem able to acquire the knowledge of how to invent new techniques themselves; they initiate nothing.

(11) To an unparalleled degree the rough cast of democracy is over us. We are 'a' Jock Tamson's bairns'. We are appallingly overdominated by 'the Burns type'. It is disastrous when a whole national culture is circumscribed by one figure – one type of thought and feeling – in this way. The result in Scotland has been an almost unanimous deprecation of 'mere intellectuality'.

The list is by no means complete, or adequately detailed; and to document it from the enormous mass of writing (mainly in short-lived periodicals, or local papers) to which the movement has already given rise (I have a collection of over 300 columns of newspaper articles on the Revival of Scots alone) is impossible here. But it will be obvious that it represents a wholesale revaluation for the results of which – in creative, rather than critical, output – it is still rather too early to look. It cannot, therefore, be said to have failed; it implies a call for a tremendous reorientation of the Scottish spirit, which must, in the nature of things, be slow. For the justification of the indictment recourse must be had to other sources – to such books as George Malcolm Thomson's *Caledonia: or, the Future of Scotland*, and *The Rediscovery of Scotland*; to Edwin Muir's *John Knox*; to the essays in the *Scots Observer* and elsewhere of William Power; to the files of such periodicals as the *Scottish Nation, The Scottish Chapbook*, the *Northern Review*, the *Scots Independent*, the *Pictish Review*; to the Scottish P.E.N. Centre's pamphlet *The Present Condition of Scottish Arts and Affairs*. So far as Scots poetry is concerned, the testimony of older critics, such as Sir George Douglas and Mr John Buchan, agrees in deploring its general and comparative condition, its decline from the great standards of its past, and its increasing circumscription to a mere 'dialect verse' level. In such circumstances any and every species of experimentation was obviously commendable.

(It may be interpolated that what Professor G. Gregory Smith says in his *Scottish Literature* became a key passage for those in the Renaissance movement specially concerned with the Scots vernacular, namely: 'It should be unnecessary to say that there cannot be any quarrel with the patriots about the richness of the Scottish vocabulary, its frequent superiority to English in both spiritual and technical matters of poetic diction, its musical movement and suggestion, and, generally, what have been called the "grand accommodations" of the art of writing as well.' That is a remarkable tribute from an adverse pro-English critic. Shared as it is by almost all competent authorities on the Scots language, it naturally prompted the question, If Scots is all this, why has it produced so little and inferior a literature? It seemed absurd to acquiesce in the relinquishment of such potentialities without taking all possible pains in trying to fathom the psychological, political, or technical reasons necessitating or justifying that abandonment.)

Having framed their indictment, what were the remedial proposals of *les jeunes Ecossais*? They may be tabulated, very roughly, as follows:

(1) We must cease to be all John Thompson's children. Aristocratic standards must be erected. We must develop an *intelligentsia*.

(2) We must recover our lost Gaelic and Scots traditions in their entirety, and realise and take up the potentialities they had when English influences submerged them.

(3) The emphasis has been for far too long on the potentialities of our resemblances to, our affinities with, the English; it is high time to shift it to our differences from the English.

(4) We must refecundate Scottish arts and letters with international ideas and tendencies congenial to our national genius – importing them direct, not *via* England, and without let or hindrance from England or the automatic filter-screen of the English language.

(5) We have been singularly destitute of those conflicts and successions of groups and movements which have done so much to diversify and enrich the art traditions of most European countries. Can these not be artificially created, to start with? Can tendencious criticism not precede, and engender, creative

developments? There were plenty of precedents in European literary and artistic history where that *had* happened.

It may be pointed out in passing that an exceedingly small percentage of what Mr Spence calls the 'riper manhood of Scotland' (to whom he says the Renaissance movement has failed to appeal) have any or, at all events, much knowledge of either Scots vernacular or Gaelic literature, and a still smaller percentage have any knowledge of both. Mr Power, for example, says: 'The impression I got from my parents and teachers was that Scots literature consisted mostly of Burns and Scott and the songs of Lady Nairne, and had come to an end long before I was born. Barbour, Dunbar, Henryson, Ramsay, Fergusson were hardly known to me even by name.' He describes how he has now come by the Scots tradition in its entirety (but not yet by the Gaelic), and concludes: 'Even to me, who neither spoke nor read it in youth, the Scots vernacular has become the language of the soul.' Mr Power has no doubt as to the reality of the Scots Renaissance. Elsewhere he tells how the new school has 'vindicated the right of Scots poets to rise above the Kailyaird and use the vernacular as a medium for metaphysical or any other ideas', and of its 'astounding revelations of the subtlety and power of the Scots tongue'. Is Mr Power or Mr Spence right? Other critics of note agree with Mr Power. Mr Edwin Muir declares that the new school has produced 'the only important Scots poetry since Burns'; Senator Oliver St John Gogarty has said that it is the 'most vivid and most vital poetry produced in English or any dialect thereof for many a long day'. Such testimonies could be multiplied.

A great deal of confusion has arisen in consequence of the term 'synthetic Scots'. Of the small percentage of Scots who have any vital interest in poetry (Mr Spence himself has said that not more than ten Scots understand the nature of poetry, and claims to be one of these himself by virtue of 'second sight'), and the still smaller number who are interested in Scots poetry, the majority are timid souls whom the term 'synthetic Scots' frightens away. They will not give the horrible thing a trial. As a matter of fact, though much has been made in controversy of the need for synthesising Scots and fashioning a medium similar to the Norwegian *landsmaal*, the new Scots poets realised that they could do little towards this as individuals – it must be, if at all, as in Norway, a co-operative effort of a representative body of scholars and creative writers – and there is actually very little experimentation of this kind in their work. They have scarcely gone further than Burns himself did, for Burns used a species of 'synthetic Scots'. 'Burns is by universal admission one of the most natural of poets,' says Mr Buchan in the preface to his anthology *The Northern Muse*,

> but he used a language which was, even in his own day, largely exotic. His Scots was not the living speech of his countrymen, like the English of Shelley and – in the main – the Scots of Dunbar; it was a literary language subtly blended from the old 'makars', and the refrains of folk poetry, much

> tinctured with the special dialect of Ayrshire, and with a solid foundation of English, accented *more Boreali*.

Mr Spence takes a great deal upon himself when he ventures to assert that the use of such an eclectic vocabulary cannot become second nature to a poet and accommodate him as freely and 'naturally', once he masters it, as any more easily acquired literary language; and to suggest that great poetry cannot be written in such a medium simply because the 'riper manhood' of a nation will not, in turn, take the trouble to learn it is on all fours with suggesting that French is an impossible literary medium because the majority of the Scots people do not understand it. Poetry has been, and can be, created in all manner of ways, sometimes coming almost spontaneously to the poet, sometimes being pieced together with endless ingenuity and difficulty; and 'dictionary-dredging' is by no means an impossible or unlikely method. Just as Mr Spence has leapt at a suggestion and condemned as 'synthetic' to the point of unintelligibility work that is, as a matter of fact, very little synthetised at all, and has been found perfectly comprehensible by Irish, English, and American readers, so most Scottish opposition to the new poetry is not due to any difficulty of language or form, but to the fact that it expresses kinds of feelings and ideas at variance with post-Reformation and post-Union Scottish traditions. It is condemned as bad poetry because it runs counter to established prejudices. Mr Spence suggests that the 'exclusiveness' of the new school is an *arrière-pensée*, but surely these young poets would have been optimists indeed if, knowing, as they must have known, that poetry of quality has a very limited public in any country, they started writing in Scots, and occasionally in a Scots which still further restricted its small public by being experimental, and beyond that, in technique, temper, allusion, and to some extent in vocabulary, borrowed, on the one hand, from Gaelic (which is a closed door to all but a handful of the specifically vernacular public) and from 'ultra-modern' European poetry on the other, and still had no foreknowledge that they must have curtailed their public almost to vanishing point. But that has obviously nothing whatever to do with the quality, as poetry, of the work they have produced.

It is not my present purpose to contend that the quality of this work has justified the experiments made: I am content to refer readers to what such Scottish critics as Mr Edwin Muir, Mr Robert Bain, Mr Compton Mackenzie, Mr William Power, Mr Neil Gunn, Mr Lewis Spence (in all his previous writings on the subject), and many others have written about it, and to such outside testimony as that of 'A.E.' (George Russell), Professor Denis Saurat, and Gordon Bottomley – all diametrically opposed to Mr Spence's view – but to point out that, although Mr Spence writes as if his efforts and mine were all that had been made, that is not the case. The effort has by no means ceased, and is, indeed, steadily making headway. Associated with the purely linguistic side of it is an increasing repudiation of the 'Burns mentality' and an endeavour to relate Scots to modern ideas, and modern life, instead of to the past. 'There's a *naïveté*,' Burns wrote in a letter to George Thomson (26 January 1793), 'a pastoral simplicity, in a slight admixture of Scots words and phraseology, which is more in unison – at least to my taste, and, I would add, to any genuine Caledonian taste – with the simple pathos or rustic sprightliness of our native music, than any English verse whatever.' Giving these words a wider application – Burns was speaking only of songs to be set to old airs – Mr Buchan says:

> It is to be noted that in some of the greatest masterpieces of our tongue, in the Ballads, in Burns' *Ae Fond Kiss*, in Scott throughout – in *Proud Maisie*, in *Wandering Willie's Tale*, in the talk of Jeanie Deans – the dialect is never emphasised; only a word here and there provides a Northern tone. I can imagine a Scottish literature of both verse and prose based on this 'slight admixture,' a literature which should be, in Mr Gregory Smith's admirable phrase, 'a delicate colouring of standard English with Northern tints.' In such work, the drawbacks of the *pastiche* would disappear; because of its Northern colouring it would provide the means for an expression of the racial temperament, and because it was also English, and one of the great world-speeches, no limits would be set to its range and appeal.

But it is not necessary to have 'one of the great world-speeches' in order to write literature, and, while from the Renaissance point of view Scottish life and letters are to be stimulated at every point and any developments along the lines Mr Buchan suggests would be welcome, it must be pointed out, first, that these are not occurring, and, secondly, even if they were, the results would be less Scottish than those accruing from the methods actually finding favour. Although it has an enormous vocabulary of words for which there are no equivalents, or no precise equivalents, in English and many writers have drawn up long lists of words which the latter language might very well have taken over, and which, in view of its wholesale borrowing propensities, it is rather surprising it has not taken over, Scots has in actual practice proved almost wholly unassimilable to English. The psychologies behind the two languages are vastly different and quite incompatible. The profitable affiliations of Scots lie, not with English, but with Gaelic. In any case, as Mr William Grant, the secretary of the Scottish Dialects Committee, and other experts have recently shown, the tenacity of Scots, in all the circumstances, is remarkable. The present writer had proof of that not long ago, when he read several poems, written in Scots of such a density that Mr Spence would undoubtedly have declared them unintelligible to all but specialists, to a class of elementary school children. These children knew over 80 per cent of these supposedly obsolete words. Teachers all over Scotland tell of the difficulties they have to face owing to the linguistic atmosphere of most of the home being very different from that of the schools – Scots in the one case and English in the other – and admit that to force English on these Scots children in the way that it is done is a psychological outrage, which must be largely responsible for the paucity and low level of creative literary work in Scotland. My main point here, however, is that it were surely better, in view of the continued wide currency of Scots, and the fact that it really presents few or no difficulties not only to Scottish people themselves, but to English readers in general, to practise such a 'slight admixture' of lapsed or unusual terms upon it rather than upon English. In the latter case the context is adverse from the introduction of such terms and phrases, which would stick up out of it like stones in a stream, or, at best, currants in a pudding, whereas in the former the practice would be in harmony with the way in which a literary language naturally develops in any tongue.

This, in fact, is what the 'synthetic Scots' school do advocate, and the extent to which it is commending itself to younger Scots writers, and the reasonableness of the proposal, may be gauged from what one of the most interesting of the younger poets, Mr Albert David Mackie, says in the introduction to his *Poems in Two Tongues*, namely:

> The poet was born in Edinburgh. Scots was not his mother tongue, but neither, for that matter, was English. What he spoke from earliest infancy was a bastard lingo, compounded of rudimentary Scots on the one hand, and mispronounced English on the other, and developing, with the aid of the Scottish educational system, into a nameless language, English in vocabulary and Doric in idiom... But for the purposes of poetry he early realised he must find a language – so he proceeded to teach himself English, as Scott and his contemporaries had attempted to do, by purging his tongue of the national elements called in England 'Scotticisms'. But this process only left him with a greater regard for the discarded national elements, which he now realised to form at least the rudimentary frame of another language, which came, if anything, easier to his tongue. The kind of English in which he had learned to write was not spoken by any but the rarest, most casual, acquaintances, whereas he could find in the hinterland, and indeed in the streets of his own town, a whole world of people who spoke this Scots with remarkable purity. Two living tongues! One spoken, in its entirety, some three hundred miles from where he lives; the other a matter of no miles worth considering! He acquired a greater facility at Scots, and not only because of this propinquity, but also because of its suitability for the expression of his own un-English moods and instincts. [Let readers compare this statement with Mr Spence's opinion that composition in Scots *must* needs be more difficult.] He learned the language, it is true, dialectally, – he still speaks, and tries to write, with a Lothian pronunciation – but there have accreted round this main dialect terms originally outside it, though never incompatible with the spirit of it. This is how a dialect may become a full-sized language, and how a standard Scots may naturally come into being. We seem to be at the beginnings of a national literature...

The experiments suggested by Mr Spence, myself, and others have not failed, then. It would be truer to say that they have scarcely been tried yet. The younger men are taking them up. The hope and purpose expressed by Mr Mackie are widely shared. The drift away from the literary use of Scots during the past two or three centuries cannot be reversed in a day, but the process has been inaugurated and is gaining ground. If a few poets, at variance with the general characteristics of contemporary Scotland, and intent upon endowing Scots poetry with *kinds* of poems in which it is especially deficient, and which in the nature of things cannot have more than the most restricted public in any language, have failed to appeal to the 'riper manhood' of their country, they will perhaps have more influence with their fellow-poets, and their divergence from normal practice may be fertile in unexpected directions. All along they have clearly recognised, and stated, that they might serve to stimulate creative activity in antagonism to, rather than in imitation of, their own, and this is undoubtedly happening, and accounts in large measure for the increased output and heightened quality in all departments of Scottish poetry today. This Renaissance propaganda has, at least, succeeded in one of its aims – it has created a multiplicity of schools and cross-currents in a literature long characterised by a flat uniformity. And it must be remembered that not only have its protagonists regarded themselves as mere pioneers, but they have realised that, apart form its purely literary bearings altogether, their insistence upon Scots was a species of useful anti-English propaganda, tending to foster the feeling of opposition and to create a heightened sense of difference. They have, also, themselves questioned the value of Scots in the last analysis.

> The latest development of this many-sided and widespread national movement [says the P.E.N. pamphlet already referred to] is an effort at synthesis and the establishment of a united front amongst the various political and cultural organisations, so that these may be brought into a definite and progressive relationship to each other, and effectively related to the Gaelic background into which, it is felt, a return must be made before a foundation can be secured for the creation of major forms either in arts or affairs.

The present writer, in a pamphlet entitled *Scotland in 1980*, puts the matter thus:

> Writing in Scots has, of course, become quite a minor element in the literary output of Scotland – 80 per cent of all the creative literature of any value published in Scotland last year was in the new standard Gaelic, approved by the Scottish Academy of Letters in 1969 – but, nevertheless, in its refined form it has distinctive qualities of its own, and Scots literature would be the poorer if this subsidiary element were to disappear altogether, just as the beauty of the sickle moon is enhanced by a star at its nether horn.

Even the most extreme experimenters in 'synthetic Scots' may console themselves with (and Mr Lewis Spence ought not to have forgotten) what Laurie Magnus, in his *Dictionary of European Literature*, says of such Gongorism.

> Gongora's most contagious vice [he says] was to play with the words themselves; to introduce strange words; to invent new ones; to employ old ones in new surroundings; to invert the order of words; to use forced constructions; somehow, and, ultimately, anyhow, to cause surprise by unexpectedness and thus to attain to a style so obscure, so allusive, and so much involved as to perplex even the learned audience of cultivated linguists to whom his poems were addressed. What was the object of it, in the first place? Plainly no poet of genius would practise Gongorism out of sheer malice; and Gongora's purpose was clearly enough to supple and diversify the resources of the literary language of Spain. Every great writer who is dissatisfied with the powers of the language which he uses, who finds some words worn by use and others inadequate for emphasis, and who tries to supply such shortcomings by new formations or new combinations, is doing work which will bear future fruit, however much ridicule it may arouse in the present by its more or less violent breach with current usage.

Perhaps no language in which great literature had been produced had been so hopelessly degraded as Braid Scots before the synthetic method began to recondition it a few years ago; and if contemporary English poets feel a need to assail 'that regressive flight towards a cosy home-made art which for nearly two decades has debilitated both theory and practice in England,' Scots poets may be condoned their inability to put right all at once the more than century-old debasement Scots poetry has undergone from the time Burns himself had sufficient occasion to cry: 'My success has encouraged such a shoal of ill-spawned monsters to crawl into public notice, under the title of Scottish poets, that the very term Scottish poetry borders on the burlesque.'

That, in brief, is the case for 'synthetic Scots'. The hopeless poverty and ineptitude of the sort of thing it is belatedly reacting against (admirably illustrated in the majority of Mr Spence's *pièces justificatives*) are ample warrant for a period of far more violent, ingenious, and intensive experimentation than has yet been tried.

C. M. Grieve (*Hugh M'Diarmid*), October 1929

Vox
1929–1930

The BBC Yearbook, 1930

There might very well be a law forbidding any one, under heavy penalties, writing to the Press criticising the BBC unless the person in question had first of all undergone a special course of study, with the BBC *Year Book* as text book, and passed an examination on the contents thereof. It is safe to say that, could this be done, 'Letters to the Editor' on radio subjects would have undergone a tremendous transformation for the better. A perusal of the 1930 issue (published by the BBC, Savoy Hill, W.C., at 2s net), which has just appeared, is enough to render the merely personal prejudices and silly little points which form the staple of most newspaper correspondents' criticism simply intolerable. Nor should the great majority of leader-writers and contributors of special articles on radio topics be excluded from the obligation of undergoing such a test. Their writings betray little cognisance of the immense range of the BBC's activities, and a failure to give credit where credit is due which it is only charitable to attribute to ignorance rather than deliberate misrepresentation. The person who still believes that radio is a mere toy or hobby – who questions its educational influence – who dismisses the entire programmes with the single adjective 'dull' – who thinks that it is wanton stupidity on the part of the BBC not to suppress elements in broadcasting of which he or she disapproves and gives far more prominence to the features he or she prefers – these, and most of the other established types of radio critics, are seen in proper perspective (and may even see themselves in proper perspective and desist from their captious, one-sided, and unreasonable complaining) in the light of this many-sided an admirably-ordered volume which so effectively reflects the progress and problems and policy of this huge and ever-increasing factor in our civilisation.

This is not to deny, of course, that the BBC programmes frequently *are* dull, and that there is boundless scope for improvement in every direction – technical, administrative, and aesthetic. But do not let us emphasise the dullness of the BBC in such a way as to suggest that dullness is peculiarly associated with radio and does not appertain to older media of education and entertainment. Aren't most of the critics duller than the BBC? Isn't nine-tenths of current fiction worthless? Yet we do not find a constant stream of letters to the newspapers complaining of the dullness of contemporary fiction. Sensible and experienced people accept it as inevitable that only a moiety of the vast mass of reading-matter pouring without intermission from the printing-presses is other than ephemeral and destitute of any real or permanent value. Similarly, most plays – most films – most musical compositions – most works of art are very poor stuff. If a large proportion of wireless programme-matter is dull, radio sins in this respect in the company of Literature, Drama, Music, and Art, and not more heinously than these. Its offence is light in comparison with that of journalism. What proportion of the people who constitute the insurance-and-advertisement-bloated circulations of the leading daily papers, for example, read a hundredth or a thousandth part of their diurnal contents? Most people going on a railway journey have to lay in a stock of a dozen or so varied papers and periodicals to ensure their having anything to read at all, and they are lucky if, out of such a selection, they find anything to hold their attention for the first half-hour or so. After that, the bundle is tossed aside and the traveller has to be content with the landscape or the possibility of a doze. Newspapers should be the last medium in the world to complain of the dullness of radio or the proportion of worthlessness in the daily programmes.

In conversation the other day, an educationalist assured me that he and his colleagues regarded radio as quite worthless as a teacher's auxiliary. But I quickly discovered that he was thinking of the educational effect of radio in a very narrow and 'professional' fashion. He was making no allowance for the great effect radio is undoubtedly having on adults. There is ample evidence of this. Wireless discussion groups are multiplying all over the country. The case cited by Miss Hilda Mathieson in a recent article of a North Country miner impelled by Miss Sackville West's reading of a descriptive passage from Mrs Woolf's *Orlando* to 'walk out into the country for miles and miles', and his subsequent craving to possess the book which had so profoundly affected him may be an exaggerated example. But librarians' statistics reflect the tremendous educational influence that is being exerted and the extent to which big sections of the public are 'reading with radio'. This follow-up reading is changing the direction of the demand for books in many ways, and, on the whole, leading to more purposive and effective reading and higher standards of taste. It is impossible to believe that this influence on adults will not speedily change for the better the cultural background of an ever-increasing proportion of their children. This is the point; most people forget that radio has only just celebrated its seventh birthday. It is a prodigious youngster. Let us be fair to it.

These random reflections do not constitute a review of the *Yearbook*. But it is not a book that can be reviewed. It is a veritable encyclopaedia in petto. Professor A. S. Eddington writes on 'Space and Ether'; Sir William Bragg on 'Rays and Waves'; Professor E. V. Appleton on 'Atmospheric Electricity and Wireless Transmission'; Mr R. L. Smith Rose on the phenomena of 'Lightning and Atmospheres', Professor J. A. Thomson discusses the question of 'Natural Wireless', as explaining the peculiar powers of bees and the problems of bird-migration, and Professor A. V. Hills explains the interrelationships of electricity and the human body. But the scientific and technical section is only a fragment of the whole. The book contains a wealth of official statistics and reports of the utmost interest to all educationalists, sociologists, art-workers, and publicists generally. Scarcely a phase of our national life is unaffected. Mr Charles Morgan writes on 'The Future of Entertainment'; Mr Filson Young on the vital topic of 'Intelligent Listening'; and other articles review the development of radio in Europe and America and canvass its problems in relation to drama, music, education, and religion. A wealth of interesting photographs and drawings illustrates the letterpress; the book is indispensable to every intelligent listener and, at 2s., represents bumper value for the money. No one can rise from a perusal of it without a new sense of the enormous range of the BBC's activities and its incalculable potentialities. If this is accompanied with a determination to react to radio in a worthy way, and to eschew fatuous and ill informed comment, in the future, that is only what is due – and overdue!

A. K. L., 16 November 1929

More about the Regional Scheme

In last week's *Vox*, Captain P. P. Eckersley showed that the common identification of the Regional Scheme with a policy of increasing centralization and the curtailment or closing-down of local programmes is wrong. The Regional Scheme need not lead to anything of the sort; it can just as easily have the opposite effect. That depends entirely upon how it is used. Nor, on the other hand, should the self-appointed defenders of provincial or local values be taken at their own valuation; they may only be stressing relatively unimportant aspects to the detriment or denial of more important elements and potentialities. The newspapers which have been so full of the protests of indignant regionalists have, significantly, avoided any real analysis of the fundamental issues at stake. They have dealt in prejudices and counter-prejudices; but the competing claims of metropolitanism and provincialism, of centralization and decentralization, have not been threshed out, and there is no evidence that most of the opposition to the much-advertised menace of standardization is more than instinctive, and very partial at that. In other words, the trouble is that those who are protesting most vigorously against the seeming trend of BBC policy have advanced no opposite policy and it is difficult to devise an effective answer to a case that has not been put forward. If the BBC has come to considered conclusions on these issues, the public ought to know exactly what they are, and if these conclusions, after thorough exposition and debate, do not secure an unmistakable public mandate, they are either premature or unjustifiable and ought accordingly to be postponed or abandoned. On the other hand if, after a clear statement of BBC policy, it is found that the public are overwhelmingly in favour of an entirely different policy, it ought to be remembered that the facilities of the Regional Scheme lend themselves just as readily to the latter as to the former. The technicians have not sold the pass, and the BBC must not be allowed to pretend that technical considerations favour one policy rather than another. If, however, the BBC has not come to such considered conclusions, the sooner it does so the better. The future of our culture should not be monkeyed about with by those who are unable or unwilling to gauge and justify the effect of their actions.

THE MINORITY QUESTION

Apart from the crucial question of centralization versus provincialism, and the possibility that only the least valuable and essential elements of either are irreconcilably opposed, the development of the Regional Scheme raises many other important points. The Scheme provides for five stations – London, Midland, Northern, West, and Scottish – each to operate on twin waves and each transmitting (*not necessarily providing*) two programmes. Once these five stations are established, the BBC will administer a long-wave service capable of reaching about 96 per cent of the population, and an alternative service available to about 80 per cent. This creates a minority problem. The West Highlands of Scotland and Central Wales are two areas ruled out by their mountainous character. The untouched area in the Highlands is a large one, though the population, meantime, is small. But these areas cannot be left out of the range of wireless. Investigation should concentrate upon some means of making provision for them as soon as possible, and of rendering the alternative programme available to as large a proportion of the population as the long-wave service.

IMPROVING THE INTERVAL

The Regional Scheme is planned for completion about the beginning of 1932. Surely, this is a prodigious length of time, considering that two stations (5XX and 5GB) are already complete and another (that at Slaithwaite, near Huddersfield) definitely begun! The Engineers' Department grinds exceedingly slow. The BBC should utilize the interval to give the public a thorough training in the utilization of the coming facilities. Wireless is not taken as seriously by the listener as by the BBC, and no prior knowledge of wireless, or interest in it, should be taken for granted. It should not be delegated to young technicians with apologetic manners to try to give the mass of listeners a superfluous and impossible interest in the technicalities which mean so much to themselves. All the public wants or needs is the shortest cut to the programmes. The BBC should cease to assume that many people are interested in wireless for its own sake rather than for the programmes. Once it does this it will also appreciate that most people know infinitely less about wireless than is generally assumed by those in whose own minds the subject bulks so largely that they simply cannot conceive the wide spread ignorance of the most rudimentary and essential details. The BBC's task is less to promote technical interest than to show people how to get all they want of the programmes with as little technical knowledge as possible. The way will then be clear for the BBC to act effectively as its own impresario.

IMPRESARIO TO WHAT?

Impresario to what? The alternative principle as presently applied by the BBC may yield a clue to its intentions – or rather its lack of adequate and defensible intentions – for the future. At present 2LO provides a series of programmes intended to appeal to all sorts and conditions of listeners and to cover as wide a field of interest as possible. Whether uniformity of method, and a general sameness of the personnel engaged, does not greatly contract this seeming variety is another question; the 2LO programmes are far narrower in their appeal than their apparent diversity may suggest. The alternative consists of taking each individual programme item from 2LO and putting on an item from 5GB which will contrast as far as possible with it. It there is an opera from London, there is vaudeville or a military band from 5GB; if a talk from 2LO, there is light music from Daventry Experimental, and so on. This arrangement is surely on the mental level of a child threading coloured beads on a string, making a pattern by never threading two beads together of the same colour. The programme builders spend all their time arranging these jig-saws. They forget that the majority of listeners have not time to piece out and appreciate such ingenuities of variation and balance. The programme service is so huge and complicated, and will be by 1932 so much more huge and complicated, that it will become a nightmare if these lean-brained subtleties of arrangement are not swept away in favour of some clear and simply stated policy. The counter-items of 5GB are planned for the most part in the same spirit that is responsible for the 2LO programmes; the contrast is consequently merely superficial. To secure real and effective contrast, the two programmes – or successive evenings' entertainments from both stations – should be prepared by people of mentalities and tastes as entirely different as it is possible to secure. If such strongly differentiated minds were at work, the programmes from the two stations would be radically and refreshingly diverse without any need for this silly and artificial balancing of item against item, which, if the 2LO programme makes an artistic unity, necessarily makes the 5GB one an unholy mess. All the subtlety the BBC possesses at the moment goes into the intricate arrangement of the programmes; it would be far more satisfactory to put the subtlety into the material broadcast.

THE PROBLEM OF LOCAL BROADCASTS

So far as local broadcasts are concerned, the trouble is that they have to be fitted into odd corners of the programmes after allowance has been made for the regular features. The local material is not considered of equal value with that from London. It has no position of its own, it is pushed into a corner and often out of the door altogether. Inevitably it drops in quality; but when every regional station has two wavelengths the regional broadcasts can easily be given a dignity of place which will help them to gain quality in conception and execution; and all those who are interested in definite local values should be organising to that end. Local values must be saved, not only from their enemies, but from their friends. At the moment only the menace from the former is clearly apprehended; once the regional scheme is fully in operation it will become progressively clearer that the latter are infinitely the more dangerous. However great the outcry against Londonised entertainment and the neglect of local talent, the latter has only to be given a regular fixed place in the programmes of one of the regional wavelengths to demand on the part of its protagonists a prodigious effort for which they have so far shown little or no capacity. Much of the outcry about local material not being broadcast is due less to the small amount presently given than to the spasmodic and hole-in-corner manner in which it is presented. If the material is considered of sufficient value to be broadcast at all, then it should be done boldly and without fear and favour. Local features must be placed on the same level and under the same conditions, and must justify themselves in competition with the other elements of the programmes. If this is done it is safe to predict that the 'inferiority complex' elements responsible for much of the present outcry about local values will be even less satisfied than they are at present. They will have lost their grievances and gained nothing in exchange except opportunities they will be hard put to utilize.

NATIONAL WAVELENGTH

I have just heard rumours that the BBC intends to use one of the 2LO wavelengths as a 'national' wavelength. I presume this means an increase of power over all other regional wavelengths; and that, on this wavelength, all items of national importance will be broadcast. This is a dramatic but essentially elementary conception, and one that involves a lot of pitfalls. What *is* of national importance? The BBC must take care not to make itself ridiculous by making a great fuss over a national wavelength and then using it to broadcast a talk on the prevalence of gnats in limestone areas. Even a Prime Minister's speech may be so emptily platitudinous as to be little, if any, better. Provincialism in the worst sense is not limited to Auchtermuchty or Llanfairfechan; it is as rampant in London as anywhere. The objection to over-centralization is that this is not equally true of provincialism in the best sense. The House of Commons can be worse than any parish pump. The real danger of the 'national' wavelength is that it may be used (may be used, from a sheer lack of better material) for programmes more provincial than any ever put on the ether from Aberdeen to Newcastle, which, indeed, failed simply because they were not local enough and because the BBC had no policy for the *development* (instead of the mere weary repetition) of local talent. Real talent of any kind is so rare that with the increased programme requirements under the Regional Scheme no one possessing it need fear exclusion from the microphone. The Regional Scheme is an insatiable monster and the BBC are still showing no inclination to make any other provision for it than to feed it upon its own tail. But in that event it is likely to devour its keepers and forage for itself in unforeseen directions.

Stentor, 16 November 1929

The Film Finds its Tongue

If *Vox* is to cover the field – or rather that phenomenon of today and tomorrow which is ending the ascendancy of Gutenberg and, paradoxically, just when the danger of a machine-ridden age becoming wholly robotised is being most loudly proclaimed, restoring the paramount importance of the human voice – indicated by its title, it must deal, not only with radio and the gramophone, but with the Talkie. The Talkie is, perhaps, the most important of the three in this incalculable displacement of the visual by the aural appeal. The radio public may be numerically greater than the cinema public: but it is very questionable whether anything like so large a percentage of people give the attention to the broadcast programmes that the films command. The artistic standards of radio in turn are still very much lower than those that have been established in gramophone music; but here again what proportion of the public are interested in the recordings of worth-while music? Of the tremendous popular influence of the films, however, there can be no question. The best gramophone music may be caviare to the general – nine-tenths of the BBC programmes may be completely over the heads of all but the 56,000 cultivated people H. G. Wells ascribes to these islands (and how many of these listen in?), but the films have a thorough grip of the masses. Sir Henry Wood may tell how difficult it has been to keep the standard of good music flying in England, and how what little he has contrived to do has been due to a faithful fifteen hundred – always the same fifteen hundred – while the rest of London's seven millions have remained completely indifferent. Good literature – good art – appeals to and is sustained by similar small fractions of the public. The cinema has a virtual monopoly of the remainder.

It is not my purpose to discuss this phenomenon here, nor to argue the case of the talkie against the silent film, nor to debate the ways and means by which the cultural effects of the cinema can or should be controlled or its artistic standards raised. I think the Talkie has come to stay and will largely, if not wholly, displace the silent film, and I note that Charlie Chaplin so far agrees with me that, although he has refused to become vocal in his films, he has consented to sound-effects (one of them enabling audiences to hear the approaching shuffle of his famous broken shoes for several minutes before his inimitable figure comes into view) while, in his next film, all the characters will speak except himself – and he will take the role of a mute.

In the meantime, my purpose is to draw attention to a remarkable book – *The Film Finds Its Tongue*, by Fitzhugh Green (Messrs Putnam, $2.50). The book is written in an American fashion which I do not like; but it tells an absorbing and important story. The publishers' note on the jacket indicates both.

> Here is the story of Talkie pioneering, the parts played by Thomas Edison and the Western Electric Company in its development, and the history of the four Warner Brothers, Sam, Harry, Jack and Albert. How the Warners had the courage to put it across after all the big film companies had turned down the talking picture, their triumph, the revolution in Hollywood, and other strange results of this new miracle, make a timely and fascinating story.

When the first talking picture began to be shown on the screen of a New York movie theatre on the night of 6 August 1926, the Warner brothers had sunk over 500,000 dollars in that one picture, invested nearly three million dollars in all in a gigantic gamble that the American public would like moving pictures that talked, and struggled for twenty years that that night might be a success. An even greater drama than that on the screen was taking place in the lives of the Warner quartet as they sat well back in that audience awaiting the verdict of the public. Despite his execrable style, Mr Green makes us feel and share their tense anxiety, their tremendous ambition, their desperate fears. This is the merit of his book. But it has another merit. It shows us by a concrete example, and in full detail, how difficult it is to put across a new invention in the teeth of interests vested in processes it would displace.

> It was the first great triumph of the 'Talkies', as the public instantly named them. And it was a glorious tribute to the vision of the men who backed them. But, alas, it was a triumph and a tribute tempered by the fact that, though Talkies had come to be a reality, there was no immediate way they could be distributed to the American public. Special projection mechanism was required to put a Talkie on the screen. The whole moving picture world was determined that there should be no such volcanic eruption in their business as this new sound film implied. They were determined that theatres should not get projection apparatus for it. They were determined to snuff out the commercial lives of the men who had dared to start it all. Not for nearly two years was the triumph to be made secure. Not until 1928 did the other motion picture titans capitulate. The final convulsion – not too strong a term either – came at a time when the movies were already in a state of turmoil. In 1927 an economy wave had swept Hollywood. Companies were retrenching. Salaries were cut from top to bottom. Long term contracts began to be denied the stars. Studios were being shut

> down. The big lots were silent for the first time in years. Could it be that the movies' golden flow could not go on for ever? Then, like a bolt of lightning, came the Talkies. The biggest men in the movies began to sit up and rub their eyes. This thing they had one and all condemned – except the little group of the Warner brothers – was riding like a genii from the lamp of one company and bewitching the public. The Talkie boom was on!

This story of the competition of big businesses is graphic and complete; the financial details are amazing. It is easy to criticise the talkies, but in view of the enormous difficulties by which their emergence was beset, delayed, and handicapped, and the short time that has yet elapsed since their final victory, it is not surprising that they are still, for the most part, so crude and unsatisfactory. Give them time. Give their promoters time to recoup themselves for some of the great capital invested in them. Mr Green is not oblivious to their defects. 'The Talkie is here,' he says,

> and here for the rest of the century. It has followed Radio into being. It is the offspring of the Radio and the Theatre, through Warner Brothers, who have made it into mass amusement. It has come a long way, but it is still very new. It will presently acquire all sorts of refinements, all sorts of flexibilities, that are now lacking. The microphones that require the actor to stand near them will be displaced in time by instruments that will give him freedom of motion. Some day someone will take the cameras out of the booths, and it will be worth more than a million dollars to him… There is no use carping at the Talkie for its crudities… The highest form of dramatic entertainment will for a long time continue to be the stage. It plays to a selective audience. The Talkie will be the mass entertainment; its level will be the mass level. It will be average. But it will be better mass entertainment than the movies were, because it is about three times as hard to make any Talkie as it is to make the best movie. It takes brains. Lots of 'em, from start to finish. No one gets a chance to sluff anything. It sharpens things. You can't make a Talkie as you go along, as so many pictures were made. The script and the dialogue all have to be worked out ahead of time and they all have to hang together.

I believe Mr Green is right in spite of the way in which he expresses his views.

Stentor, 23 November 1929

Drama of the Week: *Typhoon*

THE probably transitional phase of Radio drama, which is rather a new form of book illustration – and, as such, has, of course, a place and function of its own of no little value and consequence – owes much of the success to which it has been brought to Mr John Watt and Mr Peter Creswell, and their collaboration in giving us the radio adaptation of Conrad's *Typhoon* which was broadcast from 5GB Tuesday night and from 2LO and 5XX on Wednesday night, guaranteed a certain success and interest in advance to these productions. This they certainly did not lack, and my purpose here is simply to define the nature of the achievement exemplified in this radio version of *Typhoon* and to discriminate between it and what may legitimately be termed radio drama. The official notice in the *Radio Times* made the distinction clear when it stated that 'though there may be some doubt as to who is the hero, one thing is certain beyond any shadow of doubt. The "villain of the piece" is the storm, the dreaded Typhoon.' But the storm, despite its importance, is *not* the most important thing about Conrad's story of the China Seas, nor, mutable and mysterious and menacing as the sea is in Conrad's prose, can Conrad's sea be suggested by any mere manipulation or combination of sound effects. It depended upon Conrad's comprehensive and strangely experienced intuition of the sea, which he conveyed in a way unparalleled in English, and perhaps in any literature, by means of a prose style which owed a great deal to his own foreign antecedents and the unusual processes he employed in his use of English. Imponderables such as these cannot be distinguished by the microphone, and they constitute the very essence of Conrad's work.

Piling chaos upon chaos of weltering waters is no substitute; a means must be found – and cannot be found – for establishing in the very heart of the tempest that haunting apprehension of reality, that spiritual attitude to the circumambient fury of the gale, upon which the quality of Conrad's descriptions depended. The microphone can give us the sound but not the secret – a storm at sea, but not *the* storm; and this, indeed, was what Mr Watt and his colleagues provided.

Criticism such as this, of course, in no way suggests that the production had not values of its own. The point is simply that it did not, and could not, reproduce, or suggest in any adequate and effective measure, the peculiar distinctions of Conrad's story. But that is not to say that it failed in comparison with other forms of book illustration. It would be difficult to think of any artist who could give the particular quality of Conrad's storm, nor, short of genius, is it easy to conceive of any drawing or woodcut, which could present that night of fury and ruin better than this broadcast sound picture. The voices of Rout, Captain MacWhirr, the Second Engineer, the Bos'n, and others maintained a literal relationship between the Radio version and its original; but it is no discredit to those responsible that they did not succeed in achieving the impossible by re-establishing in this new form even a ghost of that amazing organic relationship between the human characters and the encompassing tempest which is so quintessentially Conradian. The radio version, despite all its remits, remained to the original very much as a bald summary, shorn of the subtleties of spirit and style, is to a masterpiece. But after all, this is only to say that a great poem cannot be translated into prose without loss. Neither can literature into a radio drama. But in the latter case, as in the former, the translation may to a greater or less extent make up for that loss by qualities of its own which were not in the original. Such compensations were not lacking in the broadcast version of *Typhoon*.

The theme was one admirably suited to Mr Watt's technique – a series of sound pictures fading one into the another with a minimum of connecting dialogue. *Typhoon* is in a very different category from *Carnival* or *Journey's End*; and the difference in technical treatment was fully adapted to the difference in literary character. Whether a bolder series of transitions, and such an employment of surprise lulls in the storm (corresponding to sudden close-ups or the spatch-cocking of dream scenes in film-craft) might have afforded means for qualifying the appalling racket of the storm which lacked nothing in verisimilitude with such profound and elusive suggestions as Conrad's style imported into his verbal descriptions of it, is another matter. As it actually was, this radio version of *Typhoon* – *Typhoon* without the Conrad – was a wonderfully 'realistic' sound-drama of men striving with the elements on the furious night at sea.

I am no sinologue; and am quite prepared to take the chanting of the coolies on trust, but, while I felt that the version had little enough to do with Conrad's tale on the one hand, on the other hand I should have liked to have had good outside broadcasts of scenes on board ship during loading operations and during a storm at sea for purposes of comparison.

Within the limits of his art as a radio adaptor, Mr Watt scored another success to set alongside the score or so which have given him a place of his own as one of the most active exponents in Great Britain today of this new and vital form of dramatic entertainment; and Mr Peter Creswell, as the producer, again showed his admirable technical resource in the manipulation of natural effects.

Whether Conrad is a 'radio author' or not is another question, despite the success of Mr Cecil Lewis's earlier production of *Lord Jim*, and the selection of authors for utilisation in a way which rules out their especial characteristics is, of course, to be deprecated. This criticism may not apply to the same extent to the proposed production of *Romance*, as the next of the Conrad series, since that book is not so characteristic of Conrad but will lend itself far more readily to conventional dramatisation. But – in the present state of radio drama – hands off *Nostromo* and *The Nigger of the Narcissus*!

A. K. L., 23 November 1929

Professor Trevelyan's National Lecture

I am very glad that I did not listen to Professor Trevelyan's National Lecture on 'The Parliamentary Union of England and Scotland' alone, and that the others present were all English. I would have been afraid otherwise that my feeling that the lecture was definitely 'below par' in every respect was due to personal prejudice. Happily, I was reassured. The exclamations – 'But this is too boring for anything!' and 'How hopelessly elementary' – were not mine. The dissatisfaction was general, and Professor Trevelyan would have been switched off at an early stage if I had not insisted upon hearing him through.

The unanimous opinion was that the lecture was simply a dreary rehash of the 'official' story of the Union of the Parliaments, which anybody could have put together from school history books, and destitute of all the qualities that ought to go to the making of a 'National Lecture'. The *Radio Times* made a great song, in its advance notes, about Professor Trevelyan's wit. There was no evidence of it from start to finish. In the recurrent stress he laid on oatmeal and the like, however, he came perilously near 'Scotch Comedianship'. The lecture was as lacking in grace of style and charm of delivery as in any evidence of original research, power of definitive statement, high impartiality, or any of the other attributes one might legitimately have expected. I fully sympathise with the *cri-de-coeur* of the Liverpool reader who complains 'that the BBC, which has taken on itself the task of distributing news to the public, told us nothing about the Carnera-Stribling fight. Instead, at the moment when this international event, watched by the whole world, was beginning, the BBC was sending out Professor Trevelyan's Lecture from 5XX, and 5GB was putting on the air of song from *The Geisha*.' 'Far be it from me to say a word against *The Geisha*', he continued. He did not venture to say what he thought of Professor Trevelyan's address!

Space will not allow any detailed reply to Professor Trevelyan here. Perhaps Mr Compton Mackenzie may devote one of his leaders in a subsequent issue to the 'tendentious' matter of this kind, which is continually being foisted on the ether, or to the actual value of these so-called National Lectures, supposed to be devoted to important and conclusive statements by authorities of international repute, and to have a certain exceptional and permanent value. That Professor Trevelyan found it necessary to deal with this subject at this time, and in the way he did, is not without significance, and shows his awareness of new interest in it, and the extent to which other views than his are gaining ground. In the meantime, I can only make a few points to show the way in which he abused his opportunity. At the beginning he expressly eschewed any expression of opinion, by implication or otherwise, on the desirability of any measure of Scottish Home Rule, but his did not prevent him from suggesting at a later stage that if there had been any decline in the quality of Scottish Nationality, it was not due to the Union of Scotland and England, but one of the causes was perhaps 'the Irish invasion of Scotland'. He gave no warrant for this suggestion, but it certainly showed the cloven hoof of propaganda, of which he assured us his address would be innocent but which, as a matter of fact, was in evidence from start to finish. There was an obvious discrepancy between his claim that the Union was founded on justice and equality, and was an early and signal example of the virtues of conciliation – and his subsequent admission that the safeguarding clauses of the Union had since been largely abrogated and

Scottish opinion overridden by the English majority at Westminster. There was a like discrepancy between his claim that the Union was endorsed by the Scottish people, and his insistence upon the completely undemocratic character of the Scots Parliament, i.e., the people had no say. It was surely a curious form of conciliation, too, which necessitated the Union, because, in Professor Trevelyan's own words, the increasingly efficient and independent Scots Parliament was 'becoming too good'! Professor Trevelyan's omissions were as significant as his admissions. He said nothing about bribery and corruption. He did not suggest that there might very well have been, given a desire for equality and justice, a fairer method than one designed to establish the hegemony of England. He affected to pretend, as most of the apologists for the Union do, that but for the Union Scotland would never have shared in the developments of the Industrial revolution, and would have remained in a state of hopeless backwardness and barbarism. All the benefits of civilisation were ascribed to the English connection. He even trotted out the stale old platitude about the Scots being a race of scholars and metaphysicians – a hoary legend on a level with that of mean Aberdonianism. He did not give so much as a passing glance at the tendencies of Imperial reorganisation today, or the extent to which the Empire and European civilisation have been jeopardised by the determination of England to retain its central and controlling place. A reconsideration of the Union – and of the alternative Scottish policy (the so-called 'Southern Policy') to that of English ascendancy in the British Isles – in the light of the present position, might have been singularly timely and illuminating. But Professor Trevelyan evidently felt that he had given a comprehensive wind-up to his lecture when he left us with a bibliography of four volumes with which, if we so desired, to pursue the subject further. The veriest tyro in Scottish history must know that the books in question may be all very well for use in elementary schools, but that a very different and much longer list, including none of these four, is indispensable to any serious study of the subject.

The character of Professor Trevelyan's address may be best shown by pointing out a few details that were highly questionable, and leaving his general attitude out of account for the time being. Take his three statements that the Scottish peasantry before the Union 'lived in rags', were 'housed in hovels', and 'fed on oatmeal' – 'on oatmeal alone', as he said in another sentence.

As to the first, it may be asked where all the 'rags' came from to serve as habitual clothing. In this respect things cannot have altered much in a generation; consider, therefore, what John Ray, 'Ray the Naturalist', Fellow of Trinity College, Cambridge, writing of Scottish peasants about 1663, said: 'They lay out most they are worth in clothes, and a fellow that hath scarce ten groats besides to help himself with, you shall see come out of his smoky cottage clad like a gentleman.'

The change in attire between the beginning and the end of the eighteenth century amounts to this, that, at the former stage, the country people dressed in homespun, at the latter in cloth imported from England and other fineries. (Cf. *Stat. Account*, passim.)

'Hovels' is perhaps an inevitable description. But on this it is worth while considering what is said by Ramsay of Ochtertyre in his work published as *Scotland and Scotsmen in the Eighteenth Century*, which is a useful set-off to the more lurid and sensational descriptions.

'Oatmeal alone' is nonsense and impossible. There was 'kail', with 'water-kail', and 'kitchen', i.e., cheese, butter, fish etc. Meat was not unknown, though the peasantry in the south were probably just as vegetarian as Cæsar's soldiers, to whom food was *frumentum*. The highland peasantry was in large part flesh-eating, and had abundant opportunities for using game. Witness the provision in contracts between servant and employer of salmon only so many days a week. Hear what another Englishman, Captain Burt, says in his *Letters from the Highlands* (*c*. 1729): 'In some remote parts of England I have seen bread for the field labourers and other poor people, so black, and so heavy, and so harsh, that the *bannack*, as they (the Scots) call it (a thin oatmeal cake baked on a plate over the fire), may by comparison be called a pie-crust' (Letter xiii).

'The Highlands', declared Professor Trevelyan, 'were in a state of tribal barbarism.' Martin's description of some part of the 'barbarism' induced Dr Johnson to make his visit. Among other barbarian features were churches, schools, trading burghs, and a native, traditional culture, of which the tales and music still attract rather refined intelligences. Martin (1695) notes that, in South Uist, 'Fergus Beaton hath the following ancient Irish manuscripts in the Irish character; to wit, Avicenna, Averroes, Joannes de Vigo, Bernardus Gordonus, and several volumes of Hippocrates.'

Ramsay of Ochtertyre points out that the Highland coast was a place (and the only one in the British Isles at the time we know) where shipwrecked mariners could expect humane and honest treatment. So much for the 'barbarians'.

The immediate effect of the Union on Scottish industry – and it lasted for a generation or more – was a serious economic set-back. Glasgow and neighbourhood reaped the earliest benefits in the opening of the colonial trade. But the manufacturing concerns and the Forth ports were ruined. This is a big question, but the main features are admirably sketched in W. M. Mackenzie's *Outline of Scottish History* – not one of the four books recommended by Professor Trevelyan.

These few random notes show that in matters of detail Professor Trevelyan's address left a great deal to be desired and fell far short of the standard that may reasonably be expected of a National Lecture. With regard to the bigger issues, it does not constitute a document of the slightest value in relation to its subject, and this negligibility is in the circumstances a serious reflection on contemporary English scholarship.

A. K. L., 30 November 1929

Radio and Oratory

In a recent speech Mr John Buchan, the novelist, and one of the MPs for the Scottish Universities, complained that 'all the advantages of the orator have gone when he broadcasts – the Gladstone voice, the Gladstone emotion, the impassioned appeal. In broadcasting the only thing that matters is that a man should be able to speak good sense clearly; listeners judge the matter, not the manner.' Mr Buchan himself is an MP whose matter is immensely superior to his manner, and who has certainly no pretensions to be regarded as an orator. His complaint, therefore, must be regarded as bearing out the psychological rule that most people tend to envy the qualities they lack and depreciate those they have. His lament attracted little attention, but one of the few who joined the issue with his contentions was another Scottish ex-MP in the person of Mr Rosslyn Mitchell, who has won a certain little reputation in Scotland as an exponent of the old-fashioned oratorical arts in question. Mr Mitchell is unquestionably right in so far as his contention merely implies that a broadcaster's personality and delivery do count, and that a 'good speaker' has even greater advantages in using the microphone than in ordinary public speaking, if only because of the immensely greater public he is enabled to address.

AVERSE TO SPELLBINDING

But this scarcely counters Mr Buchan's complaint that broadcasting is averse to spellbinding; nor does it deal with the essential question as to whether the elimination of the 'Gladstone voice, the Gladstone emotion, the impassioned appeal' is a thing to be deplored, or to be attributed to radio. The outcry about the decline of oratory is older than the advent of wireless, and is mainly manifest today in directions unaffected by broadcasting.

DEBATING SOCIETIES

The steady decline of debating societies is one example; the widespread eclipse of sermon-interest is another; and a third, and most conclusive, instance may be drawn from the inter-related fields of politics and journalism. The notoriously small proportion of the electorate who attend political meetings and listen to the speeches is one aspect of this; and a corollary is the extent to which newspapers have ceased to give extended reports of addresses. Compare this with the Gladstone period, when verbatim reports were the order of the day in all papers, local and national, and 'heckling' and other evidences of popular interest were in salient contrast to the apathy of today.

This change is not attributable to broadcasting, however, and it is very questionable whether it is a bad thing. The ever-increasing complexity of life – the growing realisation of the artificiality and futility of 'mere politics' – the changing emphases on human interest, due largely to modern developments of the scientific spirit – are among the factors responsible for the change; and in seeking to estimate its good or evil effects, it is necessary to remember that the extent to which the influence of Mr Gladstone and his like depended upon rhetoric and appeals to emotion rather than upon reason, accounts for many of our most pressing social and political problems, and, in particular, the reaction against democracy which is so marked a phenomenon today.

MOB PSYCHOLOGY

But Mr Buchan gives his own case away effectively enough when he says that 'listeners judge the matter, not the manner'. Radio will prove an unmitigated blessing if it transforms an ever-increasing proportion of the public into critical thinkers in this fashion. It is already doing this in a substantial degree. What Mr Buchan really means is that broadcast speakers cannot depend on mob-psychology; they have to address an enormous audience of isolated – and consequently far more critical – hearers. If the quality of broadcast speaking is already affecting other public speakers to anything like the extent Mr Buchan contends, that shows a developing sense of intellectual responsibility which must be accounted one of the most salutary factors in public life today, and one in very happy contrast to the irresponsibilities of the 'stunt Press'.

EFFETE STANDARDS

It must be remembered that an exceedingly small proportion of speakers have had – or ever can have – access to the microphone and its tremendous opportunities. Too many even of that small number are still dominated by effete standards of oratory and prove dull and ineffective broadcasters as a consequence. But when a man has something very neat and important to say, and a sufficient knowledge of radio technique to 'put it across' effectively and unencumbered by 'a pulpit voice' or other old tricks of public speaking, he scores an unqualified success. The varied quality and results of the broadcast address by divers political leaders at the last General Election gave sufficient proof of this.

A. K. L., 28 December 1929

Programmes and Problems of 1929 and the Prospects for 1930

FLEET STREET AND SAVOY HILL

Perhaps the principal event of the year that has just passed, in relation to radio, has been the increasing disappearance of 'Fleet Street's resistance to the notion that an entertainment appealing to millions of people deserves as much critical attention as a minor concert in an empty hall'. But the majority of newspapers still do little more than give space to the current programmes (baldly set out, in small type, with no guidance or auxiliary information) and, in certain cases, technical articles. Only a few criticise the actual broadcasts, and that in a very scrappy fashion, comparing poorly with the attention given in the same columns to art exhibitions, films, dramatic and musical performances, lectures, and book-reviewing, although the number of their readers who actually see, hear or read any of these is exceedingly small in comparison with the enormous listening public. Nor has the general journalistic attitude to the larger issues of broadcasting ceased to be hostile. The tone of newspaper references to the fare provided and policy pursued by the BBC is captious and derogatory ninety-nine times out of a hundred. They tell us 'with damnable iteration' that the BBC is 'not giving the public what it wants', but they do not explain why, in that case, the number of licence-holders is constantly increasing and the advertising space taken in their columns, by radio manufacturers, alongside these attacks on the 'dull programmes', steadily extending. The majority of 'letters to editors' on broadcasting matters remain querulous and trivial. But the newspapers cannot exculpate themselves for their failure to provide such articles and explanatory matter as would prepare their readers for the programmes provided and enable them to take better advantage of them. In no case is any systematic and detailed criticism given or any attempt made to create a comprehensive and progressive attitude to this stupendous new cultural force. Such a state of affairs cannot continue, and there are signs that it will speedily pass now. But it will inevitably take a considerable time yet for a body of writers to emerge capable of dealing journalistically in an effective fashion with the tremendous daily range of broadcast material. What is unquestionably the case is that radio has made available to something like fifteen million listeners in Great Britain programmes of music, addresses, literary and dramatic criticism, and all sorts of educative and entertaining material of a kind to which the mass of people (especially those living outside the great cities) have never previously had access. The newspapers in general have recognised this by condemning the 'Highbrowism' of the programmes and declaring that the BBC ought to give the public what it wants and has no right to try to educate the public. This contention is a sufficient commentary on the standards of contemporary journalism. It secures a certain justification in the doubt that remains as to what percentage of listeners do give ear to the higher quality broadcasts as compared with those who only listen to the more popular items. But surely the newspapers do not so underestimate their influence as to pretend that by supporting articles, comment and criticism, they cannot help to raise the standards of public taste and enable an increasing proportion of the public to enjoy the better material. And, assuredly, they cannot justify a refusal to essay such an educative and progressive rôle, or any attempt to impose a like anti-educative policy on the BBC.

WHAT THE PUBLIC LIKES

It is precisely where this question of 'what the public likes' arises that the available evidence is most baffling. The *Radio Times* tells us, for example, that no fewer than 195 separate items or artists were single out by its readers as the most enjoyable feature for them of the programmes of 1929 – preferences forming an amazing list, varying from the Berlin Philharmonic Orchestra's recent concert to the song of the nightingale, and from the 'Points of View' series of talks to the Fat Stock Prices. Isn't the BBC in this respect in precisely the same position as the newspapers themselves? A plebescite of newspaper readers would show very similar divergences, and if the invariable test were to be the maximum appeal to the maximum number, how many literary, dramatic, and musical critics would survive the test and how many football or racing commentators fail to emerge at the head of the poll? The newspapers provide various features – some of them with a relatively very restricted appeal – for their various types of readers, and the BBC is entitled to pursue a similar policy. The BBC can actually claim to do it better – and for an immensely greater public – than any newspaper or group of newspapers. To take one item alone, what newspaper last year had any series of articles of a general interest and value commensurate to the 'Points of View' series? The newspapers were glad enough to reproduce long extracts form these in their columns and to comment extensively upon them in their leaders. The disappointing thing, however, is that this carping disparagement of the BBC's policy continues, without, in a single case, any attempt to deal with the big question of public policy involved. A parallel would only be obtained if a campaign of pin-pricking attacks were to be conducted in the Press against the general principle of popular education.

BIG QUESTIONS OF POLICY

More extensive journalistic publicity has been given to other public questions connected with broadcasting. The fear of centralisation, and the need for preserving and developing local cultural values, has been widely canvassed and there has been ample evidence of a determined opposition to Londonisation in all the provinces. What has received less attention perhaps than it deserves is the extent to which the development of the Regional Scheme will prevent listeners 'touring Europe' for fare more to their liking. Here again the newspapers cannot be exonerated for failing to give their readers more indication of, and guidance to, the wonderful variety of the European programmes. Nor have the implications of the BBC policy in their hearing on 'good Europeanism', or internationalism as opposed to insularity, been threshed out to anything like the extent their importance deserves. The question of Empire broadcasting is another issue that has not been adequately canvassed. An excellent example of misplaced criticism was that which alleged that the Socialists had had disproportionate access to the microphone as compared with Conservatives or Liberals. The BBC's reply was shattering and final so far as this particular allegation was concerned. But no doubt a great deal more will yet be heard about 'propaganda in the programmes', in connection not only with politics, but with religion and other controversial matters; and in this connection the principles of British broadcasting require far more precise consideration and definition than they have yet received. So also with the question of radio advertising, which is coming into ever-increasing prominence, and the relation of the revenues of the BBC to programme quality. These and other inter-related issues will doubtless bulk more and more largely in the discussions of broadcasting policy during 1930, and the whole question of the constitution and powers of the BBC, and of the extent to which, in the last analysis, there is an essential antagonism between it and the interests of the Press and other established interests, will steadily develop as the time draws nearer for a renewal or revision of the Charter in 1935. Perhaps the most important issue of that type is the restriction placed on the broadcasting of news. It is inconceivable that the newspapers can indefinitely maintain their monopoly in this respect. Sooner or later it must become possible to broadcast news as and when it happens without reference to the interests of the newspapers, and when this happens the primary functions of the latter will be revolutionised. These questions are of such far-reaching consequence that the need for their thorough exploration and public discussion cannot be over-stressed, and undoubtedly great progress will be made in ventilating them and making the electorate alive to the issues involved during the current year.

THE BBC AND THE RADIO TRADE

There can be no question that 1930 is going to mark another tremendous stage in the development of the incalculable potentialities of radio, and it is significant that 1929 closed with the announcement that the BBC is to co-operate between the 12th and 18th of this month with the entire British radio industry to carry through a successful National Radio Week. For the week in question, we are told, the BBC has arranged to double its normal expenditure in order to broadcast a whole week of favourite items and special programmes of a predominantly light and entertaining character.

> Everything that the mass of listeners like will be put over, so as to make each programme as popular and as light as possible. For one night, the Sunday evening programme will be extended, and close at midnight instead of 10.30. Stars and famous artists whose names are guaranteed to attract and interest even indifferent listeners are being booked for these programmes. The object of the BBC in this is to please the non-listeners rather than the regular listeners. In plain words, the BBC is out of a boost – to gain more listeners. The idea comes from the leading wireless firms, who feel that a stimulant such as this National Radio Week will not only do the whole industry an immense amount of good, but will prove advantageous to the BBC.

The RMA and the BBC are to be congratulated in advance on a scheme which cannot fail to be another great landmark in the development of British radio, and the extensive sums which are being spent on advertising and publicity in the Press should go a long way to complete the breakdown of that 'Fleet Street resistance' referred to in my opening paragraph and induce a general journalistic response to broadcasting in future which will be far more commensurate with its stupendous social and cultural significance than the 'dog in the manger' policy which has hitherto characterised the attitude of most of the newspapers.

OUTSTANDING BROADCASTS OF 1929

Space does not permit any discussion here of the great issues which underlie the new departure – the surprising extension of a Sunday programme; the concentration on 'light programmes' on the assumption of their superior popularity; the relations in the past between the Radio industry and the BBC and the fashion in which these should be developed in the future; and so on. But, in conclusion, let me briefly recall some of the outstanding broadcast achievements of 1929 – *Journey's End, St Joan,* the revival of *Carnival*, the Schneider Trophy air race commentary, the Delius Festival; the Thanksgiving Service at Westminster Abbey for the recovery of the King; the explanatory speech of the Chancellor of the Exchequer on his return from the Hague Conference; the National Lectures by the Poet Laureate and Dr A. S. Eddington; the 'Points of View', 'While London Sleeps', and 'The Day's Work' series of talks; the season's Promenade Concerts and Covent Garden Operas; the Contemporary Music Concerts; the experiments in radio drama – and so on, *ad infinitum*. It is a wonderful retrospect, and tremendous technical developments have accompanied it and made it possible.

TECHNICAL PROGRESS AND OUTLOOK

For example, the year has marked the gradual introduction of Continental broadcast programmes relayed by telephone cable as regular items in the BBC programmes. These relays have carried a practically unqualified guarantee of success owing to the development in Europe of a comprehensive system of telephone cables which comprise circuits specially designed for broadcasting. A few years ago the possibility of the provision of telephone lines between Great Britain and the Continent of Europe which could be considered as suitable for the transmission of music was little else than a flight of the imagination. Today it is an accomplished fact. This is only one example of technical progress and the list could be almost indefinitely extended, while the potentialities of the near future are equally limitless.

It is difficult, if not impossible, to get a medium of such endless multiplicity of effect into focus in the course of a short article; but the BBC can congratulate themselves on having discharged, with general success, an enormous range of activities, the consolidation and further development of which depends largely, if not wholly, on the growth of responsible and competent criticism. And if, as the *Radio Times* claims, and all the indications suggest, 1930 is destined to be a momentous year for broadcasting in this country, let us hope that the public spirit and foresight of what Mr John Buchan calls 'the interpreting class' will be equal to the occasion, and the obligations it involves.

A. K. L., 4 January 1930

Mrs Grundy at Savoy Hill

MR SQUIRE'S MISTAKE

Mr J.C. Squire was mistaken about the demise of his second cousin, Mrs Grundy. She is by no means dead; she has merely transferred herself out of the world at large and taken up her abode at Savoy Hill. Her influence occasionally extends to the programmes, but for the most part is not – at all events readily – to be discerned by the listening public, in whose lives broadcasting is only one ingredient amongst many others, most of which are nowadays happily of a character which more than counter-balances any Mrs Grundyism in the radio programmes. But she has found a congenial sphere in this last refuge in making miserable the lives of the cohorts on the Corporation's staff, and can easily console herself for the shrinkage in her area of influence by affecting that it is of her own free will that she keeps herself unspotted from the outside world, and by exercising her authority all the more mercilessly on the little population still subjected to it.

FEMALE IMPERSONATORS

Mrs Grundy was always a protean lady and seldom had the courage to appear *in propria persona*; and at Savoy Hill she continues to affect a variety of disguises – chief among them, a disconcerting habit of impersonating some of the principal officers of the BBC. The unfortunate staff cannot tell the difference, and are apt to blame their innocent superiors for the atmosphere of insecurity and suspicion Mrs Grundy disseminates wherever she moves and the unconscionable punishments she metes out whenever she can. The 'heid yins' are not really to blame (unless for too compliantly acting as her instruments at times); they are themselves her victims, and spiritually, if not materially, perhaps even more hardly victimised than the perpetrators of the little peccadilloes upon whom she pounces.

LIKE AN EARLY VICTORIAN NOVEL

It is like the plot of an early Victorian novel and not an actual circumstance of the post-War years; but employees of the BBC must not have any domestic complications – or they are sacked on the spot. They cannot divorce their wives and keep their jobs. They are not allowed to stray a hair's breadth off the straight and narrow path of monogamy. And married and un-married alike must walk very circumspectly. 'Who were you with last night?' is the BBC anthem. The slightest breath of scandal attaching to their intimate affairs is apt to lead to trouble. Like Potiphar's wife 'they must be above suspicion.' Lady employees who marry cannot retain their posts; at any rate they lose them for a year or two until 'the offence is purged'. Male employees do not yet (as in the Army) have to secure the Commanding Officer's permission before they marry – but that rule may be enforced any day now.

CAP IN HAND

A variant of this is the way in which employees are prohibited from giving the Press any details of their personalities or careers, or supplying them with photographs. They cannot move without going cap in hand to their superiors and securing permission – and the necessary permission is not to be had in all kinds of directions. To men and women of any spirit such a regime is, of course, unbearable. What really dictates this tin-pot Mussolini-ism? It can only be a consciousness of weakness, of inadequacy, in higher quarters – a determination to 'prosecute a basis of not giving the public what it wants, but should want' – in a word, by-products of Mrs Grundyism.

NEGATIVE EFFECTS

I have said that Mrs Grundy has had little influence on listeners. Her effect on the programmes is not positive but negative. But a good deal of their colourlessness and timidity is undoubtedly due to the sense of the need to be very very proper and uplifting all the time with which she so completely hagrides the BBC staff. The prevailing spirit inhibits all initiative and *joie de vivre*, and has led to the progressive elimination of all employees with any personality of their own. This is the real significance of the long tale of resignations from Savoy Hill. No free play of intelligence is permitted. Everybody and everything must be reduced to a dead level. The sooner listeners realise that the main reason for the unsatisfactory character of the BBC is, in the last analysis, the intolerable conditions of service at Savoy Hill the better.

THE MESSIANIC DELUSION

The insistence on standards of 'ultra-respectability' which are completely out-of-date and at variance with the spirit of the age creates a cleavage between the BBC staff and the overwhelming majority of their listeners, and makes the point of view informing the programmes very frequently a sheer anachronism, as is splendidly exemplified in the Sunday programmes, for example. Hypocrisy, superiority, what Mr Mencken calls 'the Messianic delusion', 'hush, hush', and all the other characteristics of the BBC follow in logical sequence.

WANTED – A PSYCHOLOGICAL REVOLUTION

What Savoy Hill needs is a psychological revolution. The autocratic system which crushes all the individuality out of subordinates and imbues them with a perpetual fear of losing their jobs must go. So long as members of the staff do their work properly there should be no interference in their private affairs. But the change must be effected from outside. There seems to be nobody left on the staff with sufficient backbone to try, although, as the frequent resignations show, there is continual dissatisfaction and any amount of internal intrigue. Either that – or, if the Director-General succeeds in giving effect to his policy of not giving the foolish public what it wants, but what he, in his all-wisdom, knows it ought to have, let him carry his relations with his staff a stage farther, too, and insist upon them not only having no minds of their own, but no bodies either. A BBC run by a corps of carefully selected, disembodied spirits – under his sole direction – would surely realise the dream of Sir John Reith's heart, and of Mrs Grundy's, too.

A. K. L., 1 February 1930

The Scots Observer
1928–1934

What Irishmen Think of Ireland: some prominent literary men

I have just returned from a holiday as the guest of the Irish Nation on the occasion of the second Aonach Tailltean, the ancient Irish Games. Going on that footing, I had exceptional opportunities, of which I took the fullest advantage. I toured over a considerable portion of Ireland by aeroplane, automobile, shanks's nag, and jaunting-car. I had tea at Fairy Hill with Mr Desmond Fitzgerald, the Minister of Defence, and met most of the other members of Mr Cosgrave's Cabinet. I had an interview with Mr de Valera, and talks with many other Fianna Fail and other deputies. I sat at the feet of 'A.E.' in his studio-library-drawing-room in Rathgar Avenue, conversing with him, Mr Montgomery, the Film Censor, 'Seumas O'Sullivan', Mademoiselle Simone Tery, the brilliant young French authoress of a couple of books on contemporary Ireland, and others. I had a long discussion with Senator Yeats, terminating in a perambulation through the streets of Dublin in the 'wee sma' 'oors'. And I was constantly in the company of Senator St John Gogarty (the 'Buck Mulligan' of Joyce's *Ulysses*), surgeon, senator, sportsman, airman, poet, and wit.

What conclusions have I brought back with me in regard to the position and problems of the Irish Free State?

THE LIGHT OF COMMON DAY

Yeats expressed the opinion that Saorstat Eireann is at present in the trough of the wave. The impetus that led to its establishment, and to the Irish Literary revival has spent itself. The objective has for the most part been attained. What remains to be done is less inspiring than what has been accomplished. The abnormal efflorescence of Irish genius could not be maintained: the immediate future must be relatively mediocre. What are needed now are not poets and fiery propagandists and rebel leaders, but administrators, economists, and practical experts. Ireland is tired of sensations: the assassination of Kevin O'Higgins did not mark the beginning of a still more sinister phase of Irish politics, but the end (for the time being, at all events) of the 'troubles'. There is an uneasy feeling in the minds of many intelligent Irishmen that autonomy is a delusion as long as there remains financial over-control by a junta of international financiers. This leads a certain type of mind to depreciate what has been achieved; it leads another to assert that the Irish Movement has been short-circuited and that it ought to have been carried out of the ambit of English control or influence altogether. There was a considerable measure of enthusiasm for the revival of Gaelic prior to the Treaty; but the Gaelic encouraging policy of the Government has practically killed that enthusiasm. It could only thrive in an atmosphere of opposition. From the economic standpoint, it is of moment to note the headway Major C. H. Douglas's Credit Reform proposals have made amongst the Fianna Fail party.

NEED FOR ECONOMIC RECONSTRUCTION

Ireland is sharing in the general reaction from democracy. It used to be thought that Irish self-government would resolve itself into virtual control by Dublin Corporation. But the present administration have replace Dublin Corporation by a triumvirate of Commissioners. A straw shows the way the wind blows: the future of the Irish literary movement undoubtedly lies along the line of Gaelic integralism: the most important Irish poet since Yeats is F.R. Higgins, an out-and-out Republican, whose work owes much of its strength to its resumption of old bardic technique. But, politically, in the meantime, the brains are emphatically with the Government, and the immediate need of the country is for just that patient, thorough, unspectacular work which its able young Ministers are doing – above all, Mr Hogan, the Minister for Agriculture. If, on a deeper analysis, the consolidation of Ireland depends upon a break-away from 'orthodox economics', the necessary 'strong man' will probably emerge from Mr de Valera's following. On both sides I found eager interest in the new Nationalist developments in Scotland and in Wales, and the feeling that through these might lie a solution of some of Ireland's most subtle difficulties.

C.M. Grieve, 8 September 1928

What Irishmen Think of Ireland: a visit to the Free State

It is only natural that Ireland should have tremendous problems to face, considering the policy pursued during the Ascendancy, and the long period of unrest, terminating in open rebellion, and, as a final phase, civil war. But, for her size, Ireland is one of the most generously endowed countries in the world. Her ultimate economic prosperity is beyond doubt. Prior to the establishment of Saorstat Eireann, Ireland – like Scotland – contributed a huge sum annually to the Imperial Exchequer, and received back only a moiety of it in the shape of grants for Irish purposes. Now, large sums that formerly would have been dissipated in the sands of Irak or on some other area of Imperialism are being spent in home-colonisation. From 1890 to 1922, only 9000 houses were erected by local authorities or by private persons under Government schemes. Since 1922, practically 14,600 have been erected, and it is hoped to increase this activity. An analysis of prices, accommodation, etc., justifies Irish control of Irish affairs in this connection up to the hilt. In regard to roads there is the same story to tell – and, incidentally, the millions spent on road-making have helped to solve the unemployment problem. There is no dole.

On the debit side, there has been since 1921 a closing-down of several scores of industrial concerns of all kinds; but this is partly due to the severance of old business ties – a matter which will slowly but surely right itself with the establishment of new affiliations – and partly to causes from which England, Scotland, and other European countries are suffering in common with Ireland.

THE GREEN WILDERNESS

In regard to the costs of the new administration, and the effects of a separate coinage, developments of the tariff policy and the like, all that can be said is that the new Ireland is still in a transitional phase. Much will depend upon rural developments. A recent writer says:

> Visitors from Continental countries are always amazed at the obvious waste of good land under grass. The growing of corn and root crops would provide not only an adequate supply of food for the Irish people, but would give employment to our emigrants and unemployed, and enable them to live in decent comfort at home. The continuity of British policy since the 'forties of last century is to make Ireland a grazing ranch to supply John Bull with cheap beef, butter, and eggs. This is also the declared policy of the Free State Government, and in whatever direction the intelligent visitor travels, the beautiful but terrible wilderness of green grass oppresses his spirit with the silence of unlaboured fields!

BENEFITS OF SELF-HELP

Rome was not built in a day – and even the Free State Ministers can justly claim that they have not yet had reasonable time to apply their policy so as to allow of its being fairly judged. Anyhow, the Irish people are free to attempt to make their country prosperous and overcome its economic difficulties. At the very worst, there is no reason to imagine that they will be less successful in this than the English were; and if they find that their success is being restricted by over-controlling forces in world-finance, they will be at liberty to challenge these forces and to unite with other elements in seeking to throw off this incubus. I talked to Irishmen of the most diverse kinds, but I found none who wished to restore the Ascendancy; and, going up and down the country, I certainly found innumerable reasons – too intangible and complex to detail in a short article (I have not even found space in which to mention the Shannon Scheme) – to rejoice that the destiny of Ireland was again in the hands of Irish people, and to envy them their opportunities in the light of what they have already achieved.

C.M. Grieve, 15 September 1928

Scotland's Greatest Poetess: Mairi nighean Alasdair Ruaidh

It is an extraordinary fact that nine Scots out of ten have never heard so much as the very name of Scotland's greatest poetess – Mary Macleod, or, as she was popularly known, 'Mairi nighean Alasdair Ruaidh'. And fewer still know anything of her poems or of the nature of the achievement which makes her perhaps the most remarkable poetess the world has ever had. Few women have had any influence on the evolution of poetical technique; no other woman in any literature has effected a change so revolutionary and far-reaching. It was essentially a feminine thing and led directly to those subsequent characteristics of the Gaelic muse which are connoted by the phrase, 'the Celtic twilight'. The younger Irish poets today – poets like Austin Clarke, F.R. Higgins and Michael O'Connor – are consciously trying to get back to the 'Gaelic sunlight' which preceded this long spell of mellifluous decadence and shadow-worship; to return to the virile objectivity, the classical qualities, of the ancient bards. But I do not propose to initiate here any relative evaluation between the ancient methods and the modern; it is an aspect of the contest between classicism and romanticism which cannot be effectively entered upon in a brief article. The actual fact that in Mary Macleod we had a literary innovator of supreme genius who completely overturned a tradition of poetry which had preserved itself intact for many centuries and introduced elements which have since been so successful that the very term Celtic in all its literary associations has long been almost exclusively bound up with them, and few people appreciate that they represented a radical divergence from the historical culture of the Gaels, is enough for my present purpose.

In the chapter entitled 'Rise of the New School' – four chapters after one headed 'Four Centuries of Decay' – in his wonderful *Literary History of Ireland*, Dr Douglas Hyde says:

> We now come to the great breaking up and total disruption of the Irish prosody as employed for a thousand years by thousands of poets in the bardic schools and colleges. The principles of this great change may be summed up in two sentences: first, the adoption of vowel rhyme in place of consonantal rhyme; second, the adoption of a certain number of accents in each line in place of a certain number of syllables. These were two of the most far-reaching changes that could overtake the poetry of any country, and they completely metamorphosed that of Ireland.

THE COLOURS OF THE RAINBOW

'Almost in the twinkling of an eye,' he continues,

> Irish poetry completely changed its form and complexion, and from being,

> as it were, so bound up and swathed around with rules that none who had not spent years over its technicalities could move about in it with vigour, its spirit suddenly burst forth in all the freedom of the elements, and clothed itself, so to speak, in the colours of the rainbow. Now, indeed, for the first time poetry became the handmaid of the many, not the mistress of the few. Now the remnant of the bards – the great houses being fallen – turned instinctively to the general public, and threw behind them the intricate metres of the schools, and dropped, too, at a stroke, several thousand words, which no one except the great chiefs and those trained by the poets understood, whilst they broke out into beautiful and at the same time intelligible verse which no Gael of Ireland and Scotland who has ever heard or learned it is likely ever to forget. This is to my mind perhaps the sweetest creation of all Irish literature, the real glory of the modern Irish nation, and of the Scottish Highlands; this is the truest note of the enchanting Celtic siren, and he who has once heard it and remains deaf to its charm can have little heart for song or soul for music. The Gaelic poetry of the last two centuries both in Ireland and in the Highlands is probably the most sensuous attempt to convey music in words ever made by man.

These sentences express Dr Hyde's personal taste. There has been profound change in European literary tendencies during the quarter of a century that has elapsed since he wrote them. To 'make poetry the handmaid of the many, not the mistress of the few', is a slogan that the widespread reaction against democracy in recent years has robbed of its potency; the sensuous appeal has its place, but we are less inclined today to accord it priority over intellectual values. And to 'convey music in words' is a phrase which involves one of those confusions of one art in the terminology of another from which all the arts today are striving to liberate themselves. We know a great deal more too than was known in the beginning of the century about ancient bardic poetry and its technique and traditions, and are more inclined than Dr Hyde may have been to question whether the new system which disrupted the prosody employed for a thousand years will itself remain potent for anything like so long, or whether by and large, this feminisation of Gaelic poetry has been altogether a good thing and a return to a masculine spirit not long overdue.

THE GREAT CHANGE

But the paragraph to which these passages of Dr Hyde's leads up is as follows: –

> The Scottish Gaels, if I am not mistaken, led the way in this great change, which metamorphosed the poetry of an entire people in both islands. The bardic system, outside of the kingdom of the Lord of the Isles had apparently scarcely taken the same hold upon the nobles in Scotland as in

Ireland, and the first modern Scottish Gaelic poet to start upon the new system seems to have been Mary, daughter of Alaster Rua Macleod, who was born in Harris in 1569, and who appears to have possessed no higher social standing than that of a kind of lady nurse in the chief's family. If the nine poems in free vowel metres, which are attributed to her by Mackenzie in his great collection (*Sár-obair nambórd Gaelach*) be genuine, then I should consider her as the pioneer of the new school. Certainly no Irishman nor Irishwoman of the sixteenth century has left anything like Mary's metres behind them, and, indeed, I have not met more than one or two of them used in Ireland during that century. No one, for instance, would have dreamt of vowel-rhyming thus, as she does over the drowning of Mac'Illachallun:

My *grief* my *pain*
Relief was *vain*
The *seething wave*
Did *leap* and *rave*
And *reeve* in *twain*
Both *sheet* and *sail*,
And *leave* us *bare*
  And foundering.
Alas, *indeed*
For her you *leave*
Your brothers' *grief*
To them will *cleave*,
It was on *Easter*
Monday's *feast*
The branch of *peace*
  Went down with you.

'The sweetest creation of all Gaelic literature, this new outburst of lyric melody', says Dr Magnus Maclean, in his *Literature of the Celts*,

> was a wonderful arrangement of vowel sounds, so placed that in every accented syllable, first one vowel and then another fell upon the ear in all possible kinds of harmonious modifications. Some verses are made wholly on the à sound, others on the ò, ù, è or ì sounds, but the majority on a unique and fascinating intermixture of the two, three, or more; as, for example, in Mary Macleod's vowel-rhyming over the drowning of MacIlle Chalum in the angry Minch between Stornoway and Raasay.

Before Mary's day the Gaelic poets were, as he says,

> bound by the rules of their order, and to excel within the very narrow limits of the old-world prosody, hedged about as it was with so many techni-

calities, required years of severe bardic study and preparation. Mary apparently without any tuition, without even the power to read or write, suddenly burst these unnatural bonds asunder, and gave to the spirit of her poetry the freedom of the elements, unhampered and unfettered by the intricate metres of the schools. She invented rhythms of her own, often making the music of sound an echo of the sense. Orgill Mackenzie of 'The Beauties' appraised her as the most original of all our poets, who borrowed nothing. Her thoughts, her verse, and rhymes were all equally her own; her language simple and elegant; her diction easy, natural, and unaffected. There is no straining to produce effect; no search after unintelligible words to conceal the poverty of ideas. She often repeats rhymes, yet we never feel them tiresome or disagreeable, for, more than most of her Gaelic compeers, Mary was mistress of the poetic lyre.

BEST KNOWN WORKS

Perhaps the ode she wrote in Mull *Luínneag Mhic Leod*, when she was exiled from Eilean-a-Cheo by the proud chief of Dunvegan, who, it is said, 'objected to the scope of the publicity he and his menage received at the hands of the family nurse, exercising, as she freely did, the privileges of the poet,' is the most widely known of her poems. It has been translated into English verse both by Pattison and Blackie, the former's rendering beginning:

Alone on the hill-top, sadly and silently,
Downward on Islay and over the sea,
I look, and I wonder how time hath deceived me –
A stranger in Scarba, who ne'er thought to be.

The biographical details concerning her are very scanty. She lived to be 105 years old, dying at Dunvegan in 1675 and being buried in her native isle of Harris. Another peculiar fact is that it was not until she was advanced in years that she became much addicted to the making of poetry; at all events, it was late in life that she composed those pieces which have survived and rank among the glories of Gaelic literature. 'It needs some of Mary's own imagination', as Dr Maclean says, 'to picture her going about in after days wearing a tartan *tonnag*, fastened in front with a large silver brooch, and carrying a silver-headed cane', and indulging in those propensities for gossip, snuff and whisky, to which she is said to have been greatly given when long past the natural span of years. Altogether an amazing figure – unparalleled in any literature, save by Sappho. Whether or not it is time now for a studied reversal of her influence, and an attempt to return to the *status quo ante,* she certainly deserves recognition as one of the master spirits of our people.

Hugh McDiarmid, 27 March 1930

Blasphemy and Divine Philosophy Mixed: Hugh M'Diarmid's extraordinary poem

There is much in Hugh M'Diarmid's new long poem, *To Circumjack Cencrastus* (Messrs Blackwood, 8/6), which most people will deplore and a great deal that, surely, no one can justify. There is a super-abundance of needless personalities – scurrilous vilification of great Scotsmen past and present with whom the poet happens to disagree for political or other reasons or for none to all appearances except gratuitous ill-will. Scarcely anybody of any consequence escapes the lash of his rancour. That much of this invective is very effective goes without saying, but it is impossible to condone an Ishmaelitism which has its hand against everybody in this way. Knox, Burns, Lord Rosebery, Neil Munro, Sir Harry Lauder, Will Fyffe, J. J. Bell, Dr Lauchlan Maclean Watt, are only a few of the targets of his wholesale abuse. Another outstanding blemish on the poem is its excessive preoccupation with forms of political propaganda with which few can sympathise. Anti-English sentiment of the most virulent kind abounds and along with it violent depreciations of British Imperialism and a rank hatred of America. This element culminates in an inexcusable attack on the Royal Family. All these features are reminiscent of the brutality for which 'Maga' was originally infamous. A pretentious pedantry is another large ingredient. The author revels in all manner of obscure allusions, unintelligible, collocations, of obsolete or abstruse words, and an intricate linguistic apparatus which involves Scottish and Irish Gaelic, German, French, Italian, Spanish, Latin, and Greek. The best that can be said of all this is that whatever its object may be it is non-materialistic. If the author were concerned with anything in the shape of commercial success or popular favour, he could not persist in so extraordinary a medium. But this point in his favour is more than offset by his intellectual arrogance. He even goes to the length of deriding poetry concerned – not with what he conceives to be ultimate issues – but with all that has constituted poetry's subject-matter since Homer. Love, patriotism, the beauties of nature, all the normal pre-occupations of mankind are explicitly dismissed; the author cannot bring them – and thinks they cannot be brought – *sub specie aeternitatis*.

It is this that gives the poem a peculiar interest from the religious standpoint. This general impossibilism is, moreover, given direct and pointed expression in terms of religious philosophy in a multitude of passages which, whatever one may think of their 'content', go a long way to counter-balance what Mr John Buchan has well called the failure of Scottish poetry during the past five hundred years to concern itself with religious ideas in the true sense of the term rather than mere orthodox opinions or conventional pieties. The author shows an astonishing knowledge of the whole range of modern European philosophy and religious speculation, and has obviously been profoundly influenced by Nietszche, Bergson, Soloviev, Husserl, and others. This is a familiarity which is sufficiently unusual in lay circles in Scotland today to constitute a merit in itself. Many of the shorter poems dealing with religious matters are essentially blasphemous or will affect readers who lack the writer's intellectual background as blasphemous. But M'Diarmid's concern with ultimate issues goes much deeper than that, and all the blasphemy and cheap sarcasm are no more than the froth on the surface of the depths of essentially religious speculation of which the poem recurrently vouchsafes most astonishing – if frequently appalling – glimpses.

Pteleon, 2 October 1930

What is the Book of the Year?

I have read several hundreds of books published during the past twelve months, and – since I am careful in advance – practically none of them below a certain high level in its kind. Yet I have probably missed 'the book of the year', the one (if any) which will stand out as a landmark to posterity. And here, I suppose, one is more or less confined to the best book of the year in English. An impossible task! How can one choose between such incomparables, in poetry, as C. Day Lewis's *Feathers and Iron* and John Collier's *Gemini*; in fiction, *The Waves* by Virginia Woolf and *Sado* by William Plomer; in other kinds, *The Shaw-Terry Correspondence*, Allan Ross MacDougall's *Gourmet's Almanac*, and Norman Douglas's *Paneros*. And yet I have no hesitation in singling out Ezra Pound's *How To Read* (Desmond Harmsworth), a wonderful little essay which in a few devastating paragraphs clears away mountains of the rubbish under which pedants, propagandists, and journalists obscure this vital matter, and brilliantly outlines the essentials of a worthy attitude to letters. It is full of sense on a subject generally monopolised by nonsense, and packed with much of the most concentrated and profound literary criticism of our time, and since 'how to read' naturally takes precedence over 'what to read', this is my choice. Mr Pound has rendered many invaluable services to modern arts and letters, but none greater or more available to the public at large or witnessing better to the truth of the saying that 'guid gear gangs in sma' book' than this splendid little essay. It outweighs nine-tenths of the year's publishing.

C.M. Grieve, 24 December 1931

Is the Scottish Renaissance a Reality?

Is the Scottish Renaissance a reality? The phrase 'Scottish Renaissance Group' was applied first of all by Professor Denis Saurat, in an article he wrote in a French review, to the group associated with me in *Northern Numbers* and *The Scottish Chapbook*. What has happened during that interval?

The term 'Scottish Renaissance' has been wrested away from its original significance and applied loosely to all manner of activities directed towards 'a national awakening'. I deprecate the confusion that has thus been caused. My purpose here is not to deal with the existence or prospects of a Scottish Renaissance in that wider sense, but to claim that on the lines initiated or suggested by the group to whom the phrase was originally applied a genuine movement has developed and now has a considerable achievement to its credit.

The programme that was announced ten years ago was that the time had come to develop a literature based not on Scotland's affinities with England but its differences from England; that to do this involved a thorough revaluation of our literary past and a species of psychological *kultur-kampf*; and that among our main tasks must be a systematic exploration of the creative possibilities of Braid Scots and a recapture of our lost Gaelic background. Many other points emerged almost at once, but these were roughly stated, the main lines of the proposed development. To what extent have they been realised?

REVALUATION

The process of revaluation has been exemplified in such books as Mrs Carswell's *Robert Burns*, Donald Carswell's *Brither Scots* and *Sir Walter Scott*, Edwin Muir's *John Knox*, George Malcolm Thomson's *Caledonia, The Rediscovery of Scotland*, and *Short History of Scotland*, and the books, pamphlets and innumerable journalistic writings of Ruaraidh Erskine of Marr, William Power, William Bell, Dewar Gibb, Moray MacLaren, myself, and others, together with the occasional speeches of people like Compton Mackenzie, Cunninghame-Graham and Naomi Mitchison.

Whatever may be any reader's view of the justice of the revaluations conducted in this direction or that, it can scarcely be denied that the net result has been new and fruitful angles of approach and an increase in the vital interest and contemporary applicability of the subjects involved. That indeed was foreseen and one of the main objects of the movement. The necessity of being provocative was realised and, if it has been carried too far in certain directions to suit all tastes, it has on the whole abundantly justified itself. Amongst other things it has brought out a far sharper realisation of the Scottish tradition as a whole and its differences from the English tradition. If Scott and Burns have been 'attacked' they have also been defended, and the discussions evoked have concentrated more and more on vital issues. In my view, the whole process has merely begun, but in the attack on the Burns cult, the call for a return to Dunbar, the insistence upon the necessity of an all-in view of Scottish Literature which will not exclude the great Gaelic poets on the one hand nor on the other Scottish writers who are too commonly regarded rather as part and parcel of English literature, in the research work proceeding in many directions, and in the increased thinking about Scottish cultural and psychological matters of all kinds, a very marked and many-sided development has been registered, which will have definite bearings on the future of Scottish consciousness.

There is no need here to discuss some of the deeper issues that have been touched upon – the relations of politics and economics to culture; the profit of Scotland's attachment to England, Europe, and the Empire respectively; the search for a master-idea or sense of a historical national mission which will bring Scottish genius right into the mainstream of modern consciousness; the difficult problems of the relations of speech to psychology; the call for an effective re-Scoticisation of our educational system; the concern with the problems and potentialities of religion in Scotland, and so forth. All these are at work. It is difficult to get a clear view of such a complex process, let alone – even if that were desirable – embody it in any definitely organised fashion. The time for national synthesis is not yet. We are still more concerned with the breakdown of old traditions than with the consolidation of new.

PAUCITY OF OUTPUT

This is inevitable. But it is a profound mistake to regard the process as merely or mainly destructive. The necessity for it largely arose from the gulf between the old traditions and the actual conditions and prospects of Scotland today; and, from a cultural standpoint at least, if not from a politico-economic one too, its ample justification lay in the paucity of creative output in the period of Scottish history dominated by the ideas that are now being so comprehensively, if insidiously, assailed.

NEW SCOTTISH NOVEL

Leaving these deeper elements to look after themselves, the heightened national consciousness, the 'return to Scotland' spirit, the new creative use of the vernacular and Gaelic backgrounds linguistically and otherwise, the sense of a separate Scottish tradition with a continuity of its own and qualities and potentialities very different from that of the English tradition, are all exemplified in the new Scottish novelists. Here we can join issue at once with any Didymus who wants to put his finger on the spot. It is not a question of the permanent or relative value of these novels, but of their increasing number and the very definite tendencies they represent. They all stem directly and obviously from one or more of the planks of the original renaissance programme I have outlined above, and most of them are thesis novels, very markedly propagandist of 'the new Scotland'. This proves the creative impetus the programme supplied. Apart from propaganda of ideas or questions of comparative value, what can be very definitely maintained is that Scotland never at any previous time possessed so numerous a corps of novelists; that the general level of its novelistic ability was never higher; and that the 'native content' of its novels was never greater or keener. Whether in a purely literary sense the new Scottish novel is entering upon a distinctive evolution, and how it compares in technique, quality, and tendency with the novel in England, Ireland, and elsewhere today are questions not essential to my immediate purpose; but in such writers as Neil Gunn, George Blake, Adam Kennedy, 'Fionn MacColla', F. Marian M'Neill, Edwin and Willa Muir, Olive Squair and others we have, at least, a remarkable number of novelists reconcentrating on Scottish life, landscape, language, history, and prospects in an unprecedented fashion and all manifesting in their measure or that some aspect or other of the renaissance programme as originally defined.

POETRY AND DRAMA

The same thing is true, but to a much smaller degree, of poetry. We have far fewer poets of any quality than we have prose-writers; the majority of them are less at variance with established traditions, less sharply differentiated from their English equivalents, less united in a common concern for one or other of the Renaissance desiderata, less important in a purely literary sense, less influential with the reading public, and less productive even of their own work such as it is. Nevertheless good work has been and is being done, although it is very disappointing to find that such new trails as have been blazed are not being followed up and that few, if any, young poets under, say thirty are treading on the heels of those a little over that age who have secured some small reputation.

It is in drama as it is in poetry, though here again a small body of definite achievement may be claimed and the point stressed that whereas Scotland had at least some novelistic and poetic past it had no dramatic one, so that even the little that has accrued has at least a special pioneer value.

PERIOD OF INCUBATION

Ten years after all is not long in the history of any literary development, and especially one that in any way preludes, and is dependent upon, a national 'change of heart', and Scotland has nothing to grumble about in this connection. The Irish literary revival, the *Aüfklarung* in Germany, the developments (latest of all great literatures) in Russia – none of these got really under-weigh in so short a time; and in them – as in Scotland – there had to be a long period of preparation, of the propaganda of 'new ideas'. That process is perhaps far more apace – far more radical – in Scotland today than most people imagine, and its more sensational and substantive fruits may not be long delayed; but, even as matters stand, our ten years' showing is no mean one having regard to the previous literary productivity of our country as a whole, and will rank in our literary history as a definite turning point and a phase of much hard work, of a changing of standards, of a quest for new means, and of a certain amount of real gold.

C.M. Grieve ('Hugh MacDiarmid') 4 February 1933

Not Merely Philosophical Piety: Communism means a clean sweep

A Reply to Rev. J. W. Stevenson and Mr Middleton Murry

Mr Grieve, who is a well-known Scottish poet and critic, is the author of two 'Hymns to Lenin'. One of the founders of the National Party of Scotland, he has been debarred from membership of that body since his return to Scotland some months ago on account of his avowed Communism – although, as he says 'Surely Mac-Lenin is a good Scots name'! Mr Grieve is a member of the British Section of the Revolutionary Writers of the World, a Communist body controlled from Moscow.

Most of the talking and writing about Communism going on in Great Britain today is being done by non-Communists for an audience which has read little or nothing about Communism except in non-Communist papers. If, as a communist, I am allowed to follow up the articles by Rev. J. W. Stevenson and Mr Middleton Murry which have appeared in these columns, I must begin by saying that I disbelieve in the intelligence of those who fail to recognise the great crisis confronting humanity today and in the integrity of anyone who, recognising it, professes to be interested 'in the great experiment that is going on in Russia' (to quote one of the many current catch-phrases to like effect) but not sufficiently to trouble to read *Das Kapital*. As Sidney Hook points out in his study, *From Hegel to Marx*, it could not have been 'merely philosophical piety which led men like Lenin to turn aside from the exigencies of revolutionary civil war and advise fellow-Marxists to constitute themselves into "a society of materialistic friends of the Hegelian dialectic".' The Hegelian terminology with which all classic Marxian literature is shot through is not to be regarded by non-Communists as only a curious verbal fixation. Messrs Stevenson and Murry purport to discuss Communism in non-Communist terminology. It cannot be done. Similarly, Mr Stevenson devotes several paragraphs to Social Credit doctrine, but does not mention Major C. H. Douglas. The name is of the very essence of the matter. The convenience which it suits to drop his name in this way simply denotes a determination to substitute something else, no matter how closely resembling it, for Douglasism. People who really swallow camels do not boggle at gnats.

FASCIST PANTHEON

We have been familiar in Scotland far too long with professed 'extreme Socialists' who, except in some of their political assertions, were hopeless reactionaries in every other respect – and have naturally proved so politically too. It is no matter for surprise that Carlyle developed (largely owing to a pre-occupation with 'religious values' which kept him from looking realistically at events) from the early scourge of liberal Whiggism into an exponent of oppression until today, as Mr Neff tells us, he is one of the gods of the Fascist pantheon. Messrs

Stevenson and Middleton Murry – both infinitely smaller figures – equally fail to understand the pertinence of the virtues they preach, and are both headed in the same direction, though they may seem to be going in the opposite one. Ideas are known by the company they keep. Mr Stevenson can learn nothing from Communism – any more than Mr Murry can teach Communism anything – without becoming a Communist.

In their determination to face up to Communism and declare either for or against it, but to discuss Communism in terms of other ideas which they are determined to hang on to at all costs – and which, instead of Communism, are what they are really writing about – Messrs Stevenson and Murry are forced into some extraordinary positions.

Mr Stevenson is obliged to confess that he regards the great majority of professing Christians as purblind – as manifestly opposed to 'the divine will' – but he does not seem to regard that purblindness and opposition on their part as being also 'divinely willed'. He thus gives the 'divine will' a curious intermittence to suit his own fixed ideas. He even goes so far as to suggest that a modern miracle may suddenly make Communism obsolete as a method of social reconstruction. Humanity may be decimated, of course, or even entirely blotted out at any moment by a great natural upheaval; but scarcely for the purpose of re-ordering the world to prevent the spread to other countries of the type of society which is now to be found in Russia. That Mr Stevenson is obliged to insist in this way on the indubitable fact that 'anything may happen' throws sufficient illumination on his inability to justify his attitude on any nearer and more rational ground.

Mr Stevenson's is rather a tall order. Mr Middleton Murry goes even further. He finds the psychology presupposed by, and implicit in, Marxian Communism, more Christian than the psychology of the Christian Church itself today – and by today he means always. In order to call himself a 'Christian Communist' he has himself to refuse the 'crowning act' which would enable him to become a Communist to Communists; he has also to deny the Christianity of practically all the professing Christians, past and present.

MYSTICAL FORM

Mr Murry's patter about Marx and Hegel may impress a few of those who know nothing about Communist doctrines (or prefer to learn what they can about them from anybody and everybody but the Communists themselves) but, as Marx himself wrote to Kugelmann, 'Hegel's dialectic is the fundamental principle of all dialectic only after its mystical form has been sloughed off. And that is precisely what distinguishes my method.'

To establish Mr Murry's claim that Communism and Christianity are not essentially incompatible, the tenets of Marx and all the Marxians, and the anti-God measures taken in Soviet Russia, must be dismissed as an unfortunate misunderstanding on the part of all these people of the implications of their own doctrines – a misunderstanding similar in kind but opposite in effect to that which leads the majority of professing Christians to imagine they are anything of the sort. And now in the fulness of time Mr Murry arrives to put them both right! This is even a more incredible manifestation than that which Mr Stevenson takes as the outside chance of his faith!

THE RICH YOUNG MEN

The collapse of traditional civilisation is no temporary phenomenon, susceptible of any reformist patching-up. No return of economic prosperity will solve the problem. As Briffault says,

> It is not the economic structure of Western civilisation alone which has become dislocated; it is not its political structure; it is not the sentiments of confidence, of respect, of loyalty, with which it was regarded that have wilted. It is the entire mental fabric, its authority, the authority upon which the whole edifice of Western civilisation rested, that has collapsed – completely, and forever.

Like Briffault, I do not pretend to be competent to judge how far the methods of organisation adopted by Soviet Russia are likely to prove the best that can be devised and I greatly doubt the competence of anyone else to judge of the matter. The proof will be in the results. It is sufficient for me that these methods have so far accomplished more in five years for the protection of human existence and the abolition of hunger and insecurity than the traditional civilisation has accomplished in five thousand years. I align myself with this new civilisation in unmistakeable terms. The repudiation of Capitalist culture must be complete. Trying to save odds and ends from it and carry these forward into the new order is as futile as trying to carry a top hat and kid gloves into the world beyond the grave. That is what Messrs Stevenson and Murry are doing. They are like the Rich Young Man who could not give up what he already had. The call however, is for a complete, unequivocal rejection of this decaying civilisation and all its values; to have the moral courage and intellectual honesty to recognise things as they are and to fight for a new society in which the human race will emerge into a more advanced stage of existence.

As Briffault says:

> We are engaged upon the lunatic occupation of trying to run the world in terms of things and values that no longer exist as a belief in any human soul. In politics we think in terms of strategic reasons of State that are echoes of a history that is past, a tale that is told; socially, we deal in terms of a configuration that is only prevented from flying asunder by brute force; economically, with wealth that only exists on paper; ethically, with moral values to which no human 'conscience' any longer corresponds; intellectually, with a truth which has become 'pragmatic'; artistically, with

> the self-expression of a soul that no longer believes in itself. Rulers – leaders we have none – are never converted. Psychological miracles do not happen. It is all sentimental nonsense to say that truth wins; on the contrary, the fact is that lies are *never* put down. What does actually happen is a very much more radical catastrophic process – not the lies, but the whole social superstructure, empires, states, civilisations founded on them go down. Let us have no illusion; talking, arguments, logic do not count – directly. They only count by sharpening the pikes of the brute barbaric forces that are the instruments of the intrinsic Nemesis of the logic of the Universe. To entertain the idea that a profiteer chaos can be mended by our rulers – that is, by profiteers and men with profiteer principles – by advising *them* what to do is, sanely considered, the most ludicrous imbecility. Of the two alternative issues to our present situation – a decent effort towards veracity, or the deluge – we need have no expectation whatever of the former. The Bolshevists, not the Profiteers, will win, because they have the motive power, belief in their ideals, which our profiteer civilisation has not. And it is no use fancying that the deluge will be a pleasant thing to look upon...

Nor will it split to let any of the Israelites pass over dry shod!

C.M. Grieve (Hugh MacDiarmid), 25 February 1933

The Future of Scottish Poetry

There are scores of poets who have lived during the past fifty years whose work and qualities as important elements in the evolution of the human spirit should be known to all who profess a serious concern with poetry.

Few of them are English; none Scottish or Colonial; none American except T. S. Eliot and Ezra Pound (both expatriates to Europe); only one, Yeats, Irish; and with the exception of these three, and of Gerard Manley Hopkins and Charles Doughty, the rest of the English ones are relatively very 'small beer', while all the major figures belong to other European literatures.

'You may dislike the English,' it is frequently claimed, 'but you cannot deny that we have produced the greatest body of poetry in the world.'

The claim is seldom made except by those who know little or nothing of any other – except 'the classics'. It is true that one of the greatest bodies of poetry in the world has been produced in the English language, but not by English people. The great majority of its producers have been wholly or partly Celtic. Even so, since Shakespeare and Milton, I am disposed to say that English poetry is 'great, unfortunately', as the Frenchman said that the greatest French poet was 'Victor Hugo – unfortunately!' It is not my purpose to deal with these particular issues here, but I would add that I believe it is the recoil of the Celtic spirit – its desertion of English literature for a renewed concern with Irish, Welsh, and Scottish literature and the Gaelic languages, I hope and believe, in the long run – which largely accounts for the insignificance and anaemia of modern English poetry. Whatever the explanation, however, this relative triviality is one of the reasons that make it deplorable that English poetry (which is likely to have as poor a future as it has a rich past) should occupy so disproportionate a place in Scottish education and Scottish reading generally.

It would be ludicrous, in considering the novel, to promote English fiction to such a role and ignore Dostoevski, Tolstoy, Stendhal and a score of other Europeans whose work must be known to anyone whose opinions on the subject are of the slightest value, but these are never ignored as European poets of similar status are. It would be grotesque to discuss the drama in terms of the English theatre and not realise the far greater importance of Ibsen, Strindberg, Pirandello and others. It is equally, and even more, absurd in poetry. Just as with past poetry an insular dismissal of Homer, Vergil, Dante and other great European poets would be absurd, so it is with contemporary poetry.

There might be good reasons for confining our school children first of all to the Scottish poets (but not to those Scottish poets of whom they are at present taught anything!), no matter how poverty-stricken the course of Scottish poetry may be to that of many other countries, but it is ridiculous to bring them up on Walter de la Mare and other recent English poetasters, or even on Tennyson, Browning, and Mrs Hemans, not only in preference to our own very different writers, but to far more important European figures, and especially to those elements in European poetry which have a far greater bearing on the position and potentialities of Scottish poetry than almost any English poetry has. Much European poetry has positive bearings on Scottish poetry; most English poetry only negative bearings; and an over-concern with the latter is likely in the future, as in the past, to be extremely misleading and unprofitable.

I was, I think, fortunate in being not only an omnivorous reader determined to get into touch with vital contemporary poetry no matter in what European country or language it was being produced, but, from the beginning, instinctively 'cool' to English literature, which has never had any disproportionate place in my reading, and which I have all along recognised as far less closely related to my own spirit than many elements of European literature for which English literature has, if not an actual distaste or constitutional incapacity to assimilate, at least no equivalents. But as a Scotsman, under our deplorable modern dispensation, I was naturally unduly influenced for a long time by types of poetry which, if I have not yet out-grown them in my actual practice, I now set aside critically as far less worthy of study with a view to the ultimate realisation of any of the greater latent potentialities of the

Scottish genius than certain other types.

Broadly, if I were asked what kind of poetry young Scots seriously concerned with this matter ought to concentrate upon, I would quote Professor Faesi's general description of Carl Spitteler's qualities: 'Certainly love is not the basic feeling of Spitteler or the *primum mobile* of his self-created world. Courage, patience, self-assertion, unyieldingness, energy, and (above all) a steel-like and combative virility are the most important sources of his inspiration.'

The almost superhuman problem of creating even yet a worthy Scottish poetry demands like qualities – a similar conjunction of daemonic will with poetic genius. Or, as I have recently written elsewhere of our own Gaelic poet, Uilleam MacDhunleibe (William Livingston):

> He did not write 'love poetry'. He did not address himself to any of the infantile themes on which ninety per cent of versification depends. He stood clear of the tradition that insists that the substance of poetry must be silly vapourings, chocolate-box-lid pictures of nature, and trite moralisings; penny novelette love is all right, but not politics, not religion, not war, not anything that can appeal to an adult intelligence. He is a splendid masculine poet, who 'put away childish things'. The irresistible verve of his utterance, the savagery of his satire, are abhorrent to the spineless triflers who want pretty-prettifyings, and not any devotion to matters of life and death.

What recent poets, then, would I put into the hands of any young Scot who sought my guidance? All I have space to say here is that, for the above and allied reasons – since, of course, some of these poets are very far from the epic and militant vein or from any concern with the most crucial problems of mankind today, but have other qualities scarcely less vital to the end proposed – I should recommend them to give a wide berth to all modern English poetry save that of Doughty, Hopkins, Eliot, and Yeats' later work, and to devote themselves to a thorough study (such as I myself expended on Rimbaud and Blok and others I now realise to be far less germane to such a purpose as I have indicated than those I now name) of Carl Spitteler, Stefan Georg, Rainer Maria Rilke, and Paul Valéry. Without a knowledge of these, anyone professing a serious concern with modern poetry is in a position similar to that of a would-be scientist who has not grasped the work of Planck, Bohr, and Einstein, or a political aspirant who has no effective knowledge of Lenin, Mussolini or Hitler.

So much for the trend of poetry at large with reference to its bearings on the possibilities of a greater Scottish poetry; for the rest, what is wanted is on the one hand, an informed concern with the vital problems of Scotland and the Scottish spirit which will give the work of our poets a dynamic function, and, on the other, an intensive concern with the problems of, or (in rhythmic and other respects) associated with, our lapsed languages – Gaelic and 'Braid Scots'.

Hugh MacDiarmid, 24 June 1933

Behind the Scaffolding: an unusual sidelight on current Scottish literature

'The period of acute pioneering controversy being over, the foundations of the new edifice of Scottish literature being laid and the design sketched out, the majority of our writers', a friend said to me the other day, 'have passed to its material construction, to the giving of substance and volume to their plans. But, as we know, the execution of a plan is always slower than its theoretic conception, and it is also less brilliant from the point of view of success. Until the new edifice is finished our artists run the risk of being considered builders and workers of no great pretensions.'

I agreed that this figure pretty well represented the position of Scottish literature at the moment, but I also insisted that, 'while fools should never be allowed to see a thing half-done', there was no excuse for intelligent people (even when they might have no idea of how the whole thing would appear finally) failing to appreciate the really solid work that had already been done, and the multitudinous activity that was now in evidence. And then I commented on an aspect of the matter that I have not so far seen commented upon anywhere else.

Provincially-minded people are still generally of the opinion that water-tight compartments should be (and can be, by really active intelligences) maintained between, say, poetry and politics, or poetry and science, or, generally, between the various arts and sciences and departments of practical affairs. My own instincts and practice have always been entirely opposed to this. Much of the criticism to which I have been subjected has been on this score. There is a general distrust of versatility, a belief that the 'shoemaker should stick to his last.' But even leading scientists like Professor Whitehead are now condemning excessive specialisation which is not counter-balanced by a sense of totality – by the broad organic appreciation which is best exemplified in aesthetic perception; and surely, even so far as the majority of folk are concerned, recent international conferences and political performances, generally, have largely disposed of the fetish of 'experts'. However that may be, I find that in the course of my own literary career, I have not only written a very large amount of poetry but also of short stories, plays, essays in literary criticism, and articles, books, and pamphlets on politics and economics. With the exception of a very extensive output of essays and reviews concerned with the description and sympathetic criticism of ultra-modern tendencies in the literatures of most of the countries in Europe (on which for over four years I wrote some thousands of words per week) I find that even Scottish Nationalism comes as a long-way second in my total production to my articles on economics, with which I have been intensively concerned for over ten years. I was rather surprised to find this. I suppose I am generally regarded as a poet, but my poetical activities have certainly been very subordinate indeed to my intromissions with 'the dismal science'.

* * *

The point of this short article, however, is that a like versatility and even a like preponderance of work other than that in connection with which they are most generally known characterises all the other contemporary Scottish writers of any consequence. The veteran R. B. Cunninghame-Graham not only had his phase as a Socialist agitator and MP, and still retains the Scottish Nationalist activities he has pursued for so many years, but his literary work falls into the diverse categories of fiction, the essay, biography, history, travel and literary criticism. In addition to that he has emerged as a defender of the ultra-modern sculpture of Epstein, has served the War Office in respect of his expert knowledge of horses, and writes in Spanish as well as English. Compton Mackenzie's activities have been even more many-sided. To his long tale of novels, short stories, and children's stories, must be added his volumes of memoirs, his work for the microphone, and in radio-criticism and book-reviewing, his volumes of miscellaneous essays, his writings on Scottish Nationalist and other political themes, his plays, and his historical interests exemplified in his splendid little study of Prince Charlie. Norman Douglas is equally versatile; it would be difficult to characterise many of his books, the subject-matter of which moves so inimitably from one literary kind to another, but, certainly, personal reminiscence, travel, fiction, and politics are four of the principal ingredients of his work.

* * *

'Ah!' someone says, 'that is true of these three famous writers who – whatever you may say – really belong to English literature and not to the new Scottish literary movement. The younger writers associated with the latter do not show anything like a similar range.'

Don't they? Let me just quickly run over the works of six of them. Take 'Lewis Grassic Gibbon'. Most people only know him by his two Scottish novels, *Sunset Song* and *Cloud Howe*, the first two volumes of a great trilogy which will soon be completed by the publication of *Granite City* [*sic*]. But under his own name of J. Leslie Mitchell he has published a historical novel *Spartacus*; three novels – *Image and Superscription, The Thirteenth Disciple,* and *Stained Radiance*; four imaginative romances – *Persian Dawns, Egyptian Nights, Three Go Back, The Lost Trumpet,* and *The Calends of Cairo*; and the following general and historical works – *The Conquest of the Maya, Ancient America,* and *Hanno, or The Future of Exploration.* And he is still only thirty-six!

Take George Blake. How many readers can say off-hand how many novels he has now published? His clever and voluminous journalistic work is widely known, and then there are his plays, his editorship of *The Strand Magazine*, his broadcasting, and his work as a publisher.

Take Edwin Muir – four volumes of brilliant literary criticism, three volumes of poetry, four novels, a biographical study of John Knox, a critical study of the structure of the novel, and, in addition to a tremendous amount of book-reviewing and miscellaneous literary journalism, the co-translatorship with his wife of many of the most important German novels of recent years.

Mrs Muir shows a kindred versatility on her own account. She has published two novels, some delightful translations from the Auvergnat into Scots poetry, a brilliant essay on 'Woman', and her book-reviewing is well known to readers of the *Scots Observer*.

Naomi Mitchison's brilliant work ranges through the fields of historical reconstruction in fictional form, novels, plays, poems, essays, a 'Russian Diary' and an active interest in political, social, scientific, and educational matters.

The last of the half-dozen I propose to mention here is Winifred Duke – half-a-dozen novels, a collection of short stories, a number of poems, an excellent historical monograph on *Lord George Murray*, a couple of volumes in Hodge's studies of Scottish crimes, and, again, all sorts of miscellaneous literary work.

* * *

Leaving Cunninghame-Graham, Compton Mackenzie and Norman Douglas out of account, these six younger writers have between them been responsible for well over a hundred volumes, and their uncollected work would fill as many more. None of them can be properly considered as literary figures unless all their work is taken into account. The trouble is that for most people their latest publications is about all that is borne in mind. It is not studied in relation to their work as a whole. Only reviews of their current publications appear – and these seldom call up any picture of their total output or relate the new book effectively to what has gone before – while I have nowhere seen any balanced study based on all their books of any of these half-dozen writers. It is for this reason, amongst others, that most people only have a very partial glimpse of our writers, and fail to form any adequate notion of the very intensive and many-sided literary activity that is proceeding in our midst. I hope these few notes will at least serve to show that behind the scaffolding, and for the most part out of sight of the topical notices, a new book may run, and then evoke a very substantial edifice indeed is being erected, and one the nature and proportions of which will be very different from what may be anticipated by those who think mainly in terms of current fiction.

Hugh MacDiarmid, 16 December 1933

Sean O'Casey's New Play

I regret that I am away up here in the Shetland Islands at this juncture and cannot see the London production of Sean O'Casey's new play, *Within the Gates*.

Its arrival on publication in book form was for me the outstanding literary event not only of last year, but of many years. It affected me profoundly – alike by the magnificent triumph of its form, which led even *The Times* to declare that 'by no new play has the theatre been given such an opportunity in our time', and by my sense of the most crucial problems of humanity today. The theatre in the hands of Ibsen, Shaw and others has been a great propagandist force, but things have moved so rapidly in recent years that the issues with which they were concerned are already as insignificant as the Fabian Society. No matter what attitude one may take up to the questions with which O'Casey deals, one must admit their overwhelming importance and urgency. Personally, I am satisfied that O'Casey has been true to himself, and to his class, in a way that amply bears out Shakespeare's 'To thine own self be true;/Thou canst not then be false to any man.' That is the foundation of O'Casey's Communism, and it affords no orifice for any revenge-complex to enter in. As he himself wrote a few months ago in reply to a critic:

> I don't hate the middle class, and, even if I did, I should strive bravely and conscientiously to give them a fair deal in any play I should venture to write about them, or in which they would be called upon to enter. In my own opinion, under the present political and social polity, the upper-class, the middle-class, and the working-class suffer and are lost to the race in their own several ways. I am a Communist because I know that the injustice done to the working-class strikes in a different, but none the less deadly, way at the middle-class, and that the upper-class is dragged into the suffering and ruin that comes upon the race.

Technical resemblances apart – and I am not denying in the least the brilliance and diversity of Strindberg's gifts and his major significance technically for the theatre of today and tomorrow, which shunts Ibsen and Shaw on to a side-line – Strindberg, with whose name O'Casey's is today being coupled, is a dramatist of disease and disintegration; O'Casey of health and reconstruction.

The material of O'Casey's play is realism, not mere actualism – he employs exclusively the imagination which penetrates to the reality in the fact, not the bald fact and not mere fancy. In a word, he is a poet, and a major poet. Another critic has said that he is 'one of the very few dramatists in the world who are aware that the actualities and not conventional notions of human society are the raw material of social drama', and of these few, 'the most uncompromising, vital, and powerful'. That is the simple truth; and he has brilliantly resolved the technical problems involved in handling such material. It is only necessary to compare the masterly blending of the transitions from colloquialism to plain prose, from plain prose to intoned rhythms, from these rhythms to declared lyric, in the orchestration of *Within the Gates* with the handling of similar transitions in T. S. Eliot's *Waste Land* – which has had an enormous literary influence, and been recognised as a quintessential report of contemporary consciousness over a wide field – to realise O'Casey's immense superiority. His foundations are infinitely deeper and broader and he rises correspondingly higher. Incidentally it should be pointed out that Eliot's poem was a document of the acutest phase of post-war disillusionment; O'Casey's shows, despite the extreme intensification of our problems and the absence of any substantial grounds for hope in the sphere of public affairs so far, a splendid moral recovery. Dr Leavis has said of one of the younger poets that although intensely sensible of the disabilities besetting the conscious in this age, there is a positive energy in his rhythms even when he speaks of frustration and undirectedness. The content of much of O'Casey's play similarly fails to disguise – even accentuates – a magnificent determination and assurance of ultimate victory. I am not going to summarise the plot or story of the play here; everyone concerned with what is vital in modern literature (and not only literature but life) will inevitably read it and, if possible, see it. I agree with *The Modern Scot* in saying that O'Casey's earlier plays 'brought English theatre-goers nearer the world of the Elizabethans than any play written by an Englishman in the past two hundred years. *The Silver Tassie* showed him enriching his technique; *Within the Gates* shows him a dramatist of European stature.' I know something of the difficulties of finding a means of orchestrating dramatic dialogue in the fashion in which O'Casey has now succeeded – to do it has been the major problem of poets and dramatists now since long before Strindberg's death in 1912 – and I know O'Casey personally and a little of what this terrific effort, a miracle of personal integrity, must have cost him. I can only hope that, as has not infrequently happened before in prophetic literatures, but more speedily, his signal success may have its counterpart in public affairs.

Hugh MacDiarmid, 17 February 1934

The Scottish Educational Journal
1928–1934

Paul Valéry

Paul Valéry – regarded by many as the greatest of French, and, perhaps, of European, poets today – is a 'difficult' poet; a highbrow of highbrows; or – to put it more exactly – a 'poet's poet'. No writer ought to be obscure – it is his duty to himself and his readers to be as clear as he can possibly make himself – but being unintelligible is another matter. If the things he is concerned with are essentially inexplicable, of an order of which only a select and specially trained public can have any cognisance or appreciation, he may well be unintelligible to everybody or almost everybody without detriment to his art. But his attitude to such subject-matter will include a faith or a hope that it will prove increasingly amenable to his art and that ultimately he – or, thanks to his pioneering efforts, some successor – will succeed in 'making the unknown known' and thus extending the field of human consciousness. This is the primary function of art. But in these democratic days it is customary to confound obscurity and unintelligibility as if they were synonymous, and in approaching the work of such a writer as Valéry the distinction cannot be overemphasised.

Over-democratisation is also responsible for the idea that the great writer is necessarily he (or she) who 'gets through' to the greatest possible public, and for the still more harmful notion that the writer ought to do all the work and demand nothing from the reader. In Science or Philosophy a sharp line is drawn between 'mere popularisers' and those great figures whose work is necessarily unintelligible to the lay mind. Why should it be otherwise in the Arts? Is it? My space here permits me merely to raise these questions – not to essay any answers. But, taking somewhat lower ground, is an author not entitled to choose his public – and if he prefers a company that is fit and few, is he necessarily a poorer artist than one whose appeal is popular and promiscuous? And, again, is he not entitled to demand of those who would approach his work a certain preliminary equipment? Children have to be taught from the A B C upwards. One does not derate a great writer because he means nothing to those who lack an ordinary education. Why, then, be suspicious of a writer who writes in a highly allusive way that can only be understood by those who have a certain familiarity with his predecessors in a given literature or with the great literature of the world in general? Must every writer begin at the very beginning again instead of starting where a certain line of forerunners left off? Paul Valéry's work raises all these questions, and a host of others. It is emphatically – and designedly – 'caviare to the general'. Why then bother about it? Can a writer of this kind legitimately complain if the public proves to be a dog that refuses to be wagged by its tail, and does the public suffer if it refuses to be so wagged? Surely, it may be argued, there is a balance in things, and any individual's excessive development in a given direction can be disregarded. There is no need to go to extremes. If a writer gets too far ahead of human consciousness as a whole, he must not be surprised if, instead of following him, the main body switches off in another direction further down and leaves him 'high and dry'.

Apart from the fact that in every department of human art and activity progress has always depended upon individuals running the aforementioned risk, in Valéry's particular case it is only necessary to read such a highly-critical and, in many respects, antipathetic essay as that of the Right Hon. H. A. L. Fisher – last year's Taylorian Lecture at Oxford University – to see that in Valéry we have a poet who, despite all the questions I have indicated, and despite (if not because of) the excessive difficulty of his work, demands and amply repays, the attention of all who want to be *au fait* with the most significant and influential elements in contemporary world-literature.

After discussing Valéry's discipleship of Mallarmé, his relation to the Symbolist movement in general, and, in particular, the consequences of his espousal of 'La Poésie Pure', Mr Fisher says:

> The admirers of Valéry have found in his work an original and inventive quality which, apart from an unusual sense for the niceties of French prosody, gives him a special place among the poets of this age. His critics admit the excellence of his technique, but complain that his verse is cold, strained, and difficult, and to them M. Valéry would at once concede that neither in his choice of themes nor in his treatment of them is he concerned to stir the common heart of man. If he ever thinks of his readers, which may be gravely doubted, it is certain that he does not view them as lost souls to be saved by his verse. His gift to them is not ethical improvement, but the kind of subtle and intellectual enjoyment which is excited by delicate chamber-music. Some of the audience will discover deep meanings in the music, others will simply enjoy the sounds, to others the whole performance will be unintelligible. To all critics the author's reply would be that he is giving them the deepest part of himself in the form most satisfactory to his artistic conscience, and that if they do not like it they are under no obligation to listen. But even the reader who finds little pleasure and profit in introspective verse will be compelled to concede that M. Valéry is a master of musical French.

In proof of this, Mr Fisher cites single lines like: 'Sage Sémiramis, enchanteresse et roi' and 'Te voici, mon doux corps de lune et de rosée.' Quotations like this from the *Cantique des Colounes*:

Pour affronter la lune,
La lune et le soleil,
Ou nous polit chacune
Comme ongle de l'orteil

and odes like *L'Aurore*, which begins thus: –

La confusion morose,
Qui me servait de sommeil,
Se dissipe dès la rose
Apparence du soleil,
Dans mon âme je m'avance,
Tout ailé de confiance;
C'est la première oraison!
A peine sorti des sables,
Je fais des pas admirables
Dans les pas de ma raison

Valéry has had an unusual career. Born in 1871, he began writing about 1890, producing, in ten years, two slender prose works and a few poems. These verses showed that Mallarmé had secured a worthy successor: but instead of continuing to develop his art – or, rather, to exercise it – Valéry kept silence for fifteen years, during which he principally concerned himself with the study of higher mathematics. He broke this silence in 1917 with *La Jeune Parque*. Four years later, the review *La Connaissance* having organised a referendum to designate the foremost poet of the present day, the majority of the votes went to Valéry. Since then he has maintained a very small output of poems, essays, and dialogues; and his reputation has steadily extended. The fact that Mr Fisher chose him as the subject of his essay is in itself, no matter what he might say of him, a conclusive testimony to his international importance.

It is an axiom of good criticism that its function is to determine what an author's intention was, and what success he has had in endeavouring to carry it out. Mr Fisher seizes upon the heart of the matter when he writes:

> To earnest inquirers the author with a smile vouchsafed the information that *La Jeune Parque* was a *cours de physiologie*, seeing that it portrays a series of psychological changes which affect a human consciousness in the course of a night. The other poem, *L'Aurore*, is less ambiguous in its message, and may with reasonable probability be described as a picture, true as the exigencies of a delicate lyrical metre may allow, of the psycho-physical processes of sleep and awakening. It will be admitted that as themes for the poet neither physiology nor psycho-physics is *prima facie* alluring. Lucretius, however, and, later, Dante, had succeeded with matter hardly less tractable, but then neither Lucretius nor Dante was French. The French genius, so essentially rhetorical, had shrunk from the marriage of

> science and verse. 'Our poetry,' writes M. Valéry, 'ignores or even fears all the epic and pathetic of the intellect... We have not among us the poets of knowledge.' The time had come to fill the gap.

Valéry's intention could not be better described. How far has he fulfilled it? If his aim has been to write 'a very different kind of poetry from that which the world has valued since the days of Homer', is it not likely that, if he has succeeded, most of Mr Fisher's strictures may arise from the latter's retention and use of preconceptions belonging to the other kind of poetry. So Valéry's enthusiasts – and I am one of them – will contend. It is significant of much that Mr Fisher should parenthetically exclaim, when speaking of Valéry's concern in a certain dialogue with the difference between mechanism, life, and personality – 'a theme with regard to which the prudent reader will prefer to have recourse to Dr J. S. Haldane'! Mr Fisher's criticisms of Valéry are subject to a very considerable discount in the light of so English, so nineteenth-century, a partiality. And when he goes on to say: 'The attempt to express in a lyric as musical as Schubert, as formal as Hérédia, such minute psychological changes as fill Proust's operose and interminable novels, this, if a gallant, is surely a forlorn enterprise', the reply will be let those, who have eyes to see, see, and those, who have ears to hear, hear, for Valéry has accomplished this very miracle.

But whether that high claim can be conceded or not, surely there are few poets in the world today so well worth reading as one who can draw from an ironically, if suavely, hostile critic this concluding tribute:

> Geometry and Poetry are old allies; and this poet, who is also a geometrician, has already given us a small body of poetical work at once so intellectual and so melodious that the jealous portals of the French Academy have been opened for his reception. His verse is confessedly difficult, but, perhaps for that very reason, and because it evades the clear concrete lines of everyday life, it has a curious power of transporting the reader into a magical world of its own in which there is nothing common and nothing definite, but only a phantasmagoria of haunting images passing before the eye to the sound of delicate unearthly music and with just so much of consistency and permanence as belong to the scent of flowers in the night breeze or to the ethereal tissues of a dream.

A. L., 10 August 1928

An Irish Poet: Oliver St John Gogarty

Ireland has produced an astonishingly rich and varied crop of men and women during the past fifty to seventy years – a brilliant and restless generation of whom, for want of an effective Boswell, an all too inadequate record will remain, despite such monuments as the established fact of the Irish Free State and the products, above all in poetry and drama, of the Irish Literary Renaissance. Think of these people – Yeats, 'A. E.' (George Russell), George Moore, J. M. Synge, Lady Gregory, Michael Collins, Arthur Griffiths, James Connolly, Lord Dunsany, Maud Gonne, Eamonn de Valera. The list could be multiplied by ten or twenty without exhausting the number of extraordinarily interesting figures in letters or politics or both whose work is an essential element of what the term 'Ireland' or 'Saorstat Eireann' connotes to world consciousness today. And, as usually happens in such a case, no matter how complete one tried to make the list, one would omit some name to which the future will attach far more significance than the present can. It is exceedingly difficult to guage who will seem most pivotal and indispensable to such a movement a century later. Posterity has impredicable selective instincts. Its tastes differ from today's; there is no need to assume that they are better. And so far as the making of modern Ireland is concerned so much of it has depended upon brilliant talk, unrecorded by any Boswell, that the material for future estimation must do sad injustice to many of the personalities involved. Despite Moore's *Ave Atque Vale*, Joyce's *Ulysses*, Yeats' reminiscental writings, and other material, a huge amount of most vital, lovable, varied, diverting and dynamic 'personality in action' is already irrecoverable, and most of what is left is in process of falsification through change of atmosphere and emphasis, the operation of *arrière pensée*, and the lack of disinterestedness. Much of the best that modern Ireland has produced in wit, imagination, and dialectic is irretrievably lost already. They were great talkers, these significant Irish. I have been told that one of the best of them is Stephen McKenna, the translator of Plotinus, and have had described to me the amazing spate of his talk varying in the course of an evening through half the gamut of human emotions. Yeats and 'A. E.' too, are great talkers and have given much of their best in this way. And the work that has taken permanent shape is but an attenuated emanation from a wonderful background of personality. Who, for example, would not like to know a great deal more of the life together in Ely Place of the Seven Mystics of whom the young 'A. E.' was one – seven mystics who, in various parts of the world, are today heads of great businesses or government departments? 'A. E.' himself behind his literary personality shelters a practical economist who has done a vast amount for agricultural co-operation. Well may Yeats marvel at the rich harvest of gifts thrown up by the Irish people in his lifetime and comment (as he did to me in a recent conversation) on the fact that all those concerned in this Renaissance were so intimately connected with each other. And one whose name is insufficiently known out of Ireland itself, one of the most fascinating and versatile of them all, is Oliver St John Gogarty.

Gogarty is a Senator, a surgeon, a sportsman, an airman, a wit and a poet – reminiscent of one of the many-sided personalities of the Italian Renaissance. His jokes have been one of the features of Dublin life; his satirical and Rabelaisian verses are one of the spiciest elements in its secret literature. He has been a boon-companion of all the personalities of modern Ireland; he lived with Joyce for three years in a round tower at Kingstown. He was cycling champion of Ireland a quarter of a century ago; now he is carrying off gold medals for poetry at the Tailteann Games. His house is a cosmopolitan resort. He keeps a 'gleg eye' on all the world's art, affairs, and athletics. Versatility such as this is always suspect, and as a consequence his remarkable qualities as a poet have not yet received anything like their due recognition. But within the past year or two his work has been appearing increasingly in the anthologies. It is distinguished from that of the other and better-known poets of modern Ireland by its classicism, its intellectuality and its range. Yeats is a marvellous verbal musician – but tastes change, and while the reputation of having been a great poet will, of course, remain, it may well be that as in other cases (Swinburne's, for example) little or nothing of his work may be popularly known or readily quotable a quarter of a century hence, or what is preserved may be a few poems outwith his predominant manner. It is something with a tougher fibre – more intellectual, didactic or epigrammatic – that survives. How many *jeux-d'esprit* are immortal and how many epics forgotten! Poets who develop a manner and mode of their own can, in any case, be adequately savoured in the future by one or two examples. It is the poets who are more various and who touch life at a greater number of points who are more difficult to 'place', and who frequently come to occupy a larger place than their contemporaries – too much taken up by one dominant tendency or fashion – could readily credit. I have no doubt that this will prove the case with Oliver Gogarty and that he will come to occupy a much larger space relatively to Yeats, 'A. E.', Seumas O'Sullivan and the others than may seem likely to those too much taken up with the 'Celtic Twilight' note which has been overwhelmingly characteristic of the accepted products of the Irish Literary Revival. There are already signs that he is at last coming into his own. This is partly due to the reaction against the 'Celtic Twilight' business. Gogarty's work in its variety of appeal (even within a single poem) – its mingling of moods – is (paradoxically enough) more in keeping with the poetry of the old Irish bards, the poets of 'The Hidden Ireland', than a great deal of the main output of the earlier phases of the Irish Literary Movement. It is a mistake to imagine that these poets all sang in one key – that Irish poetry is all of this fine-spun, tenuous, shadowy stuff, and lacking in variety and virility. The younger poets are trying to get back, through the twilight, to the Gaelic sunshine; and Gogarty's work is more in keeping with their desires than a great deal of the work of such poets as Yeats and Seumas O'Sullivan, against which they are necessarily reacting.

Gogarty's accessible published work consists of two volumes – *An Offering of Swans, and Other Poems* (Messrs Eyre & Spottiswoode), and *Wild Apples* (Cuala Press). Few volumes of poetry in the history of literature can owe their titles to more dramatic circumstances than the first of these. It commemorates Gogarty's escape from summary execution at the hands of the Republicans –

and the wonderful inspiration which led him to get his revenge on his would-be slayers, not by savage denunciation and a demand for reprisals in the Senate, but by ceremonially gifting a pair of swans to the river Liffey through which – when it was in full spate – he swam to safety amid a hail of bullets. President Cosgrave and Yeats assisted at the ceremony; and now the swans are multiplying on the Liffey. Visitors can see them sailing up and down in ever-increasing numbers. Was there ever a happier thought?

'I wonder', says Yeats in his preface,

> if it was the excitement of escape that brought a new sense of English lyric tradition and changed a wit into a poet. The witty sayings that we all repeated, the Rabelaisian verse that we all copied, rose out of so great a confused exuberance that I, at any rate, might have foreseen the miracle. Yet no, for a miracle is self-begotten, and, though afterwards we may offer swans to Helicon, by its very nature something we cannot foresee or premeditate. Its only rule is that it follows, more often than otherwise, the discovery of a region or a rhythm where a man may escape out of himself. Oliver Gogarty has discovered the rhythm of Herrick and of Fletcher, something different from himself and yet akin to himself; and I have been murmuring his 'Non Dolet', his 'Begone, Sweet Ghost', and his 'Good Luck'. Here are but a few pages, that a few months have made, and there are careless lines now and again, traces of the old confused exuberance. He never stops long at his best, but how beautiful that best is, how noble, how joyous!

The three poems Yeats mentioned, and others such as 'Golden Stockings', are now secure of their place in the anthologies. But Gogarty has not ceased to develop and perfect his late-found gift. His 'wild apples' are slow in ripening, but they have a wonderful flavour that is all their own.

Here is the Crab-tree,
Firm and erect,
In spite of the thin soil,
In spite of neglect,
The twisted root grapples
For sap with the rock,
And draws the hard juice
To the succulent top:
Here are wild apples,
Here's a tart crop!
No outlandish grafting
That ever grew soft
In a sweet air of Persia,
Or safe Roman croft;

Unsheltered by steading,
Rock-rooted and grown,
A great tree of Erin,
It stands up alone,
A forest tree spreading
Where forests are gone.

A. L., 21 September 1928

The Nature of the Physical World

This is not a 'bedside book'. Professor Eddington is the gentleman who recently made a statement to the Royal Society on the dynamics of the electron – calling for the radical modification of the existing conception, itself only thirty years old – and making the confusion of contemporary physics worse confounded by admitting that even he himself could not say what he meant or be sure that he meant what he said on the matter at issue. An extraordinary change has come over science in the last few years. From being 'materialistic' it has swung to the opposite extreme of an incomprehensive mysticism. But after all, there is nothing very new about that, for as Sir James Jeans, in his report on Radiation and the Quantum Theory has pointed out: 'The history of science teaches that each great advance towards ultimate reality has shown this reality to lie in an entirely unexpected direction.'

Dr Eddington, Plumian Professor of Astronomy in the University of Cambridge, is widely known by his works on the structure of the universe and his discovery of the two main star drifts; and this book [*The Nature of the Physical World* (Cambridge University Press)] is substantially the course of Gifford lectures he delivered in the University of Edinburgh two years ago. Although he may find the latest conclusions to which he has been forced inexpressibly incomprehensible or incomprehensibly inexpressible, Dr Eddington is a deft and delightful writer and expounds his subject here with a wonderful clarity, however strange and difficult these new conceptions of the physical world may remain, when all is said and done. This sense of strangeness is mainly due to the necessity, foreign to the pre-conceptions of most of us, of realising that science is not concerned with the real constituents of the world. It may elicit laws from the 'pointer readings' with which it is concerned; but the 'relata' themselves disclose nothing as to the actual nature of things. Again, it is necessary to realise that the physical world is not the only world that might have been selected by mind in its constructive capacity. How profound and far-reaching is this fact that we can choose what we think; and that if we do not choose that is in itself a choice, confining us to a particular line out of innumerable lines all equally possible and valid, although utterly different in their results! The conscious mind today is a place where parallel lines meet; call it Pyhronnism, if you like – a weakness for seeing several sides of a case at once and being unable to choose between them – or go a stage further and realise with contemporary science that we live in a world in which mutually contradictory facts are equally true and in which, like Dostoevski, we can both believe and disbelieve at the same time. Physical theories do not reach ultimate realities; we fashion them in our own image. Contemporary science calls for an amazing disinterestedness – a profound scepticism. As Professor Eddington himself puts it: 'We have found a strange footprint on the sands of the unknown. We have devised profound theories, one after another, to account for its origin. At last, we have succeeded in reconstructing the creature that made the footprint, and lo! it is our own.' This beats Daniel Defoe hollow. The cosmic Crusoe is on an altogether different and far more thrilling 'island' than his prototype Robinson.

The aim of this book is to make clear the scientific view of the world as it stands today, and to describe the philosophical outcome of the recent changes of scientific thought. In the first part the author describes the new physical theories, the reasons which have led to their adoption and the direction in which they appear to be tending; in the second part he considers the position which this scientific view should occupy in relation to the wider aspects of human experience, including religion.

> Science aims at constructing a world which shall be symbolic of the world of commonplace experience. It is not at all necessary that every individual symbol that is used should represent something in common experience or even something explicable in terms of common experience. The man in the street is always making this demand for concrete explanation of the things referred to in science; but of necessity he must be disappointed. It is like our experience in learning to read. That which is written in a book is symbolic of a story in real life. The whole intention of the book is that ultimately a reader will identify some symbol, say Bread, with one of the conceptions of familiar life. But it is mischievous to attempt such identifications prematurely, before the letters are strung into words and the words into sentences. The symbol A is not the counterpart of anything in familiar life. To the child the letter A would seem horribly abstract: so we give him a familiar conception along with it. 'A was an Archer who shot at a frog.' This tides over his immediate difficulty; but he cannot make serious progress with word-building so long as Archers, Butchers, Captains dance round the letters. The letters are abstract, and sooner or later he has to realise it. In physics we have outgrown archer and apple-pie definitions of the fundamental symbols. To a request to explain what an electron really is supposed to be we can only answer, 'It is part of the A. B. C. of physics.'... The frank realisation that physical science is concerned with a world of shadows is one of the most significant of recent advances... If you are not prepared for this aloofness from familiar conceptions you are like-

> ly to be out of sympathy with modern scientific theories, and may even think them ridiculous – as, I daresay, many people do. It is difficult to school ourselves to treat the physical world as purely symbolic. We are always relapsing and mixing with the symbols incongruous conceptions taken from the world of consciousness. Untaught by long experience we stretch a hand to grasp the shadow, instead of accepting its shadowy nature.

A science of shadows!

'The world', said W. K. Clifford, 'is made of atoms and ether, and there is no room in it for ghosts.' Isn't there? How far science has travelled from the so-recent days of such crude determinism is to be seen from Professor Eddington's statement: 'The Victorian physicist felt that he knew just what he was talking about when he used such terms as matter and atoms. Atoms were tiny billiard balls, a crisp statement which was supposed to tell you all about their nature in a way which could never be achieved for transcendental things like consciousness, beauty, or humour.' But the scene is changed! 'The physical atom is, like everything else in physics, a schedule of pointer readings. The schedule is, we agree, attached to some unknown background.'

More recently Dr Eddington has said that the electron is only a 'dummy' – an imagined assistance to the imperfection of the human intellect – and commenting on this Professor Wolf, of the Chair of Scientific Theory in London University, says: – 'Even in ordinary life, when you talk of "things" – of tables and chairs – there is no difficulty; but when you come to talk of rain you do not talk of just rain or of rainfall. Habitually we say: "It is raining." What is this it? The dummy! So with physics." In other words all that science can give us is a series of measurements of a thing; it cannot tell us what the thing is in itself.

There is no clash between science and religion; the one is concerned with the schedule of pointer readings, the other with the unknown background to which that schedule is attached. 'Digging deeper and deeper into what lies at the base of physical phenomena,' says Dr Eddington, 'we must be prepared to come to entities which, like many things in our conscious experience, are not measurable by numbers in any way.'

> The word 'reality' is generally used *with the intention of evoking sentiment*. It is a grand word for a peroration. 'The right honourable gentleman went on to declare that the concord and amity for which he had unceasingly striven had now become a reality (loud cheers).' The conception which it is so troublesome to apprehend is not 'reality' but 'reality (loud cheers).' Let it be understood that the truth we seek in science is the truth about an external world propounded as the theme of study, and is not bound up with any opinion as to the status of that world – whether or not it wears the halo of reality, whether or not it is deserving of 'loud cheers'.

And, towards the last paragraph of his delightful book, Dr Eddington says: –

> Scientific discovery is like the fitting together of the pieces of a great jig-saw puzzle; a revolution of science does not mean that the pieces already arranged and interlocked have to be dispersed; it means that in fitting on fresh pieces we have had to revise our impression of what the puzzle-picture is going to be like. One day you ask the scientist how he is getting on; he replies, 'Finely. I have very nearly finished this bit of blue sky.' Another day you ask how the sky is progressing and are told, 'I have added a lot more, but it was sea, not sky; there's a boat floating on the top of it.' Perhaps next time it will have turned out to be a parasol upside down; but our friend is still enthusiastically delighted with the progress he is making. The scientist has his guesses as to how the finished picture will work out; he depends largely on these in his search for other pieces to fit; but his guesses are modified from time to time by unexpected developments as the fitting proceeds. These revolutions of thought as to the final picture do not cause the scientist to lose faith in his handiwork, for he is aware that the completed portion is growing steadily. Those who look over his shoulder and use the present partially developed picture for purposes outside science do so at their own risk.

It is good to learn that this book – now in its third impression – is still selling at the rate of fifty copies per day.

A. L., 8 March 1929

Anglo-Irish Literature

Dr St John D. Seymour has filled a gap in literary history by this account of the non-Celtic literature of Ireland – comprising prose and verse written in Norman-French, Latin and English – between the years 1200 and 1582 [*Anglo-Irish Literature 1200–1582* (Cambridge University Press)].

As the author points out in his introductory chapter:

> The reader may not unnaturally ask the question, Was there any non-Celtic literature in Ireland in this period? To which it might be answered that even if not a single fragment survived, it might yet be assumed with safety that something in the form of literature must have existed. One cannot imagine Anglo-Norman nobles and barons dwelling in semi-kingly state in their castles, or citizens and merchants living their busy lives in walled towns or flourishing seaports, or monks in the seclusion of the cloister, or lads and lasses making holiday, without the solace of literature... Such a literature did exist and flourish, and of this so much is extant, either as entire pieces or as fragments, as to make us realise that we have but a

> tiny portion of the whole, and that the greater part has been irretrievably lost. This literature consisted of original pieces, of adaptations, and of translations. It looked to England, and even further afield, for its form and its inspiration – there is hardly a portion of it but finds a parallel in contemporary English literature – and does not appear to have been influenced at all by the native literature of Ireland. But this is only what is to be expected. In its very earliest stages it was the work of Anglo-Norman *trouvères*, its intermediate stages came into being in monasteries founded by the invaders, or in cities whose inhabitants cut themselves off by walls mental and material, from the Irish-speaking people who surrounded them; while its final stages developed at a time when the English language and outlook was restricted to a small part of the country, namely, to such places as Dublin, Kilkenny and Waterford, which had always been strongholds of the English interest. It could only find an audience amongst those who spoke and wrote the language of the invaders.

Dr St John Seymour has done his work very thoroughly. Little can have escaped his small-tooth comb. The literature with which he is concerned has little intrinsic, and probably no comparative, importance. It is, almost entirely, the smallest of small beer; yet as a study in a remote bypath of literature, and in difficult inter-linguistic and cross-cultural connections, it is full of interest. Of special value, alike to students of English and of Scots, for example, are the notes on the peculiarities of the English literary dialect in Ireland between the years 1300 and 1600. These peculiarities include the confusion of *th* with *t* and *d*; the confusion of *w* with *u* and *v*; the omission and erroneous insertion of *h*; and the substitution of *t* for the final *d*, of *sh* for *s*, and *ss* for *sh*, i.e., *fisse* (for *fish*), *schame* (for *shame*), *is* (for *his*), *hit* (for *it*), *ispend* (for *ispent*).

> Furthermore, in these poems occur peculiar and unusual forms, such as *apan* (for upon), *throg* (through), *streinth* (strength), *neldes* (needles), and *axin* (ashes)… On this dialect Stanihurst has some interesting information in his *Description of Ireland*. He says that in Wexford and Fingall were to be found at this time 'dregs of the old, ancient Chaucer English.' He gives some of the peculiar words then in use, e.g., *attercop* (spider); *meanie* (household, or folks); *leech* (physician); *eeth* or *eefë* (easy)… Not long before he wrote, an English nobleman was sent to Wexford to examine some grievances. He listened affably to the peasants making their complaints, and 'conceived here and there sometimes a word, otherwhiles a whole sentence.' At this he was agreeably surprised and pleased, and told one of this followers that 'he stood in good hope to become shortly a well-spoken man in the Irish' – he actually supposed that the peasants were addressing him in Gaelic, while in reality they were speaking archaic English!

In successive chapters we have exhaustive accounts of the Norman-French *Song of Dermot and the Earl*; the sprightly 'Entrenchment of New Ross'; the early prose writings of Jofroi or Godfrey of Waterford, whose *Secreta* was not the least important of the sources from which the scientific knowledge at the disposal of intelligent laymen in France from the twelfth to the fourteenth centuries was derived, and of Father Malachy of Limerick, and Richard Fitzralph, Archbishop of Armagh, and the account of the proceedings taken in Kilkenny against Dame Alice Kyteler and her associates for witchcraft and heresy by Richard de Ledrede, Bishop of Ossory – a *cause celebre* of which a fairly full account is given here, and which no one interested in such matters can afford to miss; and in turn, religious poems, secular poems, and satirical poems, outstanding amongst the latter being *The Land of Cokaygne,* which Heuser has described as 'the airiest and cleverest piece of satire in the whole range of Early English, if not of English poetry'. Then we have chapters on 'The Religious Drama' and on 'Fifteenth Century Prose Writings', full of quaint and curious things.

The most interesting chapter, however, is perhaps the tenth, and last, for it deals with that extraordinary character, Richard Stanihurst (born in Dublin in 1547), and well described as the 'oddest of English writers, odd enough in his prose and eccentric in his verse productions'. A full account is given of his career, character and compositions. In his 'Introduction to the Reader' of his poems, Stanihurst

> developed the theory of English prosody of which Gabriel Harvey was the champion, maintaining that quantity rather than accent ought to be the guiding principle of English as of Latin metre. He rendered Virgil into hexameters by way of proving that proposition. The result was a literary monstrosity. The Latin was recklessly paraphrased in a grotesquely prosaic vocabulary, which abounded in barely intelligible words invented by the translator to meet metrical exigencies. Frequent inversions of phrase heightened the ludicrous effect.

Here is an example (for better – or worse – but unfortunately, longer, the reader must refer to the book): –

> Much like as in cornshucks singëd with blasterous hurling
> Of southwind whistling; or when from a mountain a rumbling
> Flood rakes up furrows, ripe corn, and tillage of oxen.
> Down tears it windfalls, and thick woods sturdily tumbleth,
> The crack rack crashing the unwitting pastor amazeth.
>
> (II, ll. 304–8)

This is nothing, however, to the frenzied dictionary, it is of most of it; and of Stanihurst's translations of the *Psalms*, Dr St John Seymour well remarks: 'Tate and Brady's' metrical version of the Psalms has been termed a "drysalter". Such an expression could not be applied to Stanihurst's work – the use of it would have moved any congregation to tears of laughter!'

'Those oddities of style which have raised Stanihurst to a bad pre-eminence in English literature' may be epitomised, perhaps, in that line of his own poem on the death of Lord Affaly, which runs: 'Maynooth lamenteth, Kilkea and Rathangan are howling.'

A. L., 6 September 1929

The Sense of Glory

In his new volume of critical studies, *The Sense of Glory* (Cambridge University Press), Mr Herbert Read brings together a series of essays which originally appeared in the *Times Literary Supplement*, but, read singly there and not in consecutive issues, did not disclose the impressive relationship to each other, the cumulative significance, they now manifest.

'The sense of glory', he says is his short forenote,

> is perhaps a phrase that has grown stale on our lips, and it may be a vain ambition of mine to reanimate it. As my excuse, I might repeat a saying of Renan's which Matthew Arnold once quoted; 'Glory, after all, is the thing which has the best chance of not being altogether vanity.' Glory may be only one form of romanticism; but so is every kind of idealism. Romanticism, whether we like it or not, is always with us. But though we cannot escape from the multitude of sentiments to which it gives rise, introducing among those sentiments an order whose integrity is this very sense of glory.

He goes to Traherne's *Centuries of Meditation* for the true definition of the glory with which he is concerned, and quotes the following key-passage:

> The noble inclination whereby man thirsteth after riches and dominion is his highest virtue, when rightly guided; and carries him as in a triumphant chariot to his sovereign happiness. Men are made miserable only by abusing it. Taking a false way to satisfy it, they pursue the wind; nay, labour in the very fire, and after all reap but vanity. Whereas, as God's love, which is the foundation of all, did cost us nothing; so were all other things prepared by it to satisfy our inclinations in the best of manners, freely, without any cost of ours. Seeing, therefore, that all satisfactions are near at hand, by going further we do not leave them; and wearying ourselves in a long way round about, like a blind man, forsake them. They are immediately near to the very gates of our senses. It becometh the bounty of God to prepare them freely; to make them glorious, and their enjoyment easy. For because His love is free so are His treasures. He therefore that will despise them

> because he hath them is marvellously irrational; the way to possess them is to esteem them.

And again: 'It is of the nobility of man's soul that he is insatiable.' And: 'To think well is to serve God in the interior Court.'

Mr Read's essays win no little share of the noble quality with which they are concerned. The are confined to literature, or culture. But the theme, the need for the sense of glory, could well have been applied in other directions where it is still more sadly to seek in the modern world. It involves a general denunciation of 'commercial Calvinism'; of that so-called materialism of which we are so often accused but which, as Aldous Huxley has reminded us, arises from the fact that we are not nearly materialistic enough; of all those ruts of convention, conservatism and cowardice which shut mankind off from 'life, and that more abundantly', and of all mean satisfactions and ruinous thrifts. 'Something for nothing.' The 'psychological blindness' that gives a twist to the human mind, making it distrust any proposal to make things more easy – to disnecessitate drudgery and the earning of bread by the sweat of the brow – and to abolish the horrible system of 'rewards and punishments' which constitutes our conventional morality, debars glory from our vision. Mr Read would fain break through this stupid film of prejudice, sadism and fear.

His essays deal in succession with Froissart, Malory, Descartes, Swift, Vauvenargues, Sterne, Hawthorne, Bagehot, and Henry James. 'Froissart's pages', he writes,

> are vivid with the personal radiance of men who achieve glory. There is no question here, as in Malory's case, of an author idealising a forgotten age. Froissart is the matter-of-fact reporter of events that happened in his own time, often under his own eyes. Naturally, he was conscious of the glory of the deeds he recorded; but not as we are. For Froissart, glory was the measure of all things, the crown of all virtues. For us it has become something remote and elusive; even something romantic and literary. We have lost the sense of glory because we have lost the habit of faith. We neither love deeply enough nor feel deeply enough, nor think deeply enough, to enjoy life's most impressive sanction.

Whether Mr Read's preoccupation with this sense of glory has not cast a transfiguring effulgence over some of his subjects, or certain aspects of them, and made him fail too, in complete comprehension – whether, in other words, his thesis has not at times led his admirable judgment a little astray, and his concern with a quality which is not exclusively literary led him to speculations and conclusions concerning the authors of whom he is writing which a more purely literary criticism cannot always endorse – I shall not discuss here. Sterne may, or may not, have been 'the precursor of all psychological fiction', as he contends. There can be no question that he is pre-occupied with values which are of immensely more consequence, and especially so today, than literary exactitude. A host of errors in detail may well be excused to one who has had the essential rightness to choose so timely and illuminating a theme, and to present it in a series of essays as vital and vivid as these.

Of particular interest to Scottish readers, in view of the tendencies in current Scottish letters, may be the passages in the essay on Hawthorne where he deals with puritanism and provincialism. 'It is not fair', he says,

> to call him a Puritan, even a rebellious one. In no sense is his art what the psychologists call a compensation – in no sense a reaction to environment or education, a working-off of repressions, a rationalisation of fixed ideas. Hawthorne was born with a lively sensibility and that freedom of mind which best conduces to a temperate art; and there seems to have been no attempt to interfere with his natural development. The only necessities that ever seriously galled him were economic. He led a strangely secluded life in his adolescent years, but not stranger than that of any youth of his temperament born into the dreary waste of provincial life. His defects (which have often the appearance of inhibitions) are really defects of education – as is most obviously shown in his aversion, later in life, to the nude statues he found everywhere about him in Rome. His remark that 'man is no longer a naked animal; his clothes are as natural to him as his skin, and sculptors have no more right to undress him than to flay him', strikes us with the force of its crudity rather than its prudery. It was not so much a strange, vague, long-dormant heritage of his strait-laced Puritan ancestry as a simple lack of experience.

I will not seek to argue how much of what some of younger Scottish writers attribute to our Calvinistic past is really due to that, and how much to simple ignorance of life and art; but the discrimination Mr Read exercises so admirably and so convincingly in his analysis of Hawthorne is certainly one that might be applied very effectively in the discussion of certain cultural topics which have recently been intensively canvassed in Scotland and of which a great deal more is likely to be heard in the very near future.

On the one hand, although he can write such a phrase as 'the dreary waste of provincial life', Mr Read can be scrupulously fair to the real values of true provincialism. Dealing with Henry James's definite conclusion that Hawthorne's art had suffered, and suffered disastrously, irremediably, from the thinness and insipidity of the atmosphere he had been compelled to live in, Mr Read contends that Henry James

> failed to appreciate at its true value what we might call Hawthorne's provincialism. A province, though it lacks many of the positive virtues of a metropolis, has some rather negative virtues of its own. It is more confined in its outlook, but tends to send its roots deeper into the soil with which it

> is, moreover, in directer contact. Much of the best of our literature is essentially provincial – Sterne and the Brontës, and even Wordsworth.

And he carries the matter to its logical and triumphant conclusion in the final passage of his essay on Henry James which ends the book, and which I quote in full as a last proof of the noble eloquence, the splendid reason, the imaginative fire which characterise these important essays: –

> In another place, Henry James says: 'I think it is extremely provincial for a Russian to be very Russian, for the simple reason that certain national types are essentially and intrinsically provincial.' Perhaps he would have made that overworked label suffice as a connecting-link between his antipathies. Perhaps nowadays we can see stronger and more essential links; such links are being forged by events, and the process of 'Americanisation', which carries with it all the determinate forces of materialism and mechanism, nowhere seems so irresistible as among the comparatively traditionless peoples of Russia. Is not the deepest significance of the revolution in Russia to be found in its renunciation of Europe? Its force and endurance can only be explained by a recognition of this historical truth: that there has been no suppression of the national ethos, but rather a renewal. Russia has retreated to her own fastnesses. The political doctrine with which the new *régime* is identified, although of European origin, is one which even its European adherents would admit to be totally disruptive of the cultural traditions of the West. And if today we wished to take from the world of literature two antithetical types representing the dominant and opposite forces of the modern world, we could not find two so completely significant as Dostoievski and Henry James. In the one is all energy, all evil, obscenity and confusion, the dreadful apocalypse of a conscience that has lost all civilised sanctions and has no foundations in its world; and in the other a calm, dominant, reticent and fastidious intellect, ordering the gathered forces of time to a manifestation of their most enduring glory.

A. L., 6 December 1929

The Art of Compton Mackenzie

The significance of Compton Mackenzie's *Gallipoli Memories* (Cassell) has been apprehended in many quarters. It is a timely and important book, marking a turning-point, not only in War Literature, but, one would fain hope, in post-war mentality in this country. For its significance lies in its complete break with the cataract of whining self-pity which has almost wholly submerged us. That is its general significance; its particular significance is its author's victory over the campaign of detraction which has beset his reputation. The success of *Carnival*, of *Guy and Pauline*, of *Sinister Street*, made it inevitable perhaps that their author should endure a period of depreciation. It was said that his subsequent novels were not as good as *Carnival*. Perhaps not: but what author continuously betters his best? Can he, or should he, keep on repeating it? The real point should have been not whether he was writing more *Carnivals*, but just how good was the *Carnival* he had written. The answer to that is only now being re-appreciated, and so far from Mr Mackenzie being regarded as a novelist who has not redeemed his early promise it is being realised that, contrary to the advice of the literary tipsters, his work has worn much better than that of many of his contemporaries and even younger authors who have had vogues of sorts while he has been in seeming eclipse. No British writer of Mr Mackenzie's generation occupies anything like so strong a position. Others who seemed as likely as himself to win lasting honours have somehow petered out. The War killed them; but Mr Mackenzie's work held something that, unlike theirs, has survived all the chances and changes of the War, and now, with unabated zest and vigour and endless wit and high spirits, he has all the War and the Post-War period behind him and is breaking out in new directions. He is the youngest of our distinguished writers; H. G. Wells, Arnold Bennett, John Galsworthy, are all old men in comparison and show no signs of opening fresh founts of fertility. But who of his own generation can be set alongside Mr Mackenzie? Frank Swinnerton, Hugh Walpole, Francis Brett-Young, Sheila Kaye Smith – the question only needs asking to show that he stands alone. The younger authors of some established repute are still older in comparison; world-weary, morbid, cruel. The very latest newcomers, who are reacting from the horrors, the 'realism', the jazz, of war-time and post-war reaction can look to no one except Mr Mackenzie for leadership. This position Mr Mackenzie owes not to his wit, not to his exquisite prose style, not to his wide experience of the world – but to something far deeper that is part and parcel of his philosophy of life; something that cannot be dismissed by calling him a romantic (as if these so-called 'realists' were not just jaundiced romantics themselves). He has been true to a deeper humanity than most of his contemporaries and successors. He has been no less acute an observer than they of the special characteristics of our own time; but he has not allowed these to preoccupy him into forgetting the fundamental things which appertain, not only to our own time, but to all times and places. And the result is that, returning to his early work after all these apparently changeful years, one finds it as fresh and vital as at first. It has mellowed like good wine; most of what has been esteemed above it in the interval has, on the contrary, gone rotten. And the re-discovery of the undiminished – nay, the increased – vitality of a novel such as *Carnival* leads to a reconsideration of Mr Mackenzie's work as a whole. He has written close on thirty novels – not one of them unworthy of him although he has been conscious in writing most of them that he could not hope to turn out masterpieces at the rate of two or more a year? But all of them contain passages – of wit, of description, of knowledge of the world – that, gathered into an anthology, would be more than sufficient to confound anyone who ventured to suggest that Mr Mackenzie is 'not a serious writer' (meaning by serious, a creative artist of integrity and importance); and to show that such a view, and the diverse variants of it common, until the day before yesterday, in literary circles, has been merely 'something in the air' – a bit of the intriguing for the position that is always going on among authors. These ups and downs in literary reputation are artificially created; but, where there is real substance, the reputation of the author cannot be permanently eclipsed, no matter how intensive the campaign of belittlement that is carried on by the literary cliques of the moment. It is amusing to find how many of Mr Mackenzie's more or less subtle detractors are now hastening to welcome him back into the limelight of serious consideration – thereby seeking to maintain the suggestion that they have a place in it themselves. Mr Mackenzie can remain as indifferent to their present patronising as he has done to their past disparagements. He can afford to smile at their anxiety to align themselves again with the back number suddenly transformed into the master of the situation.

For it is this transformation that *Gallipoli Memories* has disconcertingly illuminated. At the very moment that Arnold Bennett and all the rest of them are lauding the hysterical revelations of Continental writers – pictures of the War just as one-sided as would be the pretence that the existence of a continual terrible death-roll in child-birth and from cancer, phthisis and a hundred other ills in a modern city make life an unalleviated hell – Mr Mackenzie has presented a many-sided picture of Gallipoli, extenuating nothing, sparing us nothing of its real horrors and tragedies, but setting these in their proper perspective amidst an abundance of comedy such as produced the marching-songs of the Tommies, of wit without equal in contemporary English literature, of wonderful word-paintings of Medditeranean scenes, of brilliant portraits of scores of famous men. It is a remarkable book, subtle and sane and salutary – a testimony not only to his great and versatile powers as a master of the whole range of expression in English, but to his qualities as a man. What poor, dehumanised stuff these over-rated melancholy tomes from the countries of the conscript armies are, and imitative authors of the conscript period among ourselves! Mr Mackenzie expresses instead, the Volunteer spirit – the spirit of men like Julian Grenfell and Rupert Brooke. Compact of thumb-nail sketches, of marvellous vignettes of landscapes and incidents, of anecdotes innumerable, of conversations, serious and gay and ludicrous and pathetic and incredible and terrible, it is a book of inexhaustible variety – as various as the kaleidoscope of the campaign with which it deals – and the Book Society have rightly honoured it by making it their choice for the month. *Gallipoli Memories* is to be succeeded by *Earlier Athenian Memories*, *Later Athenian Memories* and *Aegean Memories*. If the next three are similar in quality to this, they will constitute a quadruple achievement in their kind without any equal in English literature. Hugh Walpole need not say that Mr Mackenzie has at last found a subject worthy of his many gifts and a medium in which he can harmonise them all. He has found that before more than once; he has simply found another subject and another medium in which he has done it once again, demonstrating, alone among his contemporaries, the unexhausted fertility of his genius.

A. L., 21 March 1930

Ash Wednesday

In his triple capacity as a critic, a poet, and editor of *The Criterion*, Mr T. S. Eliot is unquestionably the most influential man of letters writing in English today. I do not mean that he is reaching the largest public; he is reaching a very limited public – but that he is producing in each of the diverse categories in which he is operating work which, by its concentration on major issues, gives him a very special and superlatively important significance at this juncture and is likely to be regarded as a turning point in literary evolution. Mr I. A. Richards, in his *Science and Poetry*, observed that Mr Eliot

> seems to me by his poem, *The Waste Land*, to have performed two considerable services for this generation. He has given a perfect emotive description of a state of mind which is probably inevitable for a while to all meditative people. Secondly, by effecting a complete severance between his poetry and *all* beliefs, and this without any weakening of the poetry, he has realised what might otherwise have remained largely a speculative possibility, and has shown the way to the only solution of these difficulties (a sense of desolation, of uncertainty, of futility, of the groundlessness of aspirations, of the vanity of endeavour, and a thirst for a life-giving water which seems suddenly to have failed, the signs in consciousness of a necessary reorganisation of our lives). 'In the destructive element immerse. That is the way.'[1]

Elsewhere Mr Richards says that not only are many readers finding in Mr Eliot's poems 'a clearer, fuller realisation of their plight, the plight of a whole generation, but also through the very energies set free in that realisation a return of the saving passion.' These are typical tributes and seem to me justified. The probable effects upon love-poetry in the near future of the kind of enquiry into basic human constitution exemplified by psycho-analysis, and upon nature-poetry and metaphysical and philosophical poetry of the collapse of traditional world pictures under the unpictureisable concepts of relativity, the quantum theory and the other new ideas which have revolutionised the world of science, together with parallel manifestations in other departments of human thought and feeling, are preluded to an extraordinary degree in Mr

1. A misquotation from Joseph Conrad, *Lord Jim*, chapter 20. [Eds.]

Eliot's poems. But he is still immersed in the destructive element and has not found the way out. In his recent poems he is obviously concentrated on the task of mobilising to commensurate ends the energies freed in his very profound realisation of the plight in which human consciousness is involved. The destructive work of *The Waste Land* is complete; but he is not yet able to proceed beyond that to a constructive work. He still shares the plight which he has expressed and knows his limitations with extraordinary clarity.

> Because I do not hope to know again
> The infirm glory of the positive hour…
> Because I know I shall not know
> The one veritable transitory power…

And again, 'Teach us to care and not to care.' But if all the old beliefs have become untenable, he is still either craving for some new belief to take their place, or has learned like Dostoevski to believe and disbelieve a thing at one and the same time. At all events, he has not got to that complete severance from all beliefs which Mr Richards thinks is the only possible basis for the poetry of the future, as is shown by the prayer in such lines as

> Lord, I am not worthy
> Lord, I am not worthy
> But speak the word only,

and the reminiscences of Roman Catholic terminology and the expression of neo-Catholic sentiments scattered through these six short poems. Apart from that we know that Mr Eliot in his recent critical work has aligned himself with what is now a well-marked tendency in advanced literary circles in France and elsewhere – as Catholic, Royalist and neo-classicist. But unless these positions are only a confession that any belief is temporarily tenable, or a temporary pretence of beliefs of various kinds in which he can rest awhile prior to continuing the battle, the gleams he discerns of a fountain of life in the depths of the desert are only a mirage. It is difficult to tell whether he thinks it is really a fountain he sees afar off, or whether he knows it is only a delusion, or is concerned to borrow a little strength to continue under the conscious pretence that it is a well of living water or the feeling that it might have been, the wish that it had been, or the hope against hope that by the time he arrives at the spot at which he thinks he sees it gleaming, it may after all prove to be so. In any case, I am sufficiently aware of the dangers of reading personal confessions into Mr Eliot's poems, when perhaps he is making nothing of the kind but only postulating possibilities, or trying out tentative hypotheses. These verses, despite the delusive gleams of an impossible certitude that appear in the remote distance now and again, are still located in and descriptive of the waste land – the wilderness of the modern mind. But their technical organisation is marvellous; they are full of an illimitable, haunting suggestiveness and recurrent echoes of Catholic liturgy that are extraordinarily moving whether they prelude a new religion or a self-deceiving relapse upon the old.

> Strength beyond hope and despair
> Climbing the third stair.

By the third stair I take it that Mr Eliot means the Third Convention – The Metaphysical Convention which will follow the completion of the Material and Moral Conventions. But that is not yet. The subtle use of end and internal rhymes, the little-adjectived bareness of the lines and the simplicity of the wording, and the deft employment of devices of repetition, are features of the new poem which are well worthy of study, and taken together with the altogether exceptional profundity of the problems with which Mr Eliot is exclusively concerned, make this little volume, if not a successor in importance to *The Waste Land*, at least a straw to show the way the wind is blowing. Mr Eliot, in penetrating deeper and deeper into the heart of things, only leaves us a little indication here and there to show the direction he has taken. We are none the less grateful for them; they enable us to follow him; and we are still thrilled by the feeling that at any moment we may either find no further trace and lose him altogether, or make up on him and find that it is impossible for either us or him to advance any further along these lines, or that he has come upon a major discovery, supremely revealing and rewarding. It is impossible to tell which, but Mr Eliot's course is certainly the most profound and impredicable in contemporary literature in the English language.

A. L., 23 May 1930

Anabasis

Anabasis, a poem which Mr T. S. Eliot has translated from the French in collaboration with the author, M. St J. Perse, and which Messrs Faber & Faber publish in an attractive format at 10s 6d., is undoubtedly one of the most remarkable poems produced during the present century. It has already been translated into several other languages, and here the French text appears side by side with the English version, so that readers may judge for themselves of the merit and accuracy of the translation (which is not without its defects, though these are due rather to the difficulty of the poem and of rendering many of the French phrases into precise or satisfactory equivalents), and of the beauty of the original. Mr Eliot supplies only a very short prefatory note, which is explanatory rather than critical, remarking that he is 'by no means convinced that a poem like Anabasis requires a preface at all. It is better to read such a poem six times, and dispense with a preface.' The manifold reading and re-reading of the poem, however, need not conflict with the perusal and profitability of a preface and it is regrettable that Mr Eliot, who goes on to remark that

> one of the best Introductions to the poem is that of the late Hugo von Hofmannsthal, which forms the preface to the German translation; another by Valery Larbaud, prefacing the Russian translation; and there was an informative note by Lucien Fabre in the *Nouvelles Litteraires*,

does not follow the example set in Russian and German editions, or at least equip his English version with a digest of the commentaries of the three writers he mentions.

He contents himself with pointing out that the word *anabasis* has no particular reference to Xenophon or the journey of the Ten Thousand, or to Asia Minor, and that no map of its migrations could be drawn up. 'Mr Perse', he continues, 'is using the word *anabasis* in the same literal sense in which Xenophon himself used it. The poem is a series of images of migration, of conquest of vast spaces in Asiatic wastes, of destruction and foundation of cities and civilisations of any races or epochs of the ancient East.' He follows M. Fabre in suggesting that any obscurity in the poem, on first reading, is due to the suppression of 'links in the chain', of explanatory and connecting matter, and not to incoherence or to the love of the cryptogram; and justifies 'such abbreviation of method' on the ground that the sequence of images coincides and concentrates into one intense impression of barbaric civilisation. There can be no quarrel with this or with the accompanying suggestion that if such an arrangement of imagery requires just as much 'fundamental brain-work' as the arrangement of an argument, it is to be expected that the reader should take as much trouble as a barrister reading an important decision on a complicated case. The story of the evolution, relationships, comparative values, and decline and disappearance of a particular civilisation, or sequence of civilisations – an effort to seize the quintessence of such a mighty movement or series of movements in human history and to consider the whole process *sub specie aeternitatis* – is a task of sufficient magnitude and importance surely to make this demand a very moderate and reasonable one. For that is precisely what M. Perse does – he synthesises the quality of whole epochs, of vast tracts of human experience, of mighty vistas of oriental life and landscape, into a series of phrases which for sheer concentration have few equals in any literature. He does not achieve these effects by any exclusion of all but what are conventionally regarded as the grand aspects of such matters. On the contrary, he constantly secures – or reinforces – his most powerful effects by seizing upon what are commonly regarded as the meanest and most trivial details. It is this power of fusing the sublime and the petty, of seeing the eternal behind the ephemeral and vice versa, that is the outstanding characteristic of his work; and such an imaginative range, such a rapidity of transition from the things under one's nose to the uttermost ends of the earth, requires a corresponding agility on the part of the reader.

More questionable to many will be Mr Eliot's statement that:

> It would be convenient if poetry were always verse – either accented, allit-

erative or quantitative; but that is not true. Poetry may occur, within a definite limit on one side, at any point along a line of which the formal limits are 'verse' and 'prose'. Without offering any generalised theory about 'poetry', 'verse' and 'prose', I may suggest that a writer by using, as does M. Perse, certain exclusively poetic methods, is sometimes able to write poetry in what is called prose. Another writer can, by reversing the process, write great prose in verse.

Without pursuing Mr Eliot's further remarks on this score into the recesses of precise definition (if that, indeed, is possible), the questionability of the essence of the position for which he is contending will, for intelligent readers, whatever they may think of the terms in which he states his case, be one of which the actual text will speedily dispose. There is no question that M. Perse's work, though it is cast in what is generally called prose, is poetry and great poetry. 'Preein'' is the test in such matters. Who can deny that passages such as these belong to the category of great poetry?

'L'idée pure comme un sel tient ses assises dans le jour.' (I give the French here in preference to the English – 'the idea pure as salt holds its assize in the light time.' Why *light time* instead of day or daylight? This is only one of innumerable instances of the English rendering which dissatisfy me.) 'Vous ne trafiquez pas d'un sel plus fort quand, au matin, dans un présage de royaumes et d'eaux mortes hautement suspendues sur les fumées du monde, les tambours de l'exil éveillent aux frontiers l'éternité qui bâille sur les sables.'

Or again,

'Et le soleil n'est point nommé, mais sa puissance est parmi nous.'

Or, to take the English versions,

'Solitude! the blue egg laid by a great sea-bird... Yesterday it was! The bird made off.'

Or, finally,

'And the earth in its winged seeds, like a poet in his thoughts, travels...'

These are only two or three of the tremendous profusion of great imagery sown everywhere throughout the poem, but even to quote all the most powerful and pregnant phrases, all the descriptions which condense into a few syllables enormous vistas of the earth or illimitable odysseys of the spirit or complexes of psychological 'reactions', conjuring up simultaneously the most diverse and yet apposite associations, revealing the unsuspected relationships of the most widely sundered circumstances or conceptions, or compelling all our five senses at once, would not do anything like justice to this extraordinary poem, for its highest quality is its perfect unity from beginning to end. It is a 'seamless garment'. To quote any part of it is to do violence to an indisseverable content. It is this complete fusion of all the elements of the poem in its quality as a whole – the success with which M. Perse can disengage in a couple of lines a complete impression such as can only normally be conveyed by an elaborate history which, in its cumulative process, cannot give us with anything like the same immediacy a sensation of having seen a vast tract of history whole, of having, as it were, lived through it ourselves, experiencing in a second all that in reality occupied a period of centuries – which sets it on a plane of its own, justifies Mr Eliot's claim that it is perhaps the most remarkable poem of this generation, and makes his rendering of it into English one more of the many great services he has rendered in recent years to English literature and the English-reading world.

It is a summary of whole civilisations – of an entire aspect of nature, and insuperable limitations, of life on the earth, past, present and to come, as it has been lived, is lived, or will be by countless millions of human beings under Oriental conditions – given with a concision and completeness as if the determining factors which can only be apprehended after the experience of centuries wee suddenly made manifest beneath the chaos of superficial facts. A parallel feat would be to discern the ultimate outcome of the diverse tendencies of contemporary life as clearly and completely as (to our own satisfaction) we can sum up the significance of some particular phase of past history. But M. Perse's work is in a higher category than that. He has reconciled his divination of the essence of the times and conditions with which he is concerned with the highest demands of imaginative truth, by making his statement in terms of great poetry, which is a far harder test than the most brilliantly omniscient reconstruction of a historical period where Clio is the only muse who is served.

A. L., 18 July 1930

Literature and the Occult

In *La Littérature et L'Occultisme – Etudes sur la poésie philosophique moderne* (Les Editions Rieder, Paris), Professor Denis Saurat, formerly of Glasgow and now of the French Chair at King's College, London, has written a singularly comprehensive and valuable volume. The poets with whom he is principally concerned are Spenser, Milton, Blake, Shelley, Emerson and Whitman in English literature; Goethe, Heine and Nietzsche in Germany; and Hugo, Vigny, Lamartine and Leconte de Lisle in France. He draws attention in his opening sentences to two outstanding points – first, the very curious phenomenon in modern literature from the Renaissance to the Nineteenth Century, of the existence in most of the great poets, many of whom have otherwise little or no relation to each other, of a common, non-Christian basis of ideas; and second, even more curious than this common basis of ideas, the persistence of certain myths or symbols which seem to have a particular and perennial attraction for poets. He leaves aside the question of the Poet's real belief in these ideas; what he is concerned with is the ideas in themselves, and their propagation and development in great literature. 'Spenser and Lamartine apart (and even in them the most interesting religious elements are not orthodox), the poets named are not Christian in thought', he says. 'One might classify the conceptions of Milton and Emerson among the heresies of Christianity; but that would be to singularly contract their outlook. Milton in his dependence on the Cabbala, Emerson in deriving his inspiration from India, definitely abandoned Christian thought.'

The scientific thoroughness of Professor Saurat's analysis of the works of these poets is strikingly exemplified in a table in which he sets out twenty-seven of the principal conceptions of occultism, such as the noumenal God; the idea that in God, and in all beings, there is an evil element; the theories of reincarnation; the conception of forbidden knowledge; the Divine 'retreat'; the Schekhina or female counterpart of God, and so forth. The next eight columns of the table show what proportion of these twenty-seven ideals are drawn from, or are common to, folk-lore, Egypt, India, Ancient Greece, neo-platonism, L'Hermès Trismégiste, the Bible and the Zohar. The Hermes has all but four of them; the Zohar all but five; the Bible fourteen, neo-platonics twelve; while sixteen feature in folklore. Of the three countries ancient Greece has fifteen; India thirteen; and Egypt four – a curious sidelight on the geographical distribution or provenance of occult ideas. But the most excitingly interesting feature of this remarkable table is the next ten columns, in which professor Saurat shows what proportion of these ideas is to be found in the great poets with which he is concerned. Blake heads the list; he contains the whole lot. Hugo comes second with twenty-two; Milton has seventeen; Spenser and Goethe, have each eight, and Neitzsche nine. It is fascinating to see the ideological resemblances and differences of the major poets set out in this graphic way; and to do so in detail in relation to the full list of twenty-seven leading conceptions, and in the light of Professor Saurat's lucid and most exhaustive explication, with ample illustrative quotations, of the doctrines in question, rouses profound speculations on the reasons for the fixation of great poetry to this very primitive basis of ideas, and its precise function and effect in thus running counter to our intellectual evolution in general. Carried further, to embrace all the world's great writers, the method would provide us with an extraordinarily interesting species of intellectual stock-taking. It affords, in fact, the technique for a census of ideas and their relative value in respect of longevity of influence and both quantitative and qualitative dissemination.

Professor Saurat might have carried his examination one stage further. He points out that the sources of these ideas – folklore, the Zohar, the Hermes, and so forth – are even yet practically untapped. The world's writers have for the most part followed each other like so many sheep, and the twenty-seven occult ideas with which he deals represent only a very small percentage of the doctrines from which they are drawn. It would have doubled the interest of this section of the book if Professor Saurat had given us a list and some account, of, say, other twenty-seven occult ideas which none of his great poets have drawn upon at all, and which might quite as well have been utilised as those actually and almost inexplicably, taken. If writers imitate each other to such an extent as the facts he adduces show – without, in other words, going back themselves to the original sources of these ideas, and exercising any original selectivity but simply 'living by taking in each other's washing' – the provision of such a list might well give contemporary writers a ready means of realising and getting away from this curious circumscription of ideas in the great poetry of the past. The general effect of this narrow derivative habit on human thought opens up an enormous field of speculation; and seems amply to confirm, from a very different angle of approach, Professor James Harvey Robinson's contention in *Mind in the Making*, that mankind has barely begun to think yet, what is commonly regarded as thinking being almost entirely a process of rationalising very dubiously derived preconceptions. These notes do no justice to Professor Saurat's range of erudition, exact analyses, and powerful generalisations. His books on Blake and Milton are well known; but it is good news that Messrs Bell are shortly to publish all his books in a uniform edition in English. *The Three Conventions,* his most concentrated philosophical work, has been published in America but not yet in this country, while *Tendances*, a series of brilliant literary essays on Proust, Valéry and others, and *La Religion de Victor Hugo*, have, like *La Littérature et L'Occultisme*, only appeared in French so far. The absorbing interest of this last book and the certainty of its wide appeal to English readers and its importance from the standpoint of English Studies and *Weltliteratur* alike, makes one hope that it will be one of the earliest to appear in Messrs Bell's series.

A. L., 19 September 1930

Scottish Music

There has been ample justification for the complaint recurrently made during the past year or two that Scotland alone of European countries had failed to develop a distinctive art-music – a school of composers working in a national idiom. but apparently the reiteration of this complaint has had its effect. It was accompanied by several misunderstandings or erroneous assumptions. The first of these was that this distinctive art-music when it did come in Scotland must be on the basis of our folk-music. This did not necessarily follow, although in the case of most of the European national schools of composition it had been so. Scotland's delay in following their example had perhaps allowed that stage to pass and a phase had come in the evolution of music when it was no longer profitable, desirable, or even possible to operate from that basis. In the second place the established musical bodies and movements – e.g. the Orpheus Choir, and the Musical Festival Movement – were attacked as standing in the way of the real task in Scottish Music. Even the recently-formed Scottish National Academy of Music was opposed and condemned, although sufficient time had not been allowed to elapse to see what effect it was going to have. These oppositions proceeded from too simple and impatient a point of view. It was wrong to assume that the curious indifference to the problem of creating a distinctive Scottish music could only be overcome by frontal attack on all that seemed apathetic or otherwise-directed and by a too-narrow concentration on this single objective. What could not be gained directly might be gained indirectly. It was even wrong to assume that when a distinctive Scottish art-music came it would be at once recognisable as such instead of deriving its distinction from being an art-music created in Scotland, but a case of Scotland anticipating other European countries in the next musical phase rather than belatedly imitating their nationalist developments. The most distinctively Scottish national feature might be a repudiation not an acceptance, of nationalism – an elision of that portion of musical development as too belated to be profitable, just in the same way as in a definitely nationalistic development it might now be necessary to dispense with any recourse to the folk-music basis.

Mistaken in many such details, this propaganda has, nevertheless, borne fruit. Scotland is definitely making up its leeway at last and taking a place of its own in the field of modern music. A valuable distinction has been drawn between Scottish Music and music in Scotland. The marked progress now to be recorded is in both of these fields. It is a double movement that is at work, each side of which is stimulating and vying with the other. This is not surprising. Those who condemned the cry for a distinctive Scottish school of composers as a piece of 'narrow nationalism' too readily forget that it is precisely where distinctive nationalist tendencies are liveliest that the keenest interest is taken in contemporary foreign tendencies. True nationalism and true internationalism are complementary and indispensable to each other.

The literature of Scottish music remains very meagre – so meagre that a little brochure lying on my desk ranks as a positive landmark in it. It is a concert programme. That it should have such significance reflects our musical poverty. But it is a very remarkable concert programme and its existence shows the rapid progress we are at last making. This prospectus of 'the Active Society for the Propagation of Contemporary Music' provides for twelve concerts in Glasgow this winter, at which the following composers will give recitals of their own work, viz., Medtner, Hindemith, Casella, Van Dieren, Sorabji, W. Gillies Whittaker, F. G. Scott, Ian Whyte, Erik Chisholm, and J. Hunter Macmillan, while among the artistes appearing are Leff Pouishnoff, Frida Kindler, John Goss, Luigi Gasparini, Robert Burnett, and A. Parry Gunn. A well-known London music critic has commented on the 'remarkably comprehensive nature of the scheme'; Mr William Walton, the composer, says that these programmes are 'quite the most interesting I have seen for a long time'; and greetings have been received by the promoters from Sibelius, Bartok, and many other famous musicians. The scheme has been rendered possible by the splendid propaganda work of Mr Erik Chisholm and his associates. Full particulars may be had from the Society's office, 63 Berkeley Street, Glasgow, C.3. Circulars have been sent out by Mr John Tonge, 36 East Haddon Street, Dundee, in an effort to secure sufficient support to have four or five of these concerts repeated in that city. It is to be hoped that like efforts will be made in the other leading centres of the country.

The scheme represents the fusion of all the active musical interests in Scotland in touch with the latest Continental developments. Nationalist and internationalist elements commingle to their mutual advantage. It is in the light of this programme that we see how mistaken was the attempt to insist on a single tendency and attack all the others. Due tribute was paid to the splendid pioneer work towards a distinctively Scots idiom of Mr F. G. Scott, but this was unfortunately associated in certain quarters with a premature attack on Professor W. G. Whittaker and the Scottish National Academy of Music. Professor Whittaker and Mr Scott are happily in co-operation here and the venue of the twelve concerts is in the Stevenson Hall at the Academy of Music.

Space does not allow me to draw attention to the extraordinarily progressive character of the international programmes, but along with this goes most heartening evidence of the growth of an able school of young Scots composers. Mr Scott no longer stands alone. There are now, associated with him in these concerts, Mr Henry Gibson, whose 'Gaelic Sketches' were first introduced by Sir Thomas Beecham as interludes during the Russian Ballet Season in London in 1928 and whose Gaelic 'Pipe March' was performed at the International Festival at Liège this September; Mr J. Hunter Macmillan in his own Reel Arrangements; Mr Gavin Gordon with his 'Fantasia Quintet'; Mr Erik Chisholm with his 'Second Piano Concerto', and Mr Ian Whyte with his 'New Quintet for Strings'. In addition to these, Professor Whittaker, whose compositions have been performed at the International Contemporary music Festivals at Salzburg and elsewhere with great success and whose 'Piano Quintet' received a Carnegie award in 1922, is giving a recital, while one of the outstanding items in the winter's work will be the first performance of Kaikhosru Sorabji's latest and most important work – the 'Opus Clavicembalisticum', a very notable contribution to the literature of the piano, consisting of several fugues (double, triple and quadruple), with cadenzas, fantasia, and interludes interspersed between them. The fact that this great composition is dedicated to Mr C. M. Grieve provides a happy point on which to close this inadequate notice, for Mr Grieve has been the 'stormy petrel' of Scottish music (as of other departments of Scottish arts) for several years, and it is good to find all the active elements in Scottish music harmonised and pulling together at last in such a programme as this.

A. L., 10 October 1930

Scottish versus Irish Jacobite Poetry

A curious point – or set of points – with regard to the differences between Scottish and Irish Jacobite poetry, which has not perhaps been appreciated yet at anything like its true value by Scottish critics and practitioners of poetry but deserves searching consideration at what is obviously a turning-point in Scottish letters, is admirably discussed by Mr Daniel Corkery in his fascinating and far too little-known study of the Munster bards of the Penal Age, *Hidden Ireland* (Gill & Son, Dublin, 1925).

'The Scottish Poems', he points out,

> are simple, homely and direct; and if they have life in them to this day, as many of them have, it is because they were written to and about a living man on whom living eyes had rested with affection. Warm affection is the note of them; the warm affection of a simple, homely, rather unbookish people for kings of their own race; and as the years pass, and the Old Pretender gives place to the Young Pretender, this note of warm affection becomes one of warm love. 'Bruce's heir', as one song names him, was, after all, a gallant figure, bonnie, chivalrous, daring, beset by a sea of troubles, yet not 'dauntoned' by them. Prince Charlie's own person it certainly was that brought so much of Scotland to his colours; and Prince Charlie himself is frankly the inspiration of all that is best in Scottish Jacobite poetry.

There can be no quarrel with these statements, except to question the phrase about one 'on whom living eyes had looked with affection' if this is intended to convey that the actual writers of most of these songs had ever themselves seen the Prince, and to query whether the note of affection or love was really that instead of a literary convention in keeping with the Scottish 'love of the diminutive' and our general domesticising tendency. But these questions aside, Mr Corkery certainly describes the kind of Scottish Jacobite songs exactly enough. He goes on to point out that the *aisling* poems – the Irish Lyrics – had no such close inspiration.

'The Irish Gaels, since the going away of Sarsfield, whom they loved, were a people with no leader', he says.

> Nothing so surely tells us of the desperatenes of their cause than that the name of no political leader of their own is found in their songs from the fall of Limerick to the rise of O'Connell – a wilderness of more than a hundred years. And of this they were not unconscious: 'Gan triath ach Dia na Gloire' ('Without leader save the Glory of God') is a commonplace in their verse. In this despair, the only banner that promised another fight, if not a reversal of their hard doom, was that of the Stuarts. Moreover, Bruce was a name in Irish history as well as in Scottish, and the Gael was the Gael. For all that, the Stuarts were far away. On the Continent, Irishmen had

> intrigued for them – it took an Irishman to find a wife for the Pretender – and of the Seven Men of Moidart who, venturing all, landed with Prince Charlie in Scotland, some books reckon four to have been Irish. Yet still, for the Gaels of Munster, the Stuart cause lacked the warmth of flesh and blood; only surreptitiously could the young men of Kerry slip away in their smuggling craft to join the adventure; while the fighting itself, when there was any, was also beyond the sea – in a place whether Scotland or England, with which the Gaels of Munster had little or no traffic. The whole struggle then was cold with distance.

The effect of this on the Irish as against the Scottish poems is most effectively shown.

> The Scots wrote of 'My Laddie', of 'Jamie the Rover', of 'Charlie Stuart', of the 'Blackbird'; and in 'Cam ye by Athol' we have 'King of the Highland hearts, Bonnie Prince Charlie', and King of the Highland hearts in truth he was – 'His very name our heart's blood warms.' To anyone who lingers on these songs and who, at the same time, recollects how surely genuine affection tends to the use of diminutives, the story of Flora Macdonald is no miracle. Unlike the Scottish the Irish song-writers took none of these affectionate liberties with the names of the Stuarts. They wrote of 'Saesar' ('Caesar') – their most frequent 'endearment' – of 'Charles Rex', of 'The Lion', and they likened him to Angus Og, to Conall Cearnach, and to the other heroes of the myths, names they never made free with, names that still stood for the heroic rather than the beloved in their imagination.

What moods are barren and what fruitful today? An effort is being made to raise the standards of Scottish poetry – to get out of the 'Kailyaird' rut and back to the high levels of the Art. Mr Corkery's conclusions then deserve to have the attentions of all concerned this great effort. 'If one inclines', he says, 'not to the splendour of art, but to its intimacy, its warmth of feeling, one turns to the Scottish songs.' But this has so long been the tradition of Scottish song – this direct human appeal, this simplicity of expression – that its development and enrichment today may well depend upon a breakaway from its past and an attempt to utilise a very different technique. It is here that what Mr Corkery says of the very different qualities of the *aisling* poems has its great significance.

> They do not move us; they dazzle us. Or if one is at all moved by them it is not by or for the Cause they sing. If, for a moment, as we read them, we admit thoughts at all extraneous and away from the wonder of the verse itself, it is never a thought of Prince Charlie or his endeavour that visits us. What is imperative in these songs is the art of the singer. A beautiful thing is being wrought out before our eyes, and it is through the beauty of it we are moved, or not at all. Indeed their own beauty, not Prince Charlie, is

> their theme, whereas in the Scottish poems to leave out the 'Bonnie bird' is to leave all out. It is curious how little else except warm affection for the Prince himself is in these Scottish sons – the poet has but scant thought for anything else, little for Scotland, not much for the Cause. On the other hand, Ireland is in all the *aisling* poems; and the only lines in them that strike fire from us are those of her sorrows – her princes dead, her strongholds broken, her lands in the possession of churls, her children scattered across the seas. The place that the Stuarts themselves occupy in the Scottish poems is occupied in the Irish poems by Ireland herself.

Is it not time that Scotland, the Cause of Scotland, was coming to its own in Scottish poetry? And is not that precisely the time which is coming and of which the omens and auspices are all about us today?

A. L., 7 November 1930

To Circumjack Cencrastus

The publication a few weeks ago of *To Circumjack Cencrastus*, Mr Hugh M'Diarmid's new poem – his first since the publication four years ago of *A Drunk Man looks at the Thistle* – is an event of no small consequence in Scottish literature. To start with, it is the longest poem by far in the Scots vernacular. *A Drunk Man* was an unusually long poem; *To Circumjack Cencrastus* is four times as long. While it is based throughout on the Scots vernacular it is highly modernistic in its multi-linguistic character; it embodies elements of Greek, Latin, German, Italian, French, Spanish and Scottish and Irish Gaelic. It is also highly 'literary'. Whole sections of it will be unintelligible to readers who are not *au fait* with the very latest schools in Russian and German literature, and with such recent tendencies in French literature as are represented by Apollinaire, by Maritain, by Paul Valéry, and by Julien Benda's *Trahison des Clercs*. While sections of it therefore may be condemned as 'narrowly nationalistic' – and as embodying a very specialised view of Scottish nationalism depending upon an intimate knowledge of 'our Gaelic background' – other parts can be assailed on the opposite ground as far too dependent upon a specialised knowledge of contemporary foreign literature and politics. Both these 'faults' – if such they be – can at least be equally well approved as breaking with the habits of over-domesticity and the exclusion of 'highbrow' interests and foreign influences which have too long been the characteristics of Scots poetry.

Apart altogether from these 'trimmings' – these frills and falalls – Mr M'Diarmid's new opus claims consideration on very varied grounds. If there are sections which are caviare to the general and which indeed run T. S. Eliot close in the field of 'brilliant unintelligibility', there are others which are stark and unmistakable enough in their utterance. Like the ancient Gaelic poets to whom he makes such frequent reference, Mr M'Diarmid has passages of scathing personalities, of ribaldry, of direct political incitement. These, too, though they may attract undue attention in certain quarters, are not of the veritable essence of this long, involved, and many-facetted poem. The final qualities upon which the whole thing turns are a kaleidoscopic humour, a recurrent lyricism which suddenly springs into wonderful accesses of beauty quite dissociated from any didactic purpose or programmatic scheme, and deep religious and metaphysical ideas.

'Cencrastus' is an ancient Gaelic snake symbolising the fundamental pattern of life, while 'to circumjack' means 'to encompass'. Mr M'Diarmid's title roughly means 'to box the compass' – and in attempting to do so he spurns any mere logical consistency and comes to a variety of conclusions incompatible with each other which are nevertheless beautifully balanced against each other in his flexible and enigmatic verses. it is this adroitness in refusing to take a fixed shape – to subscribe to any intellectual position while repudiating any attitude which is not highly and very subtly intellectual – which is the essence of the poem.

This is accomplished by means of an astonishing paraphernalia of allusion, variation of modes and moods, and translations from various modern European poets – notably a very long translation from the German of an elegy by the late Rainer Maria Rilke apropos a highly-cultured young woman who died in childbirth. If a poet's range is a criterion of his quality then critics of Mr M'Diarmid's work will have to consider a poem which ranges from abstruse metaphysical speculation, parodies of music-hall songs, terse epigrams modelled on *The Greek Anthology*, transpositions into Scottish terms of the fiercer type of Irish political poem, and, in and between these, perfectly idiosyncratic and unclassifiable essays in pure lyricism, satire, and pathological confession. The transmutations are bewildering. Nevertheless the poem is a unity. Recurrences of theme and cross-references of all kinds abound throughout.

Some of the most remarkable poems are in English – these include the Rilke translation; a sequence of five poems dealing with a soaring bird, and the long poem entitled 'A Moment in Eternity' which Professor Denis Saurat has analysed in a series of philosophical essays and regards as the intellectual counterpart of Francis Thompson's 'Hound of Heaven'.

The extremely, and even vindictively, 'personal' elements in this poem are apt perhaps to attract more attention than its fundamental qualities, but of far more consequence is the sequence of beautiful, if wilful, tributes the poet pays to the great Gaelic poets of Scotland and of Ireland – to Alasdair MacMhaighstir Alasdair, Aodhagan O'Rahaille and many others – and his insistence upon the 'values' of ancient Gaelic culture.

The poem rings the changes on most of the leading ideas in contemporary

European arts and affairs – the return to 'the Scholastic Philosophy'; the doctrine of the 'Defence of the West' as promulgated by Henri Massis and others; the search for 'neo-classicist' developments; the philosophy of Husserl; the multi-linguistic experiments of James Joyce. But its deepest notes are struck in the realms of pure philosophy and religion. The influence of Hulme, Whitehead, James Harvey Robinson and others is obvious. The poet wants to break with 'nature' and to follow 'science' as far as it can possibly lead him, and this involves all manner of repudiations of all historical precedent and democratic values.

> A' men's institutions and maist men's thochts
> Are tryin' for aye to bring to an end
> The insatiable thocht, the beautiful violent will,
> The restless spirit of Man, the theme o' my sang,

he cries, and again:

> It's no' the purpose o' poetry to sing
> The beauty o' the dirt frae which we spring
> But to cairry us as faur as ever it can
> 'Yont nature and the Common Man.

The basic ideas of such a poem cannot be dealt with in a short article. Enough has been said here to show it is a *rara avis* in Scots letters and to indicate its extraordinary scope.

A. L., 14 November 1930

The Destiny of Cities

Mr Paul Banks is well known as one of the most penetrating of English dramatic critics today – the only one, to my mind, comparable to our best contemporary art critics and music critics. The reason for this is that he is always concerned, not with ephemeral and still less with merely commercial or personal considerations, but with fundamental values.

He is less well-known outside specialist circles, perhaps, as one of a group of writers who have put together a remarkable body of constructive political thought and whose concern is to 'redeem the whole sphere of politics from indifference, and the citizen from that sense of powerlessness and despair of any real influence which are undermining the belief in democracy.' The group includes, in addition to Mr Banks, Hilderic Cousens, Phillippe Mairet, V. A. Demant, Maurice B. Reckitt, and W. T. Symons, and in addition to individual and collective books, they run a quarterly magazine named *Purpose* which ought to be better known, containing as it does some of the most intelligent, critical, and constructive writing presently appearing anywhere in this country. Mr Banks has now published a noteworthy little book, the first entirely his own instead of in collaboration with others, *Metropolis, or the Destiny of Cities* (Messrs the C. W. Daniel Company), in which he criticises metropolitan standards of civilisation in the light of what he believes to be the creative standards of the future. He claims that only the voluntary expression of responsive citizenship and community-consciousness can enable Britain to do without the rule of a Mussolini, a Hitler or a Lenin. He appeals to the British knack of seizing from the continental extremes what is worth while and applying it practically, pointing out that Britain has contributed nobly in the past to the formation of European culture, in the poetry, drama, and novel, in parliaments and councils, and in mechanical invention, industrial processes and scientific discovery, and appealing to it again at this world crisis to set the example of putting her old house into new order, to merit the perpetuation of her prestige in the world.

The timeousness and value of the book are out of all proportion to its size. It deals with essentials throughout and is full of concentrated food for thought. 'Unless', he says in his final paragraphs,

> a body of mentally influential citizens, with far-seeing love of their folk as a whole, will constitute themselves the advisers of Parliament and call directly upon the folk to insist on the application of their advice, there seems no prospect of Britain's attainment in the future world of the prestige it is her duty to attain. Britain's past, inventive and colonising, poetic and scientific, can neither damn nor save her. Her future depends upon her future contribution. At present her Parliament is discredited, her people discouraged, and in spiritual and economic disorder. The metropolis alone prospers, and to the present has given nothing to the smaller towns and countryside but paper admonition and suggestions which do not postpone their troubles to the day after next. The state of affairs in which metropolitan cities flourish and flow with milk, honey and wine, while countrysides ruin their cultivators, has to be ended; preferably for culture's sake, by an awakening of responsibility among metropolitans. Thus only could Metropolis gain a destiny and escape a fate.

He argues his thesis with a wealth of ungainsayable facts, drawn from an intimacy of knowledge of Britain as a whole and a breadth of sympathy and understanding with all classes which free the trenchancy of his indictment from any suspicion of mere stunt-mongering. His intellectual integrity, deep concern, and thorough competence are manifest throughout. What is the position of London today in comparison with the Metropolis he disiderates? 'It seemed to me', he says in his introductory chapter,

> to augur ill for the country's future that economic disaster should not be evident in the metropolis at a time when it was strangling many boroughs

> and industries in the country. Bankrupt farmers apparently made no difference to the prosperity of Covent Garden. Immense strikes produced no effect on London, which, I realised, had no real sense of its responsibility as a Metropolis to the community as a whole. While fish and food are wasted and ill-distributed in rich London, the countryman and the fisherman live in want and the fear of famine. Transporting their goods to the city, paying an agent there, supporting a horde of inefficient merchants and retailers, in far too many shops, they are robbed without scruple, so that, when everybody else has been paid, the man who persuaded the earth or sea to deliver this food has nothing for himself. It costs so much to put food into the Londoner's mouth that it discourages the farmer from growing it. For the sake of Metropolis, not only English land has been misused, but the planet. It would be foolish to pretend that more than a very small portion of the enormous increase in productiveness of the last 150 years has been consumed in the country or even in the smaller towns, which are much as they were apart from mere multiplication of inhabitants. As regards the quality of what is consumed outside the metropolis the people are in many ways worse off... Americans and Europeans take their surplus over their living expenses to New York, London, Paris or Berlin. Through the agency of the Press the meaning of each country for the others is the capital. France means Paris, America means New York, England means London. For these cities no form of natural wealth has been secure against criminal squandering. Earth is being stripped of its forests to provide paper for the circulation of city advertisements. Most of this has been done by men for whom honour has meant no more than to become rich in their own lifetime, without a thought for the future. In the worst possible interpretation, the cities have taken no thought for the morrow. They have considered neither the lilies of the field nor the fowls of the air. The morass in which English agriculture struggles is due to the urban course of civilisation during the last century and a half.

The concomitant has been a false culture due to the Metropolis's misinterpretation of its proper relationships to the rest of the country. The facts and figures with which Mr Banks supports his case, the earnestness with which he pleads for a higher sense of responsibility and a resolute confrontation of the situation, and the extent to which his prescience (for the material of this book was written a year or two ago and originally published in a weekly review) has already been attested by the march of events and the growing realisation of the perilous divorcement of our urban policy from the self-support possible on our depopulated and uncultivated countrysides makes this a veritable tract for the times, and one which deserves a large circulation amongst responsible citizens. Given that, it cannot fail to have a very stimulating and reconstructive influence.

A. L., 26 December 1930

August Strindberg

'If ever a man lived and wrote in a hell of his own creating', says a note on the cover of this big and fascinating volume, [V.J. McGill, *August Strindberg* (London, Noel Douglas)] 'that man was August Strindberg. Here is a vivid and convincing portrait of that macabre, brilliant, contradictory man, always on the brink of madness, who adored women only to deride them, who was by turns atheist and fanatical Christian, hailed as a prophet today and indicted as a blasphemer tomorrow – and yet writing – always writing.' The paragraph sums up the man adequately enough with two important exceptions – it fails to indicate that he was primarily a dramatist and that in drama, and other departments of literature as well, he attained to unquestionable genius and has had a profound and widespread influence.

> On May 19, 1912, a great procession moved down the streets of Stockholm toward the poor section of the new Church Cemetery. It was eight o'clock in the morning, a time when the streets are usually deserted, but here in sudden evidence were thirty thousand people… The man in the hearse had been a scourge to them all. He had reviled them, betrayed their secrets, blasphemed their ideals. He had attacked the family, marriage, love, with ruthless concentrated fury. He had satirised schools, universities, art, science, business. No person or institution had escaped his hatred and evil tongue… He had written fifty-six plays, nine novels, numerous autobiographical works, lyrical poems, historical and scientific treatises. He had given Sweden a literature. No one before had written with such music and grace nor with such rapid brutal energy. In his fury and energy he resembled a natural force, striking institutions and men with desperate blows, careless of the odds or of his own danger. Once, when all Sweden was ready to accept him, he wrote, as he admits, 'a terrible book', a vicious and calculated attack on society. At one stroke his reputation was lost and his admirers turned away in aversion. For this book, *Black Flags*, and for *The Red Room*, he will probably never be forgiven; they were too convincing, too insulting to be borne. In his plays he made such brutal disclosures that people left the theatre with a sense of personal insult. His critical novels brought forth such bitter protests that Strindberg stopped reading the papers.

Yet, as the biographer says – and Mr McGill has given us an admirable biography in every sense of the term – at the end

> they paid homage to him, this enemy of society, marching thirty thousand strong to his grave, in a demonstration which has seldom been accorded to a private man. The outcast had become a god. This procession which celebrated his apotheosis was no less than a national event… This man who had burnt himself out with thought, whose very soul had gone into his

works, will be a contemporary of many generations. He has become one of that company of minds which hovers over time and history, menacing with his passions and invective, evoking his suspicions and despairs in other minds distant from him, elevating them with his mad energy, causing them to think and feel and breathe as he did. It was perhaps with a realisation of this high destiny that he spoke his last words: 'Now everything personal has been obliterated.'

Not quite! A fit few throughout Europe early recognised his amazing genius and appreciated its exact nature and effects and their number is steadily increasing. But there are still vast numbers of so-called educated people for whom it is sufficient to dismiss him as a 'madman' – who shake their pious heads over his lamentable excesses, who deplore his revolutionary influence, who believe that all great art must be 'sane' and respectable. Writing of Strindberg's reception in other European countries than Sweden, Mr McGill says: 'In England a certain niceness and prudery drove him out – critics thought him too gloomy, too mad and vicious – and it is only recently that he has made any headway among English speaking people.' While it is probably true that there are many aspects of Strindberg's genius peculiarly unsuited to English appreciation and likely to remain so, we have since made many amends for our slowness – to recognise his unique powers, and in devoting his Nobel prize-money to a foundation for publishing English translations of Strindberg's works, Bernard Shaw made a very notable gesture – all the more so in that Strindberg in drama is far removed from Shaw and represents indeed a pivotal influence which is radically different from, and in recent years has largely superseded, that of Ibsen of whom Shaw himself is a derivative.

Strindberg was a demoniacal genius and his intense and incredibly chequered career is, as it were, a microcosm of all the more extreme psychological and spiritual developments of modern Europe. In dramatic technique he was an extraordinary innovator and his output in this connection will long remain a reservoir upon which European drama will draw and which is thus far barely tapped. His personal life was a tragic tangle if ever there was one, but, as Mr James Agate has said, apropos a recent production of Strindberg's *Spook Sonata*:

> To explain away this piece would probably be easier than to explain it: indeed the upshot seemed to be that Strindberg at one time inhabited a lunatic asylum and that this play proved it. But that cock will not fight since the author's sequestration was in the early nineties, and this play was not written until ten years after his return to complete health… None, I think, could doubt the existence in Strindberg's mind of some centre to his circle, for without it the play must have been chaos, and chaos it undoubtedly was not. Behind the most utter-seeming nonsense there was mind, declaring itself in riddles and incomprehensible symbols, but still mind.

Mind – and one of the most vital and significant minds in modern Europe! That must be the verdict at every point of his life and work – no matter how antipathetic to us, no matter how obscure and blasphemous. He may have been, to quote the sub-title of this book, 'a bedevilled Viking', but there can be no question of his many-sided and dynamic genius. In 1899 a man calling on Ibsen expressed his surprise at seeing a portrait of Strindberg above his writing desk. 'Yes,' said Ibsen, 'that picture hangs there not because I am friendly towards Strindberg, for I am an enemy of his – but I cannot write a line except when this bold man with his mad eyes looks down on me.' Through the medium of this book he now looks down upon the entire English-reading world. Although most of his plays and other works are now available in excellent English translations, this is the first full-size biography. 'Tout comprendre c'est tout pardonner', and this volume should perform that service in respect of its subject for a very wide public and in so doing render them *au fait* with a great range of the more extreme manifestations of modern consciousness and their attendant social, political, and aesthetic consequences.

A. L., 27 February 1931

The Poems of Gerard Manley Hopkins

Gerard Manley Hopkins whose work, after long and almost inexplicable misprisal and neglect, has at last come into its own, was not the 'major poet' certain enthusiasts, swinging to the opposite extreme, are inclined to claim, but he was a true poet of a very rare and valuable kind – a metrical and verbal experimenter of unquestionable genius. The Oxford University Press have just issued a new edition of his poems, originally published by the late Poet-Laureate, Dr Bridges, in 1918, with a most illuminating and interesting preface and a full apparatus of notes. The new edition reproduces all that was contained in the earlier volume, together with an appendix of additional poems and a critical introduction by Mr Charles Williams. The same publishers have issued a life of Hopkins by Father Lakey, which gives a welcome account of his ecstatic and dedicated personality. Mr Williams puts his finger on the essence of Hopkins' poetry when he says: 'Other poets have sung *about* their intellectual exaltations; in none has the intellect itself been more the song than in Gerard Hopkins' and Dr Bridges in a sonnet to his friend, had the same quality in mind when he bade him: 'Go forth: amidst our chaffinch flock display/Thy plumage of far wonder and heavenward flight.'

In many ways Hopkins anticipated the experiments of our contemporary 'ultra-moderns'. The technical interest of his work is enormous. Dr Bridges does complete justice to it in his preface and notes, and all who wish a new and vital insight into the values and varieties of 'Running Rhythm', 'Sprung Rhythm', 'Reversed Feet', 'Counterpoint Rhythm', 'rests', 'hangers or outrides', and the like may be commended to these. Without such guidance the average reader will find 75 per cent of Hopkins' work unreadable. In addition to these technical issues, the outstanding interest of this poetry lies in its use of language. This frequently runs into unintelligibility, ugly and cacophonous inversions, and other grave faults, but at its best it results in an immediacy, a magical seizure of the *mot propre*, and phrasings of an almost inconceivable felicity. Yet, as Mr Williams reminds us, 'Gerard Hopkins was not the child of vocabulary but of passion', and time and again in his work it is

> as if the imagination, seeking for expression, had found both verb and substantive at one rush, had begun almost to say them at once, and had separated them only because the intellect had reduced the original unity into divided but related sounds. The very race of the words and lines hurries on our emotion; our minds are left behind. They are like words of which we remember the derivations; they present their unity and their elements at once. Just as phrases which in other poets would be comfortably fashioned clauses are in him complex and compressed words, so poems which in others would have their rising and falling, their moments of importance and unimportance, are in him allowed no chance of having anything of the sort. They proceed, they ascend, they lift us (breathlessly and dazedly clinging) with them, and when at last they rest and we loose hold and totter away, we are sometimes too concerned with our own bruises to understand exactly what the experience has been.

Hopkins' work is poetry for poets. It will have – is already exerting – a profound influence. But when all has been said of its overwhelming technical interest, of its frequent difficulty, and obscurity, there is a residue which is a vital and unquestionable contribution to the staple of English poetry and should delight all poetry-lovers. If he had lived longer he might have found himself more fully; he was aware of his faults, and already looking forward to surmounting them and beginning to abandon his eccentricities of expression. But the great 'might have been', implicit in his work, need not affect our appreciation of what he actually achieved. There can be no gainsaying the quality of phrases such as: –

> This darksome burn, horseback brown.

or

> A windpuff-bonnet of fawn-froth.

or

> Didst fettle for the great drayhorse of the world
> his bright and battering sandal,

or passages such as these: –

Flesh fade and mortal trash
Fall to the residuary worm; world's wildfire leave but ash;
In a flash; at a trumpet clash,
I am all at once what Christ is, since He was what I am, and
This Jack, joke, poor potsherd, patch matchwood, immortal diamond
Is Immortal Diamond!

or, above all, this: –

We are leaf-whelmed somewhere with the hood
Of some branchy bunchy bushy bowered wood,
Southern dene or Lancashire clough or Devon cleave,
That leans along the loins of hills, where a candy-coloured, where a gluegold-brown
Marbled river, boisterously beautiful, between
Roots and rocks is danced and dandled, all in froth and water-blowballs, down.

In conclusion let me quote one poem complete, a typical and delightful poem, not, to my mind, one of his best, but, I think, the best I have space left to give entire: –

Pied Beauty

Glory be to God for dappled things –
For skies of couple-colour as a brinded cow;
For rose-moles all in stipple upon trout that swim;
Fresh fire-coal chestnut-falls; finches' wings;
Landscape plotted and pieced – fold, fallow, and plough;
And all trades, their gear and tackle and trim.
All things counter, original, spare, strange;
Whatever is fickle, freckled (who knows how?)
With swift, slow; sweet, sour; adazzle, dim;
He fathers-forth whose beauty is past change;
Praise him.

A. L., 27 March 1931

Whither Scotland?

I

The new Scottish Movement – using the term in its widest sense, to include not only its political but cultural and other manifestations – deserves more careful study than it has yet received. Powerful – or potentially powerful – forces are at work, but these have not yet been properly defined, and, with scarcely an exception – as I hope to show in the course of this series of articles

– even those who are most actively embodying them, though they may be 'building better than they know', have hardly begun to work out the implications, and provide for the consequences, of the positions they have taken up. On the other hand, the criticism they have evoked has been on a much lower level than their propaganda. Professor Denis Saurat is right when he says that one of the misfortunes of the Movement is the puerility of its opponents. There is so little for its protagonists to sharpen their wits upon. Their crying need is for foes worthy of steel.

It is no part of my purpose here to argue the case for Scottish Home Rule, which, in fact, is generally conceded. Over sixty members of all parties of the present Scottish representation at Westminster have declared themselves in favour of it. During the past half-century successive Bills for various forms and degrees of Scottish Home Rule have been supported by an increasing proportion – and latterly by a considerable majority – of Scottish MP's of all parties, and that so many of them have not yet made up their minds how far devolution ought to go is not to their credit at this time of day. The history of the question, and a great mass of relevant statistics, is available in the Rev. Walter Murray's *90 Points for Scottish Home Rule*, and other publications obtainable from the offices of the National Party of Scotland, 131 West Regent Street, Glasgow. The more recent concentration on Scotland's economic position and prospects – and how these compare with conditions in England and elsewhere – is most adequately reflected in the files of the *Scots Independent* (the Party's monthly organ), and it is there too that most of the very scrappy and tentative attempts to adumbrate the ideas at work behind the many manifestations of the rising tide of Scottish national consciousness, or to enunciate ideas 'towards a new Scotland', are to be found. No one who wishes to understand Scottish tendencies today can afford to ignore the four annual volumes of this periodical already published or the fifth which is now in progress, while the files of previous periodicals, such as *Freedom*, *The Thistle*, *The Scots Review* , *Scottish Home Rule*, *The Scottish Nation*, *The Scottish Chapbook*, and *The Northern Review*, ought also to be consulted. Other indispensable books are George Malcolm Thomson's *Caledonia*, C.M. Grieve's *Albyn* (both in Kegan Paul's Today and Tomorrow Series), William Bell's *Rip Van Scotland* (Cecil Palmer), and A. Dewar Gibb's *Scotland in Eclipse* (Humphrey Toulmin). Special reference must also be made to the many excellent articles on various aspects of Scottish nationality and Scottish arts and affairs by William Power, 'Enterkin', and 'Looker-on', in the *Glasgow Evening News*. The publication of a selection of these in book form is highly desirable. Note must be taken, too, of the five issues so far available of the quarterly *Modern Scot*, which represents an entirely new and higher level in Scottish journalism, and is especially valuable for its profound concern with the ideas behind the Movement (or the provision of ideas of an adequate calibre where these have not already been formulated), the frank extremism of its political and cultural positions, its European purview, and its espousal of Douglas economics. Apart from the political and economic aspects, the books indispensable to an understanding of the revaluing and renascent forces at work in Scotland today include G.M. Thomson's *Short History of Scotland* (Kegan Paul), C.M. Grieve's *Contemporary Scottish Studies* (Leonard Parsons), Edwin Muir's *John Knox* (Cape), Catherine Carswell's *Robert Burns* (Chatto & Windus), and Donald Carswell's *Brither Scots* and *Sir Walter*. To these must be added the work, in fiction, of Nan Shepherd, George Blake, Adam Kennedy, Neil Gunn, and A.J. Cronin; in drama, of Murray M'Clymont, George Reston Malloch, and 'James Bridie'; in poetry, of Lewis Spence, Marion Angus and 'Hugh M'Diarmid'; and, in history, Major Hay's *Chain of Error in Scottish History*; Hon. R. Erskine of Marr's *Mac Beth*, and other writings in *The Pictish Review*, *Guth na Bliadhna*, *An Rosanach*, and elsewhere, and the work of Dr G Pratt Insh, Miss Irene Deane, Miss F. Marian MacNeill, and others. The list is far from comprehensive, but is calculated to put the reader in possession of the basic data. What should be observed is that the new Movement is operating simultaneously in practically every department of Scottish arts and affairs; the books and writers I have named illustrate this.

Counter-writings are to seek. While the literature of Scottish Nationalism and its cultural counterpart, the Scottish Renaissance Movement, is rapidly increasing (in quality as well as quantity), I have seen no work by any of the opponents of either which can be set alongside the books I have named. Thomson and Grieve have been furiously assailed in the press, but there has been no book countering their arguments – or the facts and figures upon which their arguments are based – from the anti-nationalist standpoint. There has been no defence of the English connection – no attempt to deny the case for Scottish Home Rule, let alone the need for what Mr Power has called 'an independent national culture in Scotland, absorbing only the congenial best from outside, and earning and claiming equal rank with any other national culture'. A recent writer has said: 'The extent to which revolutionary ferment was working in Spain is illustrated, long before the collapse of the monarchy, by the fact that almost every Spanish writer of note had "gone Republican".... Among the younger generation of Spanish writers it would be hard to find a single one who has not long been a Republican.' An analogous position obtains in Scotland today. The great majority of Scottish writers are either members of the National Party or not members of it simply because they are in favour of a more extreme policy. Older writers of established reputation, like R.B. Cunninghame-Graham, Compton Mackenzie, George Blake, and Lewis Spence, are among its most active leaders. So are younger writers like 'Hugh M'Diarmid', Neil Gunn, Wendy Wood, and F. Marian MacNeill. In regard to both the more moderate and more extreme of these, the time has gone by for arguing about Home Rule for Scotland. They are all opposed to any measure of devolution. 'Rights are not given; they are taken.' Indeed, alike from the official National Party standpoint and that of the 'Scottish Sinn Feiners', the danger of Westminster trying to short-circuit the whole movement by granting some measure of Home Rule is clearly apprehended, and every effort will be made to precipitate it beyond that possibility. In this connection the influence of the increasing series of books on England's downfall is of no little importance. Books like Seigfried's *England's Crisis* and Renier's *The English: Are They Human?* are being avidly seized upon, and proving very suggestive and useful in the process of 'deepening the issues' which all the live minds in the Movement realise is now of paramount importance. Scotland's curse for centuries has been its habit of domesticating everything. The leaders of the new Movement are fully alive to this and out to stop it at all costs.

In these initial notes I have only been able to touch upon the fringe of a profound and many-sided Movement, which may be fraught with incalculable consequences not only for Scotland (and England) but for Europe and the Empire; and in my next article – as a necessary preliminary to study of basic ideas – I must enumerate the many agencies which have sprung into being in connection with the Movement. Most people have heard of the National Party and of Mr Grieve's 'Clann Albann', but these are only two of many, most of which have so far received little or no publicity.

19 June 1931

II

The principal agency of the new Scottish Movement on the political side is the National Party of Scotland. A non-party political body, open to Liberals, Conservatives, Socialists, and others alike, provided they are prepared for the time being to sink their sectional differences for the common cause of Scotland, it was brought into existence between three and four years ago, and represented a fusion of the Scottish Home Rule Association, the Scots National League, and the Glasgow University Scottish Nationalist Association. The near-success of Mr R.B. Cunninghame-Graham over Mr Stanley Baldwin in the Glasgow University Rectorial Election gave it a great send-off. For various reasons, however, the Party was unable to take anything like full advantage of this, the initial sensation and world-wide publicity proved little more than a nine-days' wonder, and progress since has been slow but steady. The position today is that branches are multiplying rapidly, not only in all parts of Scotland, but in the United States, Canada, and elsewhere. Five Parliamentary elections have been contested; the last two of these show that the Party has secured a steadily increasing percentage of the votes polled. The results compare favourably with those obtained by the Labour Party in its early years, and the National Party has actually as many branches in Scotland today as the Labour and Socialist Party (110 as against 140). Its activities have hitherto been restricted by a lack of competent speakers, but, thanks largely to a well-conducted Speakers' Class, this difficulty is now being surmounted, and no fewer than 45 speakers were active on the Nationalist side in the St Rollox by-election. The relative calibre of these is another matter; the Party is at a disadvantage with the English-controlled parties in speakers of national note and high intellect. It has not yet produced a real leader – a commanding figure. Much will depend upon its timeously doing so. Of statesmen – as apart from mere politicians – it shows no sign. But, leaving aside the handful of well-known writers who have so far headed the movement, it has an increasing number of able, if not first-class, exponents, who are, so to speak, its own products, and whose activities are more or less monopolised by it – men like John M'Cormick, Oliver Brown, D.H MacNeill, T.H. Gibson, Arthur Donaldson, T. Douglas MacDonald, J. Balderstone. T. M'Nicoll, and Robert Gray, and women like Mrs N.K. Wells, Miss Elma Campbell, Miss Mary Fraser, and Miss M'Intyre. These represent a new type of Scot – a kind of Scottish consciousness at sharp variance with that which is regarded as 'typically Scottish', and which has dominated Scottish affairs and dictated their course, and, in particular, our attitude and relationships to England for the past two hundred years. They represent a definite morphological advantage into a region of activity where the old principles (or rather Anglophil assumptions) not only do not hold but are expressly repudiated.

The paid-up membership of the Party has increased during the past year (May 1930 to May 1931) from 3000 to 8000. The paid-up membership of any Party is always very small in relation to the support it can command. The National Party can rightly clam that it is the only political body in Scotland today which is on the up-grade. These membership figures do not include affiliated societies, such as the Nationalist Associations in the Universities. A footing has now been obtained in all four Scottish Universities. In addition to running a monthly periodical, *The Scots Independent*, and maintaining a regular programme of meetings throughout the country, the Party has developed a number auxiliary organisations. These include a Nationalist Dramatic Club which has produced plays by John M'Lellan (the Club's producer), Neil Gunn, J.A. Ferguson, and J.M. Paterson, a Choir under the supervision of Mr Francis George Scott, a Research and Information Bureau for the benefit of propagandists, which is doing valuable spade-work in making good the appalling leeway in Scottish economic, commercial and industrial documentation, and a Scottish Press-Cutting Agency, which has met a long-felt want, and, admirably run, is being increasingly used not only by Scots but by clients all over the world.

The Scottish National Party is, like most political parties, far from being a homogenous body. Its membership ranges from old-fashioned 'sentimental nationalists' and believers in the need for some petty measure of devolution to full-blooded Separatists and Gaelic exclusivists, but on the whole it is found that very milk-and-water adherents speedily develop once they join the Movement into much more extreme Nationalists than they could have imagined possible before they actually joined. While the Party is officially committed to agitate for its ends along constitutional lines, a study of the evolution of its tenets and activities as reflected in the proceedings of its successive annual delegate conferences shows a steady trend to the left wing. This was particularly pronounced at the last Conference (May 1931). A motion put forward in the name of the Stirling Branch, asking the Party to adopt as its policy the mild devolutionary proposals put forward by the Duke of Montrose, was defeated by 52 votes to 4. Another motion which, in certain eventualities contemplated the setting-up of a Provisional Government, and gave the National Council of the Party authority to organise the signatories to the National Covenant into sections capable of taking over the essential services of the country, was carried with practical unanimity. Mr Grieve – who is an avowed militant – characterised this as a 'splendid step forward in the Party's development, though still far short of the requirements of the situation'. I should explain that the National Covenant is an oath pledging its signatories to take any necessary step to re-secure Scottish Independence in the fullest sense of the term at the earliest possible moment, and that it has already received over 10,000 signatories, while the number is still mounting daily.

While the inclination of the Party as a whole is unmistakably to the left wing, there is, of course, a movement within the movement, and it is this 'inner circle' or 'cell' which holds the clue to imminent developments, and in all probability to the future of Scotland. I am not referring here merely to Mr Grieve's 'Clann Albann', nor to 'Fiann na h-Alba', nor to the 'Scottish Republican Brotherhood' (all of which I shall deal with later), though the personnel of these and various other bodies which have recently come into existence are for the most part also members of the National Party. The 'inner movement' is definitely militant and anti-democratic – but believes in working through or behind the official Party programme – and comprises the dynamic personalities of the Movement, between whom there exists a thorough understanding which is in advance of the Party as a whole, though, as I have already said, the general body of members is continually moving (or being moved) in that direction.

Among the other subsidiary agencies of the National Party may be mentioned the Scottish Secretariat. This was brought into being some years ago (under the auspices of the old Scottish Home Rule Association prior to the formation of the National Party) when it was found that the majority of the Scottish daily papers were anti-Nationalist and imposing a 'conspiracy of silence' or misrepresentation. The Secretariat's *modus operandi* was to send out for over two years some four to five columns of special articles on Scottish issues weekly to local papers all over the country. Over 30 of these used this material (which was supplied gratis to them) regularly, and this had a very considerable effect in improving the quality of public attention to Scottish affairs and creating a new national consciousness. The Secretariat has since altered its methods – mainly because a more or less open platform is now available in several of the leading dailies and in such organs as *The Modern Scot* and *The Scots Observer* but it is still maintaining a regular output of effective articles on Scottish topics of all kinds.

26 June 1931

III

'To put Scotland on the map of Europe' again is one of the principal aims of the new movement. It is agreed that our cultural plight, and national plight generally, is largely due to the severance of our contact with Europe, in relation to which at large, and in regard to France, Holland, the Scandinavian countries, and Russia in particular, Scotland for centuries played a very important and distinctive role. A great deal has been written of this, but much research and co-ordination remains to be done. The value of such work as that of Professor Baxter in mediaeval Europa-Scottish studies, can hardly be exaggerated. From the political point of view the matter has a profound bearing on the vital question of 'Europe or the Empire', and resolves itself in more extreme Scottish nationalist minds into the declaration that 'England has betrayed Europe'. Mr William Power expresses this from another angle when he declares that England has betrayed England to the Empire and asks what, in view of its great opportunity, it is doing 'pandering to colonials and Yankees, and coming down to their level'. The connection of this with the great questions of the 'Defence of the West', the conservation and furtherance of European civilisation, and the continuance of white supremacy, has been the subject of much writing by the Renaissance group in various newspapers and periodicals. It is related again, to the attitude of our advanced Nationalists to Chauvinism, Kailyardism, and provincialisation in general, and to what they condemn as the false internationalism – the reduction to the lowest common denominator – of the Labour Party; and is reflected in an increasing preoccupation with foreign literatures and tendencies, the definition of Scotland's particular function in relation to Europe, and the effort to create new European affiliations congenial to our national genius, and irrespective of English commitments.

Many Europa-Scottish societies are in existence. The most important of these is the Scottish Centre of the P.E.N. Club – the international society of authors, which has now centres in over forty countries, numbers several thousands of the leading writers of the world among its members, and holds an international congress in a different country annually. When one contemplates that important congress coming in due course to Scotland, the shameful condition of our country and the low place accorded to letters in popular and governmental esteem, is brought home. It would be impossible to conduct the congress in Scotland in a way even remotely approaching that of any other European country. We are insufficiently civilised; money (available for professional footballers and golfers) would not be forthcoming; governmental facilities would at best fall disgracefully short; and in every respect a lamentable state of affairs would be revealed.

Despite these difficulties, it is high time it was realised that the Scottish P.E.N. is playing a very important part in the P.E.N. International. The action taken by Mr William Power, the Scottish delegate, at Oslo three years ago in insisting upon Scotland's right to representation entirely independent of England, has had results which may have far-reaching and decisive effects on the whole organisation and direction of cultural work in Europe. This problem of cultural minorities – of dialect literatures – of regional versus centralised developments has since become one of the most engrossing and crucial issues in European literary politics. It arose in a still more acute form at Vienna two years ago, when Mr C.M. Grieve, the Scottish representative, together with Dr Hans Blunck, the Low German protagonist, and Jugo-Slav, Checko-Slovak, and other smaller country delegates, made common cause and successfully resisted the 'Big Nation' trend of the P.E.N. Movement. At Warsaw last year, and at the Hague this year, Mr Power was again active in this matter, and it has unquestionably become the most important issue in the whole continental literary field. That it represents a real contribution on Scotland's part to European literary tendency, and not merely Mr Power's personal attitude, is shown by Professor W.J. Entwhistle's recent address on 'Some Spanish Experiments for the Decentralisation of Literature' to the Scottish P.E.N., and Mr Grieve's long article on 'English Ascendancy in British Literature' in the *Criterion* (June 1931). The Scottish attitude has aroused the ire of some of the leaders of the French section, who are particularly enamoured of centralisation, but, while the French may have a genius for, and special need of, centralisation, if they endeavour to inhibit the opposite tendencies in other and very differently constituted countries, they must be prepared for the Scottish leaders carrying the warfare into their own camp and endeavouring to use the relationships they have already established with the Breton, Provençal, and other elements, to secure the establishment of autonymous or, at least, subordinate centres at Rennes, Bordeaux, and elsewhere with profound and incalculable consequences to French literature.

This 'battle' is being fought out on a very wide and complicated front. Another aspect of it was the establishment of a Gaelic Section of the Scottish P.E.N. Centre in order to ensure Scotland's autonomy in case it were decided that the title to have an independent P.E.N. centre and international voting powers was taken as a separate language. For an allied reason, Mr Grieve was largely responsible for the formation of the Irish P.E.N. two years ago.

Apart from this issue, Scotland's re-emergence as a distinctive national entity in the European field *via* the P.E.N. is illustrated by its representation at the successive European conferences, the friendships its delegates are making with leading writers in other countries, the part Scottish writers are playing in translating European works and writing about European literary tendencies, and the useful function the P.E.N. is occupying as a means for welcoming, helping, and suitably entertaining distinguished writers from other countries visiting Scotland. In the last-mentioned respect it has had on occasion the co-operation of the Franco-Scottish Society; this should be extended in the future, and the Scottish-Russian, Scottish-Spanish, Scottish Italian, and other societies may well follow suit.

Professor Patrick Geddes's re-establishment of the Scots College at Montpellier is another case in point, and may lead to the revival of Scotland's other inter-European educational ties, while it is also suggested that the Scottish elements of such organisations as the 'Friends of Russia' Society should be entirely separate from the English bodies in question, since Scotland's interests differ greatly economically, politically, and otherwise from England, engendering an entirely different attitude to the countries in question. In other directions – notably in relation to Ireland, India, and Egypt – the Scottish National Movement is establishing its own appropriate affiliations. In a word, contact with Europe has been effectively re-established, and this is one of the most significant aspects of the whole movement.

The poetical expression of all this is found in such a verse of Hugh MacDiarmid's as: –

Let's hear nae mair o' Tir-nan-og
Or the British Empire! See the fog
Is liftin' at last, and Scotland's gi'en'
Nae bletherin' banshee's but Europe's een,

while the same poet's declaration that

... I'd help
A' Earth's variety,
And to the endless challenge leap
O' God's nimiety

points behind the revolt against standardisation or submission to majority tendencies to some such underlying philosophy as that of Leontiev, who hated 'the democratic, levelling tendencies which destroyed the complex and varied beauty of social life'. 'The imperfection of earthly life was what he loved above all things, with all the variety of forms implied in it', Prince Mirsky says – and this, too, is one of the root-feelings of the Scottish movement, with profound bearings on politics, religion, science and other matters which I have not space to work out here, but which, in one form or another, are manifest in all recent Scottish writing of any consequence.

3 July 1931

IV

This active internationalism, coupled with an insistence on Scotland's own distinctive traditions and creative potentialities, is, in addition to the P.E.N., shown in the active Society for the Propagation of Music; the affiliations of one or two groups of our younger artists, some of whom recently gave a very successful exhibition in Paris; and – to a much less degree – in the occasional productions of modern European dramas by the Scottish National Players and other companies. Despite their value, societies such as the Franco-Scottish do not come into the same category, for the simple reason that they are merely educational or social – not creative. Creative interaction – vital give-and-take – is the essence of the more important activity. Its stress is laid not only on what it can derive from Europe, but what, in turn, Scotland can give; and it is because a body such as the P.E.N. consists of writers, and that, as a consequence, its stress is on originality, on reciprocal initiative, that it is far more important than those societies which are receiving on a very different plane from that on which they are giving – receiving the fruits of genius, of creative artistry, of initiative in the determination of cultural tendencies, and only returning assimilation. It is not in keeping with Scotland's history or its potentialities that it should be confined to this passive role. Realisation of this is the vital element in the international connections the new movement is making; and Europe has already reciprocated by showing a greater interest in the Scottish Movement and its possibilities than has yet been manifested in England or elsewhere in the English-speaking world.

This whole question of the development of literary and artistic movements – instead of each writer or artists 'ploughing his own furrow' and refusing to co-operate with his fellows – has evoked condemnations in Scotland on the ground that it leads to mere coteries, to little 'mutual admiration' societies, and that 'he travels furthest who travels alone'. The sorry history of Scottish arts and letters during the past century and more should, perhaps, have shown that many who have insisted in this way on travelling alone haven't got so very far that a little company would have appreciably reduced their mileage; nor are some of the older writers who have held aloof, somewhat ostentatiously, from the new groups, of such a stature that their anxiety to remain uncontaminated by their competitors can be regarded otherwise than derisively. Arts and letters have flourished far better in most other nations where there have been a constant succession of movements and groups; and, if Scotland has singularly lacked these in the past, it is perhaps high time it was making up for lost time by having a regular epidemic of them. 'But,' says someone, 'they are natural in France and elsewhere, but alien to our Scottish temperament.' The answer of their promoters in Scotland is simply that in that case it is high time the Scottish temperament was being changed (which is what seems to be happening), and they boldly declare that they are 'out to effect a psychological revolution'. So far as those older writers and professional platitudinarians are concerned, who have inveighed against the new cults and the alleged log-rolling and self-advertising propensities of those who are promoting these developments, there is no getting away from the admirable words of la Bruyère:

> False greatness is shy and inaccessible. Conscious of its foible, it hides away, or at least never shows an open face, letting be seen only as much will make an impression and save it from being revealed for what it really is, something mean and small. True greatness is free; it can be touched and handled, and loses nothing when seen at close quarters. The better you are acquainted with it, the more you admire it. It bends out of goodness of heart to its inferiors, and returns to its own level without effort. Sometimes it lets itself go, neglecting and surrendering its natural advantages, but never ready to recover them and put them to use.

On the wider issue involved in this question of tradition and innovation, nationalism and internationalism, the best word (and it has been splendidly apprehended by the leaders of the Scottish Renaissance Movement) is with André Gide when he exclaims (and his remarks are as applicable to Scotland as to France):

> It is well that France should have conservative elements reacting and taking stand against what savours of foreign invasion. But what justifies the existence of these elements if not this fresh contribution, without which French culture would ere long be nothing but a hollow form, a hardened shell? What do they know of France's genius? What *do* we know, except its past? It is the same with national feelings as with the Church. I mean the conservative elements often mete out to genius the same treatment as the Church to her saints at times. Many who were rejected, repulsed, denied in the name of tradition, are become its very corner-stones. My opinion of intellectual protectionism I have often voiced; I believe it presents a great peril; on the other hand, any essay in intellectual denationalisation involves a risk no less considerable.

Finally, in regard to the reciprocity – the necessary give as well as take – of which I have spoken, it is one of the most promising signs in the Scottish Movement as a whole to find it so effectively imbued with a realisation of the truth of Dostoevski's declaration that:

> No matter how fertile an idea imported from abroad, it can only strike root here, become acclimatised, and prove of genuine use to us if our national life, spontaneously and without pressure from without, made the idea grow up, naturally and practically, to meet its own needs – needs which have been recognised by practical experience. No nation on earth, no society with a certain measure of stability, has been developed to order, on the lines of a programme imported from abroad.

These three quotations reflect, so far as the whole of this aspect of the Scottish Renaissance Movement is concerned, the new spirit which is so ubiquitously at work in our midst, and still so little understood, so much the target for stupid criticisms. On the formal development of the literary and artistic wing of the movement this spirit issues in three principal results: – a new stress on intellectualism, since a wide purview of foreign arts and affairs, a knowledge of languages, a faculty for comparative criticism, and original creative ability are the prerogatives of a very small minority, no matter how they may subserve the higher interests of the population at large; a realisation of the need for concentration in order to register results – since a contemplation of the heterogeneity of cultural tendencies inevitably leads to a recognition of the limited potentialities of any particular country and generation and the need to avoid dispersion of energy by purposeful organisation and disciplined endeavour; and, thirdly, as a corollary of these two factors, a trend towards authoritarian positions.

Multiple bearings of all three elements are manifest in the new Scottish Movement. The reaction against democracy is seen, in the light of the first, as more than an accessibility to the fashion of the moment in certain continental literary and political groups, and more than an effort to swing Scotland from one extreme to another. In regard to the second, when Rev. W.H. Hamilton, in the preface to *Holyrood*, says that some of our younger poets 'have endeavoured to evoke (but also, we have feared, to confine) a revival of song', the question arises 'Yes, but isn't it necessary to confine to evoke? – Isn't there such a thing as advancing in all directions, and in none? – And isn't there something in the very nature of things which confines the significant period within very narrow lines?' The third element is likely to be most importantly displayed in the religious sphere, and here the little infiltration of the doctrines of Otto and Barth, which certain elements in the Scottish Church are using to reinforce the emotional appeal of their tenets, is perhaps one of the less desirable importations from Europe, since religion in Scotland has long been too emotional and too little intellectual, and any attempt to further accentuate this hypnotisation is certainly not in line with our new political and cultural tendencies nor with the claims to Scottish hard-headedness and metaphysical disposition which have been so curiously belied by our history during the past century and more that the cry of the Renaissance leaders to their countrymen is a version of the Nietzschean admonition: 'dare to be what you are.'

10 July 1931

V

Writing of the P.E.N. Movement, Mr William Power says: –

> The amazingly spontaneous world-response to the idea seems to herald the development of P.E.N. into a world-parliament of literature. What is the real secret of it all? It was suggested to me by a recent study of the

Unanimist French group of writers, represented by Jules Romains, Georges Duhamel, Chennevière, Durtain, and others – significantly termed the 'Abbey Group'. Their central idea is, very roughly, that what happens to one person happens to the whole human race; that the most intense individualism has for necessary complement the most intense universalism; that any person may at any moment become the intellectual trustee of all humanity, and any group or crowd be roused by individual inspiration to revolutionary creativeness; and that, in short, apart from active and creative love, there is no meaning in life. That is the literary and philosophical expression of essential religion.

'It was', he concludes, 'the universal feeling among writers everywhere of something like Romains' "Unanimism" – the feeling that literature, even as pure art, is the spirit of the whole human race – its essential inspiration and *raison-dêtre* – that brought these 45 centres of the P.E.N. into being' and, now that the preliminary stages of organisation are complete, has led it to the new phase when this 'literary league of nations' will consider big questions of intellectual liberty, the reaction of literature upon public life, and so forth. The Scottish Movement – literary and political alike – is not yet at the stage of participating effectively, and presenting considered and constructive attitudes, in such discussions. It is still in the preliminary stages of organisation. The sooner these are completed and the bigger questions tackled the better. In the meantime, the main thing is to keep these bigger issues clearly in view and not allow them to be lost sight of in dealing with the immediate matters and doing the necessary 'donkey work'.

Mr Power, Mr Grieve and others tell me that – though it is largely based on our past and not a product of anything we have done in recent times or, to foreign eyes, have given any promise yet of doing in the future – there is, in intelligent quarters, a very considerable amount of discrimination throughout Europe between 'English' and 'Scottish'. Continental people react very differently to the two adjectives, even although it is in many cases a reaction against the first, the 'content' of which is well understood, and a welcoming of the second, if only because it is a term which, while suggesting a difference, conveys little or nothing to them, since, in actual connotation, it has been for all practical purposes, almost entirely absorbed into the first. The object of the new Scottish Movement must be to give a vital and progressive reality to the difference between these two.

In this connotation, the following passage from the Knight of Cromarty – Sir Thomas Urquhart – may well be borne in mind:

> Then was it that the name of a Scot was honourable over all the world, and that the glory of their ancestors was a passport and safe-conduct sufficient for any traveller of that country. In confirmation whereof, I have heard it related of him who is the το ου ενεκα of this discourse, and to whose weal it is sub-

ordinated, that, after his peragration [*sic*] of France, Spain, and Italy, and that for speaking some of these languages with the liveliness of the country accent, they would have had him pass for a native, he plainly told them, without making bones thereof, that truly he thought he had as much honour by his own country, which did contrevalue the riches and fertility of those nations, by the valour, learning and honesty, wherein it did parallel, if not surpass them: which assertion of his was with pregnant reasons so well backed by him, that he was not much gainsaid therein by any in all those kingdoms. But should he offer now to stand upon such high terms, and enter the lists with a spirit of competition, it fears me that instead of laudatives and panegyrics, which formerly he used, he would be constrained to have resort to vindications and apologies; the toyle whereof, in saying one and the same thing over and over again, with the misfortune of being the less believed the more truly spoke, hath proved of late almost insupportable to the favourers of that nation, whose inhabitants in foreign peregrinations, must now of their own merit, with an abatement of more than half of its value, by reason of the national imputation; whilst in former times, men of meaner endowments would in sharper extremities, at the hands of stranger-people, have carryed thorrow with more specious advantages, by the only vertue of the credit and good name of the country in general; which, by twice as many abilities as ever were in that land, both for martial prowess and favour of the muses, in the persons of private men, can never in the opinion of neighbour states and kingdoms, be raised to so great hight as publick obloquy had deprest it. For as that city whose common treasure is well stored with money, though all its burgers severally be but poor, is better able to maintain its reputation than that other, all whose citizens are rich without a considerable bank; (the experience whereof history gives us in the reduction of the wars betwixt the Venetians and Genois): even so will a man of indifferent qualifications, the fame of whose country remaineth unreproached, obtaine a more amicable admittance to the societies of most men, than another of thrice more accomplished parts, that is the native of a soyle of an opprobrious name; which, although, after mature examination, it should seem not to deserve, yet upon the slipperiest ground that is of honour questioned, a very scandal once emitted will both touch and stick.

The aim of the Scottish Movement is to reproduce that *status quo ante* of Scotland in Europe of which Urquhart writes, and it is not surprising that, in doing so, it should espouse that type of Scotsman of whom Urquhart was himself enamoured – gallant, learned, high-spirited, no stranger to lofty ideals, and, above all, *fier comme un Ecossais* (a phrase that Mr Grieve has made one of the slogans of our Movement). The contention is that the Union with England and other factors have favoured the wrong type of Scotland and promulgated on that basis – to the detriment and practical elimination of the finer elements of our race – a false and unworthy myth. It is this that yields the principle upon which the process of revaluation in Scottish history and literature is now proceeding. From the point of view in Europe, and our rehabilitation there, it is contended that we must give up the kailyaird glorification of petty poetasters such as Tannahill, Motherwell, and hosts of others, and qualify the cult of Burns by recognising his limitations in the light of comparative criticism, the extent to which his work has already 'dated', and the egregiousness of most of the habitual sentiments of January 25th. On the other hand, it is contended that writers like Dunbar, the Knight of Cromarty himself, and the great Gaelic poet, Alasdair Mackmaighstir Alasdair – all of whom, not least in Scotland itself, are far less known and esteemed than these poorer figures – should be raised to their proper place and presented to Europe as the types of our true national genius, just as, to bring the argument down to the present day, it is grotesque that an R.L. Stevenson or a J.M. Barrie should 'stand for Scotland' instead of a Norman Douglas or a Cunninghame-Graham.

It has been observed that of necessity a far livelier and more profitable interest is taken in foreign literatures by a country which is actively nourishing its own distinctive genius, and one of the welcome concomitants of new Scottish movement is to be found in such books as Norman Macleod's *German Lyric Poetry*, Jean Stewart's *Poetry in England and France*, many of Edwin Muir's essays in *welt-literatur*, and the translations of the contemporary European poets by Professor Alexander Gray, Sir Donald MacAlister, 'Hugh MacDiarmid', and others, including Professor H.J.C. Grierson whose ability, at a recent international banquet at the Hague, to rise in the name of Scotland and prove himself the only one of the twenty-four foreign speakers who could address his Dutch hosts, eloquently and wittily in their own tongue, was splendidly in keeping with a fine old Scottish tradition which cannot be too widely renewed. Mention should also be made here of Mr J.H. Whyte's 'Abbey Bookshop' in St Andrews – the only really European bookshop in Great Britain with the exception of Bumpus's in Oxford Street, London (which, *nota bene*, is also run by a Scotsman, Mr J.G. Wilson). Mr Whyte has admirably reconstructed the interior of this fine sixteenth-century house, and here all the important books and periodicals of Europe can be seen as they appear. It is already becoming a focus for all the active intellectual interest in Scotland – an ideal forum of all the vital tendencies in Internationalism and Scottish Nationalism alike. In this connection – no matter how much truth there may have been in the strictures recently passed on the teaching of foreign languages in Scotland by Professor Sarolea (nor how much he was the last man who ought to have made them) – the cultural tendencies of the new Scotland will be splendidly helped by our scholastic equipment, and – added to that – the divers agencies which are, on the one hand, promoting more and more Continental travel, among our young people especially, and, on the other, bringing more and more visitors to Scotland from other countries.

17 July 1931

VI

Apart from the effort to overthrow the 'false myth' of the canny Scot, with its subsidiaries, the mean Aberdonian and the egregious highlander of the Clans MacSporran and Macspurtle, and to create a new myth by emphasising the higher values in our national tradition, an essential corollary to 'putting Scotland on the map of Europe again' is to rediscover it ourselves. It is one thing to appreciate and accept European standards; it is quite another thing to apply these to Scottish literature, history; and all the other departments of arts and affairs, and calls, in the first place, for a thorough knowledge of the latter. This is almost entirely lacking, and it is one of the biggest and most difficult tasks of the Scottish Renaissance Movement to 'rediscover Scotland'. It calls for intensive research in every direction. The promulgation of the 'false myth' is largely, it must be recognised, the work of Scots themselves – not only Sir Harry Lauder and other comedians, who have given world-wide currency to travesties of certain of our national types, but to our general public. They, although they may resent these caricatures, actually do correspond very closely to them and, just as in the very nature of the case, those who are callous by nature do not know they are callous, so most Scots, while resenting any exaggeration of their kind, are at least equally resentful of legitimate criticism of such attributes as thrift, canniness, and the other attributes of the 'debased myth', and quite incapable of conceiving that the very opposite values to those which for the past century and longer have determined the nature of most of our people are of a higher order and, not only essential if we are to re-establish a better name for ourselves throughout the world, but, at one and the same time, in better keeping with our true national genius as it existed prior to the Union, and our subsequent progressive Anglicisation, and, as the present condition of Scotland shrewdly indicates, in better keeping with our urgent national deeds today. It is this insistence on the dual strain in Scottish character which is one of the main features of the Renaissance Movement. On the one hand there have always been the flashing, brilliant, cultured types, the Mary Queen of Scots, Bonnie Prince Charlie, Sir Thomas Urquhart, William Dunbar, type running down the ages till we come to its contemporary manifestation in such fascinating and picturesque personalities as those of R.B. Cunninghame-Graham, Norman Douglas, and Compton Mackenzie – and, on the other hand, there have been the hodden-grey hordes of douce Philistines. It is putting it too far to say that the Movement's aim is to effect a 'psychological revolution' if by this is meant any hope or attempt to transmute the base metal of the vast majority into the fine gold of the favoured few. That can not be done; but what can be done – and what the Movement is really trying to do – is to alter the attitude of the majority to the minority, to destroy their false gods, to inculcate a better appreciation of the finer figures of Scottish history, and to change over the relative values attached by most people to sport and other matters which are overwhelmingly popular today to literature, music, and art instead. This cannot be regarded as a hopeless task. These things are given their proper place (and incidentally their practical value as well is clearly appreciated) in other countries where the general level of intelligence is lower than in Scotland; and this better incidence of interest prevailed in Scotland itself in former times. It would, however, be a fatal mistake to underestimate the difficulties of creating such a *kulturkampf* in the contemporary conditions. Failure to appreciate the cardinal necessity for it lies at the root of the failure in many quarters to understand what the more extreme protagonists of the Movement mean when, for example, they welcome the so-called 'Irish invasion', speak of 'reconditioning Scotland with the Irish', advocate Anglo-phobia, and pin their hopes to the 're-Catholicisation' of Scotland. But, after all, 'ideas are known by the company they keep', and the Protestant pro-English Scotland, that has forgotten its Gaelic background and lost its connection with Europe, has come to a pass today which is forcing many people to dig down beneath their traditional prejudices and enquire what exactly are the subtle and complicated connections between all these particular cultural and political and religious positions and this process of national degeneration. And this question naturally involves speculations as to what the effects would be in the various departments of our national life if we swung over to the opposite positions to those we have so long entertained. Put at its very lowest level, it can hardly be denied that Scotland has been subjected to undue influences in many directions, and that it is high time the balance was restored even by, for a time, going to the other extreme. The instinctive resentment of most Scots when they encounter these new anti-English, pro-Irish, anti-Empire, pro-European Scottish nationalists is to call them 'un-Scottish'; but this is to place upon the term 'Scottish' a connotation that appertains to a very limited period of Scottish history (and one that has led to results in our relative national condition which are far from recommending it), and to deny our national genius freedom to change and develop. Conventional Scots are also apt to resent the over-throwing of established national idols and to ask what these so-called nationalists mean by 'filing their own nests' and indulging in adverse criticisms of Burns, Scott, Stevenson and others; but this is a kind of chauvinism which cannot withstand the claim of the new nationalist that they are not going to accept anything as good merely because it is Scottish, but are going to apply European tests of value to it and determine whether (1) it is really good (2) really Scottish, and (3) really good for Scotland today and tomorrow. If this triple attribute is borne in mind, much that is puzzling to most conventional Scots about the new Movement will disappear.

In my last article I said that our educational equipment in Scotland was adequate enough to the task of re-establishing and developing our contact with Europe. Whether it is anything like equally adequate, or disposed, to facilitate the rediscovery of Scotland itself is another matter. The usual anti-Nationalist claims that 'the nationalists have no monopoly of Scottish nationalism but only an inferior and distorted kind of it', that pride of country is widespread among us, and that we cherish our history and literature and our national heritage generally in a truly patriotic fashion, cannot withstand for a single second the fact that Scottish literature is actually not taught at all in our schools and Universities. It is – or rather parts of it are – *referred to* here and there. But it is not *taught*, and our children grow up with only the scrappiest knowledge of a few outstanding writers and no appreciation whatever of the course of Scottish literature as a whole. No other country in the world has ever subordinated its own literature to that of another country in this way; and the inferiority of Scottish literature to English must be largely attributable to this cause. It is an absolutely indefensible state of affairs. The full ignominy of it is reflected in the fact that in our two Chairs of Scottish Literature the subject is conjoined to Scottish History (and, to all intents and purposes, lost in it). Why should Scottish Literature be associated with Scottish History in this way rather than with Scottish Geography or any other subject? In connection with the forthcoming Sir Walter Scott centenary celebrations, one of the proposals put forward is for the creation of a Lectureship in Scottish Literature in Edinburgh University – but this has been included in the scheme more because it 'looks well' and is an appropriate sort of proposal to make, than because there is any hope of realising it. And 'even if it were realised', one of these dreadful new nationalists would say, 'it would be given to an Englishman – or what is practically the same thing, to a Scotsman who had had the sense to complete his education at Oxford or Cambridge!' That is undoubtedly the case.

24 July 1931

VII

I only use the lack or inadequacy of the teaching of Scottish literature as an example. My argument – which is that of the Scottish Renaissance Movement as a whole – is not primarily concerned with literature because it realises that an effective concern with many other things must precede an effective concern with literature. Short-sighted people are apt to mistrust and jeer at a movement led by 'poets and novelists', and there is today in addition to that a widespread feeling that the relative importance of literature is greatly exaggerated, but these attitudes are found in company with an aversion to fundamental thinking of any kind; business men for example, who are most apt to be aggressive in deriding 'high-brows', are for the most part demonstrably the antithesis of business men in any real sense of the term content to operate a routine and so unwilling or unable to confront the basic issues of their own affairs that they can admit without shame that 'they have no knowledge of economics – that sort of thing is beyond them – they do not pretend to understand the intricacies of high finance', and so on, and in short, it is even truer of life as a whole than it is of schools and universities in particular that (as was said in the article on 'Empire Universities', in the *Scottish Educational Journal* of 17th July), 'to shape a pupil's whole school training in order to serve a definite vocational end is a policy that in the long run is sure to defeat itself.' It is this policy in the widest sense that is the cause of Scotland's parlous condition today; the sentence quoted is only a paraphrase of the old dictum that without vision the people perish.

The truth of all this matter is splendidly phrased in James Elroy Flecker's *Hassan*, where the Caliph says: 'Ah, if there shall ever arise a nation whose people have forgotten poetry or whose poets have forgotten the people, though they send their ships round Taprobane and their armies across the hills of Hindustan, though their city be greater than Babylon of old, though they mine a league into the earth or mount to the stars on wings – what of them?' and Hassan truly replies: 'They will be a dark patch upon the world.'

It is therefore one of the most significant and promising of things that this new Scottish movement should be headed by poets – there could have been no movement without them – and that they 'have returned to the people' to the extent they have done in taking this active interest in politics, trade and industry, and every aspect of national affairs. The only real reason for apprehension is the extent to which they are being crowded out of the movement they have created by so-called 'practical men'. The main criticism, for example, to level against the Scottish Trade Development Council is precisely that it does not include a single one of even such relatively insignificant creative minds as Scotland yet possesses, and that, even if it did include either or both of these, they would be unable to make themselves heard in the din of nonentities who constitute its overwhelming majority.

To revert in this necessary digression (for which there is no reason to apologise in these columns of all places) to the sphere of higher education in Scotland, there is a passage in Dr Abraham Flexner's *Universities: American, English, German*, which cannot be too thoroughly pondered by all those who are inclined to depreciate or segregate and nullify the creative faculty, or, failing any manifestation of that, the higher cultural categories in general in favour of mere 'practical experience and sound common-sense'.

'The biographer of the late Dr Stresemann', we read,

> calls attention to the fact that his doctor's thesis was entitled 'The development of the Bottled Beer Trade in Berlin.' One can imagine what an American would have made of this topic; but Stresemann saw in it an evidence of the decline of the 'independent middle class'; and it is from this point of view that his thesis was written. (Before this he had published two scientific papers of some importance. The one, which appeared in the supplement of the Cologne *Allgemeine Zeitung*, dealt with questions of currency; the other, in the *Zeitschrift für die gesamte Staatswissenchaft*, on 'Big Stores, their origins, development, and economic importance.') His career is an excellent example of the legitimate way in which universities may play a part in public life. He received, first, a sound secondary education; then, at the university, a general education on the philosophical side without any '*ad*

> *hoc*' reference. Leaving the university, an educated man, he embarked in business. The War and the post-War situation created new problems, to deal with which no one had been trained or could have been trained. But the lack of *ad hoc* training was no obstacle: 'Chance', as Pasteur said, 'favours the prepared mind.' And in the deepest sense Stresemann had been prepared by training in method. It does not matter that 75 per cent of German university students subsequently enter practical careers. Their education has enabled them to bring minds trained through teaching and research on the problems they encounter. The uncritical even in Germany cry out, more or less, for *Fach* training; but thus far fortunately without much success.

And Dr Flexner calls attention to the superiority of such education 'over the *ad hoc* training by which education in America is being blocked'.

In such Scottish boards as the Development Council, where it is not hopelessly discounted or lacking, the education employed is merely of this sort, and education of even the Stresemann sort is, where it infrequently appears, suspect and stultified. So far as Scotland is concerned, this distrust of real education in relation to affairs, coupled with an unparalleled lack of interest in, and knowledge of and research into, specifically Scottish issues of all kinds, has consorted during this period of Scotland's increasing denationalisation and degeneration with allied tendencies in the Scottish Universities, though I am not sure that in regard to Scotland (which has a special genius for education to take into consideration) the emphasis is correctly placed where Dr Flexner speaks of universities where an excessive proportion of the students become teachers, and remarks: 'To be sure, teachers need to be educated, but a point is soon reached where a university is saturated with prospective teachers; beyond that point, leisure and inclination for research suffer, and the university tends to deteriorate into a teacher-training establishment, though, of course, the right man will win through.'

Rather the question is whether Scottish teachers are really Scottish, in their tradition and tendencies, and the consonance of their work with the best interest of Scotland, and why they are so overwhelmingly merely teachers (routine workers instead of active agents in the development of the creative aspects of Scottish education), and fail to pull their full weight in all the arts and affairs of our country instead of leaving these almost wholly to people of inferior training and abilities.

In other words, even without the radical change in the policy of our universities and the general national *kulturkampf* predicated in any attempt to bring about a state of affairs in keeping with Dr Flexner's recommendations, a great deal might be done within the limits of the existing system if Scottish teachers could be brought to a realisation of their national duties and responsibilities and made their influence felt all along the line in the manner indicated.

So much for the universities (I will recur later to the question of a Gaelic university). Let us now look at the actual working out of all this in Scottish schools and resultant citizenship.

31 July 1931

VII

While admitting that in certain respects the system of popular education in Scotland has been in advance of that in certain other countries in developing efficiency in teaching what it has taught, the Scottish Renaissance Movement has not only deferred raising questions concerning the content of that curriculum but the subject of education as a whole, for a variety of reasons, the principal of which are (1) that the Movement is so opposed to the whole of our so-called education – as distinct from our educational system – that those interested in it realise that any comment is useless while the present political system obtains; (2) that the credit which has been given to Scotland, and which, in a much lesser extent, Scotland has claimed, for its forwardness in regard to education is so generally vitiated by the confusion in regard to what does and should constitute education, that here again, for the time being, discussion is practically useless; and (3) that so far as the entire public which can be usefully addressed on any Scottish subject today goes, or will go for the next decade at least, it is better to concentrate on the increasing number of other agencies which are more and more supplementing what the schools have done, or undoing that and substituting something very different.

This exclusion of the schools from the argument for the time being is the natural consequence of the exceedingly slow progress that is being made in the schools in respect of anything in which the Movement is interested. Some time ago a Vernacular revival movement, backed by the Burns Federation and otherwise influentially supported, was launched, and a good deal of space was given to it in some of our leading newspapers which otherwise keep their columns closed to these newer Scottish tendencies. What has the result of that been so far as our schools are concerned? Negligible. Going to the other end of our national scale, in commenting editorially on a recent radio address by Mr Evan Barron, the *Modern Scot* says: 'Mr Barron is content to express satisfaction that fifty schools in the County of Inverness should give elementary instruction in Gaelic, but that is very different from giving instruction *through* Gaelic, which is what we would insist upon.' The principle for which the *Modern Scot* contends is 'that children who have been brought up to speak Gaelic at home should be taught through the medium of their native tongue.' Doubtless the same principle would be applied to all those whose native tongue is not that linguistic medium of our schools which Mr Donald Carswell calls 'non-Scottish English' but 'Scottish English'. The concession of this principle in both cases would, of course, only represent a beginning so far as the leaders of the Scottish Renaissance Movement are concerned. They would insist upon compulsory Gaelic for all in the Gaelic areas as the primary language, and upon the compulsory tuition and use of a full canon of Scots in the rest of Scotland, with Scots as a compulsory second language in the first case and Gaelic as a compulsory second language in the other. There is no reasonable argument against their case; those who would seek to oppose it would have, logically, to admit that if the Germans had won the War, and invaded and subjugated Britain, they would have been right to proscribe English and make German compulsory and the general medium of education, or, to take another illustration, say that they see no reason why French should continue to be taught in France or Spanish in Spain when, but for the political accident that these countries have remained longer intact than Scotland, German might have been *de rigeur* in France and, say, Arabic in Spain.

It may seem that, so far as Scotland (alone in Europe in this respect) is concerned, these ideas are not only, as those who entertain them admit, hopelessly outwith the bounds of practical politics in the meantime, but that they must always remain so. A little reference to history, however, shows that that is not the case. Stranger things have happened often, and will again, and may well do so in Scotland, too, and perhaps very soon. In other such cases, prior to the event, precisely the same arguments were advanced by many people, as most people in Scotland today would advance against compulsory Gaelic or Scots, either as primary, media, or second languages; but, after the event, it has been invariably proven that life has not as a consequence been unnecessarily complicated, that 'economic internationalism' and the comings-and-goings and business and other relationships of peoples can quite well co-exist with any number of linguistic differences, and that, on cultural and other grounds, the change has produced results which either represent a decided improvement on the *status quo ante*, or are so different from those which obtained before that comparison is virtually impossible (in which case recourse must be had in justification of the change to the general criterion which underlies the fact that although the English and the French have, for example, very different traditions of poetry and drama, there is no good reason why the English should abandon English in favour of French or the French French in favour of English).

The progress that is being made by what may be called these 'extreme doctrines' in regard to Gaelic and Scots is being made in various indirect but none the less important ways; (1) the general 'crying-down' of Scottish education as it presently exists; (2) the post-school alienation of an increasing proportion of our more intelligent people, leading them to take part in the destructive process above-mentioned, on the one hand, and, on the other, to make good the deficiencies of their education by learning Scots and Gaelic (and our educational authorities would be surprised if they knew the very substantial headway that is being made in this direction); (3) the adoption of attitudes in other directions which will render it easy later on to capture the machinery of Scottish education; and (4) the creation of movements in regard to Scots and Gaelic, in literature and otherwise, of sufficient significance to be effectively justificatory of the first two points.

Of the growth in numbers, but, far more importantly, in political and cultural power of the minority who are concerned with this swing-over, there can be no doubt; and the fashion in which like movements have developed in other countries should at least prevent any under-estimation of the likelihood that, within a relatively short time, what nine hundred and ninety-nine Scots in a thousand would, if the question were put to them, regard as impossible and undesirable, will actually happen.

The reason for this lies in the facts that (1) education is compulsory, i.e. its control is in very few hands and the 'democracy' can be 'manipulated' by whatever clique contrives to seize power, and (2) the apathy of the overwhelming majority of people to such matters. The policy, therefore, of the Scottish Renaissance Movement in relation to education is governed, like their policy in other respects, by a disbelief in the value of popular discussion, a repudiation of democratic principle, and the conviction that an 'adequate minority' can 'seize power'.

All this can be represented as a conspiracy against the existing 'ethos' of Scottish education. It involves no criticism of the teachers as such, or of the success of the existing system. The Scottish Renaissance Movement wants to produce entirely different kinds of people to those turned out by our schools as they are today; and its propaganda to this end is many-sided and indefatigable. There is no answer to it on the part of Scottish education as it exists; the two are incomparable. The whole issue depends upon 'power'. Whether – pending the decision of that – any compromise between the two is possible or desirable is another question; and the schools are in this respect 'advancing' a little to meet the requirements of the Movement by giving more and better instruction in Scottish history and in other ways, while the Movement itself is always agitating for further advances of this kind. But these advances made are of little value; where agitated for not really desired; and serve to confuse rather than to clarify the issue.

14 August 1931

IX

The extent to which Scottish Education is under the control, or 'biased', by outworn elements, repudiated by the nation in other spheres but contrived to retain still in the schools an influence out of all proportion to their continuing influence outside the schools, is a matter which raises serious and far-reaching questions. Those who most doggedly and indefatigably champion the influences in question, and, at the same time, pay lip-service to the ideals of democracy, are also, it should be noted, generally the most suspicious and vociferous opponents of what they call 'propagandist prostitution of the schools'. It is, in their view, right to promulgate anti-alcoholism in the schools but would be a heinous offence to promulgate communism. It is right to observe Empire Day, but would be wrong to encourage anti-Imperialist sentiments. It is right to promote School Savings Associations, but out of the question to allow any discussion or study of unorthodox economics. So far as very large elements of the population in Scotland are concerned, an imperialist bias is given to the children of Socialists and Communists in direct opposition to their parents' views; the children of those who have thrown religion overboard are still having their mentalities coloured by religious teaching; the insidious propaganda of the temperance faction is still more marked. The sum effect of all this is an adscription of the school-system generally to ideas that have been generally overpassed. There is always a time-lag between the schools and the general temper and tendencies of the times. Those interested in this matter should read such a book as Dr Norman Wood's *The Reformation and English Education* (Routledge). Writing on this, Mr E.E. Kellett recently said:

> I have often thought what a terrible time a schoolmaster must have had between about 1530 and 1560, when the State religion altered every five or six years, and when, whatever it happened to be, the schoolmaster had to teach it. Even your Latin grammar might turn out to be heretical all of a sudden; and woe to you if you were caught teaching from it! Not every teacher could be as accommodating as Dr Perne of Cambridge, who contrived to please Henry VIII, Edward VI, Mary, and Elizabeth in quick succession, and even, for a time, changed the word turn-coat into Perne-coat. All Governments have seen the importance of the schoolmaster, and of the desirability of enlisting his services on their side. The Kaiser, for instance, demanded that German schoolboys should be taught how wonderful the Hohenzollerns were; and, even now, in America the school histories somewhat idealise the Fathers of the Republic. And much more keenly is this necessity felt at times like that of the Reformation when each State does its utmost to keep out dangerous doctrines. The nation must be united, and, therefore, it is imagined, there must be uniformity in religion. The teacher, then, must teach what the State desires, or out he goes. This was emphatically the principle of Elizabeth and her counsellors. From the chiefs of Oxford and Cambridge down to the village Holofernes every educator had to teach what the State taught him.

The system still obtains and in many respects to a worse degree than ever, as may be appreciated from a perusal of Professor James Harvey Robinson's *Mankind in the Making*, with its devastating analysis of what may not be taught – economics, sexual ethics, etc. – and the extent to which this lack of freedom in education, this adscription to Government policy, has been responsible for the incalculable aggregate retardation of human development. So far as issues such as those we have been concerned with in Scotland are affected, it is interesting to read in Dr Douglas Hyde's *Literary History of Ireland* of the methods taken by the ruling class to disseminate the idea that Irish Gaelic and its literature were not worth learning. Promulgated in a much subtler way, precisely the same idea is entertained by most Scots regarding the value of Scots Gaelic and its literature and the development of native and idiomatic initiatives of all kinds again. In the light of this – and the history of Europe abounds in other examples of the same sort of thing – Scots may well ask themselves how many of their conventional assumptions have no basis in reality whatever but are simply the product of the biasses which English policy has given our educational system. The progressive falsification of ideas induced by processes of this kind are well illustrated in Major Hay's *Chain of Error in Scottish History*. Only teachers willing to be the blind fools of such polices and having no sense of their duty to their country and no basic attitude to the question of freedom in education, can be indifferent to these issues, and a thorough consideration of them in relation to Scotland is long overdue.

The more obvious questions with regard to Scottish Education under Westminster rule have been adequately debated in the literature of the National Party of Scotland: and most teachers are fully aware of the extent to which our educational system (in view of the Scottish attitude to education compared with the relatively very backward position it has always had in England) is disadvantageously affected by being thirled to England and financially rationed in proportion to the English demand. But this realisation has not yet produced any practical coefficient. There has been among teachers generally too little or no recognition or application of its political implications. It is high time there was. In this connection too much attention cannot be concentrated on what is said in the admirable leading article in the *Educational Journal* the other week. For example,

> The Commissioners either did not know, or they considered it a matter of no consequence, that Scotland has an education system of its own, differing from that of England in its organisation, its grant system, and its method of fixing the remuneration of its teachers. The sole questions considered are English ones. The solitary reference to Scotland is that in Scotland the State pays into the Education Fund 11/80ths of its contribution to the salaries of teachers in England and Wales.

The Commission's attitude to Scotland is only the latest example of what is inevitable under the existing system and bound to recur until Scotland regains its independence. It is hardly creditable to teachers that they should only manifest any interest in the matter when it threatens to affect them professionally.

The BBC, the great instrument of adult education, is similarly thirled to the existing political system, while its capacities as an instrument of adult education are greatly restricted by the outcries of some of the large-circulation newspapers over the proportion of distinctively Scottish matter broadcast is no more than the regulation 11/80ths imposed in other connections, while the choice of even what is broadcast is open to the severest criticism. Most of the specifically

Scottish cultural tendencies of the slightest significance today are 'denied the microphone' in favour of 'Scotch coamics' and kailyaird stuff generally. Apart from the over-riding political considerations, the root of the trouble in Scotland is the absence of competent and responsible control. It is absurd that an instrument of such potentialities should not be directed by a Scotsman of established reputation, mature judgement, and acknowledged fairness. The irresponsibility – the lack of a policy in keeping with our highest national standards and distinctive potentialities – is perfectly appalling. It is instructive to compare Scotland's position in this respect to that of Wales.

28 August 1931

X

The new Scottish movement has not yet made any organised effort in the field of adult education, though the importance of this has been repeatedly recognised and definite forms of activity suggested. That these have not taken shape except in the case of classes in Gaelic, Scots language and literature, history and economics, run in connection with a few of the branches of the National Party – and, prior to that, of the Scottish National Movement, the Scots League, and the Scottish Home Rule Association – including a week-end school experiment at Dundee, is mainly due to the fact that such activities have been under a cloud in Scotland, and elsewhere, in recent years, and that the movement has been waiting for the growth of an adequate public demand before intervening in this direction and joining issue with existing adult educational bodies, most of which either run counter to or are irrelevant to, its requirements.

Prior to the war literary and debating societies, and mutual improvement societies, flourished all over the country, and Burns clubs, churches, political organisations and other bodies had little difficulty in securing the necessary audiences for series of lectures. The war changed all that. Since the war efforts to revive activities of that kind have met with little or no response; socials, dances, and whist-drives have monopolised attention instead. There is at last every sign that this epidemic of thoughtless and trivial hedonism is about to disappear and that a revival of serious interests may be expected.

It is to be hoped that steps will be taken to organise this on a national scale and in a fashion that will afford due scope to the agencies that are working for a new national consciousness. One of the weaknesses of the old state of affairs was that too much dependence was placed on the availability of local speakers. Considerations of relative quality went by the board. The possibilities of co-operative action were ignored, and the result was a multiplicity of footling little bodies, each ludicrously jealous of its own corner of the vineyard. No circulatory system was established. If all these bodies had been affiliated to a national organisation their activities might not only have been systematised and related to a central scheme covering the country as a whole, but speakers of a higher calibre than they could individually command would have given their services and a method of pooling expenses would have made their utilisation by all sorts of little local bodies financially practicable.

There can be no question that as a result of the work that has already been done there are now large numbers of people everywhere in Scotland who would welcome a course of instruction in Scottish subjects – language, literature, and history – and, if the potentialities of the movement are to be developed, no time should be lost in organising the necessary classes. The services of most of our young Scottish writers, artists and composers would be available, and it is highly desirable when a far-reaching cultural change of this kind is taking place that the creative workers should be kept in as close contact as possible with the masses of their compatriots. The gulf between the creators and the public is responsible for most of the unsatisfactory features in modern arts and letters. So much depends upon free give-and-take between them, and in this connection Scotland should certainly seize every chance that offers of direct action and inter-action between them without the intervention of any unnecessary middlemen of the 'interpretative class'.

The idea that has been generally canvassed is the creation of an SEA on the lines of the WEA, but devoted to a different set of subjects. Those who are advocating this contend that the overwhelming interest that has been devoted during recent decades to sociology, economics, and related subjects is gone; the emphasis has shifted; and what Scotland now needs first and foremost is the revival of an intensive concern with its own distinctive spiritual values and potentialities. Such an organisation would certainly be an ideal complement to the Scottish Development Board, and would put the whole question of the 'New Scotland' on a broad and promising basis. Existing organisations like the Churches and the Burns' Societies could, so far as their literary and debating bodies and lecture schemes are concerned, be effectively affiliated to it, and the schools would play an appropriate part, both in the way in which local teachers would naturally be associated with the work and the way in which such general activities would sooner or later be reflected in changes of the fare furnished in evening continuation schools and elsewhere.

Mr William Power, Mr George Malcolm Thomson, and other writers, have recently testified to the attitude of expectancy with which Scottish affairs are being watched throughout Europe today, and, more particularly, by Scots abroad. 'Scotland', says Mr Power in a recent article,

> is not merely the possession 'in fee' of the Scots who live in it. It is an inheritance which we hold in trust for the millions of Scots throughout the world. They look to us to make the best possible use of it; to develop our economic resources unitedly on a firm national basis; to take our rightful place among the nations in science, literature, art, and culture generally; in short, to keep the flag of Scotland flying high… We are rebuilding the Zion of ten million Scots.

This is the spirit that is at work, and it is high time it was being facilitated by the creation of suitable educational auxiliaries. Text-books, editions of Dunbar, and other authors, and like literature are sadly to seek; publishers will not risk producing them as matters stand – but call such an organisation into being as is indicated here, and the opportunity will quickly be seized to make good this disgraceful leeway.

4 September 1931

XI

The London Institutes, with their wonderful array of educational and social activities of all kinds, are unique in the whole world, but, in view of the traditions concerning our people, once reputed to be the greatest readers especially of serious literature, credited with argumentative dispositions and an inappeaseable lust for knowledge, and (further back in our history certainly) endowed with *joie-de-vivre*, love of song, dance, and social life in all its phases, and vigorous and dramatic livers, it is perhaps more surprising that equivalents to these Institutes are lacking in Scotland than in any other country. Many other countries – notably Germany and Russia – have distinctive organisations of their own fulfilling a somewhat similar purpose. Scotland alone lacks anything of the sort. Why? Is the heart of the British economy, London, still relatively robust, and our decadence seen progressively the further we go away from it, into the provinces, on to the numbed and bloodless extremities. Even Wales with its manifold organisations, its big Young Welsh Movement with all its cultural activities, its successful maintenance of the Welsh language, its numerous periodicals, is much more alive than Scotland. Hiking in Scotland has developed by leaps and bounds. There are innumerable rambling clubs. But the growth of these has been singularly unaccompanied by cultural developments of any kind. Their members hike physically – but not mentally or spiritually. They exercise their bodies but not their minds. What a miserable, meaningless thing it all is in Scotland in comparison to the Youth Movement in Germany and elsewhere in Europe, the Young Welsh Movement, the part the Young Irish Societies played in securing autonomy and since the establishment of the Irish Free State in the reconstruction and reorientation of Ireland, the regimentation of young Italy under the Fascist regime, and, above all, the purposive concentration of the young people throughout the USSR. Is it only in Scotland that the young people are infused with no sense of all-round responsibility to their country, fired with no intensive regard for its past, present, and future, lacking in *corps d'esprit*, destitute of intelligent direction and serious purpose? Comparisons have frequently been made between the part student groups all over Europe have played in political and cultural movements of all kinds and the lack of drive, the indifference to vital issues, the utter frivolity and emptiness, of our Scottish students. But that is only one instance. The thing runs through the whole fabric of our population. A real grip is being taken nowhere amongst us. It is all just drift.

Reverting to the London Institutes, take the case of the City Literary Institute – started ten years ago with two hundred students, and now with over six thousand. Besides courses of lectures on English and Continental literature, notable books and plays, art, history, philosophy, and science, to mention but a few general subjects from a prospectus which runs into thirty-six pages of close type, there are within the institute a great variety of circles and clubs, all contributing in various ways to the fostering of a corporate life. There is a theatre in which students produce operas and plays, some of them original works of their own. There are circles and clubs for art, dancing, and French and German literature, a league of friendship, a library, and a canteen. There is no vocational teaching and there are no examinations and tests. Can Scotland – Edinburgh, Glasgow, Dundee and other large centres – not evolve similar popular universities? Doubt may be expressed whether they would succeed. The same doubt was generally entertained when the City Literary Institute started. Given a little courage, the venture would probably succeed in Scotland as in London. Above all, it should be stressed that there is no propaganda – the thing is purely cultural and social. The like cannot be secured by anything that is under the shadow of officialdom of any kind, the Churches, one or other of the political parties, or is in any was adscripted to any accepted standards. It must be free to develop as it likes. There is no room here for people who 'want to do good', to 'keep the young people off the streets', to 'guide them into right channels'.

From the purely Scottish point of view, with which I am concerned here, it is a remarkable fact surely that, under the charge of a well-known Scottish writer, Miss Agnes Mure Mackenzie, the City Literary Institute actually has a course in Scottish Literature. This is summarised in the syllabus as: 'A brief general survey of the non-Gaelic literature of Scotland, with special regard to its relations with Scots history, and to its influence upon the literature of the English language generally, and, if time serves, upon that of the Continent.' Where is anything of the sort available in Scotland itself? There is also a course in Scottish Gaelic, viz.: 'For elementary stage: Phonetics; Elementary Grammar; Accidence of the Language; Sentence Formation; Practice in Sentence Building; Reading and Translation Exercises; Simple Conversation. For more advanced students: Reading and Conversation; Exercises in use of idioms and in Syntax; Reading from recognised Gaelic authors.' This class has been run successfully for several years. The teacher is Mr J. MacIver, M.A.

Surely at least as much can be done, and should be done, in these respects in every city and burgh in Scotland as is being done in this little street behind the Holborn Town Hall in London?

18 September 1931

XII

I referred in my article before last to the need or desirability of keeping the young creative writers and artists in a country undergoing a cultural change in as close contact as possible with the masses of their compatriots, and suggested that if something in the nature of a Scottish Educational Association could be formed their services would be readily available as lecturers and tutors. But, especially in a small country like Scotland overshadowed by a much greater one by which it is dominated politically and economically, this is a far-reaching and many-sided matter, and I am glad to see that one of the most distinguished of living Scottish writers, Mr Edwin Muir, has had the courage to deal with certain other aspects of it in an important article in the *Glasgow Evening News*.

Asking why Scots writers emigrate, Mr Muir puts the matter plump and plain when he says:

> It [i.e. to live in Scotland] was possible for the eighteenth-century literary group whose headquarters was in Edinburgh, for that group consisted mainly of professors, lawyers, ministers, librarians and gentlemen of private means. But for the writer without private means and with no skill in any other profession it has never been possible to live in Scotland since the Scottish Stewart dynasty began to lose its power; since the death of James the Fifth in other words. Without extraneous aid it is impossible for a writer to make his living in Scotland today. I fancy that almost every other country in the world gives its writers a chance to live in it; Scotland does not. If this state of affairs is not changed, then we must soon say goodbye to the Scottish Renaissance, which is at present promising so well. It is a movement for which there is literally no support, which rests on nothing but itself; a movement in a vacuum made by Scotland's effective refusal to lift a hand to help it. And this is the reason why I have always felt somewhat sceptical about the Scottish Renaissance, and still feel sceptical about it, in spite of its achievements. A national literary revival cannot be carried on entirely by emigrés, with the help of an occasional writer so fortunately circumstanced as to be able to continue living in it.

Proceeding to ask how means can be found to support Scottish writers in Scotland, Mr Muir says:

> Those means exist just as plainly and indubitably there as anywhere else in the world. It is not a matter of inaugurating any vast scheme of charity; it is merely a matter of using machinery which is already in existence. There are the universities, the libraries, and the newspapers, and there are many rich people sufficiently interested to start a weekly review. Now these simple means are the main support in other countries of writers whose work in itself is not remunerative enough to support them. I have nothing to say against professors, librarians and journalists; but I am certain that the universities, the libraries and the newspapers would not lose but rather gain by the inclusion of an occasional outsider who is trying to add to the sum

of literature. Other countries recognise this; I think it is urgent that Scotland should do so too.

There can be no gainsaying this. What other countries – even small countries like Norway and Sweden – do for their young writers would be absolutely incredible to 99 per cent of Scottish people. They see no reason why writers should be helped in this way; the very fact that they see no reason is one of the very strongest reasons for it. Mr Muir meets this point. 'It may be objected', he says, 'that the making of a livelihood is the writer's own job and nobody else's. But the more civilised a nation is the less it will insist on such a purely economic consideration, knowing that the best work in literature is rarely the most remunerative.' The endowment of genius is a difficult problem, but it is becoming more and more clearly recognised by the most far-seeing brains in all civilised countries that it is an increasingly important one. Mr Muir's immediate practical proposals do not trench on that question, nor does he refer to the political side, although the re-establishment of an independent Scottish Parliament would bring about incidentally a re-orientation of journalism and book publishing, the centralisation of which in London is one of the main causes of the state of affairs he deplores. But short of that, a great deal could be and should be done along the lines he suggests. One of the gravest aspects of Scotland today is the utter lack of national responsibility in matters of this kind on the part of our leading Scottish newspapers. Not only do they, like most papers everywhere, hate significance and seriousness and wish to roll everything in a mindless welter, but they are specifically anti-national. The universities, pending a big political change, are beyond hope. The libraries are perhaps the most hopeful of the three. Ireland was able to do a great deal for its young writers by giving them library appointments. But the attitude of Colonel J.M. Mitchell, of the Carnegie Trust, is not encouraging in this respect. He has recently been making remarks on the high standards – practical and cultural – of modern librarianship. We have heard all that before; it is the old game which first one class then another plays – ice-cream practitioners will be the next, just as accountants were the last – of 'acquiring professional status'. Butchers, bakers and candlestick makers can all get together and resent the privileges and superiorities of 'more dignified callings' and insist that their particular trade requires not only probity and experience but 'a high educational standard' and is 'as important a public service as any'. The whole thing depends upon a dexterous confusion of terms. Nobody will deny that most librarians are far from illiterate; they may be 'great readers' (whatever that means). But just as it has been pointed out that 'an MA' is not necessarily educated, so it is unquestionably the case that most librarians 'know nothing' about books and that for them to pose as 'authorities on literature' and claim to 'guide the reading tastes of the public' is rubbish. But librarianship is becoming highly professionalised; it is impossible to get a job in a library unless you go through the mill and have the necessary diplomas and certificates. The point to insist on is that it is in the national economy where for any job two men equally competent to do it apply for it that it should be given for preference to the man who, thus economically secured, is most likely to do not only his job but something of creative value. That is why these professional qualifications should not be too rigidly insisted on; the system should be kept elastic enough to admit the exceptional case. And there is no young man or woman likely to do good creative writing for Scotland who will not fill any ordinary library job at least as well as those who do get these appointments and have 'nothing more to them'.

2 October 1931

XIII

There is one marked element in the Scottish Nationalist party propaganda that is certain to be fostered by the present economic crisis in Great Britain; that is the application to Scotland of the Douglas Economic Proposals. A good deal has been heard concerning these in the inner councils of the Scottish National Party, and over a year ago it was remitted to a special committee, under the convenership of Mr C.M. Grieve, to consider the economic policy of the Party, with special reference to the Douglas Proposals. This committee reported back at the last Annual Conference that by a majority they favoured the adoption of Douglasism as the economic policy of the Party, but, in view of the general ignorance of the subject and the desirability, when the time came, of having an informed vote on such an important issue, they recommended that for another twelve months branches and individual members of the Party should be asked to study the subject carefully, that every possible facility ought to be given at meetings and in the organs of the Party for the exposition and discussion of the New Economics, and that a final decision with regard to the adoption of Douglasism as the official economic policy of the Party should be made at the end of that period.

The significance of all this has been thrown into high relief by recent events. The challenge to orthodox economics and the existing currency and credit system has been sharply defined. Most people have been compelled at last to give some consideration to banking practice and its relation to the standard of living. 'Bank ramp' has become a general catchword, and whether its existence be asserted or denied, it is obvious to almost everybody that things are heading towards a general crisis – a complete collapse of the existing order – in relation to which the present crisis is a mere preliminary skirmish.

What is not by any means so generally known is that the inevitability of this trend in affairs, with all the hardships it involves, was foreseen years ago by a group of original economic thinkers headed by Major C.H. Douglas, and that events now, not only in this country but all over the world, are verifying their conclusions in a most remarkable fashion. Declarations that when made seemed to be the naïve ideas of a few fanatics, are now seen to have been extraordinarily shrewd divinations of the course affairs have taken. In the interval, the Douglasites have maintained an intensive propaganda under incredible difficulties. 'Conspiracy of silence' is a weak phrase to indicate the measures that have been taken by the interests affected to keep all reference to the Douglas analysis of the existing system and proposals for an alternative system out of the newspapers and other media of publicity. For years it was virtually impossible to get the matter mentioned. Force of circumstances has now broken down most of these barriers, but although the term 'Douglasism' is to be frequently encountered, the newspapers are still very far from permitting any real discussion of the subject. What references they do permit to it are almost invariably superficial and misleading, and a great deal of space that should be occupied by the serious discussion of these momentous issues is given over instead to shallow articles on nationalisation of the banks or other half-way or quarter stages, or to mere blind alleys. That years ago Douglas and his colleagues should have foreseen with such uncanny accuracy the course events must take should surely entitle them now to the thorough consideration of every intelligent person.

From the standpoint of the Scottish Movement it is highly significant that many of its leaders should have been early Douglasites and that New Economic propaganda should have been part and parcel of its *material* right from the start, since, in the light of the circumstances that have now arisen, this is seen to mean not only that the Party was equipped from the outset with a deep foresight into these crucial issues but was aligned with something of basic consequence in world tendency generally.

Apart from the National Party itself several of the other Nationalist organisations are definitely Douglasite – e.g. Fiann na h-Alba and the New Scottish Constitution; definite Douglas Groups exist in Glasgow, Edinburgh, Dundee and elsewhere, and *The Modern Scot*, the intellectual organ of the Renaissance Movement, has devoted considerable space to the matter and had contributions from Major Douglas himself, Mr H.M. Murray, and other leading exponents.

I have said nothing here of the Douglas Proposals in themselves, but I fancy that current events will be forcing most people – and above all the teaching profession – to go into the matter at last. When they do that, apart from the purely economic bearing, they will be compelled to realise the profound nationalist implications. That a Scotsman should have been the genius in economics to hit upon the great new equation and show how civilisation may free itself of the vicious artificial, arbitrary and totally inadequate financial system in which we are 'potbound', surely means that Scotland is once more making an independent and vitally important contribution to world-affairs. Thus we have a basis for no mere 'petty nationalist' movement. And when the nature of this contribution is considered in relation to the characteristics hitherto regarded as officially Scottish (I am not referring here so much to the part Scotsmen have played in inventing and building up the existing financial system, as to Scottish Calvinism generally and its relation to the capitalist system), the profoundness of the re-orientation upon which we are embarking reveals itself in an immensely exciting fashion.

I shall deal with Douglas's actual proposals in a subsequent article, but a few facts and figures with regard to Scotland's actual and relative position in financial matters will not come amiss here. Scottish gold has just been removed to the vaults of the Bank of England. Why? We are told that its transference thither will not affect the clients of the Scottish banks. Then why transfer it? Are the clients of the English banks on a different footing? If not, then the transference will not affect them either. If it makes no difference to them that this trifling sum is now in London instead of Edinburgh and no difference to the Scottish depositors either, what is the sense of the operation? Apologists of the existing system are driven to such absurd expedients. As matters stand, the fact is that four out of eight of the Scottish banks are under direct English control, the others retaining a purely nominal independence under the Bank of England. The Scottish banks under English control charge a higher rate of interest to Scottish industrialists than to firms in the South of England, thereby making the Southward trend of industry inevitable.

Scotland is now taxed to the tune of £17 per head of the population. If her taxation were at the Irish Free State level (£10) she would save about £35,000,000; if at the Danish level (£5), she would save about £60,000,000; at the Dutch level (£8) the saving would be about £45,000,000; at the Norwegian level (£7) it would be about £50,000,000. With these immense savings she could either reduce taxation greatly or finance great schemes of national development.

Although she pays disproportionately, she receives almost equally less in return. Every maternity hospital in England is subsidised by the Government, but no maternity hospital in Scotland receives a subsidy. In 1927 the number of babies dying under the age of one year in Glasgow was twice the number of babies who died in London in proportion to the population.

Similar disparities between the treatment accorded to England and to Scotland apply to unemployment relief, housing grants, education grants, library grants, and in every other connection.

9 October 1931

XIV

The essential thesis of the New Economics is set forth succinctly in the following declaration: –

> Supporters of the Social Credit Movement contend that under present conditions the purchasing power in the hands of the community is chronically insufficient to buy the whole product of industry. This is because the money required to finance capital production, and created by the banks for that purpose, is regarded as borrowed from them, and, therefore, in order that it may be repaid, is charged into the price of the consumer's goods. It is a vital fallacy to treat new money thus created by the banks as a repayable

> loan, without crediting the community, on the strength of whose resources the money was created, with the value of the resulting new capital resources. This has given rise to a defective system of national loan accountancy, resulting in the reduction of the community to a condition of perpetual scarcity, and bringing them face to face with the alternatives of widespread unemployment of men and machines, as at present, or of international complications arising from the struggle for foreign markets.

So much for the diagnosis of the existing trouble. How about the remedy? Major Douglas's proposals can be best studied in his own books: *Economic Democracy*, *Credit Power and Democracy*, *The Control and Distribution of Production*, and *Social Credit*. Mr H.M. Murray's sixpenny pamphlet, *An Outline of Social Credit* is an admirable outline. A relation of the subject to the theme of Scottish Nationalism in particular is to be found in Mr William Bell's *Rip Van Scotland*. The complexity of the existing financial system is admitted on all hands, but most people ask that, in contra-distinction, Douglasism ought to be capable of short and simple exposition and are as intolerant of any difficulty of understanding its proposals as they are tolerant of the difficulty of comprehending existing practice, which they are content to leave to so-called experts. Most people frankly confess that they do not understand the present system; how then without thoroughly studying and mastering that can they hope to understand proposals for an alternative system? Perhaps the best thing I can do here is to reproduce what seems to me the simplest and most successful effort I have yet read at getting over in minimum space the essentials of the Douglasite position. It is from a recent issue of the *New Age*, and runs as follows: –

1. Wealth is goods, not money.
2. As a result of the Industrial Revolution there need now be no shortage of any of the goods we want. Machinery, rapid communications, modern organisation, etc., have made it possible to abolish poverty altogether.
3. It is ridiculous to talk of over-production whilst there are still people who want goods. What is wrong with the world is under-consumption.
4. The link between production (i.e., industry as a whole) and consumption (i.e., the wants of all of us) is money.
5. Money is merely a device for transferring the goods which are there to the people who want them. In quantity it should be an exact reflection of the prices of consumable goods (i.e., the goods we all want to buy) on sale at any given time. In other words, money should be subordinate to the productive capacity of industry and the wants of the consumer. As matters stand, industry and the consumer are subordinate to money.
6. Nearly all the money in circulation today is 'credit', i.e. cheque money. This credit is credit by the banks out of nothing and comes into existence as loans or overdrafts to industry. The banks control absolutely: –

(*a*) The amount of money in existence.
(*b*) To whom it shall be issued.
(*c*) For how long it shall be issued.
(*d*) Its recall and cancellation.

7. By this control of money the banks have absolute power in principle over industry, the political government (which is always in debt to the Bank of England), and the lives of the whole community.
8. As a result of the bank's method of issuing and recalling credit there is never sufficient money in circulation to meet the prices of consumable goods on sale. The situation is similar to that of a community whose total incomes are £100 whilst the total price of goods available at the same moment is £250.
9. Because there is always a surplus of goods (i.e. £150 worth in above example) which cannot be sold within any industrialised community we have: –
   Unemployment, i.e. an attempt to reduce the surplus by reducing the output of industry.
   'Economy', i.e. an attempt to reduce prices of goods regardless of the fact that incomes are correspondingly reduced.
   Struggles for foreign markets in which to sell the surplus, with the consequent grave danger of war.
10. Major Douglas's social credit proposals would make total prices equal to total incomes. The process is automatic and depends entirely on the total production and consumption of goods over a given period.
11. His proposals do not involve any sacrifice from anybody. They would abolish poverty without taking anything from the rich. The only change would be that the banks would lose their power to decide national and international policy. For this reason the banks do all they can to suppress the Social Credit proposals. They have never attempted to refute their technical accuracy.

How are the Douglas Proposals to be applied in any country? Rapid headway is being made towards this end in Australia, and at a recent Conference in Sydney, of delegates from about a hundred Douglasite Societies and Associations, the following Agenda was the subject of consideration, the object of the promoters being to formulate practical proposals to be submitted to the Federal and State Premiers as the groundwork for what they call the 'Douglas Sales Equation Act' (an agenda which equally affords a working model for a practical approach to the matter in any other country): –

1. A National Credit Authority shall be constituted by the Government of the day.
2. The power to grant loans and overdrafts on security shall be taken from Private Trading Banks. These banks shall, however, have power to look

after individual current accounts.

3. A National Balance Sheet showing all national and commercial Assets and Liabilities throughout the Commonwealth shall be taken out. This Balance Sheet to show the total value of unconsumed goods (goods that may be used for human and animal consumption and for any branch of building or manufacture).
4. The National Credit Authority to inform the Government of the day, after considering the Balance Sheet, the amount available for distribution as the National Dividend. The Government of the day to declare the National Dividend, specifying amount and time of payment.
5. All primary producers, manufacturers, wholesalers, retailers shall sell their goods at 50 per cent of 1928–1929 values, and shall be reimbursed the other 50 per cent, after proved sale, by the National Credit Authority per medium of their regular banking accounts.
6. Income taxation will exist as at present, but the sums recovered in taxation will be used in cancellation of credit.
7. The Treasury, in conjunction with the National Credit Authority, shall control the currency.
8. All exports and imports shall be cleared through the National Credit Authority.
9. Legislation to be passed that the portion of the National Dividend equal to the declared Basic Living allowance shall not be available for sequestration or other legal processes.

With regard to point 3 above, an Australian National Balance Sheet has been issued by the Douglas Social Credit Association showing, on Social-Credit principles of accountancy, a distributable surplus (actual or potential) of £800,000,000; and they propose that this be distributed as a National Dividend. Not a bad beginning!

James Maclaren, 30 October 1931

Scotland and the World of Today

This has been a notable year for Scottish novels. The increasing output and improving quality has demonstrated the reality of the Scottish Renaissance movement. But we have still a long way to go before we have a school of fictionists exploiting Scotland as comprehensively and competently as like schools are exploiting practically every other country in Europe; and still further to go perhaps before a sufficient diversity of ability at work begins to show, apart from individual qualities, some distinctive trend giving Scottish fiction a place of its own in (and an influence on the evolution of) modern fiction in general. What has been done of any note so far, has been unrelated not only to the other contemporary Scottish products of any like quality but to the problems and requirements of the age at large. The four outstanding recent Scottish novels are Neil Gunn's *Morning Tide*, A.J. Cronin's *Hatter's Castle*, Adam Kennedy's *Orra Boughs*, and Edwin Muir's *The Three Brothers*. The first two were laureated as books of the month. *Morning Tide* was not an improvement on the short story of which it was an expansion, and, admirably written though most of it was, it avoided its essential problems and can only be regarded as another corner of the kailyaird – the flower border, perhaps, but still in the same old kailyaird. *Hatter's Castle* was a rechauffé of threadbare themes of melodrama, and represented no advance on *The House with the Green Shutters*, to which, indeed, it was definitely inferior. A very penetrating critic recently wrote that he had read most of what is accounted best in modern English poetry, not without much pleasure, but, after doing so, he suddenly felt impelled to ask himself: 'But is this the product of the highest intelligence of a great nation, with tremendous literary traditions', and was compelled to answer that, so regarded, it was simply pitiable. A similar question relegates both Gunn's and Cronin's books to negligibility. Kennedy's and Muir's have more value – the first for its experimentation with Scots and its subtle and independent psychological analyses, and the second as part of the process of historical revaluation that is going on in Scotland. Both are, in other words, definite contributions to the new Scottish movement.

Now Mr Muir's wife – Willa Muir – who has been his associate in the long series of translations of vital European novels they have translated from the German – has published a first novel, *Imagined Corners* (Secker), which is far and away better alike as a novel and as a contribution to the Scottish movement than the other four books I have mentioned. First novel though it is, there is nothing amateurish about it. It deals with a large number of perfectly particularised people, abounds in witty dialogue and splendid descriptions of Scottish scenery and penetrating analyses of Scottish traditions and characteristics and, above all, is concerned throughout with really vital questions. In other words, it is a mature book, concerned not with little arbitrary and artificial constructions but with actual life, and the work of a competent person with a wide experience of men and affairs and an adequate intellectual background. It can sustain comparison, therefore, with the serious products of other countries, and deserves to be recognised as the first novel of adult intelligence dealing with Scotland and by a living Scottish writer. This is a sufficiently significant achievement coming at this juncture and it is to be hoped that all other younger Scottish writers will carefully perpend the difference between this novel and all other recent Scottish novels in this most important respect. It is time we were ceasing to be a nation of literary Tooley Street Tailors or Peter Pans who won't grow up, and manifesting an adult concern, with an effective equipment, in all the fields of Letters.

I do not intend here to summarise the story of Mrs Muir's novel. Every intelligent person interested in Scotland will read it for himself or herself. But I may briefly indicate, not the dexterity with which the diverse characters are displayed, the constructive power of the whole book, or its range and readability, but Mrs Muir's dialectical ability and epigrammatic quality on the one hand, and the economy and force of her descriptive work on the other hand by quoting two short passages.

Take this, for example, illustrating the first of these.

> There is an undercurrent of kindly sentiment that runs strong and full beneath many Scots characters, a sort of family feeling for mankind which is expressed by the saying: 'We're all John Tamson's bairns.' It is a vaguely egalitarian sentiment, and it enables the Scot to handle all sorts of people as if they were his blood relations. Consequently, in Scotland, there is a social order of rigid severity, for if people did not hold each other off, who knows what might happen? The so-called individualism of the Scots is merely an attempt on the part of every Scot to keep every other Scot from exercising the privileges of a brother. It is not everyone who can live without embarrassment in a Scots community.

And in the second respect this vignette from an Angus seaside burgh:

> The wind had veered a point or two towards the north; the grey clouds were breaking up and blowing over a pale, cold-blue sky; only the puddles with their ruffled surfaces told of the morning's rain that had driven in from the North Sea. It was towards the shore of the North Sea that the two women now turned as if by consent, although hardly a word was spoken. Salt spindrift and an occasional fan of sharp sand stung their faces when they came out on the dunes. The sea was choppy and fretted with white caps; no whale-backed billows heaved from the horizon as on that day when Elizabeth had exulted in their power; the water looked cold and ugly, except towards the north, where the broadening space of clear sky spread a greenish light over the bay and outlined the headland above it.

The book does equal credit throughout to Mrs Muir's head and heart. A £100 prize is, I believe, to be given to the best Scottish novel of the year. If the standards of choice are not wholly frivolous, no other book but this is so far in the running, for Mr Buist's[1] was too specialised in its interests, the best things in Mr Muir's do not belong to fiction but to the essay, religion and the art of criticism, and both Mr Gunn's and Mr Cronin's are little more than 'idle reading'.

A.L., 17 July 1931

1. J.S. Buist used the pseudonym Adam Kennedy when publishing his novels *Orra Boughs* (which was published as a 'Special Supplement' number of *The Modern Scot*, vol. 1, no. 3, Autumn 1930) and *The Gleam and the Dark* (Oxford: George Ronald, 1954), as well as the short story 'One Bright Day' (*The Modern Scot*, vol. 2, no. 2, Summer [July] 1931) [Eds.]

Common Sense about Poetry

Mr L.A. Strong, who has himself achieved distinction as a novelist and a poet, has written an admirable little book, *Common Sense About Poetry*, published by Victor Gollancz Ltd, at 2s. 6d. There has been a spate of these books lately. In a recent issue of *The Scottish Educational Journal* I reviewed three of them, but all these, like most of their kind, consisted more of conventional commonplace – than of common sense – about poetry. None of them touched the heart of the matter. Here, however, is a little book which deals with poetry from the inside – not with mere pedantries and other externals.

Dealing in his initial chapter, 'Clearing the Ground', with the prejudice against poetry – a prejudice, he points out, not necessarily attributable to unreasonableness and an obstinate shutting of eyes to facts but to an instinct which is arguably unsound and unfortunate – Mr Strong writes:

> Nobody buys books of poetry. Few publishers accept them. I remember an audience of working men being shocked into silence when they heard the terms on which poetry appears in magazines and newspapers. This can only mean one thing, that poetry is avoided and ignored by an overwhelming majority of readers. It is not that they read it and dislike it. The sales of the poetry books, the handful of copies taken by the circulating libraries, prove that. They simply let it alone; and that is why, without offence, I speak of the prejudice against poetry.

Mr Strong's analysis of this prejudice against poetry is extremely able and convincing, and he concludes: 'To approach an unfamiliar method of expression, especially if it connotes memories of boredom or dislike, requires genuine effort. The golden rule is, therefore, *Never read nor allow yourself to be persuaded into reading anything that bores you*. It is the golden rule for approaching or starting to learn any subject.' Mr Strong proceeds to accept this test in respect of the remainder of his subject matter, and succeeds splendidly. I cannot imagine any intelligent reader, no matter how indifferent to poetry hitherto, who will not derive a great deal of enlightenment and interest from these pages.

Following a brief and wonderfully satisfactory discussion of rhythm and rhyme – pointed with excellently chosen quotations from a wide range of poets – and a specially welcome chapter on 'The Limerick', Mr Strong goes on to analyse the general objections to poetry, and in the course of this chapter observes, *inter alia*,

> First of all the ground is often spoiled in the very places which should best prepare it, and a natural approach to poetry is made well-nigh impossible. In a great many schools, poetry is 'taught'. There are many ways of 'teaching' a subject, almost as many ways as teachers; but upon one point mod-

ern educationalists are agreed; and that point is, that you want a really good teacher *at the beginning*. The attitude of mind in which the subject is first approached is all-important. We are past the bad old days when children were made laboriously to learn by heart poems which they could not understand, and which no one told them how to say. We are almost past the criminal practice of setting *good* verse to be learned for a punishment. But there are still too many schoolmasters to whom a poem is valuable (in the classroom), not for itself, but for what they can get out of it in the way of questions, answers, and marks. There will usually be 'notes' to the poems studied. These will, often quite properly, afford information about the personal, historical, and other allusions in a poem. They will tell us when it was written, and what So-and-so said about it. They will elucidate an odd word or so, point to a device, rap the poet reproachfully over the knuckles for an irregularity in scansion, and so forth. *The purpose of such notes is to enable the reader to understand and appreciate the poem.* Yet to many schoolmasters they are just something to get hold of. They make their classes learn them by heart; see if they know them; enter the results into their markbook; set an imposition or two; and pass on to the next poem. In the course of a year they burn their destructive trail across a considerable stretch of country; leaving behind them, in their pupils' minds, the ashes of many a poem they might otherwise have come, quite naturally, to enjoy. This is bad enough, but, as everyone can see its badness, it will not last much longer. There is another practice, more insidious, used by certain teachers who have an enthusiasm for poetry. They read a poem aloud, or set their class to read it: and then ask the class to rewrite the poem 'in their own words'. This sounds harmless enough, and I have been quite unable to convince many schoolmasters of the very real mischief it does. The writing of such paraphrases does not produce any disgust with poetry – except in so far as it makes work of it; in fact, classes often like the task. Yet it gives rise to a fundamental misapprehension, a misapprehension which is at the root of half the popular prejudice against poetry. *It encourages the wholly false belief that poetry is an artificial way of saying something which can be said equally well in prose.* The truth is that a poem can never be paraphrased. The differences between poetry and plain prose statement are not just differences of language. The *thought* is different. The approach to reality is different.

On this essential difference, on metrical and other basic elements, and on poetry as against prose – illustrated with apt and conclusive quotations in each case – Mr Strong has invariably a great deal that is sensible, suggestive, and practically useful and timely to say. He is a master of his subject – a difficult subject, not for every man even to attempt to expound, and for few at any time to write so effectively and helpfully about, for, as Mr Strong says, poetry is necessarily an exceedingly difficult subject, being the fruit of the rarest and most complex of all human faculties.

A.L., 5 February 1932

Burns: the Next Step

I

NOW that the Burns celebrations are over for another year, shall we take stock? Little of the slightest consequence, and much that was grossly stupid, was said or written apropos the annual occasion. In this it did not differ from any of its predecessors. Again most of the speakers and writers were of no literary or even journalistic consequence. They would scarcely venture, and would certainly not be invited by any responsible society or journal, to express their views on any other poet. There were a few exceptions. Mr F.W. Thomas, the humorist, in the London *Star*, had an entertaining paper on the amount of sheer repetition of whole lines in Burns's works, and pointed out that if this padding were removed the Bard's corpus would be reduced by about seventy-five per cent. A glaring case was a stanza of four lines created by the multiple repetition of only seven words. Criticism of this sort, even from the standpoint of a 'silly billy' columnist, is far more valuable than 90 per cent of what has ever been written or said about Burns. Then there was another London evening paper, with the caption 'Bur-r-rns' Nicht, And We're No' Forgettin'' over half a column of information about the night's memorial arrangements in Cockney Scots. But the rest was a dreary waste of empty platitude and egregious exaggeration. None of the regular literary journalists of any standing took the theme for their current article. The total effect is well summarised by a journalist in the following table: –

	Tons	Souls	Miles
Haggis	4,000,000	–	–
At the Nappy	–	2,345,654	–
Speeches	–	–	862,765
Poetry	–	–	–

In other respects the year has been better. It marked the appearance of Mrs Catherine Carswell's *Life of Burns*, and of Professor de Lancy Ferguson's edition of Burns's *Letters*. The former did a great deal to bring Burns the man – as distinct from the poet – into a better perspective and evoked a storm of condemnation from orthodox Burns' enthusiasts which was all to the good. The anti-Carswellites were so in inverse ratio to their own standing as literary critics or creative artists. A salient example of this was the tirade on the subject by Dr Lauchlan Maclean Watt in the current *Burns Chronicle*. On the other hand more reputable writers in various quarters were moved apropos Mrs Carswell's book to express themselves on a subject that does not commonly come under their purview in terms which show how it stands with cultivated regular-reading people. 'An idiotic piety has heavily whitewashed Burns... The one thing to do is simply to accept him, whole; and I find it the chief merit of a biography which has many that Mrs Carswell has quietly done so', wrote Mr T. Earle Welby, but he went on to say that:

> She might have made it a still better book by remembering, oftener than she does, that what matters most in the life of a great poet is after all his poetry. It is not that she is not quick to note and, sometimes just a little too fancifully to expatiate on the circumstances in which an autobiographical poem came into existence, but that she frequently passes by poems which, telling us nothing of outward event, tell us essential things about the temperament of Burns. Then, she surely ought to have made it clear that Burns was not only a great individual poet, but, in a way probably unparalleled, the embodiment of the precedent popular lyrical poetry of his country. From memory, and subject to such slight correction as would not affect the argument, I may say that only two or three of his finest songs are without obligation to predecessors.

The significance of this indebtedness may be left aside for the moment, but Mr Earle Welby is, of course, right. A very obvious example of the consequences of the general ignorance of the historical background of Burns's work is given in the article on Scottish Literature in the *Encyclopaedia Brittanica* (16th Edition) where it is pointed out that in 'the non-Chaucerian material' in the manuscripts of Asloan, Bannatyne, and Maitland

> the historical student will find anticipations of the manner of Ramsay, Fergusson and Burns, which criticism has too often treated as the expression of later Scotticism. It would not be difficult to show that the reaction in the 18th century against literary and class affectation (however editorial and bookish it was in the choice of subject and forms) was in reality a re-expression of the old themes in the old ways. It is impossible here to do more than to point out the leading elements and to name the leading examples. These elements are, briefly stated; 1. a strong partiality for subjects dealing with humble life, in country and town; 2. a whimsical elfin kind of wit, delighting in extravagance and topsy-turviness; 3. a frank interest in the pleasures of good company and good drink. The reading of 15th and 16th century verse in the light of these will bring home the critical error of treating such poems as Burns's *Cottar's Saturday Night*, the *Address to the Deil*, and *Scotch Drink* as entirely expressions of the later poet's personal predilections.

But when the need to resume Burns into his proper historical setting, to consider his work as a whole, and to study it in its proper relationships as part and parcel of Scots Vernacular Literature has been satisfied, the task of critical appreciation has barely begun, as the very phrase 'non-Chaucerian material' shows, since, as Mr George Malcolm Thomson observes (in his *A Short History of Scotland*, Kegan Paul, 1930):

> It is as absurd to put Henryson and the greater Dunbar into the pigeon-hole labelled 'Chaucerian' as it would be to dismiss Chaucer as a 'Petrarchan'. The men of this time were Scottish poets, writing, it is true, in an English tongue and with English models before them. But they cannot persuade us to believe that they are anything but Scottish: the note, the final essence escaping analysis, of Henryson's *Testament of Cresseid* is profoundly and unanswerably different from the poem of Chaucer's to which it is a sequel. Its very intensity is utterably un-English; we must conclude that it is as Scottish as are Dunbar's subdued moral absorptions and troubled spiritual core. A portrait from a narrative poem by Dunbar placed beside one from the *Canterbury Tales* is as a figure from Breughel set beside one from Hogarth. The poetry of this Scotland was Scottish poetry and no apprehension of its peculiar qualities can be attained while it is tacked on to a foreign shore. Henryson and Dunbar – like Burns – decline to be 'placed' in English categories.

Mrs Carswell was unfortunately – though perhaps necessarily as a clearing of the ground – concerned with Burns the man, not with a thorough critical study of Burns the poet. Her friend, the late D.H. Lawrence, was greatly attracted to the latter task. He would have been a splendid man to tackle it and whatever exceptions might have been taken to his work he would have lifted the whole question of Burns on to a higher plane than it has yet occupied and given it the literary influence, the vital significance, it lacks. But on mature consideration he gave up the idea because he came to the conclusion that it could not be done save by a Scotsman. Now a distinguished poet, of Scottish descent, Mr Roy Campbell, is about to give us a study in Messrs Faber & Faber's 'Poets on Poets' Series. May he succeed in doing what Lawrence decided not to attempt!

Critical revaluation of Burns is long overdue. Mr Augustine Birrell put the matter too mildly a year or two ago when he wrote: 'Very little of the criticism to which Burns has been subjected can today be read throughout with pleasure.' It would have been truer to have said that Burns has been subjected to extraordinarily little criticism, and that the overwhelming mass of the writing about him has been a tiresome rehash of the story of his life, and of the stock tributes of his anniversary celebrants.

Mrs Carswell's *Life* and Professor Fergusson's edition of the *Letters* has put us in general possession of a great mass of new material; and has done the further service of exposing to some degree the extraordinary machinations of the Burns Federation in denying access to this. 'The situation created by the official

Burns cult is hardly credible', Mrs Carswell wrote in *The Spectator* in reply to certain criticisms.

> More than any poet of modern times Burns has suffered from deliberate destruction and suppression of biographical material. To this day such M.S. sources as remain are very considerably preserved for the private delectation of a circle of privileged persons who approve one another as 'Burns students' and determine among themselves just how much and how little shall be revealed to outsiders. New material of importance is held up, it may be for years, or it may be for ever. Not only the contents but the very existence of documents may be withheld from general knowledge. On the eve of publication steps were even taken by the Burns Federation to have my book suppressed or mutilated.

She concludes by looking forward to the day when 'access to Burns sources is made free and safe'. From my own knowledge that one day will release several sensations, and in particular, one relating to certain business transactions of Burns's which will only be properly dealt with in a fashion similar to Mr Donald Carswell's deft and dispassionate disentangling of the tortuous courses of some of Sir Walter Scott's business dealings.

12 February 1932

II

My purpose here is not to inquire closely into the composition and quality of Burns's alleged world-fame; nor to discuss who actually are the world's greatest poets and precisely how Burns stands in relation to them; nor to ask why the corpus of Burns's work is far less thoroughly taught and studied even in Scottish schools than that not only of Milton and Chaucer and Tennyson, but of a whole host of relatively unimportant English poets, while it has scarcely any place at all in the curricula of schools outwith Scotland in the English-speaking world, let alone elsewhere; nor even to deplore that the Burns Clubs at home and throughout the world are for the most part charitable and social organisations which have little or nothing to do with Burns the man, still less with Burns the poet, and scarcely anything with the continuance of those particular interests in Scottish life, literature and language which came first and foremost in Burns's own life, made him what he was, and but for which there would undoubtedly (no matter how it has been diverted into inappropriate and relatively unworthy channels since) have been no Burns cult, since the fact that Burns had a titanic personality and a complicated life would never have transpired, had he not been primarily and principally a poet. All these matters would form subjects for other articles and ought to do so, because, if Burns is the great Scottish national and world-figure he is claimed to be, all that bears upon and extends the influence of his work ought to be intensively canvassed from every point of view – which is, in fact, what happens with all the other great poets of the world, whereas, in regard to Burns, there is for the most part only an orgy of repetition of unessential stock phrases. What little genuine revaluation work has recently been done has infuriated the Burns enthusiasts, and there could be no better condemnation of the Cult as a whole than the stupidity, venom, and utter lack of critical standards shown in the such occasional controversies.

The great majority of professed Burnsians can be ruled out with contempt. They have no knowledge of Burns, no understanding of his work, no humanist and literary perspective, and that Burns needs the vociferous defence of such partisans only shows that the Burns they are concerned with is a figment of their own petty imaginations and has nothing whatever to do with the real Burns, either as man or as poet. They are more concerned with the sale-price of holographs and association material of all kinds than with genuine and useful research; and are on a level with those who peddle or prize the shirt in which King Charles was executed or a lock of Arabella Stuart's hair. But, after all, intelligent interests belong to intelligent people, and the pitiful antiquarianism in which the Burns movement is bogged would not matter very much if those who run it were not also perpetuating misrepresentation of all kinds and withholding letters and other material throwing a new light on Burns, and one very naturally at variance with the official legend, from those who are competent to use it.

All that stage – the completest disclosure of the ins-and-outs of the lives of Burns and those associated with him; the definitive editing and annotation of his works and correspondence; the exploration of his methods of working, his intellectual background, the influences upon which he drew, his 'borrowings' from his predecessors, the sources and correspondences of his modes and metres, and so forth – should have been over and done with long ago, and would have been if Burns had secured the serious service most of the great figures and other literatures have secured from the literary historians, biographers, editors, commentators, and critics of their own and other countries. Actually, in the case of Burns, all these elementary studies are in a state of incredible incompleteness and chaos. I am referring here only to attempts to discharge these duties; if they have been or had been done at all another issue would arise – to wit, the question of finality and quality in the performance of them. As a matter of fact, bibliography is the only department in which as yet Burns has been at all adequately served. I say this with the profoundest respect for Mrs Carswell's biography – a very valuable and timely piece of work, despite certain important handicaps under which, as I have indicated, she wrote it, some inaccuracies, and the possibility of (and even the need for) very different interpretations of Burns' life and psychology than hers. I should like, for example, to see a consideration of Burns in terms of 'the new psychology', like Baudouin's book on Verhaeren. But that, and biographical studies of many other kinds, will come; and they will not displace Mrs Carswell's book. The views of Burns of writers of very different mentalities are needed – and the further away from any previously expressed the better. Far too many of those who have written of Burns have been broadly speaking of the same type of mind. They did not approach him from sufficiently divergent angles. The consequence is that most of the books about Burns have been only 'cauld kail het again'.

Far too much has been, and is being, written and said about Burns by people of no vivid personality or literary standing. But even if books of this kind multiply in the near future, and help to make up the deplorable leeway of Burns' studies in books of real value as apart from 'dud material', in which they are perhaps the richest in the world, Burns' studies in the sense in which we speak of 'Shakespeare studies', or 'Goethe studies', or 'Homer studies', will barely have begun. But, I hear someone say, is Burns the simple ploughman poet, susceptible of such studies? 'Simple ploughman poet' gives the question away. Burns was nothing of the sort. My hypothetical questioner only illustrates the vicious misconception of Burns which is still generally entertained, thanks largely to the deplorable direction in which the Burns Cult has developed. I hope to show, in my next article, that the next, and long-overdue, step in regard to Burns is to initiate such studies and to demonstrate how and why this should, and must, be done.

19 February 1932

III

The main thing, of course, is adequate discussion of the values of Burns' poetry. There is need for technical analysis and research, and in regard to the language he employed, it is vital – the crux of the whole Burns question – to consider why, and precisely under what impulse and in what spirit, he reverted from the stilted 'poetic diction' of eighteenth-century English to the racy Vernacular. He brought (belatedly) a certain attitude to bear upon the use of Scots. Was that an attitude capable of exploiting its potentialities to the full? What feeling for sound had he – what acquaintance with the full canon of Scots, not only with its vocabulary, but with its idiom, and with the work of his predecessors in it – and how did deliberate choice or the accidents of his upbringing and environment dictate the kind of Scots and range of vocabulary he used? Did his previous use of English for poetical purposes, and his continuing epistolary use of it, in any way vitiate, de-limit, and colour with an alien element his usage of Scots? All these questions require to be thoroughly threshed out and a beginning has hardly been made to do so. There is the further point as to the extent to which, reverting to Scots in language, his forms and rhythms remained English rather than native. Burns is frequently described as the representative Scot, but was he anything of the sort? Was his knowledge of Scotland, of Scottish history and Scottish literature, not extremely circumscribed? Was he capable of taking an all-in view of his country – or constitutionally inhibited to a very narrow and strongly prejudiced groove? Ideas are known by the company they keep. I am not referring here to his inconsistencies – his espousal of one opinion in one poem and his voicing of an opposite sentiment in another. Nice questions came in there, not only of the chronology of composition, and the relation of the poems to particular circumstances, but of the extent to which a man's poems can be held to voice his own opinions rather than represent a mere manipulation of opinions suitable to the type of poem he happens to be writing or a species of dramatisation of ideas which may not be his at all, but those of a hypothetical character he is temporarily assuming. All Burns' expressions of opinion and their incidence require to be carefully schematised. It would be extremely interesting to see a table setting forth the proportion of his interest in different subjects – i.e., religion, politics, the land, conviviality, history, and so forth – and to compare it with similar tables in respect of other great poets. It would be equally interesting to take such a table as that which Professor Denis Saurat gives of a dozen or so of the leading poets of Europe showing the relative incidence in them of a whole range of ideas which have furnished the material of a very large proportion of great poetry, and see how Burns comes in there. The late Hugh Haliburton (J. Logie Robertson) and others have gone into the question of Burns' borrowings from his predecessors, but a great deal more requires to be done in this connection, and not only in so far as subject-matter, spirit, similarities of phrase and the like are concerned, but with regard, also, to stanza-forms and metres. An important consideration here is the extent to which Burns adapted his words to pre-existing tunes, and the question of his musicality as a whole. Then there is his improvement of old-material by the elimination of bawdy elements. Opinions on such matters amongst intelligent people have changed considerably since Burns' day, and there may be considerable divergence of view as to whether he really did improve on the originals or not. It would be interesting to have them set out side by side with a competent commentary.

But more important than all these is to consider first of all what, in general agreement, constitutes great poetry and what proportion of Burns' work comes into that category and at what qualitative level. All sorts of issues arise. There is, for example, the question of how far the 'content' of Burns' work was derived from certain dominant tendencies of his time and has consequently 'dated'. His preoccupation with rural conditions, for example, has been largely outgrown in these highly urbanised days. Much of his work refers to dead controversies. Some of his main impulsions are related to ideas of democracy, the federation of mankind, and the like which are being comprehensively challenged and to a large extend discarded by contemporary consciousness. The same thing applies to his notions of 'romantic love'. In these days of highly specialised sciences, and of 'the new psychology', his landscape and national history passages seem very vague, generalised, and transpontine and entirely lacking in that exact notation which has been a progressive feature of subsequent literature, while he sings of all his loves in almost identical conventionalised sentiments, so lacking in either physiological or psychological discrimination that it would be impossible to distinguish the one from the other. Most of his love-songs are just the same thing over again, and might have been addressed to any of his sweethearts, so completely destitute of particularisation are they. I am not blaming Burns for not doing something he not only never tried to do but which would have been foreign to his aesthetic altogether, nor am I perpetrating the anachronism of accusing him of not having developed certain very modern attitudes which were out of the question altogether in his day. But these are issues that must affect the continued currency and influence of his work. What I am suggesting is that a great body of his work has no vital significance for us today, and can only be properly appreciated if it is resumed into its right historical setting and seen in that – in terms of the past, and a particular period of the past, and not of the present or future. Burns did not inaugurate a new phase in Scottish poetry; he summed up and ended an old tradition.

But there is another question, and that is the penetration and power of Burns' own critical and self-critical faculty, and his opinions of his own work. These run counter to the opinions of most Burnsians for the simple reason that Burns had a different conception of, and method in, poetry to that which most of them entertain or can comprehend. This is intimately related to his methods of composition. He was by no means the spontaneous singer of popular imagination. There was a decided dichotomy here between his practice and his professions, and his gibes at 'college learning' are at variance with his own predilections to such an extent as to constitute mere 'sour grapes.' His contemptuous reference to 'a man's a man for a' that' (so far as its poetical quality – or lack of quality – goes) should be pondered by all who entertain the notion that Burns was a poet of simple, heartfelt utterance. Nothing could be further off the mark. This duality in Burns has never received the attention it deserves, nor has the relative value of his satirical work to his inordinately popular songs been properly considered.

Other issues that require attention are the reception of his work by his own contemporaries and the development of subsequent opinion about him in this country and elsewhere – the growth of the myth, in other words; the paucity of references to him in modern books on poetry compared with the unparalleled phenomenon of his annual celebration; and the lack of influence of his work on the evolution of poetry. These are some of the gaps in Burns' studies to be filled, and suggest angles of approach to his work which may give it a more practical and intelligent significance for humanity than it has yet developed.

James Maclaren, 26 February 1932

Colour and Literature

The Ulysses Book Shop have rendered a real service by issuing in book form Mr Havelock Ellis's essay on 'The Colour-Sense in Literature', which appeared in

The Contemporary Review for May 1896. It is too important an essay to be left buried in the files of a periodical, and curious that its warrant to separate republication should have gone unrecognised for thirty-five years. In his prefatory note, Mr Ellis says that his essay

> may have been the earliest attempt to put on an impersonal and objective foundation the study of the reactions experienced by poets to the colour of the world in which they lived. But the way for such a study had been prepared. Darwin in 1871, in his *Descent of Man*, had suggested how colour may have had an influence of considerable importance in the evolution of species. Various writers, notably Grant Allen in 1877, in his suggestive book, *Physiological Aesthetics*, had pursued the matter further by indicating the presence of the physiological element in our tastes in literature and in art. The way had been made smooth for entering the psychological field and seeking to show how widely poets vary in their reactions to the colour world.

Mr Ellis brings together the fruits of a great erudition. He recalls an English writer's essay some fifteen years earlier than his own dealing with the precise parts played by the various senses in the work of Shelley and Keats, and then mentions a short French study of the colour-sense in literature, but says that this writer 'approached the matter as a physiologist's holiday task', and by taking a few pages from five authors, nearly all French, and noting the number and nature of the colour-words they used, he reached the conclusion that the predominant colour in literature is always red; but his data were too small and his methods too careless to carry full conviction. The only other investigation into this field Mr Ellis knew when he conducted his own was Dr Thebussen's paper on 'Lo Verde', in the *Espana Moderna* for March 1894, in which the writer, by a detailed though not numerical study, showed that Cervantes has a special predilection for green, making the eyes of Dulcinea *verdes esmeraldas*, going out of his way to clothe his favourite personages in green, and otherwise dwelling on this colour (to which, Dr Thebussen further argued, there is a certain general repulsion) in a manner not common to his contemporaries.

Mr Ellis undertook a much more comprehensive investigation, and assembled a mass of very curious facts by studying a series of imaginative writers, usually poets, from the beginning of literature to the current year, from this angle.

He finds, for example, colour used copiously, usually as the repetition of a formula in the 'Mountain Chant of the Navajo Indians'. 'It is evident that colour among the Navajos is highly symbolical; black, which occurs most frequently, stands for man, blue for woman.' The sixth-century Irish 'Wooing of Emer' manifests for the first time the predominance of red and white. 'Colour here is not used as a formula; it has been clearly seen; and it is largely this characteristic which gives life and charm to the tale.' In the Icelandic *Volsunga Saga* there is singularly little colour, but red predominates exclusively, whether as red blood, red gold, or more variously. 'Homer's colour terminology, and that of the Greeks generally', we read,

> is very vague; but in these respects they by no means stand alone; thus Hindostani, spoken by a highly intelligent people possessing a fully developed colour-sense, presents precisely similar peculiarities. 'Black' means 'dark' both in Homeric Greece and modern India; in both countries also the same word might be applied to gray things and green things; just as in Brittany also the word *glas* can be applied alike to a pale blue cloth, a green field, and a dapple-grey horse. I have made some examination of the Greek Anthology, as representing a later period of Greek aesthetic feeling, and find a similar absence of blue and green, and slightly greater prevalence of red, while black has receded into the background to give place to yellow and white. Green predominates both in Job and the Song of Songs; simple red and white (frequently in conjunction) in Chaucer; Shakespeare uses red epithets about eighty times to fifty times that he uses green. Shakespeare's use of colour is very extravagant, symbolical, and often contradictory. He plays with colour, lays it on to an impossible thickness, uses it in utterly unreal senses to describe spiritual facts. Colour seems to become colourless algebraic formulae in his hands. It may safely be said that no great poet ever used the colours of the world so disdainfully, making them the playthings of a mighty imagination, only valuing them for the emphasis they may give to the shapes of his own inner vision.

The prominence of brown is remarkable in Thomson's *Castle of Indolence*; black and white, and golden-yellow, predominate in Blake; Coleridge 'at once continued the eighteenth-century movement in favour of green, and united it with Blake's revival of yellow, bringing in at the same time, as his own contribution, a return to white and corresponding repugnance to black, which has ever since characterised English literature.' The chief character of Shelley's colour is that it is always mingled with light and movement; for him, as for Heraclitus, the world was a perpetual flux. Keats' colour is very largely verbal – his colour-words are not epithets of colours he has seen, but words that have appealed to his ear; vague, exotic colour-words, found in books, that no one would think of using in the presence of actual colour.

Wordsworth, Poe, Baudelaire, Tennyson, Swinburne, Rossetti, Walt Whitman, Pater, Verlaine, Olive Schreiner and Gabriele D'Annunzio are also analysed. Though a great deal has been done in this field since 1896, the essay remains a valuable introduction to a fascinating subject and raises many very subtle and important issues, which readers may well perpend before they go on to consider the more complex problems of the role of colour and in relation to so-called 'decadence'.

A.L., 18 March 1932

Social Credit

'We disregard knowledge which we possess, though we are unaware of that disregard', says Sir Norman Angell, author of *The Great Illusion*, in his new book, *The Unseen Assassins*.

> We do not *desire* to create social or economic evils, to impose injustice and bring about wars, but we apply policies in which those results are inherent because we fail to see the implication of the policies. Those unperceived implications are the unseen assassins of our peace and welfare. Yet they would be visible to quite ordinary mental eyesight if it had not been artificially distorted or rendered defective from entirely preventable causes.

This is nowhere truer than in relation to the financial system, but the present widespread and intensifying economic crisis is compelling concentrated attention to its root-causes, and one of the consequences of this has been the collapse of the general boycott so long maintained in this and other countries against the Social Credit proposals of Major C.H. Douglas. References to these proposals, and even to Major Douglas himself, by name, are increasingly frequent in all sorts of newspapers and periodicals; there is a very general trend of opinion in the direction he advocates; and in Australia and elsewhere, Douglas Social Credit Associations are multiplying rapidly. It is only a question of a little time now before the whole issue forces itself into the open. The question, however, is whether it will do so speedily enough to avert a general economic smash-up with disastrous consequences to humanity at large. The resistance to the promulgation of these new ideas has been so long and so desperately maintained that even in the opinion of some of Major Douglas's most active supporters the smash-up (of which the present economic crisis is a very small forerunner) cannot now be avoided, and all that Douglasism can hope to be seen as in the course of time is as a background against which the smash-up could occur and upon which a re-forming can eventually take place.

'We have got a bankers' Government,' Lord Morley said recently, 'carrying out a bankers' policy, to meet a bankers' crisis, caused by bankers' management.' Major Douglas has just published two excellent new books which prove that statement up to the hilt, and show how an alternative system can be brought into being, eliminating all the needless poverty and misery caused by the existing order. In the first of these – *The Monopoly of Credit* (Chapman & Hall) – he asks:

> How is it possible for a world which is suffering from over-production to be in economic distress? Where does the money come from? Why should we economise when we are making too many goods? How can an unemployment problem, together with a manufacturing and agricultural organisation which cannot obtain orders, exist side by side with a poverty

problem? Must we balance our budget? Why should we be asked to have confidence in our money system, if it works properly?

His answers to these questions deserve the earnest attention of every intelligent person. The book contains as an appendix a statement of the evidence Major Douglas submitted to Lord MacMillan's Committee on Finance and Industry. The second book – *Warning Democracy* (C.M. Grieve) – reprints a series of addresses delivered and articles published by Major Douglas between 1920 and 1931, one of the advantages of their collection being that 'as the test of science is prophecy, the correspondence between the course of events as they have developed, and are developing, and the arguments embodied in these papers, approaches solid ground for optimism. Difficult as the present times may be, and worse as they may become, we know that the monetary system is the cause of our discontents, and we are for that reason so much the nearer a cure.' One useful feature of the volume is an illustration in the form of a graph showing the close relation between suicide and bankruptcy statistics; and in one of his chapters Major Douglas sums up his proposals as follows: –

> To summarise the matter, the principles which must govern any reform of the financial system which will at one and the same time avoid catastrophe and reorientate world economic policy, are three in number: –
>
> 1. That the cash credits of the population of any country shall at any moment be collectively equal to the collective cash prices for consumable goods for sale in that country, and such cash credits shall be cancelled on the purchase of goods for consumption.
> 2. That the credits required to finance production shall be supplied, not from savings, but by new credits relating to new production.
> 3. That the distribution of cash credits to individuals shall be progressively less dependent upon employment. That is to say, that the dividend shall progressively displace the wage and salary.

And he goes on to say:

> It is becoming fairly well understood that the banks have the control of the issue of purchasing power to a very large extent in their hands. The complaint which is levelled at the banks is generally that they pay too large a dividend. Now, curiously enough, in my opinion, almost the only thing which is not open to destructive criticism about the banks is their dividend. Their dividend goes to shareholders and is purchasing power, but their enormous concealed profits, a small portion of which goes in immensely redundant bank premises, etc., do not provide purchasing power for anyone, and merely aggrandise banks as banks. But the essential point in the position of banks, which is so hard to explain, and which is grasped by so very few people, is that their true assets are not represented by anything actual at all, but are represented by the difference between a society func-

tioning under centralised and restricted credit, and a free society unfettered by financial restrictions. To bring that perhaps somewhat vague generalisation to a more concrete form, the true assets of banks collectively consist of the difference between the total amount of legal tender, or Government money, which exists, and the total amount of bank credit money, not only which does exist but which *might* exist, and is kept out of existence by the fiat of the banking executive.

That is the issue. *Warning Democracy* is packed full of most important material dealing with the crucial problems of modern life, and, prompted by diverse occasions and addressed to very various audiences, states the Social Credit case in a variety of ways, so that it constitutes a guide to the subject accessible to all, and not designed for the understanding of experts alone.

A.L., 25 March 1932

A Female MacGonagall

The editor of MacGonagall's poems rightly claimed that MacGonagall was unique and that there could never be another of him. His particular brand of badness as a poet was inimitable. There have been bad poets before him, as delightful anthologies like Wyndham Lewis's *Stuffed Owl* remind us, but the proportions of mis-education, illiteracy, capacity for malapropisms and the like are never twice the same, and the resultant 'poetic' product varies accordingly. Messrs Desmond Harmsworth Ltd have been fortunate in securing in a Soho charwoman, Lucy Watkin, one of the most amusing of the breed who has turned up for many years, and have issued in pamphlet form a delectable selection of thirty-six poems culled from over two thousand she has written. Most of these are printed without editorial interference, and these are not only rich in *gaucheries* of many kinds, but exemplify the poetess's *forte* – a weird and wonderful genius for mis-spelling. As an editorial note says, 'both Donne and Poe might well envy her the horror-holding *wormbs*'!

In her 'author's introduction', the poetess writes:

> To the Author who has purchased for Harmsworth for Publication certain Poems from my Pen, and is disirous to know the saurce and insperation they have sprung from – My Spiritual Topical and Instructive Poems have all passed into and through my mind channel as naturally as I eat or drink and with no more effort of will power than mankind obeys nature's instinct.

Mr W.L. Henchant, who prefaces the pamphlet with an admirable essay, says,

> Southey began the business. Or perhaps it was Mrs Hannah More, with

her enthusiasm for Lactilla, the Milk Woman of Bristol, rather than that dull Laureate with his interest in certain low and untaught rhymers, whose works have now run through their little hour and now are sleeping with the trunkmaker. 'Uneducated poets' was the indefensible phrase whose lack of definition caused that contemporary confusion which has become our legacy. Uneducated poets, indeed! What has education to do with that idle and unprofitable trade? For the versifier's education is enough, your poet is controlled or uncontrolled (I resist the temptation, you will note, to talk of *pseudologia fantastica*); so there are good and bad poets and there are those who prefer a bad poet to a writer of verse however able. And Lucy Watkin is almost a poet. Certainly she is not sealed of the tribe of Woodhouse, Bennet, Bryant and the rest, not even of the poet MacGonagall (whose cards announced 'Poetry Promptly Executed'); there are resemblances to Mrs Yearsley, or Lactilla, if you prefer it, but if Lucy Watkin is to be linked up with a tradition then it is that of the writers of the street 'ballads on a subject', dying speeches and confessions and the rest from Autolycus' pack – She writes one or two poems a day and sometimes three or even four: she cannot escape her impulses, a newspaper paragraph, a visit to the cinema, an obituary notice, a shopping expedition, almost anything. This selection is barely representative of the two thousand poems of which it is made; each poem is merely one of a large group and all, Lucy contends, hold thoughts to which the world would do well to listen.

It is, indeed, difficult to exemplify in short quotations the quality of the poetry of this lady who 'is a charwoman in Soho by day and by night a Pillar of Fire in Hyde Park'. Their effect is cumulative and it is the broad result of her egregious communings, her absurd inconsequences, her grotesque mis-spellings, which is so epically diverting. As she herself says in the verses entitled 'There is Room for All in Poetry Lane':

There is no Royal way to Poetry upspringing,
There are various turnings to Fame road winning
And the World is wide with plenty of room
For every Idia to Blossom and Bloom.
So Poetical Minds compose to your liking,
You lover of prose stop all this biting,
The Road would be blocked and minus the Find
If Poetical Mortals were all of one mind.

So she sings of 'Holladay Faces in August in Town'; of 'Wondorious Hyde Park with its Mixed thousands'; in praise of the improved quality of London vegetables due to the increased 'swiftness of the freightage'; 'to our local butcher, the all-round'; to a wine-bar where a friend paid a last earthly visit;

and to 'The Stiff Neck'.

> One of the most distressing ailments of the common thype
> Is the very painfull stiff neck
> When you cannot turn that offending organ at all
> Of your body neither right not left...
> If I were a Member of the Parlement sprigs
> I would take a few lessons to learn how to bend
> My stiff-neck until it would turn any way
> Then I know that Member would be a real friend.
> My eyes may see through the corners and glints
> My legs could carry me on
> My arm could strike the object I saw
> But my neck is the turning anchor in the storm.

Her 'ancistril mansions', the sea's vast 'mesterious power', her 'Spirit of Controversity', and her animadversions against the 'unholy music' of wireless with

> It's grumpy, it's bumpy, and oftimes ends in a scream
> Never heard in the Victoria Piano,
> And when the Song's sang it's a creapy clang,
> An óppology for the once sweet Saphorino

need no 'oppology'. These are perfect in themselves and constitute a real find.

A.L., 29 April 1932

The Course of Scottish Poetry

I

Scotland has produced extraordinarily little poetry – if by poetry is meant something more than verse. The statement holds good both absolutely and in comparing Scotland's achievement in this respect with that of other countries. What little it has produced has been in relatively unimportant categories, and Scotland has had no great poet. It is strange that the etymology of the word 'ποιητησ' – 'a maker', so called in old Scots – should have been so consistently forgotten in Scotland of all countries. It has been said that in so far as he is imaginative the poet creates what has not been, at all events as he sets it out, and gives it to us as what might have been, or might be going to be. 'He clothes it in a reality even more convincing than the reality of what we call "fact"'. He is the *maker*, not the *follower*, of fashions. How do the long line of Scottish rhymesters answer to this test? It is a test that cannot be over-insisted upon today when belated new departures in Scottish poetry are being savagely assailed, or stupidly misprized, by 'stick-in-the-muds'.

Scotland has had no great poet? What is meant by great poet? What combination of qualities constitutes supreme poetic art? It has been said – and I accept the definition – that these qualities are three, viz.: (1) Robustness of thought; (2) felicity of expression; (3) comprehensiveness of view. Many poets possess all of these qualities in *large* measure, many more possess one or other of them in *full* measure, but exceedingly few possess all three in *full* measure. The purely lyric poet, by the very character of his muse, is incapable of excellence in the first quality – robustness. Scottish poetry has been overwhelmingly lyrical, and is abnormally destitute of intellectual content. Recent poetry in most countries has suffered the same fate. Writing of contemporary English poetry, Mr H.P. Collins has said that he

> has gone scrupulously through the whole of a widely-acclaimed volume of *Georgian Poetry*, not without pleasure, and afterwards reflected with consternation that never for an instant had he the sensation of being in contact with the serious creative intelligence of a great modern nation. The quality of the thought embodied seemed immeasurably inferior to that which goes to the making of a high-class review of letters, or philosophy, or scholarship. There was nothing to recall or suggest the impressive intellectual and moral traditions of English literature.

What is there in Scottish poetry to bear out the claims made for our scholarship, metaphysical bent and international status?

The poverty of Scottish poetry is what one would expect to find in a country that has put on record so incredibly little thinking about poetry. Where are our poetics? Has Scottish poetry, such as it is, 'just growed', like Topsy? The attitude – or lack of attitude in other than a negligible sense of the term – of the entire body of Scottish poets to their art is in keeping with the paucity and low level of their achievement. They did not take it seriously; there is a conspicuous absence of fundamental brain-work throughout. And in the rarest quality of all – comprehensiveness of view – no Scottish poet comes into the world-reckoning at all. Professor Otto Schlapp, in a recent lecture in Edinburgh, has reminded his hearers of similar criteria of supreme poetry expressed by Seeley – who, as he said, has the credit for fixing Goethe for the British reader in the front rank of poets. 'The sovereign poet', said Seeley, 'must be not merely a singer, but also a sage; to passion and music he must add large ideas and abundant knowledge; he must extend in width as well as in height; but *besides this he must be no dreamer or fanatic*; he must be as firmly rooted in the hard earth as he spreads widely and mounts freely towards the sky.' I have italicised one of these clauses in view of certain recent much-discussed Scots poems. It is well to note in this connection – not only the relationship of *Hymns to Lenin* today with Burns's welcome to the French Revolution – but the significance of such an assertion of the young Marxian critic, L.L. Auerbach (in connection with the Soviet celebrations of Goethe's centenary), viz. 'our artists need neither the subjectivism of

Schiller nor the objectivism of Goethe, neither prejudice nor impartiality, but the Party passion of struggle for communism.' Or, as Lenin himself said, 'Literature must become party literature.' But the full significance and potentialities of this in relation to Scotland we will develop in the proper place later.

Lacking any poet of the first rank then, into what category, or categories fall the best poets Scotland *has* produced? (Let these best poets of ours go unspecified for the nonce. Many may find my choice of these a challenging one, and much of my subsequent notes must be devoted to explaining it.) Ezra Pound, defining great literature as 'simply language charged with meaning to the utmost possible degree', says, looking back over the whole history of literary activity, that this charging has been done by several clearly definable sorts of people, and by a periphery of less determinate sorts. And he classifies them as follows: – (a) *The inventors*, discoverers of a particular process, or of more than one mode and process (e.g. certain methods of rhyming, new forms, original usages of language, etc.); (b) *The masters*, a very small class, and with very few real ones (the term being properly applicable to inventors who, apart from their own inventions, are able to assimilate and co-ordinate a large number of preceding inventions – they either start with a code of their own and accumulate adjuncts, or they digest a vast mass of subject-matter, apply a number of known modes of expression, succeed in pervading the whole with some special quality or some special character of their own, and bring the whole to a state of homogeneous fulness; (c) *The dilutors*, those who follow either the inventors or the 'great writers' and who produce something of lower intensity, some flabbier variant, some diffuseness or tumidity in the wake of the valid; (d) the men (and this class produces a great bulk of all writing) who do more or less good work in the more or less good style of a period – add but some slight personal flavour, some minor variant of a mode, without affecting the main course of the story; (e) those, not exactly 'great masters', who can hardly be said to have originated a form, but who have nevertheless brought some mode to a very high development; and (f) a supplementary or sixth class of writers, the starters of crazes (e.g. Ossian MacPherson, says Mr Pound), whose wave of fashion flows over writing for a few centuries, or a few decades, and then subsides, leaving things as they were. It will be seen, Mr Pound adds, that the first two classes are the more sharply defined; that the difficulty of classification for particular lesser authors increases as one descends through the list, save for the last class, which is again fairly clear. The point is, that if a man knows the facts about the first two categories he can evaluate almost any unfamiliar book at first sight; he can form a just estimate of its worth and see how and where it belongs in this scheme.

Let us consider the poets of Scotland from this standpoint.

1 July 1932

II

But before going on to do that, let me make one or two additional points which ought to be borne in mind of all I must subsequently write. Just as there have been many decent books – Renier's, Seigfried's and others – dealing with the character of the English people and none dealing with the very different character of the Scottish people, not to say instituting the exact and thorough differentiations between English, Scots, Irish and Welsh, which are long overdue, so, in the realm of poetry, not only has there been an enormous library devoted to all the aspects of English poetics and poetical achievements, but there has been practically no literature at all on these matters in relation to Scottish or Welsh poetry and, proportionately, little more devoted to Irish poetry, but the distinctions and differences of Scots, Irish and Welsh poetry have received practically no expiscation and study. So far as Scottish poetry is concerned, I only recollect the pregnant passages in Daniel Corkery's *Hidden Ireland* – that wonderful monograph on the Gaelic poets of Munster in the Penal Age – in which he stresses the human element of the Scottish Jacobite poems, with their intimate insistence on the 'golden-haired laddie' and 'Bonnie Prince Charlie', as against the formalism of their Irish counterparts, where no such endearing term, but 'Caesar' is used instead. These passages should certainly have the careful consideration of all students of Scottish poetry. And then there is Thomas Davis's *Essay on Irish Songs*, in which we read:

> War, wine and women were said to be the only subjects for song, and England has not a dozen good songs on any of them. One verse of the 'British Grenadiers' and a couple of tolerable ballads are no stock of war songs. 'Rule Britannia' is a Scottish song. Bishop Stiff's 'Jolly Old Ale' is almost the only hearty drinking song of England, and that is an antique. As to all the English love poems – they are very clever, very learned, full of excellent similes, but quite empty of love. There is a cold glitter and a dull exaggeration through the whole set, from Marlow and Jonson to Waller and Turnbull, that would make an Irish or a Scots girl despise the man who sang them to her… Contrast such English songs with any of the hundreds of good Scottish songs. Or rather let us take a sample from the early tunes of Scotland:–
>
> *The Ewe Bughts, Marion*
> Will ye gae to the ewe-bughts, Marion,
> And wear the sheep wi' me?
> The sun shines sweet, my Marion,
> But nae half sae sweet as thee…
> Sae put on your pearlins, Marion.
> And kirtle o' cramasie,
> And soon as my chin has hair on
> I shall come west, and see ye.

And then, skipping over such names as Ramsay, Burns, Scott, Campbell and Hogg, and the often nameless and obscure authors of the Jacobite minstrelsy, to come on such songs as Cunningham's 'Nannie O', 'My Ain Countree', 'Phemie Irvine', or the fine ballad song of 'My Gentle Hugh Herries': Oh! *That* Scotland is worth a hundred Englands! The Scots songs evidently are full of heart and reality. They are not written for the stage. They were the slow growth of intense passion, simple tastes and a heroic state of society. Love, mirth, patriotism, are not the ornaments but the inspiration of these songs. They are full of personal narrative, streaming hopes and fears, bounding joy in music, absolute disregard of prettiness, and, then, they are absolutely Scottish.

There are other passages in this pregnant essay – more especially in regard to the gaps and deficiencies in Irish (and alike in Scottish) song – which should have the close attention of students of Scottish poetry. Apart from Corkery and Davis, what else have we in this line? I can only recall a lecture on the 'Poetry of Three Nations' – English, Irish and Scots – by Robert Bain, that close student and admirable reviewer of poetry. But in his remarks on Scottish poetry he seemed to me always to fall into that danger of using 'poetical' language which is least fitted to express criticism and has as little relation to its subject as the description of a musical composition as 'frozen architecture' (being a hopeless confusion of the arts) has to the purely musical and quite non-literary processes involved in such a composition, and he had the further fault of trying to establish an equation between England's relatively domesticated, well-cultivated, and 'green embosomed' landscape and the sudden transitions, and comparative wildness, of Scottish scenery. And this reminds me of a paragraph in Dr Ernest Curtius's recent book, *The Civilisation of France*, in which, noting how strongly French histories and school-books insist upon the beauty of France – which probably does not contain a greater sum of beauties of all kinds than any other country – he observes that 'to extol one's own land as the most beautiful and beloved country on the face of the earth is only the natural expression of love of country; but when, over and beyond this, the French discover in their land – in the formation of the soil and in its river system – geometrical regularity, or aesthetic elegance, or providential guidance, we can only describe such views as idealistic.' Although the conception of France as containing a golden mean, a natural order. a coast facing the warm Mediterranean and another facing the wild Atlantic, produce from the Pas de Calais to the olives of the Alpes Maritimes but not anywhere too great extremes, is so general amongst Frenchmen that it must have some of the attributes of spontaneity, the insistence on the 'unconstitutionalism' of Scotland, its mixture of kinds, its position as the frontier of Europe against America, and so forth, are equally irrelevant, misleading, and dangerous, and, except in so far as they may be leading to the development of a much-needed new *mystique* (though the recognition of that need and the determined avoidance or transcending of it are still more needed), have been an unwelcome feature of recent Scottish poetry. For the essential differences between Scottish, English and Irish poetry, one must dig deeper and depend upon exact analyses of the poems themselves.

English comment on Scottish poetry has been for the most part worthless. Witness Robert Graves's stupid remarks, and J.C. Squire's belief that Burns might have as well – and probably better – written in English. Remark has already been made of the absence in relation to Scottish poetry of essays on poetics, manifestoes of new schools, technical theorisings and the like. Practically all that is of value are two passages (which students should look out for themselves) of Allan Cunningham's and Joanna Baillie's respectively in *The Letter Book of Sir Walter Scott*; a few items in the correspondence of Robert Burns; certain paragraphs in Professor Millar's *Literary History of Scotland*; the whole of the late Professor Gregory Smith's *Scottish Literature*; certain notes in John Buchan's *Scottish Garland*; one or two essays by Edwin Muir, and some elements in C.M. Grieve's purposely very biassed and tendencious *Contemporary Scottish Studies*. Compared with the endless harvest of like material in regard to English – and most other – poetry, it is a poor gleaning.

8 July 1932

III

Miss Jean Stewart has written an interesting book on *Poetry in France and England* which effectively brings out the salient differences between the poetries of these two countries; and Mr Norman Macleod, in his *German Lyric Poetry*, institutes similar useful comparisons between German and English poetry. 'The history of German poetry', he observes,

> is strangely unlike that of English. England has had, since the time of Chaucer, a succession of poets, each of whom has been aware of the work of his predecessors, if not indebted to it. Thus Spenser calls Chaucer his master; Dryden modernises him; Wordsworth goes back to the original, and William Morris is again a confessed disciple of the old poet. Even where an author like Pope writes in a new style, he is still in the succession. Pope admired Spenser and edited Shakespeare, and only the most extravagant of nineteenth-century critics failed to perceive the greatness of Pope's own work. In German literature there is a lack of great names between the thirteenth and eighteenth centuries, and, not only so, but there is an absence of continuity. In the twelfth and thirteenth centuries there is a great school of Minnesingers. These are succeeded by the Meistersingers, but then there is something like a collapse. In the seventeenth century Opitz attempts a revival on French and classic lines; late in the same century other writers attempt another revival on Italian models. Neither attempt produces much of permanent value. In the eighteenth century Klopstock, with more success, follows Milton, but it is not till the

> coming of Goethe, late in the century, that German poetry again achieves freedom and mastery, and it is only since Goethe's day that there has been a continuous development.

In regard to French poetry, again, Mr T.S. Eliot has written:

> It is difficult for us, naturally wasteful, to understand the economy of French literature; to understand that the unity and uniformity of the French mind is such that what appear traditional or revolutionary are only movements within one tradition; and that therefore one poet can be approved by all parties, as uniting the innovations made by an adventurous generation with the traditional merits of French classical poetry.

Superficially, there may seem to be similar differences between English and Scottish poetry. The latter has certainly never had any continuous development. There is a like lack of continuity, a like lack of great names over long periods, a like lack of connection between the major achievements. But the Scottish case vis-à-vis the English is far more complex than the German. The latter, after all, has a great poetry not incomparable to the English, and has contributed in reasonable proportion to the evolution and treasure of world poetry. The disparity between English and Scottish – close neighbours, operating for centuries very largely in the same language and sharing to a great extent the same culture and other influences – is extraordinary and not susceptible of easy explanation. One must dig deep for the causes.

This is rendered the more difficult by the extent to which most students, even of certain aspects of Scottish poetry, have failed to take the other necessary aspects into consideration. As Mr C.M. Grieve has said in his 'English Ascendancy in British Literature':

> The phases of Scottish poetry – the lets and hindrances of its evolution – cannot be properly understood if the fact that great poets like Alasdair Macmhaighstir Alasdair, Duncan Ban MacIntyre, and Iain Lom, wrote gloriously of Scotland and Scottish matters in a language of which the great majority of Scottish people know nothing, but against which they are still deeply prejudiced, is not taken into consideration, and, along with it, the facts that at a certain period the best Scottish poets wrote in Latin, and that, again, later, even those who were continuing or interested in Scots vernacular poetry were practically ignorant of the 'Auld Makars' and unable to see its distinctive course in proper sequence and perspective, while on the other hand, modern Scots vernacular poetry has been sadly parochialised by a tendency to regard 'Scottish' and 'Kailyaird' as synonymous and to stigmatise the work of a John Davidson, or a Rachel Annand Taylor, or a Frederick Branford as 'un-Scottish'.

Not only is it necessary to have this 'all-in view' for which Mr Grieve pleads, but it is also essential to get rid of certain entirely fallacious generalisations which have achieved a wide acceptance. A typical one of these is the belief that 'a congenial mythology is needed for poetry'. This recently led a Scottish essayist to say that

> Ireland's wealth in mythological figures is unquestionably the main reason for her remarkable achievements in poetry and drama. Is it not curious that Scotland, the home of the original Ossian, and the focus of the great Ossianic cult of the eighteenth century, should have no current eponymous mythology, and should have had to concentrate her mythological impulse, not without danger of idolatry, upon Burns? That danger, and the difficulty with which Scots poetry climbs up out of post-Burns tracks on to the uplands and summits of imagination, suggest the part that Gaelic 'culture' may play in our literary future – not by producing another 'magnificent mystification', but by bringing into the general national heritage the whole crock of gold with a few grains from which, artfully alloyed, Macpherson changed the imaginative currency of Europe.

Did Macpherson do anything of the sort? See how Pound places him in his scheme. His work will be discussed in his proper place. What is said of Gaelic 'culture', the whole crock of gold, and the literary future of Scotland is valid enough – but not in the writer's sense. To put it bluntly, his contentions are nonsense. More of the world's great poetry has been devoid of mythological material than indebted to it. And so far as Ireland is concerned, what is its poetry worth? Precious little, and what is of value, by the standards we have laid down, has been precisely that which has eschewed the mythological stuff. This is equally true of the work of Yeats and of the ancient Irish Gaelic poets. Besides, there is a time-factor in these matters, and we have got beyond the point where mythologies are of help in poetry, just as we have got beyond the point in music where we can profitably develop from a folk-song basis.

Then there is the ubiquitous democratic fallacy. Mr Norman Macleod says that 'the Scottish working class is the only proletariat in Great Britain which has expressed itself in poetry.' This is nonsense. Even if they had, it would far more likely have been imitative stuff, like Burns's early modelling on Shenstone and others, instead of proletarian poetry in any real sense of the term, but the fact of the matter is that most of the Scottish poetry of the slightest value has been written by professors, divines, aristocrats, and the like, and very little, if any of it, by 'horny-handed sons of toil'. It is sometimes wrongly contended that the difference between Scottish and English poetry is largely due to the comparative wealth of England and the extent to which Scottish poetry has been written by working class people. The latter is only true on a quantitative – not a qualitative comparison. Great poets come from all classes; second- and third-rate poets from the wealthier and more leisured classes; and bad poetry again from all classes. This is true of all countries.

Not only, however, should 'the doctrine of historic patience' to which Hugh MacDiarmid refers in his *To Circumjack Cencrastus* be carefully borne in mind in considering the Scottish output compared with the English, but, in regard to what is best known to an Anglicised public of Scottish poetry, it ought to be recollected that it is equally true of Scottish poetry as Mr T. Earle Welby says of French: 'The English reader fastens on the things that in a sense are not truly French – the patches that most directly appeal to English taste; but the value of those patches to Frenchmen is in their delicate or violent contrast with the periodically exploded but recurrent national ideal of which we are not possessed.'

Having made these preliminary points, we can now proceed to consider the poets of Scotland in relation to Mr Pound's scheme, and the poets with whom we have mainly to deal are (in addition to the balladists, the writers of traditional songs, pasquils, bothy songs, etc), Mary Macleod, Alasdair Macmhaighstir Alasdair, Duncan Ban MacIntyre, William Livingstone, William Dunbar, Robert Burns, Sir Walter Scott, 'Ossian' Macpherson, Lord Byron, James Thomson ('B.V.'), Alexander Smith, and John Davidson. (Living poets are excluded from this study.)

22 July 1932

IV

In a recent lecture on Scottish Nationalism Dr A. Boyd Scott said that

> the variety of the current movements are almost baffling to those who would seek to co-ordinate them. He considered that the root of the confusion lies in the vagueness that attends the 'image' of Scotland towards which the prevalent movements devote their slogans and energies. A perplexing plethora of 'Scotlands' dances before the imaginations of those several groups. A requisite of the time is a popular history of Scotland which would endeavour in its compass to co-ordinate the various interests and loyalties which have taken new life to themselves in the jostling movements of this vigorous but rather muddled renascence.

This objection to operating on a diversity of planes at once – this plea for uniformity and a common goal – is antipathetic to the real Scottish spirit, and a typical example of a general mood analogous to that thinking of Scottish poetry in terms of English or Anglicised tastes to which I referred in the previous chapter, while it is also largely informed by 'the democratic fallacy', and that false internationalism and belief in increasing interdependence, which have characterised Scotland in its poorest period. The opposite spirit has produced all the Scottish poetry of any value; and our need is not for co-ordination but for the widest recognition and acceptance of our fertile fissiparousness.

Since Mr C.M. Grieve first proclaimed, some ten years ago, the necessity of recovering our ancient Gaelic background as a pre-condition of our ability to work on major planes again – and in his *Scotland in 1980* anticipated Gaelic re-ascendancy in our literature, with Braid Scots remaining 'like a bright star at the nether horn of that sickle moon' – this has become one of the slogans of the Scottish Movement. The study of Gaelic and of Gaelic literature has had a great impetus. 'Looker-on', in the *Glasgow Evening News*, says:

> Clearly neither Scott nor Burns was the representative Scotsman. Nor could full representativeness have been achieved by a blending of their personalities and endowments. A mere composite of contradictions is unthinkable… Dunbar stood for a greater number of fundamental and enduring Scots qualities than Burns or Scott did – but he had little in him either of the real or the conventional Celt. Even Dunbar, therefore, was not the representative Scot. But he came nearer to it than any other Scot one can think of.

Ian Macpherson, author of *Shepherd's Calendar*, asking if the Highlanders have sold the Gaelic heritage, says:

> It was the most eminent Highlander of his day, the impostor James Macpherson, with his pseudo-epics, his Miltonic-cum-Homeric-cum-Isaianic bombast, his Fingals and Ossians and Deirdres, who gave the initial impetus to false views of his country. He did it for reward, and was buried in Westminster Abbey, whereby his native land was spared the shame of hiding him. It was William Sharp's lady-like Muse and feminine rhymes which set Scotland gazing at the Highlands and talking of the soul of the Celt, the mist on the hills, and the breaking heart. Mrs Kennedy-Fraser used her talents to corrupt Hebridean rhymes of genuine, though frail, beauty, and made them fit for hikers and music halls… Macpherson was not alone in selling his country not for a song, but for the price of bad poetry. William Sharp and the many poetasters, who rhymed while Victoria ruled, occupied the public ear so well that the complaints of evicted crofters were unheard. It has ever been an English hobby to pay lip-service to a country's culture while it destroyed the springs of that country's life. The Irish comic dramatists, Sheridan and Congreve and Goldsmith, were greatly admired while Ireland ran with peasant blood. But never, except in the Highlands, was England aided by so many native Judases to kiss its hand to the past while it crucified the present.

Sharing to an extraordinary degree this false Celtic romanticism and writing out of a spirit completely antithetic to Dunbar's, Rachel Annand Taylor produces a study of that poet which has been justly characterised as the worst book evoked by any phase of Scottish poetry, while, on the opposite side, almost equally biassed and absurd is the contention of an essayist in *The Times Literary Supplement* that

> there is nothing in Dunbar of that consciousness of nationality, that active patriotism which is conventionally ascribed to the Scot; even in a poem like

'The Thrissil and the Rose' there is no explicit pride in his country. Dunbar's ancestry in part explains this. His ancestors were as often found on the English as on the Scottish side in troubles between the kingdoms. It may be in part also due to Chaucer's influence, but we are more aware of it in Dunbar than in others of the group; Douglas, referring to his choice of languages for translating the Æneid, writes of

> Kepand na Sudroun, but our own language;

while Dunbar writes of Chaucer,

> Was thou nocht of *our* Inglis all the licht.

Dunbar's racial antipathy was for the Celt; his gibes at the Highlanders were many and pointed. It is a chief weapon against his rival poet Kennedy in the 'Flyting', he calls him 'Ersch bribour bard'; he has a scathing poem on Donald Owre, a West Highland rebel; while in the late poem, 'Ane Arisoun', after Flodden, he has nothing to say of the national enemy; his prayer is: –

> Lord hold thy hand, that stricken has so sore;
> Have of us pity after our punition.

The canvassing of these opposite points of view – without solid scholarship behind them – marks the rudimentary phase the Scottish Movement has only so far reached in this connection. The quibbling over 'Suddroun' versus 'Inglis' is merely a question of terms. Little definite work has yet been done in exploring the relations between Gaelic and Scots – the extent to which the latter represented the Celt's compromise with circumstance – and the way in which both have been almost wholly excluded from any infiltration into English, despite its availability to the influence of almost every other language under the sun. The actual history of Scottish Gaelic literature has also been little explored and very poorly and scrappily presented. Nor have due comparisons and relationships between it and Irish Gaelic literature been adduced. In other words, all these comments on Ossian, Dunbar, 'Fiona Macleod' and the others reflect a predominantly English or Anglo-Scottish background, uncorrected by any complete apprehension of the Gaelic side itself. As Mr Grieve says in his 'English Ascendancy in British Literature':

> The Gaelic literature of Scotland is still practically a *terra nullius*. We have no study of it a thousandth part as good as Corkery's or de Blacam's or Douglas Hyde's or Eleanor Hull's books on Irish literature: and non-Gaelic readers can still only approach the best Scottish Gaelic poems through such inadequate and distorting translations as were those, in Ireland, of Sir Samuel Ferguson, and the beginners of the Irish literary revival, which have only to be compared with the re-translations, far 'harder' and truer to the

original Gaelic spirit and free of the 'Twilight' nonsense, of such recent translators as Professor Bergin, Mr Robert Flower, or Mr James Stephens, to show how much has still to be done. Space does not permit me to indicate here what inter-relations of Scots Gaelic and Scots vernacular are today leading writers in the latter to the former again, and causing them to realise that they cannot get back to major forms until they recover their lost Gaelic background; nor can I discuss the kindred movement in Wales that is proceeding under the leadership of Professor Saunders Lewis. But in both Wales and Scotland the services of such re-translations and literary historians as I have named in connection with Ireland are still sadly to seek; and it may be further suggested that the whole movement will not take its proper shape or get into effective grips with the English ascendancy traditions until the younger groups in Ireland, Scotland, and Wales make common cause. The attitude of the Irish bards of the Penal Age to that 'easier mode of writing' – the abandonment of the strict rules and elaborate techniques of the Colleges – is at least an influence which would be a salutory importation into the contemporary literary atmosphere. All I would add is that the two deepest issues involved in this matter are: (1) the possibility of 'getting back behind the Renaissance', and (2) its bearing on 'The Defence of the West'.

The Scottish Movement is developing rapidly now, however, and the first sound of this authentic hard Gaelic note in modern Scottish literature is to be found in Fionn MacColla's *The Albannach*, where such a passage as this occurs: –

'Is it not the queer language the English?' says Duncan Lachlan Iain of the Squint, 'There's a great gabble of long words in it to be sure, and there's a great number of people that will be speaking it (though I never met any myself that had anything much to say that was worth the saying), but there's no music in it at all that I could ever bear, and the queerest thing in it is that the words seem to have no meaning to them.

'Now in our own Gaelic a man can't tell his name itself without every man will know his whole history and his people's before him; and the name of every place will be a picture of what will be there, so that a man will almost know a place on its first seeing by its likeness to the name that will be on it.

'Say Achadh nam beith to a Gaelic man and he will be seeing in his mind a level place and the birch trees growing here and there, and they white and slender.

'Say Achadh nan siantan and he will be seeing a little plain between great mountains and the rain driving down on it. But will a man of you tell me what Achbay or Achnasbeen will mean in the Beurla, or what kind of place is in Lowestoft or Dover?'

Hugh MacDiarmid, in a poem, 'The Vital Fact', in *The Scottish Educational Journal* (11/3/32), emphasises the same point about Gaelic, and cries: –

> Wha looks at Scotland through anither leid
> Goams through a wa' o' fog. If we'd gane on
> And thocht o' a'thing else as sheerly as
> Oor forbears did in gi'en places names,
> Cleavin' to the vera core o' a' they saw!...
> Ten thoosand names cry shame upon oor minds
> And are to maist o' oor thochts as stars to mud.

His *To Circumjack Cencrastus* is full of the Gaelic background – praise of and allusions to the old Irish bards, attacks on Mrs Kennedy Fraser, stresses on the o-hill-i-has of Gaelic, the English attempts at them, and the ancient technical poems, and poems like 'Staoiligary', 'To Alasdair MacMhaighstir Alasdair', and 'To Mary Macleod'. Having sketched in the general background thus roughly, it is to the latter – whom Mr Grieve has called 'the only woman who has had a decisive influence on the evolution of any literature' – we must turn; and she must have a chapter to herself.

29 July 1932

V

Bearing in mind that writing from an Irish standpoint (a militant Irish standpoint at that) and frankly admitting the lacunae of, and difficulties in, Scottish Gaelic scholarship – and that his contentions have to be qualified accordingly – the best approach to the whole field of Scottish Gaelic poetry, and to Mary MacLeod in particular, is perhaps through this passage in Aodh de Blacam's *Gaelic Literature Survey* (Blacam has himself Scottish Hebridean connections and the blood of the Maxwells, Leipers, and others in his veins); and the passage has, as the various parts I have italicised shows, shrewd bearings on my contentions in previous chapters in regard to the differences between Irish and Scottish poetry, the fact that most of our poetry has come from the upper classes, and so forth.

'We have observed', he writes,

> many traces of close intercourse between Highland Scotland and Ireland – in the tales of Cuchulain and Deirdre, in the life of S. Columcille, and in the careers of the bards from Murray Albanach O'Daly to Fearghal Og Mac-a-Ward. We might have considered further how multitudes of Scottish warriors were brought to Ireland as galló-gláigh, and settled in Ireland. We might have read, too, the story of that academy of piping maintained for centuries at Boreraig by the MacCrimmons, where the pipers of the whole Gaelic world learnt their craft in a great sea cave, under a clan reputed to be of Italian origin. Irish literary culture dominat-

ed Gaelic Scotland down to the middle seventeenth century. In this fact, as in the dominance of Irish mythology in Old Welsh literature, we recall days when Ireland was an overflowing source of energy. That state of affairs ceased in the seventeenth century, and, with the dethronement of Irish culture, Scots Gaelic developed a national school parallel to the provincial schools that then arose in Ireland. Whether or not there was a popular, native culture in Gaelic Scotland in former times, the Scottish MSS that survive from the sixteenth century or earlier are virtually all recensions of Irish literature, written in standard Irish. A forerunner of the native literary tradition, however, is found in the Dean of Lismore's Book, an anthology of poetry compiled in Argyle in the early sixteenth century. This work contains many classical Irish bardic poems; similar poems by Scots bards, *who practise, however, the looser kind of syllabic verse*; and a considerable bulk of Ossianic lays. We owe to this codex many semi-bardic poems which are links in the Irish literary tradition – as, for example, the dánta grádha of Earl Gerald, and that lovely Fenian fragment, Binn guth duine i dtér an óir, 'Sweet is the voice in the land of gold'. The book shows us Gaelic Scotland as cherishing Irish classics in the same way that the British colonies cherish English classics, and as working in the same tradition. *It manifests a racial independence, however, in three ways. In the first place, we see the Scots Gael favouring the more popular kind of poetry* – the semi-bardic poems of courtly love, and the Ossianic lays – *a century before Ireland deigned to give such poetry place beside the poetry of the schools. In the second place, the Scottish poets freely use local dialect. In the third place, the standard Gaelic orthography is abandoned.* The Dean of Lismore writes down his poems as he speaks them, giving English values to his letters. While this so-called phonetic spelling enables us to conceive the Scottish accent of the time, it renders the text exceedingly obscure, and reconstruction has perplexed the best scholars, native and Irish. A similar compilation, called the Fernaig MS (1688–1693), was made by Duncan Macrae, chief of his name, nearly two centuries later. This work has been printed in recent years, with a transliteration from the difficult 'phonetic' script; it is particularly interesting as illustrating the life and culture of a Highland gentleman of the seventeenth century. Macrae, *chieftain, soldier, mechanic, poet, Jacobite, and Episcopalian*, is remembered as a fine type of his class. It is interesting to note that *full half of the fifty-seven* poems that he gives are traceable to *authors who were gentry* – Sir John Stewart of Appin, Bishop Carswell, lairds, factors, and ministers. The poetry, in effect, is of the type that we have called semi-bardic, although it includes pieces in the stressed song metres. The poems are religious, political, and elegiac. Lighter forms of poetry are few. The first poem – we may note in passing from a work which is interesting more for historical than literary reasons – is Bonaventura O'Hosey's rendering of

> the mediaval hymn, Cur mundus militat, here called Crosanachd Ghille-Bhríghde; and the difficulty of understanding Macrae's phonetics may be judged from the first verse: –
>
> Troú korr chlaind Ahú
> Aiwghlick kaird i chowlain
> Doimbhoin doy í deoreire
> Gloir ghoiwhoin donan.
>
> The first book ever printed in Gaelic was the version of the *Book of the Common Order*, commonly called *John Knox's Liturgy*, made by Bishop John Carswell of the Isles, and published in Edinburgh in 1567. The Bedell-Daniel Irish *Bible* was transliterated into Roman characters and published in London, for circulation in Scotland, in 1690. We have seen how the adventures of a Scottish Macdonald in the Confederate war in Ireland were chronicled by a Scottish historian (a MacVurrich, and therefore of Irish bardic descent) whose Gaelic, as late as 1700, was little different from the Gaelic of Ireland. Thus down to the end of the seventeenth century, the Irish tradition persisted, although, as we see from the dialect of the native poems in the Dean of Lismore's Book and the Fernaig MS a local tradition was gathering strength for two centuries. We now come to consider a great school of popular poetry that then arose. A remarkable poet was Mary Macleod, who made *bardic poetry* for the Macleods, *but in the accented metres* during a life-time of over a century. Her work is richly musical, and is racy of Scotland. Some critics have represented her as the pioneer of the popular schools of the two countries.

It is a reflection on Scottish Gaelic scholarship that there is no thorough biographical and critical study of 'Mary of the Songs' and that the attribution of some of her work is still in debate; and it is a reflection on Scotland generally that a poetess who is the only woman who 'has affected the evolution' not of one literature but of two, the greatest of Gaelic women writers, and who, moreover, had a life of exceptional biographic and psychological interest should be so little known. She was born in 1588 and died in 1693. The only account of her I have read recently was a long article by Mr C.M. Grieve in *The Scots Observer* a year or two ago, but Hugh MacDiarmid has written a long poem about her beginning:

> Auld Mary Macleod in her tartan tonnag
> Has drunk her whisky and snuffed her snuff
> But the Lord has put a new song in her mouth
> – Hallelujah, that's the stuff.

But he goes on to point out that the 'new song' is no longer new and that it is time to embark on a very different course from that along which she impelled Scottish and Irish poetry – a typically feminine impulsion, abandoning the consonontal basis of the old Bardic poetry and introducing that wonderful vowel music which constitutes perhaps the most exquisitely sensuous use of words the world has ever had. All this is fully dealt with in Hyde's *Literary History of Ireland*; it was, indeed, Dr Hyde who first reclaimed Mairi Nighean Alasdair Ruaidh for the marvellous innovator she was – an achievement which, be it noted, brings her into the first class, the inventors, in Pound's scheme as set out in my first chapter.

Elsewhere Mr Grieve has urged that the time has come to reverse this influence and get back to the preceding conditions of the consonontal basis. He asks us to consider carefully the results of this 'feminisation' and the fashion in which it has led 'from the Gaelic sunshine to the Celtic twilight' – from the hard classical qualities of the ancient bards to the shadowy softness of 'Fiona Macleod' and the earlier Yeats. And in this he is, of course, in line with the newer tendencies in Irish poetry exemplified in the work of Daniel Corkery, Austin Clarke, Fred Higgins, Frank O'Connor, and others, but is significantly re-echoing in these days when we are in search of 'a new classicism' the laments that were voiced at the time of Irish bardic decay towards the end of the sixteenth century. He quotes Fearfeasa's *Mór do-ghníd daoine dhíobh féin* on the cheap cynics of his age – the scoffers at the bardic art in the Ireland of conquest and plantation: 'It is a great deal that some people make of themselves: with petty detraction, with a silly sapience, with brilliant words that yet are not clear, in quest of a name that is not to be had by them.' Or, again, O'Heffernan's equally passionate poem, *A mhic ná meabhraigh éigse*, warning his son not to study poetry: 'A vulgar doggerel – "soft" vocables with which 'tis all-sufficiency that they but barely be of even length – concoct such plainly, without excess of involution, and from that poor literary form shall thy promotion be the greater.'

But before the point of such reminders can be appreciated and the merits of the two techniques fairly weighed, one must have a full knowledge of the ancient Bardic technique and of the revolution which Mary Macleod wrought. Her place is one of cardinal significance and students ought to read Hyde's account and put themselves in possession of such accounts of her life and times, and translations of her poems, as are yet to be had, while it is to be hoped that modern Scottish scholarship will speedily do greater justice to a poetess who – in respect of her influence if not the qualities of her own work – ranks as one of the unique women (a small band!) in the whole range of literary history.

5 August 1932

VI

Scottish Gaelic poetry suffers – and has always suffered – from an over-conservatism, a stereotyping of manner and material. It is precisely this excessive traditionalism – particularly in technique – which makes its faults equal and opposite to those of Scots vernacular poetry, and suggests that these two have a great deal to teach each other if their complementary and corrective functions as parts of a single Scottish tradition can be effectively realised. The outstanding significance of Alasdair MacMhaighstir Alasdair lies in his great range, which frees him from these narrow conventions of Gaelic verse. It is one of the chief of our many lacks in Scottish books today that we have no volume of good translations of his poems, let alone any biography or adequate critical study, since with the exceptions of Dunbar and Burns he is the greatest of all Scottish poets.

About the time of the unveiling of the memorial to him in the old churchyard of Kilmory, of Arisaig, on 8 October 1927, a number of articles about him appeared in various Scottish newspapers and Gaelic periodicals, written by Liam Gille Iosa, the Hon R. Erskine of Marr, C.M. Grieve, Miss M.E.M. Donaldson and others, while since then he has been the subject of an elaborate thesis (unfortunately not yet published) for a Sorbonne doctorate; but it is unfortunate that advantage was not taken of the occasion by the writers in question and a few others to issue a collection of essays about him which would have been a truer – and more longer overdue – memorial to his genius than the bronze tablet in question. The extraordinary indifference to – or ignorance of – his value, even amongst his own countrymen, is illustrated by the fact that three-quarters of the total cost of this tablet was subscribed by a few Jacobite supporters in New Zealand! He has achieved no whit of international recognition yet; Dr Laurie Magnus's *Dictionary of European Literature* does not accord him so much as a bare mention. The status of Scottish poetry will not be effectively established – not its course seen in true perspective – till this appalling disregard is rectified.

Aodh de Blácam, in his *Gaelic Literature Surveyed*, while curtly stating to us that Alasdair MacMhaighstir Alasdair, Mary Macleod, Ian Lom, and others were 'but petty poets', does not seem to realise his relative stature either, and only gives him a single page out of the 390 of his volume, although it is equally unquestionable that he is among the half-dozen most important writers with whom it deals, and that on a basis of respective worth he should have had at least twenty pages devoted to him. 'He was the son of a clergyman', says Blácam,

> and was educated at Glasgow University. He became a schoolmaster, and in 1741 published the first dictionary of Scots Gaelic. Ten years later he published a book of Gaelic verse, which was the first native Scots Gaelic work to be printed. He had become a Catholic and had fought under Charles Edward, from the raising of the standard to the dreadful day of Culloden. One of the best poems was made on the day after Culloden, when he and his brother were hiding in a cave: a poem of defiance and undaunted hope. His 'Morag' is a curious lilting love-song, playing on the woman's name that was given to the Prince when he went disguised in woman's attire.

> *'S ioma óigear a ghabh tlachd dhiot*
> *Eadar Arcamh agus Manuinn*
> *Agus hó Mórag, na hó-ró*
>
> From the Orkneys south to Manann
> Many a man adores you dearly…
>
> as some translator has rendered the lines, catching the indented rhyme. Songs to incite the clans, and sonorous lines imploring divine blessing on the Jacobite swords, spears, axes, and other weapons, exhibit MacMhaighstir as the Homer that might have been of the epic of the last Jacobite campaign. He has love songs, too, and poems in description of scenery and of singing birds that recall the genius of Old Irish. He is the most individual, the boldest of Scottish singers. Ten editions of his poetry have appeared.

That is all, except that, passing on to other matters, Blácam says: 'Macdonald (his Anglicised name was Alexander Macdonald) was haughty, mettled, elegant, a poet recalling the Irish bards, but inspired, perhaps, more by his classical reading than by the Gaelic literary tradition.' It is curious to note that the paragraph does not so much as mention his masterpiece, 'The Birlinn of Clanranald', one of the greatest sea-poems in all literature. Nor does it even barely indicate the romance and interest of his chequered career, which should yet make the subject of an enthralling biography. Some of the details of that, and some indications of his significance in Scottish history, are afforded by Miss Donaldson in the article mentioned above. 'Just as in the wars of Montrose,' she says,

> Charles I's greatest assets in the Highlands, next to his great lieutenant, were the fierce incitements of the Bard of Keppoch, the soul-stirring and martial poems of the Clanranald Bard were of equal value to the Jacobite cause. 'The Year of Charles', 'Health of Charles', 'Song of the Prince', and 'The Ark' roused to the highest pitch the war spirit latent in every Gael, and inspired them also with the same zeal as that with which their author was aflame… Present at the raising of the Standard at Glenfinnan, it is said that he was introduced to Prince Charles, and that, when he was set on the knee of the Bard, Alexander forthwith extemporised the spirited lines known as 'Tearlach Mac Sheumais.'… Nothing is known of the actual part taken by the Clanranald Bard in the Jacobite campaign, but such privations did he endure as a hunted fugitive that after one intensely cold night Alasdair woke up to find that the side of his head that had rested on the ground had become grey. When the Act of Indemnity was passed in 1747 the poet received from Clanranald – probably as a reward for his services – the office of steward of the Isle of Canna… Not only to Alasdair MacMhaighstir Alasdair belong the honour of being the first Gaelic author

> to publish an original work, but probably he is the only Gaelic writer who ever had a volume burnt by the common hangman. This was the fate of *Ais-eiridh na Sean Chanain* (*The Resurrection of the Old Language of Alba*) in Edinburgh in 1751, because the book, published the previous year in the capital, breathed too passionate a devotion to the exiled royal house for the authorities to tolerate… It is perhaps not surprising to hear after this that the Bard was not successful in obtaining a teacher's post in Edinburgh, so once again he returned to Moidart, where he appears to have been largely dependent once more on the kindness of his chief. Clanranald gave his clansman the farm of Eignaig, high above the lonely and beautiful shores of Loch Moidart, but, unfortunately, the Bard forfeited this by a return to his savage style in poetry. His chief moved him to Arisaig, and there at Sannaig, off the alluring road that winds round Loch nan Cilltean to Rhu Arisaig, he succeeded in recovering and retaining the esteem of his neighbours. At Sannaig in 1780 the Bard died, and naturally was to have been buried, like his family, on Eilean Fhionnan. A violent storm, however, made this impossible, so his remains were laid to rest in Kilmory of Arisaig.

One gets exciting glimpses there of his versatility and turbulence, and the ups-and-downs of his variegated and adventurous career.

Now let us turn to his poems.

26 August 1932

VII

'Though it is impossible to fix the dates of Macdonald's various poems, they may be easily classified', says Magnus Maclean, 'in three groups: – (1) love songs; (2) descriptive poems; (3) patriotic and Jacobite songs.' In each category he wrote some of the best work in the whole range of Scottish poetry. With 'Mi-mholadh Moraig' an 'Cuachag an Fhasaich' in the first category; 'The Birlinn', 'The Sugar Brook', 'Hail to the Mainland', and the 'Odes to Summer and Winter' in the second, and 'Song of the Clans', 'A Call to the Highland Clans', 'Health to Charlie', 'The Year of Charles', 'Song to the Prince', 'The Ark', and the incomparable 'Morag', he produced a body of work which for diversity of kind, general excellence, and historical purpose and effect challenges comparison with that of any Scottish poet, not excepting Burns himself.

'"The Birlinn"', says Dr Maclean,

> is acknowledged on all hands to be his masterpiece, and probably the most unique production in the Gaelic language. 'No poem,' says Pattison, 'is ever spoken of in the same breath with it, except the "Coire Cheathaich" or "Ben Dorain" of Duncan Ban; and even these are perhaps not always looked on with quite the same pride; though being easier understood, and composed altogether in a more elegant style, they probably impart fully as

> much pleasure both to hearers and readers. Yet if all Gaelic poems were to be destroyed, and one only excepted from the general ruin, I believe the voices of the majority of Highlanders would fix on "The Birlinn of Clan Ranald" as that one. It is the longest poem in the language, excluding the Ossianic pieces, and has been translated by Sheriff Nicolson, Thomas Pattison, and, in part, by Professor Blackie.

None of these translations approximate even faintly to the savage exultation of the poem, its technical particularity, or its verbal magnificence and power. It is one of the greatest sea poems in European literature and is unique in its fusion of imaginative splendour, emotional gusto, and hard realism.

'Anglo-Saxon sea-poetry', says a recent essayist on 'Sea-Thoughts of Two Races',

> represents reality imaginatively, Celtic sea-poetry escapes from reality through the imagination. In the latter the centre of interest is not the voyage but the strange adventures, the wonderful sights and experiences which may be the lot of the man who ventures forth on the sea. *La race Celtique s'est fatiguée à prendre ses songes pour des réalities at à courir après ses splendides visions. L'élément essentiel de la vie poétique du Celt, c'est l'aventure, c'est-à-dire poursuite de l'inconnu, une course sans fin après l'object toujours fuyant du désir.* The different attitude towards the subject is seen when we compare the pride in ships and seamanship shown by the Anglo-Saxon poets with the casualness of the Celtic voyagers. They occasionally take some pains in preparing the coracle with 'well-stretched skins,' but having put out to sea, after a preliminary effort they seem to let the boat drift where it will or be guided by some supernatural power; 'thereafter their voyage was left alone,' and 'three days and three nights were they and found neither land nor ground' till they heard 'the voice of a wave against a shore.' It is only when the voyagers reach some fantastic shore that the imagination of the writer awakes and gives us descriptions strange, vivid, and sometimes beautiful.

This essayist supports his contention by quoting the voyages of Bran, Maelduin, Hui Corra, and others and the 'Cath Finntraga, or Battle of Ventry' – but he makes no mention of 'The Birlinn', which completely disposes of his argument, which, indeed, is based on 'Celtic Twilight' stuff, but not on many of the more characteristic elements of ancient Gaelic poetry or the work of a classic poet like Macmhaighstir. 'The Birlinn' is sheer realism, packed with intense knowledge of the sea and of seamanship to a degree far beyond what can be found in any Anglo-Saxon poem, and, indeed, in the whole literature of the sea it sustains comparison only with some of the splendid passages of the work of another Scot – Hermann [*sic*] Melville in *Moby Dick*.

Of Macmhaighstir's other two most famous poems – both very different in kind and exemplifying his amazing range – Miss M.E.M. Donaldson gives the following admirable accounts:

> On the hillside above the rugged and beautiful shore there are still to be seen the ruins of the farm (at Coire-Mhuilinn) which the Bard occupied, and beside it flows the stream of which he has so exquisitely sung in his 'Allt an t'Siucair', perhaps the most beautiful of all his poems. The poem describes in animated and appreciative language the charm of a lovely summer morning in the setting of his secluded farm. The Bard misses nothing in his walk abroad. He hears the varied songs of the birds, notes the dew glittering as diamonds on blade and leaf, the bees sucking sweetness from the flowers, and the cattle peacefully grazing. There is joy everywhere in the sunshine; the burn dances, the fish leap, the calves and kids frisk in sportive fashion, the herdsman and milkmaid are busy in unhurried labour; the ground is gemmed with flowers of every hue, and on the sea, ships, white-winged, speed on their courses. Today, except that the activities of farm-life are no more, one can go to Coire-Mhuilinn on a fine summer day and, with 'Allt an t'Siucair' in hand, find that it still perfectly pictures the scene… Of all the genuine Highland Jacobite songs, the Clanranald Bard's 'Morag' is the most famous. It is written in praise of Prince Charlie, who is cryptically represented as a maiden with flowing yellow locks, wooed by the Highlanders. 'She' is implored to return with other 'maidens', to dress the red cloth, under which simile the thrashing of English redcoats is to be understood. This song is still used in the Outer Hebrides as a waulking song by the women when fulling their home-spun tweeds.

That a poet of such calibre – with poems so full of diverse genius and so related to the course of Scottish history, Scotland's natural beauty, and our continuing political and psychological problems – should be so little known, and not yet available in adequate translations and accorded his due place in our educational system and in our culture generally, is a national scandal of a type which could happen in no other country in the world. He is beyond all question one of our three or four greatest poets and it is disgraceful to reflect on the disproportionate fame of one or two of these in relation to his comparative neglect. Nor, in the wider field of European literature, have we more than three or four poets who ought to be better known or as highly esteemed, while the character of his work, and the circumstances of its production, give him a historical value as a representative Scottish writer which is singularly lacking in one or two of the others who, on purely literary grounds, are perhaps his equals.

16 September 1932

VIII

Of the other Gaelic poets the only ones who call for more than the merest passing mention in these articles are Duncan Bàn MacIntyre, Dugald Buchanan and William Livingstone, while Donald Sinclair could have come into the same category and demanded considerably more space but for the fact that his demise (a month or so ago) is too recent to enable him to be regarded as other than a contemporary poet and so outside the reach of this series.

'What Burns is to the Lowlands of Scotland,' Robert Buchanan wrote in *The Hebrid Isles*,

> Duncan Ban is to the Highlands, and more; for Duncan never made a poem, long or short, which was not set to a tune, and he first sang them himself as he wandered like a venerable bard of old... His fame endures wherever the Gaelic language is spoken, and his songs are sung all over the civilised world. Without the bitterness and intellectual power of Burns, he possessed much of his tenderness; and as a literary prodigy, who could not even write, he is still more remarkable than Burns. Moreover, the old simple-hearted forester, with his fresh love of Nature, his shrewd insight, and his impassioned speech, seems a far completer figure than the Ayrshire ploughman, who was doubtless a glorious creative but most obtrusive in his independence. [*sic*] Poor old Duncan was never bitter. The world was wonderful, and he was content to fill a humble place in it. He had an independent mind, but was quite friendly to rank and power wherever he saw them, for after all what were they to Coire Cheathaich with its natural splendours? What was the finest robe in Dunedin to the gay clothing of the side of Ben Dorain? In the life of Burns we see the light striking through the storm-cloud, lurid, terrific, yet always light from Heaven! In the life of Duncan Ban there is nothing but a gray light of peace and purity, such as broods over the mountains when the winds are laid. Burns was the mightier poet, the greater human soul; but many who love him best, and cherish his memory most tenderly, can find a place in their hearts for Duncan Ban as well.

It is indeed unfortunate that so many lovers of Scottish poetry are largely restricted to the former and have no knowledge of the latter. He wrote beautiful love lyrics like 'Mairi bhan òg' – perhaps the finest in the Gaelic language; and Jacobite poems like 'Falkirk Field', and 'Another Ode to Falkirk' (withheld from publication during his lifetime on account of its pronounced Jacobite sentiment), but his greatest works are his nature poems, the masterpieces of which are 'Ben Dorain' and 'Coire Cheathaich'; these are essential to any anthology of the kind our country has produced. Duncan lived till his eighty-ninth year, died in Edinburgh, May 1812, and was buried in Greyfriars' Churchyard.

Dugald Buchanan (born 1716) is the greatest religious poet Scotland has produced and his poem 'The Day of Judgment' is the greatest Scottish achievement in a kind of which Scotland has been singularly destitute. 'The Skull', another masterpiece, is better known: but it lacks the 'sublime and terrible realism' of 'The Day of Judgment'.

Oh! canst Thou cast me from Thy face
Where Thou shalt never hear me cry?
Is there in hell so dark a place
As hide me from Thy piercing eye?

Canst Thou in blessedness complete
Hear Thy poor creatures' mournful tones –
Father, have pity, ease the heart
That boils the marrow in my bones!

Hear, O my God, my wretched prayer,
And hear the groans that tear my breast,
And for the sins I have to bear
Grant me, O Lord, this sole request –

When I shall weep in flaming fire
Until ten thousand years go by,
Till even torturing demons tire,
Grant then, O Lord, that I may die!

Buchanan died at Rannoch in 1768. The great majority of Scottish poets of a religious time have been mere hymn-writers or platitudinous versifiers; Buchanan alone soared to something approaching the Dantesque and his gloomy religion, his literality of interpretation and illustration and the intense, if narrow, nature of the ideas which obsessed him studded his work with passages and with many isolated lines and images of quite extraordinary power. Judged against his work, the trite moralisings which constitute the bulk of Scottish 'religious poetry' sink at once into their proper insignificance.

William Livingston was born at Gartmain in Islay, in 1808. So far, he has received extremely unjust treatment on account of his Scottish Nationalist and anti-English views, but, with the great change in Scottish opinion in recent years, is at last coming into his own. He died in Glasgow in July 1870, and was buried in Janefield Cemetery, where his admirers erected a freestone obelisk to his memory. 'Livingston', says Magnus Maclean, 'never gained breadth of view', and, as if the two things were synonymous, continues:

> He was an Anglophobe of the deepest dye. In this spirit he wrote in English a *Vindication of the Celtic Character* and a *History of Scotland*, which he tried to publish in parts, but failed to complete for lack of publishers. Five parts only appeared. From his blind, unreasoning hate of England and all things English, he was absolutely incapable of taking an impartial view of historical questions. The depopulation of his native island through changes in the tenure and use made of the land sorely exercised him. His delightful poem, *Fios thun a' Bhaird*, in which he deprecates the passing of the old order, can hardly be surpassed for its sad pathos.

Yet even Dr Maclean is forced to admit that: 'As a bard Livingston undoubtedly ranks high. The most forceful poetic personality of the Gaelic poets of the nineteenth century, this son of the muse is equally powerful in the expression of ruthless fierceness and tearful sorrow.' We are better able to see in their proper perspective today the ideas which the Anglophil Dr Maclean regarded as harmful and deplorable prepossessions on Livingston's part, and can appreciate that, whatever may be said of them on other grounds, they not only did not lessen or lower the force of his work, but were the very mainspring of his genius, while the fact that he was so different in this respect from most Scottish poets – as in certain other respects, notably the fact that he never sings of love, and is the only Highland bard who has produced a dramatic poem – give him a unique place and attach a special interest to his life and writings. The Rev. Dr Blair, in 1882, edited his poems with a memoir. Such of his work as is available in translation suffers, as did his 'Duan Geall', one of his best, of which Dr Nigel Macneill says: 'As much of its beauty consists in a sort of proverbial form of expression of which the bard was a consummate master, and in a rhythm of consonantal rhymes, much of what is powerful in the original becomes quite prosaic when rendered literally in English.'

14 October 1932

IX

To bridge over from these preceding articles and establish the deep connections underlying Scottish Vernacular and Scottish Gaelic poetry calls for a few general remarks before going on to deal with the three or four Vernacular poets who alone, of the unconscionable multitude of our Doric versifiers, seem to me to call for consideration; but it is by no means so difficult as is generally assumed by those who have no full view of both fields.

Let us first consider certain resemblances which underlie all the superficial differences of language and technique and those discrepancies in historical incidence which complicate comparison.

The first is that both Gaelic and Scottish Vernacular poetry are alike in their failure to produce long, let alone great, poems. On the whole, in this respect, Gaelic has the best of it; the Scottish Vernacular has nothing on such a high plane and so sustained as Alasdair MacMhaighstir Alasdair's 'Birlinn of Clan Ranald'. Burns's 'Tam o' Shanter', Ross's 'Helenore', Beattie's fantasy of the kelpie in Glen Finella, are all on a far lower imaginative level. But apart from mere length of poems – although the absence of sustained works of any kind in either tradition is a serious matter – the percentage of poems either in Scots or Scottish Gaelic on great subjects or in great moods is extremely small in comparison with that which obtains in the poetry of any other European country. Prosaic subject-matter, pedestrian treatment, a prevalence of fancy and a lack of high imagination, an eschewing of those themes which in all literatures have contributed most to the staple of great poetry, characterise both traditions.

Both are short-winded, local in their appeal, deplorably domesticated. The extent to which both derived directly from 'life' and not from 'literature' is equally notable, and accounts for the relative absence of phases – of periods characterised by different styles and informed by spiritual changes. They exhibit a remarkable sameness of manner and matter through the centuries; they have undergone little or no evolution. They are both similarly constrained in range – confined to a few 'kinds', and lacking many of the departments of poetry which appertain to all fully developed traditions. They are alike in their lack of traffic – action and interaction, influences – with other literatures.

Exceedingly few poets in either – and then only to a very limited extent – manifest any development in their output. With most of them anything they wrote might have been written so far as the character of the poetry is concerned at any other period of their careers as easily as at the particular date when it was produced. Little or no interest attaches to the psychology *qua* poets of any of them. They had no intellectual or artistic growth. Just as 'phases' are absent from both traditions as a whole so are they absent from the output of the individual poets. Most of the poets, too, produced no considerable body of work – probably because they had neither the stimulus of personal growth nor the helps towards development they might have derived in an atmosphere of more varying activity. If a country is happy that has no history, a literature assuredly is not – it needs its vying coteries, its reactions of one generation against another, its phases of tradition and of experiment. Exceedingly few of the poets in either developed any personal flavour – they did not 'find themselves', but kept for he most part within established traditions (if conventions so humble and unenterprising can be dignified with that title) that if the bulk either of Scots or Scots Gaelic poems could be put before a competent critic who had no previous knowledge of either literature he would be exceedingly hard put to it by all the devices of 'textual criticism' and internal evidence to distinguish the work of one author from that of another. A few topical allusions, the chronology or geographical distribution of word usages and the like might enable him to split them into certain groups; but the kind of the poetry – no!

How is this to be accounted for? Why should Scottish poetry – equally in Gaelic and the Vernacular – be singular compared with the poetry of any other people in this respect? It is not as if we were considering only a limited period – say a century or half-a-century – during which a single convention might well hold unchallenged sway, especially in so small a country. Where a convention has so held sway elsewhere the ultimate *kulturkampf* has only been the greater – and between the supremacy of the one and its overthrow by the other the interval has seldom been so long as fifty, let alone a hundred years. Nor has it been with us the iron rule of a dominant convention but rather the absence of any convention at all – the failure of any convention to emerge and hence the continuance of a natural anti-literary output.

It is this natural, anti-literary character – this dependence on 'life' rather than 'literature' – this lack of artistic autonomy and inner developments which has prevented Scottish poetry challenging the course of affairs – which has made it influenced by, but never a real influence on, our history – and hence, despite all the linguistic and technical differences of Gaelic and Scots Vernacular verse, has given the overwhelming bulk of the poetry in either the same appalling accessibility to dull moralisings, cheap sentiment, and the attributes of the kailyaird generally. This resemblance overrides all the superficial differences so completely – and has led both to a culmination which is better described as a collapse – as to show that they have shared a common fate which transcends their divisibility into either Gaelic or Scots Vernacular and depends upon factors which are national, and peculiar to the Scottish nation as a whole. As to the future if a failure to realise their relationships as parts of a national whole has served both Gaelic and Scots Vernacular poetry so ill in the past and brought both to a like end in brainless doggerel, an insistence upon what they have (or lack) in common now, rather than upon non-literary considerations of race or language and the like, may serve both in better stead, no matter how belatedly.

16 December 1932

X – WILLIAM DUNBAR

Surprise is expressed in certain quarters at the abandonment of Burns and return to Dunbar of the younger writers associated today with the new tendencies in Scots Literature.

> Dunbar was an efficient versifier and breathed freely on many places of poetic inspiration, but he had neither the warm-hearted humanitarianism of Burns nor the broad-minded humanity of Sir Walter Scott. Reading over 'The Flyting of Dunbar and Kennedie' one tries hard to repress the suspicion that, after all, Kennedy got the better of the argument, and that Dunbar was made to look rather small. It is Kennedy who starts out as the protector of Scottish national pride, and it is Dunbar who is made to appear rather anglified, and contemptuous of his own people. Burns is nearly always a big man; Dunbar is almost all the time what Kennedy called him – a dwarf – and often one feels tempted to echo 'Ignorant elf'.

The best that can be said of observations such as these is that they are typically Scottish – typical of those characteristics in Scottish life which have so gravely restricted our literary development and against which, necessarily, the younger writers today are reacting vigorously. If Dunbar disliked the Gaels so have many very characteristic Scottish types since his day; if he preferred the English so have a very large proportion of subsequent Scotsmen; and it is worth noting that while this criticism of Dunbar appears in a Scottish paper, one of the leading English literary weeklies emphasises his true qualities and in particular insists upon the absurdity of classifying him as a Chaucerian. 'Nothing', says this writer,

> can curb the dreary prolixity of the writers commonly known as the English Chaucerians. 'The moral Gower', Lydgate, and the rest give a new meaning to the term unreadable. But there in Scotland Dunbar never writes lengthy poems and scarcely ever one that flags. The English Chaucerians drone and drone; Dunbar is awake, active, concentrated except when deliberately digressing into Rabelaisian or other extravagances. The English Chaucerians have none of the salt of Chaucer's humour, none of the April freshness of his poetry; but though we shall not, except to a small extent in Henryson, find the master's temper in the Scottish Chaucerians, we have in Dunbar a poet as awake as Chaucer. His mere variety of stanzaic form marks him out as a master of technique.

All this is admirably said but it is necessary to join issue with the general anti-Dunbar and pro-Burns attitude so common in Scotland on other grounds. The fact that Dunbar was Anglophil means little; the political situation has changed since his day; his expression is none the less racily Scottish, nor are his qualities of satire and humour any less in the direct line of the Scottish tradition and very different indeed from anything appertaining to English literature. To suggest that he is less Scottish than Burns on account of his anti-Gaelic and pro-English proclivities is on a level with suggesting that Scotland ought to be prouder of, say, Joseph Laing Waugh than of Norman Douglas, or of Joe Corrie than of R.B. Cunninghame Graham. This refusal to accept purely literary standards has cost Scottish Literature a great deal. Part and parcel of it is the insistence on Burns's 'warm-hearted humanitarianism' and Scott's 'broad-minded humanity'. These have done very little for Scottish literature as such – indeed the extent to which attention has been focused on these kinds of subject-matter is intimately related to the lack of development in Scottish Literature. The tendency to think that great writers must also be great men – to consider their moral qualities of more consequence than their artistic abilities – is to be deplored. A great proportion of the world's best literature has been produced not by exemplary but by scandalous characters, and if Dunbar was petty-minded he is in the good company of many famous writers. At all events it was imperative that our younger writers, if there was to be any Scots Literary Revival, should make a stand against this sort of thing and insist for a change on the relative importance of form to substance – of the manner of saying rather than the matter. A re-concentration on pure technique was long over-due and in this connection young writers had nothing to learn from Burns and a great deal to learn from Dunbar. Not only in this respect but in others Dunbar is actually far more modern than Burns; much of Burns's work is hopelessly dated – eighteenth-century conventionalism, the expression of types of completely uninteresting or even repellent today. A still more important fact is that the unbalanced enthusiasm for Burns has obscured a proper view of the distinctive Scots tradition as a whole, of which, when all is said, he is only a part, and a part not to be properly understood unless in relation to the whole. Burns gave no new impetus to Scottish poetry; he was the terminus of a particular line of development. Nothing further can be done in that direction. Young writers were forced to look elsewhere for their outlet. It is not surprising that they were forced back on Dunbar – the more especially since Burns's great popular vogue is scarcely more disproportionate than the corresponding neglect of Dunbar. Dunbar when all is said and done is by no means so relatively small a poet as to warrant the comparative neglect to which he has been subjected any more than Burns is so great as to justify his monopoly of public interest. It was high time that the balance was being redressed. It was also high time that issue was being joined with the particular attitude to poetry predominantly associated with the Burns Cult. Dunbar was not only a lesser poet than Burns, but he was a very different poet – and it was time for Scottish poetry to shift its concern to other kinds of poetry than are to be found in the Burns corpus. The movement away from Burns and back to Dunbar was not an adequately studied one – it was at first largely instinctive, a defensive gesture of the spirit of the Scots Muse. The lack of proper attention to Dunbar and to Scots literature and language generally in our schools handicapped these young writers at the outset; so did the lack of competently-edited moderately-priced editions of the Scots classics; so did the chaos in Scots philological studies. The last-mentioned is being made good now by the dictionaries of Professor Craigie and Dr William Grant; so is the second by such volumes as Dr W. Mackay Mackenzie's Porpoise Press edition of Dunbar; a little improvement in regard to the first is slowly filtering through, but the organised Burns Movement could have secured the necessary changes here if it had been imbued with a proper attitude to the matter – an attitude in keeping with that which would undoubtedly have been Burns's own attitude. That may come yet; if it doesn't, the Burns Movement itself will pay the penalty of its indifference. In the meantime, despite all the handicaps, the effort to re-envisage Scots literature as a whole, as a continuous and distinctive tradition, is making small but yet vital headway and has already yielded better results than the whole dreary period of post-Burnsian imitation.

17 February 1933

XI – William Dunbar (continued)

With a side-reference to a likeness between Dunbar and Byron, to which I shall return when I am elucidating later the continuity of the distinctively Scottish vein which makes not only Byron so Scottish, but John Davidson so much more so than R.L. Stevenson, for example, a writer in *The Times Literary Supplement* stresses the difference in excitement, in tempo, of Dunbar and Chaucer with whom Dunbar is so frequently and fallaciously bracketed as if he were a mere Scottish follower of the latter.

As this writer points out, Dunbar's methods testify to this radical difference.

Even his pentameters are dynamic, rapid, like Byron's in *Don Juan*

> Thow callis the rethory with thy golden lippis:
>   Na, glowrand, gaipand fule, thow art begyld,
> Thow are bot gluntow with thy giltin hippis,
>   That for the lounry mony a leish has fyld...

But it is those metres which combine the regularity of French versification with the excited crunching of the old alliterative verse which make the difference between Dunbar and Chaucer as metrists and between the moods of their music. It is the excited rhythms, the tom-tom alliterations of Dunbar that make him a poet worth having in such an edition as this (Dr Mackay Mackenzie's), cheap as such editions go, handy and pleasantly printed. Skelton has had his new coat, two or three of them indeed in the last ten years. And at least as important as Skelton is Dunbar, important for the need of the times. The English poetry of the twentieth century seems to be seeking further and further back for the rhythms it wants to hear and speak. Mr Eliot went back to the blank verse of the late Elizabethan drama, and in Mr Auden's work there is obviously a catching up again of the alliterative metres which have always been a subtle influence behind English verse, but which have seldom since the sixteenth century been a power: –

> Which of you waking early and watching daybreak
> Will not hasten in heart, handsome, aware of wonder...

These words would have sounded like a strange piping dialect to Dunbar or Langland, but the drumming of them would have had immediate meaning.

This is what is really behind the return to Dunbar. Scottish music has as much to gain as English from a like recapture of its older rhythms; but in content and form and quintessential spirit, too, it has lessons to learn from Dunbar still which are not for the English, and cannot be dissociated from the Scots Vernacular medium, for, as the same critic says, '*pace* Mrs Rachel Annand Taylor', 'There is a good deal in Dunbar which is unmistakably Scottish. In the poem beginning "In secreit place this hynder nycht", for example, Dunbar is almost Burns at his best, and we know were the best Burns came from. And in the matter of Latinized diction, the "aureate" diction, Dunbar is characteristically a Scot, though Henryson is even more Latinized.'

Another writer has effectively focussed and put into their right perspective other aspects of his work, which show that despite Chaucer's influence the independent Scottish character remained, and that, after all, it was not a question of wholesale derivation from the English, but of a give-and-take between the two literatures.

Dunbar's claim to be the greatest poet between Chaucer and Spenser rests on his skill as an artist, the remarkable ease and felicity with which he handles metre, the variety and beauty of his verse forms. He was a poet of splendid capacity, but, save in the matter of prosody, without literary conscientiousness; almost all his poems are occasional; they preserve a passing mood or a striking incident; he never collected his powers in one supreme effort, never enshrined in a single poem all the fine qualities of his art; his poems show single facets of his genius, but no one poem adequately represents him. His versatility is surprising; it is difficult to recognise in the 'Dance of the Seven Deadly Sins' with its sardonic glee and reckless abandon, the courtly poet of 'The Thrissil and The Rose', with its jewelled compliments; or to associate the author of the 'Lament for the Makaris' with the ribald 'Dance in the Queen's Chamber'. That Chaucer's influence, so paralysing in its effect on his English followers, should have been so fruitful in Scotland, is *perhaps* explained by the difference of race and literary tradition. The Scottish poets had their own way of seeing life, and they had behind them in literature the homely historical romance of Barbour and Blind Harry with its intimate human interest, and also the Northern English and Scottish alliterative poems, rich in colour and in vocabulary; these things modified Chaucer's influence, they helped the poets to study and imitate his work without losing the individual and racial qualities which are essential elements in their poetry.

This is excellently said, and there is no 'perhaps' about it.

James Maclaren, 14 April 1933

New Bearings in English Poetry

It is no valid criticism of Mr F.R. Leavis's *New Bearings in English Poetry* (Chatto and Windus) to complain that it is 'for first-class passengers only', and exclusively concerned with modernist and 'difficult' poetry to the complete exclusion of all that most readers regard as poetry at all. Yeats is put in his place, the value of his later and far harder and more intellectual poems being appropriately emphasised in comparison with his earlier romantic escapist work, though whether Mr Leavis is right when he says that 'No Englishman could have profited by the sources of strength open to Mr Yeats as an Irishman and no such source is open to anyone now' is very questionable. Scotland and Wales may yet afford such sources to Scottish and Welsh poets; Ireland is continuing to do it in poets like Austin Clarke and F.R. Higgins to whom Mr Leavis makes no reference although their work gets clear of the 'Celtic Twilight' and into the sunlight of ancient Irish classical art; and England did it to some extent in the work of Charles Doughty, while in his notes on the relationship between politics and poetry and the abandonment since Skelton of 'native English' modes

Mr Robert Graves has perhaps indicated other sources which may be utilised by poets yet.

This is not to quarrel, however, with Mr Leavis's next remark: 'No serious poet could propose to begin where Mr Yeats began.' He is right when he contends that

> Poetry matters because of the kind of poet who is more alive than other people, more alive in his own age. He is, as it were, at the most conscious point of the race in his time. He is the point, as Mr I.A. Richards says, at which the growth of the mind shows itself. The potentialities of human experience in any age are realised only by a tiny minority, and the important poet is important because he belongs to this (and has also, of course, the power of communication).

The substance of Mr Leavis's book is accordingly confined to T.S. Eliot, Ezra Pound, and Gerard Manley Hopkins. Walter de la Mare and the Georgians are dismissed with scant courtesy; the Sitwells, we are told, 'belong to publicity rather than to poetry'. But it is unfortunate alike that Mr Leavis should devote considerable space at the end of his book to young Mr Ronald Bottrall and have nothing to say of such poets as Mr C. Day Lewis, Miss Laura Riding, Mr Robinson Jeffers, Mr Norman Macleod, and others, who better deserve mention in this specific connection.

'A Poem', says 'A.E.' in his 'Song and Its Foundations', 'is the most intricately organised form of thought, and in the coming into being of poetry there is the greatest intensity of consciousness.' 'When a man complains', says Mr L.A. Strong,

> that a poem is unintelligible, he usually means that he personally cannot understand it; and that is quite a different pair of shoes. The ordinary reader (not always, by any means, the man who has read no poetry) cannot get out of his head the idea that it is a poet's business to make his meaning clear to *him*. If he has read poetry, he complains of contemporary poets. If he has once or twice looked at it, he complains of all poetry. The assailant of contemporary poetry usually says he can understand the *great* poets (of the past) but that these modern fellows, who make their stuff as obscure and ugly as they can, have only themselves to thank that he does not read them. The answer to him, as Miss Edith Sitwell has so untiringly and courageously pointed out, is that he understands the poets of past centuries (if and when he does understand them) because the community to which he belongs has had a hundred, two hundred, three hundred years in which to become accustomed to their vocabulary and ideas: or to accept thoughtlessly and 'on authority' the repeated assertion of the few that So-and-so and Such-and-such were great poets. The contemporaries of these poets (except the very few) did not understand them, and raised the same

objections which he is raising today against their successors. This is a matter of history. The reader of today who quotes Keats and Shelley against contemporary poets is forgetting that none were more vilified in their own day than these two poets. The reader of today may understand Keats and Shelley; but it is the wildest arrogance to assume that they are responsible. If they did not trouble to make their meaning clear to the mass of their contemporaries, it is unlikely that they were looking down the centuries for him. In the realm of abstract thought, of beauty, with which the lives of ninety per cent and more need never practically be concerned, the pioneer may wait a very long time for understanding.

The merit of Mr Leavis's book is its concentration on contemporary English pioneering of this kind at its most difficult, and his detailed commentaries on poems like Eliot's *Waste Land*, Pound's 'Hugh Selwyn Mauberley', and Hopkins's amazing technical inventiveness and verbal power are extremely lucid and illuminating, while his grip of the potentialities of these new tendencies and his analysis of the current situation in poetry generally could hardly be bettered. Readers who find difficulty with any of these three poets should immediately repair to this excellent book. In conclusion Mr Leavis says:

> It does indeed look as if respect for poetry were mainly a vestigial habit. All traces of it, almost, have disappeared in the vast masses catered for by the popular press. The ordinary cultivated reader is ceasing to be able to read poetry. In self-defence amid the perpetual avalanche of print he has had to acquire reading habits that incapacitate him when the signals for unaccustomed and subtle responses present themselves. He has, moreover, lost the education that in the past was provided by tradition and social environment. Even the poetry of simple sensibility, if it is not superficially familiar, seems incomprehensible to him. And the more important poetry of the future is unlikely to be simple. The important works of today, unlike those of the past, tend to appeal only at the highest level of response, which only a tiny minority can reach, instead of at a number of levels. On the other hand, the finer values are ceasing to be a matter of even conventional concern for any except the minority capable of the highest level. Everywhere below, a process of standardisation, mass-production, and levelling-down goes forward, and civilisation is coming to mean a solidarity achieved by the exploitation of the most readily released responses.

This – the short-circuiting of human consciousness – should be a matter of urgent concern to teachers in particular, and Mr Leavis's book may be specially recommended to them.

A.K.L., 23 September 1932

The Significance of Calvalcanti

Ezra Pound – the most many-sided and diversely influential spirit in the world of contemporary poetry – has crowned one line of his creative interests by giving us a magnificent volume, *Guido Calvalcanti Rime* (Genova: Edizione Marsano S.A.), which, together with his friend T.S. Eliot's *Dante*, in Messrs Faber & Faber's 'Poets on Poets' series, immediately takes rank as one of the all-too-few contributions in English to the study of Italian literature of any real value. It is in a sense a counterblast to Mr Eliot's book, and still more so to the conventional British view exemplified by Dr Laurie Magnus's declaration that Dante 'was aware, by the insight of genius, that the Sicilian nest of singing birds' (of whom Calvalcanti was the greatest) 'was destined to be surpassed by the native notes in the Tuscan "vulgar tongue", which he was founding by his critical studies and his own magnificent example', and that he did surpass it. Or, as Dante himself put it: –

> So has one Guido from the other taken
> The glory of our tongue, and he perchance
> Is born, who from the nest shall chase them both,

the 'he perchance' being, of course, Dante himself, and the two Guidos, Calvalcanti and Guinicelli respectively.

These opposing attitudes are especially worth the close consideration of Scottish students today, when the issues bound up with each are variants of the vital elements involved in the reconsiderations of the past, present, and potentialities of Scottish culture which are proceeding today. There can be no disputing the importance – and the significance for Scotland of a thorough understanding and local application of it – of Dante's *De Vulgari Eloquentia*, rightly characterised by Saintsbury as 'a document of the very highest value', but in one of the poems of his, *To Circumjack Cencrastus*, Mr Hugh M'Diarmid leaves the two diametrically opposed attitudes to it from a Scottish standpoint balanced in a most equivocal fashion, and it is well to have it off-set by Pound's insistence that:

> The mediaeval poets brought into poetry something which had not been, or not been in any so marked and developed degree in the poetry of the troubadors. It is still more important for any one wishing to have well-balanced critical appreciation of poetry in general to understand that this quality, or this assertion of value, has not been in poetry *since*; and that the English 'philosophical' and other philosophical poets have not produced a comparable *Ersatz*... They (the Troubadours) are opposed to a form of stupidity not limited to Europe, and a belief that the body is evil. This more or less masochistic and hell-breeding is always accompanied by bad and niggled sculpture (Angoulême or Bengal). Gandhi today is incapable

of making the dissociation that it is not the body but its diseases and infirmities which are evil. The same statement is true of mind, the infections of the mind being no less hideous than those of physique. In fact, a man's toothache annoys himself, but a fool annoys the whole company. Even for epidemics, a few cranks may spread wider malefaction than anything short of plague universal. This invention of hells for one's enemies, and messy confusion in sculpture, is always symptomatic of supineness, bad hygiene, bad physique (possibly envy); even the diseases of mind, they do not try to cure as such, but devise hells to punish, not to heal, the individual sufferer. Against these European-Hindoos, we find the 'clean mediaeval line' as distinct from mediaeval niggle.

In a word, Calvalcanti as against Dante! Guido's canzone, *Donna mi Prega*,

may have appeared about as soothing to the Florentine of A.D. 1290 as conversation about Tom Paine, Marx, Lenin and Bucharin would today in a Methodist bankers' board meeting in Memphis, Tenn. The teaching of Aristotle had been banned in the University of Paris in 1213. This prejudice had been worn down during the century, but Guido shows, I think, no regard for any one's prejudice; we may trace his ideas to Averroes, Avicena, he does not definitely proclaim any heresy but he shows leanings, towards not only the proof by reason, but towards the proof by experiment. I do not think that he swallowed Aquinas. It may be impossible to prove that he had heard of Roger Bacon, but the whole canzone is easier to understand if we suppose, or at least, one finds a considerable interest in the speculation, that he had read Grosseteste on the Generation of Light. In all of which he shows himself much more 'modern' than his young friend, Dante Alighieri, *qui était diablement dans les idées reçues*, and whose shock is probably recorded in the passage of Inferno X., where he finds Guido's father and father-in-law paying for their mental exertions. In general, one may conclude that the conversation in the Calvalcanti-Uberti family was more stimulating than in Tuscan bourgeois and ecclesiastical circles of the period.

There can be no question as to which of these two types of conversation Scotland needs. The open, speculative, experimental mind, full of intellectual interests, abreast with the times, is the desideratum of the Scottish Renaissance movement, not Dante's 'looking forward backwards'; and what Pound has to say of 'hell-making' has a peculiar relevance to our Scottish situation in these days when we are freeing ourselves of the curse of Calvinism, and, more especially, when some of the more active minds amongst us have seized upon the implication of Major Douglas's new economics in their challenge to the whole system of 'rewards and punishments', and their insistence upon the economic insanity of poverty in the midst of plenty, and drudgery within the potentiality of the Leisure State.

This admirably produced book, equipped with full Italian text, English translations, bibliography, photographic facsimiles, explanatory essays and an elaborate apparatus of notes, exemplifies anew the rightness of Guido's claim when he wrote: –

> Thou mayest go assured, my Canzone,
> Whither thou wilt, for I have so adorned thee
> That praise shall rise to greet thy reasoning
> Mid all such folk as have intelligence;
> To stand with any else, thou'st no desire.

A.L., 10 February 1933

Fish in Scottish Poetry

'Fishing', says Mr John Buchan in one of the notes to *The Northern Muse*,

> which in England has had a literary atmosphere since Dame Juliana Berners, did not acquire one in Scotland till Scott's prose and the songs of Thomas Tod Stoddart and George Outram. So I will supplement my tiny collection with Meg Dod's *Apologia*, which every angler should have by heart, and a taste of Zachary Boyd's preposterous ichthyology. The first is from the opening chapter of *St Ronan's Well* – Meg on the life of the fisherman. The second is from Boyd's *The English Academie*, in MS in the library of Glasgow University: –

> God's might so peopled hath the sea
> With fish of divers sort,
> That men therein may clearly see
> Great things for their comfort.
>
> There is such great varietie
> Of fishes of all kind,
> That it were great impietie
> God's hand there not to find.
>
> The Puffen Torteuse, and Thorneback,
> The Scillop and the Goujeon,
> The Shrimpe, the Spit-fish, and the Sprat,
> The Stock-fish and the Sturgeon;
>
> The Torteuse, Tench, and Tunnyfish,
> The Sparling and the Trout;
> And Herring, for the poor man's dish,
> Is all the land about.

The Groundling, Gilt-Head, and the Crab,
    The Gurnard, Cockle, Oyster,
The Cramp-fish and also the Sea-Dog,
    The Crefish and the Conger;

The Periwinkle and Twinfish –
    It's hard to count them all;
Some are for oyle, some for the dish;
    The greatest is the whale!

In literature, too, the whale is the greatest, for it produced a great prose masterpiece, *Moby Dick; or, The White Whale*, by Hermann [*sic*] Melville, an American writer of Scots descent; while the Biblical story of Jonah and the whale has had an exceptional attraction for contemporary Scottish writers, exemplified in the play by James Bridie and the poems by Edwin Muir and W.D. Cocker on that subject.

English poetry has in this, as in practically all directions, completely outdistanced Scots poetry in particularity and fullness of detail, and we have nothing to compare either with Rupert Brooke's poem on 'The Fish':

In a cool curving world he lies
And ripples with dark ecstasies.
The kind luxurious lapse and steal
Shapes all his universe to feel
And know and be; the clinging stream
Closes his memory, glooms his dream,
Who lips the roots o' the shore, and glides
Superb on unreturning tides.
Those silent waters weave for him
A fluctuant mutable world and dim,
Where wavering masses bulge and gape
Mysterious, and shape to shape
Dies momently through whorl and hollow,
And form and line and solid follow
Solid and line and form to dream
Fantastic down the eternal stream;
An obscure world, a shifting world,
Bulbous, or pulled to thin, or curled,
Or serpentine, or driving arrows,
Or serene buildings, or March narrows,

or any of the many splendid pictures of fish life in the poems of Edmund Blunden. But the tradition is an old and fully developed one in English poetry, and we remember many such an exquisite vignette as Tennyson's

They vanished, panic-stricken, like a shoal
Of darting fish that on a summer morn
Adown the crystal dykes at Camelot
Come slipping o'er their shadows on the sand,
But if a man who stands upon the brink
But lift a shining hand against the sun
There is not left the twinkle of a fin
Betwixt the cressy islets white in flower.

As distinct from sporting or humorous poetry there is little serious poetry about fish in our Scottish literature. A few images like Mark Alexander Boyd's 'Lichter nor a dauphin with her fin', and Burns references in 'Tam Samson's Elegy' to

the stately sawmont,
And trouts bedropped wi' crimson hail
And eels weel kenned for souple tail,

and John Buchan's *Fisher Jamie* are all, until we come to Hugh MacDiarmid, who has written of a diseased salmon in one of his fine earlier lyrics, and in a recent long poem not only excels Zachary Boyd's catalogue quoted above, but manifests a thorough knowledge of all the fishes and crustacea of the Moray Firth. Compare the following verses with Zachary Boyd's – and remember that here the ichthyology is absolutely accurate: –

Wha kent ocht o' fish alang that grey coast,
Save herring and haddock and cod and a wheen mair
That folk could eat – the only test applied?
Tam saw and studied day after day there
The Sandsucker and the Blue-Striped Wrasse,
Six kinds o' Gobies, the Saury Pike,
Yarrell's Bleny, and the Silvery Gade
(Lang lost to science), and scores o' the like.

The Bonito, the Tunny, the Sea-Perch, the Ruffe,
The Armed Bull-head, the Wolf-fish, and the Scad,
The Power Cod and the Whiting Pout,
The Twaite Shad and the Alice Shad,
The Great Forked Beard, the Torsk, the Brill,
The Glutinous Hag, the Starry Ray,
Muller's Topknot, and the Unctuous Sucker,
– These, and deemless ithers cam' his way.

A great deal of fish-life, and water-life of all kinds, seems to have come Mr MacDiarmid's way, and apart from a catalogue-poem such as the above, he frequently rises in his references to these 'denizens of the deep' to higher kinds of poetry, as when he writes of Tam that

> Lang by his douce fireside he'd sit
> Studyin' an Equoreal Needle-Fish
> Ane o' his lassies fund; or watchin'
> An anceus or ensirus in a dish
> Wi' a care that took in ilka move
> ... o' these peerie things,

or of how he

> frequented the haunts
> O' the Leptoclinum – that green Ascidian –
> And Drummond's Echiodon, and often longed
> To traverse the untrodden caves of the deep
> For the inconceivable things wi' which they thronged.

James Maclaren, 18 August 1933

English in the Melting Pot

It is not surprising that in some of his recent long poems Mr Hugh MacDiarmid should have turned from his preoccupation with 'Synthetic Scots' to a little experimentation with 'Synthetic English'; since most of the greater creative artists writing in English in recent times have been driven to one form or another of verbal experimentation – witness Hardy, Meredith, Coventry Patmore, Gerard Manley Hopkins, James Joyce – while others who have practically confined themselves to the orthodox vocabulary of 'King's English' have been compelled to complain of its 'anaemia', of the difficulty of doing new creative work in it. Only a very tiny proportion of the words listed in any ordinary popular English dictionary are part of our ordinary literary language, and since all these words represent definite shades of meaning, it follows that the non-use of nine-tenths of them represents an equivalent circumscription of the subject-matter of literature and of the psychological, musical, and other effects at which it aims. Why should an endeavour not be made to treble or quadruple our ordinary vocabulary? If an important body of English writers – constituting a sort of equivalent of the French Academy – were to set themselves to the task, there would surely be in the course of a few years a better approximation of our usual linguistic medium to the ever-increasing complexities of differentiation in modern knowledge and the bottle-neck of signification which insists that all these new shades of meaning shall pass through the narrow limits of the established canon of our speech or, as the only alternative, be relegated to the limbo of specialist terminologies which are not to be 'understanded of the people', and are therefore useless for literary purposes, would be destroyed. Why should only the merest fraction of the resources of our language be used? Why should all writers – whether for the cultured public or for the big uncultured public – depend upon substantially the same vocabulary, and, eschewing all but a thousand or so of the scores of thousands of available terms which do not overlap but denote separate things, make this limited list of approved words serve all their very different purposes? Is it not a case of an equivalent to 'poetic diction', and is it not high time the orthodox vocabulary was demolished for the artificial and restricting convention it is?

Whatever may be the answer to these important questions, it is interesting to observe that they raise problems with which our greater creative writers are more and more insistently confronted, and a few notes on the diverse ways in which a few of these have tackled the issues involved, and the reasons behind their verbal departures, may be useful. Of Coventry Patmore, Professor Ifor Evans says:

> His themes were unusual, and even when his vocabulary was simple the words were often fashioned into such strange symbols and thoughts that his meaning was difficult to unravel. Though no word is strange, the content cannot be revealed without some knowledge of Patmore's whole philosophy. In a few of the poems Patmore uses unusual words ('shaw', 'photosphere', 'prepense-occulted', 'draff'), but although the vocabulary is more involved than in *The Angel*, difficulties arising directly out of vocabulary are infrequent.

Let us turn to George Meredith.

> Meredith's poetry grew intricate in his endeavour to express these new elements of thought. He develops a vocabulary, individual, unexplained, and often uncouth. 'Yaffles on a chuckle skim' is his method of describing the laughing cry of the green wood-pecker. 'Heaven a place of winging tons' is his description of the primeval cosmos. Such examples are not difficult in themselves; they suggest merely an individual approach to vocabulary, simple in its elements but fanciful and involved in its effects. Combined with these difficulties of phrase are found almost every possible grammatical inversion. Beyond all these complexities lie Meredith's specialised philosophical vocabulary and his use of allegory. 'Heart', 'Brain', 'Blood', 'Common-Sense', 'Comedy', all represent newly-devised concepts, and their full meaning is only revealed when they are studied in relationship to his whole thought. The value of Meredith's poetical method is difficult to estimate. Occasionally it seems to be a mere wantonness in words. As in the novels, he sometimes creates deliberately difficult passages, signposts for the dull-witted to proceed no farther, so in his poetry he appears to delight in verbal convolutions. Such an exercise in dexterity is intellectual revelry, a harlequinade of the mind. These metaphysical fan-

> cies account, however, for but a small part of Meredith's vocabulary: the real source of difficulty is more deep-rooted. He has related his spiritual affirmations to all that knowledge and experience have shown him of life, and demanded not unnaturally a fresh vocabulary for their poetic expression. Consequently the perplexing elements, once they have been unravelled, render a rich yield of thought which could not have been otherwise fashioned. They serve, too, to colour the philosophical poetry with an atmosphere not inappropriate to its content, a suggestion of quick energy, violent at times and explosive, but never inert. It is the poetical counterpart of the torrential eloquence of Carlyle.

Take Thomas Hardy:

> In vocabulary, too, Hardy is individual; he has revalued words for himself, but his selection adds no sudden revelation of verbal beauty to his poetry. Strange words intrude significantly but frequently with harshness. Words such as 'adze', 'cusp', 'ogee', though most of them have been used in poetry before, are employed by Hardy. Apart from this architectural vocabulary one finds other groups of hard, unusual words in Hardy's poetry. Such words as 'lewth', 'leazes', 'dumble-dores', 'spuds', 'cit', 'wanzing', and many others. Poetic diction, in its more rhetorical and decorative phases, he consciously avoids. The total effect of his vocabulary is that of expressiveness and dignity without sensuous beauty. His vocabulary is, in one instance, impelled by the requirements of an experience that is new to poetry. He sees man frequently as a determinist sees him, the helpless plaything of forces outside himself. To express this view of the world poetically Hardy is forced to use words such as 'automaton', 'foresightlessness', 'mechanise', 'fautocine', 'artistries in circumstance', 'junctive law'. These words are not new in themselves, but their application to human life suggests new angles of vision.

Turn to – any significant modern English writer you like. They are all doing the same sort of thing. The most comprehensive innovator of this sort is James Joyce; in poetry, the most successful Gerard Manley Hopkins. And why should there not be an individual approach to words as to anything else? Is there any virtue in adherence to stereotyped diction? Are there not worse things, even when they are no more than that, than such exercises in dexterity, intellectual revelries, harlequinades of the mind?

The verse of Mr MacDiarmid's I had in mind when I began this article is a very simple and straightforward description of one of the Shetland Islands, rendering with perfect exactness not only its exact coloration but its physical structure of shingle and peatland. It begins as follows: –

> In shades of lastery and filemot and gridelin,
> Stammel and perse, our chesil and turbary lie.

James Maclaren, 25 August 1933

The Drowned Man

The Drowned Man is one of the most important characters in English poetry, in which he occupies a place out of all proportion to the incidence of death by drowning in our mortality statistics. And yet if the question were put in an examination paper how many students would be able to cite and compare half a dozen of the best examples of passages dealing with the drowned man? I propose to give a few here, but do not pretend to have made any exhaustive collection of them, and readers may well be able to provide still more interesting quotations relevant to this subject than I have chanced to hit upon. Death by drowning has perhaps a peculiar pathos which accounts for the relative frequency and power with which it has been taken as a subject for poems; and of course the symbolical possibilities of the theme are infinite. Apart from that, just as a place where a suicide has taken place often becomes a regular venue for suicides, so much poetry is the imitation of past models, and a great deal of the poetry that deals with the Drowned Man is undoubtedly in direct descent from the first poem which dealt effectively with this subject. It may be added that in this respect, as in most others, Scots poetry is extremely poor in comparison with English poetry. Only two examples from the former occur to me at the moment of writing. The first of these is from Logan's 'Braes of Yarrow':

> He promised me a wedding-ring –
> The wedding-day was fixed tomorrow –
> Now he is wedded to his grave,
> Alas, his watery grave, in Yarrow!
>
> They sought him east, they sought him west,
> They sought him all the forest through;
> They only saw the cloud of night,
> They only heard the roar of Yarrow.

And my other example deals with the same haunted stream, and is from the anonymous 'Willy Drowned in Yarrow':

> She sought him up, she sought him down,
> She sought him braid and narrow;
> Syne, in the cleaving of a craig,
> She found him drowned in Yarrow.

But these two examples show very little – though within its narrow limits very effective – variation; and have nothing of the peculiarity, the precise detail, of the best English specimens.

In English poetry I would begin with Shakespeare's immortal 'Sea Dirge':

Full fathoms five thy father lies;
Of his bones are coral made;
Those are pearls that were his eyes;
Nothing of him that doth fade
But doth suffer a sea-change
Into something rich and strange.
Sea-nymphs hourly ring his knell:
Hark! now I hear them –
Ding, dong, bell.

Second on my list comes Milton's elegy for a friend drowned in the Irish channel, 'Lycidas', in which for the first time the possibilities of the theme are adequately explored:

Ay me! whilst thee the shores and sounding seas
Wash far away – where'er thy bones are hurled;
Whether beyond the stormy Hebrides,
Where thou, perhaps, under the whelming tide,
Visitest the bottom of the monstrous world;
Or whether thou, to our moist vows denied,
Sleep'st by the fable of Bellerus old,
Where the great Vision of the guarded mount
Looks towards Namancos and Bayona's hold,
– Look homeward, Angel, now, and melt with ruth;
– And, O ye dolphins, waft the helpless youth!

Just as Collins, in borrowing from Milton the stanza form for his 'Ode to Evening', took over a very little-used pattern of verse which, as Professor Garrod and others have observed, has yet blessed all who have subsequently attempted it with a measure of success that seldom attends the appropriation of commoner forms, so Milton may be imagined to have been prophetic of the subsequent successes in dealing with this theme which stem directly from his own great treatment of it. It may seem difficult to ring the changes effectively on such a subject and win other high successes on a claim already so magnificently pre-empted by Shakespeare and Milton in their very different ways, and yet not a few other English poets have essayed the task and produced passages which amply sustain comparison with either the 'Sea Dirge' or 'Lycidas'; nor, as I shall show, is the notable succession ended.

Take, for example, this great example from Cyril Tourneur's *The Atheist's Tragedy* (I quote according to the critical text of Professor Nicoll, but for convenience and familiarity the modernised spelling and punctuation of the *Mermaid* text is used): –

Walking next day upon the fatal shore,
Among the slaughtered bodies of their men,

Which the full-stomached sea had cast upon
The sands, it was my unhappy chance to light
Upon a face, whose favour when it lived
My astonished mind informed me I had seen.
He lay in his armour, as if that had been
His coffin; and the weeping sea (like one
Whose milder temper doth lament the death
Of him whom in his rage he slew) runs up
The shore, embraces him, kisses his cheek;
Goes back again and forces up the sand
To bury him, and every time it parts
Sheds tears upon him, till at last (as if
It could no longer endure to see the man
Whom it had slain, yet loth to leave him) with
A kind of unresolved, unwilling pace
Winding its waves one in another (like
A man that folds his arms, or wrings his hands
For grief) ebbed from the body, and descends;
As if it would sink down into the earth
And hide itself for shame of such a deed.

Swinburne sang the theme with a difference, for he imagined himself the Drowned Man: –

Ah yet would God this flesh of mine might be
Where air might wash and long leaves cover me,
Where tides of grass break into foam of flowers,
Or where the wind's feet shine along the sea.

The desire for sea-burial is a fairly common theme of minor poetry, but I cannot recall any instance in which it has found great expression. Tennyson was particularly interested in the death by drowning of wounded men, whose flowing blood 'incarnadined the waves' and deals with morbid particularity on colour effects so secured in certain passages. But we return to the mainstream of our subject with the following magnificent passage from Charles Doughty's *The Dawn in Britain*, dealing with the drowning of young Lepidus, the son of Priscus: –

Recounts that soldier, how the Roman dead,
He, on the chesil banks, beheld, row-laid.
Himself, he saw young Lepidus' cold corse;
That comely lapped, when he was taken up.
Wild tangles of the sea, from head to feet,
Like fair *praetexta*. In shole tide he lay;
Where lifting, every billow, his bright locks,

Seemed kiss his cheeks. Men say, did nereids rise,
Beating their bosoms, from the guilty waves,
On him to gaze; and that the sea-maids sought,
Clipping, in their white arms, his clay-cold corse,
How him to chaufe, with their delicious breasts.
Closed his quenched eyes, they plaited his bright locks.
Bearing him, in their horny hands, to land,
Out of the brown-pitcht bark, rude fishers wept.

That the tremendous imaginative possibilities of the theme are by no means exhausted yet is shown by such recent dealings with it as that of Gerard Manley Hopkins, whose 'Wreck of the Deutschland' rings with such vivid eloquence as this:

For the infinite air is unkind,
And the sea flint flake, black-backed in the regular blow,
Sitting eastnortheast, in cursed quarter, the wind;
Wiry and white-fiery and whirlwind-swivelled snow
Spins to the widow-making, unchilding, unfathering deeps.

Or, again, the same poet in his 'The Loss of the Eurydice':

Three hundred souls, O alas, on board,
Some sleep unwakened, all unawarned, eleven fathoms fallen,
Where she floundered! One stroke felled and furled them,
The hearts of oak! And flockbells off the aerial downs' forefalls
Beat to the burial.

James Maclaren, 3 November 1933

Færöerne

I

The teaching profession was very much in evidence during the recent quadrennial visit of the Shetlanders to their kinsfolk in the Faroe Islands – on both the Shetland and the Faroese sides. The Lerwick party included Mr A.T. Cluness, Rector of the Anderson Institute, and half a dozen other teachers, while prominent among our Faroese hosts were Johan M.F. Poulsen, Headmaster of Strandur Public School, Esturoy – who at the early age of thirty-nine is President of the Lagting (or Parliament) of Faroe; Simun av Skarthi, Headmaster of the People's High School in Thorshavn and a well-known folklorist and philologist; and Johan Dahl, the Dean of Faroe, who, apart from his clerical duties, has done a great work for Faroe in writing the grammar of the Faroese language (in 1908) for use in schools, and translating the New Testament into Faroese. Educational interests were predominant in other directions. On a trip to the Norduroyar we had the company of Miss Erasmusson, a graduate of Copenhagen University, who is making a special study of Faroese folklore, while at Klakksvig we were met and guided round the sights by Mr Alex Enniberg, the headmaster of the school of 250 pupils there. These Faroese-Shetland inter-visits, which alternate every two years, were initiated in 1929 – mainly on Faroese initiative, inspired by the sense of racial relationship, affiliations in language, traditions, and the regional economy of fishing and crofting common to both groups of islands, and, above all, the gratitude of the Faroese to the Shetlanders since it was from the latter that they learned, some eighty years ago, the smack fishing for cod in the East Iceland and Greenland waters, which is now their staple industry and accounts for the remarkable progress and increasing prosperity of the Faroes since then. The positions are now virtually reversed, and the Shetlanders may now have even more to learn from the Faroese than the latter learned from the former. The question is whether they will show an equal readiness to learn and a like enterprise, courage, co-operative enthusiasm and farsightedness in applying the available lessons. That remains to be seen. Economic matters apart, the Shetlanders have not, despite the pioneer work of Mr J. Haldane Burgess, Mr John Nicholson, and others, yet developed the most elementary beginnings of such a cultural renaissance – linguistic, literary, dramatic, and historical – as is now so far advanced and vigorous in the Faroes, though there is no reason why, on the basis of their old Norn language and kindred traditions, the Shetlanders should not make a relatively favourable show. There is no sign yet of any such purposive application, but the germs of it are there if only in the insistence of the Shetlanders that they are not Scots and have more in common with the Faroese than with their Southern neighbours, and it has been interesting to see how this Foroyar-Hialtland rapprochement, though it is still restricted, so far as the great majority of the Shetland contingent are concerned, to a mere football, badminton and general holiday-making footing, is steadily expanding to higher planes of interest. On this occasion quite a number of the Shetlanders showed an active interest in the relationships between their own lost Norn language and their ancient place-names and the terminology of the old *haaf*-fishers with the Faroese vocabulary, in the physical and psychological and other resemblances of the two peoples, in the points of resemblance and difference in the practical economy and standards of living of the two groups of islands, in antiquarian issues, in bird-life, and in other matters; and if it did not seem to occur to any of them to wonder why nationalist politics (and a species of economic nationalism) should be so vastly in the ascendant in the Faroes and, not content with ridding itself of the crushing Danish monopoly, should be proceeding more and more in the direction of complete separation from Denmark, while the Shetlanders have been unable to engender anything of the sort or to secure any measure of local initiative let alone comprehensive regional planning, or to speculate on the poor little kailyaird attempts at a

Shetland local literature in comparison with the vigorous and many-sided Faroese revival which has developed during the past half-century or so, and is associated with such names as those of Niels Finsen, Rasmus Effersöe, and, amongst the living authors, Hans Djurhuus (a Thorshavn schoolmaster), all that may come; the movement is still in its infancy and is capable of tremendous developments.

One thing is certain. If it does develop a great deal will depend on the Shetland teachers and, though it would be invidious to mention names, I have reason to know that many of these are increasingly interested in the matter. It was particularly interesting in the Faroes to note how the politico-economic and cultural movements have gone hand in hand and what a part the teachers play in every phase of public life. This is as it should be, and as it has been in periods of national reconstruction and material and spiritual efflorescence in practically every country in Europe. Only our own insular country exhibits a singular divorce between education and public and practical affairs, and the latter are conducted without regard to the due place and authority of the nation's teachers and authors. To be a scholar or a poet with us is regarded as almost *ipso facto* a disqualification for practical affairs, and the latter are relegated to 'hard-headed business men'. There is no trace of this strange spirit in the Faroes, and as a result material and spiritual advancement go hand in hand and one of the most remarkable reconstructive and forward movements ever exhibited in any European country has been consummated within a couple of generations, and today the Faroes have an almost entire absence of the crucial problems besetting most other civilised peoples and a general atmosphere of prosperity and progress of a most enviable character.

II

The Faroes are seldom visited by foreigners except on business connected with the fishing industry, and have developed nothing in the nature of a tourist traffic. It is, indeed, surprising how little is known of them in Great Britain, despite the fact that proportionately to population they are our best customers, the ratio of British goods in their imports being exceptionally high. I was amused on the voyage up to be asked by several of the Shetlanders whether it was true that there are still lingering traces of leprosy in the Faroes – since that is a question that has been put to me several times in relation to the Shetlands themselves. Needless to say, there are not. The notion that there are all manner of dreadful things in these remote islands is only part or parcel of the general attitude to the unknown and misconceived, and equates with the feeling entertained in the South at such distant places (not to mention nearer ones like the Orkneys and Shetlands, or even Scotland itself north of the Highland line) must needs be barbarous and well-nigh uninhabitable or at most occupied only by some kind of Esquimaux. Nothing could be further from the mark. The Faroes enjoy all the amenities while suffering few of the disadvantages of modern civilisation.

The nature of the country makes them permanently free from industrialism; they have no traffic problem, no unemployment, no serious poverty, no emigration, no rent-paying (since every man owns his own house – commodious wooden bungalows in the Norwegian style), practically no crime. On the other hand they are 'masters in their own house'; they operate their industry without the intervention of foreigners or middle-men, and the entire proceeds accrue to the islands themselves – a centripetal policy reflected in the general well-being. They have abundant hydraulic power and as a consequence electricity is very cheap and ubiquitously used. They are the greatest telephone-users outside the United States of America. They are a genial, cultured people, fond of dancing, music, and drama, and – all of them at least bilingual – they have a fully European standard of life, which seems almost a paradox against their background of pointed volcanic mountains. In a general absence of Philistinism – in town-planning, in the cordialities and courtesies of social intercourse, in their love of colour, in the appointments of their homes, in the amazing range and wonderful quality of their cuisine, and in all other directions, so far from being backward and poverty-stricken, I know scarcely any part of Europe (and certainly none in the British Isles) to compare favourably with the Faroes let alone to excel them.

But certainly one's first glimpse of the Faroes, and one strange spectacle after another as the vessel slowly makes up to the land, are calculated to confirm one's worst apprehensions. There is an indescribable nightmarish quality about these initial views – almost as if one suddenly found oneself, not in some familiar hill-country, but in the mountains of the moon. Especially is this the case if the eye, searching the horizon, first picks up the monstrous shapes of Litla Dímun and Stóra Dimun. These become more not less incredible on closer approach – fantastic and fearsome stacks of sheer rock. They are a true index to all the subsequent vistas. The Faroes are indeed weird and wonderful freaks of Nature. There is nothing else in Europe at all like them. The Shetlands have a similar lack of trees which at first gives an impression of barrenness and monotony until closer acquaintance shows that, despite this strange lack, there is no absence of variety of colour and form and the landscape, however different to that to which one has been accustomed, has its own completeness and complexity. The Shetlands, however, present a very moderate aspect indeed in comparison with the Faroes; the latter present all the peculiarities of the former, heightened and intensified to an extraordinary degree and with all sorts of *outré* and *macabre* features of their own. The Faroes are 'a world apart' – a strange and stupendous world of great cliffs and ocean caves and ex-volcanic mountains tortured into unbelievable shapes; pyramids rising to needle-points, bastions of basalt, gaunt skerries and stacks of all kinds, and ridges edged like the blade of a knife. An impossible country to live in, it appears; and, indeed, inland it is so; the shapes of the stony, sparsely-turfed hills are such that there are (except in the two small, and flatter, islands of Sandoy and Vaagar) no inland valleys, and all the towns and villages and isolated cottages and strips of cultivation are confined to the water's edge, and across country there are and can be virtually no roads, all locomotion from point to point necessarily being by boat. But if the essence of a holiday is a complete change, a trip to the Faroes cannot be bettered. It is totally different from anything within easy reach of European, and particularly British, travellers, and the haunting views of those strange acclivities, rising on terrace after terrace of stony ridges from the water's edge to heights of between two and three thousand feet and culminating in freakish and forbidding pinnacles, is well worth going far to see. It does not cost much. There is a regular service from Leith on a well-found and speedy steamer, and in Thorshavn and other towns there are excellent hotels or pensionats, while the shopping and other facilities leave nothing to be desired, and matters are facilitated by the surprising number of the Faroese who speak a little English. The cost of an excellent ten days' or fortnight's holiday need not exceed a couple of pounds a day.

12 January 1934

III

It is best to make a visit to the Faroes coincide with the annual celebration there of the National Festival of St Olaf, to whom this year's was the 903rd yearly commemoration. That also coincides with the opening of the Lagting, or Faroese Parliament, one of the oldest, if not the very oldest, of such institutions in the world. At that time Thorshavn has its normal population nearly doubled by the influx of visitors from all the islands and from further afield. We were a cosmopolitan party this year: Scots, Shetlanders, Orcadians, Norwegians, Danes, Spaniards, Icelanders and Germans. Everywhere the natives are in their national costume (which many of them wear regularly and not only on special occasions) – to women in garb not unlike the traditional attire of the Newhaven fishwives but in finer materials and richer colours, and the men in their brown or navy tunics with rows of clear metal buttons, their close-fitting knee-breeches with coloured gaiters, their bright-buckled shoes, and distinctive caps of striped material with the tasselled top dipped over on the right side. The whole place is *en fête*. Concerts and dances of all kinds are arranged, and visitors should not miss the Faroese National Dance, executed hour after hour to the singing of many hundreds of verses which have been transmitted orally generation after generation, and are only now in the process of being committed to writing, just as the *Kalevala*, the great Finnish epic, which extends to 22,793 verses, was taken down from the lips of the peasantry and pieced together by Dr Lönnrot of Helsingfors as recently as 1835. To join in this dance is a most enjoyable experience, although to weave in and out in its serpentine movements in a tightly-packed hall from nine o'clock one night till five or six the next morning is not for everybody. It certainly brings one into close contact with the people, and a delightful, gay, hospitable and courteous folk they are. On this occasion they let themselves go; their complete abandon is a joy to watch or share – and it is not surprising; it is only twice a year, at the Festival of St Olaf and at Christmas-time, they forgather thus; in a day or two again they will be dispersed to all the lonely corners of their nook-shotten isles and the carnival spirit surrendered again to Spartan abstemiousness and hard work. Let me mention here that the Faroes are prohibitionist. Only light, non-alcoholic beer can be bought in the hotels and konditori. Residents can import wines and spirits for their own use, but not for sale. There is no duty on tobacco, however, and smoking mixtures, cigars, cheroots and cigarettes of splendid quality can be obtained for a fraction of what they cost in this country.

St Olaf's Day is celebrated on the last Sunday of July, not in memory of King Olaf Tryggvesson of Norway, whose short reign, beginning in 995 (he died in 1000 AD), as devoted to the Christianising of Norway, but in memory to one of his successors, Olaf the Saint, who became king of Norway in 1016, and by his remarkable life, but still more tragic death, succeeded as Olaf Tryggvesson had really failed, in establishing the supremacy of the Christian religion, for which he died fighting against countrymen of his own in July 1030. St Olaf's Day was the most important festival of the Norwegian Church in the Middle Ages. The religion confessed by the majority of the Faroese is still, as it has been since the Reformation, Lutheran, and while all Scandinavia and Scandinavian dependencies had dropped the celebration as a Church festival of St Olaf's Day until Norway revived it a couple of years ago, the Faroes have all along maintained it and made it their national fête.

The vigorous nationalism in the ascendant in the Faroes is responsible for the invitations to Icelanders and other kindred peoples to be present at this time, as it has been for the beginnings of the reciprocal Foroyar-Hialtland movement. The Faroese people themselves are a healthy and happy lot – the men lean and athletic, and the women merry and well favoured. It is difficult to distinguish the national type of beauty among the latter. Although lint-white hair and Nordic colouring prevail, there is a splendid sprinkling of dark types, just as in Marseilles we find the opposite, and among the swarthy Mediterranean majority there crops up here and there a flaxen beauty no less wholly Latin in blood.

IV

My comment on the relative absence of local initiative and soundly-based and successful economic and cultural activity in the Shetlands did not altogether please some of my Lerwick friends, and they were inclined to call my 'strictures exaggerated'. But the only Shetland press-man who accompanied our party, in the article he contributed to the Thorshavn *Dimmalaeting*, 'gave the game away' as completely as I could have desired in the following passage, and in the phrase I have italicised struck the keynote of Faroese life and revealed the reason for the success and happiness of the Faroes today.

'Your older men', he wrote,

> are never tired of reminding us that it was the Shetland men who taught them to fish, and that it is therefore to Shetland that Faroe owes its present remarkable prosperity. But you have been more than apt pupils, and the way in which you have developed and now conduct your great fishing industry and have built upon it a full and up-to-date life alongside all your old customs, is the wonder and admiration of every Shetlander who comes among you. You had, of course, the incalculable advantage of retaining what we were deprived of centuries ago – the old Norse laws and liberty. Hence the independence of nearly every man among you; *hence your essential quality, with differences that raise no envy*; and your bold spirit, as well as your love of the past and your widespread culture. In your old laws, your Faroe dance, national costume, and most of all in your language, you have kept a firm hold, such as perhaps we could not keep, on a great past. In your management of industry and business, notably your fishing and your own steamship company; in your political, cultural, and general life, with your Lagting, your growing literature, your magnificent library and museum, your anti-tuberculosis organisation, and many other things, you have, without exaggeration, outstripped us Shetlanders. You have done this in less than two generations, and in doing it have shown a spirit of comradeship and unity which we envy. As we see it in the natural features of your islands a Shetland heightened and intensified, so also we see in your whole life something to look up to and admire.

Exactly! The essence of the whole situation is there. Not only the Shetlands, but Scotland too, compare miserably with the Faroes today, and can only retrieve their position by a like concentration on true values. I have referred to the place teachers, scholars, and poets are accorded in the national life. Their activities are not regarded as something apart – as highbrow specialities, polite accomplishments, amenities apart from the real business of the community; but are integral with the national life at every point. This is indispensable, and cannot be too strongly stressed. In Scotland, and the Shetlands, teachers, scholars and writers cannot 'pull their full weight'; they occupy an equivocal and unassured place; their due influence has been thrust aside by relatively unintelligent forces. Any real reconstructive and renascent movement must depend upon a realisation of real values – upon the establishment of a hierarchy of true standards. This is only a paraphrase of the old (and generally misunderstood) admonition: 'Seek ye first the kingdom of God and all other things shall be added unto you.' There could be no more impressive object-lesson of the proper place of education, scholarship, and the creative spirit in a national life than the Faroes today present, and no more devastating condemnation of the neglect of a true perspective in these matters than the relatively appalling condition of the Shetlands and of Scotland. '*Such as perhaps we could not keep*' – there is no cause of failure to retain or recover except lack of understanding and determination.

The Faroes laboured under far greater natural and imposed difficulties than burden Scotland or the Shetlands. Following the decimation of the population by plague in 1349–50, the lively intercourse with Orkney, Shetland, Norway and Iceland completely ceased; the trade of the islands passed into the hands of continental merchants; swift decline set in in all directions; and the Faroese entered on five hundred years of seldom-relieved misery, lasting to within the memory of some men still living. After the Black Death the trade passed into the hands of the Hanseats of Bergen – with the possibility that the Faroese might some time recover it. But in the second half of the sixteenth century, when Norway became a province of Denmark, the trade became monopolised, and after changing hands several times during the following two hundred years, became in 1709 the State monopoly of Denmark and remained so for nearly a century and a half.

We get a vivid picture of the results in the *Reminiscences* of Christian Ployen, Chief Sheriff of Faroe a century ago. The Faroese were allowed neither to buy nor sell to foreigners on their own initiative but had to sell only what the Danish State thought fit to buy, and buy only what it thought fit to offer them. The consequence was the complete strangling of all enterprise among the islanders and the prevention of any improvement in the standard of living. Ployen is never tired of girding at what he calls, in the concluding sentence of his book, 'the all-industry-strangling, all-profit-absorbing monopoly'.

The vast change that has been affected during the past fifty to seventy years is one of the great romances of modern Europe and calculated to inspire the nationals of any country concerned with its present grievous problems. The monopoly has been completely broken; the industry of the country is in the hands of the people themselves, and has not only been prosecuted with an energy and vision which has carried it to great prosperity but along such lines that practically the entire work is carried out on the islands themselves and practically the entire proceeds reverts to them to the benefit of every phase of the national life. The Lagting was restored, the Danish ascendancy broken, a large measure of autonomy obtains, and the largest political party is pressing for complete independence. The rise, within little more than half a century, from the verge of destitution to comparative affluence is reflected in all directions, and not least of all in education. In 1872 schooling was made compulsory up to the age of fourteen, as was simultaneously done in Britain. The educational facilities of the islands are now varied and excellent, and, while a satisfactorily high proportion of the pupils proceed to Denmark to complete their University careers, the splendid work of the Faroese units of one of the most distinctive of Danish institutions – the People's High Schools, residential schools for the adult education of fishermens' and farmers' sons in the winter and their daughters in the summer – is worthy of special study. I had the pleasure of being present at a students' cabaret show in the Sjonleikurhus and of witnessing the performance, in Faroese, of the Norwegian satirical play *To Heimith Mitt* ('My Sweet Home'). While they all know Danish, the Faroese habitually use their own language, but many of them are excellent linguists, and it was a matter of no little surprised comment to find that the majority of the Shetlanders knew, as a Faroese teacher put it to me, 'no language but English – and that not too well!'

19 January 1934

V

While it has been said that 'the Faroese, like the Shetlanders, are fishermen and crofters too – they know the toil of land and sea both – and, again like the Shetlander, the Faroe islander is a fisherman with a croft and not, like the man from Orkney, a crofter or farmer with a boat', the nature, conditions, and scale of the principal Faroese fishery – the cod-fishing, which is the mainstay of the life of the islands and dwarfs everything else to practically negligible proportions – are entirely different from anything that obtains in the Shetlands.

The whole business is of recent development. 'As early as the first half of the fifteenth century,' writes my friend, Mr T.M. Manson,

> French, German, Dutch and English fishermen exploited the Faroe waters while the Faroese themselves fished only for home consumption. The Dutch came to be the principal fishers, as in Shetland waters; but in the course of the sixteenth and seventeenth centuries Holland's sea-power was wrested from her by England, and as a result in later years the British fishermen came to be in the majority. This had an important result through the Shetland Faroe smacks of the later nineteenth century, but meantime the first impetus to the export of fish by the Faroese was given by the lifting of the Danish monopoly in 1856. The monopoly had dealt only with wind-dried, that is, 'stock' fish, and that on a small scale, while it exported the fish only to Copenhagen. Almost immediately after 1856, however, Faroe began to open up direct commercial relations with Great Britain, and beginning the export of salted fish, received the favour of British and foreign markets for that commodity. Then in the years round about 1860 and 1870 came fishermen from Shetland to the handline fishing in cutters of 70 to 80 tons. The kinship of the Shetlanders and Faroese in race, language and occupation, and the use by Shetlanders of Faroe harbours and stores, led to the frequent employment on the Shetland cutters of young Faroese men, some of whom later bought Shetland cutters and became pioneers in a native fishing industry; while the curing processes were improved, very largely through contact with the Shetlanders, whose methods of work had been studied at first hand on behalf of the Faroese by Ployen as far back as 1839. Thus, while in 1870 the total number of decked vessels in Faroe was only 16, small ones at that, in ten years they

had increased to 26. The growth of the industry went on unchecked after the Shetlanders gave it up. In 1890 there were 24 Faroese cutters; but by 1911 the number had risen to 125, and in 1927 to 157, since when the fleet has been further substantially augmented. Besides cutters, there were in 1927 183 motor boats and 1505 pulling boats, the total number of fishermen engaged being no less than three thousand; and the annual value of the industry to the population of 24,500 (few or no foreigners participating) is now about £400,000.

The chief buyers now are the Spanish. The most modern methods of curing have been established, and trials have also been made with some success to export iced fish, and an extension of refrigerating facilities on shore, and vessels specially fitted out for transporting iced fish will undoubtedly lead to important developments in the near future; but in the meantime 'klip-fish', or 'spit-fish', are – and must remain – the main consideration. The fishing is prosecuted mainly in the East Iceland and the Greenland waters, and lasts from the beginning of May until August – trips home being made to unship the catches (which have been preserved in salt) for curing on shore, thus keeping for the islands themselves this important part of the industry which provides the staple female industry and yields those employed in it – the wives and daughters of the fishermen themselves – a wage of 5s to 7s per day. It is a touching sight to see small flags flying at the homes of the families concerned to signalise these return visits of the smacks from the distant fishing-grounds.

During the absence of this fleet in Iceland and Greenland waters, however, a large fleet of some 1700 smaller boats prosecutes cod fishing off the coasts of Faroe itself. These boats begin working in the beginning of March and carry on the spring fishing till the beginning of May, while, of course, they conduct a summer fishing too. They work from sixteen to twenty-four miles off the coast, chiefly off the north-west of the islands, where there are great spawning beds, and they produce coalfish and a cod which is even superior to that caught off Iceland, though it is smaller, and has the reputation of being the finest cod in the world.

A voyage in one of these Faroese smacks is a most interesting experience. The method of fishing followed on the Iceland grounds is such that a great number of men find employment on comparatively few boats. Each smack requires eighteen to twenty-two men, and they stand at the gunwale of the boat, each tugging at a line on which, in good seasons, two to four cod at a time will be hauled in. An important point is that as the fish are hauled in each one individually is killed at once, for this gives them a very superior quality in comparison with fish caught by the long line, fishing-net or trawl, as these die or are strangled to death long before reaching the deck. This work goes on throughout the day, and when the day is done the smack retires some distance from the fishing ground. The cod is then ripped open, its guts taken out, and its head and bowels cut and thrown overboard. The bodies are carefully washed with sea-water both before and after being split open, and the 'klip-fish', as they now become, are put into the hold for salting, so that the smack need not return home till a full shipload has been obtained. Some idea of the work entailed in all this can be gained from the fact that though each individual fish is handled as described above, a not unusual catch for the three months' spell on board a single smack is between 20,000 and 30,000 big cod.

It must also be remembered that in the Faroes every fifth man is drowned at sea – a greater proportion than that of any other nation even in times of war.

VI

Subsidiary industries include the sheep and wool industry; the hosiery industry, similar to the Fair Isle industry in the Shetlands, and bird-fowling and egg-collecting. Since St Kilda has been evacuated and these industries are no longer prosecuted – at least to any extent – in the Hebrides or the Shetlands or even on Foula, visitors should not miss viewing the expert rock-men and fowlers at work in the Faroes on their precipitous coasts. I spent a most interesting day with the bird-catchers on the cliffs of Nolsoy, the island which lies at the mouth of the Thorshavn harbourage. In the Faroes about 280,000 puffins, 100,000 loons, and 30,000 kittiwakes are killed every summer by the men who are neither farmers nor fishermen but professional fowlers, whose dexterity on these great rocky surfaces over which they run in their 'rivelins' (or hide shoes) nimbly as antelopes is a sight worth seeing. A good hunter kills up to 1000 birds a day. The annual harvest of eggs is over 60,000, chiefly from the Stóra Dímun. The daring fowlers work in pairs, or in fours if projections cannot be found on the cliff-top to which to fasten the rope, one man descending while the other or others tend the rope; while, of course, the cliffs are also scaled from below.

There are two methods of catching the birds. One, employed chiefly for the puffins, which burrow for their nests, is to probe the burrows and holes with a stick called a 'lundacrook', by which the birds can be hooked and hauled to light.

The other, and more spectacular, method is to use a long fourteen or fifteen foot pole with a fowling net at the end of it. The fowler climbs to a suitable ledge, and standing there swings the net about him, catching one or more birds at every stroke. However the bird is caught, it is quickly put to death, by having its neck wrung, and is either hung on a noose from the hunter's belt or thrown into the sea to be picked up by associates in row-boats.

The puffins sell for about 2d each. Only the breasts are eaten. The feathers are of some commercial value, and a large proportion of the birds are preserved in salt for winter use or hung outside, nailed through the beak, to dry like fish similarly treated in the Shetlands.

Large quantities of the eggs – the gathering of which involves the same danger as the catching of the birds – are preserved for winter use.

VII

I wish my friend, Miss F. Marian MacNeill, author of *The Scots Kitchen*, had been with me, to interpret the secrets of the wonderful Faroese cookery and give me the necessary notes on the enviable domestic economy practised by the island women. The Shetland ladies were certainly amazed and loud in their praises of the superb housekeeping, the excellent cuisine, and the perfection of the domestic appointments, which included the very latest electrical appliances. 'The Faroese housewife', said one of the Shetland ladies, 'has out-Yanked the Yanks in labour-saving, easily-run houses, probably due to the intercourse with Copenhagen and to the excellent domestic training in the finishing schools there, and we could take many a leaf from her notebook' – as could our housing authorities from theirs. Certainly, thinking of the sumptuous and endlessly varied fare with which we were regaled, the boundless hospitality, and such special dainties as that wonderful sweet dish, 'Den hoide Dame' (the white lady), the Shetland ladies have cause to wonder how, when the time comes for the Faroese return visit, they are going to make anything like an equal show, a problem by no means disposed of by merely recalling the old verse: –

We'll ha'e trunchers full o' craapin,
And bannocks o' barley meal;
We'll ha'e stap and liver muggies,
And a keg o' blaand as weel.

Hugh MacDiarmid, 26 January 1934

Orthodoxy at Odds with Itself

Kenneth Ingram, *Modern Thought on Trial* (Phillip Allan, 8s 6d)

'Modern Thought on Trial' is an ambiguous phrase which can mean quite a variety of very different things. It might mean a digest of the findings of modern thought on the subject – procedure of – trial in the law-courts sense. It might mean – a very tall order, but what, at first blush, the words will probably suggest to most people – an assayment of the value of modern thought, in which case it might either be a systematic account of contemporary schools of thought, or a broad treatment of the content and tendencies of modern intellection at large; and 'modern' in either case might mean post-war or go back to Francis Bacon and the beginnings of 'modern' science. And, thirdly, it might mean 'trying, or sampling, modern thought', and that in fact, in a genial discursive and quite unacademic fashion, is what – roughly – it does mean. The note on the cover defines the nature of the book much more effectively than the title.

Most studies of modern thought are either strongly partisan, designed to

> shock the orthodox, or else are wholly antagonistic to the modern mind. Mr Ingram is sympathetic but critical. He deals with present-day developments in religion, morals, and politics, and he offers many interesting constructive suggestions, the gist of which is that orthodoxy can take new forms and can adapt itself to the spirit of the age, without losing its principles. It is not a 'heavy' book; it is entertainingly written throughout. And it provides a useful guide as to what is happening, and how it should be met.

This is a fair enough description, but at the risk of seeming a stickler for exactitude in the use of terms (justifiable enough, since logic depends on the initial fixing of terms), I must point out that it ought to have been said that 'orthodoxy can take new – and *frequently unrecognisable* – forms' and that the importance of whether orthodoxy loses its principles in so evolving or not ought to be one of the first and most important questions for a thinker and not, as here, simply taken for granted – on orthodoxy's side. Again, the book undoubtedly deals with present-day developments in religion, morals and politics – but rather in popular practice and opinion than in 'modern thought' in any strict use of the term – and provides only a useful guide as to *a few things* that are happening, and how *they may*, or *granted the writer's assumptions should*, be met.

There can be no question of the need, or wisdom, of recognising the processes of syncretism at work – the extraordinary transformations orthodoxy can undergo.

It is precisely this difference between formal legal recognition or proclaimed belief in all manner of ideas, and actual practice, that Mr Ingram confuses throughout. He treats professions of opinion as equivalent to practice, and assumes the reality of attitudes which in most cases are mere survivals, or camouflages for radical changes, or more or less consciously misleading. His book suffers from a general absence of objectivity; many of the subjects with which he deals – divorce, irregular unions, the prevalence of abortion, the prevalence of prostitution, the growth of homosexuality and so on – cannot be effectively dealt with in the absence of statistics. Personal impressions or one man's reading and reflection are not material enough on which to base conclusions on such matters. On political issues he is as a rule out of date; events are moving too rapidly – and besides, he belongs to too old a generation and there is no bridging the gulf, no possibility of mutual comprehension even, between him and the younger people with whom the issue lies. An example of this out-of-dateness is his failure to realise that the crux of affairs is no longer in the sphere of politics but in that of finance – that 'credit power precedes and determines political power'. This is not the only instance in which he betrays his years by treating with the old respect what were a decade or so ago regarded as substantial issues and are now generally relegated to the role of mere shadow-play. The book is full of the debris of superseded controversies – of a failure to recognise that emphases have shifted tremendously in the past few years. The general impression one derives is of an earnest, well-meaning, somewhat elderly man of no special expert knowledge in any field but a fund of shrewd commonsense, a width of general experience, and all manner of 'wise saws and modern instances', deluding himself – and trying to delude his readers – that he is keeping fully abreast with the changed times. It is rather pathetic. But once the necessary allowances are made, there is a considerable amount of homely wisdom voiced in the book in regard to many of the most complex and crucial problems of the day, and the subjective character of the book has at least the merit of illuminating many of the issues from angles of personal experience which probably few readers share and which have therefore a corrective value in relation to more purely contemporary impressions.

Hugh MacDiarmid, 26 January 1934

Scotland and Europe

I

In view of the forthcoming important International Congress of P.E.N. Clubs in Scotland this summer – the sign and seal of Scotland's successful re-emergence as an independent entity in the field of European culture – there are two aspects of the relationship of Scotland to Europe which seem particularly worth discussing.

In her *Historical Survey of Scottish Literature to 1714*, Dr Agnes Mure Mackenzie devotes a large proportion of her prologue to our wandering scholars in the Middle Ages and such facts as the existence of two Scots booksellers in Paris in 1324; Michael Scott's services at Oxford, Paris and Toledo and at the brilliant Sicilian court of *Stupor Mundi* (Emperor Frederick II); Scottish soldiering in Italy, Spain, Denmark, Germany, France and so forth; the existence, even as late as 1878 of a Scots colony, the descendants of the soldiers, near Tours, and the possession still by Orleans of a Street of the Sword of Scotland.

In a footnote she shows that this foreigneering tradition 'did not cease with the Middle Ages; the civil wars of the sixteenth, seventeenth, and eighteenth centuries did much to strengthen it. A full account, even in outline, would need a largish book.' And among the interesting facts she lists are the following:

> The Russian navy was created by a group of Scots, and in the eighteenth century had several Scots admirals. Admiral Elphinstone destroyed the Turkish fleet in 1770, with three Scots officers in command of his fireships. Admiral Greig defeated the Swedes in 1788. As late as 1877 an English traveller in the Caucasus came on a *Schottlandskaya Koloneya* there, and was addressed in broad Scots by a man of pure Russian blood.

As a matter of fact, it has in no way ceased or even abated yet. There is an impression in many quarters that Scotland has become provincialised; that may be true in so far as Scotland's own political status and the quality of attention given to Scottish affairs by her own people and by others is concerned; but in so far as it is taken to mean in regard to either the extent or the quality of her intercourse with Europe it is simply not true.

I do not propose to cite the ramifications of Scottish trade and industry; the part Scots are still playing in political, military, naval and aerial matters; the maintenance of Scottish Churches abroad, or the active inter-relationships between our Scottish ecclesiastical leaders and their compeers in all European countries; the fact of Scotland's effective representation in European conferences of all kinds; the cosmopolitan range of our leading scientists, engineers, educationalists, and so forth. The allegation of Scotland's provincialisation is generally narrowed down to the contention that Scotland is no longer making a distinctive contribution on the highest levels, the levels of creative art, to the common stock of European culture, and has lapsed away from the mainstream into a petty backwater of its own.

Now it is undoubtedly true, for a variety of reasons, that the Scottish contribution is no longer so emphatically recognised as such, or even the salient character it had of yore – or, perhaps, it would be better to say, has subsequently acquired as the result of historical research, since it is very questionable if the nature and magnitude of Scotland's Continental intromissions were anything like as clearly appreciated contemporaneously as they are now. In the same way Scotland's relations with Europe today may only emerge in similar relief after a like passage of time. But a rapid glance round is sufficient to show that even in these limited fields of creative effort (and I admit their relative importance over all other contacts) Scotland's international activity is being at least adequately maintained and is of no less a distinctive character than before.

Among the names that immediately occur to me in various arts are those of Charles Rennie MacIntosh in Architecture; Duncan Grant and J.D. Fergusson in Painting; Joseph Hislop and Mary Garden in Singing; Frederick Lamont in Pianoforte Playing; the late Isadora Duncan in Dancing; Professor Crew in Genetics; Professor J.B.S. Haldane in Biology; A.S. Neill in Pedagogics; and the late Professor Patrick Geddes in a score of directions, ramifying all over Europe, including the re-establishment of the Scots College at Montpellier, and ending with his presidency of the New Europe Group in London. That is not a bad beginning – and it is only a beginning.

Let us look in another direction – at the activities of Scottish writers today, a matter of special moment in view of this P.E.N. Conference. Can they hold an equal footing amongst delegates including the leading authors of forty different countries? Are their interests equally international? Assuredly, Cunninghame-Graham, for example, is confined to no 'kailyaird', but writes in Spanish as brilliantly and pungently as in English, and his subject-matter ranges over many countries. There is nothing provincial surely about Norman

Douglas? Or Compton Mackenzie? And no one man, unassociated with any Government or any big Corporation or Society, has such a wide and challenging international reputation today as Major C.H. Douglas, whose ideas have called into being strong movements in most of the civilised countries of the world and constitute perhaps the most crucial problem that has ever confronted all rulers, chancelleries, financial interests, and established authorities of all kinds in the history of mankind.

The international proclivities of Scottish writers have been particularly manifest in recent years in the literature of the English-speaking world, and to them many of the great European writers who will shortly visit Scotland owe their introduction to that vast public. Perhaps our most distinguished exemplars of the translator's art are the late C.K. Scott-Moncrieff, who was responsible for the translation of Marcel Proust, and Edwin and Willa Muir, to whom we owe the translations of Feuchtwanger, Hans Carossa, Hermann Broch, Franz Kafka, and many other German writers. Just as a Scottish translator, Thomas Common, gave us our first translation of Nietzsche, so another, John Linton, recently gave us Rainer Maria Rilke's fascinating autobiography of his *alter ego*.

In Scots literature as apart from the wider field of British literature, it is well to remember that the recent developments here have been the subject of pamphlets in French by Professor Denis Saurat and in German by Dr Reinald Hoops, and that our writers have displayed an astonishing knowledge of *welt-literatur*. We have had translations into the Scots vernacular of German poems by Professor Alexander Gray and Norman Macleod, of French poems by Margaret Winefride Simpson, of Dutch poems by Professor H.J.C. Grierson, of Russian and modern Greek poems by Hugh MacDiarmid (who has also translated a Spanish novel), of Norwegian poems by R.L. Cassie, and of poems from the Auvergnat by Willa Muir, while Scotland furnished, in the late Sir Donald MacAlister, one of the most amazing polymaths of recent times, who published excellent verse translations from fifteen different languages. Surely such facts as these dispose of the charge of provincialisation against us, whether in the wide field of British Literature or the narrow one of Scots Letters, in their dealings with *welt-literatur*.

30 March 1934

II

In this second article I wish to consider a very different aspect of our relationships with Europe. It resolves itself into asking whether in certain matters of literary judgment the Europeans are all wrong and only the British (and the Anglo-Scots) right, or, in other words, whether everybody is out of step except John Bull. The matter can perhaps be most easily approached by recalling that I mentioned in my last article that excellent pamphlets on the Scottish Renaissance Movement had been published in France and in Germany. Can anyone imagine that happening in England? Full-dress articles on the subject had, in fact, appeared in periodicals in most of the European countries and in America before any serious account appeared in any English paper, and even then the article in question did not appear in any of the London press but in *The Manchester Guardian*. Most of the references to this movement that have appeared in the English papers have been of a slighting and belittling order; most of the references in the European press of an adequately critical, yet distinctly welcoming type. Here again it would seem there is an illustration of the truth of what Dr Agnes Mure Mackenzie says: 'It appears that the resentment of our Senior Partner against our old refusal to be annexed has lasted longer than she cares to admit' – or troubles to conceal.

This, however, only brings me to the fringe of my subject. There are certain outstanding instances of divergence between European judgment as a whole and English judgment in literary matters, and perhaps the classic case is the European fame of Edgar Allan Poe – who had, by the way, Scottish connections and lived in Scotland for a time – and the English deprecation of him. The issue may be briefly revealed by the following quotation from Theodora Bosanquet's study of the contemporary French poet, Paul Valéry. 'Valéry was fascinated by the devices of Edgar Allen Poe. "I am absolutely unable to shake off the intoxication of that mathematical opium: Poe, Poe", he wrote, adding, "Poe is the only flawless writer. He never makes a mistake."' In that unequivocal statement Valéry unfurls the flag of his country. The excessive admiration for Poe characteristic of Baudelaire and his spiritual descendants has never ceased to puzzle English critics, who grope their way about literature with the attennae of a sixth sense rather than with their eyes and ears, and find their aesthetic justifications after instinct and prejudice have thrown them into an attitude.

English readers are led by that instinct and prejudice to suspect something spurious about Poe's mathematical magic, but extremely intelligent French readers have no doubt he is a first-class poet. It may be, as Aldous Huxley suggests, that they pay their tribute not to the printed poem, but to the very great artist who perished on most of the occasions when Poe wrote verse. 'Not being English they are incapable of appreciating those finer shades of vulgarity that ruin Poe for us, just as we, not being French, are incapable of appreciating those finer shades of lyrical beauty which are, for them, the making of La Fontaine.'

Without stopping to discuss the relative Europeanism of the Scottish as against the insularity and extra-European Imperialism of the English, or the testimony of many keen students of national differences as to those qualities of the Scottish mind which are more like the French than the 'muddle-through' spirit of the English, I would point out that there is a consideration on a far lower level which ought not to be overlooked, and that is simply the fact that Poe was an American writer. English literature has always grudged to admit the claims of American and Colonial writers to a place in its higher ranks without some stress on the bar sinister, just as, with all its multi-linguistic borrowings, it has borrowed extremely little from Gaelic or from Scots, and in fact, apart from familiar dialect terms appertaining rather to the 'stage Irishman' than to the general article has, as a recent writer in *Studies* points out, only twenty Irish loan-words in all. I would suggest that the deprecation of Poe is not due to his artistic peculiarities but to his provenance, since the same belittling spirit is shown to other writers who did not belong to England proper, which is apparently the first essential passport to a place in the central tradition, or canon, of English Literature. There is the case of Hermann [*sic*] Melville, an American Scot, for example. Mr T.S. Eliot went so far as to declare the claims of Mr W.B. Yeats to be regarded as the greatest living English poet could not be admitted without some dubiety, since he is an Irishman. A certain amount of lip-service is paid to Burns by Englishmen, but does the average English literary man really regard Burns as one of the world's greatest poets to the extent of reading him thoroughly? There is a suspicious disproportion of discussion about Burns as compared with discussion about, say, Keats or Shelley, and are English schoolboys and students taught anything like a fair proportion about Burns and other great Scots poets to what Scots schoolboys and students have to be taught about many far inferior English poets? It may be suspected that the English admission of Burns's greatness is almost a purely formal matter, unimplemented by any real knowledge of or interest in the matter.

But it is when we extend our inquiry on the basis of these instances that the operation of this dog-in-the-manger policy is seen most clearly, for in the outstanding cases in which there is a very marked divergence between European estimation and English estimation of writers who wrote in the English language we find that without exception the writers in question belong to the Colonies, America, Scotland or Ireland. So far as we in Scotland are concerned the principal cases are Ossian and Byron. Both of these had and have an enormous Continental vogue and influence, but there is no Englishman so poor as do Ossian homage, and depreciation of Byron has been carried to incredible lengths in English criticism. To not quite the same degree the same thing applies to Carlyle, whose books have had an enormous post-war vogue in Germany, and elsewhere in Europe. If this is the principle that is really at work it is unnecessary to stress the unfortunate character, and real danger, of the over-attention paid to English literature in Scotland, especially in the absence of any general attention to – and particularly school and University teaching of – Scottish literature itself. This is not said in any sense of instigating reprisals against England in the matter; but simply because if England is thus ruling out of its canon the products of distinctively Scottish qualities then we must be on our guard against a subtle changing of our national psychology.

Unfortunately, the case against England can be borne out by looking in other directions, in addition to that of recruitments to the English vocabulary to which I have already referred. Scottish Gaelic and Scottish Vernacular studies are still very largely centred in European countries, and our linguistic interests and the by-paths of our literature are the subjects of innumerable theses in Germany and elsewhere – but who can imagine any English student deeming it worth his while to devote himself to Henryson or Sir David Lyndsay rather than to Richard Rolle or some other minor writer of the true bulldog breed?

James Maclaren, 6 April 1934

Purpose
1930

Allen Upward and the Facilitation of Genius

> It may be true that acute intellectual fastidiousness or artistic sensibility can find no enjoyment in the second-rate but most of us have this advantage over genius… that we can find a definite place in the world for what entertains but does not edify, what gives us passing pleasure without adding greatly to our knowledge or appreciation of life.

Thinking of Allen Upward and his great idea of a self-elected senate of genius in Europe, I come upon this typical passage in an article on current fiction by a well-known reviewer. The phrases following the ellipsis are adroitly euphemistic. There may be – there are – forms of entertainment which elude any too-narrow definition of edification; passing pleasures which do not seem to add much, if anything, to our 'knowledge and appreciation of life' in the restricted senses commonly attached to these terms. It is questionable, indeed, whether a concentration upon 'the first rate', which had no room for these things, would not defeat itself; but the point with regard to the passage itself is its failure to realise that these secondary matters (if they *are* secondary) need not necessarily be opposed to the primary ones. They are not mutually exclusive. The vicious element is the assumption that mediocrity has *any* advantage over genius – that mediocrity is other than an arrested stage of the development of its content to the pitch of genius. All the implications of the passage sin against the light. It is typical in this of the overwhelming mass of all public utterance on cultural and spiritual matters. The only defensible attitude is that which insists that baser aptitudes or appetites must not impede, or triumph at the expense of, higher ones. But can any species of human consciousness or predilection be dismissed on the ground that, however inferior it may be at the moment compared with certain specified preoccupations or psychological or spiritual developments, it cannot ultimately lead, *along its own line*, to results qualitatively higher than the latter? Of course not. The habit of tendencies to over-refine themselves out of existence – the necessity for literature, for example, to relapse from any elaborated diction and draw fresh strength from the reservoir of vulgar expression – need not be stressed. Was Allen Upward sufficiently conscious of all this, or was he thinking in terms of a particular civilisation, of certain conceptions of culture and human destiny, without taking into consideration the possibilities of entirely different kinds of civilisation debarred by the existing one? I am afraid that in the last analysis his standpoint was vitiated in this way. It needs restating in terms of infinitely wider conceptions. Its value lies in the fact that it is susceptible of such restatement.

Janko Lavrin has said that,

> instead of growing, our age prefers to 'enjoy itself', and its vulgar epicureanism is assuming more and more alarming aspects all over the world. Another sad fact is that all our tremendous activities have no creative vision or direction; they are only productive, and the mass of this production grows at the expense of creation, at the expense of life. Hence the pessimism and 'nothing is worth while' among those who still keep their eyes open. To make things worse, the whole of modern humanity has accepted and even canonised the most crippling kind of fatalism – that of one-sidedly understood 'economics'. The dogma that man is a product of his environment and of economic conditions is one of those convenient (and therefore dangerous) half-truths which can be accepted only on the plane of Fate. And since the whole of European and American consciousness is drifting back on to that plane it is bound to become a victim of economic fatalism, which eventually makes humanity an appendage to its own system, and lowers the individual to the level of the standardised Robot.

He contends that 'the Promethean impulse is responsible for everything great on earth, and great is only that which makes man inwardly free; that, in short, liberates him from Fate and raises his existence above "external conditions".'

But this, too, is at most a half-truth, and the absurdity to which it may lead is exemplified in such a verse as this:

> Love of the world with the years increases.
> Beauty of women and strength of men,
> But to dream my dream for an hour again,
> I'd smash the world in a million pieces,

while a different point of view is effectively illustrated in Santayana's complaint in *The Poetry of Barbarism* that Browning leaves no room for the higher work of reason. 'The passion he represents is lava hot from the crater, in no way moulded, smelted, or refined. He had no thought of subjugating impulses into the harmony of reason.' Had he seen the world through the intellect,

> he would not have been able to cry, 'How the world is made for each one of us!' On the contrary the 'Soul' would have figured only in its true conditions, in all its ignorance and dependence, and also in its essential teachableness, a point against which Browning's barbaric wilfulness particularly rebelled. Rooted in his persuasion that the soul is essentially omnipotent, and that to live hard can never be to live wrong, he remained fascinated by the march and method of self-consciousness, and never allowed himself to be weaned

from that romantic fatuity by the energy of rational imagination.

All who, on the one hand, realise the deplorable retardation of human development (that ubiquitous rationalisation against which, as James Harvey Robinson's *Mind in the Making* so clearly shows, thought has never been able to make any real headway) – the extent to which the great mass of mankind are incognisant of all arts and sciences, as relatively barbarous today as the brutes of Neanderthal who were still at large when Socrates listened to Plato – the hatred of 'highbrowism' – the decline of free intelligence – the need for the subsidisation of genius – the danger of civilisation being undermined by its 'sub-men' – and, above all, the persistent effort in every direction 'to bring things to an end', short-circuit human consciousness, and realise Dostoevski's Legend of the Grand Inquisitor – and, on the other hand, the likelihood that any attempt to alter all this will prove in the long run just another manifestation of the same human tendency and result in a like conspiracy to circumvent still higher and more difficult and perilous developments – should certainly be deeply concerned today with Upward's great idea.

The problem boils itself down to this: How to reconcile in an effective fashion, Coleridge's cry, 'From a popular philosophy and a philosophical populace, good sense deliver us', and the passage in which he deplores 'the long and ominous eclipse of philosophy, the usurpation of that venerable name by physical and psychological empiricism, and the non-existence of a learned and philosophical *public*', with Mr D.S. MacColl's observation that

> The visitor to the Arts and Crafts Exhibition would find there plenty of emotion, but, *instead of a public motion*, he would find a feeling of an intensely private order. Instead of pride, dignity, cheerful self-possession, lusty vigour, heroic force, instead of *the public virtues aimed at wherever men are associated and drilled together, formed into armies and other institutions by the beliefs and claims of the State*, he would find the emotions of the recluse, the fugitive, the pilgrim, the mystic, the rebel… *The hope of the future, wherever it may lie, does not lie here.*

The best angle from which to approach Upward's idea is perhaps that suggested in Orage's remark that all other exercises in culture are 'elementary in comparison with the master problem of disinterestedness'.

> No word in the English language is more difficult to define or better worth attempting to define. Somewhere or other in its capacious folds it contains all the ideas of ethics, and even, I should say, of religion. The *Bhagavad Gita* (to name only one classic) can be summed up in the word. Duty is only a pale equivalent of it. I venture to say that whoever has understood

the meaning of 'disinterestedness' is not far off understanding the goal of human culture.

And as to the *modus operandi* of the self-elected senate, the word is again with Orage – the need to realise the true interpretation of the misunderstood saying, *De gustibus non est disputandum*. 'The proof of right taste is that there is no real dispute about its judgment; its finality is evidenced by the cessation of debate. The truth may be simply stated: a judge – that is to say, a true judge – is he with whom everybody is compelled to agree, not because he says it, but because it is so.'

C.M. Grieve, April–June 1930

The Modern Scot
1931–1932

Irish Lessons for Scottish Nationalists

Under the title of *An Ulster Protestant Looks at His World: A Critical Commentary on Contemporary Irish Politics*, Captain Denis Ireland, of Belfast, publishes a series of very important extracts from his journal of 1927 to 1930. I am not concerned here with Irish politics, or the relations – and future relations – of Irish to English and Scottish politics but with the lessons which the growing body of active Scottish Nationalists may derive from these pregnant pages. A critical and creative spirit is slowly developing in Scotland, but it is not too much to say that even the best writing and speaking which it has yet produced are pitifully puerile in comparison with Captain Ireland's comments. Scottish Nationalists should use this book as a guide to how to give really nationsired consideration to our country's issues. If they carefully review what has been said and written of Scottish questions during the past few years in the light of the balanced purview, the intellectual integrity, the grasp of fundamentals, and the constructive power of these reflections, they will speedily – and not before time – develop a due understanding of the professional advertisers' *clichés*, the Rotary and Publicity Club spurge, the instinctive and insuperable avoidance of first principles and hatred of real ideas, prevalent even in S.N.P. circles, and still more so in tourist and trade development quarters and in journalistic directions where an enthusiastically superficial but totally inadequate and misleading 'boost Scotland' spirit is manifesting itself. They will even get the ideas of the Duke of Montrose, Mr A. Dewar Gibb, and Mr George Malcolm Thomson into perspective – and here I am not relegating the two last-named to the intellectual category, or lack of category, of the first-mentioned but discriminating between the excellent work they have done in various ways and their purely political ineptitude and the egregiousness of their so-called constructive proposals. 'When we say that two men are talking *politics*,' says Mr F.W. Robertson, 'we often mean that they are wrangling about some mere *party* question.' Captain Ireland is exclusively concerned with the former. The trouble in Scotland still is that there are scarcely more than two men who can do this in relation to Scottish – as distinct from English – *politics*; and probably not a score who can talk *politics* at all instead of mere *party* questions. Apart from the quality of its thought, Captain Ireland's book is peculiarly valuable to Scottish Nationalists for all the purposes I have indicated because it deals in large measure, and very clearly and convincingly, with many deep-seated and difficult problems which present themselves in Scotland under very slightly different guises and few of which have yet been more than most dimly apprehended by any of the writers and speakers of the new Scottish Movement.

Does not this passage about Ulster apply very largely to Scotland too? –

> The real inner drama of the North is that, blinded by his own nineteenth-century industrial success, misled by a false and inadequate system of English education, and torn by a new industrial revolution which as yet he only partly understands, the Protestant Ulsterman remains unconscious (or, more disturbingly still, only half conscious) both of his own historical background and the depths of his own nature. Unconscious of his history, he finds himself without bearings in a swiftly changing world, and his difficulty in orienting himself in the new century is correspondingly increased.

Trade Development Board boomsters and critics of the role artists are playing in the Scottish Movement should note this quotation:

> Practical people are excessively bored by any discussion of principles; they hate abstractions. The result is that their mutual understandings hardly ever get to the root of anything. They like to take up each question as it comes along and decide it superficially and temporarily in respect to its immediate material consequences. Abstract principle is left behind. The result of this propensity is that large questions left in the hands of practical people are almost invariably tangled into hopeless snarls.

On the need for a revolution in the outlook of those controlling industry and banking, just as applicable to Scotland as to Ulster, he quotes this vital passage from Professor Henry Clay's *The Post-War Unemployment Problem*:

> In Germany the co-ordination and capitalisation of related industrial activities is undertaken largely by the banks and in the United States by merchant bankers and issuing houses. In England these agencies are not available; the joint stock banks concentrate upon deposit banking and the London merchant bankers have their eyes turned abroad rather than at home. There seems to be a clear failure of private enterprise at this important pivotal point in English economic life; the capital requirements of the depressed industries are not met at a time when there is abundant liquid Capital available for investment.

The short chapters on 'Irish Versus English Ideas of Political Sovereignty' and 'Imperialism and the Workings of the English Mind' are especially suggestive and the latter ends:

> During the nineteenth and early twentieth centuries the Englishman almost infallibly arrived at temporarily and (from his point of view) perfectly sound political conclusions without the trouble of thinking – exercising in place of his mind that extraordinary instinct which warns him of the

presence of something unfavourable to his system. This instinct brought the Englishman to the front in the confusion of the nineteenth century – that age of Anyhow – while other people wasted time in thought. Whether it remains an equally potent instrument for dealing with the twentieth century – or whether the excessively logical Irishman is not more attuned to the spirit of the age – is still an open question.

I have only space left in the meantime to recommend my readers to give special study to the chapter on 'Dualism of the Irish National Outlook', i.e. the Gaelic question – it raises questions vital to Scotland too – and in conclusion I must refer to two other matters. The first is raised by the chapter on 'An Irish Front Door to Europe', which is preceded by a prophetic quotation from Cardinal Newman, who wrote: 'I am turning my eyes towards a hundred years to come and I dimly see the island I am gazing on become the road of passage and union between two hemispheres and the centre of the world.' Protagonists – and opponents – of the Mid-Scotland Canal should study this. The second point concerns the religious issue. All Captain Ireland says about it in its relation to politics is worth the study of Scottish Protestants and Catholics alike, and note may be taken here (and with this I must leave a volume of the most penetrating psychological, political, and economic commentary) that

> Irish dissent has often manifested a curious sympathy for, and understanding of, Gaelic and Catholic Ireland; in the person of John Mitchel, a Unitarian, it produced one of the great national leaders of the nineteenth century – as if the extremes of the religious scale were in reality nearer to one another (when left to their own devices and not politically distracted) than to the compromising creeds in the centre.

Gillechriosd Moraidh Mac a' Ghreidhir, Spring (April) 1931

A Study of T.S. Eliot

Mr Thomas M'Greevy's *T.S. Eliot: A Study* (Chatto & Windus) is a very personal, discursive, and in many respects tentative and naïve study by a young Irish writer, domiciled, I think, in Paris as secretary to Mr James Joyce. It is full of interesting, if frequently irrelevant, matter. It is dominated by its writer's Roman Catholicism as when, dismissing Mr Eliot's early work as merely social comment on a spiritually bankrupt society, garnished with modish 'doing Europe' elements, he contends that 'Mr Eliot's verse has purified itself of merely social elements as he moved towards Catholicism, even the bastard, schismatic, and provincial, if genteel, kind of Catholicism (Anglo-Catholicism) that, for the time being, at any rate, he has, somewhat New Englishly, stopped at.' He is on sounder lines (but Mr Eliot, whose chance early gibe at Mr Yeats's fairies he is dealing with, would now agree with him on this, at least in large measure) when he contends that:

> To those who are not provincial minded, the architecture and other arts of the Celtic countries are, within their limits, of as lasting interest as any others, and all the Calvinistic sneers that Belfast and Bayswater and Boston ever have produced or ever will produce will not alter the fact that the Celtic countries have provided poetry with some of its greatest spiritual themes and with practically all its most unselfish loves. The Grail legend took shape in a Breton monastery, Isolde and Deirdre and Naoise were Irish, Tristan and Abélard were Breton, and Romeo and Juliet belonged to the country that was Cis-Alpine Gaul, as did again, that impeccable artist and lover who, when she whom he loved was stricken with plague, 'pratïcandovi al solito, se le appicò la peste de maniera, che in breve tempo nella età sua de XXXIII anni, se ne passò a l'atra vita.'

But that is a feeble enough commentary on Gaelic literature and leaves out of account all its substantive achievements.

The analyses of *The Waste Land* and 'Gerontion' are well enough, if superficial. The former he finds 'practically beyond mere literary criticism', but when he continues 'to criticise the religious and moral attitude expressed in it would be to criticise the strictest Christianity', the question arises: 'Why not?' just as when he insists on the need for a certain respect and sympathy in poetry for common humanity, he is begging a very big question. The enormous vistas of scepticism and revaluation opened in human consciousness in recent years are not to be closed by avoiding the issue in this fashion; literature cannot relapse upon its old comfortable attitudes. As a poem what matters about *The Waste Land* does not go outwith the bounds of 'mere' literary criticism. Mr Eliot's possession or lack of charity, pitiful belief in natural life, and all the other flowers that bloom in the Spring tra-la, are beside the mark and the important thing, so far as the future of poetry is concerned, is not to 'imagine how outraged Victor Hugo and Rossetti would be if they knew that forty years after they died there would be writers of genius who found the Lord God a greater source of inspiration than Marion de Lorme or Jenny' but to ask whether the Lord God really is greater – leading to greater poetry – or whether poets yet may not find greater subjects. It is quibbling with terms to contend that 'Poetry is neither romanticist nor classicist' and jejune to contend that 'to be royalist or republican is to be more worried about the means than the end' with the vague addendum that 'Russia under the Soviets is apparently much worse off than it was under the Czars' and the scarcely less questionable statement that 'the monarchist régime works so well in England that nobody but a fanatical theorist would think of questioning it.' 'It is not,' Mr M'Greevy goes on, 'a question of "isms" at all. It is a question of whether the head of a state, pope, king, or president, knows what good government means, and understands what exactly his own position counts for in helping to ensure good government in any given set of circumstances.'

There can be countless different ideas as to what 'good' means and as to what 'understanding his own position' means in such matters and the remark only convicts Mr M'Greevy of utter political egregiousness (not to speak of a democratic sloppiness which prevents him seeing the diverse artistic possibilities of different conceptions of government and the propaganda of opposed ideas). Besides which it is at variance with his own Irish attitude in which he writes of Ireland giving British Jingoism 'a tolerably resounding *coup de poing sur le visage*, and Ireland subsequently going out of fashion in London intellectual circles, which was fortunate for Irish writers, some of whom were already getting seriously corrupted by the flattery of half-educated reviewers and gushing hostesses in London.' Mr M'Greevy's idea that *Ash Wednesday* shows Mr Eliot moving towards greater poetry than *The Waste Land* and voiding his cynicism derives from his religious prejudice rather than from any valid literary considerations. Nevertheless it may be so but, as Mr M'Greevy points out, he has certainly had a period of poetic sterility, he is turning forty, and *Ash Wednesday* itself declares that

I do not hope to know again
The infirm glory of the positive hour…
– The one veritable transitory power.

Perhaps Mr Eliot knows better than Mr M'Greevy. It is unfortunate that the latter should have been so bemused by his own hopes and predilections that he has failed to give Mr Eliot anything like due credit for his critical work and widespread influence in many various and vital directions. Neither has he considered *The Waste Land* and his poetry in general as landmarks in a subtle and irreversible evolution of modern consciousness.

C.M. Grieve, Spring (April) 1931

Dòmhnull Mac-na-Ceardaich

I have been blessed in having many poets –
Yeats, Eliot, A.E., Sturge Moore – for friends.
You were so little known that having you too,
Their unfamed peer, a heightened wonder lends.
I could not know O'Rathaille or MacMhaighistir
Of all dead poets I would most have known,
But knew one of Gaeldom's greatest since, knowing you,
And being in that of living poets alone.

At the beginning of the nineteenth century quite an unprecedented number of Highland bards existed; among others Duncan Ban MacIntyre, Ewen Maclachlan, Allan Macdougall, Alexander Mackinnon, John

> Maclean, Donald Macleod, Kenneth Mackenzie, James Shaw, James Macgregor, John Macdonald, Donald Macdonald, Angus Fletcher, and Allan Macintyre. The splendid renaissance of the Forty-five had thus culminated in the remarkable result that there was scarcely a parish or clachan throughout the Highlands and Islands that had not its own poet. And yet the noontide glory had already departed, for of the great sons of the Muses, Macdonald, Maccodrum, Macintyre, Roy Stuart, Macpherson, Buchanan, Rob Dònn, and William Ross, only one was still living – the venerable hunter-bard of Glenorchy, who outlived his peers and died at Edinburgh in 1812,

Dr Magnus Maclean writes in *The Literature of the Highlands*, and, of the nineteenth-century poets dealing with William Livingstone, Ewan Maccoll, John Maclachlan, James Munro, Dugald Macphail, John Campbell of Ledaig, Angus Macdonald, Mary Mackellar, and Neil Macleod, asks:

> Is it not significant that while in the dawn of the nineteenth century every district in the Highlands had its native poet, now at the beginning of the twentieth not a single Gaelic bard of known reputation exists anywhere within its borders? Will there be a single Ossian left – even though the last of the Gaelic bardic race – to sing the praises of love and nature, of kin and country, when a new century opens ten decades hence? It is a far-reaching question; but who can answer it? The bibliographer Reid, in 1832, confidently calculated that the ancient tongue could not survive more than fifty years at the longest; yet it is still a living speech today. One thing, however, cannot have escaped us, and that is, that even in bardic effort the tuneful language of our fathers is gradually being supplanted by its rival, English, because the new poets coming up prefer the latter as a medium, and know it better.

The Highlands and Islands have certainly not produced a single poet writing in English of such a calibre as to lend any substance to the last contention; nor, whatever may be the case in Scottish Gaelic, has there been anywhere else such a dearth of true poets content to make 'great music for a little clan' as to confine the production of poetry of consequence even proportionately to the 'great world languages'. The reason for the failure of Gaelic to develop its own great and distinctive traditions and yield, as other European languages read or spoken by relatively small populations have continued to do, its quota of work which was a real contribution to the evolution of modern poetry and secure due international recognition for it, is the collapse of critical standards so deplorably illustrated in Dr Magnus Maclean himself (amply shown in such an appalling *non sequitur* as when, speaking of William Livingstone, he writes: 'Yet Livingstone never gained breadth of view. He was an Anglophobe of the deepest dye'), and that horribly moralistic miasma which leads the Rev.

Robert Blair in his prefatory memoir to the *Duain agus Orain, le Uilleam MacDhuinleibhe* – the same unfortunate poet, an out-of-season forerunner of our militant Nationalists today – to depths such as these:

> His enthusiasm for country seemed very real. We heard two anecdotes that give a ludicrous illustration of the extent to which he at times carried this enthusiasm. Once that he went to visit a friend in Argyllshire. He was in feeble health and his purse was empty. He set out to walk, fell faint on the way, and believed he was about to die. He laid him down on a bank of blooming heather and as he said when relating the circumstance, 'I believed the end was near, but I had much peace in the thought that I would yield up the ghost on pure Highland heather!' We have heard of many a false ground of hope in death, but hardly of one so unique as this. On another occasion a young Highlander took offence at one of the Gaelic ministers of the city. He was about to leave the church, but before doing so he consulted Livingstone. The advice the bard gave was this: 'Don't leave a church where Gaelic is preached. Attend the Gaelic service, and read the Gaelic Poets, and I assure you, you will be safe enough.' A peculiar ground of safety indeed!

More following of that advice, and fewer Robert Blairs and Magnus Macleans, would have given the Highlands far greater safety, both materially and spiritually than they have had. Fortunately, the subject of this brief memoir is free from the *gauche* comments of men of that type. His work is not of the sort that comes within their orbit; they are engaged, when they touch upon letters at all, in hailing geese as swans as fatuously and numerously as the late Mr Edwards or the Rev. W.H. Hamilton in respect of the plethora of Scots vernacular or Anglo-Scottish poetasters, and really in their element in welcoming a Ramsay Macdonald to the Fort William Mod. How many members of An Comunn Gàidhealach know even the bare names of the poets of varying degree listed by Dr Maclean in the above quotation, let alone possess any such knowledge of the course, traditions, and techniques of Gaelic literature as any Scottish junior student is expected to have of Sassenach literature? The real trouble is that while the lesser-known languages, such as Gaelic and Scots, have smaller publics with any reading or speaking knowledge of them, they have no greater percentage able to take any vital or intelligent interest in literature, so that if English has only a 'higher intellectual public' of, say, 30,000, the proportion for Gaelic and Scots is only a few dozen. That has nothing to do with the literary potentialities of these languages which are, in fact, as great as those of English, German, or French; nor does it make the emergence of an occasional great poet any the less possible – but it means that his work is 'beyond' even the majority of those who have any knowledge of the language in which he is writing, and that, while he is virtually unknown and unappreciated, they are busy giving bardic crowns to parish ministers and village doggerel-mongers.

Though they have, in fact, been too busy with these activities to notice Donald Sinclair's death last May, at the age of forty-six, just as prior to that any passing notice accorded to him suffered from a complete failure to appreciate his exceptional quality, and at best ranked him, as if these were equals, with a few other contemporary Gaelic writers, who were relatively of no consequence whatever, the bitter note in my sentences is one that could never have proceeded from Sinclair himself. He knew that such an attitude was an inevitable concomitant of the pass to which Scotland has fallen. That he did not make many protests and kept his work aloof from propaganda does not mean that he was not acutely enough conscious of affairs. It is not always those who are most alive to these – and most deeply critical of them – who are most obviously preoccupied with them in their work. Sinclair was no fugitive from reality, either into the past or into some fair future; but he preserved his own spirit, unsullied by alien and distasteful surroundings. Barra is at least as much a part of the world as Manchester, and, while his material circumstances were cast for twenty years in and about the latter, he preferred to maintain in his own spirit an equivalent for the former. He was, of course, a Roman Catholic, and, as Shaw puts it in *Back to Methuselah*: 'The man who was scientific enough to see that the Holy Ghost is the most interesting of all the hard facts of life, got easily in front of the block-heads who could only sin against it.' Sinclair himself, with his delightful humour – the humour of the saints – might have preferred to explain his spiritual certitude and æsthetic integrity rather in the words of Purdie in *Dear Brutus*: 'I feel that there is something in me that will make me go on being the same ass, however many chances I get.' It has been said that the human spirit is continually seeking, from age to age, to free itself from the intolerable bondage of its own civilization; to escape from the hell of complication to the heaven of simple things. Sinclair attained to one of those states which has a divine incomprehensibility behind its external simplicity. E.V. Lucas has written: 'There is no saying to what we may come or how we shall earn tomorrow's bread in this world that pitches and tosses in a gale of change. Any day might see my business of selling words fail me; might see me, instead, selling bone collar-studs and india-rubber umbrella rings. I hope I should take that change calmly.' Sinclair took calmly the duties of an engineer's draughtsman for Metropolitan Vickers, and changed back in his leisure hours as calmly to the work of a Gaelic bard, in much the fashion that, in Corkery's *Hidden Ireland*, field-workers all day regained the scholarship and subtle interests of the Bardic Colleges in their nightly gatherings. They, and he, were people of two worlds, and accepted both fully, but did not mix them. So there was no such incongruous mixture in Sinclair as May Sinclair portrays when she says of Savage Keith Rickman that he has 'the soul of a young Sophocles battling with that of a junior journalist in the body of a dissipated young Cockney… the child of 'Ellas and of 'Ollywell Street.' And Sinclair could look out from a secure and untroubled faith – knowing that *'Thig crìoch air an-t-saoghal,/Ach mairidh gaol is ceòl –'* on, all about him, a horde of 'minds crowded together, making a dense atmosphere, impervious to the piercing of truth. All this mass of stupid, muddled, huddled minds… Greedy minds, ignorant minds, sentimental, truthless minds…!'

Sinclair's work is a lovely island in this insensate welter. If it is true that Chesterton, 'like all satirical poets below the first rank treats the insignificant twitterings of minor politicians as if they were the blasphemous thunders of the Lords of Hell', Sinclair knew better, and remembering, like Cunninghame-Graham, that 'Gladstone, though in talk for fifty years, never contrived to say a single thing either original or worth remembering', took an opposite course which, if it seemed to some as if it made his attitude to current affairs like that of Hornblower, who said: 'I'm going on with as little consideration as if ye were a family of black-beetles', at least seemed to some of us a just commentary on English life and letters, 'like a steady lamp, held up from time to time, in whose light things will be seen for a space clearly and in true proportion, freed from the mists of prejudice and partisanship.'

While not guilty of thinking that a writer who claims hundreds of thousands of readers is necessarily a greater writer than one who appeals to half a dozen only, many otherwise intelligent readers seem guilty of a like delusion in imagining that there is less probability of great literature being produced in little-known languages – say Finnish or Catalan – than in the 'great world languages', say French or English; but just as in respect of the last-named a critic like H.P. Collins can brush away all modern poets in it, save, perhaps, Charles Doughty, as of little or no ultimate consequence, so a poet like Sinclair, while seemingly divorced from the actualities of modern life may be in far closer contact with its ultimate realities, and may yet be discerned as a poet of far greater significance than any twelve, put together, of those who may be most generally regarded as the greatest contemporary poets of these Islands.

There was nothing static about his conceptions of Gaelic literature – no mere 'looking back', no mere following in a conservative rut. Apart from the 'settled order in his mind', and the consequent classicality of his work, he was tirelessly alert to the problems of the present and the future of Gaelic Literature, and I had conversations of absorbing interest with him on Scottish and Irish politics, on the disintegration of the Gaelic into dialects and on the problems of synthesis that exist also in regard to the Scots vernacular, and the necessity in both of a resurrection of the great amounts of 'dead vocabulary', and the like.

I have before me as I write his *Rosg agus Rann, Bho'n Mhàigh* 1912 *gu Màigh* 1916 (from *Guth na Bliadhna*) containing his dramas: (1) *Dòmhnull Nan Trioblaid*; (2) *Suirghe Raoghail Mhaoil*; (3) *Featrann a Shinnsir*; and (4) *Crois-Tàra*, together with some of his best poems, *Cainnt Mo Mhàthair, Faoileag an Bhruaich-Chladaich, Innse Gall*, and his long *Là Nan Seachd* (over 800 lines), and such prose studies as his *A' Mhor-Roinn agus am Fearann, Canach an t-Sléibhe* and *A' Ghàidhlig agus a Muinntir*. None of these (no small tale of work for so short a life) have yet been published in any collected form, but his beautiful play, *Long Nan Og*, interspersed with delightful lyrics, was published, with an introduction on Gaelic Drama by Aonghas MacEanruig and illustrations by Stiùbhart MacGille-mhicheil, by Comunn litreachais na h'Alba (Dùneideann, 1927), while in *Voices from the Hills* (Guthan o na Beanntaibh), published as a memento of the Gaelic Rally in 1927 by An Comunn Gàidhealach, there appears an English version of the first part of *The Fiery Cross* – his best-known play, *Crois-Tàra* – by his friend, the Hon R. Erskine of Marr, under whose editorship most of Sinclair's best work appeared in the *Celtic Review*, *Guth na Bliadhna*, *An Ròsarnach*, *The Pictish Review*, and elsewhere. It is to be hoped that all his scattered work will soon be brought together, and that he may be justly appreciated in his several capacities as a poet, as a dramatist, and as a short-story writer and essayist. Donald Sinclair was never unmindful of the counsel Erskine addressed to Gaelic playwrights: 'Remember the answer which the Black Lad MacCrimmon returned to the fairy who promised him his wish. "Which would'st thou prefer," says she, "skill without success or success without skill?" The Black Lad said he would rather have skill without success, and that he got. He was a true Gael and a true artist.'

So was Dòmhnull Mac-na-Ceardaich,

One of a small band.

Hugh MacDiarmid, October 1932

Fife and Angus Annual
1933

Literary Angus and the Mearns

A map of Scotland on unorthodox lines was recently drawn up in connection with a special display in a London bookshop, and provided an interesting insight into the way in which practically every nook and corner in Scotland has been associated with some book or author. The names of well-known books and their authors were given in place of the names and towns, so that a glance at this 'literary map' was sufficient to indicate to anyone familiar with Scotland which book to read in order to find out about any particular district or locality. I did not see the map in question; probably it was only on very broad lines, and Sir James Barrie may have been the only representative of Angus. In any case, although it is true that practically every inch of Scotland has been 'written up' in some way, it is also true that few parts of Scotland have been as intensively cultivated in a literary sense as many parts of England – Sussex, for example, or Hardy's Wessex, or Arnold Bennett's Five Towns – and most other countries. They have not been endowed with a mental atmosphere – have not become the seat of a definite spiritual quality as well as a geographical expression. A very large part of the writing about England has an intimacy, a particularity, a genius of loving study and interpretative skill, to which little or no writing about Scotland yet attains. We have, of course, the Burns country, Scott's 'Borderland and Balladland', the Stevenson country, and the 'Celtic Twilight' manner of 'Fiona Macleod', Neil Munro and others applied to the Western Highlands and Islands, but these are rather myths, literary conventions, superimposed on the realities of the localities in question, than translations of their qualities into appropriate literary forms, forms, that is, in which the written expression and the reality are not at variance, but in which the former springs directly and convincingly out of the latter and is like an extension on to another plane of its naturalness, recognisably a native product of the scenes in question as if substantially the same processes had gone to the creation of both without the intervention of any strained or alien element. It is writing of this kind that other countries are so rich in and Scotland has still for the most part to acquire. And, although the fact is not yet generally known, Angus – and to a lesser extent its neighbour, the Mearns – has given Scotland a notable lead in this direction.

It is indeed surprising to find to what extent the new literary tendencies in contemporary Scotland have been related to this particular area and how much of the best work this movement has yet produced has had an Angus background; the sprit of the Angus countryside has informed the work through and through and constituted itself one of the principal characters (where fiction has been concerned) and one of the salient characteristics (where the work has been other than fiction). I cannot cover the whole subject in this brief article, of course, and since I am more anxious to deal with some lesser-known facts, I need say nothing here of Sir James Barrie's connection with the County. 'Thrums' will always be one of the most kenspeckle names in Scottish literary geography. Sir James's particular kinds of work did nothing to inaugurate anything in the shape of an Angus regional novel; that has been left for subsequent writers. The first of these – notable in several departments of literature – is Mrs Violet Jacob, a member of the famous old family of Erskine of Dun. Her *Songs of Angus* were the forerunners of the revival of Scots poetry and, in addition to their fine rhythmic qualities, vigour and often humour of treatment, and splendid grip of the vernacular, they are characterised by graphic power and exact seizure of significant detail of which Scottish poetry was long sadly in want. This precise notation of nature is one of the factors which has built up the traditions of local literature so largely in various parts of England; in Scotland we were too long content with vague generalised epithets which never acquired 'a local habitation and a name'. But Mrs Jacob's work was racy of the soil – full of idiomatic turns and evidences of sharp observation which betokened a thorough familiarity, as of one rooted in this particular soil – as, indeed, Mrs Jacob is. For it is long-established relationships with the locality, a perfect knowledge of all its ins and outs, and a passionate love for it which informs her work and gives it its high and particular qualities. For many years, although obliged for reasons of health to live in the South, Mrs Jacob has never been happy unless she could spend a few weeks in the autumn at the House of Dun and in the environs of her beloved Montrose. The settings of *Flemington* and some of her other novels, and many splendid descriptive passages in them, reflect the same knowledge and love, and, with these, an exhaustive knowledge of the history of the county, while in her history of her family, she has written one of the best examples of this fascinating *genre* Scotland has produced in recent years. It is curious to reflect that Mrs Jacob's personal appearance is known to exceedingly few of her admirers. She has consistently refused to be photographed and it is only those of us who knew her fine long-limbed figure about the streets of Montrose, or encountered her on the roads by Craigo Woods and other favourite haunts, who are able to relate her work to the actual presence and personality of its singularly reserved creator. The House of Dun has perhaps not ceased to contribute to Scottish literature. Miss Kennedy Erskine – Mrs Jacob's niece – has published some charming verse in *Country Life* and elsewhere. It would be some compensation for Mrs Jacob's quietness for the past few years if we could hope that younger members of her distinguished family have inherited a measure of her gifts. My own intercourse with Mrs Jacob, and our discussions of old Scots words and the local dialect of Angus, will remain one of my happiest recollections of my ten years' sojourn in Montrose, that delightful burgh with an air of its own as of a miniature Edinburgh.

Other notable Angus families have made their contributions to literature. Mr Patrick Chalmers, the charming *Punch* versifier, for example, belongs to the old family of Chalmers of Auldbar Castle, and the Southesk family in the person of one of its Earls gave our literature one of its most attractive curiosities in the poem of *Jonas Fisher*. Then Mrs Lindsay Carnegie of Kinblethmont was a versifier of no mean skill and one of her poems is included in my *Northern Numbers* anthology.

I think it was her love of Mrs Jacob's work that first drew Miss Winifred Duke to Montrose – but it was also love of the place itself that drew her back year after year and gave Angus themes and settings to several of her novels and many of her short stories. She was particularly fascinated by Glen Clova and made it, and the story of the Ogilvie Murder, the subject of one of her best novels, and also dealt with this famous crime in an able monograph. Miss Duke also wrote some excellent verse full of local colour on Angus scenes, and took a particular interest in the strange story and correspondence of the poet Beattie, author of 'John o' Arnha', a poem that is in the same category as Burns' 'Tam o' Shanter' and has passages of imaginative force and verbal vigour not excelled by that masterpiece. Beattie committed suicide at St Cyrus and his grave with a suitably inscribed tombstone, is in the old churchyard below the St Cyrus Cliffs. It had fallen into disrepair, and I was glad to have had some share in organising the movement which led to its renovation.

Montrose, of course, was associated with Burns himself. His ancestors belonged to 'The Mearns' and his cousin was Town Clerk of Montrose. It was to this cousin that he addressed a last pressing despairing request for a loan of five pounds from his deathbed. The graves of Burns' ancestors at Glenbervie have been a special charge for years in the Montrose Burns Club, who have a fund for keeping them in decent order.

Another Angus vernacular poet of importance in a bygone day was Alexander Ross, the schoolmaster of Lochlee, that lonely little parish at the head of Tarfside. His poem, 'Helenore: or, The Fortunate Shepherdess' is a fine narrative poem of great interest to all students of the vernacular.

To return to contemporary literature, however, Mrs Willa Muir, the co-translator with her husband, Mr Edwin Muir, of *Jew Süss* and other famous German novels, is a native of Montrose, and both her novels – *Imagined Corners* and *Mrs Ritchie* – deal with it. She wields a graphic and incisive pen and both these books hold, and are likely to retain, a high place in the rapidly developing tale of contemporary Scottish novels.

Mrs Muir is not the only Scottish novelist of today whose birthplace was Montrose. Another is Fionn Mac Colla, the author of *The Albannach*, that remarkable study of our lost Gaelic background, which perhaps is the most radical product of the whole Scots Renaissance Movement to date. Although a native of Dundee, Adam Kennedy, the author of *Orra Boughs* and *The*

Mourners lived in Montrose for a year or two, while visitors to it during my sojourn there included Compton Mackenzie, Neil Gunn, J.W. Thomson, William Jeffrey, Gordon Bottomley, J. Pittendrigh MacGillivray, Denis Saurat, Francis George Scott, and many other novelists, poets and artists.

Lewis Grassic Gibbon, the author of the widely-acclaimed *Sunset Song* and *Cloud Howe* is a native of The Mearns and both these notable novels deal with Auchinblae, Fettercairn, Luthermuir and thereabouts. Another well-known Scottish writer with a Mearns and Angus connection is William Power, the literary critic and fine descriptive essayist.

The natural beauty, country life, and characteristic vernacular of Angus frequently inform the delightful verses of Miss Helen B. Cruickshank, another native of Montrose, best known perhaps as the Secretary of the Scottish Centre of that remarkable international literary organisation, the P.E.N. Club.

The pioneer educationist, A.S. Neill, author of *Dominie's Log*, *The Problem Child* and many other books, is a native of Kingsmuir, near Forfar.

The student of the by-paths of Scottish letters should not overlook the curious books, marked with a wild humour, of R.J. Muir, a former Inspector of Schools resident in Montrose. These, and much else of Angus interest, are to be found in the Local Corner Section of Montrose Burgh Library, whose librarian, Mr James Christison, F.S.A. (Scot.), is an authority on the historical and literary associations of the area.

I must not conclude even this brief and scrappy article – which is, however, ample to show the foremost place Angus holds in he new stirrings in Scottish letters – without a reference to the charming nature studies of the Angus glens by the Rev. James Landreth, the minister of Logiepert.

It is not surprising that Angus should be finding itself such a centre of literary and artistic effort, for it is a surpassingly beautiful county, combining within itself the entire range of scenic effect from the peaks and glens of the Grampians, down the broad, cultivated and well-wooded straths, and on to the coast. The towns and villages are extraordinarily individualised and diverse in their character – Kirriemuir, Forfar, Montrose, Brechin, Arbroath; each has its separate character, traditions, and associations; and the entire area is so bound up with the events of our chequered history that it presents itself as an ideal *locale* for Scottish books of all kinds. Great as the output has been in the last few years, I feel that the resources of Angus have scarcely begun to be tapped and that it remains a mighty treasure store for the genius of our younger writers yet to 'pree'. Their elders have begun the good work; it is for them to carry it on to greater and greater triumphs; and it is for this reason, amongst others, that I welcome the establishment of this new Annual Miscellany of the province – a regional journal of a kind that has long been a desideratum and one that I hope will now receive adequate support and become a repository year after year for an abundance of new work of quality inspired by this splendid countryside of ours.

Hugh MacDiarmid, 1933

The Free Man
1932–1934

C.M. Grieve Speaks Out

'Scotland can give me nothing.'
'Mischievous and mindless' Scots.
Outspoken autobiography promised.

In a special interview with *The Free Man*, Mr C.M. Grieve ('Hugh MacDiarmid') said that he wished to make it clear, since his name had been so largely associated with these bodies, that he had resigned from the Scottish Centre of the P.E.N., of which he was the founder, and requested that his name should no longer be used on notepaper, etc., in that or any other capacity; and that under the constitution of the National Party of Scotland he was no longer eligible for membership.

OLD DEADHEADS

Continuing, Mr Grieve said that he was entirely in opposition to the Scottish National Development Council and the Scottish Watch. He had no use and no time for non-political, non-party organisations of any kind. The Development Council was founded on the impossible basis of trying to help Scottish commerce and industry by carefully avoiding any of the fundamental financial, economic, and political factors. It had been carefully 'rigged' from the outset – not in the interests of Scotland, but as a 'newspaper stunt', and most of the people associated were demonstrably hopeless. Their past records showed that. Not only so, but all efforts to put the Movement on better lines and give it the benefit of experience gained in similar enterprises, had been baulked in deference to a futile 'Couéism', a parrot-like cry that if we got all together Scotland would improve. It wouldn't. It was significant that all the old dead-heads who for decades had been responsible for Scotland's decadence had hastened to join it. Not one of them understood – or wanted to understand – Douglasism; the only real contribution Scotland had made to the problems in question.

THE SCOTTISH WATCH

As for the Scottish Watch, it was the same old thing under a new name. 'Give the people circuses.' When the idea was first conceived a militant youth organisation was contemplated. This was speedily abandoned in favour of the line of least resistance. And all the old gang again hastened to give it their benediction. What on earth could be expected of any organisation with which duds like

Rosslyn Mitchell and Hugh Roberton had to do? He was sorry some of his own friends had to be misled – people like Dr Insh and Wendy Wood ought to have known better.

RETURN TO SCOTLAND IMPOSSIBLE

Asked about his own work and whether he would ever return to Scotland, Mr Grieve replied that he was so completely at variance with practically everything that was thought and believed in in Scotland today (even by those who imagined they were promoting a National Movement) that he thought any question of his returning was impossible. 'Besides', he added, 'I must live and nobody would give me a job. They daren't even print my stuff.' As to his work, Mr Grieve said two new very long poems of his were appearing shortly, both in English periodicals – the 'Second Hymn to Lenin' in the *Criterion*, and 'The Oon Olympian' in the *New English Weekly*. Both were in Scots, and parts of his huge poem, 'Clann Albainn'. He had lots of others on the stocks. 'I expect no recognition from Scotland,' he added, 'and who is there in Scotland whose opinion is worth a damn beside that of T.S. Eliot and A.R. Orage? So long as they like my work I am not concerned over the opinion of anybody in Scotland.'

UNDER NO DELUSIONS

'Scotland will – and can give me nothing', added Mr Grieve. 'I will continue to give Scotland all I can. I know lots of young people in Scotland are following me closely – they are right. I am under no delusion as to my powers, but I am the only person who counts or can count with them. None of the rest have a spark of creative ability. No – "Clann Albainn" contains few personalities (I am reserving these for a very outspoken "Autobiography of a Scots Poet", which I am now writing), but I have taken occasion to deal very fully and in a far more devastating fashion than I have yet been able to command with the Duke of Montrose, Sir Iain Colquhoun of Luss, and one or two other people whom I regard as peculiarly mischievous and mindless.'

Unsigned, 30 April 1932

Nietzsche in Scotland

'At the outbreak of the War, Nietzsche', I read in a recent *Scots Observer*, 'attained a sudden unexpected and undeserved notoriety… This silly war-scare soon died its inevitable death, and since then his name has hardly ever been mentioned.' The writer means in Great Britain; he admits that it is otherwise on the Continent – among 'the lesser breeds outwith the pale'. *The Scots Observer*, which is doing excellent work for Scottish letters in some directions – and could, and ought to, do a great deal more – must really be far more scrupulous in its literary statements. This particular review is a bit of petty prejudice penned by one demonstrably ill-informed on the facts and constitutionally incapable of dealing with the issues involved. It is a gross disservice to the movement to raise critical standards in Scotland to entrust a subject of this kind to such a reviewer. My purpose here is not to expose his grotesque errors – he writes, for example, that 'it has seemed good to certain people to issue a pocket edition' of *Thus Spake Zarathustra* – as if this were the first such edition. And so on. But I want to join issue with his remark that Nietzsche's 'gospel of the Superman does not harmonise with his concept of Eternal Recurrence, and *neither has left any mark on modern thought*.' This is a monstrous lie. *The New English Weekly* is nearer to the mark when it calls *Zarathustra* 'the most important book of the past half century – It is inexhaustible in its richness and wisdom – The only way to understand it is to read it over and over again until it has become an integral part of one's spiritual experience.'

I do not know how any Scotsman of intellectual consequence or creative power who is not immeasurably indebted to Nietzsche, and it is a source of pride that a Scotsman – Dr Thomas Common – was one of his earliest translators. Common's work and personality have not yet received anything like the attention they deserve. He was one of the important forerunners of all that is valuable in the new Scottish Literary Movement, and it is to be hoped that some of our young men may write a worthy essay on him ere long. Edwin Muir is another Scot who has written notably on Nietzsche, and most Scots with vital minds owe a great deal to the *New Age* and to Orage, Ludovici, and others who wrote so much on Nietzsche in its columns about twenty years ago.

My own debt to them is incomputable, and through Nietzsche before the War I had been drawn to Dostoievski and other main influences on my work. F.G. Scott, the composer, will acknowledge a like debt and a like sense of the supreme desirability in Scotland in particular of an extension of Nietzschean understanding and spirit. And so the list goes on. 'Nietzsche's work has come to stay' no matter how many reviewers of the *Scots Observer* type persist in looking at him as the little girl did at the camel and crying they 'don't believe it', but it is unfortunately true that 'only a few "free spirits" appreciate its grandeur yet.' The readers of the *Free Man* should swell the numbers of these free spirits.

It is worth while pointing out that the only other place in which I have found an equally stupid and unconscionably prejudiced attitude to Nietzsche is in the hopelessly unfair and ignorant paragraph with which he is dismissed in Dr Laurie Magnus's *Dictionary of European Literature*, but when I and others protested against this, Dr Magnus defended himself by saying that his book was designed to help those engaged in 'English studies'. I can well believe that that explains any imbecility. This lack of intellectual integrity in the *Scots Observer*, too, can only be due to the fact that it belies its name and remains mainly English in its cultural outlook. The sooner it de-Anglicises itself the better.

The references to Nietzsche are not the only stupidities that stick out a mile in this particular copy. Another, which deserves a first prize for pure idiocy, is Mr G. MacIntyre Little's statement that 'Delicacy is perhaps not expected in French novels.' Scotland will make a little headway with its new movement until all that is intellectually honest in the nation bands itself together to produce a periodical which will not tolerate *gaffes* of that sort.

C.M. Grieve, 21 May 1932

Mr Eyre Todd and Scots Poetry

'If anyone may claim to have been a pioneer in the Scottish Literary revival,' writes 'Enterkin' in the *Glasgow Evening News*,

> it is Mr George Eyre Todd. The publication of his Abbotsford Series of the Scottish Poets, in the nineties of last century, brought the treasures of our old Scots poetic literature, in an admirably selected, well edited, and attractive form, to the notice of thousands of readers, many of whom acquired from those volumes a new and bigger conception of Scots literature and of Scotland. It is good news that those excellent volumes are to be republished in a new edition. They will largely facilitate instruction in Scots literature in our schools.

The best *exposé* of the Abbotsford Series is to be found in James Colville's *Studies in Lowland Scots*, and I have no hesitation in summarising a few of the main items in his indictment here if only in the hope that some of the grosser errors may be corrected in the forthcoming new editions. The question of the admirableness of Mr Eyre Todd's selections is another matter I will not discuss here; suffice it to say that I regard him as quite the wrong type of person to meddle with matters of this sort, and that the carrying-over into the new period of Scottish life and letters of influences such as his can only do harm.

'The Abbotsford Series of the Scottish Poets', wrote Mr Colville, 'has the merit of being a commendable attempt to popularise the neglected study of our old literature, not without serious faults of execution, however. From the last, and what ought to have been the easiest, of the volumes, *Scottish Poetry of the Eighteenth Century*, I select a few points of much that "comes in questionable shape".'

He points out that in Watson's droll story of the 'wee wifikie comin' frae the fair', the line 'Somebody has been felling me' is given without explanation, the reader being left to imagine the pedlar knocking her about, whereas the poor body is simply saying in her best Aberdeen accent, 'Somebody has been *feelin'* me' – i.e. making a fool of me, as the narrative bears out.

Then in Fergusson's 'Leith Races', the lines, 'The Races owre, they *hale the dules*/Wi' drink o' a' kinkind,' are given with the ridiculous gloss of *heal the pains*, which entirely misses the point of Fergusson's witty metaphor. As

Colville says, any Scottish Schoolboy ought to know what it is to hale the dules, or dulls, as he calls them.

Here is the pick of the bunch, however: –

> Few Scotsmen will admit that Burns is ever obscure to them. In the Abbotsford Series the editor very properly includes *Hallowe'en* and *Tam o' Shanter*, and here we have examples of the climax of absurd glossing to make 'the judicious grieve, the unskilful laugh'. Near the close of the former poem we read: –
>
> And ay a rantin kirn we gat
> And just on Hallowe'en
> It fell that nicht.
>
> We are here told that a rantin kirn is a 'churning in which the butter does not gather rightly'. If any unhappy Southron should have difficulty in visualising a churn ranting, he must feel grateful to the editor. In reality the poet was referring to the revelry of the harvest-home under its usual designation of the kirn.

Again, in *Tam o' Shanter* occur the hard lines: –

> Rigwoodie hags wad spean a foal,
> Louping and flinging on a crummock.
>
> The two obscure words here are thus glossed – '*rigwoodie*, straddling; and *crummock*, cow with crooked horns.' Alas! 'stands Scotland where it did?' Why hags, above all people, should have occasion to straddle, and why in that condition they should be chosen to spean foals, are known only to the editor. To discover what a rigwoodie is he should try the alternative which old Polonious was ready to face – 'keep a farm and carters'. But these wonderful hags not only straddle when speaning foals, but loup and fling on a cow with crooked horns. Poor Crummie has cruelly tossed the editor here.

And Mr Colville well concluded: –

> It must surely be the familiarity which breeds contempt which tolerates an inexact and feeble standard of scholarship where the folk-speech is concerned. There is a better spirit abroad. A favourite thesis for a German doctorate is some obscure corner of Scottish literature. Before me is a learned and exhaustive academical dissertation on the Scoto-English dialect, publicly defended before the Philosophical Faculty of Lund on 5 March 1862. Another and more recent is a curious philological analysis of verbal and nominal inflections in Burns. Yet in our educational systems there is no place for such distinctively national studies.

C.M. Grieve, 28 May 1932

An Earlier Anglophobe

No more apology is needed for Anglophobia than for liking an apple and disliking an orange; deciding that a particular piece of ground shall bear one kind of crop rather than another, or appreciating that it is constitutionally capable of bearing the former rather than the latter; or, finally, perceiving that, rightly and necessarily, one man's meat is another man's poison. Students of the implications of Douglasism need no warning against the 'interdependence of nations' and other catchwords of the existing system, but they may need reminding of what economic nationalism means in cultural and other connections. One of the signs of a real national movement is its power of drawing contributions to its developing strength from the most diverse sources; and in this sense no more valuable or significant contribution has been made to the Scottish Nationalist Movement than the cold douche Sir Arthur Keith gave to pacifists and internationalists in his Aberdeen rectorial address.

My anti-English proclivities have been railed at as mischievous – by people who did not realise how anti-Scottish in effect, if not in intention, the opposite sentiment has consistently proved since the Union. It is not a question of failing to recognise England's particular qualities; but of appreciating that these have been produced by inhibiting the development of other very different qualities. A concern for the latter is just as legitimate as a fondness for the former. Besides, the future lies with the concern in question rather than with the fondness which is generally an incurious, supine acceptance of the existing state of affairs. But of all existing states of affairs it is true that they resemble organisms and have their three stages of birth, maturity, and death. Since the latter (the stage England has now reached) is inevitable, a concern for the future implies a consideration of the stage that is likely to follow the existing one, and the law of compensations directs us most naturally for this to the particular potentialities that have been suppressed in order to let the existing dominant qualities develop. In this country the growing end is with Scotland. England in its collapse will find itself succeeded by the very different potentialities it drove underground and has continually kept in suppression in order to achieve and maintain its supremacy.

I am delighted to find an earlier Scottish Anglophobe in no less a person than David Hume, the increasing concentration of learned attention upon whom is one of the signs of the times which ought not to be missed by Scottish Nationalists concerned with the deeper significance and possibilities of their movement. 'The taste for literature', he wrote from Paris, 'is neither decayed nor depraved here, as with the Barbarians who inhabit the banks of the Thames.' London society, he declared, was 'relapsing fast into the deepest stupidity, Christianity, and ignorance', but in Paris 'a man that distinguishes himself in letters meets immediately with regard and attention.' Nor were the English of the time loth to express equally strong feelings against the Scots, and

Hume had frequently to observe their 'mad and wicked rage' against the northern race.

The violence of the English antipathy against all who do not take them at their own valuation and accord them supremacy finally disnecessitates any apology for according to them similar treatment.

So untypically broad-minded and just an Englishman as Mr A.R. Orage (who has recently had cause to emphasise the importance and literary future of the Scots vernacular), discussing the case of Ireland some years ago (and the same thing applies to Scotland of course), was constrained to say:

> Having had my own language virtually suppressed, and being compelled to speak and write in an alien tongue, charged with alien traditions, I should feel the inclination to bite my own tongue, and to curse myself for the very ease with which the Conqueror's language came to me. And when works of my countrymen, written in this alien language, were claimed for the literature of my conqueror and employed to adorn the triumph of his conquest, my indignation would begin to rise like milk on the boil.

Would that more Scotsmen felt like that! It is time to reclaim many Scots from English literature and give them their proper place in our very different tradition. Dr J.T.Y. Greig, who has written a valuable life of Hume, edited his letters, and helped to compile a calendar of Hume's manuscripts in the possession of the Royal Society of Edinburgh, is a Scot who has helped greatly to reclaim Hume for Scotland, and in reading his work it is part and parcel of a proper appreciation to remember Hume's attitude to the English and to imagine how he would have felt about an Anglicised Scotland sunk deeper even than London in 'stupidity, Christianity, and ignorance'.

C.M. Grieve, 4 June 1932

Lenin and Us

The looker-on does not always see the most of the game – especially the writer who uses the pseudonym of 'The Looker-On' in the *Glasgow Evening News*. In a recent article he condemns the 'brilliant young writers and students in Britain' who have become enamoured of Lenin – but takes care not to tell us who they are. Comparisons might be uncomfortable for his own claims to attention as against theirs. Personally I am in the habit of putting my name to my expressions of opinion. *The Free Man* is not mentioned in this article, but readers will have no doubt as to who is aimed at if they compare the interview with me published in these columns some weeks ago with the following paragraph from 'Looker-On's' article: –

> We have got to rebuild Scotland. To gird at people because they happened

to be born a few years before we were or because their political and cultural ideals are not what ours happen to be at the moment we write – to denounce development committees and so forth because they cannot change the face of the country overnight – to sneer at cultural movements which do not involve the banning of Burns Clubs, the scrapping of everything written or sung in Scotland from 1600 to 1918, and compulsory instruction in Gaelic, Russian, and Serbian – to shut one's ears to what is doing in one's own land and listen only to the 'brave music of a distant drum' – what sense is there in such an attitude? No good is done by the irritating assumption that all the people who are trying to 'do something' are fools, or duds, or renegades, or cowards. The right assumption is that 'he that is not against us is for us'; the right plan, to get behind every constructive movement, economic or cultural, back it up, criticise it, urge it forward, join it, and work for it.

Nonsense! This is the Rotary, uplift, American publicity boosting method – that's all. 'Looker-On' is so helplessly carried in the current of his own democratic assumptions that there is no hope of his seeing himself objectively, but his lubrications are so typical of most Scottish thought today that I propose to analyse them in some detail.

Note first of all, in the paragraph quoted, its ghastly loose question-begging journalese. Who girds at people because they are a few years older? What is 'Looker-On' girding at but people with different political and cultural ideas than his? Are development committees and so on denounced because they cannot change the face of the country overnight – or because they are considered useless and pernicious on other grounds? Who has sneered at cultural movements compatible with Burns Clubs, etc., if there are any such, or recommended the scrapping of everything written in Scotland from 1600 to 1918? Why should English be compulsory in Scotland rather than Gaelic, or even Russian and Serbian? Isn't 'Looker-On' just setting up straw men to knock down? Nothing has ever been achieved along the lines he recommends. One finds oneself swamped by one's hordes of mediocre fellow-members. It is the old attitude of the Church – 'Don't stand outside and criticise us – come in and help.' But that doesn't suit the case of those who do not believe the Church should be helped! All the valuable clash of mind against mind – all that prevents the short-circuiting of the restless human mind and its incalculable potentialities – would be destroyed if that advice was accepted. One must stand outside all that drivel to achieve anything. 'Looker-On' should learn from Lenin, who, as James Maxton points out (*Lenin*, Peter Davies – the best thing by far Maxton has done yet, though I question if his adoration of Lenin would be in any measure reciprocated), always took a line of his own and did not mix very much with his fellow-revolutionaries. Those of us who are really concerned about Scotland must take a similar course, and a study of human history shows that the relationships of ideas current at any time necessitate our careful reckoning with Leninism. Besides, many of us have had cause to come, like Mr C.E.M. Joad, 'to believe that what most people said and felt and thought must almost certainly be wrong.'

As my friend H.W. Nevinson says, Lenin 'was one of the most remarkable and influential men in the world's history.' This is no music of a distant drum; it is a major fact of contemporary affairs, and only fools can ignore it or fail to give it deep and patient study instead of railing against it under the spur of stupid prejudices. 'Looker-On' cannot understand how those of us who are more or less pro-Lenin can 'swallow the squalid, stupid, and sickening horrors of the Russian revolution, or contemplate a repetition of them'. No repetition of them might be necessary in this country but for the still more 'squalid, stupid, and sickening horrors' of our opponents' mentalities. Music of a distant drum!

As a writer in the *Forward* says, there is, for writers like 'Looker-On', 'no jolly hysterical thrill, no "kick" in the thought of a million, or five million, British children being slowly murdered by malnutrition, overcrowding, darkness, and ignorance. Such an immense expanse of misery has no "human" appeal – whereas the Lindberg baby…'

Dunbar wrote of our

houses mirk
Like na country but here at hame,
Think ye nocht shame?

Neither he nor Burns were the yea-sayers 'Looker-On' desiderates, nor did they hesitate to lash out with home-truths and gird at people with other political and cultural ideas than theirs.

Music of a distant drum? In view of the Dundee riots and the Kilbirnie sentences? 'Looker-On' makes a characteristically vicious appeal to the gallery by saying that British pro-Leninites aren't even playing with fire. Aren't they, in view of police persecution, prison brutalities, victimisation of all sorts? 'Looker-On' himself is determined to keep on the safe side – but it may not remain safe, even in Scotland, as long as he thinks.

C.M. Grieve, 11 June 1932

Mr Pooh Bah

Mr Cleghorn Thomson has been at it again. I am not concerned for the moment with the dispute between him and the Glasgow Choral and Orchestral Union, but the matter raises far deeper and more important issues. Sir D.M. Stevenson said that Mr Thomson's conduct or attitude had been 'positively unbearable', asked what 'could be done with a man like that', and suggested that the only possible way in the future was to see that any future negotiations they had with the BBC were made direct with London, unless there was a complete change in the present procedure. The general bearings of the matter were not discussed, however, and there does not seem to have been any realisation of the absurdity of Mr Cleghorn Thomson being in a position to act as virtual dictator of Scottish cultural interests – an absurdity which, in turn, is only a reflection of the still greater absurdity of a man like Sir John Reith controlling a great organisation which has such a tremendous bearing on education and the arts.

Sir John Reith is precisely the type of Scot the whole Scottish Renaissance Movement is reacting against and hoping to render extinct. He is the last man in the world to be entrusted with anything cultural. As technical controller of the BBC he might have served, although it is difficult to imagine that his position even as an engineer was such a leading one as to entitle him to take charge of the BBC. It has been said that the reason why Scots of his type succeed is simply because of their sheer insensitivity to finer issues of all kinds – they just forge ahead in the most unconscionable fashion while finer spirits are retarded by their wider vision and higher scruples. Surely in a matter of such moment the interests of art, music, literature, and drama should have been entrusted to figures in these several fields of really representative standing and unquestionably distinguished achievement – not to a mere engineer.

The result of Philistine dictatorship has been an enormous whittling-away of the cultural possibilities of the broadcasting medium. All the forceful personalities, all the real creative abilities, at BBC Headquarters have been frozen out in order to consolidate Sir John's dictatorship. He cannot tolerate opposition; his word must be law – and like all little hide-bound mentalities in such a position he had an infallible instinct – ex inferiority complex – for men of higher calibre than himself, and promptly gets rid of all such menaces to his supremacy. The relation of the BBC as a consequence to British arts and letters today can be seen at once by considering the BBC personnel – a snobbish set of young English Public School or University people, or Anglo-Scots of the same kidney, thoroughly unrepresentative of the great sections of BBC patrons, controlling the programmes with their own little lean-brained 'superior' ideas, erecting their pet prejudices into principles of insidious and ubiquitous censorship, and not one of them with an achievement to justify a position of such responsibility and incalculable influence.

In the last resort the strength of Sir John Reith's position – and that of his staff – lies in their willingness to allow this tremendous instrument of publicity to be 'cribbed, cabbined, and confined' by Government and financial policy and such like considerations. They are astute enough and know which side of their bread the butter is on. Hence the lack of an equal share of the ratio to all interests – the disproportionate time given to religion, the exclusion of Communist spokesmen, and so on, and, as far as Scotland is concerned, the maintenance of an English ascendancy programme. Harry Lauder, yes – but the new Scotland, no. Anything innocuous, yes – anything really creative, no. Broadcasting in

Scotland is determined by this. English matter of all kinds is predominant. A farce is made of running Scottish programmes of a kind, but care is taken to keep them subordinate to the English programmes and to restrict the specifically Scottish material for the most part to a kailyaird sort which is definitely inferior. No scope whatever is given to the vital interests of Scotland and those sorts of Scottish creative work which are seeking to re-establish separate standards capable of challenging English work, tendencies, and interests at every point on an equal plane.

Sir John Reith is a typical Anglo-Scot of the kind which has been mainly responsible for Scotland's progressive provincialisation. Mr Cleghorn Thomson is a juvenile understudy of the same role. What are his qualifications for virtual cultural dictatorship of Scotland? An Oxford education – and the fact that he is a son of the manse? It is impossible to discern any others. He is a dilettante of all the arts – but has not achieved a substantial iota in any of them. An overweening vanity is his principal characteristic. Poet, composer, dramatist, critic – he fancies himself in every sphere. Director of this, director of that, he must have a finger in every pie. Yet the man has done, and can do, literally nothing – except pose and intrigue.

Even without complete autonomy, what time is allowed to Scottish programmes might have done a very great deal to further the new Scottish Movement in literature, drama, and music (it would be too much to hope for in relation to politics and economics). As a matter of fact it has done nothing, absolutely nothing, but concentrate undue attention on the comparatively worthless work of relative nonentities, and help to perpetuate bad traditions which – but for it – would probably have been completely ousted in the fields of all the arts in Scotland before now.

Surely a post of such responsibility and power should have been given to a man of high established reputation, mature judgment, and widely representative whom any creative artist – no matter how opposed to him in many ways – could have respected, worked with, and been sure of receiving fair play from.

C.M. Grieve, 18 June 1932

The Lion Upside Down

The *Record* prides itself on its twenty years' consistency of policy in regard to Scottish affairs, but since not Scotland but its own interests are its main concern the appearance of consistency is caused by the framework of popular appeal within which it operates; apart from that it says one thing today, another tomorrow, like the rest of them. Hence – as it suits its book – what it calls 'the most vital mind in present-day Scotland' in one issue becomes transformed in another into 'a mischievous Play Boy or Handy Andy'. And it operates anonymously. Who are these people who have been telling Scotland what it ought to do for the past twenty years – whose prescience antedated the Scottish Renaissance Movement and the National Party of Scotland – who know exactly the line that must be taken between the 'extremists within the National Party' on the one hand, and 'those who think that concern for Scotland as an entity is foolish and reprehensible'? Who are these wiseacres who can dismiss other people's ideas as 'trumped up enmities and hectic theatricalities', and prescribe government by newspaper – by the *Record* and its subsidiaries – as the only sane and possible course for Scotland? Free men fight in the open – over their own names. The *Record* policy represents an anonymous group whose advantage over those who have brought the Scottish Movement to the point when it pays the *Record* to exploit certain parts of it lies simply in the fact that they have the resources of several newspapers behind them – but whose disadvantage lies in the same fact and in the fact that they are 'mere journalists' with all that that phrase implies. What does it imply? Amongst other things the mentality of which the following is a sufficient sample: 'It is characteristic of Sir Alexander McEwen's breadth of sympathy that he gives full, indeed primary, value to the ideals of thinkers... The ultimate inspiration of nationalism is not economic, industrial or political. It is spiritual... but it is a matter of business as well.'

In other words, the spiritual must be kept strictly in its place. It is all very well paying occasional lip-service to poets, but don't let them get swollen-headed; it is 'the hard-bitten business man', who is about as spiritual as a rogue elephant, who really matters. The spiritual must be ruthlessly subordinated to those who completely lack it. 'The most vital mind' carefully inhibited in the interests of stupidity. So none of your phantasies. The *Record* knows exactly how far poets can be allowed to go – and it is not going to have any of their damned nonsense!

Hence for its own sake the National Party 'has to decide that progress cannot be achieved by the revocation of the Treaty of Union with England', which 'constitutes, in practical effect, our national charter'. 'The Union must be upheld', and so forth. In other words, no blasted freedom for the Scottish people to determine their own destiny – they must be kept strictly within bounds. Why? Oh, just because! – it would never do! – every sensible man knows that – for heaven's sake let us be reasonable and leave these fancy flights to the poets we pretend to honour, but, of course, *entre nous* thoroughly despise. Douglasites know from A to Z the mentality behind 'common-sense' of this sort. At the recent Summer Conference of the Nursery School Association of Great Britain, Dr R.H. Tawney said that the function of education was 'not to impart information, impose discipline, or fit children into moulds, but to aid growth'. And it is precisely being forced into this mould or that by any established political or economic system that we are against. We may decide that our interests and England's are not incompatible – we may decide to remain within 'the British commonwealth of nations' – we may decide to retain the institution of monarchy – but Scotland ought to have full and unfettered power to decide on any course whatever. There can be no 'thus far and no further' so far as Scottish freedom is concerned. And above all we ought to remember in the field of economics that our problems have arisen under the order which joins us to England and the Empire – not under conditions of economic nationalisation – and that financial over-control in any shape or form is the first limitation upon our sovereign independence both as a people and, separately, each individual of us, which the efforts of every man should be directed to removing, since, until it is removed, it conditions our ways of living and our very thoughts to a degree which constitutes the deadliest form of slavery the world has yet seen.

The *Record's* whole policy is to make Scotland still safer for mediocrity – for all who are content to leave the decisions on the major matters which determine all the rest in the hands of an unspecified group of nonentities elsewhere – to give as much of the illusion, and as little of the substance, of freedom and self-determination as possible – and so, to maintain its circulation, since it is sedulously designed to appeal to the type of mind (or lack of mind) conditioned by this slave-morality. Compare the mental calibre of the members of the Scottish Development Council with men like De Valera in Ireland, Hitler in Germany, Gandhi in India. For heaven's sake do not let us have any ideas in Scotland – nothing that is beyond the ordinary six and five-eighths. Momentous events may happen elsewhere and we'll adjust ourselves to their effects upon us as abjectly as possible, but we are too sensible in Scotland to fight for anything – we'll leave that to the Irish and the Russians and the Indians and all the other poor devils who really believe in something so much that they are willing to die for it. But as for us, the removal of the Union Jack and the running up of the Scottish Flag at Stirling Castle has given 99 per cent of our population diarrhœa (heaven knows the state we'd be in if anything had really happened – one pistol shot would have scared us into jelly) – and the English MP who said that a platoon of English soldiers would be able to defend Stirling Castle nowadays was paying Scotland an undeserved compliment; the *Record's* junior office-boy is all that is needed. Let us take everything lying down, and confine any nationalist movement to pretending that we do so of our free will and choice, and that our brainlessness and pusillanimity, so far from being discreditable to us, as fools who do not know the particular genius of Scotland might rashly imagine, are proofs of our fine old Scottish wisdom and essential difference from our inferiors, the rest of the world!

C.M. Grieve, 9 July 1932

The Future of Scotland

Readers of the *Free Man* should not miss the current issue of *Scottische*, which is largely monopolised by a manifesto on what he calls 'Scoatch Poleeteeks', by no less a compatriot than Sir Harry Lauder, who, rightly contending that for many years he has occupied an unique position and been regarded as practically a synonym for Scotland all over the world, criticises the inadequacy of the *Daily Record's* scheme, and says, *inter alia*, that any really satisfactory plan for Scotland must recognise: –

1. The world-wide recognition and value of Scottish Humorists.
2. The necessity of not being too serious – except for the purpose of not being too serious (although, he admits, the *Record* already goes a long way to meet his views in this connection).
3. The strict confinement of the kilt to music-hall uses.
4. The adoption of his 'Safest o' the Family' as the Scottish National Anthem (a demand which he contends in no way clashes with, but rather confirms, the *Record's* insistence on the maintenance of the monarchical system).

Given these four points, he states that he will refrain from advancing against the National Party with the full force of his curly nibby.

I was glad to have a letter the other day from one of the most influential officials of the National Party in which he said that too much attention ought not to be paid officially by the Party to the *Daily Record*'s latest stunt. It should, he thought, be dismissed in a short paragraph in *The Scots Independent*, and he attributed the whole business 'to the Editor's jealousy of the progress of the National Party and his disappointment at the failure of his own Trade Development and other stunts'. Mr Compton Mackenzie is to be congratulated on his admirable letter on the Stirling Castle incident, and the essential silliness of the *Record*'s claim that it happened 'to be in the position of alone knowing the mixed motives which led to the incident at Stirling Castle' cannot have escaped the attention of those who are closely following a set of manœuvres which will ultimately form a very entertaining chapter in the history of the Scottish Movement.

Congratulations are also due to Mr R.E. Muirhead, ex-Bailie William Thomson, and, above all, Mr D.H. McNeill of Inverness, for their sturdy letters, their insistence upon points of principle and prime importance which reveal the superficiality of the *Record's* manifestoes, their refusal to allow the National Party to be over-ridden and dictated to in the fashion attempted, and the generally satisfactory manner in which within the very limited space at their disposal, they relegate the egregious intervention of the *Record* to its proper place. It is also satisfactory to find other correspondents fully alive to the way in which the terms of the Union have been violated and indisposed to 'trust England' in the way the *Record* suggests.

To get the whole thing in its proper perspective, however, so far as the issues raised are concerned (and the whole controversy so far has been limited to comparatively superficial and inessential issues, compatible with cheap journalism), it is only necessary to reflect on the fact that all the *Record*'s pother has not affected substantial opinion in Scotland. Those who may have become excited, imagining that anything the *Record* did was of vital consequence, have only succumbed to the illusion of influence it tries to create in face of all the facts. The

Record has no substantial influence, and practically all the correspondence has been evoked from unimportant quarters. Had this been a vital national affair, responsible Scots of real standing would have hastened to back up, or comment on, or oppose (in so far as their letters would have passed the editorial censorship) the *Record*'s campaign. All such have been conspicuous by their absence. Why? Because the *Record* has no real weight and cannot jump the issues involved in this facile and impudent way. The poverty of its letter-bag is a sufficient commentary on its qualitative inferiority as a newspaper.

The less said about the *Record*'s pet lion – the Duke of Montrose – the better. His intromissions with the National Party, and with the question of Scottish Home Rule all along, will not stand a moment's examination. But for his title no one would pay the slightest attention to any of his halting and boneless utterances.

The whole essence of Montrose's appeal – and the *Record*'s – is that the National Party, which has built up the only substantial Scottish Home Rule movement yet developed, should relapse upon the inadequate platform of Liberals and others which failed to do precisely what the National Party's programme has done, and give way to the alleged bulk of moderate opinion in favour of devolution, which if it was worth a rap, could have organised itself independently of the National Party and got what it wanted long ago.

Scottish Nationalism is not synonymous with the stupid prejudices of the Duke of Montrose and the *Record* and – with all its faults – the National Party had at least the merit of advancing the single issue of Scottish autonomy as one upon which all Scots could join, whether they were Tories, Liberals, Socialists, or Communists. Now the *Record* wants the exclusion of Republicans, Communists, and Direct Antagonists, and all sorts of ridiculous pledges designed to stereotype the new Scotland by forms of the over-control of its opinions and free development derived from the very period of over-Anglicisation responsible for the present plight of Scotland and the consequent development of the National Movement. Why doesn't it go further and demand that the National Party refuses membership to all who are not: –

1. Registered readers of the *Daily Record*.
2. Members of the I.O.G.T.
3. Admirers of Sir Hugh Roberton and Mr Rosslyn Mitchell.

These demands would be exactly on all fours with those it does make.

C.M. Grieve, 16 July 1932

Scotland, Hitler and Wyndham Lewis

Every one who wishes to get a ready measure of the puerilities of the *Daily Record*, the Scottish Development Council, the Scottish Watch, and the National Party of Scotland – and the extent to which generally the Scottish people are kept concerned about footling inessentials and cut of from everything that really matters – should read a little study of the works of Wyndham Lewis, just published at 3/6 net by the Unicorn Press Ltd., under the title of *Apes, Japes, and Hitlerism*. It blows the gaff with a vengeance on the contemporary conspiracy against the free man.

'The turmoil and events of an ever-changing world', writes Mr John Gasworth, the author of this admirable and timely essay, which is likely to have results out of all proportion to its size and modesty of manner,

> provide a constant source of inspiration to Lewis. It is the present that he delights to live in and think about. The political aspect of Adolf Hitler and his Nazis, with their anti-usury, anti-banks campaign, soon claimed his interest. He was in Germany at the time of the commencement of their campaign, and able to study the question at first-hand. The result of his study was a challenging book, *Hitler*; but the gage he threw down was not taken up. **The work suffered the fate all books suffer that raise questions unpopular with the political viewpoints of the Press.** It was ignored, blank disinterest shown; solely and simply because the newspapers in their discounting of Hitlerian events were wilfully misrepresenting the objects and intentions of the Hitlerian movement. Little is heard over here of the anti-capital, anti-semitic activities the Nazis are engaged upon; certainly no newspaper would call undue attention to Lewis's account of them. A general prejudice eliminated any attention that might have been paid. *Hitler* was doomed from the day of publication.

Exactly! This is just what is happening in the *Daily Record* and elsewhere in the Scottish Movement. That is why the Scottish edition of the *Daily Express* refused an article on the poetry of Hugh MacDiarmid, stating in a covering letter that 'there were reasons why it was inexpedient to boost Mr C.M. Grieve at this juncture'. That is why, the editor of that 'free forum', the *Daily Record*, writes, explaining his non-use of an article on Scottish Nationalism ordered by telegram, that he 'could only have used it in a way that would hurt you, and I have no wish to do that'.

Wyndham Lewis is a splendid protagonist of the free man; and it is just this sickening hypocrisy and endless unscrupulousness all free men must fight when, where, and as they can. Finance, he says, controls the 'organs of popular publicity', and

> in the great democracies of the West we live more or less under press government by suggestion and education of course, by absorption daily of column after column of gossip, breezy social articles, selected 'news', 'controversial' special features, 'informative pars, etc., plus Talkies. Whether openly or covertly, it is Press and cinema hypnotism that rules Great Britain and America, not the conversazione at Westminster or the White House.

In view of the recent discussion in Scotland of the necessity of militant action, readers should carefully weigh what Mr Gasworth says: –

> Hitler is as much a prophet as Mahomet, Mussolini, or Lenin, but he is an armed prophet. Machiaveili has it: 'All armed prophets have conquered; all unarmed ones have been destroyed.' Though Hitler is armed he is no militarist menace. He is a man of peace, as are his followers. Though his 'Sturmabteilung' are a private police force, well versed in the gentle art of street fighting, they carry on soberly. 'Nur legal' is the watchword they regard, keeping healthily within the law. The German 'Schupo' is almost certain then to be inattentive on the occasions when they and the 'Reds' see fit to square a few accounts…

Didn't Compton Mackenzie point the way when he remarked that one of the Stirling Castle soldiers in passing whispered approval of the incident there? Isn't there a lesson for Scotland in the fact that the whole of the Irish Rising was arranged by the IRB Executive, without more than a fractional percentage of the Irish people knowing it was going to happen – even such a 'leader' as John Redmond not having any idea of it?

'Loan capital', continues Mr Gasworth, 'is the enemy of enemies that Hitler would fight; for all peoples and governments that bow to its might find themselves inescapably bound with credit slavery.'

'Take Adolf Hitler', says Mr Lewis,

> as a point of departure, as a significant personal gesture across the face of Europe, as a political hero, as a puppet thrown up in response to an intolerable situation, as a Boulangist phantom, or anything you like. I myself am content to regard him as the expression of current German manhood – *resolved, with that admirable tenacity, hardihood, and intellectual acumen of the Teuton, not to take their politics second-hand, not also to drift, but to seize the big bull of Finance by the horns, and to take a chance for the sake of freedom.*

Can there be a better description than the passage I have italicised of what ought to be the spirit of the Scottish Movement – or anything further from the shallowness and stupidities, sheep's bleat of interdependence and moderation and general flux of the *Record*'s policy or, substantially, even the National Party's?

Mr Gasworth has given us a splendid little book on one of the most stimulating, versatile, searching and incorruptible of our living figures – almost, indeed, the only one of them who merits any of these adjectives – a man among a lot of dithering shadows, an authentic voice in a chaos of newspaper and cinema captions and radio din. It ought to be read by every one who thinks he can – or would like to be able to – stand on his own feet – 'no movement gathered here (thank Heaven!), merely a person, a solitary outlaw and not a gang', in Lewis's own words. That is to say, **a free man!**

C.M. Grieve, 23 July 1932

Gasset versus Gas

The *Record* has sunk to the last ignominy in foisting on its readers the utterly worthless 'Home Rule' interview with Ramsay MacDonald – a Scotsman who has never done anything for Scotland and who is so devoid of personal distinction or worth of any sort as to afford a perfect illustration of that hallucinatory action of politics which can invest such stupidity with an illusion of world importance. Happily the *Record*'s unscrupulous absurdity in this connection did not, as their letters show, impose on R.E. Muirhead, Lewis Spence and other nationalists, though it was, of course, eagerly swallowed by the Duke of Montrose and Mr McDowall, of the Cathcart Unionists, whom the *Record* has promoted into a 'notable Scot' and quoted as almost the only specimen of that curious breed to bear out its claim that its pronouncements have evoked widespread interest and letters of support from leading personalities. Those interested in the deeper realities of the Scottish Movement should not miss the splendid letter in the *Record* of 21 July by Archie Lamont of Glasgow University, while the letters by Hector Sutherland of Kirkcaldy and Donald Campbell of Rutherglen in the *Record* of 22 July show that up and down the country there is a growing body of men who have the whole thing in true perspective and are determined on far more radical developments than the *Record* advocates. The confused puerilities of the Editor of the *Scots Observer* on this subject equate very well with the grotesque interview with Lieut-Col T.C. Moore, MP, in the *Record* of 21 July. The absence of any grip of the facts, of any sense of political realities, of any 'adult' attitude to Scotland, in both of these, as in practically all that has appeared in the *Record*, is simply appalling and on a level with such a mentality as MacDonald's. The Lausanne farce has been referred to with appropriate contempt in these columns, but to get the whole problem bound up with it effectively into line readers should get hold of Ortega y Gasset's *The Revolt of the Masses* (George Allen & Unwin Ltd). 'Anyone', he writes,

> who wishes can observe the stupidity of thought, judgment, and action shown today in politics, art, religion, and the general problems of life and the world by the 'men of science', and, of course, behind them, the doctors, engineers, financiers, teachers and so on. The state of 'not listening', of not submitting to higher courts of appeal which I have repeatedly put forward as characteristics of the mass-man, reaches its height precisely in these partially qualified men. They symbolise, and to a great extent constitute, the actual dominion of the masses, and their barbarism is the most immediate cause of European demoralisation. Furthermore they afford the clearest example of how the civilisation of the last century, *abandoned of its own devices*, has brought about this rebirth of primitivism and barbarism. The most immediate result of this *unbalanced* specialisation has

> been that today, when there are more 'scientists' than ever, there are much less 'cultured' men than, for example, about 1750. And the worst is that with these turnspits of science not even the real progress of science itself is assured…

MacDonald is a typical barbarian of this sort. As Paul Scheffer, of the *Berliner Tageblatt* says: 'The mechanics of politics in our time seem to favour "centralised governments" in general. The men now in power in Germany do not pretend to be exceptional…' but are 'resolved to remain in power under all circumstances'. So with our MacDonalds and the like, but in this country stupid men like MacDonald and Baldwin still pretend to be 'exceptional' and are generally believed to be. Scheffer says: 'The reply of the Nazis to the tactics of the present Government will develop slowly. But unavoidably it will become clear to them that the present rulers are in fact Conservatives.' So are ours. The whole *Record* campaign with its insistence on monarchy, continued English over-control, support of the existing economic and imperial systems, etc., is a conspiracy unworthily masking itself behind a pretended interest in Scotland, to delude those great majority bodies of the Scottish electorate who are Socialist and Irish. How long will it take these to realise the callous stick-at-nothing Conservatism of the whole manoeuvre? Surely Scottish Socialists have seen through MacDonald. Surely the Irish in Scotland are not going to take the *Record*'s and *Evening News*'s anti-Irish policy – or the *Scots Observer*'s call for the repatriation of the Scottish Irish – lying down? The hope of Scotland lies in a concentration of these elements on the side of Nationalism opposed to the 'moderate' elements now trying to capture the Scottish Movement.

Scotland and England we are told are indissolubly united; the Crown must be maintained, and so forth. But why? The parrot-like insistence on these things goes on, but those who insist upon them neither analyse nor discuss nor submit to question these propositions which serve them for, they think, formidable premises. Without further investigation they start as from something incontrovertible. They have never set themselves the problems. They take them as they would take trams.

What Gasset says of Spain is equally true of Scotland.

> It would be interesting and even useful to submit to this test (of how it is organised in respect of command and obedience) the individual character of the average Spaniard. However, the operation would be an unpleasant one, and, though useful, repressing, so I avoid it. But it would make clear the enormous dose of personal demoralisation, of degradation, which is produced in the average man of our country by the fact that Spain is a nation which has lived for centuries with a false conscience in the matter of commanding and obeying. This degradation is nothing else than the receptance, as a normal constituted condition, of an irregularity, of something which, though accepted, is still regarded as not right. As it is impos-

sible to change into healthy normality what is of its essence unhealthy and abnormal, the individual decides to adapt himself to the thing that is wrong, making himself part of the crime or irregularity. All countries have passed through periods when someone who should not rule has made the attempt to rule over them, but a strong instinct forced them at once to concentrate their energies and to crush that irregular claim to exercise power. *They rejected the passing irregularity and thus reconstituted their morale as a people. But the Spaniard (the Scot) has done just the opposite; instead of resisting a form of authority which his innermost conscience repudiated, he has preferred to falsify all the rest of his being in order to bring it into line with that initial unreality. As long as this continues in our country it is vain to hope for anything from men of our race. There can be no elastic vigour for the difficult task of retaining a worthy position in history in a society whose state, whose State, whose authority, is of its very nature a fraud.*

Lord Middleton in his book on Ireland points out the ill-effects (so far as the continuance of English ascendancy was concerned) of the failure of Royalty to visit Ireland proportionately and shows how Scotland was relatively favoured – and so kept in thrall – by the cult of Balmoral and Royal Deeside. Isn't Ramsay MacDonald's occasional sentimental Scottish bletherings and frequent trips to Lossiemouth just an extension of the same dodge?

Miss Christine Orr takes me to task in a very confused and silly article in the *Record* for my talk of bloodshed. I may talk of bloodshed but she obviously doesn't know what she is talking about at all. Her whole idea of internationalism and world-peace is one of these 'incontrovertible propositions' referred to above – pieced together from newspaper propaganda and unaware of its real source, *viz.*, central banking propaganda. I need not go into that here – nor the necessity for individuals to stand on their own feet against all the current suggestioning of inter-dependence, the unimportance of the individual, the necessity of peace *at any price*, the decoying of intellectuals in favour of the mass-man. But there is one point that must be referred to. Miss Orr assumes that the peace sentiment is general and virtually contrasts my militant attitude with an assumed peace-desiring society at large. On the contrary it is the vast violence – the determination of the unfit to rule, to remain in power at all costs – that generates my attitude. I believe it is better to take any and every chance and die fighting a forlorn hope if need be than to submit to that monstrous thing. And Miss Orr and all who feel like her should carefully perpend the fact Gasset rightly emphasises.

A concrete example of this mechanism (of mass-man) is found in one of the most alarming phenomena of the last thirty years, *the enormous increase in the police force of all countries.* ... But it is foolishness for the party of 'law and order' to imagine that these 'forces of public authority' created to preserve order are always going to be content to preserve the order that the party desires. Inevitably they will end by themselves defining and deciding on the order they are going to impose… When, about 1800, the new industry began to create a type of man – the industrial worker – more criminally inclined than traditional types, France hastened to create a numerous police force. Towards 1810 there occurs in Great Britain, for the same reasons, an increase in criminality, and the British suddenly realise that they have no police. The Conservatives are in power. What will they do? Will they establish a police force? Nothing of the kind. They prefer to put up with crime, as well as they can. 'People are content to let disorder alone, considering it the price they pay for liberty.

'In Paris', writes John William Ward, 'they have an admirable police force but they pay dear for its advantages. I prefer to see, every three or four years, half a dozen people getting their throats cut in the Ratcliffe Road, than to have to submit to domiciliary visits, to spying, and to all the machinations of Fouché.'

Finally, let Scottish Nationalists remember Renan's words (and have no hesitation in risking the word I have italicised). 'To have common glories in the past, a common will in the present; to have done great things together; to wish to do greater; these are the essential conditions which make up a people. … In the past, an inheritance of glories and *regrets*; in the future, one and the same programme to carry out.'

C.M. Grieve, 30 July 1932

Communism and Literature

'Two heads are better than one', but not apparently in literature. Critics of Bolshevism have recently been emphasising that all literature is the product of individual genius – and cannot be evolved co-operatively by committees of writers, still less spring out of 'the folk consciousness'. I am not concerned in this article to defend the specific experiments with literature which are proceeding in Soviet Russia, but the essential question at issue is a much deeper one than can be disposed of merely by considering what is happening or is likely to happen there. Even if it is true that literature is there made subservient to propaganda in a fashion inimical to its best interests, and that even so it is produced by individual writers as in other countries and the idea of 'a literature by the people for the people', remains as much a myth there as elsewhere, that does not dispose of the fact that in other countries, the existing system has opposite but equal faults. Excessive individualism has led to eccentricities and an increasing gulf between the writers and the public at large. Even very moderately conservative people may well deplore the striving for sensationalism and publicity observable in many quarters and think that a greater measure of anonymity in authorship would be no bad thing to revert to, since it would tend to shift the emphasis in literary production from the personal to the general. That this would have salutory results will be at once realised by those who appreciate that great art is generally produced, as Professor Grierson has insisted, under a settled social order, and that, as Mr A.R. Orage has pointed out:

> The greatest writers and thinkers have always the jury of mankind in their minds as not merely the auditors but as the assessors of the case before them. To be sure, the greatest thinkers have also thoughts upon which it is impossible for common sense to pass judgment today; thoughts that it is perhaps not yet possible to reduce to truisms. But these the greatest thinkers refrain from putting forward as conclusions; they prefer to leave them as myths, as guesses, as poetry, or what not. Such, however, of their conclusions as can be expressed in plain terms always turn out to be the conclusions of common sense; and by that test they stand.

It is a test which can be applied to very little contemporary writing. Our judgments have been generally distorted by modern romanticism and the increasing stress on personal authorship, and we are apt to fail to take in a sufficient stretch of literary history to get the matter into proper perspective. In this connection it is useful to remember the old Celtic bardic system which reduced the personal element to a minimum and subjected the young poets to a vigorous technical training over a considerable period of years during which they graduated from the use of certain simple technical forms to the more complex ones. A revival of a similar discipline would be very healthy today.

Another useful angle of approach to this important question is a consideration of the history of our ballads. Were these works of individual authorship or communally produced? W.H. Hudson referred to the ballad 'as a form which appears to have arisen spontaneously in almost all literatures'. The late Professor W.P. Ker pointed out that the great ballad collections of Europe display many points in common, alike of subject, treatment, and metre, and are alike too in concealing the secret of their spontaneous origin, like Topsy in the story they may have 'growed'. All sorts of writers have debated their authorship and the extent to which they were co-operatively produced by the whole people, or, at least, modified into their final forms by their passage through oral tradition. The latest writer on this fascinating subject, Professor Gerould, of Princeton, on this vexed question of origins is no communalist, though he realises on how much communal material the ballad-maker worked. 'All in all', he says,

> we are forced to the conclusion that most ballads, both those which have been in circulation in later times and those of earlier date, have been composed by individuals. The qualities they possess with respect to music, to structural organisation, and to poetic style are the result of two equally

> important and inter-related factors; the development, at least as early as the twelfth century, of a traditional art in folk-song, which include the composition of ballads that were sharply focussed, dramatic, impersonal; and secondly the constant reshaping of ballads, once they were launched on the stream of oral tradition, by the co-operation of later generations, each of which learned the popular art and passed it on to the generation following.

His conclusion then is that individuals, who in some cases were fine poets, were responsible for the first draft of a ballad but in the course of its descent it received so many additions and alterations that as we have them today they may be fairly called the work of the folk-mind. My own point is that the bulk of our literature today lacks any such valuable corrective and that anything that can be done to bring artist and people together again in such co-operation is highly desirable. For the want of it writers have not only been divorced from common sense, but there has been an enormous deterioration of the general taste. In ancient Ireland the general public in their leisure hours could bring to the hearing of poems and stories a knowledge and appreciation of fine points in technique and tradition generally and a ready understanding of allusions that is sadly to seek today. In his recent paper on 'Education and the Drama in the Age of Shakespeare', Mr L.C. Knights is able to show that the greater part of the audience at the public theatres in Shakespeare's time was composed of men 'who were capable of a detached and at the same time vivid interest in words and the kind of pattern into which the dramatist might arrange them'. The significance of the want of this today, with all our alleged modern educational advantages, cannot be overstressed, and the bridging of the gulf between writers and public in this way is one of the major problems of modern culture.

Besides, there are other notable examples where the committee work of individually practically unknown men has made very notable additions to literature. Only one of these need be mentioned here and that is the outstanding case of the authorised version of the Bible. 'About the marvels of collaboration', says Orage,

> the world has not been curious enough. We all know that the Homeric poems may have been written by perhaps a score of poets. The greatest of all Indian epics is certainly not the work of one man. Yet both display unity enough; and the world speaks of Homer and Vyasa as their single authors. In Shakespeare's own time again, collaboration was a common practice. The inspired English translation of the Bible was the work of eleven obscure men. Bacon is known to have employed a good many young men in writing his works. So did Dumas. Still more to the point there is a weekly journal of some reputation of which most of the articles accepted for publication undergo an editorship, the effect of which is to make them indistinguishable from one another in style.

What can be done in one case can be done in another, and this submerging of individuality in a co-operative enterprise might in many directions be an invaluable corrective to modern literary tendencies. The communal production of literature cannot be dismissed as impossible. Authors' vanities and other things have prevented it being tried: but that does not dispose either of its practicability or, possibly, its desirability, apart altogether from the particular forms of it which are being fostered in Russia today.

C.M. Grieve, 6 August 1932

Ex Nihil, Nihil Fit

'He has not produced any new ideas and has not come nearer the solution of any great problem.' 'He cannot look a fact in the face without becoming frightened.' 'He has no real greatness.' These sentences are taken from a very outspoken and condemnatory analysis of a certain European politician who has been very much in the limelight recently, but are they not applicable to all the people, whether of the National Party of Scotland, the Democratic Scottish Self-Government Organisation, the Scottish Watch, the Scottish Patriots, the St Andrew's Home Rule Society, the Young Scots, the Cathcart Unionists, and Heaven only knows how many other bodies who are confounding counsel in Scotland today with their shameless mediocrity? Their lack of personal calibre of any kind condemns them. All their notions put together would not rank as a single substantive idea. Their democratic din is, in fact, an aspect of the very disease which has brought Scotland to its present pass – the disease of Jack being as good, if not better, than his master; the disease of a plague of vociferous nonentities who have not a single achievement of any sort to their credit entitling them to be heard on public questions, let alone, in any measure, to 'speak for Scotland'; the disease of an almost nation-wide lack of, and hatred of, distinction of any kind. *Ex nihil, nihil fit*; and out of these people nothing worth a rap can possibly emerge. If it could their individual records would have shown some measure of distinction or achievement in some direction or other before this. As it is they are 'null and void'. Before they aspire to lead national movements let them go and do something of some value themselves – let them bring some sort of prestige or evidence of quality to the movements in question.

The *Daily Record* pretended that its Plan for Scotland has evoked a wonderful response from 'leading Scots' – but was only able to give a few stupid excerpts from letters sent in by a few nobodies. Ramsay Macdonald's contribution was a characteristic 'put-off'; who else by any stretch capable of being considered a Scot of the slightest distinction contributed to the discussion? The whole movement has been prostituted to rampant mediocrity. The horrible shuffling – the fear of anything definite – the hatred of anything in the shape of a 'big idea' – is all in keeping. It is noteworthy that any attempt to concentrate on the crucial current problem of the financial system finds no favour in these stupid quarters; but that the only two organs of the slightest intellectual value the Scottish Movement has today – *The Modern Scot* and *The Free Man* – are Douglasite. So is every single individual in any branch of the Scottish Movement for whose intellectual capacity and integrity I have the slightest respect. But they are prevented by hordes of nonentities from exercising any commensurate influence on the development of the Movement. The fiat has gone forth; they must be ridiculed as cranks, dismissed as dreamers. Scotland is not to be saved by 'ideas'; but by the vast mob who haven't any.

To have established any position worth mentioning in any field of intellectual effort is enough to warrant a man's dismissal from influence in the Movement. He is at once made a target for denigratory reflections of every sort – generally anonymous or pseudonymous (let alone lacking the courage to face up to any idea these people dare not criticise their opponents even by name – they must use all the beastly journalistic arts of innuendo, suppression of replies, and so forth). To be a poet in particular is to be branded as a fool who must be dismissed from 'practical schemes'. What then? Are these people experienced public men, or have they even controlled important businesses? Not a bit of them.

Watch the names given space in the newspapers' accounts of these bodies or in their correspondence columns when Scottish issues are being discussed – and scarcely one has given any County Council, Town Council, or any public service, scarcely one of them has ever been associated with any greater business than running a whelk-stall. The few younger Scots who have done anything of any note are either 'extremists' at almost complete variance with the official voices and rank and file of these movements, or are constrained to manifest whatever sympathy they can and render whatever help they can from outside these movements. Edwin Muir seldom touches on political or 'practical' interests, but the trend of his ideas is clearly enough seen in his literary arguments on the need for a clean break with Scotland's past and a fresh start. Fionn McColla [*sic*] is another 'extremist'. Compton Mackenzie has in most directions very different ideas from those with whom he is associated in the National Party and elsewhere in Scottish movements, and must be as a rule simply appalled and disheartened by their crass idiocies and determination to do anything rather than think. So we might go round the little list of younger Scots of any achievement; they must give way to the polypseudonymous miasma of the *Record* or the *Express*, or the hydraheaded mob of nincompoops who are finding in the diversely-branching movement the chance of a little limelight for their imbecilities.

By the way, has the *Record* lost the toss – is the National Party more in Beaverbrook's pocket now? It would seem so – this municipal elections farce is his pet scheme, isn't it? Not that it matters much. The *Express* and the *Record* in this affair are pretty much six and half-a-dozen. The leader on 'Rhondda and

Clyde' in the *Glasgow Evening News* of 15th inst., is typical of the almost incredible brainlessness (even for Scotland) of the whole business. 'If there is to be recovery from the industrial depression,' we are told,

> it is the South that will most fully and rapidly benefit from it. We must face the facts that our heavy industries will be very slow starters in the recovery, and that the nature of the recovery may not favour them at all. The political situation will then be a strange one indeed. It is not difficult to imagine England ridding itself of bankrupt provinces and embarrassing the nationalists by presenting them with the freedom they want, and more. Then we should have a very troublesome baby to hold. It is to be hoped that the extremists will see the point.

It is to be hoped that the *Evening News* will. We extremists saw it long ago. The passage accurately defines what England's set policy has been and what the very probable contingency is. But we must be canny – let England make us a bankrupt province, but do not let us cut ourselves from whatever little crumbs of charity it may then be disposed to give us. And above all let us have no hatred of England – let us on the contrary be thankful to have been thus reduced to a bankrupt province and bear no ill-will, but, on the contrary, do all we can to let England continue to enjoy its ill-gotten gains and content ourselves that we have at least acted in a Christian spirit.

C.M. Grieve, 27 August 1932

D.H. Lawrence and the Essential Fact

The attention of Mr Lawrie Tod and all the other shallow brains who are deprecating any anti-English sentiments in connection with Scottish Nationalism and think they can found a realistic practical policy on that basis may be directed to certain significant passages in Catherine Carswell's splendid life of D.H. Lawrence, published under the title of *The Savage Pilgrimage*, and as fascinating an account of a genius as that wonderful account of the sculptor, Gaudier Brezka – Ede's *Savage Messiah* – which it resembles alike in title, brilliancy of writing, and permanent value.

'Perhaps from his North Midland upbringing and origin,' says Mrs Carswell – and have I not elsewhere referred to the North of England as 'Scotland Irredenta'? –

> Lawrence had a warm feeling for Scotch people. 'I don't care if every English person is my enemy,' he wrote to me once later; 'if they wish it, so be it.' I keep in reserve for the Scotch. The inexpressiveness of the Northern temper, implying, as it does, a distrust of easy verbal expression, was congenial to him. In the facile intellectualising of emotion he found

evidence of a certain poverty of nature. 'I think one understands best without explanations,' he said often. Or of those who talked and talked – 'they don't WANT to understand.'

In a footnote Mrs Carswell adds: 'Personal sympathies apart, Lawrence regarded "Celtic" influences – whether Welsh, Irish, or Scottish – as essentially destructive of the English genius and culture: this especially in politics.'

Lawrence was right, and any Scottish, Irish, or Welsh movement which fails to realise this and attempts to proceed on any other basis is not worth a damn.

Consider this in relation to the inept utterances of Mr Ian Macpherson in the *Scots Observer* on Home Rule for the Highlands, or the *Daily Record*'s appeal to An Comunn Gaidhealach – of all the boneless bodies in existence – to declare itself on this subject. The utter unreality of such expressions of opinion – their complete divorcement from 'real politik' – needs no further comment, and the sooner those who fancy that Scotland is not a unity but is portionable, whether politically, economically, or culturally, into Highlands and Lowlands, save under the distorting influence of Anglicised ideas, get rid of it the better. It is, of course, in keeping with this fatuity that the papers which are promulgating it should be anti-Irish, pro-Imperialist, and gravely concerned about De Valera's policy in particular. They have a great deal to learn. The 'Irish troubles' are not ended – they have scarcely begun. And Scottish interests are completely bound up with them and must pursue like ends.

Certain confused and confusing writers, chief among whom is the polypseudonymous gentleman who variously styles himself 'William Power', 'Lawrie Tod', 'Onlooker', 'Enterkin', and Heaven knows what else, and whose favourite cry is the adjective 'practical', wants us to be sensible – to be practical – to be businesslike. We are told that the Scottish people have always been that and will have nothing to do with fantastic schemes, but must be convinced that anything proposed clearly makes for their material benefit. It is not a conclusion that the history of Scotland since the Union, in our present plight today, seems in any way to justify. The words 'practical', 'business-like', 'sensible', and so on cut no ice in view of the facts, and are certainly far from synonymous with the conditions they imply. Nothing less resembling practicality, business-likeness, and so forth, than 'Lawrie Tod's' proposals in their name can be imagined. I am going to venture on a frank assertion; it is this – that certain things (I can think right off of twenty) are happening in Scotland today which imply a definite use of Scotland to ends not one person in ten thousand of our population can conceive; that they completely override the so-called 'practical considerations' of Lawrie Tod and his confreres; that, although their significance sticks out beyond all else in Scotland today, not one of them has yet been apprehended by any Scottish newspaper; and that their gravity entirely outweighs all the business-like matters with which such writers and the National Party are concerned, and involve such a reorientation of basic Scottish polity and functions that any argument which fails to take full account of them is *ipso facto* relegated to puerility. What are these twenty points? Ah! I could list them here in a moment, but I am not going to present the *Record* and the *Express* with material which is worth hundreds of pounds to either of them, apart from the fact that they would grossly misuse it. I have made other arrangements. But what I will do is this – I challenge Lawrie Tod or any like-minded to meet me anywhere in adequately arranged public debate and to talk about what is 'practical' and 'business-like', and I will immediately, to the complete satisfaction of any audience, dispose of their claims to represent anything of the sort, and demonstrate (without giving too much away) (1) that they do not know anything about anything of the kind, and (2) that they are utterly and irremediably ignorant of the major realities in relation to Scotland today and prospectively.

C.M. Grieve, 10 September 1932

On Standing One's Ground

An insistence upon standing one's ground is unpopular today. It automatically makes one a 'crank'. One is supposed to be ready to do anything for money, favour, or an easy life. Any refusal to take other people – particularly journalists – at their own valuation ensures one a hard time. So far as a poet is concerned, he is, of course, a 'figure of fun' from the outset – a legitimate prey for every brainless scribbler. His work can be misrepresented and ridiculed, but he has no redress – unless he is unusually resourceful and determined, as I flatter myself I am. Let me give two current examples of the sort of thing with which a Scottish writer has to contend.

I received a letter as follows from a Glasgow firm, viz.: –

> Exhibition representing contemporary Scottish literature. – An exhibition as above will be opened here by Mr Hugh Walpole early in January. In connexion (sic!) with it a Guide-Book Catalogue, which will be heavily illustrated, is now being prepared. This Catalogue will contain biographies of Scottish authors. I should be glad if you would kindly send me at your earliest convenience a personal notice somewhat after the patterns enclosed. Time is short, so the matter is one of some urgency. Please try and send a personal note by next Wednesday.

The questions this aroused to me were: – 1. Who is Hugh Walpole? 2. Who decides – unless they are all to be lumped together whether writers of consequence or mere scribbling nonentities – what relative space is to be given to various people? 3. Who determines whose photographs are to be used? 4. What 'prominent Scottish authors' (vide the Press) are to be present at the exhibition, and on what principle were these particular authors invited? And so on. Is the whole business to be 'window-dressed' by some commercial interest, and are

Scottish authors to be ranged by some bookseller's assistant? But 'the patterns enclosed herewith' settled me. They concerned John Geddie, whom we are told is 'one of the ablest and most encyclopædic of Scottish journalists', whose 'intellectual energies have overflowed into numerous books'; and A.J. Cronin, who, we are told, 'is devoted to literature, and it seems like *Hatter's Castle* and *Three Loves* will be the first of a list of remarkable works from his pen.' Rats!

I replied that I could not accede to the request, and wished nothing about myself or my writings to appear in the Catalogue in question, but, if they would not respect my wishes, I would take whatever proceedings might be available to sue in respect of any inaccuracies, omissions, etc. But I shall certainly procure a copy of the Catalogue, and look forward to no little amusement.

The other instance concerns a review of my latest book in the *Daily Record and Mail*. It is signed 'E. de B.' and ridicules the volume, contending that I am for the most part incomprehensible but, where I am comprehensible, don't write poetry. In next day's issue an unimportant rhymster was highly commended, and the following day a couple of columns was given to some crude doggerel by W.D. Cocker. 'E. de B.' says I am increasingly under the influence of James Joyce. I know too much about Joyce not to know the full absurdity of this remark. A village idiot with half an eye could see that neither in technique nor subject-matter have Joyce and I one iota in common; the silly fellow merely said so because I mentioned Joyce – which is probably all he knows about him. But why should the Editor of 'Scotland's National Paper', which pretends to be doing so much for the Scottish Renaissance, turn over my book to such a moron? He refused to publish an article of mine on Scottish Nationalism because he could 'only do so in a way which would hurt me – which he had no wish to do.' But he prostitutes his columns to the stupid venom of a nitwit and lets him dismiss with contempt work that is highly esteemed by critics and fellow-poets of the highest international repute. It does not hurt me at first hand; but it hurts himself and his paper and the cause of Scottish Poetry – and the injury to the latter's interests hurts me in a way that justifies this exposé and makes me all the more determined, and certain of my ability, to stand my ground.

C.M. Grieve, 12 November 1932

The Scots Vernacular

Mr T.S. Eliot has said that fiction – not religion – is now the opium of the people, and my friend, Mr Eric Linklater, seems to be suffering from an overdose of it. His remarks on 'The Limitations of Dialect' (extensively reported in *The Scotsman* and other papers on Friday), in his address to the Scottish Association for the Speaking of Verse (Edinburgh Branch), were singularly irrelevant to the issues with which they purported to deal. *Inter alia*, he said that Scots was not an 'adult' language, meaning, one presumes, fit for the whole range of modern expressive purposes; and contended that 'in everyday life there was a natural evolutionary process in language which tended to eliminate local characteristics, and the attempts which had been made to revive antique and vanished forms of speech were against the natural process.' Everyday life has precious little to do with literature. He is not only depending here on a false analogy between life and art, and attacking the autonomy of the latter, but his whole argument is only a variant in respect of literature of the nonsense about the 'increasing interdependence of nations', 'the trend towards a world state', etc., frequently libelled against the so-called 'narrow nationalism' which Mr Linklater inconsistently declares he supports in other connections. Just as the growth of intensive nationalism is an outstanding feature internationally today, so all European literatures are intensively cultivating dialect, archaic, and technical forms in a fashion which disproves Mr Linklater's declaration that the trend of language is in the opposite direction. It is always as dangerous linguistically as in other connections to fancy that the battle is with the big battalions. Some of the most powerful influences in modern European literature, Ibsen, for example, wrote in relatively little known languages, and that neither restricted their international influence nor stunted their intellectual growth, as Mr Linklater fears Scottish writers may do by confining themselves to what he calls 'the limited area of the vernacular, rather than by exercising themselves in the copious magnificence of English'. I know of no Anglo-Scots whose performances in the latter need abate any man's preference for the former.

The value, and certainly the relative value, of all modern English literature – in poetry, say, between Milton and Doughty – is highly debatable. Professor Saintsbury, in his monumental history of criticism, thought that major work need only be looked for in certain great established languages, and so he failed to note the beginnings of that tremendous literature in the little known language of Russia which has since been the paramount force in *welt-literatur*. It is difficult to imagine what Mr Linklater means by an 'adult' language. All languages have their particular qualities and particular limitations, and it is a radical mistake to imagine that the effects can be secured in English can be duplicated in French or German, or vice versa. The peculiar virtues of Scots produce works which are strictly incomparable, i.e. insusceptible of comparison with the very different products of other tongues, and there is no more reason why we should eschew or belittle these than there is why we should dismiss poetry altogether because few people read it, and think that we will find salvation in 'the main stream of contemporary thought', which is presumably popular fiction or the reptile press.

'The spirit blows where it listeth', and there is no more vulgar error – disproved by all literary history – than to imagine that it is aligned with commonsense (i.e. majority opinion), or that it depends on its relation with 'contemporary speech', and cannot be manifested in 'dictionary dredging'. Mr

Linklater presumes to lay down a 'must' for Scottish writers; tells us – without showing how he knows, as, indeed, he cannot – what Milton or Shakespeare could not have done, and insists that Burns was 'confined within comparatively narrow limits by the disabilities of the language he employed'. If future Scottish writers are not confined within any narrower limits, they – or their readers – will have little to complain of. It is the essence of bad criticism to refuse to consider what exactly an author tried to do, and to what extent he succeeded, and to waste time imagining what the results would have been if he had shared the critic's personal prejudices instead and tried to do something entirely different. It is absurd to say that English is a language 'in the main stream of contemporary thought'. Most people do not think; and all the significant thinking of the day is probably being done by a dozen or two people using (and necessarily so!) all sorts of different languages, whereas for all the contemporaneity of their 'thought', 99 per cent of the users of English, or the other so-called great languages, might just as well be employing Cherokee or Swahili. And so far as future Scottish writers are concerned, the poor showing our countrymen have made in English literature in the past does not support the idea that they would be better advised to continue struggling with media and traditions so radically unsuited to their psychologies, instead of reversing the process which has restricted them to so subordinate and almost irrelevant a role, and concentrating instead on Gaelic or a full canon of Scots.

The falsity of Mr Linklater's whole position is shown by his remark that 'an ardent nationalist might not be embarrassed by the Englishman's failure to understand his speech, but to find himself not understood in his own country must certainly disturb his equanimity.' But poetry is not understood by most people in any language, and practitioners of the most difficult synthetic Scots can reflect that they are no worse off in respect of popular comprehension than Charles Doughty, Gerard Manley Hopkins, or T.S. Eliot in England, Soffici in Italy, Rilke in Germany, or Kruchonyk or Pasternak in Russia, and consider it better worth while to share the disabilities of such writers than the advantages of any best sellers.

C.M. Grieve, 26 November 1932

Scotland and Race Psychology

A correspondent writes asking me to slay two 'great lions' of a certain school in the interests of the Scottish Movement. The 'giants' in question are J. Emile Marcault, Principal of the Theosophical World University, and Ivan A. Hawliezek, who have collaborated in writing *The Next Step in Evolution: a Sequel to 'Evolution of Man,' being a brief survey of the psychological evolution of the Aryan Race, with some notes on present-day world problems.* I agree with my correspondent who writes: 'I have seldom read a brochure so full of error about the Celtic peoples, and about the Anglo-Saxons and Nordic Races. Evidently, according to them, the Romans were better.' In writing direct to the authors, my correspondent said:

> Many of us have read your book very carefully. It is full of errors which I hope you may be able to correct if your brochure arrives at another edition. When you visualise England to yourselves where do you put the boundary line? At the Cheviot Hills, the Tweed, or the town of Berwick? Scotland gave its King to England in 1603, and the Crowns were united. Scotland (unfortunately) amalgamated its Parliament with that of England in 1707. But Scotland in consequence did not cease to be a nation. England's alternative name (by treaty) was South Britain; Scotland's alternative name was North Britain. England is not synonymous with Britain and should not be used as an alternative or to create a little variation. Just so you might say – as you say of Greece and Rome – Scotland and England evolved together from 1603. Then, as to races, there is again a terrible mix-up. We in Scotland are not Anglo-Saxons and not Teutons. This is an error which we must combat at all points. You mention the Irish race and the Irish. This is entirely misleading. You certainly mention the Keltic or Mediterranean people, but no other mention is made of the Celts, nor of the Gaelic language, which is supposed to be closely allied to Sanskrit. The Celtic peoples inhabited (and do still) Brittany, Wales, Cornwall, and most of Scotland. Their place-names, family names, folk lore, all show this.

What interests me most, however, and seems most suspiciously significant, is the relationship of these errors of omission and commission to general prejudices founded on the established political order; the revelation of precisely the same sort of mentality as prevented even highly intelligent people in Ireland fifty years ago crediting that (contrary to English assumptions and pro-English propaganda) – there could be anything worth recovering in ancient Gaelic literature, or, again, just the same sort of thing as prevents many Scots even yet thinking of their country's past, present, and potentialities save in terms of the English ethos. It is akin, too, to that covert biasing and control of the League of Nations by the Great Powers – and by international finance – which vitiates its entire organisation and gives its activities an entirely different meaning and effect than its declared objectives warrant. The authors are hopelessly unscientific and, consciously or unconsciously, on the side of the big battalions and propagandists of the subtler interests of the established powers all the time.

'You will realise no doubt that in a book of 84 pages, which covers fully 100,000 years of history, it is impossible to mention each nation by name', writes Mr Hawliezek to my friend. 'This must serve as a sufficient apology for not mentioning the Scottish people by name. It does not betoken a lack of appreciation on our part of their excellent qualities.' An appreciation which finds other peoples worthier of mention requires a different defence. But there is no defence. In the period in question the Scots have had a significance for humanity at large which far outweighs that of most other European nations, and it is of so distinctive a character that it ought to have had due consideration – especially at this juncture when its renewed and intensified manifestation is likely to be one of the most significant features of the next step in European evolution. Scotland has had far too much of that pretence of appreciation of its great qualities on the part of people who have lost no opportunity of leaving them out of account until objection was taken and such belated explanations and expressions of admiration evoked. Scotland's claims to recognition in all directions have been 'more honoured in the breach than in the observance', but we are having no more of this from any quarter or in any connection.

M. Marcault is even more specious. 'It would greatly serve the work of the Theosophical University we have at heart,' he writes,

> if students in each nation would seriously undertake to work out the method of approach to race-psychology which Theosophical teaching provides for us for their own people. Our booklets were partly meant as an incentive to much study, and if you would form, or induce the formation of, a group of Scottish students to elucidate in some detail the psychology of a race which I love truly I should be glad indeed.

No doubt! But a 'method of approach' which does such injustices to the Scottish people and bases itself on a preference for other races scarcely recommends itself to us. Why should we waste time dabbling with a 'race psychology' which is invalidated by its own admission that it lacks – and looks to us for – the elucidation in some detail of our own psychology? Are we a mere essential appendix to its propositions? M. Marcault and his collaborator put the cart before the horse and ask us to assume that their general theory – a monstrous abracadabra – is correct or at least useful and be good enough to adapt the facts of our own case to their framework. It is an unreasonable and impertinent suggestion and throws a flood of singularly uninviting light on the mentalities of those who advance it.

C.M. Grieve, 3 December 1932

Fundamental Issues and Party Policy

Reviewing the summer issue of *The Modern Scot*, in the *New English Weekly*, my friend, Mr A.R. Orage, said *inter alia*,

> I should like to believe that the contents of *The Modern Scot*, even when not nationalistic, are at any rate matters of interest to Nationalists and that its admirable articles and critical comments are the kind of thing the Nationalist Movement really appreciates. Unfortunately, it is difficult for

me to persuade myself that among Scottish Nationalists there is more than a fractional per cent concerned with cultural ideas. The innocent reader would derive, from any issue of *The Modern Scot*, a very flattering and a very false impression of the mentality and ideology of the Scottish Nationalist Movement.

Orage, of course, is absolutely right. The Scottish Nationalist Movement in its present form derived its impetus from a small group of writers vitally concerned with ideas and able, because of their intellectual calibre and their knowledge of various European cultures and their dynamic contemporaneity of mind and proleptic faculty, to get completely free of the entanglements of English culture and envisage a separate Scottish culture altogether on the basis of its distinctive traditions, psychology, and potentialities. To get the national arts of Scotland, cabined and confined on all sides, thwarted by the unconscionable prejudices of Anglo-Scoticism, ignored in the schools and universities, betrayed now by the sentimental duplicity of the Kailyairders, and now by the incalculable, impalpable coils of Anglicisation, into this creative perspective was no easy matter; and, when the history of the movement comes to be written, the range of reference to European writers and thinkers of all kinds used to throw light on the problems involved and destroy the English monopoly of influence, in the writings of these pioneers, will be found amazing. They brought Scotland to the bar of world thought and the creative spirit and found it virtually bankrupt. Literally they had – so far as Scotland was concerned – to make bricks without straw. A period of intense experimentalism – of a complete overthrowing of established traditions – began. It was speedily realised that an effective cultural movement of this kind was only possible under conditions of political and economic independence – and that the latter in themselves were of no account to any intelligent person except in so far as they might facilitate the former. The political movement developed rapidly – and forgot the latter fact. The vast majority of those attracted to it came in for stupid and superficial reasons and speedily swamped out the original ideas – with the aid of (probably unconscious) place-hunters and careerists playing to the gallery. As a consequence the intellectual status of the arguments and notions upon which 99 per cent of the Movement rests is not only beneath contempt, but is confined to that very framework of English culture in the broadest sense, and English party-political conceptions in the specifically political field, which it was the initial design of the Movement to knock to smithereens. The overwhelming bulk of the National Party's appeal is addressed and accommodated to the very mentality which it was the first – and ought to be the main – purpose of the Movement to destroy. And, once again, the core of really creative spirit which made the movement is struggling against an ubiquitous Englishry like the formless might of the Great Boyg in Ibsen's *Peer Gynt*.

'We must appeal to the public on their own level to catch votes.' Precisely!

The policy of the Movement has been prostituted to this – though that destroys its own *raison-d'être*. How else can the public be appealed to? Not by pandering to them in any such way. Just as these few writers and thinkers gave the Movement its initial impetus in the teeth of public indifference, so the same integrity could have carried the Movement far further and made it infinitely more valuable if it had not been diluted and adulterated in the name of so-called 'practical politics'. This is the difference between creative and conforming politics. The Movement may be gaining the greater part of the Scottish electorate, but it is assuredly losing its own soul. The very methods of organisation and propaganda – the types of schemes put forward – the continued failure to realise the bankruptcy of mere politics, and the fact that the real struggle lies in the economic field – all these are the very sign-manuals of the English system. No matter how great a measure of so-called national independence can be secured thereby it will still remain a mere Devolution of the English idea; and the bulk of its protagonists have not even their pretended Nationalism sufficiently at heart to induce them to make good their English-contrived ignorance of Gaelic, Scots, their accompanying literatures, and the real history and significance of Scotland. Their 'nationalism' is manifesting itself only on one plane – and that a very inferior and relatively unimportant one – which, of course, is dictated by the fact that they are operating within the framework of English preconceptions with only the slightest of quasi-Scottish variations. Nor can they cease to do so until they get in earnest about the business and really study Scottish literature and history. Most of their reading is still confined to English novels, newspapers, and so forth. Orage is absolutely right – and, *ipso facto*, the whole Scottish Movement is correspondingly wrong.

C.M. Grieve, 10 December 1932

Scottish Scenery

The facts brought out in the recent wireless discussion on Scottish weather between Dr A.M. Clark and Mr J.W. Herries – particularly the relative rain and sunshine statistics between Scotland and England – serve an excellent purpose in showing us how little we know about our own country, how utterly wrong many of our commonest assumptions are, and how difficult the necessary data is to come by. I have frequently pointed out that to all intents and purposes Scotland is an undiscovered country and that nine-tenths of our vaunted love for it is simply a myth through which the real facts are not allowed to transpire. Nothing confirms this more completely than the extraordinary absence of exact descriptions of scenery in our poetry, and literature generally. As many writers pointed out apropos his recent Centenary, Scott has obscured the whole of the Borders in a romantic haze which is foreign to their nature to such an extent that even yet it is extremely difficult to see the reality. His intromissions with the

Highlands were no less artificial, misleading – and inferior to the truth. The whole of the 'Celtic Twilight' business is another instance of the same thing. So is 'Kailyairdism'. Even Burns seldom gives us any graphic detail; most of his descriptions are vague eighteenth century work. The real thing seldom penetrates through the generalised epithets, the conventional jargon. The trail of the rubber-stamp is over the bulk of his work. In prose it is the same thing. Contrast Scotland's case with England's in this respect. Think of the loving and meticulous elaboration of detail in descriptions of English scenes; and of the continuous and amazing evolution of the English attitude to landscape manifested in its vast treasury of poems, essays, and novels. The same process has virtually not made a beginning in Scotland. Practically all our Scottish descriptive books are feeble, flabby things like T. Ratcliffe Barnett's or Alasdair Alpin MacGregor's – scrappy, sentimental, negligible as literature. It is an appalling thought that modern Scotland has not produced anything half so good even as Stanley Baldwin's *On England.* J.J. Bell's *Glory of Scotland* won't do – it simply isn't. A mass of guide-book stuff churned up with a little pawky humour and a petty button-holing sentimentality is a poor substitute for the book of the calibre of *Arabia Deserta* Scotland should evoke. The first man who can really write and knows Scotland – or any part of it – thoroughly, and is inspired by a spirit in keeping with its magnificent variety of scenery, its tragic and wonderful story, and its unequalled potentialities, will score a tremendous success. It is notable that such a mere journalist as H.V. Morton, though all his books on England, Ireland, and Wales have sold enormously, should have sold tens of thousands more copies of his *In Search of Scotland* – though he found nothing of the essence of it. And in Scottish poetry above all, the future lies in exact notation. Almost the only poem I know that approximates to the immediate possibilities in this direction is the short 'Inversnaid' by that wonderful descriptive artist, Gerard Manley Hopkins; practically everything else I have read looks very darkly indeed through the glass of an alien and inappropriate diction. It is time to abandon this transpontine stuff. Let us insist upon an appropriate spirit, first-hand observation, a resolute grappling with the hard facts, endless concentration on the seizure of significant details. Scotland is one of the most wonderful countries in the world; let this – not stale or silly *clichés* – be reflected in our writing. It will be no easy matter to break through the hopelessly bad traditions which are so long established. All the vital lineaments of the country are grossly overlaid with false and foolish conceptions. Nothing less than a psychological revolution will enable us to get rid of these. Linguistic and technical problems of all kinds, too, are involved. The forms suitable to the softer and more obviously harmonious character of England will not serve for Scotland; the whole tempo of our country with its far greater variety and wildness of scenery is radically different. English, without manipulations which have nowhere yet been attempted, is an impossible medium for our purpose; it is the reverse of autochthonous. Doughty had to manipulate English for Arabia. But in Gaelic and Scots we have media to hand the amazing resources of which have been hardly more exploited than the scenery of our country itself. Perhaps the two are indissolubly bound together and the realisation of the qualities of our country depends upon the true use of our lapsed languages. However that may be, it is a national scandal of the first degree that a country like England should give rise to one of the greatest literatures of the world, and that faithfully-observed and most appropriately written books of descriptive work should be being added continually to that tradition and its poetry enriched with beautifully-developed aspects of love and understanding of it, while nothing is written of Scotland that deserves a moment's notice from any critic of standing. This is the real Scottish problem. We do not love our country. False sentiment is all we manifest. The quality of our regard must, like everything else, be tested by its fruits – and a literature so qualitatively inferior implies an equally unworthy attitude.

Gray wrote of Scotland: 'The mountains are ecstatic, and ought to be visited in pilgrimage once a year. None but those monstrous creatures of God know how to join so much beauty to so much horror. A fig for your poets, painters, and clergymen, that have not been among them.'

Alas! those who have have so far been worth little more. Let us make a New Year vow – to see Scotland, to *really* see it (no easy task!), and to do what we can to wipe out this national disgrace.

C.M. Grieve, 24 December 1932

Dunbar and Burns

The Porpoise Press are to be congratulated on the publication, at the low price of 12/6, of *The Poems of William Dunbar*, edited by Dr Wm Mackay Mackenzie. No more timely or important service could have been rendered to the new movement in Scots Letters. 'A recent enquiry', as Dr Mackenzie points out in his preface, 'through the bookshops of Edinburgh disclosed the fact that there was but one copy of Dunbar's poems for sale, and that a handsomely bound, and therefore costly, example of the first collected edition in two copies.' This was a scandalous state of affairs which Dr Mackenzie's edition now helps to rectify, and it is to be hoped that it will secure such a measure of support from the book-buying public as will enable them to go ahead with other much-needed, moderately-priced and editorially up-to-date editions of our Scots classics. Little more can be done until such time as Scots Literature is accorded its proper place in our schools and universities, when editions that can be published at 2/6 or 5/- may become practicable. Within the limits of this edition Dr Mackenzie makes an ideal editor. It is a pity that the scheme could not have comprised an adequate biographical and critical study and technical analysis of the poetry and a much more detailed apparatus of notes on the historical, philological, and other aspects of his work. The condition of Scots Letters today is such that one firm having commissioned and issued a study of Dunbar – Rachel Annand Taylor's, issued by Faber & Faber – there is little or no possibility of inducing any other firm for a considerable period of years to publish any countervailing valuation, no matter how bad the first-mentioned was. Mrs Taylor's book on Dunbar was therefore nothing short of a tragedy. It was written from an angle preposterously antagonistic to Dunbar – entirely destitute of that sympathy essential to any real understanding. It was, therefore, neither more nor less than a hopeless travesty.

'Not Burns – Dunbar!' and 'Return to Dunbar' have been among the slogans of the new tendencies in Scots Letters. It is not difficult to see why. Burns – or rather the Burns cult (which is a very different thing from any knowledge of Burns' poetry, let alone any knowledge of poetry in general) – had for generations completely obscured the whole tradition of Scots poetry, of which he was only a part. Burns summed up a tradition and brought it to an end. No further progress was possible in that direction. He gave no new impetus to Scots poetry. The result was the dreary waste of post-Burnsian imitation, lit by scarcely the smallest gleam of genuine inspiration. Scots poetry had as a result been brought to a lamentable pass. If it was to be revived outlets must be sought in very other directions. It was necessary to concentrate not on what Burns had done, but on what he had not done.

Not to vie with Burns in his own field was all the more necessary since that field was in many respects already remote from current interest. Much of his work is eighteenth century junk of no value whatever; much of it is self-repetition of the most banal kind; much of it embodies moral and 'democratic' ideas which are badly 'dated'; most of it refers to conditions of rural life we have left behind and to which we have no intention of returning; his love-poetry applies the same stock phrases to all sorts of women, but psychological discrimination – anything that would enable us to identify one from the other, let alone anything in keeping with the contemporary attitude to love – of people beyond the penny novelette stage – is sadly to seek; and little he wrote has any bearing whatever on present-day problems or any vital bearing on the evolution of poetry. Even in natural description he seldom passes beyond vague general terms; detailed and specific realisation is not in his line. He is best in satire perhaps, but here the personnel and issues with which he was concerned are for the most part 'the deadest of dead meat'. From the purely poetic point of view his work is singularly uninteresting; the emphasis is almost always on the now generally demoded content and seldom on the manner; contemporary poets have little to learn from him technically; his use of Scots is not of a type likely to be helpful to those concerned now with the potentialities of that medium; and his choice of subject matter, his angles of approach, the very texture of his mind are singularly antipathetic to most people. It is specially to be noted that enthusiasm for Burns is generally most prominent in people who have little or no use for most of what is accepted as the greatest poetry of the world. These are, in fact, mutually exclusive.

Dunbar, on the contrary, is singularly modern. The interests he arouses are mainly technical. He was a superb craftsman. 'Dunbar', says one reviewer, 'was an effective versifier and breathed freely on many planes of poetic inspiration, but he had neither the large-hearted humanitarianism of Burns, nor the broad-minded humanity of Sir Walter Scott.' Precisely! That sort of large-hearted humanitarianism has run its course, and its natural fruits are such things as the Burns Clubs, Harry Lauderism, and the snivelling sentiments of men like Ramsay MacDonald; while the recent centenary farce showed what wonderfully broad minds Scott's influence has propagated in our midst. Both types are the greatest menaces to the further urgently necessary developments of the human spirit in Scotland. To call Dunbar petty-minded while admitting that he is a great poet is to invite the obvious retort that we can do with far fewer swollen but impotent minds in our midst in lieu of his like again.

One man genuinely concerned about poetic form is worth thousands with the woolly sentiments about poetry which are generally prevalent; and it is for this reason that the vital spirits in modern Scots literature are repudiating Burns and turning to Dunbar – a process that is naturally incomprehensible to those who are incapable of purely artistic interests and who regard as poetry only what reflects their own moral and ethical prepossessions.

C.M. Grieve, 28 January 1933

Poetry and Plain Talk

The idea that there are certain kinds of subject matter or diction more appropriate to poetry than others dies hard. My 'Second Hymn to Lenin' and some other recent works are taken to task in the current *Modern Scot*, and condemned for their bald prosaical character. I am told that it is not the truth or untruth of what I say in such poems that is regretted, but their irresponsibility – that Communism calls for more serious treatment than I give it; that there is a case against Gœthe, but it would require a greater philosophical earnestness than I bring to the task to establish it. My withers are unwrung; I seem to remember other poems against which precisely the same charges are made, and propose to consider their fate. The *Modern Scot*'s points are arguable enough; and are certainly made in far more allowable terms than in certain other cases recently where substantially the same criticism, were made in ways to which I took violent exception.

I think Matthew Arnold was right when he wrote:

> More and more I feel that the difference between a mature and a youthful age of the world compels the poetry of the former to use great plainness of

speech as compared with the latter; and that Keats and Shelley were on a false track when they set themselves to reproduce the exuberance of expression, the charm, the richness of images, and the felicity of the Elizabethan poets. Yet critics cannot get to learn this, because the Elizabethan poets are our greatest, and our canons of poetry are founded on their works. They still think that the object of poetry is to produce exquisite bits and images – such as Shelley's *Clouds shepherded by the slow, unwilling wind*, and Keats's *Passim*: whereas modern poetry can only subsist by *its contents*; by becoming a complete *magister vitæ* as the poetry of the ancients did; by including, as theirs did, religion with poetry, instead of existing as poetry only, and leaving religious wants to be supplied by the Christian religion as a power existing independent of the poetical power. But the language, style, and general proceedings of a poetry which has such an immense task to perform must be very plain, direct and severe, and it must not lose itself in parts and episodes and ornamental work, but must press forward to the whole.

Very well! It follows that in poems like mine on Gœthe, where I wish to express contempt and ridicule, I am not going to use a refined and dignified medium. I am not going merely to say I am contemptuous, but to show it by the very language I use – and if I am going to attack a particular philosophy it is enough to do it, not to put forward an alternative one, not to do the other the honour of carefully meeting it point by point, like a schoolboy who must not only get the correct answer to a sum but detail how he worked it out.

But there is more in it than that. I am in excellent company. I have the tradition of Scots poetry in particular behind me. As Naomi Mitchison says: 'The elders who attacked Catherine Carswell are still the people with power, but the real muse of Scotland, from Dunbar to Burns and beyond, was always crude, vigorous, unashamed of speech and of acts.' Lewis Spence has recently been writing about Sir David Lyndesay's *Satire of the Thrie Estaits*. He condemns it for practically the same reasons as my 'Second Hymn' has been condemned by the *Modern Scot* and others. 'Had it been infused by a noble wrath it might have been among the greatest of our literary monuments,' he says, 'but it employed a scurrility and baseness of method which one cannot believe even the most debased among those it lampooned would have stooped to. Worse still, from the point of view of the national genius, *it is almost destitute of intellectual argument and political merit*.' I incur practically the same strictures all these centuries later. So do all works that go with the gloves off for what they detest. We know too well these 'noble wraths' that are approved by their very targets. The *Satyre* knew its business: and Mr Spence still finds it profitable to write about it today. I would rather have written it than all our post-Burnsian lyrics put together. How many of them will articles be written about a century or two hence?

Mr Spence goes on: 'It is the method and machinery of "The Jolly Beggars."' Precisely! Burns's greatest work, I think. T.F. Henderson is right:

> Burns triumphs in spite of an almost elementary knowledge of the metrical art. Metrically 'The Jolly Beggars' is a mere disordered and incongruous medley of scraps from the old vernacular 'makaris' and the innominate rhymers of tradition, and the broadsides and penny chapbooks. It is resonant of the echoes and refrains and sentiments of a miscellaneous crowd of preceding bards, celebrated and obscure. It is wholly lacking not merely in artistic originality, but almost in individuality of metrical achievement, and never was a literary history unauthorised by the higher conventions, and, in fact, *so unpretentious almost to contemptibility*.

I am very willing to be equally contemptible. To blazes with the 'higher conventions'!

C.M. Grieve, 4 February 1933

Uilleam MacDhunleibhe

In the long overdue revaluation of Scottish Literature that is now proceeding, one of the figures most in need of recognition is undoubtedly the Gaelic poet, Uilleam MacDhunleibhe (William Livingston), and the pretentions of any one who claims to be able to view our traditions as a whole in proper perspective can hardly be put to a better preliminary test than the question of his rating. The matter is vitally important on account of the fact that he has hitherto been occluded by precisely those forces of pro-English and radically anti-Scottish sentiment which have travestied the whole course of our literature and resulted in people prating of puerile poetasters like Tannahill and Motherwell as typically Scottish (and better poets) than John Davidson, for example – magnifying Burns to the exclusion of Dunbar – and vaunting a one-sided attitude content, so long as it knew a group of petty vernacular or Anglo-Scottish rhymsters, to remain in ignorance of Alasdair MacMhaighstir Alasdair and the whole body of Scottish Gaelic poetry.

Matters are no whit better in Scottish Gaelic literature than in Scots Vernacular literature. If the latter has been reduced to a pass in which all true standards are lost and poets of real value obscured by a horde of post-Burnsian imitators, so in Gaelic literature sight has been lost of the great traditions, and the whole field is monopolised by a host of insignificant versifiers expressing Wee Free sentiments. The ministerial voice is ubiquitous, and poems are judged by their conformity to sectarian dogmas and canons of provincial respectability. The man outside this mindless ruck stands no chance. And, above all, it is insistent that the substance of poetry must be silly vapourings, chocolate-box lid pictures of nature, and trite moralisings. Penny novelette love is all right, but not politics, not religion, not war, not anything that can appeal to an adult intelligence. Finally, good poetry cannot be anti-English. It must bow the knee to Kirk and State. Anglophobia and sedition are out of the question.

These last, happily, were of the very essence of Livingston's work. He did not write love poetry. He did not address himself to any of the infantile themes on which 90 per cent of versification depends. He wrought, instead, in an epic vein, concerned with the stern substance of Scottish history. He is a splendid masculine poet, who has 'put away childish things'. Such a poet was sure of misprisal and misrepresentation in his pusillanimous and effeminate age. The irresistible verve of his utterance, the savagery of his satire, are abhorrent to the spineless triflers who want petty prettifyings, and not any devotion to matters of life and death.

A new Scotland is not to be built up on inane musings; and Livingston was a forerunner of all that is vital in our Nationalist Movement. He ought to stand a better chance of due recognition today than he did during his lifetime when a passionate love for Scotland, a detestation of the English, faculties of virile versification, and a creative concern for Gaelic were generally regarded as forms of insanity and suppressed by all the forces of pro-English propaganda. After Alasdair MacMhaighstir Alasdair, Duncan Bàn MacIntyre, and a few others of that period of splendid efflorescence, he is practically the only Scottish Gaelic poet of the slightest consequence till we come down to Domhnull Mac na Ceardaich in our own day.

Born in 1808, he died in 1870, and is buried in Janefield Cemetery, Glasgow. His grave ought to be one of the places of pilgrimage in a renascent Scotland. But we are still living in a country which has a lie in its right hand and does not know it.

Hugh MacDiarmid, 25 February 1933

Professor Berriedale Keith and Imperial Constitution

Organised Scottish Nationalism has progressively eschewed discussion of fundamental issues, and confined itself to what its opponents consider 'reasonable'. In other words, adapting itself almost entirely to the 'mentality' that depends upon newspaper snippets, its concern has been almost exclusively with minor adjustments and such shallow differences of opinion as in no wise threaten to disrupt the existing system or involve any fundamental changes. The realisation of the whole programme that has been officially proclaimed by the National Party of Scotland, let alone the Duke of Montrose's party, would only exemplify 'the greater the change the more the same'. The radical difference that alone can constitute Scottish nationality in any real or useful sense of the term is nowhere realised or sought for in these piffling proposals; and this can be best appreciated by considering the declarations that have been made by the National Party on the questions of the Empire and the Crown, in the light of the comprehensive new book on *The Constitutional Law of the British Dominions*, by Professor Arthur Berriedale Keith, of Edinburgh University (Macmillan) who, incidentally, is one of the supporters of the Duke of Montrose.

The National Party announce as their objective, 'Scottish independence within the British Commonwealth of Nations' – a self-contradictory phrase that the junta controlling the party have persisted in adhering to, although in the early days (before any concern with ideas was abandoned in order to concentrate on vote-catching) the most important debates centred on this, and several delegate conferences carried by majorities a repudiation of the absurdity, insisting instead on an Independent Scotland – that would then decide whether it was to remain within the so-called 'British Commonwealth of Nations' or not; a very different proposition to that of a Scotland the measure of whose independence was qualified by a predetermination to remain within that organisation without the reservation of any choice in the matter to the Scottish people. To pre-commit the Scottish people in this way is a negation of all the National Party claims to stand for. The progressive degeneration of the party was shown by the 'patriotic' telegram addressed to the King from Bannockburn – and contemptuously ignored by His Majesty.

We are told that this is a democratic country, with a constitutional monarchy, but Professor Keith shows what goes on behind the scenes – behind the back of Parliament itself. The special attention of those who call themselves Scottish Nationalists may be directed to the right quietly conceded to the Irish Free State in 1931, of direct access and advice to the King, together with the possession of a special Seal, to be struck, kept and controlled in the Irish Free State, for use upon documents issued on that advice. This slim manoeuvre was consummated behind the backs of our MPs. 'The vital importance of this arrangement was well understood in Ireland,' says Professor Keith,

> where it was hailed as marking the definite emergence of a Kingdom of Ireland as a distinct international unit, *though no information on the question was given to the British Parliament, which remained long wholly unaware of the vital character of the change to which the Government had assented.* What had been done by the Irish Free State can, of course, be done by every Dominion, and it is hardly possible to deny that the power to make treaties entirely uncontrolled by the British Government in any direct manner accords to the Dominions the right to claim international status as distinct states.

But observe the phrase, 'in any direct manner'! Indirect controls at variance with autonomy are maintained all right. The status – but not the substance – of distinct stateship is conceded; as a means of preventing the latter, Professor Keith disposes in no uncertain fashion alike of J.H. Thomas's characteristically egregious and misleading declaration that (as a result of the Westminster Statute), 'the United Kingdom itself is now only a Dominion like the others', and Mr McGilligan's idea that 'the King, on the advice of British ministers, could no more make treaties for the Irish Free State than could the Mikado of Japan or the King of Italy.' On the contrary, Professor Keith rightly stresses the purely 'permissive' character of the Statute, and the fact that the supremacy of the Imperial Parliament is maintained, inter alia, by the enactment of the Statute itself, which no Dominion can alter. Like Mr M'Gilligan and Mr Thomas, General Smuts was wrong when he declared, after the peace conference, that the separate membership accorded to the Dominions in the League of Nations gave them 'the position of fully sovereign states'. Professor Keith disposes of nonsense of that sort by drawing attention (1) to the protest by the British Government against registration of the Irish Treaty at Geneva; (2) the determination of the Ottawa Conference to establish the doctrine that inter-Imperial preferences are matters outside the sphere of the operation of most-favoured-nation clauses in treaties with foreign powers; (3) the fact that the foregoing involves a reaffirmation of the doctrine of the Imperial Conference of 1926 that the relations of the parts of the Commonwealth, *inter se*, are not relations of international law. The provisions for maintaining English over-control by hook or crook are, furthermore, evidenced by Professor Keith's statement that, in the event of the King receiving inconsistent advice from the 'autonomous communities within the British Empire, equal in status, in no way subordinate one to another, in any aspect of their domestic or external affairs', the proper way to resolve such a conflict 'would clearly be the advice of the Imperial Conference to the disputants'. Exactly – or, in other words, the same old thing under a different name; a new mechanism of inter-Imperial organisation, to the same old end. The amount of real autonomy that emerges from this process is negligible; and confined to minor matters. It must again be insisted that the issues which should concern the National Party of Scotland, or any other organisation professing to stand for Scottish Independence, are the Crown and the Empire – that the limitations placed upon 'independence' by either of these within the limits of the Statute of Westminster destroy the essential significance of the term – and that, above all, the retention of the Westminster Parliament as the 'king-pin' of the organisation is incompatible with anything worth contending for in Scotland. The only proper or useful stand for us to take is to claim complete independence, declaring that Scotland's subsequent relationships with England, or the Empire, or other countries, are matters for the absolute free determination of the Scottish people. The misunderstanding, or misleading, tactics of those who seek to reconcile nationalism with current Imperialism is, at all events, made sufficiently clear by Professor Keith's conclusions.

C.M. Grieve, 11 March 1933

George Reston Malloch

The Moments' Monuments, a collection of seventy sonnets by George Reston Malloch (Stirling: Eneas Mackay) evoked a remarkable tribute from a writer in *The Times Literary Supplement* the other week. 'The Shakespearian sonnet', the notice read

> invites the grand style so compellingly that even in these days, when romantic phrasing is so generally suspect, there are few who can use it uninfluenced by its first master. Yet rich as the cadences which he achieves often are, we cannot help feeling at times that in striving to recapture the pomp and pageantry of an earlier day he submerges the still small voice in himself. It is doubtful, in fact, whether the young magic of the Elizabethan sonnet can be sought after today quite so sedulously as he has done without falsifying thought and emotion through verbal extravagance. There is, however, no lack of fundamental brain-work in his sonnets, and while some of them are a little too grandiloquent, in many he eschews altogether 'the sceptical glories' of the past and yet keeps them high-pitched by virtue of his own intensity and his concentrated craftsmanship. Certainly there can be few modern sonnet-sequences of this length in which fine feeling, fine thought, and fine phrasing have been so subtly and yet harmoniously inwrought.

It is with the tribute to Mr Malloch's qualities as a poet in the last sentence that I am particularly concerned because he is one of our best contemporary Scottish poets and has not by any means received his due as such, while in other directions, and particularly as a dramatist, he has rendered notable services to the Scottish Renaissance Movement, of which he was one of the early protagonists. And that initial group, in my opinion, remains, alas! of a higher calibre than almost all who have arrived since to join the ranks of our Scottish *literati*. (Perhaps that is best indicated by the fact that there has been an altogether disproportionate increase in the number of novelists, whereas the initial group were essayists and poets but had little or nothing to do with fiction!) I agree, too, with the feeling that in this particular kind of work Mr Malloch may be 'submerging the still small voice in himself'. There are certainly poems of his in other kinds that I greatly prefer; though even these – and some of them are really excellent work – leave me with the same feeling that this is not quite what he ought to have been doing; that he has never really 'found himself'. However that may be, what wants to be emphasised is that Mr Malloch is one – and not the least – of a group of Scottish poets seldom recognised as Scottish, and whose best poems have never been presented in an anthology that would set a whole department of modern Scottish literature in a very satisfying, probably surprisingly satisfying, perspective. The group includes Robert Buchanan, 'Fiona Macleod' (William Sharp), John Davidson, John Barlas, J.B. Selkirk, Alexander

Smith, 'B.V.', Ronald Campbell Macfie, Lord Alfred Douglas, Sir Ronald Ross, and others. All of these were, or are, Scotsmen and must not be left to England to calmly appropriate, apart from the fact that their work – though in the English language – has qualities whose un-English character would be better appreciated if their best poems were brought together between one set of covers containing no work by any poet not a Scotsman.

The other point – about the sedulous search – is less well taken. The true sonneteer is the man who has made himself such by constant practice in this particular form until he has acquired *habitus*. Sonneteering is not something within the compas of any rhymster who remembers that a sonnet consists of fourteen lines in iambic pentameter with a certain rhyme-scheme. Practically every poet who has ever produced a sonnet of any value has written scores of sonnets; the latter were the condition of the former. I should say that to produce a good sonnet without considerable previous practice in the form is one of the most improbable of literary feats. Mr Malloch does not claim to have produced what is properly called a sonnet-sequence in this volume. 'The short form of the sonnet and its self-contained nature', he says, 'suggests a kinship between such a volume as this and the once-favoured collection of aphorisms; in the present case, the resemblance is strengthened by the author's design which is adequately explained in the title. These moments have, perhaps, some common significance; it is with no idea of offering a "sonnet-sequence" with a connected story that their poetic exposition has been attempted.' The Aphoristic parallel to which Mr Malloch hints is reflected in many pregnantly epigrammatic lines in these sonnets.

> Men cannot to their ghosts devise entail,
> Today and now is ours or else we fail.

Or, again:

> They are no wiser, then, who worship man,
> Denying God, than those who, man denying,
> Would credit God with such a foolish plan
> As that where man's salvation lay in dying.

Mr Malloch issues his volumes of verse at long intervals. His *Lyrics and Other Poems* appeared in 1913; *Poems and Lyrics* in 1916; *Poems* in 1920; *Human Voices* in 1930; and now these sonnets. Even so he has a more substantial body of work to his credit – has proved the possessor of a more sustained gift – than all but one or two recent Scottish poets. Many of his best poems were contributed under my editorship to *Northern Numbers* and *The Scottish Chapbook*; while he acted as dramatic critic for *The Scottish Nation*. His connection with the Scottish movement was closer then than it has been in the last few years, and it was at that time he began to write, specially for it, that series of plays which include *The House of the Queen* (a lovely symbolic drama of

Scottish nationalism), *Thomas the Rhymer* and *Soutarness Water*. These, like his other work, have somehow never won the esteem to which they are entitled. But those of us who know and prize his work, and have been sorry to hear less of him for the past three or four years than we were wont to, welcome this volume's evidence of his continuing creative activity, and, though we would fain have had his work more directly associated with the development of the Scottish Movement, rejoice that though he has taken a different course than at one time seemed likely there is no abatement of his subtle and scrupulous craftsmanship. His hand has not lost his cunning; he is once again richer in performance – and perhaps no less rich in promise than ever.

C.M. Grieve, 25 March 1933

John Davidson

John Davidson, amongst other things, initiated a development that has been little followed up by subsequent Scottish poets (none of whom has been anywhere near his stature), or, for the matter of that, by English poets either; and that is long overdue and desperately necessary.

It is admirably expressed by the reply of Kipling's engineer, McAndrews, 'the stiff-necked Glasgow beggar', to the passenger who asked him, 'Don't you think steam spoils the romance at sea?':

> Damned ijit! I'd been doon that morn to see what ailed the throws,
> Manholin' on my back – the cranks three inches off my nose.
> Romance! Those first-class passengers they like it very well,
> Printed and bound in little books; but why don't poets tell?
> I'm sick of all their quirks and turns – the loves an' doves they dream.
> Lord, send a man like Robbie Burns to sing the Song o' Steam!

Davidson repudiated the past. 'The insane past of mankind is the incubus', he said. Or again: 'The statement of the present and the creation of the future are the very body and soul of poetry.' He was determined at all costs to face facts and revalue ideas:

> These are times
> When all must to the crucible – no thought,
> Practice, or use, or custom sacrosanct,
> But shall be violable now.

The concluding sentences of Israel Zangwill's tribute are significant and undeniable. 'John Davidson', he wrote,

> is a prodigal of every divine gift, pouring out untold treasure from his celestial cornucopia. Fancy and imagination, wit and humour, fun and epi-

gram, characterisation and creation and observation, insight and philosophy, passion and emotion and sincerity – all are his. Nothing is lacking from that long catalogue by which Imlac convinced Rasselas that it was impossible to be a poet. And all these glorious gifts have found vent in the most diverse artistic or inartistic shapes – novels, dramas, eclogues, ballads, Reisebilder – some written for the market, but the bulk in defiance of it. Of these products of a somewhat riotous genius, only a few have the hall-mark of perfection – some pieces about music halls, a sheaf of ballads, a bundle of songs, a set of eclogues – but they are already quite enough baggage to go down to posterity with. And it is significant that all Mr Davidson's chief successes are won when he surrenders himself to the inspiration of the modern. This is the work that we need.

It was, of course, work for which Scotland (or England) had little or no use; and Davidson has been persistently denied the recognition and place he deserves, on political, religious, and other conventional grounds. What few pieces of his are generally anthologised and popularly known are for the most part early work, amenable to such prejudices – work he himself subsequently disowned; work far more in keeping in subject matter (but not in quality of utterance!) with the infantile bletherings of 'Surfacemen' and any of the other rhymsters who have subsequently won public favour in Scotland, than with Davidson's later and more important work, which has a far closer relationship to radicalism, anti-Christianity, the machine age, scientific developments, and the thought of Nietzsche and other modern thinkers than to the sugary sentiments and pious piffle that supply the bulk of the material for the types of versification that still appeal most to the bourgeois poetry-reading public, a public not to be confused with the masses, who have no use for that sort of nonsense at all, and are cut off from work like Davidson's, which deals with matters of concern to them, by the insidious and incessant propaganda of the schools and the press and the churches and other debauching agencies, which bolster up the existing social and economic system responsible for their being so cut of from any helpful or effective culture.

In the teeth of all these forces, it cannot be too emphatically insisted that Davidson – albeit writing in English and little concerned with Scottish scenes or subjects (although expressing throughout a very Scottish type of mind) – was one of the greatest poets Scotland has produced; secure of his place in the first dozen from the very start of our literary history; and a giant among pigmies, not only to such men as Robert Buchanan and 'Fiona Macleod', and, in fact, all the other Scots poets between Robert Burns and himself, but equally above, and very different in kind and effect to, all the other poets of the eighties and nineties in England, with whom he is generally and most misleadingly grouped.

The particular rock of offence to the 'goody-goodies' in his work was less his modernity than (unless the two terms are inseparable) his virulent anti-

Christianity, but his own statement of his position disposes of most of their superficial condemnations. 'Art knows very well', he declared,

> that the world comes to an end when it is purged of imagination. Rationalism was only a stage in the process. For the old conception of a created universe, with the fall of man, an atonement, and a heaven and hell, the form and substance of the imagination of Christendom, rationalism has no substitute. Science was not ready, but how could poetry wait? Science was synonymous with patience; poetry is impatience incarnate.

What did Davidson substitute? A profound and passionately asserted vision of life as matter seeking ever finer and more effective manifestations. And in poetry, 'the subtlest, most powerful, and most various organ of utterance articulate faculty has produced', he saw the latest emanation of what he calls the 'concrete mystery, matter', created, 'like folk, or flowers, or cholera, or war, or lightning, or light', by an evolutionary process involving all activities and states of consciousness.' As Holbrook Jackson says, 'Poetry for him was thus no scholarly accomplishment, no mere decoration or bauble, but the very instrument of thought and imagination, emotion, and passion, the finely tempered weapon of a nationalism, which he linked up with nature and endowed with her fierceness, mastery and power.'

'Nine-tenths of my time', he wrote on his fiftieth birthday, 'and that which is more precious, have been wasted in the endeavour to earn a livelihood. In a world of my own making I should have been writing only what should have been written.' On 23 March 1909, aged fifty-two, he committed suicide; a poem written the previous year anticipating this ending:

> None should outlive his power… who kills
> Himself subdues the conqueror of kings:
> Exempt from death is he who takes his life:
> My time has come.

A recent manifest against Scottish Nationalism, and particularly separatist and anti-English tendencies, was signed by the Dukes of Buccleuch, Atholl, Argyll, the Earls of Linlithgow, Stair and a score of other noblemen, who, *inter alia*, said that the movement they denounced had attracted no one of any consequence. All the holders of Scottish titles in Davidson's own day or since put together were not worth a year of his life. Yet they were all comfortably circumstanced, while he had long years of grinding struggle, which could easily, and ought to, have been prevented, by his adequate endowment, even if that had meant expropriating all the nobility in Great Britain, who, with all their undeserved advantages, have rendered no proportionate public service of any kind.

Davidson would have been one of the supporters of *The Free Man* today – a Scottish Nationalist of the radical republican type (though in the different political setting of his own day he naturally expressed certain views which may seem to conflict with that to those who cannot make the necessary allowances for the time-factor), and, certainly, a Douglasite – the man who wrote

> … the difficultest go to understand,
> And the difficultest job a man can do,
> Is to come it brave and meek with thirty bob a week,
> And feel that that's the proper thing for you.

I can only repeat what I said in my *To Circumjack Cencrastus*: –

> The relation o' John Davidson's thought
> To Nietzsche's is mair important
> Than all the drivel aboot 'Hame, Sweet Hame',
> Four million cretins mant.

He was a free spirit of magnificent endowments and splendid fearlessness of energy – a better exemplar for young Scots of today than any other writer we have produced; and one of the objects of the Scottish renaissance movement ought undoubtedly to be to instal him in his proper place and dethrone the absurd and vicious popularities of the relative nonentities of the kailyaird and later schools who still usurp it.

To think of Davidson – and then of Barrie taking 'Courage' as the theme of his rectorial address at St Andrews – is enough to make any honest man violently sick.

C.M. Grieve, 1 April 1933

Genius and Money

At a recent debate I attended in Edinburgh the hoary old theory was trotted out that authors were all the better for the pinch of poverty – if they had not to worry about ways and means they might produce less. There was nothing like a little starving to force them to turn out their best. The wolf at the door was necessary to ginger them up.

This is a very widespread idea – for the simple reason that society has always treated its writers (and other creative artists) so badly that it must find an excuse and so it falls back upon the cowardly lie that hardship is good for them. It is, at best, a false analogy from their own base incentives.

Although arts and letters are not of vital consequence to more than a tiny minority of people, and even of these not one per cent has any real appreciation of the conditions and requirements of creative production, it is impossible to deny that, however indirectly, they are the highest factors in human development and that everything else is contingent upon them. Even the stupidest Philistines are wholly dependent upon whatever moiety of the usufruct of past genius is accessible to them; and as the simplest matter of enlightened self-interest it ought to be the concern of every country to see that it facilitates the work of the creative spirit within its bounds by every possible means. A state of society that starves its few artists of any actual or potential consequence and yet is so organised that it has a large proportion of wealthy business men (too stupid to have any use for culture) is cheating itself – selling its birthright for a mess of pottage. Which country is not in that condition today? Which country has not its hordes of rich drones who have rendered no social service entitling them to fortune's favour – enabling them to trot about, as weather or inclination suggest, to Egypt, the Riviera, the Highlands of Scotland, while most of the few writers it possesses whose work is above a certain standard and is at all likely to have the slightest permanent value (when all the opulent Fat Men are blotted out as if they had never been) are desperately hard put to it to maintain the double struggle of wresting a living out of unfavourable conditions and doing their own original work into the bargain?

The real meaning of these stupid misconceptions of the extreme difficulty and tremendous value of creative work is simply that all but an infinitesimal percentage of people can never hope to do – or even to understand – work of that kind; and they revenge themselves upon the artist by pretending that it is not nearly so important as is made out and that it either ought 'to pay its own way like other forms of labour' or that if it doesn't it is the artist's personal look-out and society is under no obligation to come to his assistance. If people must write poetry and things, let them do it in the evenings after their day's work is done! It is absurd at this time of day to argue that such activities should furnish a livelihood for those who choose to engage in them!

Now that the necessity of practically all human labour is disappearing (or would disappear but for the retention of a stupid, cruel, and obsolescent economic system), the significance of creative work is not likely to continue to be as easily occluded as it has been in the past. The artist has no choice; he must yield to his *daimon* – no matter at what cost in hardship and poverty to himself and his dependants; and society's attitude boils itself down to the atrocious meanness of saying – 'Let the blighter struggle. We'll get the benefit of his work in any case – for nothing; and a little drudgery and starvation will help to "save our face" against his infernal superiority.' This attitude is actually enforced by the Law. Other forms of property are transmissible to one's heirs and successors in perpetuity. Not so an author's copyright. His dependants can only have the benefits of any proceeds from these for a limited number of years, and then they become common property. The very society that most strenuously insists that everybody must work for a living takes 'something for nothing' from its artists all right. Authors are even put to the expense of sending gratis copies of their works to the Copyright Libraries. Imagine the howl if builders, engineers, and the like had to present the State free, gratis, and for nothing with sample copies of the houses, bridges and so forth they produce!

Things are worse in this respect today than ever probably, and in every country (and Scotland is perhaps the worst in Europe) creative artists are desperately hard put to it if they are determined to be free to develop their genius and refuse to engage in forms of work they despise. Even if they don't the latter are almost impossible to get. It seems that work is remunerated almost everywhere in inverse proportion both to its actual necessity and its ultimate value to humanity. Most jobs are not only unnecessary but are filled up by – and by a preference allied to the general Philistine basis of society given to – types immeasurably inferior in social value to anyone capable of doing original work of the slightest merit in any of the arts. I can scarcely think of a young man of first-class calibre in Scotland or England in the circle of my acquaintance today who is not leading a hand-to-mouth existence and subjected to the most humiliating straits.

What humanity has lost by this stupid treatment of its artists is incomputable. Most of the great poets were only able to produce their work because they were men of independent means. A large proportion of great literature not by wealthy writers was produced in the teeth of hardship and public indifference or hostility, and it is safe to conclude that the producers' output was greatly limited and otherwise unfavourably affected by these untoward circumstances. Poor men of genius have produced occasional masterpieces despite their conditions, but no big body of work; it is safe to say they would have produced far more good work than they actually did if they had not been forced to maintain the hopeless double struggle to earn a living and live up to their highest aspirations. In this connection it is generally conveniently forgotten by the Philistines that in so far from being an easy affair that can be done in spare time after a day's work, creative production is actually, as a simple scientific fact, infinitely harder work than the vast majority of people can even imagine. More foot-pounds of energy are expended in the creation of a single lyric of first-class quality – though it may only take five minutes – than in twelvemonths' labours of a buck-navvy.

Humanity has cause for endless shame if it peruses the records of its great writers. The majority of the finest spirits mankind has produced have been reduced to the dependence on friends, begging, miserable official pittances, ignominies, and hardships of all kinds. Well may Winifred Holtby say, in her recent biography, of Virginia Woolf – 'She did not have to write for money. She could do as much or as little as she chose. She was free to work, to read, to travel. She went to Greece, to Lisbon, to Italy. It was almost an ideal form of life for an artist.' Mrs Woolf elsewhere herself says that £500 a year and a room of her own is essential to a woman writer, and, although Miss Holtby questions her sweeping statement that it is 'certain that, by some fault of our commonwealth, the poor poet has not in these days, nor has had for two hundred years, a dog's chance', by remarking that 'William H. Davies, Sean O'Casey, Lionel Britton, James Hanley, to say nothing of Dickens and his bottle-factory, all belie her', it is only to go on to quote the theory of William Blake, 'often, like all the greatest mystics, capable of the most practical common sense', who, writing an introduction to a catalogue of pictures, remarked –

> Some people and not a few artists have asserted that the Painter of this Picture would not have done so well if he had been properly encouraged. Let those who think so reflect on the State of Nations under Poverty and their incapability of Art. Tho' Art is above either, the Argument is better for Affluence than Poverty: and though he could not have been a greater artist, yet he could have produced greater works of Art in proportion to his means.

That is unanswerable. But, the generality of Philistines continue, 'if writers are in straits that is generally their own blame. They ought to behave themselves. They ought to work harder and drink less.' It is beyond question that an extraordinarily large proportion of all great writers – all really vital spirits – have found it impossible to conform to bourgeois morality, and have been guilty of excesses of all kinds. But the extent of that proportion – the persistence and completeness with which 'respectable standards' have been defied – suggests that this wildness was an indispensable condition of their genius. They cannot 'be like other people' and yet so utterly unlike them as to be capable of creative work. The matter is too complex to discuss at the tail-end of an article mainly concerned with other aspects of a state of affairs which is certainly ensuring, to a greater extent today than ever, that while all sorts of numbskulls can live in the lap of luxury, the majority of those who are adding to the real heritage of humanity are likely to have a deuce of a struggle for the barest subsistence, to be passed over like Dunbar in favour of nonentities whenever there are any sinecures going, and to perish like Burns and Dostoevski sending out desperate begging letters from their death-beds. Then 12,000 will gather at Burns's funeral and 30,000 at Dostoevski's and they received posthumously the place in human esteem which is their due – though if a little of that had been forthcoming in advance, and in practical form, they might have lived years longer and added greatly to their great achievements.

C.M. Grieve, 22 April 1933

The Exhaustion of English

At a recent debate in Edinburgh on whether English should remain a compulsory or be relegated to an optional subject in Scottish schools (a way of putting the issue that, as the leading speakers on both sides pointed out, really meant making Gaelic compulsory and virtually proscribing English altogether), there was an overwhelming anti-English vote (over thirty – scarcely any of whom, incidentally, had the slightest knowledge of Gaelic – to three). I believe that a similar result would be secured at any meeting in Scotland where the question was properly debated and an honest vote elicited in accordance with the weight of the arguments.

In the first place it is to be noted that those who would seek to defend the ascendancy of the English language in Scotland do so on the lowest possible grounds. They evade argument by assuming that 'even if it were desirable it is impossible to return to Gaelic at this time of day.' They use phrases which mean nothing, e.g. 'putting the clock back'; 'in these days of increasing independence of nations', and so forth. They say that the abandonment of English would enormously handicap our people in trade and industry. These dogmatic statements (for they are seldom or never argued out) proceed on the bases of mere assumption or base and misconceived expediency and represent attitudes of mind which are the natural products of English ascendancy. It is impossible to deal with the matter fully in the limited space at our disposal here, but let us go into a few aspects with a little of that precision and fullness which it is the very spirit of English domination to prevent by 'laughing out of court' and similar means.

I would begin by categorically denying that the gift of the English language has been of any more benefit to Scotland than any of the other so-called boons conferred on us by our association with our Southern neighbour. We must 'beware of the Greeks bringing us gifts', and in view of the disastrous effect upon Scotland in every other aspect of our affairs of our connection with England it would be amazing to find that our cult of English language and literature had, on the contrary, had beneficial or even defensible effects – and, as a matter of fact, it hasn't. It is well to remember that English *is* compulsory in Scotland – we do not adopt it voluntarily because we regard it as a superior language to Gaelic or any other tongue or for any other reason. The question we are discussing is one which only arises in subjugated countries – and Scotland (to our disgrace) is the only subjugated country in which there has not been a bitter and determined and ultimately successful fight for the retention of the national speech and a repudiation of the conqueror's.

As I have said, those who seek to defend the use of English in Scotland invariably appeal to what they are pleased to call 'common-sense'. They suggest 'grounds of expediency' – implying that for certain material benefits they think we are justified in making an abject adjustment to circumstance culturally and linguistically. Where is this alleged necessity? What has the adoption of English benefited us commercially and industrially? The present position of Scotland *vis-à-vis* England or compared with any of the smaller European countries is far from revealing any such benefits. Nor have any of these smaller European countries had to relinquish their independent languages to share in the benefits of industrial civilisation, and the advantages of the modern world generally to a far greater extent than we do. It is surely strange if the alleged over-riding tendencies that put small languages like Gaelic economically out-of-court and make it expedient to relinquish them in favour of a 'great world language' only affect Scotland. They do not appear to affect any other country. On the contrary – so far from tending to a common tongue – the whole international tendency is in the opposite direction; towards the more and more intensive exploitation of native languages, and even of archaic, dialect, and other specialised forms of them. This is in accordance with the law of life, which runs from homogeneity to ever greater heterogeneity, and not *vice-versa*. International trade does not appear to be at all handicapped by the multiplicity of languages – indeed, that very multiplicity, implying, as it does, a wealth of different tastes, tendencies, and aptitudes, is part and parcel of the very basis of that complex of different producing powers and requirements which is the basis of international trade – and the addition to the existing list of another independent language for Scotland would not noticeably increase the existing complexity.

Let us take this argument the other way round. Is it possible to imagine that Scotland would have forfeited any of the benefits of so-called industrial civilisation if it had retained its separate language? Why should Scotland be the solitary exception in this respect? All sorts of other countries have retained their separate languages – and have not thereby forfeited one iota of so-called modern progress. On the contrary, it is immediately demonstrable that Scotland has not even benefited proportionately to other countries which have retained their languages.

But, it may be contended, it is at all events not practicable to abandon English and revert to Gaelic now. Isn't it? There is nothing to hinder it really, though it may be true that the vast majority of people are too lazy or stupid or anti-nationally prejudiced to enable such a change to come about by democratic means. But suppose we had a Dictatorship and Gaelic was made compulsory and English proscribed! No one in his senses can argue that the result of this would be retrogression – that we would lapse back into barbarism and cease to play any part in international trade and industry.

As a matter of fact, though any talk of relinquishing English and making Gaelic compulsory evokes the instant appeal of that blessed word 'commonsense' and to 'grounds of expedience', and a great deal is made of the wonders of the English language and the magnificent literature associated with it, the real opposition to any such move would proceed on very other grounds. The English would fight it tooth and nail – and not because they were altruistically anxious that we should not harm ourselves economically or otherwise. We do not get anything economically or culturally or in any other way as it is by their good grace; they are ready enough to filch our trade and industries; and their real reason for foisting English upon us is, like all their other actions, not in our interest but in theirs. It is insufficiently realised that the very nature of the English language is directly and incurably anti-Scottish. It has enhanced its vocabulary by tremendous borrowings from practically every other language in the world – but not from Gaelic. The genius of the two tongues is utterly incompatible. English has not even borrowed to any extent from Braid Scots, though Braid Scots has hundreds of admirably expressive words for which English has no equivalents at all or no precise equivalents. Why has it all along eschewed Scots in this way? It means that it has similarly eschewed those qualities of the Scottish spirit which made the words in question. English ascendancy necessitates the suppression of these Scottish elements. It depends upon the stultification of all that is most vividly and vitally Scottish. It must be remembered that even to this day, despite the long period of English ascendancy, the teaching of English in our schools requires the subjection of our children to a prolonged psychological outrage. They have to be compelled to learn a language that is not natural to them. They have to learn to twist their thoughts to fit an alien mould of speech. All this has a profound effect in discouraging or extirpating their creative powers. This accounts for the relative poverty of Scottish literature to English. We are not so intellectually and spiritually inferior to our Southern neighbours that it can be accounted for in any other way. The retention of English means the permanent immense literary inferiority of the Scottish to the English.

And, after all, *is* English taught in Scottish schools? The English themselves would insist that the Scottish attempts make a very inferior show. What our Scottish pupils actually do learn and succeed in using of the English language is just that poor fringe of it which over a large part of the world serves as a kind of *lingua franca*. Those who are vitally concerned with the English language know that it has vastly outgrown itself and is becoming more and more useless for creative purposes. It has got away from its true background; the native genius of the language is no longer capable of vitalising so enormous a development. It is suffering from a kind of Imperial elephantiasis. This accounts for the vast amount of experimentation that is going on in English literature today. Meredith, Hardy, Doughty, Joyce – scarcely a writer of English in recent times who has not been brought hard up against this problem and compelled to try all kinds of verbal innovation. The future of English – otherwise than as a kind of esperanto for mere commercial and industrial use – is in the melting pot. It must get back to its own true basis and operate in its own true sphere. So must England in other respects; the sooner England gives up the Empire and its ascendancy over Scotland and Wales and becomes simply itself again the better for it (and its language and literature) and for everybody else. And the same thing applies to Scotland. It has profited us nothing to gain the whole world and lose our own soul.

C.M. Grieve, 29 April 1933

Goodbye to the National Party

The Council of the National Party of Scotland have finally rejected what they consider my application to rejoin that party. Months ago I was accepted as a member of the South Edinburgh branch, and no objections were intimated to me at the time. Subsequently in newspaper correspondence and over the radio Mr John McCormick denied that I was a member, and in one letter stated that I was a member of the Communist Party. I challenged him to prove this, and accused him of relying upon tittle-tattle, and reaverred that I was in every respect eligible for membership of the National Party. Mr McCormick stated that if I was dissatisfied I had the right of appeal to the delegate conference of the party. I promptly wrote him intimating my intention of exercising my right. Then the slim manoeuvres began which are characteristic of the junta which controls – and has now hopelessly betrayed this party. It is in vain for my friend, Cunninghame-Graham, and others to claim that the National Party is open to men of all shades of opinion – Tory, Liberal, Labour, Socialist, Communist – who are agreed upon the prime essential of securing the Independence of Scotland. So far from wanting the Independence of Scotland, this precious junta wants to carefully predetermine and condition the future status and ethos of our country in the terms of their own brainless prejudices; independence in any shape or form is the last thing on earth they are capable of conceiving; and, above all, they are determined not to allow the members of the party any. The latter was the real rub in my particular case – not my Communism, which has been made the ostensible reason. In reply to Mr McCormick's last letter to myself before his final intimation that the Council had decided to debar me from membership, I was asked, *inter alia*, to signify that I agreed with the policy of the party. I replied that I did – subject to the freedom of every member within the party to advocate and agitate for any change which he might think desirable in that policy. It is precisely this that is intolerable to those in control. Their whole aim and object is to make (or to keep, having now made) the party safe for mediocrities like themselves. But all this is not the final treachery. Although it was he himself who stated in the *Glasgow Herald* that I had the right of appeal to the conference, it was Mr McCormick who moved at one of the Council meetings that I 'be not heard'. Mr McCormick, or anybody else, may rest satisfied that they can never prevent my being heard.

I had intended this week to deal with certain slavering stupidities on the Scottish Renaissance business which appeared recently in leaders in the *Glasgow Evening News* and *The Scots' Observer* respectively. They might have been written by the same person; I pointed out in my last article their affinity with the attitude of Dr Agnes Mure Mackenzie, and there is not a nit-wit in Scotland who would not be practically certain to express himself in identical terms. Their principal characteristic is to imagine that significance is not so rare as some of us contend, and that genius is an eminently reasonable thing which would never dream of repudiating English and expressing itself exclusively in Gaelic or Braid Scots, for example, or in terms insusceptible of being 'understanded of the folk' – or, alternatively, that if it is so ill-advised as to do anything so irrational, it can be safely disregarded, there being 'safety in numbers'. Much is made of the undue consideration on the activities of an alleged small coterie of self-advisers – a little mutual admiration society, whose principal asset is an overweening conceit. But the address of this body is not given. I must confess I do not know any of the group in question. I certainly have a very moderate admiration myself for the work of one or two contemporary Scottish writers, but for the work of most of them I have nothing but contempt. On the other hand, the ruck outwith the alleged coterie – on whose behalf these arguments are advanced, the implication being that they are almost, if not quite, as entitled to recognition and encouragement as the favoured (or self-favouring) few – is, in my opinion, beneath contempt. But this plea for their admission to a share of the limelight (such as it is) shows what really lies behind all this attempt to dispute the reality of the Renaissance Movement is to 'broaden its basis', and deny that it belongs to a clique. All kinds of nonentities want a look in too on whatever is afoot – and the writer of these leaders, and all who share their views, are just nonentities. American universities cater for this sort of thing – they give degrees in dish-washing, boot-blacking, and so forth, as well as in Law and Letters, and the other departments with which such academical distinctions are traditionally associated. In exactly the same fashion in Scotland, the idea that a National Movement or Literary Renaissance calls for gifts which are exceptionally rare – and so cannot be shared in by Tom, Dick, and Harry – is utterly distasteful; and so any little good work that has been done must be skilfully scaled down by all the arts of depreciation and mean innuendo so that everybody can be assured that they have a great part to play in the New Scotland, and that it is a matter of little or no consequence whether that consists in writing an immortal poem or inducing a hen to lay two eggs when it used only to lay one. So we are solemnly told that poetry is not of prime importance, but that the future of Scotland perhaps depends more on mothers' meetings, or in that broad and catholic view which can discern the national importance of the development of hiking facilities, or any of the other matters in which the 'many-headed' engage. All that is, of course, in keeping with the process of deterioration that has gone on in the National Party.

Well! What are we going to do about it? The only thing is to redouble our own creative efforts with a complete unconcern as to whether we are reaching a public of one or a thousand or a million – so long as we know that we are doing work which appeals to those whom we regard as intelligent people. The danger is for us to compromise one iota in order to reach those whom we know to be the unintelligent mass. That is precisely what the National Party has done, and what the *Scots Observer* and the *Glasgow Evening Times* want the Renaissance Movement to do. In each case, however, that is precisely what no person of the slightest significance can possibly do – and these papers can boost what writers they like, and the National Party what alleged leaders it cares; their reward will be the same in each case – utter insignificance.

I shall never renew my application to join the National Party. I can do without it far better than it can do without me. I know that my decision will affect many others of a far higher calibre than any of the present leaders of the Party. I know that wherever Scottish Nationalism is mentioned, my name will be associated with it and will give the measure of the cowardice and stupidity of those who have ruined the party. I know that I am – and will remain – one of the exceedingly few real Scottish Nationalists who have yet emerged, and that I shall be strengthened rather than handicapped in anything I can do in the future for this great cause by my complete dissociation from its present leadership.

C.M. Grieve, 3 June 1933

A Three-legged Discourse

I JOHN HENRY MACKAY

Since I first pointed it out in my *Contemporary Scottish Studies*, Scotland's preference for its characteristic morons and its ignorance of its ablest and most significant sons has become an accepted fact in all more or less intelligent circles; but while Norman Douglas and a few others are getting a little tardy acceptance in the country to which they belong – and many stupid idols are being thrown down from the pedestals to which they should never have been elevated – the process of recovering our misprized sons of genius is proceeding slowly and is still far from complete. One of those to whom I drew attention was John Henry Mackay, the Anarchist writer, born in Greenock, but domiciled most of his life in Germany and writing his novels and other books in German. He died in May, and a short obituary appeared in *The Times* of 23 May; but I do not expect any of the Scottish papers took any notice of his death. Certainly none of them accorded him the tiniest fraction of his due as one of the most distinguished Scottish writers of recent years. Mackay knew that his death was approaching, and his latest book, *Abrechnung* (Berlin-Charlottenburg: Mackay-Gesellschaft), was written with that in view – as a sort of literary and political testament. After writing poetry and some novels, which gave him rank as a German writer of some note, Mackay took up the study of philosophic anarchism and devoted himself to the interpretation of Max Stirner, the author of *The Ego and His Own*. Mackay tells his life-story in this valedictory book and describes the way in which he was led to his position as a philosophical anarchist. This should be of no little interest to readers of *The Free Man* in particular, for what anarchism meant to Mackay was the supreme freedom of the individual from all external laws and prohibitions. The irony of fate showed him in his final years a Europe divided between Communism and other forms of dictatorship; everything he hated was more openly rampant than at any previous period of his life – yet although the overwhelming tendency of contemporary life is in the opposite direction to that which he advocated, he ended by reaffirming his complete loyalty to the ideals he had preached. The economic crisis in Germany during the past few years all but destroyed his means of livelihood; he is better dead than under the present regime in that unhappy country. His book finishes with an appeal to well-wishers to carry on his work against the tyranny of the State. Many of us will, no matter against what apparently overwhelming odds, and know that in Mackay Scotland has lost one of its noblest sons. I have dedicated to him the following poem:

First Objectives
(TO JOHN HENRY MACKAY)

Here let us vow that we shall know
No peace, no thought of compromise,
Till all false values we destroy
That true ones may arise.

Not boasts of better blood alone,
Not titles bought, nor vain degrees
Of masonic mediocrity;
These, and far more than these.

Not murderers in soldiering's name,
Not thieves of licensed usury,
But with them all who in judgment sit
Our mortal foes shall be.

All profiteers, monopolists,
And all who claim to own the Earth,
These, with the others, we'll remove;
Mankind will know no dearth.

All censors, police, and teachers who
Instead of just opening out impose –
And parents who fix their children's lives;
War to the knife on those!

All those who have power to withhold or give
Or mete life's means to other men,
Or any coercive power at all
We'll ban from human ken.

And above all the Church must go.
True values may not be ours to make,
Strive as we will, but this is sure
– The false are ours to break.

II THE HOLY WAR

Unlike Mackay, I am not a man of peace – a disbeliever in violent revolutionary means, and the organisation and plans of the Scottish Fascists who are out to drive the Catholic Irish out of Scotland and to deprive all Scottish Catholics of the rights of citizenship have my hearty approval – not because I am a Catholic or an advocate of Catholicism, and still less because I am in the very slightest degree favourable to Protestantism. My position is quite different. I do not hold a single idea compatible with even the most reduced form of the Christian faith, but I approve the Fascist policy, just as I will approve any policy (and the better the more violent) the Catholics adopt to counter it, because I believe that in the present state of Scotland anything that will shake the masses of our people out of their indifferentism will be to the good. I am out for fight, and I do not care very much what means prove useful to that end. I wrote several years ago that I looked with hopefulness to an intensification of sectarian warfare in our midst; the other policy of compromise and peace at any price which has been in the ascendant in recent years has certainly availed us nothing. For the same reason I heartily approve the decision of Inverness educationists to refuse appointments to any teachers who do not profess Christian principles. The fact that there are still idiots of that description in our midst makes me glad whenever they come out into the open in this way; when they don't it is because they are getting things all their own way by secret intrigue. I am all in favour of an open fight – a fight to the finish. Scotland is manifesting possibilities of becoming quite an interesting place at last.

The Rev. William Paxton of Liverpool, who has been protesting against the new school of Scottish novelists because of their realism, is barking up the wrong tree altogether. He complains they are exaggerating the ugly and sordid elements of Scottish life. He is wrong; these elements can't be exaggerated. They beggar all description. He is, of course, right when he says these novelists are false to the ideals of the Scottish people. They are, however, true to the facts; and because the majority of our people prefer to pretend that all in the garden is lovely when Scotland is the most barbarous country in Europe is no reason why our novelists should follow suit – is, in fact, a reason in precisely the opposite direction. Mr Paxton will be better occupied in pretending that the Scotland Street division of Liverpool is a bed of roses. In any case he should leave literature alone. Like most Scots – like all Scots who share the sort of sentiments he has been expressing – he knows nothing about it, and never will.

III THE SCOTTISH BBC

An article in the *Radio Times* on the 'sound principles upon which the Scottish region works', says, *inter alia*:

> If we put on plays of real significance in the world of Scottish letters little notice would be taken. But let us put on an entertainment which is a judi-

> cious mixture of Scots songs, Scots speech, and Scots humour, old-fashioned in that it contains no songs of recent composition, simple in that it contains no trace of what is grandiloquently styled 'wireless technique', and our postbag, like our listeners' cup of happiness, will be full. We do not put on such programmes because we regard them as the perfect flower of the Scottish muse, or because we have no other material at our disposal. We put them on because we know from experience that they are what the typical Scottish listener wants.

What a confusion! Three questions: – (1) How do they know that the Scottish listener does not want better stuff if they do not try it on him? (2) If their contention is true, what becomes of the BBC claim to be a great educational force – are children only to be taught what they like? (3) If this is true, why aren't Scottish BBC listeners confined to this precious Scottish popular stuff instead of being given also so much of the National Programme, which is designed in accordance with a very different policy?

What it amounts to is that whatever is capable of being called Scottish in the programmes must be confined to the beastly old kailyaird stuff – whatever of any higher value is given must be English, or Continental; Scotland must not be given a look-in on any of the higher spheres.

My paragraph is mis-titled. There is no Scottish BBC – there is only the Scottish region of an English Broadcasting Corporation, which treats all that is distinctively Scottish as all other English superiors have always done in politics, economics, literature, and everything else. Only a few of them have ever admitted it so frankly as this *Radio Times* article does.

C.M. Grieve, 1 July 1933

The Ineptitude of the BBC

Living at a considerable distance from Scotland, and receiving very few newspapers, I do not know whether the appointment of the Rev. Melville Dinwiddie to succeed Mr David Cleghorn Thompson as chief of the BBC in Scotland has evoked in any quarter anything other than the usual guff. I expect not. But the appointment is a thoroughly unsatisfactory one, and the way in which it was made also calls for the most outspoken condemnation. Let me say at once that I have no personal feeling against Mr Dinwiddie; I never so much as heard of him before reading of his new appointment in a paper the other day. I fancy the vast majority of people – including the vast majority of radio patrons – are in the same boat. This is in itself a damning criticism of the appointment – it ought not to have been given to anyone, who, prior to the publicity attendant upon it, was one of the great army of undistinguished ministers. It is a very important appointment – the BBC has great educational functions; its power as a propagandist organ is at present sedulously manipulated in certain interests which are not those of the people at large, and for which no mandate would ever be obtained if the matter were submitted to a referendum, and in relation to all the arts it plays a very important role, which is very far from being used in the best way. So far as Scotland is concerned, it is a branch of an English concern, with the customary English ascendancy and anti-Scottish attitude to our country of all English concerns. I have no doubt that Mr Dinwiddie will prove a very safe office holder from the point of view of those concerned to maintain these biasses of the BBC. But nothing in his past record indicates that he has any qualification whatever for meddling in literary, artistic or political matters, or being entrusted with any sort of cultural influence upon our nation at all. A man who had achieved some measure of scholarly and creative reputation of his own – who had manifested an active interest in cultural matters and was likely to be able to secure the respect, not the ruck of professionals who are always willing to earn a few guineas, but of such genuine artists and thinkers as we happen to possess – was called for. Above all, a man of high mentality and wide experience. I was a severe critic of Mr Cleghorn Thompson at times; I thought his qualifications so slender in many respects that no confidence could be reposed in his judgment. But we are out of the frying pan into the fire; however slender Mr Thompson's qualifications were, Mr Dinwiddie has literarily none. Whatever their quality, Mr Thompson's interests were cultural and embraced the whole range of the arts. Mr Dinwiddie has shown no such interests, let alone manifested an equal range. He, too, is so young and relatively inexperienced that to put him in such an important post where he will of necessity have to make suggestions to or even criticise people of serious accomplishments and real creative power, is to put him in a position where he will be unable to escape being intolerably presumptuous.

The fact that in Mr Dinwiddie the Scottish BBC has acquired the remainder of the alphabet is no recommendation. Most degrees are a device of organised mediocrity to ape qualifications that could not have been won on merit. There are thousands of BD's. What do they amount to? What does Mr Dinwiddie as BD amount to? A completely undistinguished member of the countless ruck of clergy. Ministers are desperately put to it today to eke out their waning influence as such by all sorts of expedients which have nothing whatever to do with their real business, in which they have completely and hopelessly failed. They are maintaining their prestige after a fashion – or holding on to the loaves and fishes and some hypocritical vestige of their ministerial business – by taking advantage of all sorts of side-winds. Mr Dinwiddie attributed his appointment to some very influential members of 'our Church'. The Church as a patron with the bestowal of BBC directorships and whatnot in his pocket is an interesting sidelight on its pretensions in other directions.

Mr Dinwiddie also holds the MC and the DSO. Well, old soldiers know how these were dished out. They only mean that their holder was luckier, or had more 'pull' than others – not that he was braver or rendered in any way better service than the hundreds of thousands who received no such decorations. Then Mr Dinwiddie is also an OBE. Obviously he is an inveterate picker up of letters after his name – another revealing and unrecommending trait. No man worth twopence would use or possess the OBE.

The fact that Mr Dinwiddie has been in Aberdeen for the past eight years is another regrettable fact in relation to the appointment; so far as Scotland is concerned – or, at all events, Scottish culture, even such as it is – Aberdeen has always been a bad influence. It is the greatest Philistine stronghold in Scotland. No one concerned for a New Scotland – least of all for a Scottish Literary and Artistic Movement – can expect other than the most pigheaded opposition from that 'airt'. The last thing in the world our Scottish BBC programmes need is any stronger blow of the mean wind from the Nor'-East Corner.

With all his alphabetical qualifications, Mr Dinwiddie was not the first by any means to be 'sounded' in regard to this appointment. The least said of some of the others the better; let me simply observe that bad as I regard Mr Dinwiddie's appointment to be, the job was first offered to, and refused by, others a great deal worse. It was also offered to a few slightly better. I wonder, for example, why Dr Hyslop turned it down; he would have been far better in many ways, and at least he does know something about music which bulks so largely in the radio fare. Perhaps he, like one or two others, refused it for reasons of modesty and intellectual integrity. The main point is that others again whose qualifications in every respect completely outweigh Mr Dinwiddie's, were not approached. I agree that, as the BBC is presently run and having regard to the fare it serves up, they were too good for the job. The very best that can be said for Mr Dinwiddie is that he isn't.

I am almost entirely opposed to the entire BBC policy. I object to its very constitution and to the fact that posts such as this are not openly advertised or subject to competition like Civil Service posts. I am, moreover, a thoroughly disaffected person – a political extremist, a cultural highbrow, and a rank irreligionist. And, though I cannot afford not to, there is no fee that will induce me to broadcast again unless and until I can say exactly what I want without the censorship of people like Mr Dinwiddie or any regard for any of the BBC biasses.

In any case, so far as the present business is concerned, I wish to register my strongest protest against the methods of appointment on the grounds of their detestable hold-and-corner character, which is an offence against all the standards of public life; against the appointment itself in the name of the standards and interests of all the arts involved and of Scotland generally; and against the action of Mr Dinwiddie himself in accepting such an appointment made in such an objectionable fashion and in view of his paucity of qualifications and the general uncertainty of his attitude to the very important issues involved in the exercise of such a post.

C.M. Grieve, 22 July 1933

Lewis Grassic Gibbon

This is going to be a notable autumn in the history of Scottish literature. I have not yet read (save the portion which appeared in the *Modern Scot*) Willa Muir's second novel, *Mrs Ritchie*, nor Naomi Mitchison's new novel dealing with Scottish Nationalism and Communism, a portion of which will appear in the forthcoming issue of the *Modern Scot*; but they will both be notable additions, as is Adam Kennedy's *The Mourners*, to the new Scottish novel. A fury of exposure, a savagery of satire, which will leave *The House with the Green Shutters* like a Christian Endeavour tract, is called for by the present conditions in Scotland – and will be forthcoming. A good deal of it is forthcoming in Gibbon's new book, *Cloud Howe*, which, with *Sunset Song* as the first, forms the second part of a trilogy which will be completed by a third novel, *Grey Granite*, which is now in preparation. Compton Mackenzie said of *Sunset Song* that 'the comparison with Burns is constant in the reader's mind'; Eric Linklater said that it was a 'more authentic picture of Scotland than ever Douglas or Maclaren did'; L.A.G. Strong called it 'the biggest book I know which has come out of modern Scotland'. It deserved all these and all the other tributes it received; it was racy of the soil, full of a broad humanity. *Cloud Howe* is far better; Gibbon is merely getting into his stride; his work seems to be growing as he goes nearer the heart of modern life – first, it was the countryside, now it is the village, next it is the city, and if he develops with the increasing complexity of his theme his treatment of Dundee will be a tremendous, appalling and vitally necessary masterpiece. His range is obviously enormous; he knows all sorts and conditions of people at first hand and with an amazing intimacy and completeness; he passes in the most life-like fashion from beautiful descriptions of Scottish scenery and country routine to the most brutal truth, the coarsest humour, the subtlest wit; he runs through all grades of society; he has equal mastery of the significant detail and the biggest mass effect. He doesn't need to put in twirly bits and sit back and admire his cleverness; there is no conscious writing up at all; his grip of essential reality never fails; the sheer integrity of his spirit supplies its own momentum – incident succeeds incident with perfect inevitability. All is grist that comes to his mill; not his style, which is only a by-product of it, but his character and the profound convictions natural to him, are able to absorb and use it all; here is a consciousness that can pass all Scottish life through it, without any jibbing or evasiveness whatever, but an amazing directness and gusto. *Cloud Howe* reminds me of what a man said to me on a Shetland island one day: 'I love to listen to the music of the sea, but, above all, I love to hear the roust (the tide) going through it.' The multitudinous music of Scottish life is in *Cloud Howe* all right, ringing all its changes from farce to fantasy; but there is a mighty roust going through it all the time. It is that roust which is going to tear Scotland from all its old moorings – all the old moorings by which it has mouldered and rotted and stunk so long.

Gibbon knows all about that roust. Listen to him on the village war memorial and compare the power of his satire with George Blake's in *Returned Empty*:

> An angel set on a block of stone, decent and sonsy in its stone night-gown, goggling genteel away from the Segget Arms… folk of her own, those folk who had died (thought Chris), and they set up *this* to commemorate *them* – this, this quean like a constipated calf! Robert said: May God forgive them this horror. Folk'll think it a joke when we've altered things, this trumpery flummery they put up in stone. But what kind of change, Robert (asked Chris)? Things go on the same as ever they were, folk neither are better nor worse for the War.

Listen to him on the English:

> She was only English, and they're tinks by nature – with a face like a bairn, a fool, white, with no guts.

Listen to him telling why Chris, as the minister's wife, doesn't like going round visiting the congregation:

> 'Ah, you see,' says Chris, 'I wasn't always a minister's wife. I was brought up on a croft and married on one, and I mind what a nuisance we thought some folk, visiting and prying and blethering about socials, doing everything to help us, or so they would think – except to get out and get on with the work.' And Jeannie Grant said: 'And get off your backs, you could surely have added. You're a Socialist the same as I am.'

Listen to Chris dealing with Stephen Mowat, the young laird, back from an English university and full of the New Scottish Movement:

> 'Scotland is a nation – that was the goal with its old-time civilisation and culture. Hwaw?'
>
> But Chris said: 'And what's going to happen when you and your kind rule us again, as of old, Mr Mowat? Was there ever the kind of Scotland you preach? – happy, at ease, the folk on the land well-fed, the folk in the pulpits well-feared, the gentry doing great deeds? It's just a gab and a tale, no more.'

Listen to how he ticks off Ramsay MacDonald:

> Ramsay came on with his holy-like voice and maa-ed like a sheep, but a holy-like sheep, that the country could yet be saved; and he'd do it.

And, finally, listen to his real message, as he puts it into the words of the minister:

> 'I'm afraid my wife and I think the same – *as all folk worth their salt in Scotland must think*. There are changes coming – they are imminent on us

– and I once thought the folk of some teaching would help. Well, it seems they won't – the middle-class folk and the upper-class folk and all the poor devils that hang by their tails; they think we can last as we are – or go back – and they know all the while they are thinking a lie. But God doesn't wait, or His instruments, and if these in Segget are the folks of the mills, then, whatever their creed, I'm on their side.'

The only weakness in Gibbon's book, I think, out of all its abundant wealth of life, its utter veracity, is just putting these sentiments in the mouth of a minister – not that I do not think but that there are ministers who would say as much now in our midst, but just that it doesn't matter if they do. Apart from that detail, however, *Cloud Howe* is a mighty transcript of Scottish life, and one informed by a great and noble purpose, and yet because of its brutal sexual passages and its handling of politics, religion, and other sacrosanct matters we have still plenty of slimy idiots left who will believe the hypocrites who condemn as foul and blasphemous and a libel on Scottish life this – the only really religious book Scotland has produced for a century and a half.

C.M. Grieve, 29 July 1933

Seeds in the Wind

Under this happy title has been published the third volume of poems by William Soutar, the previous two being *Gleanings from an Undergraduate*, and *Conflict*. The latter contained some notable poems in English – poems of a high philosophical order. The new volume is in Scots, and, as the sub-title implies (*Poems in Scots for Children*), most of the poems are no more than they purport to be – bairn rhymes, pretty jingles, almost meaningless trifles. They spring from certain superficial predilections rather than from deep conviction, and Soutar's work as a whole has not that consistency, that drive, that 'roust', of which I have spoken elsewhere. Yet how definitely related he is to the real aim and object of the Scottish renaissance movement is well enough known to readers of *The Free Man*, where many of his brilliant satirical and political poems and biting epigrams have appeared. In his use of Scots he illustrates what many of us do – Gibbon, A.D. Mackay, Adam Kennedy, and others – the return to, and new use of, Scots or the Gaelic or of Scots and Gaelic idiom in order to break away from inherited and Anglified habits of thought, achieve a closer contact with the objects actually around us, in Scotland here, and in relation to conscious Scottishness furth of Scotland itself, and to define the reactions of our sensibilities to our unexplored environment as Scots. And in this connection Soutar's contribution as manifested in this book and elsewhere is a very valuable one. He has a masterly grip of many phases of Scots; and the glossary to even this slim – and excellently produced – volume runs to some hundreds of words. Frequently the content and the verbal dress of his verses are in splendid keeping; the spirit of the poem is as purely Scottish as the words. And in 'Tam Teuch' I think he achieves an outstanding success of a rare kind – in the world of sheer nonsense. It originally appeared in *The Free Man* some months ago, and its perfect gratuitousness has recurred to me again and again since then and set me laughing. It runs as follows: –

There was a loonie ca'd Tam Teuch,
  Wha gat a spurtle-blade:
But it was hingin' sune eneugh
  Abune his brither's bed.
Ae nicht as Tam pou'd on his goon
  In cam' his brither Charlie;
Wi' that the spurtle-blade drapp't doon,
  An' Tammie said: *'You're early.'*

But *Seeds in the Wind* contains at least half-a-dozen short poems which ought to be included in any new edition of Mr John Buchan's *Northern Muse*, and once we are in a position to survey as a whole Mr Soutar's considerable output of poems of many kinds in English and Scots, critical and philosophical articles, epigrams and pasquils, there will be a good deal left in each of these categories of permanent value – a very definite and valuable contribution to the new Scottish Movement, and shrewdly, if not in many cases very obviously, related to the purposes which I have declared all we younger Scottish writers worth a rap have – and necessarily so – in common.

C.M. Grieve, 29 July 1933

The MacCrimmon Memorials

I have been waiting to see the faintest indication anywhere of a realisation of the enormity perpetrated in the recent unveiling of memorials to the MacCrimmons at Borreraig and in Kilmuir Churchyard, and in the speeches delivered on these occasions. There has been no such indication – no single note of protest or disgust. This is a damning reflection on the new Scottish Nationalism – a proof of the immense distance that has yet to be traversed before anything worthy of the name of Scottish Nationalism can be generated. Scotland is the most hopelessly barbarous country in Europe – so hopelessly barbarous that the ghastly insult to the MacCrimmons involved in the circumstances of these commemorative services has apparently escaped notice altogether. The attitude to the arts seems to be that to publicly 'honour' them at all is a distinguished gesture testifying to our high degree of culture; it never occurs to anyone that the manner of the honouring calls for any scrutiny – that for people whose lives are wholly divorced from artistic interests to get up in public and pay lip-service to arts of which they know nothing and care less is a diabolical insult which should be flung back in their teeth by all who are themselves creative artists or have any real sense of and regard for spiritual values. But the acceptance of the posturings of these hypocrites has reached in Scotland a degree unthinkable in any other so-called 'civilised' country. No credentials are called for; any jackass can get up and patronise any of the arts and get credit for being a wonderfully cultured person; no one dreams of pointing out that if the art or artist in question is of any consequence whatever in ninety-nine cases out of a hundred the actual spokesman at any commemoration ceremony is the last person in the world with any title to open his mouth. That he does so shows that his personal complacency completely overrides any regard he may imagine he entertains for the art or artist in question; that he is allowed to do so shows that the general public – and still more the cultured class who should be the guardians of such matters – are lost to all sense of the fitness of things. We are, alas, habituated in Scotland to these beastly befoulings of national genius by herds of unconscionable nitwits. The Burns Cult is a byword in this connection; no other country in the world would for a moment tolerate such egregious treatment of one of its great geniuses by a pack of mediocrities whose pretensions to speak on any literary or spiritual matter can only degrade what they affect to honour and who, if Burns were alive, would be the objects of his flaying contempt. The Scott Commemoration in Edinburgh was a national scandal and a disgrace to all connected with it; that not a single writer of repute, not a single Scottish writer at all, was associated with it, and that it was left for an English novelist of very mediocre merit, Mr Hugh Walpole, to walk as the solitary representative of Literature side by side with a gang of brainless Town Councillors has been the fitting subject of many scornful comments – in papers and periodicals outside Scotland. Inside Scotland I think the only appropriate protests were made by Mr Lewis Spence and myself. The new generation in Scotland seems to be no better than the old; writers are still apparently prepared to belly-crawl to any extent to a Philistine public and only too pleased to take any sort of back seat at all while the front rows are occupied by business men, clergymen, and other inferiors. A case in point was the Contemporary Scottish Authors' Book Exhibition in Glasgow. I am glad to see that a writer in *New Britain* makes a scathing reference to this ignominious farce. But he is wrong when he says that no Scottish author protested against it. I did, in the most unmistakable terms, and completely dissociated myself from it.

What should be the proper attitude of the creative artist to any sort of public patronage? My friend Kaikhosru Sorabji, the composer, puts the matter in a nutshell in a recent article in *The New English Weekly*:

> The importance of the aspect of the opera as a social function is this. It is a tacit admission that it is not possible to be a member of a civilised society and profess a total indifference to the things of the mind; and has it not

been said that hypocrisy is the homage vice pays to virtue? That, I think, as a realistically-minded person, is by no means altogether a harmful thing, namely, that people shall be made to realise, by the force of social feeling, and to dismiss music and art as of no account is just not done. And if music and art prosper by the patronage – in the financial, no other, sense, *bien entendu* – sincere or not, of modish half-wits, I should be the last person in the world to complain, provided neither myself nor the artists themselves realised, and make the modish half-wits also realise, that they, i.e., the latter, belong definitely to the lower orders, with whom an artist can no more be expected to establish personal contact than the highest cast Brahmin in the good old days with an untouchable, all is as it should be, so it seems to me.

I heartily endorse that. All true artists do in their hearts, but few of them ensue it. They are prepared to do all sorts of grovellings to pick up the crumbs that fall from Dives' table. They accept LLD's; they allow themselves to be treated as supernumeraries, as society entertainers, by people who are neither more nor less than influential enemies of all the arts and of every spiritual value. The time has come for artists to adopt a far more aggressive attitude and condone this sort of slavering humbug no longer – either in regard to themselves or to the great dead of their art. In regard to any public ceremony in connection with the latter the immediate question should be – is the spokesman a man of sufficient standing himself in the art in question? Nothing less should be tolerated; it is monstrous that nonentities with no relation whatever to the art in question should be allowed to get up and let off a lot of 'blah' on such occasions, while whatever real contemporary artists of that kind the country has should be ignored or brought on in a subordinate capacity to some mindless figurehead. That is precisely what happened in connection with the MacCrimmon ceremonies; those who spoke had no title to speak and spoke a lot of infernal and dishonouring balderdash. Let anyone who is tempted to question this just ask: – (1) What the intellectual or artistic status of the speakers in question happens to be; (2) what they have done for the art in question or for the arts in general in Scotland; and (3) whether Scotland even today has no sons who in virtue of their own creative calibre are not far more fit to speak on such an occasion. The answers would be – (1) negligible; (2) nothing; (3) certainly. Who were these particular speakers? First of all, Macleod of Macleod – the heir and representative of the chiefs to whom the MacCrimmons acted as hereditary pipers for three hundred years, eminent as composers, players, and teachers, until one of his precious ancestors, with the characteristic attitude of Scotland to the artist, tried to take away part of the land allocated to them. The MacCrimmons were having no nonsense. Has the present Laird undone that damnable insult to these great artists – has he himself acted otherwise towards the arts – has he, too, not thought it right that a nonentity like himself, of no public value whatever, should be relatively well-off and made much of while genuine artists in Scotland had to starve? Not a bit of him! Then he had no right whatever to speak on such an occasion – a resetter of the wrong done to those he purported to be honouring; a man perpetuating in his own attitude to the arts the very offence the MacCrimmons so mortally resented.

The other speaker was the Very Rev. Dr Norman Maclean. What does he know of any of the arts? What has he ever done for Scottish culture in any shape or form? He had the unholy impertinence to remind his hearers that:

> Men such as these who have enriched the generations were held in great honour in their day. They did not engage in manual toil. When the lady of Glengarry asked the family piper why he did not engage in useful work in his spare time, he replied: 'It is a poor estate that cannot support the piper without his working.' They were men of dignity, fully conscious of their own worth. When the Duke of Edinburgh consulted Donald Mackay, the Prince of Wales's piper, as to engaging a piper, 'What kind of piper does your Royal Highness want?' asked Donald. 'Oh! Just a piper like yourself,' answered the Duke. 'It is easy enough to get a piper,' replied Donald, 'but not easy to get a piper like me.'

Scotland can get any amount of Dr Norman Macleans, but creative artists of the slightest consequence are few and far between, and in these days they are not accustomed to being held in great honour in their own day. The Dr Norman Macleans see to that – but are always ready to yap about the dead who cannot exclude them from any of the current limelight. It is high time Scottish artists were getting back a bit of the spirit of Donald Mackay and putting these parasites in their place. 'They were men of dignity, fully conscious of their own worth.' Does Dr Maclean think they would regard it as any acceptable recognition to be mouthed over by one who not only has no standing whatever in relation to any art but himself embodies an attitude of society destructive of all artistic values and has no hesitation in usurping the place of the real artist and lucubrating with sheer effrontery on matters of which he knows nothing and of which his own life-practice and the utterly disproportionate place he has in the public eye is a sheer negation? The few of us in Scotland who have any trust in these matters and any artistic ability of our own, no matter how slight, must make a determined stand against such canaille no matter at what cost to ourselves. I know what the cost is – an exclusion from the very means of earning the barest livelihood for those who will not truckle to these hypocrites. It is in this these gentry show their real attitude to the Arts; the rest is all 'my eye'. There can be no compromise.

C.M. Grieve, 9 September 1933

Edinburgh University and Scots Literature

I

Let me suspend the further instalments of my accounts of recent Scots Literature for a little while to deal with a related matter. The *Edinburgh Essays on Scots Literature* require a good deal more to be said about them than the brief – but within their limits most effective – remarks recently made in these columns by 'A.A.' It is almost an established custom if one wants to pretend to do something on behalf of Scots interests – and doesn't know enough about the thing in question or want to really exert oneself very much – to call it the Edinburgh so-and-so. I hardly imagine that Edinburgh University would have allowed its name to be coupled in any way with so poor and careless a product in any other department of studies. The book is the counterpart in the sphere of Scots letters to the most wishy-washy devolutionism (say, the attitude of the Liberal Party or the Duke of Montrose or Mr John McCormick) in the sphere of Scots affairs. Apart from Professor Grierson, who provides a preface, there are seven essayists. The older men have taken the easier tasks and have resaid about Dunbar, Henryson, and other of the 'old 'uns' what has been frequently said before. These essays are rehashes of no consequence; they add nothing to such reputations as their writers already possess or to the learnings or appreciation already given to their subjects. It is difficult – if one is to avoid derogatory suggestions – to see why they were written; they are essentially purposeless – as little related to real scholarship or criticism or public education or literary purpose as are the compositions of school-children to literature. To compare them with T.S. Eliot on Lancelot Andrewes or Ezra Pound on Calvalcanti or Herbert Read on Gerard Manley Hopkins is enough. Yet some of the subjects could have – and should have – been treated on a like plane. Dunbar, for example. And in most of the essays crucial issues are involved, but the writers clearly have no realisation whatever of the relative importance and livingness of these since they devote their sentences instead to purely negligible ends. The other two essays – on very difficult and controversial subjects – are by younger men of no experience or authority and a sad mess they have made of them. Modern Scots Poetry and Modern Scots Fiction are essentially matters which not only cannot be dealt with by those who are not *inside* these movements but with which the main business and training and prepossessions of Messrs Ian Gordon and Angus MacDonald practically preclude them from dealing. They would require to be as Scottish as their names before they had an earthly chance of opening their mouths on such matters without putting their feet into them. Their main business is with English literature – and with English literature in its past forms, or where they condescend on contemporary writers at all, very highly respectabilised. I fancy both of them would hesitate before they burst into print on the subjects of T.S. Eliot or James Joyce or Hopkins or Charles Doughty. Why have they so little respect for Scots literature – and for themselves in relation to it – that they sail gaily into waters so alien to those in which they have been taught, and are accustomed, to fish? They would hardly take like liberties with any other European literature; I cannot imagine them venturing to publish essays on Paul Valéry or Rainer Maria Rilke or Boris Pasternak. Is a conviction of the relative negligibility of their Scots subjects – or perhaps a constitutional inability to have any such respect for them as they would, equally constitutionally, accord to German, French, or Russian writers – a qualification for their task? And if it is – if Scots writers desire no better than to be dealt with thus cavalierly by amateurs whose real interests lie elsewhere, and in a direction completely antipathetic to radical developments in Scots creativity – is the task worth undertaking at all, and is their willingness to undertake it not a damning criticism of their own lack of that self-respect which otherwise would necessitate their saving their powder and shot for more important game? However, these matters may be, it may be useful just to check over the articles in question and show that whatever the deficiencies of the Scots movement may be on the critical side at any rate we are not so deficient as to be easy prey to peashooters like this.

Mr Gordon devotes a fair part of his essay to myself. Unfortunately he cites only those of my earliest lyrics, which have become anthology pieces – 'The Watergaw', 'The Bonnie Broukit Bairn', and 'Crowdieknowe'. This is suspicious – for these are by no means the most important of my early lyrics on the strength of which Mr Gordon deplores my subsequent decline in poetic power. I had to spend a considerable amount of my time some years ago in educating people to appreciate some of these lyrics; the better of these lyrics I have not even yet been able to get across to their noddles – but though I managed to convince them of the quality of my early lyrics in general (and to do it I had to run the organs that printed them – no other paper would have published them) they have since revenged themselves upon me for subjecting them to that unfamiliar and painful experience by turning round and condemning my subsequent work because it does not resemble what I had taught them to admire. They even affect to have turned the tables on me; I am a dog they are feeding with its own tail. The truth, of course, is that they quickly reached their saturation level; a few of the easier of my early lyrics sufficed; the best ones were and remain beyond them, together with all the best of my latest work; and now they run after each other like sheep, each with the identical bleat about my early lyrics and subsequent decline. What a farce!

Mr Gordon is talking nonsense when he says, dropping the self-contained lyric, in my *Drunk Man*, 'several inset lyrics are still retained in the body of the poem'. Several should read about sixty! You would imagine from his references to it that *Cencrastus* has no lyrics in it. And of the contents of my subsequent books – not to mention the large number of uncollected poems I have published in all sorts of quarters these last two years – he says nothing. The fact of the matter is that he does not mention a single one of my more important poems, and in this respect is in the same state as all the other nit-wits in Scotland who are yapping about my lost lyricality, my increased propagandist tendencies and general decline, and in precisely the opposite case to the few Scots to whose opinion I attach the least importance and to every distinguished outside critic and fellow poet of whose views upon my work I am cognisant. At this stage then – before going on to discuss more general issues raised by Mr Gordon's essay – let me tell Mr Gordon and all his kind who deplore my 'falling-off' that there are not six of the lyrics in my first three books which they can name that can be set aside the very considerably greater bulk of my top-notch work contained in my last two books or published recently in periodicals and not yet collected, and that in any competent consideration of my work whatever the following poems must be regarded as major pieces, viz., 'Tarras', the first part of 'Water Music', 'Milkwort and Bog-Cotton', the second 'Apprentice Angel' poem; 'The Seamless Garment'; 'In Memoriam: Liam Mac Ille Iosa', and 'Harry Semen'.

30 December 1933

II

Let us then, as I said in my previous article, take up and consider a few details in Mr Ian Gordon's article.

On p. 138 we read: 'The greatest achievement of all is the new Scots lyric.' On p. 141 we read: 'The new lyric is probably the greatest achievement of modern Scottish poetry.' This slipshodness is characteristic of the essence – if seldom so flagrantly of the expression – of Mr Gordon's essay.

On p. 143 we read: 'For all the brilliance of "Grieve's" lyrics, synthetic Scots, lacking any but a personal basis for its concoction, is linguistically unsound.' Obviously it isn't unsound for poetry – or my poems in it do not deserve what Mr Gordon says of them; and since his subject is Modern Scots Poetry 'linguistic unsoundness' is surely irrelevant.

In any case, isn't any writer's usage of any language a 'personal concoction', and how does this differ from synthetic Scots? No one writes to an agreed vocabulary – no language has certain limits within which one is 'linguistically sound'.

On page 143 again: 'Scots can never compete with English. The main line of development has passed it by.' Nonsense! Neither can English compete with Scots in the things which are peculiarly and distinctively Scots. How can Mr Gordon assert that the latter are minor – relatively negligible – for what English can give? 'The counting of heads' means nothing in relation to literary values. 'The spirit blows where it listeth'; it does not confine itself to 'the major tongues'; the greatest influences in modern literature have written in languages so little known as Norwegian (Ibsen; Strindberg); Russian (Tolstoy, Dostoevski), and so on. The victory does not lie in this, more than in other matters, with 'the big battalions'. The decline in its value for creative purposes in English is in precise proportion to its development into a 'world language'. Even English as we know it would have treated its own Anglo-Saxon basis as it has treated Scots, and its own dialects, but for a woman – Elizabeth Elstob. What would English studies today be without the Anglo-Saxon background? What might they not be if Scots was given its proper place in our British linguistic scheme of things? It cannot be over-emphasised that we in Scotland are fighting against that English ascendancy spirit which attempted not only to disown or discredit Scots, but almost succeeded in disowning its own basis and native rhythms.

And what has all this got to do with literary values? Are Alfred Noyes and Rudyard Kipling greater poets, though they may be 'understanded of the people', than Charles Doughty, who wrote in a synthetic English every whit as archaic and incomprehensible to the man in the street as any synthetic Scots?

'And you cannot make poetry from the dictionary', says Mr Gordon. Great poetry has been made from Lemprière's *Classical Dictionary*. Burns made great poetry out of a jigsaw puzzle of antiquarian odds and ends. The provenance of many great poems has been equally unexpected. Mr Gordon contradicts himself, for he has given high praise to my lyrics – which were made from a dictionary. He must not presume to legislate for the creative spirit. It 'moves in a mysterious way, its wonders to perform'.

Has Mr Gordon reflected on the fact that all the major modern English creative writers have had to use masses of recondite words – spoken English would not serve them. Browning, Meredith, Hardy, Patmore, Hopkins, Joyce - the list goes on. Why? What is the use in face of this of trying to tie us down to 'the living Scots speech' and to (an unspecified) English. 'Revival of older Scots writers revives all the old difficulty of an aureate diction.' It doesn't do anything of the sort, but even if it did what of it? To whom was this 'aureate diction' a difficulty – and did the fact that some people found or find it a difficulty affect the literary values of what was done in it, as such?

Mr Gordon thinks Scottish writers may write in English. How does he account for the fact that recent English critics like Professor Ifor Evans and R.L. Mégroz, in example after example, show that our predecessors who tried to do so wrote poorer stuff in it than they wrote in Scots, and that there is every indication that if they had concentrated properly on the latter they would have been greater writers. These critics cite R.L. Stevenson, George MacDonald, and others quite conclusively in support of their contention. None of the Scots who write in English have established a place of any consequence in English literature. A modern critic has well observed that when Burns unwisely discards the vernacular his efforts resemble 'nothing so much as a bather whose clothes have been stolen'. Other Scottish writers present a still ghastlier spectacle, since few of them have anything like Burns's physique.

As to what Mr Gordon says of aeration, lightening of structure, and dexterity – and supports by hopeless alleged examples from Cocker and the like – he could find far better examples of the like in 'Hugh Haliburton' and 'J.B. Selkirk' and others whom he does not mention, anterior to the point from which he does 'the regeneration of Scots verse'.

P. 144. I hope Mr Gordon does not imagine that 'broukit bairn' means 'lost child'.

Finally, what is the sense of accusing me of 'inability to separate art and life' and yet have Mr Gordon conclude his essay by hoping that 'Scots poetry will be positive' and that we may 'retain our new technique and still keep in close touch with humanity'? Mr Gordon would seem to have written in what Sean O'Casey's Joxer calls 'a state of chassis'.

I said finally just above – but this is one other point. 'Above all,' says Mr Gordon, 'satire calls for clarity and a reasonable chance of knowing what the poet is attacking.' Does it, indeed? What then of not satire in particular but satire in general – just the expression of a satirical disposition? The satire to which Mr Gordon refers must have been satirical enough or he could not have recognised it for satire; that it left him not knowing precisely whom it was attacking was perhaps just its intention – to communicate a temper, and leave it at that.

I must deal with Mr Angus MacDonald's remarks on Modern Scots Novelists in a separate article.

C.M. Grieve, 6 January 1934

In Reply to Dr Mary Ramsay

One gets very tired of the old gag about 'serious and constructive criticism' as opposed to so-called 'destructive writing', and I am surprised to find Dr Mary Ramsay using it again against me. Let me just quote her Robert Briffault:

> The platitudinarian formula that one is not justified in being destructive unless one can be constructive also is an asininity. It is a very convenient formula in defence of existing infamies and atrocities, and accordingly the question, 'What do you propose to put in its place?' is the habitual repartee to proposals to abolish collective murder, typhus, religion, small-pox, or capitalistic banditry. In point of fact all human progress, if fundamentally considered, will be found to have consisted in destruction much rather than in construction. Scientific progress, for example, has been a series of destructive criticisms. Copernican astronomy did not give an account of the universe; it merely showed the absurdity of the geocentric doctrine and of the faked forgery of epicycles. The Darwinian theory has not to this day explained organic evolution; what it has done is to explode the naive legend of special creation. Einstein and modern physics have reduced physical knowledge to a muddle; their merit lies in their having destroyed the cut-and-dried conceptions of nineteenth century physics. Similarly with what social progress has been compassed. Democracy has done nothing whatever

towards building up social organisation except that it has abolished the feudal system by blowing up armoured knights with gunpowder and divine absolutism by chopping off the heads of kings. To picture progress as having been essentially constructive is bourgeois superstitious nonsense. It has consisted in destruction. To pull down the bastilles which the frauds of class cultures have built round the human mind is to liberate the human mind and human power. The question what shall be substituted for prison walls after they have been pulled down is merely silly.

Dr Ramsay is inconsistent, too, in that her rebuking of me is a variant of the fault of which she accuses me since she does not take up the critical points I made against Gordon. With Gordon as an individual I had no concern; his essay appeared under the *ægis* of Edinburgh University, on the staff of which he holds a far more important and lucrative post than Scotland will ever afford me. Why should I excuse his stupidities on the score of his comparative illiteracy and youth? As well let a man disseminate an infectious disease on the ground that once he gets a little more experience he will cease to do so. The type of opinion Mr Gordon has disseminated seems to me as dangerous as any infectious disease. If Gordon had done good work in verse I should have been very happy and very swift to recognise it; I have only seen 'The Old Miners' and one or two other short things, and do not agree that they afford me any margin for praise. I had intended to deal even more severely with Mr Angus MacDonald than with Mr Gordon. His essay was certainly much worse. But the current issue of *The Modern Scot* has said all that is necessary about it, and I am insufficiently interested in novels to wish to add anything to that, except to point out that the custom of pre-nuptial intercourse is still, happily, preserved in the Shetlands and elsewhere, with results that compare favourably with any resulting from other practices elsewhere, and Mr MacDonald has no right to refer to *White Maa's Saga* in terms which suggest that the circles in which he himself moves are either any higher in the scale of sexual ethics or any more worthy of novelistic attention.

To return to Dr Ramsay, her interest in constructive criticism does not lead her to attempt to substantiate her claim that Mr Herbert Wiseman's 'untiring and judicious work has been steadily raising the standard of musical education in Scotland' – which I flatly deny, while again inviting her or anyone else to meet the definite challenges I threw out in my article on Mr Wiseman. Here, again, is no question of personalities: I am simply and solely concerned with the facts, and if Mr Wiseman, Dr Ramsay, or anyone else will consent to deal with these I am their man.

With regard to Presbyterians let me reply to Dr Ramsay as follows: –

(1) If the office of clergyman makes such demands on men's time and capacities why do they waste so much of it trying to write novels, poetry, and what not? Our Scottish ministers always seem to have had ample time to write books

of all sorts. Only the quality has been almost invariably extremely bad.

(2) How is it that it is only Presbyterian clergymen whose literary work 'must almost inevitably be in a form closely related to their ministerial functions, viz., sermons, meditations, sacred poems', while Rome can give us great poets and great writers in other categories, and even the Church of England can soar to figures like Swift and Donne, while all the post-Reformation clerical authors Dr Ramsay cites are extremely small potatoes, against not only these, but against, say, Dunbar and Gavin Douglas?

(3) As to the need for constant contemporary restatements, and the consequent speedy eclipse of religious writings except those of great genius, I do not agree that this is the case, and believe that far more people in Scotland today have read *The Four-fold State* or *Natural Law in the Spiritual World* – not to mention the *Pilgrim's Progress* – than have read Dunbar or any other great literature in any form, or any modern religious restatement.

(4) It would be easy to show that Dr Ramsay's list of Scottish Protestant minister-authors compares very unfavourably with that of the minister authors of any other national church or big denomination in Europe.

(5) Dr Ramsay must not write of what poets may do in a Scotland restored to nationhood. Ibsen and Strindberg found it as necessary to indulge in constant invective as I do, though Norway and Sweden were politically in the case she imagines Scotland coming to.

And, finally,

(6) When I find that I cannot indulge in invective and 'more serious' work simultaneously and that my critical activities involve restrictions of certain other creative activities, it will be time enough for me to cease bothering with the former. So far they are certainly not interfering with, but rather feeding, each other, and I do not get any encouragement to think I would serve Scotland better by eschewing controversial writing of the sort in question by looking at either the quantity or the quality of the work of any other Scottish writers who have followed that recommended course. Far from it!

C.M. Grieve, 17 February 1934

Sean O'Casey's New Play

No book I have read for long enough has moved me so profoundly as Sean O'Casey's new play, *Within the Gates*, which has just been produced at the Royalty Theatre, London. It not only marks his emergence as a dramatist of European consequence, but is a triumphant solution of the most crucial problems of dramatic presentation towards which Ibsen, Strindberg, and to a smaller extent the living American dramatist, Eugene O'Neill, pointed in their most significant developments, and will unquestionably rank as a landmark in the history of the theatre. Mr O'Casey has transcended the naturalist convention and restored the drama to the plane of great poetry – supreme realism instead of mere actualism. His technical means of orchestrating contemporary consciousness and moving naturally out of plain speech into intoned speech and thence to song is an achievement only equalled by the later prose work of his fellow-Irishman, James Joyce. It has taken him years to do it; I have the privilege of knowing O'Casey personally and know what it has cost him. He has not sacrificed one iota of his personal integrity, of his proletarian fidelity, and he has treated the crucial socio-politico-economic and moral problems of the age with sheer genius. It is a book which must be read by all interested in modern drama and literature generally, and by all deeply concerned over the plight of civilisation. It is a book for Free Men everywhere – Fascists and lickspittles won't understand it. As Paul Banks says in *The Plough and the Stars*, it was O'Casey's own people – the Irish – who were stripped naked and shamed. In *Within the Gates* it is the English, the proud builders and proprietors of Empire. 'And England as an entity ought to suffer the shame and degradation, the humiliation and the heartbreak, that the work must cause in every individual beholder.' Every individual reader or beholder, he should have said, with a shred of decency left. But, bless you, there are a number in our midst who haven't that and who are therefore immune – thousands so superficial, so shallow, that a paper-boat couldn't find enough depth in them to float, let alone a modern destroyer like O'Casey's play. Catharsis – the purging power of tragedy – is far too strong a medicine for those whom the system has completely eviscerated till they have not only no bowels of compassion left but no guts of any kind. A typical example is the infernal tittle-tattler who writes the dramatic notes over the pseudonym of 'Masque' in that worst of all Scottish papers, *The Weekly Scotsman*, a paper that cultivates a sheer silliness without parallel, I think, in this or any other country. No more appalling revelation of the scatter-brained interests of Scottish people can be imagined than the Readers' Club and query columns of this weekly; they have a triviality that beggars description. 'Masque' is a suitable contributor to such an organ – his pseudonym is exactly right; the false face is all there is to it – it has completely subsumed any man or woman there was ever behind it. What 'Masque' does with O'Casey's great play is to lump it together with all these other extraordinary modernist experiments which have the impertinence to be too clever for people like 'Masque'. But 'Masque' isn't having any. 'We can point out to him', says 'Masque', 'that instead of being profound he is only perplexing, that his symbolism is merely an irritation of the nerves, and that by the end of his play scarcely a soul knows what he has been driving at.' How did 'Masque' know? Did he conduct a plebiscite of those present? Even so, why the devil didn't he ask the few exceptions who did know what it all meant! Referring to O'Casey's Down-and-Outs, who march and chant in procession, 'Masque' says: 'They are the dregs of humanity, but what they are doing in the play no one can ever guess.' Can't they, by Heavens! The whole play is a parable on the fact that we are all down-and-outs under this accursed system, or soon will be. 'Masque' gives what purports to be a synopsis of the story of the play – he doesn't mention that one of the principal characters is a young prostitute. The *Weekly Scotsman*, bless you, is far too genteel to admit the existence of such creatures. The play is a devastatingly simple, heart-searching parable of the great problems of humanity today, and this blithering nincompoop is permitted to air his incredible fatuity and petty insolence at its expense. I have devoted this article to it because – although this is an extreme example – the whole thing is so typical of Scottish newspaper criticism. *The Times* (reactionary as it is) admits the greatness of the play; *The Times Literary Supplement*, in a long, ably written review, hails it as a masterpiece of unquestionable dramatic genius; all the other leading papers – whatever their politics – are in no two minds about its signal importance. But this piffling little Edinburgh rag – this mainstay of all the hordes of curious Colonial Scots who long for bits of white heather – allows a mindless scribbler to vent his soul-destroying inanities at its expense. If there was any responsible Government with the great human interests of its constituents at heart – the *Weekly Scotsman* would have been promptly suppressed as an intolerable insult to human intelligence. (But then – if there were any such Government – O'Casey would not have needed to write such a play, perhaps! It is the Government who are ultimately responsible; the papers which debauch the minds of their readers till they tolerate the insanities of the existing politico-economic system, are merely its tools.) O'Casey's play will rank among the great works of European drama – and amongst the sincerest works of literary genius moved by the vital problems of humanity – long after 'Masque' and all his kind have passed into the oblivion from which they should never have been permitted to emerge, and the *Weekly Scotsman* is preserved in the Scottish National Museum as one of the most shameful mementos of our inconceivably simian past. And on the top of this witless attack on O'Casey's great play, the same paper, mark you, devotes a page of letterpress and photographs to the wonderful progress of the Scottish Community Drama Movement. But 'Masque' did not write these notes. It was a colleague of his – a fellow-genius – another of the amazing band of brilliant litterateurs who grace the pages of this Comic Cuts of Literature!

C.M. Grieve, 3 March 1934

Scottish Themes in Poetry

I have recently had occasion to write a long poem on the subject of Pipe Music – the pibrochs of the great period, to which all written since 1800 are hopelessly degenerate. Few people know anything of these great pibrochs, and even those who do, as a rule, fail completely to understand, even when hearing them, the tremendous altitude of the spirit which divides them from the tunes which to most people constitute music; fail to understand even if they are told what is meant by such a difference – just as they are hopelessly ignorant of the affiliations in Arabia, India, and elsewhere of this 'timeless music'. The extent to which Scotland considers the degenerate forms (which alone it knows) synonymous with its true glories need not detain us here; what I am concerned with for the moment is the way in which my preoccupation with the subject of pipe music led me to reflect again on the fact that practically none of our most distinctive features or emblems of nationality have yet evoked poems of any worth. I have dealt in a previous paper with the extraordinary failure of Scottish poets to recognise the beauties of our scenery. They have almost all been content with dull conventionalisms of treatment, destitute of first-hand observation, intimacy of knowledge, and vivid personal emotion in the presence of these great scenes. This is apart from the fact that their attitude to nature generally is either a merely escapist one, or flatly actualistic. The evolution of man's attitude to nature under the impetus of scientific knowledge is almost wholly unreflected in their sentimental outpourings, animated as these are by a vicious anti-intellectualism, a sensuous submergence of the self in nature instead of that domination of nature which is man's job, and lying pretences of a desire to return to conditions which no sane man, with a moment's thought, could pretend to entertain. But it is something other, and greater, than this unreal attitude to our national surroundings that I am dealing with now – it is the utter failure of our poets to realise any of our great national symbols, to acquire a worthy attitude to Scottish history and our present conditions and our future possibilities. Almost everything that is being expressed in verse bearing on love of country and pride in our national past is beneath contempt; it could only emerge from the minds of garrulous morons incapable of any rational attitude to either. There is a hideous lack of maturity not only in the forms of expression, but in the actual content of what is said in these outpourings that suggests that they are not the products of grown men and women who have had the benefits of a decent education, but of mentally defective children. Apart from one or two poems in the Gaelic – which, while delightful enough, are only concerned with the actual fact of the deer's beauty, not in transforming it into an effective national symbol, nor in any other intellectualisation – there is no poem about one of the noblest and most distinctive of the animal forms inhabiting our country – the wild red deer – that is worth a moment's attention. There is no passable poem about the eagle. There is no poem doing anything approaching justice to the magnificence or wildness or loneliness of any of our great mountain scenes. There is no poem of the slightest consequence written in recent years on any of the great themes of Scottish history, or interpreting the trends of that history and dealing with our national genius and destiny, or involving either any prophetic faculty or worthy hopes and ideals for the future of our country. Scotland is supposed to be a great religious country; no poem of any value on a religious theme has been written in it since before the Reformation. We are supposed to have a genius for metaphysics and philosophy – there is no literature in the world so destitute of metaphysical or philosophical poems. We have undoubtedly played a great part in the developments of modern industrialism and science; but these have had no commensurate place in our literature. We have a very distinctive sense of humour; we have produced no masterpieces of comical poetry. We have a vivid and dramatic national vitality; it has no more reflected itself in our poetry than it has in dramas. And to make an analysis of the trumpery themes our poets have devoted themselves to is appalling evidence of our national, spiritual and intellectual bankruptcy; that grown men and women should churn out such appalling tosh and manifest such an unredeemed infantilism is almost incredible. It has never happened in any other country in the world that its poets for generations in succession had been afflicted so unanimously with such an appalling puerility.

I began by mentioning pipe-music. There are very few good poems in any of the world's literatures dealing with music; the poets who try, if they do not confine themselves to mere analogics and those grandiose utterances supposed to be in keeping with the elevation of their theme, but really attempt to express an intimate understanding of the subject, generally come an infernal cropper. Scottish poets have run no such risk. The references to the pipes in Gaelic poems are almost all of a purely matter-of-fact order, or straight-forward references to their military utility. Some of the best of them are to be found in Alasdair MacMhaighstir Alasdair, as, for example

Lium a's muirneach 'n am éri,
Cruaigh sgal éibhinn do sgórnain;
Anail-beatha do chréafoig,
D'a séidid hroi d' phóramh.

But of penetration into the soul of pipe-music, as apart from the more obvious external effects, or of any consideration of the relation of the pipes to the Scottish psyche in particular, not a bit! And one of the very few references to the matter in poetry in English is Byron's: –

And wild and high the 'Cameron's gathering' rose!
The war-note of Lochiel, which Albyn's hills
Have heard, and heard, too, have her Saxon foes: –
How in the noon of night that pibroch thrills,
Savage and shrill! But with the breath which fills
Their mountain-pipe, so fill the mountaineers
With the fierce native daring which instils
The stirring memory of a thousand years...

But now they forget all that is really worth remembering, and the deeds of derring-do to which the traditional music inspires them are nothing to write home to mother about!

C.M. Grieve, 10 March 1934

English Ascendancy

The future of these islands largely depends on the rapidity now with which and the extent to which England realises – or the other elements, Irish, Scottish, Welsh, Cornish, and Manx compel her to realise – that she only stands for one element in our midst, and that not now, whatever it may have been from certain points of view in the past, in any way better or more important than the others, and allows the lot to have full play without continuing to impose on them any English ascendancy idea. It is unlikely that this vital process of liberating all the forces which in a free synthesis will make for our immeasurable enrichment and strength – and which crushed into the mould of English ascendancy are now our greatest weakness – will come to any great extent from a timely realisation of the need for it on the part of the English themselves. Nevertheless, there are signs of a little awakening to it among certain sections of the English people, if not among the public school boys or in those circles who are hopelessly occluded from seeing the realities of the English situation, let alone of any other part of the British Isles, by their preoccupation with that monstrous Imperialism which is really only an elephantiasis of the English ascendancy spirit. These awakenings are naturally to be found in the North of England, to which London centralisation is almost as much a curse as it is to Scotland or Wales, and in those English counties which still retain a large measure of native regional life antipathetic to metropolitanism. But even in less likely directions there is a welcome indication of a growing critical insight into the dangers of the English ascendancy spirit, and these indications confirm the wisdom and necessity of the growing impatience of the several elements in Great Britain with the continued assumption and enforcement of English superiority. I see, for example, an eminent naturalist drawing attention to the extent to which English field studies are spoiled by the general insularity of the naturalists in question; they are unable to – or fail to – correlate their findings to the work done on the same subjects in other countries, and as a consequence their conclusions are largely vitiated or distorted by the naive assumption that conditions in England in these respects are peculiar to England, and not, as the fact is, common to a much wider area. Again, in the very different sphere of art, the typical English ascendancy manifestation is clearly seen in what a recent critic of modern drawings says: 'The mental contribution to drawing – with or without what are felt to be aberrations', he says

> is more in evidence than it used to be in living memory. That the return is less marked in England than in the other countries of Europe, and would be so in America if it were not for the number of foreign-born artists working there, is also true. However highly selective and well-composed the typical English drawing may be, it still consists in making marks on paper to imitate the facts of the subject. That it is often done with great skill and

economy of means does not affect a difference, which helps to explain the violent assertions of older English artists that their younger colleagues will not take the trouble to draw. The truth is, of course, that in mentally digesting the subject of their drawing, they (these younger artists) are taking a great deal more trouble than did the nineteenth century trained draughtsmen, whose chief concern was to imitate the facts of appearance.

This obstinate insularity and relative avoidance of the mental is what particularly differentiates the Scot from the Englishman, and it cannot be too strongly emphasised that the more we resemble the English in any respect the more we cut ourselves off alike from Europe and our own genius – and from arriving at once at positions at which England will only very slowly and awkwardly and incompetently arrive too long at long last. It is significant that our most vocal anti-modernists in Scotland are our most typical and inveterate Anglo-Scots.

'There is', says Mr T.S. Eliot, in his *The Use of Poetry and the Use of Criticism*,

> a view of English poetry, already of some antiquity, which considers the main line of English poetry from Milton to Wordsworth, or from perhaps even before Milton, as an unfortunate interlude, during which the English muse was, if not beside herself, at least not in possession of her faculties.

Professor Herbert Read says

> The main tradition of English poetry... begins with Chaucer and reaches its final culmination in Shakespeare. It is contradicted by most French poetry before Baudelaire, by the so-called classical phase of English poetry culminating in Alexander Pope, and by the late Poet Laureate.

Mr Eliot does not agree with this view. 'What I see in the history of English poetry', he says,

> is not so much daemonic possession as the splitting up of personality. If we say that one of these partial personalities which may develop in a national mind is that which manifested itself in the period between Dryden and Johnson, then what we have to do is to re-integrate it.

There can be no question that this partial personality, which has led to the domination in our literature of that tendency which is not only opposed to all the minority elements which ought to be the true tributaries of a fully British tradition – the Scottish, Irish, Welsh, and all the regional dialect elements – but equally to the native English traditions themselves – has manifested itself for many centuries and become increasingly dangerous. The time has come when it is vitally necessary to effect that reintegration of which Mr Eliot speaks, and reassume it into its proper subordinate place in relation to the whole. Indeed the dangerous dominance it has achieved renders it necessary to stimulate every other element now instead of it, and relegate it ruthlessly to a back seat until such time as it recovers its proper modesty. As Coleridge says – in what Mr Eliot rightly calls one of the saddest confessions – in English literature as in Coleridge's own case: 'That which suits a part infects the whole,/And now is almost grown the habit of my soul.'

Mr Eliot makes a very valuable point when he observes: –

> The great work of Dryden in criticism is, I think that at the right moment he becomes conscious of the necessity of affirming the native elements in literature. Dryden is more consciously English, in his plays, than his predecessors; his essays on the drama and on the art of translation are conscious studies of the nature of the English theatre and the English language, and even his adaptation of Chaucer is an assertion of the native tradition – rather than, what it has sometimes been taken to be, an amusing and pathetic failure to appreciate the beauty of the Chaucerian language and metric. Where the Elizabethan critics, for the most part, were aware of something to be borrowed or adapted from abroad, Dryden was aware of something to be presented at home.

But elsewhere, Mr Eliot says:

> I do not believe that good English verse can be written quite in the way which Campion advocates, for it is the natural genius of the language, and not ancient authority, that must decide; better scholars than I have suspected even that Latin versification was too much influenced by Greek models; I do not even believe that the metric of *The Testament of Beauty* is successful, and I have always preferred Mr Bridges' earlier and more conventional verse to his later experiments. Ezra Pound's 'Seafarer', on the other hand, is a magnificent paraphrase exploiting the resources of a parent language; I discern its beneficial influence upon the work of some of the more interesting younger poets today. Some of the older forms of English versification are being revived to good purpose.

This is heartening hearing. The sooner England gets back to its proper native basis the better, and, supplementary to Mr Eliot's remarks, I would direct all those concerned with the true way out of the muddle in which English culture has been involved by that vaulting ambition which has so disastrously overleapt itself to what O. Vocadlo says in his paper on 'Anglo-Saxon Terminology' (in the fourth volume of the *Studies in English*, by members of the English Seminar of the Charles University, Prague), where he has hard words for those who share the prevailing sentiment that the Anglo-Saxon age was a crude and uncouth period, reminds us that *'in literary culture the Normans were about as far behind the people whom they conquered as the Romans were when they made themselves the masters of Greece'*, and emphasises the significance of Aelfric's Grammar as a test of the fitness of the West-Saxon literary language for the higher functions of science.

C.M. Grieve, 17 March 1934

'Bysshe Vanolis': A Centenary Tribute

The centenary of the birth of James Thomson, who wrote over the pseudonym of 'Bysshe Vanolis' (which commemorates his admiration of Shelley and Novalis), occurs this year. An admirable account of his work appears in Professor B. Ifor Evans's *English Poetry in the late Nineteenth Century*, and from that I may extract this brief account of his life.

'He was born', says Professor Evans,

> at Port Glasgow in 1834. His mother died when he was six, and from her close evangelicism he was later to revolt. His father was a sailor stricken with paralysis, and some of Thomson's unstable characteristics have been traced to his influence. Thomson was found sufficient schooling to qualify him for an army-schoolmastership, and from 1854–1862 he served in army schools in Ireland and England. Like Leopardi, who influenced his poetry, he loved unsuccessfully; the one woman to whom he was deeply attached died in 1853, and in the most ambitious of his prose essays, 'A Lady of Sorrow', he has commemorated the attachment in language influenced by De Quincey. His years as a schoolmaster were the most untroubled in his life. He had worked to gain a knowledge of Italian, French, and German, and had read widely in English literature. It was then that poetry began, and as yet the poverty and self-inflicted distress of the later years had not mastered him. He was dismissed from his post in 1862, for a breach of discipline which appears to have been of a trivial character. In his early days as a teacher, he had met, at Cork, Charles Bradlaugh, the rationalist politician, who carried his atheism so aggressively into English public life. His influence on Thomson was profound, and it was to Bradlaugh that he turned after his dismissal. Bradlaugh found him work on his paper, *The National Reformer*, and from 1862–1874 Thomson wrote regularly for the rationalist press. His satiric prose in such pieces as 'The Story of a Famous Old Jewish Firm' has an assaulting power; the work that Swift might have produced had he been an atheist and not a Christian. Unfortunately his rationalist associations and his poverty barred him from the society and the literary journals where his poetical works might have found acceptance... Apart from one visit to Colorado and another to Spain, a garret in London was the centre of the rest of his life, and the dim gas-lit streets of London appear frequently in his poetry. Melancholy possessed him with the strength of physical disease, and he grew into a habit of drinking, which he

was powerless to control. It was towards the close of this period that 'The City of Dreadful Night' appeared in *The National Reformer* March–May 1874. In 1875, Thomson quarrelled with Bradlaugh, and his association with *The National Reformer* ceased. He struggled to gain other journalism, and some of his work appeared in that most curious Victorian periodical, *Cope's Tobacco Plant*, in which a Liverpool firm advertised its tobacco by printing reputable literature. These were temporary exploits, and Thomson's condition was frequently not far from destitution. He had the good fortune to gain the friendship of Bertram Dobell, bookseller and publisher, who arranged for the appearance of his first volume of verse, *The City of Dreadful Night and Other Poems*, in 1880. The title poem had already gained the attention of George Eliot, George Meredith, and Philip Bourke Marston, and the volume was in every way successful. Later in the same year (1880) appeared a second volume, *Vane's Story, Weddah and Om-el-Bonain and Other Poems*. Recognition had come at last, and had Thomson had settled health, or temperate habits, he could have developed the openings offered him in periodicals such as *The Fortnightly* and *The Cornhill*. But dipsomania possessed him, until even his friends found difficulty in associating with him. He died in 1882 in University College Hospital, where he had been taken by Philip Bourke Marston and other friends. After his death, a third volume of verse, *A Voice from the Nile and Other Poems* (1884), was published with a memoir by Bertram Dobell, and in 1895 the collected *Poetical Works* were issued.

Such is a brief account of the life of one of the very few Scottish poets – not more than three or four all told – since the death of Burns, whose work is of great interest to any intelligent reader today. Incidentally, it may be remarked that there is no periodical in Great Britain today where a poem of the length and quality of *The City of Dreadful Night* would have any chance of appearing, nor does any commercial firm today run any magazine in which, as in *Cope's Tobacco Plant*, literature of a quality above contempt is published. Thomson is for the most part only known by that sombre masterpiece, but he was a poet of wide range, by no means limited to the expression of this single vein of profound pessimism, while, as Professor Evans observes, his prose essays were marked by wide literary enthusiasm and discrimination. His prose work is contained in three volumes, *Satires and Profanities* (1884), *Essays and Phantasies* (1881), and *Biographical and Critical Essays* (1896). The sources of some of his inspirations are worth nothing – the excellent narrative poem, 'Weddah and Om-el-Bonain', in which he 'consolidated the elements of fable, satire, and description into one impressive whole', derives its story from a brief prose incident in Stendhal's 'De l'Amour'; 'The Doom of a City' (1857) foreshadowing his great poem, and describing a voyage to a city of stone people, is derived from the Tale of Zobeide in 'The Three Calendars' in *The Arabian Nights*; 'Vane's

Story' at one point involves a recital of Heine's 'Ich bin die Prinzessin Ilse'; and *The City of Dreadful Night* has, as a culminating episode, a verbal rendering of Albrecht Dürer's *Melencolia*.

Two editions of Thomson's great poem, each with a selection of his other pieces, appeared in 1932, one with a preface by Henry S. Salt, and the other with an introduction by Edmund Blunden. Mr Blunden compared Thomson's poem to T.S. Eliot's *Waste Land*; Thomson was certainly, with his fellow Scottish poet, Alexander Smith, in advance of any English poet in dealing with those phenomena of urban life which bulk so largely in modernist poetry, but it was stupid of a *Times Literary Supplement* reviewer to remark, apropos Mr Blunden's comparison, 'Mr Eliot ploughed through his waste lands to a sanctuary. Over the bourne of Thomson's city we abandon hope.' Most of us would prefer to remain in Thomson's city to making a fantastic escape to Eliot's Royalist and Anglo-Catholic position. It is true, however, that 'the tragic vision is possible only to a nobler conception of life and destiny than Thomson's view of lost man's defeated hedonism could rise to.' That does not justify – but on the contrary! – the same writer's reflection: 'Thomson accepted entire the implications of the scientific theories of his day – implications barely admitted by the scientists themselves; and if today science may seem to be changing places with mysticism, this dolorous lamentation should be outmoded and its poignancy lost for ever.' Although science has moved away from 'crude determinism', and its latest positions are well nigh ungraspable to the lay mind; it has moved in an opposite direction entirely to any return to 'mysticism' in the normal religious sense. However that may be, 'from a distempered gloom of thought the magic of a poet's creative energy made a thing of beauty.' What might be a horror of darkness is transmuted into fadeless night, although 'the sun never visited that city.' If there is no shining symbol of promised ease, there is, even in the city of night, a nobler one of courage and endurance. Or, as Professor Evans says:

> The mood of despair penetrates deeper than the spiritual nostalgia of the romantics or the prayer for life's cessation of Swinbourne's 'The Garden of Prosperine.' Life is here an aching and inescapable futility, like the maddening wakefulness of insomnia. The strength of the poem lies in the imaginative quality that has sustained these dark phantoms without monotony; and it increases in the later sections, so that the fallen statuary and the transcript of Dürer's 'Melencolia,' and the description of the Sphinx amid shattered statuary, are among the most marked and individual passages in the whole of Thomson's work. Despite uneveness, he has poetic integrity, and not infrequently poetic power. His contacts lay closely with the earlier nineteenth century discussion of faith and disbelief. He caries on that theme where Arnold left it, in self-frustrating doubt. He penetrates deeper than Arnold and arouses from his scepticism an image of despair.

If he had had the still greater misfortune to live during those years in Glasgow or Edinburgh, his work would almost certainly have acquired a few still deeper hues of darkness. However slow or loath Scotland may be to welcome to her bosom her disreputable sons of genius, there can be no gainsaying Thomson's high rank in English literature, nor the fact that he and John Davidson, equally abhorrent in their lives to the vast majority of Scots, are the only two outstanding Scottish poets of the period, and that it is highly unlikely that any subsequent Scottish poet will do first-class work who does not follow in their footsteps, and go still further away from all the orthodox beliefs of the great mass of his canny countrymen.

Hugh MacDiarmid, 31 March 1934

The New English Weekly
1933–1934

Science and Culture

Although Wordsworth held that there was no scientific process or conception which cannot become part and parcel of the language of poetry as soon as it is thoroughly domesticated in the poet's consciousness – thus breaking with the idea that poetry is confined to any particular subject-matter instead of taking in the whole field of reality – Denis Saurat has demonstrated conclusively the surprising degree to which poets have followed each other like so many sheep, and continued, in all ages and countries, to draw an extraordinarily large percentage of their ideas from certain occult books. Or rather from these originally but for the most part through each other without independent reference to the sources. The bias that has been given to all poetry as a consequence is incredible. It would go far to justify Peacock's conclusion that:

> a poet in our times is a semi-barbarian in a civilised community. He lives in the days that are past. In whatever degree poetry is cultivated, it must necessarily be to the neglect of some branch of useful study; and it is a lamentable thing to see minds, capable of better things, running to seed in the specious indolence of these empty, aimless mockeries of intellectual exertion. Poetry was the mental rattle that awakened the attention of intellect in the infancy of civil society: but for maturity of mind to make a serious business of the playthings of its childhood is as absurd as for a grown man to rub his gums with coral, and cry to be charmed asleep by the jingle of silver bells.

But although Professor Saurat shows that the great poets have a certain common mental heritage, and how their thought is closely related to primitive conceptions which are embodied in mythology and which have lived on, side by side with Christianity in the form of occult doctrines such as those of the Cabala and the Theosophists – and does not subject to any qualitative comparison the ideas they have thus for the most part derived at second-hand or tenth-hand from these sources with those other equally available but unexploited elements to which an intellectual integrity necessitating independent personal recourse to their actual sources might have attracted their poetic genius with incalculable consequences to human mentality – he does not fall into Peacock's error. On the contrary, he quotes Renan's saying: 'Never has man when in possession of a clear idea converted it into a myth', and continues:

> The danger of taking myth seriously is obvious to all; and yet the need for it is a constant historical fact. Philosophical poetry reconciles the existence and development of myth with the knowledge that it is only myth and not reality. For in the realm of art doubt need not have a sterilising or withering effect. Poetry is carried into a region which is far beyond truth and error, which is sounder and more necessary than being beyond good and evil. In order that myths may be beneficial, they must be accompanied by two contrary convictions: one must know that they are necessary, and one must know that they are false... We find in our poets the expression, become legitimate because it has abandoned its dogmatic pretensions, of the metaphysical needs of man.

This is only another way of repeating what Matthew Arnold said:

> The future of poetry is immense, because in poetry, where it is worthy of its high destinies, our race, as time goes on, will find an ever surer and surer stay. There is not a creed which is not shaken, not an accredited dogma which is not shown to be questionable, not a received tradition which does not threaten to dissolve. Our religion has materialised itself in the fact, in the supposed fact; it has attached its emotion to the fact, and now the fact is failing it. But for poetry the idea is everything.

As a Douglasite who has had years of experience of the difficulty of getting even highly intelligent people to understand Major Douglas's proposals – the stupendous 'psychological resistance' – and as a practising poet concerned with the position of poetry in the world today, I have been constrained to take all the cognate phenomena I can find into account, and not the least of these is the recently-so-tremendously-changed atmosphere of science. Certain types of reader look forward to a world-language – really, the short-circuiting of human consciousness – and deprecate the increasing exploitation in all literatures of dialect and archaic forms, specialised vocabularies of all kinds, and the various other sorts of linguistic experimentation so prominent today and so obviously at variance with the notion of a common world-culture. But they cannot deny the ubiquitousness – and hence their coincidence with deep-seated requirements of the human consciousness – of these disintegratory literary forces; and their attitude in relation to them equates with the Victorian 'scientific materialist' attitude as compared with the present intensifyingly-complicated 'scientific mysticism'. There is an essential parallelism between the untranslatability of so much 'advanced' literary work in all languages and the growing incomprehensibility except to a specialist here and there of the new conceptions in physics, astronomy, and other sciences. Science and poetry are going hand to hand to an unprecedented degree; does this not mean that in some inexplicable way the age-long ascription of poetry to the particular 'common mental heritage' Professor Saurat describes has been overcome? Dr Whitehead in *Science and the Modern World* found himself compelled to stress 'the other side of the evolutionary machinery, the neglected side, expressed by the word *creativeness*', and to emphasise, as against narrow specialisms, the importance of art, the source of a corrective sense of totality and the means of arranging the environment 'so as to provide for the soul, vivid but transient values'. It is equally significant that perhaps the greatest contemporary poet – Paul Valéry – writing 'La Jeune Parque', which he describes as a *cours de physiologie*, and 'L'Aurore', a picture of the psycho-physical processes of sleep and awakening, found it necessary after his first few poems to silence his muse for twenty years – owing to 'a profound modification; perhaps due to a kind of substitution in the predominant hereditary functions' – and devote himself to mathematics before returning to versification.

The retardation of the introduction into industry of labour-saving and production-increasing processes of all kinds is, of course, due to the arbitrary and artificial financial system in which we are potbound, and another aspect of the same manner is the purely commercial character of most scientific journals. These are of little or no use to real experts in the subjects or to the non-specialist public; they almost al lack any general basis or background, any wide correlative character, and any forward look, and are almost wholly concerned with the exact description and marketing of particular machines or processes which are frequently obsolescent from a real scientific standpoint by the time they are thus written up. This accounts for the way in which even in so-called scientific journals in various countries 'triumphs of progress' can be hailed when all that is happening is the unconscionably belated introduction in some particular area of a device which has been in use elsewhere for donkey's years. At best these journals are only incipient textbooks, and abreast merely of what is already, or is about to come, on the market.

The relation between scientific retardation and the money monopoly, on the one hand, and the parallelism I have hinted at in between 'advanced' literary experimentation and the 'incomprehensibility' of recent scientific conceptions, suggests that it is high time in periodicals like the *New English Weekly* to cease being confined to Politics, Economics, and the Arts, and treat Science on the plane upon which these are regularly discussed. No discussion of the former or of the potentialities of mankind, which are being so stupendously restricted by the existing financial system, should any longer fail to reckon with the implications of that 'biological blindness' – that habit of human limitation – which still makes most people not only fail to absorb difficult scientific ideas, but to continue to think and feel in terms, for example, of such old and ridiculous ideas as 'light as air' or 'solid as a rock', when any rock is porous as the solar system and the greater heaviness of air keeps the earth together. Our sensations (and terminology of thought) ought to be brought abreast of our scientific knowledge and the promotion of science to treatment on the same intellectual level as politics or the arts in journals like this would to some extent supply that deficiency in scientific organs which resembles the difference between a 'merely utilitarian' and a 'humanist' treatment of their subjects, and help to reduce the extent to which, since modern scientific ideas are so different in nature from the ideas of everyday thought, 'the popular writings of physicists' (as Mr G.P. Wells recently said) 'so often give one the feeling that the real essence of the matter is not set down, but has been lost, and necessarily lost, in the popularising.'

Hugh MacDiarmid, 27 April 1933

Problems of Poetry Today

I

'There has always been a great deal of verse describing sights and sounds of "nature"', says R.L. Mégroz, 'but even Wordsworth gave us in his verse only a small portion of the genuine thing.' I not only agree with this but with pronouncements by Matthew Arnold and Charles Doughty respectively, – the former's declaration that Wordsworth, Shelley, Keats, and the rest of them, were likely to prove to have produced work of only very temporary value for the simple reason that 'they did not know enough'; and Doughty's repudiation of practically all English verse after Milton and Spenser. Almost all our living poets seem to me to know even less than any previous generation. So far as 'nature poetry' is concerned, I am in agreement with Edmund Blunden where he writes:

> I cannot for instance deceive myself that the surface of a work like Pennant's *History of Quadrupeds* (1871) is not dry and corrugated. But beneath it there is a regard for Nature's family which Pennant might claim to be much more genuine a communion with the spirit of the universe than the more ambitious reveries of those who saw men as trees walking. There is none of the mystic, or acting-mystic, in his description of animals' bodies and ways of life, but there is a most satisfying sense that the better they are known the better it must be for everybody.

A like comparison holds good between all other kinds of poetry and the scientific and other 'literature' of their subject-matter.

In the language used, and in the subject-matter alike, an appalling mumpsimus prevails, and I think the first requirement is a rigorous sumpsimus. 'In electing to write classically correct poems about metaphysical experiences', says Theodora Bosanquet,

> Valéry gives himself two major problems to solve, the problem of a laborious form and the problem of a limited vocabulary. There is a strange hybrid vocabulary used by psychologists, but most of the words it contains would have much the same effect on the texture of a poem as the addition

of a serviceable patch of mackintosh on the texture of a butterfly's wings. Valéry, poet by birth and scientist by education, knows perfectly well that most of these words are unusable. He allows himself a few of the less barbarous, and he persistently uses certain words, like 'pur', as a chemist would use them, but he takes care to keep his poems free of any really indigestible lumps of scientific vocabulary.

This, of course, is just a variant of the old insistence on a 'poetic diction' and a parallel to the old and persistent notion that certain sorts of subject-matter are inappropriate to poetry or less appropriate than other sorts. Scientific terms are coined because there are no available words to give exact expression to the significations in question; it is impossible to think about most of the latter except in the specialised terminology; 'thought begins where the pictureable ends.' Why, then, try to discuss such matters with an incompetent audience; why (verbally) 'popularise' such conceptions when that involves an inevitable loss of exactitude and the use of all manner of cumbrous circumlocutions and obliquities of technique; why – in short – attempt to express in a given language matters which are essentially, by definition, outwith its range? It is another matter, of course – and part of the poet's duty – if without falsification, loss of economy and precision of utterance, and other sacrifices, it is found (as often will be the case) that a less 'difficult' terminology will be equally (which is to say, more) effective. But the use of the phrase 'hybrid vocabulary' begs the question. All vocabularies are hopelessly hybrid; only that of the man-in-the-street is so in a different direction than that of any scientific specialist. It is time that poets abandoned the anti-intellectualist pretence that the jargon of average mentality is preferable to the latter; or that some special virtue attaches to restricting our linguistic medium to a miserable fraction of our expressive resources. (I will carry this contention further later on, with reference to the necessity – or, at least, the validity – of a multi-linguistic medium.)

This impossibility of expressing what they wanted to express in familiar words, joined to a determination like Valéry's to restrict their employment of 'barbarous terms' to a minimum, has demonstrably crippled all recent English poets, except those who had already completely crippled themselves by restricting their choice of subject-matter to what could be handled in the conventional medium. I do not propose to multiply instances; in the few of his poems Patmore uses unusual words ('shaw', 'photosphere', 'prepense-occulted', 'draff'), but elsewhere 'though no word is strange the content cannot be revealed without some knowledge of Patmore's whole philosophy'; Meredith's poetry

> grew intricate in his endeavour to express these new elements of thought – he develops a vocabulary, individual, unexplained, and often uncouth (*to whom?*) – beyond all these complexities lie his specialised philosophical vocabulary and his use of allegory – 'Heart', 'Brain', 'Blood', 'Common-

> Sense', 'Comedy', all represent newly-devised concepts, and their full meaning is only revealed when they are studied in relationship to his whole thought;

in Hardy apart from architectural terms, such as adze, cusp, ogee, one finds other groups of hard, unusual words, such as lewth, leazes, dumble-doves, spuds, cit, wanring, and many others, and, beyond that,

> his vocabulary is, in one instance, impelled by the requirements of an experience that is new to poetry – he sees man frequently as a determinist sees him, the helpless plaything of forces outside himself – to express this view of the world poetically, Hardy is forced to use words such as 'automaton', 'foresightlessness', 'mechanize', 'fantocine', 'artistries in circumstance', 'junctive law'.

But why the general attempt to express new information and conceptions, through the bottle-neck of common speech? Those who break away are condemned for their 'wanton word play', their incomprehensible terminology, in the name of the average 'common-sense' reader, but when was the latter vitally interested in poetry, and what preoccupations of his are more desirable or justifiable than any poet's adventures among the possibilities of expression? It is time to have the full courage of our intellectual interests, and to deplore that slovenliness and laziness and lack of concern which condemns all but a moiety of our language to the limbo of incomprehensibility for all but a moiety of our people. A concerted effort to extend the general vocabulary and make it more adequate to the enormous range and multitudinous intensive specialisations of contemporary knowledge is long overdue; and the problem of poetry and power which should be the prime concern of every poet (and the stature of a poet cannot be better tested than just by his concern with this) to a very large extent centres round this question of whether poetry is to be confined to obsolescent material and relatively unimportant side-issues – thus playing into the hands of those who regard it as infantilist or as a mere 'polite accomplishment', or 'luxury art' – or join issue at every point with modern intellection. It is impossible to believe that the vast majority of contemporary poets believe that poetry is vitally important, let alone the rarest and most important faculty of the human mind, or are prepared, for example, to counter the relatively enormous publicity given to some murder or divorce or stupid political 'stunt' as against the lack of 'news value' considered to attach to any good new poem. They acquiesce in the socio-economic-politico-journalistic debauching of educational interests – the organised subversion and stultification of even those beginnings of popular education on which so much public money is spent; but poetry ought to be the mainstay of these educational interests. And it is precisely here that I reinforce the line of argument I was pursuing above – it is the parasitical 'interpreting class', those who 'talk down to them' and insist that the level of utterance should be that of popular understanding, and jeer at what is not expressed in the jargon of the man-in-the-street, who are the enemies of the people, because what their attitude amounts to is 'keeping the people in their place', stereotyping their stupidity. The interests of the masses and the real highbrow, the creative artist, are identical, for the function of the latter is the extension of human consciousness. The interests of poetry are diametrically opposed to whatever may be making for any robotisation or standardisation of humanity or any short-circuiting of the human consciousness. 'Who has any respect for what he understands?' It is precisely pandering to the public that has brought poetry into its present general disesteem and impotence. 'But', I am asked, 'what of the practical side? Poetry must be published, mustn't it, and what publishers are going to put out books there is no public ready to appreciate? And what of the question of poetry as "communication"?' The answer is that there is no evidence to show – plenty of evidence to the contrary, indeed – that poetry catering for a public in this way pays any better than poetry that makes no effort to do anything of the sort; and that so far as 'communication' is concerned this is by no means synonymous with general, or, indeed, any, intelligibility. Does a statue of Queen Victoria 'communicate' better than the Sphinx?

21 September 1933

II

Spengler's contention that 'one must do the necessary or nothing' applies to poetry as to every other human activity; the trouble is that, from a variety of causes, an immense amount of poetry masquerades as, and is taken for, something, when it is really nothing; and there is little or no attempt on the part of poets, critics, or others, to define, and concentrate upon, what is 'necessary' in poetry today, with the consequence that the great bulk of verse is an entirely superfluous and indefensible imitation on an endless succession of lower levels of what has been expressed 'once and for all' before.

The incredible extent to which the issues are confused is sometimes devastatingly betrayed by critics of some contemporary sireability. I by no means regard Mr R.L. Mégroz as nearly the worst of the better-known writers on poetry in Great Britain today; indeed, I regard him as superior to Sir John Squire, Mr Desmond McCarthy, and others of similar kidney; but the slightest knowledge of the achievements of human expression – the most casual glance back over the course of great poetry throughout the ages – is sufficient to show the appalling character of the following paragraph in this year of grace 1933: –

'Ultimately,' says Mr Mégroz,

> we may come to the conviction that no poet in the first quarter of this century, not even his great fellow-countryman, W.B. Yeats, has more fre-

quently justified the admiring astonishment implied in the verdict 'Miracle!' than Mr James Stephens. Not only does reflection in his verse go tip-toe for a flight, and mystical wisdom flee into Blake-like enigma, but if he chooses to make a bird-song ('I cling and swing, on a branch'), most of our modern native poetry beside it is tame as a gentle prose essay; and there is no telling when a phrase will not transport the imagination. He has not made a poetic imitation of sea-billows in 'The Main Deep', with a handful of such phrases ending with

Chill-rushing,
Hush-hushing,
... Hush-hushing...?

But, poetry-reviewing in Great Britain today (and other countries are no better), abounds in equally – and far more – disgraceful utterances; and I will have far more hope for our poetic future when I see our responsible poets joining together to denounce such nonsense wherever it appears; refusing to allow their books to be reviewed in any quarter save competently by worthy critics; refusing to allow their work to be anthologised cheek by jowl with rubbish; and generally, by every available means, seeking to re-erect and insist upon and heighten our standards, dignity and responsibility of their art. It is one of the weaknesses of the situation that responsible poets do not league themselves together to such ends. Just as I do not believe in the 'freedom of the press', where that only means permitting a group of newspaper owners to undo public education and debauch the popular taste, and feel certain that this must yet be brought under effective control, so I do not believe that those seriously concerned with poetry should not make it their business to protest against the debasement and chaos of poetical standards, whether this takes the form of idiotic reviewing, the log-rolling of unscrupulous rhymesters and their publisher-accomplices, or the flooding of the schools with contemporary verse of no real value. An authoritarian position must be (and will be, since the preservation, let alone the furtherance, of civilisation depends upon it) re-established, and it is a matter for shame that what poets of even the slightest value we have should not be indefatigable in this direction.

A very extensive personal acquaintance with contemporary poets of some reputation in this and other countries, an omnivorous reading of contemporary poetry and writing about poetry, convinces me that the root of the trouble is the unworthy and incompetent attitude of almost all our poets to their art. Significant in this connection is the lack of technical discussion; and this is more than borne out by the alleged poems. Most of the poets seem to have had, or to have given themselves, no thorough training in their art – nothing like so thorough a training as doctors have in their sphere, for example. Any Tom, Dick or Harry rushes into print, 'pouring out his soul' with the most contemptible minimum of technical equipment. Some petty 'discovery' in the art of expression which was a commonplace to practising poets centuries ago, serves to establish a great reputation today. In the old Gaelic days, poets had to go through a long and rigorous apprenticeship in the Bardic Colleges, and qualify by arduous stages for the right to use certain metres and tackle certain types of subject-matter. It would be a god-send for poetry if a like course were compulsory today.

One of the most regrettable things is the lack of a similar internationalising of poetic achievement to that of scientific achievement. It is lamentable how scanty and haphazard is the average poet's knowledge of – or interest in – the general course of poetry. Most of them are limited to a knowledge of the evolution of the poetry in their own language. It is surprising to draw up a list of the great poems of all European literatures and to find how few of them – and then in, for the most part, what inadequate translations – are available in any particular language. This, it seems to me, should be a matter for the corps of responsible poets in every country; to see that, so far as their own language was concerned, the maximum number of the great poems of Europe in as good translations as possible, was made available, and the government of each European country might well make a grant and enable such a corps of poets to keep a continuous audit to this end. Nine-tenths at least of the money spent in publishing poetry annually would be better devoted to this purpose. Incidentally such a systematic study of the possibilities of translation in this, its most difficult, and most important, department, would serve the invaluable purpose of casting light on the deepest problems of the particular genius, and insurmountable limitations of each language. I said in my first article that I would refer later to the question of a multi-linguistic medium. This naturally arises at this point. The expressive powers of each language have these biases and lacunæ; but there can be no valid reason why each language should not take over from other languages precisely those elements in the latter in which it is deficient. This is the opposite of that 'carrying coals to Newcastle', which justifies the depreciation of using foreign terms to express what can just as well be expressed in native terms. Readers and writers of serious modern consequence usually know a number of languages, and are more or less thoroughly aware of untranslatable terms, shades of meaning peculiar to certain national consciousnesses which cannot be naturalised in certain others, and so forth, in every language they know, and appreciate the vital and increasing importance of these in welt-literatur. There is no reason why literature should submit itself to the Procrustean bed of any linguistic laziness; and as to the language pursuits, their attitude is only another variant of the insidious insistence in divers forms on some sort of 'poetic diction', while in actual practice languages do make all sorts of borrowings from other languages (and there is no reason why these should be for less worthy reasons or less systematically brought about), and the very people who object to it in poetry, themselves, in conversation, journalism, and so on, use all sorts of alien tags.

It is impossible to go into the matter exhaustively in the space available to me here; but the type of thing which such a 'continuous audit' of European poetry and a wider diffusion of a really thorough knowledge of the course of world-poetry would surely end, may be illustrated by the following passage, which I read somewhere recently:

> Who, when all is admitted, has put more of the rose into poetry than Francis Thompson with a few lines of the splendid 'Ode to the Setting Sun':
>
> Who made the splendid rose
> Saturate with purple glows
> Cupped to the marge with beauty; a perfume-press
> Whence the wind vintages
> Gushes of warmest fragrance richer far
> Than all the flavorous ooze of Cyprus's vats?

A critic of integrity wishing to establish this point should have given instances; it is highly unlikely that the writer in question making his idle comment, had in mind, and made any careful comparison between, the best passages in which the poets of the world have dealt with the rose; but if he had known – as he ought to have done – the work of Rainer Maria Rilke, he could never have made such an absurd statement.

Another audit that should be made is that of the subject-matter or content of poetry. Denis Saurat, in his *Literature and the Occult*, furnishes a surprising table showing the extent to which major poets – generally without any recourse to the originals, but simply following each other like so many sheep – have derived their main conceptions from the Kabbala and other obscure sources. Apart from the lack of recourse to the originals, it is impossible to believe that thorough intellectual workmanship would have so largely confined them to this particular strain, which is unjustifiable, and vitiates their work, from the standpoint of any serious thought on the evolution, functions, and problems of human consciousness, and the relevance and responsibility of poetry in particular. But what would a similar analysis of the intellectual content of contemporary poetry reveal? It would dispose of the claims of 99 per cent of living poets of 'established reputation' to any further consideration at all; for in that proportion at least it would reveal only shameful fatuity – an imbecile divorcement from serious purpose of any kind. It is inconceivable that with a moment's measuring of them in the light of the achievements of the past, most poets could publish their worthless effusions; or, perhaps, the crux of the problem is just that in very many cases it is not now inconceivable at all. But, at all events, in the public interest that measuring should be obligatory, public, and unsparing.

Hugh MacDiarmid, 28 September 1933

'AE' and Poetry

We see a spirit…
… wing hence the way he makes more clear.
… such living shows
What wide illumination brightness sheds
From one big heart – to conquer man's old foes;
The coward, and the tyrant, and the force
Of all those weedy monsters raising heads
When Song is murk from springs of turbid source.

A.E.'s book, *Song and Its Fountains* (Macmillan), in which he essays to 'track song back to its secret foundation in the psyche', shows a perfect concordance with the findings of science, and I have reason to believe anticipates in many valuable details stages that have not yet been reached in that analysis of the so-called 'unconscious self', and tracing and exposing of its whole physical organisation, which has been developing since the beginning of this century on the basis of the brilliant discoveries of Sir Henry Head, the late Dr Rivers, Sir John Parsons, and others. The reason for that is precisely that which led Browning to place his real trust upon monologue rather than dialogue, since, as William Sharp put it:

> To one who works from within outward – in contradistinction to the Shakespearian method of striving to win from outward forms 'the passion and the life whose fountains are within' – the propriety of this dramatic means can scarce be gainsaid; the swift, complicated, mental machinery can thus be exhibited infinitely more coherently and comprehensibly than by the most electric succinct dialogue.

In other words, A.E. knows what he is talking about; most scientific writers on such subjects do not, having had no personal experience of the processes or phenomena in question. This is really what is wrong with *The Road to Xanadu*, of which A.E. merely says: 'the logic of that analysis would almost lead to the assumption that when the palette is spread with colour, it accounts for the masterpiece.' A.E. confines himself almost wholly to his own work – to aspects of the evolution of some of his own poems. I could wish he had written a much bigger book in which he could have detailed the bearing on his work of such matters as physical location, state of health, courses of reading and personal contacts that influenced the production of poems, and given various rough drafts – trial shots – of some of his poems. And I could have wished that he had used much of the abundant material that is available to compare notes in these matters between himself and other poets – a work that calls to be done but cannot be usefully tackled save by a poet of considerable rank. Such amplifications, however, would only have confirmed the accuracy of the observations he does make – as, indeed, it is in all essentials corroborated by the testimony of many other poets, and only becomes questionable when he forgets that it is song, and, in particular, his own song, that he is tracing to its source, and not processes which issue in various kinds of mystical and other expression, the correspondence of which with his own work is often merely verbal, as, in fact, his use of phraseology already adscripted to mystical and religious and other dubious matters, obscures his theme at least as often as it expresses it.

It is true of Browning that 'his position in regard to the thought of the age is paradoxical, if not inconsistent. He is in advance of it in every respect but one, the most important of all, the matter of fundamental principles; in these he is behind it. His processes of thought are often scientific in their precision of analysis; the sudden conclusion which he imposes upon them is transcendental and inept.' There is no such paradox or inconsistency in A.E.; it is not his conclusions, but only the terms he uses, that are frequently transcendental and inept. I regret, of course, that his mind, while open to all the acquisitions of the understanding, 'retains some degree of sovereign interdiction, and closes its vast horizon precisely where its light ceases' – that the odours of hypotheses are so often to be detected amid the sweet savour of his indestructible assurance – that he lacks that profound inquietude which, as Saint-Beuve says, 'attests a moral nature of a high rank, and a mental nature stamped with the seal of the archangel' – and that he too generally forgets that 'with God there is no lust of Godhood', and 'there can be nothing good, as we know it, nor anything evil, as we know it, in the eye of the Omnipresent and the Omniscient.' But that is only to say that he is A.E., and tells the truth about A.E. here in a characteristically modest and kindly little book. I personally find it a great deal easier to follow such discussions couched in the jargon of psycho-analysis than in that of the Salvation Army, but in this case, to use an unhappy phrase, I am able to 'make the necessary allowances', knowing A.E. personally, and having an intimate knowledge of his work.

Apropos Professor A.E. Housman's recent 'revelations' (which got a publicity scandalously greater than A.E.'s), of the genesis of his poems, and the effects of poetry upon him, the *Times Literary Supplement* observed that such personally-conducted tours of the poet's workshop were unfortunately seldom to be had. This is not the case; we are in possession of extraordinarily-detailed information as to the processes of many great poets and the inception and stage-by-stage development of many great poems. (Judges depend to a great extent upon their sense of the credibility of different witnesses – a matter, of course, susceptible, if time allowed, of corroboration from other sources and even of scientific ascertainment. But I mention my personal knowledge of A.E. and high regard for his work, because I not only think Professor Housman a poet of little or no consequence, but a witness in this matter who is not borne out by the bulk of far more competent and important evidence. For in Professor Housman's case – and in Shelley's, and in A.E.'s, – the 'not' no longer holds good in Browning's remark on the second of these, apropos charges against his moral nature, that 'we are not sufficiently supplied with instances of genius of his order to be able to pronounce certainly how many of its constituent parts have been tasked and strained to the production of a given lie, and how high and pure a mood of the creative mind may be dramatically simulated as the poet's habitual and exclusive one.') What could be more 'unscientific' – more the antithesis of A.E.'s book in this all-vital respect – than for a writer addressing himself to the task of formulating a psychology fitted to explain, in so far as explanation is yet practicable, the evolution and present status of the most refined spiritual faculties of humanity, to act as if the *Times Literary Supplement*'s egregious observation were true and make no levy for illustrative material upon the great poets, and other great writers, but to prefer to draw upon his own petty, personal experiences or to suggest hypothetical cases which only show his deplorable poverty of invention? I am referring here to the irritating faults of a very great and perhaps epoch-making book – G.B. Dibblee's *Instinct and Intuition*. With all its abundant knowledge and extreme dialectical ability, it illustrates to a lamentable extent how the growth of civilisation can yet leave the spiritual stature of man not increased by one iota, and Mr Dibblee's inept illustrations, jejune personal recollections, and lack of recourse to the very people who embody these 'most refined spiritual faculties', remind me of Edward Berdoe's comment: 'Caliban is a savage with the introspective powers of a Hamlet, and the theology of an evangelical churchman.' I am afraid that A.E. too, occasionally gives us merely what Goethe calls *schwankende Gestalten*, and that he has a feeling, at conflict with his very purpose in this book, that this passion for 'dissecting a rainbow' is harmful to the individual as well as humiliating to the high office of Poetry itself, and not infrequently ludicrous, and so falls back upon something akin to Joubert's declaration that 'it is not difficult to believe in God if one does not worry oneself to define Him.' But, regretting its limitations, what it actually does divulge is scientific, as much of Mr Dibblee's material is not.

> Bid shine what would, dismiss into the shade
> What should not be – and there triumphs the paramount
> Surprise o' the master.

The prophetic character of much poetry is of course well-known and amply attested. I do not know if anyone has previously noted the most precise prophecy of the Great War – and a wonderful picture of it – in Francis Thompson; surely one of the most extraordinary instances of this phenomenon. But – since I have a very great admiration for Mr Dibblee's work, despite the defects I have noted – let me redeem my strictures by directing him in reference to his important passages on the sense of smell, its direct passage alone of all sensory messages to the cortex, and his demonstration that instead of being decreasingly important and obsolescent in civilised man, it is actually becoming more important, to the remarkable corroboration of this to be found in modern literature, and poetry in particular, though – like the general belief in the decreased significance of the function of smell – this has commonly been misunderstood and dismissed as one of the unhealthy prepossessions of literary decadence. That is only one illustration. I could multiply them. Paul Valéry, for example, made a present of his speculations in *L'Idée fixe* to the medical profession. What has the medical profession made of this important gift from a man of an intellectual stature to which few of its own members ever aspire? Does it, like Mr Dibblee, prefer to rely upon the evidence of inferior minds and coarser sensibilities? In regard to many far obscurer mental phenomena of which Mr Dibblee again and again says, 'we are not yet in a position to say' or 'we do not know enough', I should be happy, if he cared to correspond with me, to give him references to relevant European literature – in many cases supplemented by my own experience, which carries with it a very rare faculty of entertaining along with my ideas complete picturisations or other detailed awarenesses of the physical processes involved.

I have another reason for mentioning Dibblee's book in this notice of A.E.'s. They are related in a much more important matter. 'It is by no means uncommon', said a writer on Dibblee,

> to find in the classic philosophies a difference not only of degree but apparently of kind also, between the germinal idea and the ultimate consummation which never fails to impress us afresh with a sense of its magnitude. It seems at first sight to savour of the inconsequent that the humble Socratic endeavour to convince mankind of invincible ignorance should culminate in the uncompromising Platonic intellectualism, and to be scarcely less astonishing than Spinoza's modest quest for the good life for man should find final expression in the starkest affirmations of the metaphysical categories with which the armoury of thought is equipped. Mr Dibblee's work presents us with an example of the discrepancy referred to. It leads up to the single, supreme problem of the nature and limits of fundamental dualism, and it seems, at any rate on a perfunctory view, to be a far cry from the idea with which he starts – that of the economic, or, at least, the material, definition of 'value' – to his final task.

It is so only on a very perfunctory view indeed. The far cry is by no means far at all to anyone who understands the implications of Douglasism, which has indeed 'knocked the bottom out of economics', and will render it impossible for people who fail to embody effectively in themselves the acropetal strivings which are the specific feature and function of mankind to survive even physically, let along indulge in that orgy fools fear will be most people's life when they no longer need to work. Just as Dibblee confesses that 'an inquiry into the nature of instinct, and inferentially into an analogous mental phenomenon entangled with it, intuition, was urged on me from my having come to a full stop in my researches into fundamental questions in the basis of another subject, economics', so it is entirely natural that A.E.'s mysticism should issue a concern for agricultural organisation, and such fine political books, consubstantial with his poetry, as *The National Being* and *The Interpreters*. If a congress of representative poets – of, in other words, the supreme realists – were convened to offer guidance on the crucial practical problems of the nations today (the true test of poets), Ireland would be very effectively represented by A.E. and Yeats. Valéry's political prescience was manifested in his 'La Conquête Allemande', Russia, Germany, Spain and Czecho-Slovakia, could all be represented by practical seers; but England has none, nor has America, nor, since Ibsen and Bjornson, have the Scandinavian countries, nor has Italy, nor has Holland, nor Greece, nor Austria.

A.E. has a great deal to say about dreams, whence he got many of his poems, as Mozart got the *Zauberflöte*, Professor Kekule his discovery of the 'dance of the atoms', and Srinivasa Ramanudjan his mathematical solutions, and this fully bears out the conclusions of modern science. 'The organisation of emotion about an object is the normal mode of working of the waking mind. The organisation of objects about an emotion, is, on the other hand, a normal mode of working of the dreaming mind.' But all that Dibblee says of the co-existence of thalamic with cortical consciousness, and of the fact that, contrary to general belief, the former is not only holding its own but gaining ground, even physiologically, not only bears out all that A.E. says, but is of the utmost value in considering the future and relative status of poetry. We cannot be simultaneously 'outgrowing' Poetry and maintaining, and, in fact, extending, our 'thalamic consciousness'.

Hugh MacDiarmid, 5 October 1933

Poets, Consider!

Why shouldn't there be (when every other section is congressing – unless that is just why not!) such a congress of representative poets as I suggested in my recent article on 'Æ and Poetry'? (And, by the way, when I said that neither England nor America had anyone to represent them at such a gathering, I was thinking in terms of established political states – I regard T.S. Eliot and Ezra Pound as supra-national, belonging neither to England nor America. But such a congress without them would be absurd.) The idea behind my suggestion does not originate with me; it has been promulgated in one form or another by Carlyle, Allen Upward, and many others; the latest perhaps is Karl Jaspers who, in his 'Geistige Situation der Gegenwart', if there seems to be no hope in present circumstances that the nobility of human existence shall persist in the form of a ruling minority, at least ventures to whisper something of a dispersed *élite* gathered, as it were, in the mystical body of an invisible Church. Of those who would constitute such a congress, whatever their minor differences of political opinion might be, one thing is certain – they would all substantially share the view expressed by T.S. Eliot:

> About certain serious facts no one can dissent. The present system does not work properly, and more and more people are inclined to believe both that it never did and that it never will; and it is obviously neither scientific nor religious. It is imperfectly adapted to every purpose except that of making money; and even for money-making it does not work very well, for its rewards are neither conducive to social justice nor even proportioned to intellectual ability. It is well adapted to speculation and usury, which are the lowest forms of mental activity; and it rewards well those who can cozen and corrupt the crowd.

This general position was illuminated from another angle by J.S. Collis in his article in these columns on Havelock Ellis, when he said:

> He is the greatest living English writer... By all the laws of life that we know of intellectually and by intuitive grasp, it is impossible that in occupying that position his stature could be generally recognised; for to be greater than the great and lauded ones calls for the possession of qualities that cannot even be seen by the multitude.

Translated down to the current British political system, this prevalent falsity – this usurpation of a place to which they are not entitled by inferior spirits – results in the state of affairs described by the editor of *New Britain*:

> The great mass of the people of this country has probably no respect for the present Government, and there are few intelligent people, outside those enjoying the fruits of office, who find any real satisfaction in contemplating what the Government is or has done.

Again, it is a state of affairs which issues inevitably in such a declaration as that of J.M. Keynes:

> I see us set free, therefore, to return to some of the most sure and certain principles of religion and traditional virtue – that avarice is a vice and the exaction of usury and misdemeanour, and the love of money is detestable; that those walk most truly the paths of virtue and sane wisdom who take least thought of the morrow. We shall once more value ends above means, and prefer the good to the useful. We shall honour those who can teach us how to pluck the hour and the day virtuously and well, the delightful people who are capable of taking direct enjoyment in things, the lilies of the field, who toil not, neither do they spin. But beware! The time for all this is not yet. For at least another hundred years we must pretend to ourselves and to everyone that fair is foul and foul is fair; for foul is useful and fair is not. Avarice and usury and precaution must be our gods for a little longer

still. For only they can lead us out of the tunnel of economic necessity into daylight.

Mr A.J. Penty made all the necessary comment on this:

> Surely there is something perverse about this. It puts the peculiar intellectual vice of our age in a nutshell – a capacity for self-deception without parallel in history, a capacity for persuading ourselves that black is white when it happens to be successful. What hope can there be for a nation when its intellectuals to whom it looks for guidance so betray their trust? It explains why, today, we are as a nation facing the present crisis intellectually bankrupt. If intellectual activity has any validity it can only be because it upholds a standard of right thinking, that it seeks to keep alive the flame of truth in the hostile social and economic environment in which we have the misfortune to find ourselves.

My point here is that this is primarily and most powerfully the poets' task and that the failure of modern poetry to anticipate this crisis and to abate or traverse with rays of penetrating exposure this miasma of false standards is a damning criticism of its quality and of the integrity of its practitioners. Tolstoy's *What is Art?* was greeted with howls of derision and dismissed by our decadents as a Philistine tirade; but it should be 'read, marked, and inwardly digested' by every young person interested in literature today. No one who does not realise that it is infinitely more valuable, more packed with truth, than all the other books of literary criticism which have been produced since its appearance, and for long enough before that – or who (without knowing anything about it) does not, at least, arrive independently at most of its essential conclusions, will contribute anything of the slightest consequence to the literature of today or of the future. His chapters on the vices of 'luxury art' of all kinds – his realisation that 'our exclusive art, that of the upper classes of Christendom, has found its way into a blind alley' – should be re-read. Again and again he drove home conclusions which must be accepted and acted upon if we are to find the way out of our present *impasse*. Poetry, in particular, has gone deplorably astray along the lines he indicates, and its impotence has been the inevitable result. Yet the great instrument which can destroy the ubiquitous falsities of our times belongs to poetry and must be recovered and used by poetry. The future of poetry depends upon it. I refer to satire. And the subject is Money. The great traitor of poetry was Goethe. See *Faust*, Part II, Act I, where he goes fully into the matter:

> The hoards of wealth untold, that torpid sleep
> Within the Empire's borders buried deep,
> Lie profitless. The thought's most ample measure
> Is the most niggard bound of such a treasure.
> Not fancy's self, in her most daring flight,

Strain as she will, can soar to such a height;
Yet minds that worthy are to sound the soundless
A boundless trust accord unto the boundless.

Then he falls to the level of Ramsay MacDonald and his message to humanity becomes:

I hoped for heart and will to new endeavour,
Who knows ye though will lightly read ye ever,
Well do I see, though treasures on ye pour,
Ye still are, after, what ye were before.

It was one of the most appalling and deliberate betrayals in the history of human consciousness. It is still the attitude of most people. All the other modern poets echoed it, or dodged the great issue – dodged, in other words, poetry's main task. The challenge to 'minds that worthy are' remains; Douglasism has, however, long since taken the measure of the Goethe attitude. Burns with all his defects came nearest to it of all the poets until recent years; then we had men like John Davidson and D.H. Lawrence with his satirical cry: 'Make money or eat dirt', and hints and tentative efforts in others, but no sign of any one fit to bend his bow of Ulysses. Poetry cannot redeem itself until it successfully addresses itself to this task.

Curious, by the way, how little poetry – how very little good poetry – the Socialist Movement has produced in any country. (Not that one would look there – the very last place – for poetry inspired by a sound economic conscience! But surely for burning social indignation, for scathing political satire, for inspirations towards a better order!) The British Labour and Socialist Movement produced practically nothing that was not sheer doggerel and the pettiest emotionalism. What little with a vital spark in it there was, the British Labour and Socialist Movement has ignored as if deliberately. Francis Adams' *Songs of the Army of the Night*, for example – far and away the best of the lot. This is not mentioned at all in Eva Walraf's recent monograph, *Soziale Lyrik in England* (Leipzig: Tauchnitz) which has a very meagre gleaning – echoes of the 'Arbeiterproblem' from Crabbe onward to William Morris, John Davidson, Ford Madox Hueffer and a few others; Wilfred Gibson's new line with the theme of the 'Arbeiterseele'. Some of our younger poets – Spender, Auden, Day Lewis – are Communistic, I am told. We will see what we will see. I have seen nothing so far germane to my present concern. Ezra Pound's passages in defence of Douglasism (Cantos XIX, XXII) are another matter, a solitary exception.

The path was pointed out to English writers years ago in terms upon which I cannot improve by Gilbert Cannan; and I conclude this article with the following quotations from his splendid little book on *Satire* in the hope that they may be more effective today in inducing the long-overdue reorientation of our literary – and, above all, poetical, activities, than they have proved since he penned them nearly twenty years ago:

> Common-form religion in England now calls for no satire, unless the national god, Humbug, should suffer a sea-change and clothe himself in it once more. Turn the satiric vision upon English life, cut it open like a pigeon's crop, and you will find only two facts, money and sex, and those disguised. The ideas of all other facts have long since been thrown by the board, and these two, which are essential for the movement towards stagnation as may be. Set the ideas of them clear, and at once other ideas, and the recognition of other facts, become necessary. That is work for satire to do, and it will be done as soon as the lively fellow of genius is squeezed out of the ferment which like mud underlies the stagnation. Until it has been done it is very certain that nothing else will – neither in art, nor in politics, nor in social reform, for English fathers will go on lying to their sons about money and sex so that they must either spend their lives in a hectic floundering reaction or subscribe to the current cant about those two all-important facts, and so come to a disastrous atrophy of all their faculties… If the community be so far gone that its poetry is dithered with metaphysics, its tradition in the applied arts almost faded out of memory, its political institutions congealed into a mechanical routine, its drama sunk into cold fantasy, its satire diluted to a genial quipping of successful persons, its religion broken up to sectarianism, so that nothing can move men but money or sex, and those being unilluminated by poetry or art or statesmanship or drama or religion, then genius, which, of its nature, cannot despair, must take refuge and the offensive in laughter… A modern poet could thus apply the logic of his genius to the idea of money or the idea of sex, if it could find either idea pure enough. A great poet will one day arise to apply his sturdy logic to the two impure ideas of money and sex, and he will arrive at satire, and his work will prove the release of ideas for the genius which comes after him. In a way he will be lucky, if it be luck to find your job lying to your hand and easy of performance, and easy this will be, because of all things genius is less bound by money and sex than by any other, has no respect for them, can go for them without excess of hatred, and, as the ideas of them are easily identifiable, will be able to pick them out of men's brains, wipe them clean, and replace them without any serious shock to the human constitution. When that operation has been performed, then money and sex will begin to exercise their natural function of gravitation towards all other acts, will establish connections with them again, and once more human energy will begin worthily to express itself, and, incidentally, English life will become dramatic instead of theatrical and hypocritical.

Hugh MacDiarmid, 7 December 1933

Insular Internationalism

This *History of European Literature* will recommend itself perhaps to academic persons; it can be of little value to anyone with an interest in European literature as a living thing. Dr [Laurie] Magnus has frequently cause to show how the mistaken ideas of a previous generation were rectified by their successors in the period he surveys; he is very far from realising that he is almost always speaking from a point of view which has long been similarly rectified. Practical considerations of the probable public for such a book might have led him to consider that, as I have previously pointed out in these columns, the great majority of those who are interested in foreign literature are interested in contemporary foreign literature, and comparative studies in literature, in the light of the present and the future. None of these interests will be served to any extent by this volume; most of it consists of precisely that sort of pedantry antipathetic to those who entertain any of these interests. It is merely scholarly enough in the worst sense of these terms. That is not to say, alas, that practical considerations were not taken into account – this is precisely the sort of book which will be used educationally. It is most safely fossilised. It ends with this quotation from Saintsbury: 'It is not at all impossible that, in the immediate or at least the near future, there may be something of a return to that comparative study of European literature, that absence of sharp national divisions, which existed to some extent in the Middle Ages, and was interrupted, partly by ecclesiastical, partly by literary causes, at and after the Renaissance.' And Dr Magnus hopes that his book may prove some slight contribution to the cause of international union! This high-and-dry Toryism characterises it throughout. The fact of the matter is that there has been a steady increase of the give-and-take of European literatures and their interest in each other; thanks largely to the break-up of a common culture and the accentuation of those national differences which gave them all the more to compare. We go to foreign countries for their differences – otherwise we might as well stay at home. So with literature. And the quotation invests the whole performance with the most singular unreality at the present time when the tendency of the most significant work in all countries is in precisely the opposite direction to that desiderated by Saintsbury. It is well to remember that Saintsbury's 'Big Five' attitude enabled him to treat Russia in his monumental *History of Criticism* as a barbarous country which had never produced literature of any consequence and was never likely to – although Tolstoy and Dostoievsky had already written their great books and Russia was on the verge of becoming the greatest influence in world literature. A similar blindness afflicted the late Dr Magnus at every turn. Indeed, his treatment of Russia is almost identical with Saintsbury's. He calls the section of five-and-a-half pages he devotes to it 'The Russian Movement'; a page to Pushkin; half-a-page to Radiskchev (not because of his literary importance, but to illustrate the hazards of Russian authorship in Tsarist days); half-a-page to Lermontov; half-a-page each to Gogol and to Goncharov; the rest to odds and ends. What of Tolstoy and Dostoievsky? Only this: 'The brief winter sunshine of Russian fiction, reflected at first from foreign climes, is an afterglow of European literature. Gogol's *Dead Souls*, Goncharov's *Oblomov*, Turgenev's *Fathers and Sons*, Dostoievsky's *Crime and Punishment*, Tolstoy's *Anna Karenina* and *War and Peace*, are supremely great novels, the stature of which is not diminished by the shortness and lateness of that wintry sun.' Incredible, isn't it – even in England? A great poet like Blok is not mentioned; nor is Chekhov, nor any Russian dramatist; the 1917 Revolution is mentioned as if it had put an end to everything. But when it serves his peculiar purposes Dr Magnus can be so up-to-date as to quote us from James Truslow Adams's *The Epic of America* (London, 1932): '"America's dream and ideal," says the modern historian, "rest on the Jeffersonian faith in the common man."'

The whole book is, in fact, a curiosity of sterility, and might well be dismissed as such without further ado were it not that in our academic circles there are so many who resemble Dr Magnus to a greater or lesser degree, and who, in their obstinate blindness to the realities of modern literature and their inveterate political, religious, and other prejudices, are thwarting, by their virtual monopoly of educational influence, that very interchange and comparative study of European literature they profess to be serving – and which has undoubtedly all the urgent desirability they proclaim and prevent. So let us look at this particular example a little more closely. Much of the book could have been compiled quite easily out of the *Encyclopædia Britannica* and similar sources; all the older stuff is served up in stereotyped way. Indeed Dr Magnus tells us he does not know Russian – he does not tell us how far he had read other literatures in the original. But he certainly does not communicate one man's experience of European literature; and a recommendation of the value of a comparative study of European literature on any other basis is worthless. We can all have recourse to reference books: and the sort of information they contain is none the better for being reproduced, freaked with a few personal eccentricities, and extraordinary ineptitudes. Take this example:

> The Heritage from Greece and Rome. And now for one sentence written about them. Sir Richard Jebb, an indisputable authority, writing in the *Cambridge Modern History*, says of this age of Petrarch and Chaucer: 'The pagan view was now once more proclaimed that man was made, not only to toil and suffer, but to enjoy.' It is essential to our purpose thoroughly to understand Jebb's meaning. If we can get that clear it will help considerably to simplify and to co-ordinate the history of European literature.

It would have saved space if he had done that first and given it to us, *tout court*, without bothering about Jebb, whose authority is by no means indisputable, instead of giving three sentences to the matter which is a good deal more than he devotes to many very interesting and important European writers. But he is obsessed by Professors – not unorthodox ones like Professor Herbert Read, but D'Arcy Thompson, Walter Raleigh, W.J. Courthope, F.J. Snell, and so on, and 'a quotation may be permitted, limited though our space is, from Mr Stanley Baldwin's Introduction to Messrs Longman's "English Heritage" series' and 'all we will subscribe to Sir Frederick Pollock's estimate' (of the secret of Spinoza for Goethe), and, apropos an absurd quotation from him applied to Russian fiction, a footnote tells us that Stephen Phillips's 'oblivion is as undeserved as the excess of praise which he encountered in the eighteen-nineties.' Again we read:

> It is recorded that Tennyson succeeded Wordsworth as Poet Laureate in November 1850, and that he prefixed to the seventh edition of his *Poems* in March, 1851, the noble stanzas addressed 'To The Queen'. One of these stanzas, never reprinted, had been worded as follows: –
>
> She brought a vast design to pass
> When Europe and the scattered ends
> Of our fierce world did meet as friends
> And brethren in our hall of glass.
>
> Why did he excise and suppress it? Was the union of Europe too brittle and the brotherhood too fierce for friendship? Or did the poet's sense of a beauty not of this world refuse the bleak glare of halls of glass? We cannot say.

This is typical of the egregious rubbish, which along with a mass of dry-as-dust stuff of no consequence to the evolution of European literature or to any vital interest in it, is encountered at every turn in a book which makes no mention of (to confine ourselves for the moment to French literature) Verlaine, Baudelaire, Rimbaud, Taine, Ste Beuve, Mistral, or any living French writer. Mention of Mistral reminds me that the 'Big Five' attitude, here as in Saintsbury, has no time for minority cultures – Scotland, Ireland, Poland, the Balkan countries; pshaw! British literature itself is dealt with in a queer way too. 'Watts-Dunton, a very competent critic', we read – but Middleton Murry, T.S. Eliot, the brilliant translation work, and general *welt-literatur* services of Ezra Pound, and indeed, almost everything of any value in recent critical revaluations and biographical studies and in inter-literary work (the work in English literature, for example, of Cazamian, Legouis, Saurat, and other French scholars) are ignored. But space is found for quotations from General Smuts, and for Sir Alfred Ewing's declaration that: 'In the slow evolution of morals man is still unfit for the tremendous responsibility' entailed by the progress of discovery.

Behind all these defects is the intrusion of all manner of odds-and-ends of non-literary considerations, which in the absence of a proper treatment of literature in the light of philosophical and political and religious spheres from which they are drawn are simply irrational and futile. The conspicuous exception to this is the absence of any such waifs and strays from the domain of the Marxian conception of literature. This is only another illustration of the principal object of the book – the fact that it is not conceived with an eye either to the present or the future but simply to the past.

The book that is really actuated with the ostensible purpose of this book will go about the business in a very different spirit; the emphasis will fall very differently all the way through and for the most part on other men, or on other aspects of the unavoidable men (and very largely – to the extent of a quarter at least of a book on this scale) on men not mentioned in this book at all; it will be really European in its stance – and not dependent on illustrating the course of European literature to an altogether disproportionate degree through the comments of English professorial writers to the exclusion of great European critics (Brandes and Croce are alike unmentioned); it will concern itself with what have been and what still are the lets and hindrances to the freest and fullest international literary give-and-take; and, above all, it will recognise that the only way to discharge its declared task is by seizing on those interests in European literature which are vital at the time it is produced and endeavouring to increase them and extend them backwards into the past instead of following the method here adopted – of turning a blind eye to all that is of real international literary interest and professing to endeavour to stimulate such an interest by a general exhumation of dead bones and a rigid exclusion of all that is alive. If you are concerned with Strindberg or Wedekind or Carl Spitteler or Arne Yarborg or Gabriel D'Annunzio or Padraic O'Conaire, or Alasdair MacMhaighstir Alasdair, or Rainer Maria Rilke, or Adam Ohlenschläger, or Sören Kierkegaard, or Zygmunt Krasinski, or Verhaeren, or Hölderlin, or – but what is the use of going on? – you will find nothing about them here; but if, on the contrary, you are interested in Jacopo Sannazaro or Francesco Molza, 'whose blank verse translation of the *Æenid* passed into the translation of Tudor poetry' (Pound's Calvalcanti or his 'Seafarer' – oh, no!), or Jorge de Montemayor, a Portuguese who wrote in Spanish, you will find scraps of information about them here, and there are, of course, plenty of encyclopædias available where you can secure the full details if you desire. Perhaps what accounts for the whole thing is Dr Magnus's belief that 'enjoyment is the chief aim of literature', and, though a person with a different sense of what is enjoyable, like myself, may imagine that a book like this should concern itself with relative literary values, there is no gainsaying the applicability here as elsewhere of Dr Magnus's ingenious plea against any attempt to supersede the sonnet sequences of Sir Philip Sidney in favour of, say, George Meredith's *Modern Love*, that neither the one nor the other 'has been disproved to express certain modes of personal experience and an individual point of view'.

Hugh MacDiarmid, 1 March 1934

The Poetry of Ruth Pitter

In any discussion of contemporary English poetry a shrewd test, alike of critical ability and of mere integrity, depends on the answer to the question (apart from the extremely rare case where the name comes up without being asked for in this way): 'And what about Ruth Pitter?'

In my opinion much of the best literature produced in English this century lies buried in the files of the *New Age* (whose traditions the *New English Weekly* has brilliantly resumed); but it is subjected to a conspiracy of silence while vastly inferior work is almost everywhere proclaimed the cream of the period. Of this occluded group who have nowhere got a tithe of the recognition they deserve is Miss Ruth Pitter. She is represented in few anthologies; the annual selection of the 'best poems of the year' invariably passes her over; I have seen no good study of her work – in significant contrast to the reams of discussion given to very inferior poetesses like Edith Sitwell, Dorothy Wellesley, Vita Sackville West, or even Fredegonde Shove and Mrs Daryush; and in discussions of contemporary poetry it is seldom that her name crops up. Yet she is demonstrably the greatest poetess who has written in English since Christina Rossetti and Elizabeth Barrett Browning, and while susceptible owing to her virtuosity, her intellectual strength, her classical quality, of far less popularity than the latter, a greater poetess in almost the same proportion that Mrs Browning is superior to Ella Wheeler Wilcox or Wilhelmina Stitch.

Mrs Browning owed her popularity to those elements in her work which are essentially of the same kind, if they differ in degree, to those which characterise these ladies' effusions; but she owes any continuing literary significance she has to the emergence at the other end of the scale in her work of a few elements not dissimilar in kind but greatly inferior in quality to those of which Miss Pitter's poems are solely composed. In certain respects there is a considerable superficial resemblance between Miss Pitter's poetry and that of 'H.D.'; only the latter is fake-Greek and Miss Pitter's is the genuine article. But there is no need to dwell further on these comparisons. Hilaire Belloc puts the matter in a nutshell in his introduction to Miss Pitter's new volume, *A Mad Lady's Garland* (The Cresset Press, 3s 9d post free) when he says:

> I could wish to be younger in order to mark the moment when talent of this very high level reaches its reward in public fame. It must come. But the day in which we live, having no standards and having apparently forgotten what verse is – and, indeed, what the art of writing is – may keep us waiting some time. However, I don't feel that that matters much for stuff which is clearly permanent can wait as long as it likes. The obvious truth that the other kind of stuff washes away like mud, and that automatically the earth is purged of it, is the one consolation we have for living in the chaos we do.

'A.E.' says of the present volume:

> I would shrink from the grotesque poetry in *A Mad Lady's Garland* with all the shuddering with which we remove ourselves from the vicinity of cockroaches or earwigs, only Miss Pitter makes the creatures of her fantasy – spiders, fleas, cockroaches, worms, mice or whatever else – speak so classically, with so exquisite an artifice, that I am stayed to listen to them, and admit into my house of soul thoughts I would have closed door upon if they had come dressed in so courtly a fashion.

I do not share 'A.E.'s' shudders and hesitations, however. Miss Pitter has indeed employed these crawling things in the fashion he describes – as ingeniously manipulated properties of the Gothic convention. It is a long worm that has no turning, and Miss Pitter gives even the coffin worm an acceptable little twist; but her creatures are used in fables, they are humanised till they retain little or nothing of their real nature. We are a long way here from the 'channering worm'; still further from 'Christ the worm', that tremendous fusion of diving philosophy and physical incongruity which should yet become the subject of a marvellous poem. It seems to me that there is a far greater creative potentiality in a more realistic angle of approach – that 'sheer statement of what a thing is', which, as Professor Whitehead says, also goes a long way to 'explain why it is'. I wish Miss Pitter had applied her great powers to this harder task of showing how the shape, and nature, and movement of these things are related to our own structure in the most intimate, if unflattering, fashion.

This realistic approach can coexist with the most diverse temperaments; compare Baudelaire's treatment of the delousing of a head with Burns's 'To A Louse'. D.H. Lawrence plumbed deepest perhaps into some aspects of this matter; but he confined himself to tortoises and so forth, and scarcely ventured into the insect world. Even in regard to earwigs, cockroaches, and the like, however, Miss Pitter's treatment lies only half-way between Don Marquis's *Archy and Mehitabel* and my own exploits with my beloved 'horny-golochs', 'switchables', sclaters, wireworms and similar small game. Nor in the form of her poems does she attempt in any way to communicate the actual movements of these creatures or the instinctive repulsions they excite or the 'feel' of their presence on or about one. None the less for its almost incredible restraint, however, the greatest success here is undoubtedly her 'Maternal Love Triumphant, or Song of the Virtuous Female Spider':

> Ere long the sorry scrawny flies
> For me could not suffice,
> So I prepared with streaming eyes
> My love to sacrifice.
> I ate him, and could not but feel
> That I had been most wise;
> An hopeful mother needs a meal
> Of better meat than flies.

And ending,

> I look not here for my reward
> But recompense shall come
> When from his toilsome life and hard
> I seek a heavenly home;
> Where in the mansions of the blest
> By earthly ills unmarred
> I'll meet again my love, my best
> And sole desired reward.

On the whole, however, the many deft thrusts, the verbal skill, the satirical, comical, witty, and epigrammatic qualities, and the invariable technical expertise of these poems only makes me wish the more that Miss Pitter had been perfectly ruthless and that it might be said of her as she says of her Virtuous Female Spider: 'The tenderness did all depart/And it is better so.'

Turning from these insect poems we find a poem of a very different order, with an almost magical beauty, in 'Fowls, Celestial and Terrestrial'; and Miss Pitter's astonishing range is exemplified in the contrast between the Cockroach's:

> Moderns? Oh, yeah, you call yourselves moderns?
> Well, I've been as modern as you
>   Any time these many million years,

The beauty-parlour ballyhoo of 'The Nymphs, That They Would Confess the Pre-eminent Beauties of Pyrrha' raised to enchanting eloquence and slowly deflated like a slyly pricked balloon, and lines such as these, of the Swan: –

> Ah, then she bridled up her lordly head,
> Spread forth her silver plume in clean array,
> Arched her queenly neck, and with her red
> And polished bill down her sleek sides made play…

or, of the Bird of Paradise: –

> She clapped her blinding wings and straight up flew
> To the high summit of a cedar green;
> A beam of dazzling silver from the blue
> Lighted on her, that now was no more seen
> As earthly fowl, but even as she had been
> One of the awful burning cherubim;
> Upon a fiery cloud her breast did lean,
> With heaven-assaulting gaze she pierced the dim
> Azure, and *holy, holy, holy*, was her hymn.

This is Miss Pitter's finest vein; which leads 'A.E.' to speak of the serene mood and stellar loveliness of much of her work, and Hilaire Belloc of her exceptional twin-gift of perfect ear and perfect epithet which produces 'verse of that classic sort which is founded and secure of its own future'. She is not speaking ex cathedra in these bizarre pranks with insects and vermin – unfailingly amusing and gently horrifying as they are; but when she stands forth in her real singing robes she is one of the purest and most praiseworthy voices in poetry today.

Hugh MacDiarmid, 4 October 1934

Denis Saurat: supernatural rationalist

'To C.M. Grieve who will criticise, but also for MacDiarmid who will approve' is how Professor Denis Saurat inscribes a copy of his latest book to me [*Histoire des Religions* (Paris: Denoel et Steel)]. I am afraid it is the other way about; the poet in me entirely disapproves, while my lean-brained *alter ego*, Mr Grieve, can join in the intellectual game with considerable appreciation (just as it is to the latter almost exclusively that Saurat's studies of Milton, Blake, Hugo and other poets appeal while the former laments a singular inappreciation of poetry as such). For it is a most ingenious game. French intellectuals can carry the gentle art of sitting on both sides of the fence at once – of keeping a foot in two opposing camps – to a pitch of incredible dexterity; and Saurat is a past master at this.

But a poet has no time for these bourgeois agilities, and from his point of view the performance is a dangerous piece of cultural-fascist equivocation, seeking on specious grounds to give an extra lease of life to religious humbug, just as the Kabbalistic element in to much great European poetry, the result of sheep-like imitation and unconsciousness of, let alone first-hand recourse to, its sources (see Saurat's *Literature and the Occult*), is an incredible fixation largely responsible for the gulf between poetry and the people, for poetry's lack of relationship to crucial human issues and of that centrality indispensable to great creative work, which must inevitably result in a vast scaling down of the 'so much great European poetry' referred to.

Saurat's motivation here – if the underlying class-war significance is not taken into account – is an amazingly slim manoeuvre, like producing Hamlet and leaving out the Prince of Denmark; for he himself is anti-clerical, he repudiates Christianity, although he regards the teaching of Jesus as the highest yet vouchsafed to humanity (but in his exposition of it significantly avoids any reference to the Sermon on the Mount) because it demands efforts contrary to man's nature, and he attaches prime significance to the practically unbroken Kabbalist liaison. But the cloven hoof is seen even more clearly in other directions – his avoidance of any reckoning with the social consequences, and political and economic affiliations, of the various religions; his failure to institute any inquiry into the reality of the nominal religions of the vast masses of their adherents; his avoidance of any discussion of the extent with their professions, and the consequent suspicion that the latter, either consciously or unconsciously, merely mask their real activities; his anti-Oriental attitude which leads him to define the essence of Buddhism as at the furthest remove from Western mentality, modern mentality (as if the two were synonymous) – the 'dark side of the human intelligence' (whence surely spring these deep instincts in Western Man to which he contends the Kabbala so curiously continues to appeal): and, complementary to that, his French provincialism which, *inter alia*, leads him to speak of 'les esprits les plus puissants et les plus subtils de notre époque, Hamelin, Bergson, Brunschvieg, Proust, Alain et Valéry', who 'malgré leurs variations de zéro a l'infini dans leur vocabulaire et dans leurs précautions, n'ont donc pas reconcé à l'idée de Dieu.'

These are certainly superior tight-rope-walkers to Sir James Jeans, Professors Eddington and Whitehead and their like; but it is disappointing to find T.S. Eliot excluded; surely his super-subtle pleas that 'a whole generation might conceivably pass without any orthodox thought', that the Inner Light is 'the most deceitful guide that ever offered itself to wandering humanity', that 'reasons of race and religion combine to make any large number of free-thinking Jews undesirable', entitle him to his place in the diverting little list. But no! Eliot is not quite expert enough. Does he not characterise Lawrence as a prime heretic given 'a lust for intellectual independence' by 'his deplorable religious upbringing' and declare that 'individual writers can be understood and classified according to the type of Protestantism which surrounded their infancy'? I do not go so far as to say that Saurat is like Eliot, a very meticulous priest of the devilry which arises as the class struggle develops; denial of mind, resurrection of cult, and so forth – all so overwhelmingly in evidence today; but I do find something absurd in the writing of a History of Religions from so extraordinarily narrow, so peculiarly French, so essentially irreligious, an angle. An all-round survey would certainly have necessitated the appearance in the index of at least as many names, actually excluded, as those which in fact appear. I am sure that almost any one who might consider writing a book on the ostensible subject of this one would regard seventy-five per cent of those Saurat mentions as irrelevant and be almost wholly concerned with men Saurat either does not refer to, or barely refers to. The Fascist bearing of the whole book clearly emerges in the statement that today 'pour la première fois depuis l'époque de la Grèce ancienne, les penseurs s'attaquent directement aux problèmes sans autre préoccupation que de chercher la vérité.' More of the Ivory Tower business! It reminds me of Mrs Franklin D. Roosevelt's statement: 'It is rare to find an Englishman who does not know the classics, because they look upon a knowledge of Greek and Latin as essential.' And invites the same response: Oh yeah!

Maritain is mentioned here, for example, but not Marx; there is no reference to the attempts that have been made at 'supplementing' Marx by Thomas Aquinas, as in the writings of Wilhelm Hohoff and others, or to the fact that there are to be found among Catholic socialists in France some who admire both Marx and Aquinas. Only a couple of sentences are devoted to Nietzsche. Shestov and the other Russian religious thinkers are not referred to either. Feuerbach gave the name of 'cud-chewers' to the thinkers who wanted to revive the elements of the old philosophy, and thought Saurat is not engaged in the process with the blatancy of a Jeans, there is a distressing amount of mere cud-chewing in his book; a deplorable dependence on such as Sir James Frazer of whom it has been truly said

> his methods of correlation have been as crude and unregulated as his industry and the cultivation of his erudition have been immense; the confusion of savage and primitive states of culture commenced by Tylor and his school has been carried to excess in his works; from the point of view of the social historian attempting to disentangle the story of man's coming and growth upon this planet he is one of the most calamitous phenomena in modern research

and an extraordinary disregard of Freud and the finding of modern psychology generally. These are not the only inexplicable omissions. Many of his sections are curiously inadequate and behind the times; notably those on German Philosophy and on Scientific Materialism (confined to three short paragraphs as against nearly thrice the space given to Le Panthéisme Occultists – Hélène Blavatsky and Victor Hugo). He even falls back on the conventional cliché: 'Si la matière n'existe pas, le matérialisme pèche par la base; et la science tend de plus en plus à détruire l'idée même de matière.' After that we can hardly sympathise with him over the *Times Literary Supplement*'s verbal quibbling which asks, apropos Saurat's declaration that 'Rien d'aussi divin que la parole de Jésus n'a jamais touché l'humanité', 'why, if the teaching is so divine, Jesus himself should be denied divinity, and also why, if the teaching is so divine, it should be rejected.'

Saurat's whole position naturally leads him to his eulogy of Mohamedanism (which, nevertheless, is certain to play as negligible a role in Europe in the future as it has done in the past and which one assuredly cannot picture Saurat himself seriously trying to propagate – the measure of the unreality of the whole thesis):

> L'Islamisme est une religion simple dans ses grands principes et relativement rationelle, moins encombrée de théologie officielle que le Christianisme ou le bouddhisme. C'est aussi une religion plus complète; elle n'est pas séparée de la vie politique des peuples qui s'en nourissent, contrairement au Christianisme. Ausse elle inspire un attachment plus universel peut-être, en leur demandant moins d'efforts contraires à leur nature.

It is to appear shortly in English in which it will cut an even odder figure, but this is largely due to the fact that it follows on from Saurat's previous books, all of which unfortunately are not yet available in English. It is to be hoped that this may be speedily rectified. If the present book contains little of what one would expect in a book with this title and much that one would not, it abounds in out-of-the-way information of all sorts, in pregnant reflections, and in admirable synopses of vast tracts of knowledge; there is nothing that Saurat can possibly write that is not better worth publishing and reading than at least 90 per cent of all that does appear and find readers in English. All the same the *Times Literary Supplement* is right: 'It must be understood that, although anti-clerical, Dr Saurat is no pedestrian materialist.'

Hugh MacDiarmid, 18 October 1934

New Britain

1933–1934

The Shetland Islands

The Shetlands have been well described as 'the skeleton of a departed country'. Geologists will tell you that these islands are 'full of the ghosts of minerals'. The population is rapidly declining; scores of crofts are falling into desuetude; the fishing has dwindled to vanishing point – soon there will be nothing but the bare stones left. Frequently a Shetland vista gives one the illusion of not being on part of the habitable earth, but of some burnt-out star. The end of the world; well, it will come to that some time, won't it? As well, perhaps, to reckon with a foretaste of it now. Why wait in parts where infinitely more irrelevances have still to be shorn away before the true goal of all this complicated terrestrial process manifests itself?

A LAND OF STONES

'Out of this stony rubbish, what grows?' Very often, it would appear, nothing at all. Finally you may pick out an isolated cottage or two – or are they cottages, or just cairns of stones? – practically indistinguishable from their stone-grey setting; and a scratch or two of tillage little different from striae on the rocks. And there may be the tiny black shape of a man or woman – or ant? It is difficult to tell. What life of trolls – of pigmies in underground dwellings – can people lead in such parts? Does their life, too, match its surroundings with an almost imperceptible difference from death? Is that why you – a poet – live here, dismissing everything else as the stones which are the beginning and the end of the earth dismiss all the multifarious proliferation and evolution of life? Do you live here because you realize – and are content to realize – that it is only, in the most literal sense, if at all, through these stones that mankind and all the rest of terrene creation can win to God?

Yes; that is the reason. This bare prospect – without trees, without running water, with a minimum of life of any sort – lacks nothing. Strangers cannot get used to it; they experience a sense of incredible deprivation. It is only by slow degrees that they realize that the addition of trees, streams, and other features familiar to them in other regions would add nothing to the Shetlands – that they are complete as they are, and lack nothing to be found anywhere else in shape or colour. These take different and for the most part far less obtrusive forms; the patience and understanding necessary to detect and appreciate them under such changed conditions are not easily acquired. Stupid people distrust and fail to learn technical terminologies of all kinds; thus disabling themselves from thinking about – even from seeing – everything that is not expressible in the poor little stock vocabulary.

THE ESSENTIALS ARE HERE

Therefore they are completely at a loss in a country like this and think it bare and desolate and destitute of all the rich variety to be found elsewhere. They are wrong – there is no less variety, there is no monotony, if only they had eyes to see. All the essentials are here – all that is hidden in most other places under a multiplicity of secondary forms, a welter of transitional appearances, a chaos of vain imaginings.

Appearances are deceptive here too, where they are reduced to a minimum. Go into these little isolated cottages and you will find a life there practically identical with the life to be found in the houses anywhere else in Great Britain. The picture-paper – the radio – all the rest of it. Similar hopes and fears, joys and sorrows. The same language. But appearances are very deceptive. These people seem just the same as most people in Scotland or England or Ireland or Wales. You would not think they were utterly different in regard to one of the most essential and contentious of all matters – that they are guilty of or connive at what the vast majority of the mainland people would denounce as 'utter immorality', 'living in sin'. Yet it is so. Why is it difficult to tell? Nothing in their aspect, in their health, in their apparent relations to each other, suggests such an extraordinary deviation – such an easy, unselfconscious acceptance of what almost everywhere else would be regarded as heinous, unthinkable, lewd, and abominable. Nor is there any conscious concealment; it is so taken for granted, so natural and time-honoured, a part of their mode of life, that they seem unaware of their appalling departure from the standards accepted elsewhere. There is, I say, no sense of guilt – but ask them about it and they will blandly deny that anything of the sort obtains.

EXPERIMENTAL MARRIAGES

The simple fact is the lads go with the lassies certain nights of the week – the lads, in other words, go to the lassies' homes, and with the full knowledge and approval of the parents, to bed with them. It is taken for granted that if 'anything happens' marriage will ensue; it generally does. Mishaps are few. How much of the misery of adolescence is thus avoided, how many complexes resolved and unfortunate inhibitions prevented! There is a delightful understanding – a lack of tension, difficulty, and the divers morbidities of sexual dissatisfaction – between the young people; a delightful absence of false pretence. And a doctor with whom I discussed the matter thought it had other important advantages: 'For one thing, it makes both the lads and the lassies more particular about washing themselves.' It is certainly fine to see them tidying themselves up on these particular nights.

REAL CHRISTIANITY

The so-called 'beliefs' of the Shetlanders – which, of course, no one really believes – are identical with those of the mainland people; yet there is a subtle underlying difference which can only be illustrated by one concrete example. There was a Shetland minister who was an epileptic – he used to fall about all over the island – if he came in to visit you or you called at the Manse he would sometimes fall into fit after fit. It was very distressing to watch but one soon got used to it. It became as natural as anything else. In the pulpit he'd take half-a-dozen seizures in the course of a sermon. As he came out of them he'd forget where he was at when the fit came on – and carry on from a different point of his manuscript altogether. His sermons were hopelessly disjointed; it was impossible to make head or tail of them. But one soon got accustomed to it and thought nothing of it. What did it matter? The acceptance of that war-injured minister is the nearest thing to real Christianity I ever encountered.

No doubt lots of people on the mainland feel exactly the same about all they see and hear, but they do not admit it to themselves quite so completely. It is impossible to imagine their tolerating an epileptic clergyman constantly 'losing his place' and going off at a tangent; they still demand a certain appearance of continuity and sense and it is not publicly admitted and acted upon that God manifests himself not less effectively through such an 'unfortunate' as through an ordinary rational person. No; this is the sort of thing that can only happen in the Shetlands, and one must look close to see it and know exactly where to look. I could tell you of many far stranger things, but you would not believe me or, if you did superficially credit what I told you, you would not really understand it. That takes time and patience and perfect integrity and is not for everybody – at least on this side of the grave.

I love the Shetlands – the end of the old world; and the beginning of the new!

Hugh MacDiarmid, 18 October 1933

What the unemployed could do

There are two lines of action which can be easily and inexpensively taken by those throughout Great Britain who are already members of the various New Britain Groups and Social Credit organizations. The first of these is to prevent all further dumping and destruction of foodstuffs or other consumable goods of any kind. Vigilance committees ought to be appointed to keep their eyes and ears open for anything of the kind and as soon as they get wind of any such intention there should be a central body to which they could pass on the word, and that central body should have a small Mobile Squad at its disposal.

PREVENTING DESTRUCTION OF FOOD

That Mobile Squad, which should consist of perhaps twenty to thirty carefully selected and intelligent unemployed, should be sent at once to the area where the sabotage was threatened, with instructions to prevent it. To keep within in the law as far as possible, a nominal sum ought to be offered for the goods in question in lieu of their destruction, together with the promise that if that sum is accepted and the goods handed over, the latter will be distributed for nothing to the necessitous unemployed and their dependants in the nearest appropriate centre. If the offer is not accepted and all attempts at persuasion fail, the Mobile Squad should then, by every possible means of obstruction and resistance, try to prevent the intended destruction – but without resorting to violence.

It would be the duty of the central body to look after the interests and dependants of those of the Mobile Squad who might be arrested and to arrange for their defence. The effect of action along these lines would be, I think, to draw additional attention to all these cases of anti-social sabotage, and in the event of proceedings against arrested men to throw an increasing onus on the authorities to defend the indefensible in circumstances which would range public opinion generally more and more strongly against them.

ARTIFICIAL UNEMPLOYMENT

But the second, and far more important, line of action I would suggest concerns the unemployed. My first concern is to stress – and to insist upon the need everywhere for stressing – that their release from wage-slavery is in the great majority of cases not temporary but permanent. They will not be reabsorbed into industry, but an ever-increasing proportion of those presently employed will year after year become like them 'surplus to economic requirements'. The fools, knaves, or combinations of both, who are endeavouring to perpetuate the present tottering system, are thinking in terms of the past and failing to realize (or deliberately shutting their eyes to the obvious fact) that the enormous volume of so-called 'unemployment' is the inevitable and highly desirable result of scientific labour-saving and production-increasing devices.

Whole masses of people are forced to starve or semi-starve and to stint themselves in all manner of ways in the midst of unparalleled abundance owing to this blind adherence to an obsolete system and the rooted prejudices it produces, and all the organs of publicity are manoeuvred to stress the illusory need for 'economy'. There is no need for economy. On the contrary an enormous extension of prosperity for everybody is immediately practicable.

In these circumstances it is above all else 'up to' the unemployed to realize their own position clearly and to see that the power of a small class to continue to oppress and dehumanize them in this way cannot last long – and that they, the 'unemployed', can help materially to shorten it. How?

There are two things they can do; cure their unemployed fellow-workers of the idea that the unemployed are any burden on them or menace to them (ideas which the authorities in control of the existing system ubiquitously foster for their own ends), and, secondly, to show that though released from wage-slavery they are not unemployed, but are willing and able to use all their faculties for the general good.

There are heaps of works they can engage on; but first and foremost they must absolutely refuse to have anything whatever to do with all the false self-help schemes, all attempts to divert attention from the main issue and to bolster up the existing system in some way. The attitude which says: 'Why should we work for nothing?' – 'Why should we do anything for ourselves or other people unless we get paid for it?' – won't help them either; it plays into the hands of those who control the existing system. A complete reversal of that attitude on the part of the unemployed themselves will go a long way to help to destroy the effete system which is interposing between them and nature's abundance on the onc hand and the incalculable increase of producing power on the other.

OFFER THEIR SERVICES

'But what can we do?' Everywhere – in every community – there are desirable public improvements or increased amenities not provided because the Councils say: 'We must economize – we have not the money for these just now.' Let the unemployed say: 'Very well – we'll give all the necessary labour absolutely free.' Let them thus throw the onus on the authorities of refusing that unpaid public service. Let them go further and embarrass all public authorities still more by offering to do for nothing all the schemes they are presently proceeding with. And do not let them take a narrow destructive class-view of the matter. Let them say: 'Here's a big landowner who reckons that owing to heavy rates and taxes he can't keep his estates in proper order – can't afford to have his woodlands properly forested, and so on. He's no friend of the unemployed. Let us heap coals of fire on his head. Let us go to him and say: "It's a pity to see all your estate going to rack and ruin, and all your forests reverting to jungle because of lack of labour. These are really great public assets in the long run. We are public-spirited enough not to want to see *our* country going to ruin like this. We will do all the necessary work for you – free, gratis, and for nothing."' Imagine the faces of our great territorial magnates faced with offers like these!

CONQUER THE SYSTEM

If along with that intelligent public service the 'unemployed' combine a clear appreciation of the utter inadequacy of the existing economic system, and a knowledge of the Douglas Social Credit proposals which will throw it on the scrap-heap and so open the way to plenty and leisure for all, which spreads its glorious prospect just beyond the bottle-neck of High Finance, so much the better.

Morally justified in all men's eyes and mentally equipped to expedite the breakdown of the present system and help to usher in the new order their position will be unassailable. They can transform themselves from being the victims of the existing system to being the victors over it. They can turn their very difficulties and humiliating experiences into the most potent weapons for the overthrow of the anti-social forces responsible for them. Great poetry is generally the product of suffering conquered and transcended; the 'unemployed' can perform an analogous feat. Let them realize they are not the offscourings of the economic system, but the advance guard of the greatest forward movement in human history, and rise, and gird their loins, and acquit themselves like men, and they will speedily turn their personal circumstances into a tremendous asset to humanity in its fight against vested interests and purblind prejudice.

Hugh MacDiarmid, 22 November 1933

Poet and People

As a practising poet I find myself increasingly exercised over the – we are told, widening – gulf between art and the people; in other words, between poetry and the man-in-the street. I emphasize man-in-the-street rather than woman-in-the-street because the mass of bad poetry, and the ubiquitous obstacle of a wrong approach to poetry, is, like the wrong sort of religion, the sentimental escapist religiosity, mainly supported nowadays by women.

Let me say right away that I am in complete agreement with T.S. Eliot when he says: –

> When all exceptions have been made, and after admitting the possible existence of minor 'difficult' poets whose public must always be small, I believe that the poet naturally prefers to write for as large and miscellaneous an audience as possible, and that it is the half-educated and ill-educated, rather than the uneducated, who stand in his way. I myself should like an audience who could neither read nor write. The most useful poetry, socially, would be one which could cut across all the present stratifications of public taste – stratifications which are perhaps a sign of social decadence.

HIGH FALUTIN NONSENSE

Why do I think it is vitally important to re-connect the poet and the people? It is not only because it is increasingly difficult to publish poetry and secure the right public for it. It is not only because I am revolted by the petty cliquism and absurd rites of the ladies in green and purple *djibbahs* who attend poetry-reading enterprises and the high falutin nonsense and artificiality of the Verse-Speaking Movement which in any case has its special repertoire (in no way corresponding to the real situation and tendencies of poetry today), its own parasitical breed of 'interpretative artists', and is by no means a 'fair field with no favour'. It is not only my disgust with those poets who have allowed themselves to be thrust into little niches where they can make up for the paucity of their readers by a sense of spiritual superiority – die-hards of a lost, but glorious cause. It is because I have a different conception altogether of the future and functions of poetry.

I must not be taken as agreeing altogether with Mr I.A. Richards when he says: –

> The most dangerous of the sciences is only now beginning to come into action. I am thinking less of Psychoanalysis or of Behaviourism than of the whole subject which includes them. It is very probable that the Hindenburg Line, to which the defence of our traditions retired as a result of the onslaughts of the last century, will be blown up in the near future. If this should happen a mental chaos such as man has never experienced may be expected. We shall then be thrown back, as Matthew Arnold foresaw, upon poetry. Poetry is capable of saving us.

POETS *VERSUS* PARSONS

But I certainly think that the very dubious attitude of Poetry to these traditions all along – its extraordinary non-Christian or anti-Christian attitude (even in those poets who, apart from their poetry, were most 'Christian' and conventionalist in character or profession), and the occult provenance of its leading ideas – supports this idea, just as the apparent determination of the poetic spirit to resist all mere patching-up and compromise designed to halt modern consciousness at the Hindenburg or any other line does. In the meantime, however, I am content to express the view that it is absurd and dangerous that we should have thousands of pulpits filled in Great Britain weekly by pastors depending mainly on a species of bastard poetry and so few poets either regularly or at all in direct touch with the general public.

Most people only come into contact – under the most unfavourable auspices at that – with poetry in their school days. Space does not permit me to discuss that here; suffice it to say, that one of the stand-bys of teaching poetry in schools is that vicious thing, paraphrasing, which instils a totally wrong idea of the nature of poetry to begin with. A general but quite erroneous idea of the nature of poetry persists thereafter, but only a small minority subsequently read much, or any, poetry and the agencies at work to debauch the public intelligence persistently disseminate false ideas of poetry, as a thing remote from the practical consideration of life, a species of 'mere dreaming', a thing which 'doesn't pay', and whose long-haired practitioners are figures of fun.

THE 'MINDLESS MOB'

All this vast public seldom or never comes in contact with an actual poet or hears from him at first-hand what he is about. They only get an idea of this poet or that through stray reviews – and the papers they read give scant space to poetry-reviewing. The very small minority who read poetry constantly and follow its 'movements' and belong to poetry clubs and such like are hardly in any better case. They, too, scarcely ever meet poets fact to face, and still more seldom poets of the slightest consequence who, naturally, have no time for such hole-and-corner affairs.

It was not always thus, however, and in my opinion it is high time to get back to a very different state of affairs. It is not a question of making poetry easier; the public do not want 'talking down to'. That habit of pandering to the supposedly mindless mob which characterizes modern mass journalism, pulpiteering, and other kinds of general appeal is three-quarters of the trouble. Unscrupulous journalists are always declaring that modern poets are too intellectualist, too recondite, too allusive. The Greek dramatists, Pindar, Shakespeare, the old Irish Gaelic bards, were far more so, and the public took their points all right.

DEBAUCHED PUBLIC TASTE

We have, at the present time, to undo a tremendous debauching of the public mind that has accustomed it to be fed on sops and snippets and to think that anything calling for mental effort is 'over its head' and not for it. Long ago, in Scotland, as Agnes Mure Mackenzie tells us, 'to illiterate and therefore uneducated peasants things like *Chevy Chase* and *The Bonnie Earl o' Moray* took the place of such things as the diary of an unpleasing specimen of the gigolo, lately killed in a squalid row with his protectress, which the newspaper with the largest sale in England is advertising as a star attraction on the day on which this sentence is written. But compulsory education is, of course, a blessing…'

How are those of us, conscious of this ignominy and its fateful implications, to get back to a healthier state of affairs and re-connect poetry and the people in an effective fashion? I have concrete proposals to make for the consideration of young poets, New Britain Groups, and others in my second article next week.

Hugh MacDiarmid, 7 February 1934

Let Poets Meet the People

The start must be made by the poets themselves and by those with something really to say and determination to find ways and means of saying it. Most of them still, however, prefer to flourish in holes and corners; they are too high and mighty – or too cowardly, too conscious of the invalidity of their pretensions – for the 'game in hand'. I knew an artist on his 'beam ends' in London, but he began to go round the pubs. His *modus operandi* was this. He spotted whom he thought a likely customer and sat down and made a lightning portrait of him. He then either found ways and means of letting the subject see what he had done and offer to buy it, or he did it in such a way as to attract the attention of other customers who in turn wanted to be done too. And he did very well out of it.

POETRY A VOCATION

But who ever saw a poet hawking his wares in a pub – a real poet? That is left for the most part to those miserable individuals who tramp round with a dolorous bit of war-verse on a postcard, or to a few tramp poets who go up and down the country selling pamphlets of their poems, picture postcards of the 'ex-Navvy Poet', and so forth. I know some of them and financially they do quite well out of it, but without exception their verse is dreadful doggerel. I do not believe for a single moment that really good poems, cheaply but attractively printed in pamphlet form or on long sheets, would not sell as well and a great deal better, and if the sale of them were coupled with open-air expositions of his work by the poet himself which really took the people into 'the poet's workshop' and brought them into direct touch with the creative processes, not only would a highly lucrative business develop, but it would be immensely good for the poet as well as for the people. Incidentally it would help to break down the vicious idea that poetry isn't a full-time job, a real and all-engrossing vocation for a man, but only a polite accomplishment, one of the minor amenities of life, to be relegated to one's spare time and not depended on for a living.

THE PUBLIC NOT AN ASS

A poet who took this course, relying on no eleemosynary appeal as an 'ex-Navvy' or an unemployed ex-soldier, but solely on the vital merit of his poems, would have a very strenuous time of it if he allowed 'heckling' at his meetings (as some modern composers have recently done after performances of their works). The illusion of 'talking down' to the public would be speedily dispelled; he would find them quick on the uptake and searching in their questions, and just as anxious to get the 'hang' of the creative process as he could possibly be to communicate it. For the public at bottom is not really deceived; it knows it is being systematically doped, and it is eager for the real thing.

Poets who go back to the people in the way I suggest will quickly find that they can 'cut little ice' with their own pretty little ideas carefully worked up overnight. The emphasis will be on their technical ability, readiness of wit, address, and, above all, on the extent to which, having these, they really do have something to say. If they have something to say people will listen all right, but it must be straightforward man-to-man dealing – no hanky-panky, no monkey-tricks, no overt or covert eleemosynary appeal of any kind, and no pandering to notions of what the people think poetry is. What would be developed if this practice became general would be a true correlation of poetry and the people. The oral poet would acquire the genius of hitting upon the vital needs of the people. Those who are in the habit of public speaking know the wonderful feeling of swaying an audience – all the more wonderful when the speaker is not delivering a prepared address, but speaking spontaneously, carrying his audience with him, and responding as he goes to the feelings he senses in them. This is infinitely better than any experience your 'literary closets' can vouchsafe.

NATURAL DICTION

The poets who go to the people in this way need not fear that as a result of the improvisatory method their work will be all planless and occasional; purposes, tendencies, will manifest themselves all right, but they will be those of the spirit of the people, not the *voulu* constructions of the isolate *littérateur*. Contact with the 'great miscellaneous public' will compel the initiation of new techniques – not little lean-brained coterie manœuvres corresponding to no reality and meeting no general need – and, above all, will profoundly affect the language question. Such improvisatory poetry cannot be screwed up to false standards of speech like the scriptive stuff into which most modern verse has degenerated; it will adapt itself to and utilize the natural modes of utterance of the mixed public which recognizes no 'King's English', but has its own racy, dialect, and infinitely various media. The verbal imperialism of 'correct diction' will immediately collapse.

A POETS' GUILD?

At first there may be few ministers who will give a poet the freedom of a pulpit; few poets who dare carry the propaganda of poetry to the street corner. That is where the New Britain Groups come in. Can we not form Groups who will insist upon talks about poetry and readings of poetry by poets themselves – not by non-creative people acting as interpreters? My idea is that the Groups themselves should try to spur one or more of their members to the higher level of public discourse and so initiate the recovery of the oral tradition. Once a beginning is made – once groups meet regularly up and down Scotland, England, and Wales with this object in view and study the history of oral literature and get some of their members to essay improvisatory work of this kind – I am certain that there will be very speedy and salutary developments. My idea is that the groups which have developed members capable of successful improvisatory poetry should then appoint these members to represent them on a central Poets' Guild, which could carry the matter a great deal further, arrange for its best improvisers to go round the various groups in turn, and conduct open-air meetings and other methods of propaganda.

Hugh MacDiarmid, 14 February 1934

Rainer Maria Rilke

When Rainer Maria Rilke died in 1927 there were no paragraphs in the

British newspapers announcing the fact. The death of a great poet – the birth of a great masterpiece of human expression – has no 'news value'. Most people have been so debauched that they need to keep themselves posted in the tittle-tattle of all the ends of the earth – the crimes, the divorces, superficial, and generally erroneous, gossip about political and social tendencies; and one who disavows any interest in such matters is regarded as a queer chap, a narrow-minded crank. So is anyone who takes – and ventures to suggest that most people ought to take – any interest in current foreign philosophy and literature and art and music. We remain in all important matters hopelessly insular.

All this notwithstanding, Rilke is receiving attention much more quickly and adequately in British literary circles than is usually the fortune of foreign contemporaries. How much of Blok, for example, is yet available in English translation, though Blok died in 1921? How much of Boris Pasternak? Only a few translations in advance-guard American reviews. How much of Stefan George – next to Rilke the greatest of modern German poets? Carl Spitteler, the Swiss poet, had to wait a long time for English translation and discussion. Paul Valéry has fared better; several of his works have been excellently translated. And Valéry, like George and Pasternak, is still alive. An enormous literature in most of the languages of Europe has grown up about Rilke since he died, and though what is yet available about him in English is a mere moiety of what is to be had in the other leading languages, it is clear that he is going to be the subject of a very great deal of interest in English too.

Rilke was born in Prague on 4 December 1875, the descendant of an old aristocratic Carinthian family. After five years in the Kadetten Korps, he studied in Prague, Munich, and Berlin; lived in Paris for a number of years, and was for a time Rodin's secretary; and subsequently travelled to Italy, Sweden, Algeria, Tunis, Egypt, and Russia. He finally dwelt in the Canton of Valais, where he died and was buried on 2 January 1927, in the cemetery of Raxon. He published a very large body of poetry, and a considerable quantity of extremely interesting and individual prose. His earliest work was published in 1890; but his great work is – though all the intervening books show steady progression and contain a wealth of splendid poetry – his *Requiem* (1909), his ten *Duineser Elegien*, written during the winter of 1911–12 in the Castle of Duino, which stands on a precipitous, solitary piece of the Adriatic Coast, and published in 1923; the series of fifty-five sonnets, *Sonette an Orpheus*, composed in the Château de Muzot and finished in February 1922; and his prose story of his *alter ego, The Notebook of Malte Laurids Brigge* (Hogarth Press).

The earliest translations of Rilke poems in English were those of Jethro Bithell in his *Contemporary German Poetry* in 1911. A sumptuously produced translation of the ten Duino elegies was published by the Hogarth Press in 1932, the translators being V. and Edward Sackville West. But as Dr Otto Schlapp and other German authorities and Rilke enthusiasts pointed out these were extremely bad translations. The translators themselves said they were only a 'crib'; but their method of 'literal accuracy' was inapplicable to Rilke of all writers, for his usage of German is extremely novel and difficult, and literal translation simply lands one in a mass of ludicrous misreadings. In this untranslatable usage of German, Rilke is, of course, in line with advanced literary artists in all European languages today.

Others who have published translations of the Duino elegies in part or in whole include Hester Pickman and the present writer, but these, too, are extremely poor approximations to the originals. Happily various other translators are busy upon them, notably Mr R.C.T. Hull, whose draft translations of these, and of the still more difficult Orpheus sonnets I have been privileged to see, are infinitely better than anything that has yet appeared. As Miss Pickman has finely said: –

> Keats, Shelley, Blake, and many others have never been given to the un-English world. They escape translation as taste and perfume escape vocabulary. Now Rilke is such a poet as they, and as such it is folly to think of him in another language. We can get neither the music nor the mood, nor the precision of emotion that lie in his words… It is only the qualities of thought that we can study in him, and the material out of which that thought is made and what it helps us to see. Rilke divested of his magic is still important because he was one of those rare people who follow thought as far as it will lead them. He was still able to perceive at a point of inner experience where most men lose their bearings and come back to the surface. His poetry takes us carefully and surely through well-defined curtains of illusion to a reality that is as unmistakable as daylight.

Miss Pickman continues: –

> It would be interesting to compare him to Joyce and Proust, who have both gone far in the same direction. It seems to me that Rilke, though his work is on a smaller scale than either of theirs, has had the courage to go on where they turned back. Perhaps the metaphysically minded German in him found a reality in thoughts that seemed tenuous to them. He lives and breathes easily in a world of double reality where death never seems less beautiful or less important than life. It is a world full of fears because he must constantly deal with mysteries that have no solution and which our human constitutions seem designed to ignore.

Rilke is in many superlatively important directions by far 'the furthest point yet' of human consciousness and expressive power – a lone scout far away in No Man's Land, whither willy-nilly mankind must follow him, or abandon the extension of human consciousness.

Hugh MacDiarmid, 28 February 1934

A Letter from Scotland

In this article the writer – former Publicity Officer to the Liverpool Organization, the largest civic publicity and trade development organization in the world – criticizes all such bodies for their 'hopeless avoidance of basic questions'.

The transformation of Scotland into Britain's Playground – for which large tracts of it are undoubtedly well fitted – which is the declared objective of the Scottish Travel Association, is not a worthy objective apart from – and still less if substituted for – the creation of a true national economy.

The movement implies a dangerous and altogether unnecessary acquiescence in the dereliction for all purposes of local rural economy of vast areas of cultivatable land, in the collapse of Scotland's basic industries, and in that 'Southward trend' which is removing important and large labour-employing Scottish concerns, and, to a lesser extent, their employees, to the South of England. Taking all the factors into consideration, and with them the personalities and records of many of the men prominently associated with the Scottish Travel Association and kindred stunts, it is very questionable whether the real aim and object is not just to divert attention from the main problems. Certainly most of the men in question are closely associated with those economic, political, industrial, and commercial interests centralized outside Scotland which have brought about Scotland's major problems in these connections – problems which the Scottish Travel Association, the Scottish National Development Council, and other bodies carefully avoid.

BLINDNESS TO SCOTLAND'S PROBLEMS

In these circumstances it cannot be too strongly insisted that the leading personnel of these movements have been largely responsible for, and have always shown a significant blindness to, the development of Scotland's crucial problems, and that whatever the visitor-increasing and other projects of these question-begging associations do, they cannot, even at the very best, do more than touch the merest fringe of these problems. In Scotland's condition today agencies which ignore the substance of our national situation and divert – or tend to divert – public attention to the mere frills require at least to be very carefully scrutinized, and when it is found that their chief promoters are men who have all along been hand in glove with the forces which have brought Scotland to its present critical pass, are directors of English centralized banks and other big concerns which have operated to Scotland's detriment, and have the bulk of their own personal interests outside Scotland, it is inevitable that it should seem that the real objects of such associations are scarcely in harmony with, if not directly opposed to, their declared purposes.

WASTEFUL OVERLAPPING PROPAGANDA

One thing that may also be pointed out is the increasing overlapping of tourist propaganda. All sorts of countries are doing the same thing and making the same, or similar, claims for their attractions and facilities. Travel 'literature' has a horrible sameness, and where tourism develops in this way it reproduces the same features, until the interesting and attractive distinctive features of the various countries are all smeared over with the same vulgar veneer of cosmopolitanism and popular entertainment. It would be useful to have the actual statistics of the money spent on propaganda of this sort and such definite figures as to the results achieved as are ascertainable.

In any case it is obviously a form of advertisement which involves wasteful competition and an increasing artificialization and trivialization of the scenic and other grounds upon which it battens. This is accentuated where there are, in addition to a national travel association, all manners of local holiday associations, issuing rival literature and making precisely the same sort of claims. The great bulk of this money could be far more advantageously spent if it was devoted to promoting the real economic interests of the places concerned, on the basis of thorough regional surveys.

BASIC QUESTIONS IGNORED

The Scottish National Development Council aspires – or pretends to aspire – to the latter role, but the claims made for it by the Earl of Elgin and his colleagues are singularly disproportionate to anything it has actually effected. The reasons for this are not far to seek. The present writer has been Publicity Officer for the largest and most successful trade development and regional publicity association in the world – the Liverpool Organization – and there as elsewhere it was impossible to do much because the leading personnel were all men whose interests were bound up with the existing order and as a consequence fundamental considerations were ruled out from the start. The existing order has to be accepted; the organization has to do what it can within them – and is consequently limited to the fringes.

The actuating motive of these bodies is, consequently, the very antithesis of a scientific principle. It is only the application of the scientific principle that disregards all existing interests and is simply and solely concerned with the maximum potentialities of such an area, and its most profitable functional relationships to other areas, that can effectively discharge the ostensible objects of such bodies.

A DESERVED LACK OF SUPPORT

Everything germane to a thorough consideration and possible solution of Scotland's essential problems was ruled out of the consideration of the Scottish National Development Council from the outset. Even if they had not been, the constitution of the body was such that it would have been without executive power to carry into effect the requirements it discerned. It is not a question here of one opinion against another – say the Earl of Elgin's against mine. The 'literature' produced by the Council is its own most complete give-away. Fundamental issues are nowhere condescended upon; basic principles are simply taken for granted in the most unscientific fashion; and the consequence is a series of the woolliest documents imaginable.

Happily, the shrewd general public of Scotland, either because of native wit or the inexorable pressure of the actual facts which these bodies ignore in favour of exploitable frillings, are not impressed either, and the Scottish Travel Association and Scottish Development Council have been poorly supported, financially and otherwise. They will contend that their failure is largely due to that want of support; in my opinion the want of support has been a shrewd commentary on their failure to deserve it. There is no sense in throwing good money after bad.

Hugh MacDiarmid, 21 March 1934

The Eleventh Hour
1934

The Sense of Smell

Empyreumatic, alliaceous, hircine – the English language is extraordinarily deficient in words for sensations of smell, and the few that it has are seldom used, most people falling back on general terms like 'fragrant', 'pleasant', 'stinking', which convey nothing of the specific quality of the odour in question. What do the three I have given mean? Empyreumatic means 'acrid like the smell of burning vegetable or mineral matter' (though different vegetables and minerals have all manner of different smells for which we have no discriminating terminology whatever); alliaceous means 'like garlic'; and hircine 'having a strong goatish smell'. We are practically destitute of words for comparing all kinds of perfumes. This may not seem an important matter, but what it means is that we are incapable of discussing, or even effectively thinking about, one of the factors that bulks most largely in our lives.

All the words we have are blind windows to the magic tower that stands central in our consciousness. This is one of the directions in which English could profitably have drawn upon Scots. Scots contains all sorts of words for which there are no equivalents at all in English, dealing with or describing the complex sensations that affect the nose and tongue, separately or jointly. The various degrees of rottenness that can affect meat or fish or sour lard, for example, or the feelings we have on touching or smelling these. Why has English which has borrowed such a tremendous vocabulary from all the other languages of the world eschewed its nearest neighbour in such a matter? It is because Scots has an entirely different psychological background and 'direction'. Just as there are certain continental qualities that cannot be reproduced in English, and that we can only refer to by their native foreign names – the German *weltschmerz* and the French *naiserie*, for instance, so nearer home English must turn a blind eye to elements of consciousness antipathetic to its own limitations and essential bias. But this is only another way of saying that each language has its own genius – its own qualities untranslatable into any other – no matter how fondly some people may hope for a world language. Any such general medium is impossible without a wholesale sacrifice of subtler perceptions of all sorts.

ACHILLES' HEEL

Yet in the tremendous change in world consciousness which is now proceeding this lack of olfactory terminology may prove the chink in the armour, the Achilles' heel, which will bring the whole fabric of the cultures of languages which have so ignored or belittled or maligned this sense, and excluded it from effective thought and expression, into disrepute and ultimate desuetude if they cannot overcome these 'blind spots'; and it is highly unlikely that they can since this misprizal or ignorance of the powers of smell is essential to their present character in a multitude of connections, and to promote smell now to the attention and verbal prominence its overwhelmingly important relationship to our consciousness deserves, would involve a tremendous transvaluation of values.

The older languages which have evolved to their present power and prestige in step with the general 'myth' of consciousness which found it necessary to ignore smell in this way can hardly execute such a *volte-face*. The bearing of this can be seen in the fact that it is customary in English and German and French to deprecate too much literary attention to nasal phenomena as morbid, a sign of decadence; while in all western Europe it is the general belief that the sense of smell is a decreasingly important factor in civilised life. Yet modern science not only shows that precisely the contrary is the case, but puts those who pin their faith to nationality – to 'cortical understanding' – in the quandary of having now to explain why then they attach so little importance to the only sensory messages which have direct access to the cortex and the most powerful – and frequently annihilating – effect on the consciousness. This little-known (or rather little-appreciated) fact is an extraordinary criticism of human reasoning power.

THE FUNDAMENTAL FACT IN INTELLIGENCE

In one of his letters, W.H. Hudson comments on Professor Elliot Smith and Dr Henry Head's researches, and quotes the declaration that: 'The fundamental fact in evolution of intelligence is the significant part played by the sense of smell.' In a footnote to his edition of Hudson's letters, Morley Roberts makes some curious observations apropos this quotation: –

> To what extent the decay of the sense of smell in civilised people, if indeed it has decayed in those who are healthy, is due to the development of other senses, is extremely doubtful. It is true that the whole forebrain has sprung from the great development of the primary ganglia connected with the ancient olfactory nerves, but that affords no great reason for saying that the olfactory centre has in any way degenerated… But when we discover that the usual condition of the nasal mucous membrane in northern districts is actually morbid, and the pocket-handkerchief is a medical appliance, there can be little doubt that such constant nasal trouble must disorder the sense of smell. I may remark that when in dry tropical and sub-tropical countries I am happily unconscious that I possess a nose at all. These facts suggest forcibly that the human race evolved in hot climates and is not yet adapted to a damp one.

THE SPHINX BETWEEN OUR EYES

The most important discoveries have been made, however, with momentous implications for all students of psychology and philosophy, since Hudson and Roberts conducted that correspondence. In *Instinct and Intuition* (Faber and Faber, 1929), G.D. Dibblee made for the first time a systematic attempt not only to analyse the so-called 'unconscious self', but to trace and expose its whole physical organisation. The unconscious self is, in his view, a question-begging term for the unconscious operations of the Instinctive and Intuitive faculties. His theory rests primarily on the evidence for the fundamental duality of the human sensory system, accumulated in the first quarter of this century through the brilliant discoveries of Sir Henry Head, Dr Rivers, Sir John Parsons and others. Here I am only concerned with his important findings regarding that 'Sphinx between our eyes – the sense of smell', the only sense with direct access to the cortex, the seat of the rational intelligence, whereas the messages of all the others pass to the thalamic region, the seat of the instinctive intelligence, where they are divided into protopathic and epicritic and a proportion then relayed to the cortex.

FASHION *VERSUS* FACT

Olfactory impulses, says Dibblee, are comparatively simple and almost as few in character as those of taste. They break into our serious life on only rare occasions and we usually give them very little overt attention.

> It is fashionable to conclude that they are of slight specific importance and that the olfactory sense is a receding one from the evolutionary point of view. There probably could be no greater mistake. We do not often consciously accord it our notice, but in spite of the usual faintness of its impressions their effects on our general feeling are spasmodically powerful. They are linked in an emphatic way with our affections and our suspicions. They have a peculiar hold on the memory. They are decisive in their qualities of attraction or repulsion, exquisite in their fragrance and horrifying in their capacity to disgust… It is curious that in spite of its real range and delicacy, the content of olfactory material seems small, while we make so much fuss over the coarser sense of taste… Most of us avoid the solicitations of odours, bad or good, on account of their disturbing qualities. We prefer to keep a 'tonus' or bracing of the nervous system, a healthy rigidity of self-defence by automatic abstention from pleasant or unpleasant odours. The tobacco habit, perhaps, is the cult of olfactory indifferentism. Smell gives us only a few rare facts; but they are of vital import, because so often hate and love and more often the love of children is fostered by them.

Hugh MacDiarmid, 19 December 1934

New Verse
1934

Answers to an Enquiry

1 *Do you intend your poetry to be useful to yourself or others?*
2 *Do you think there can now be a use for narrative poetry?*
3 *Do you wait for a spontaneous impulse before writing a poem; if so, is this impulse verbal or visual?*
4 *Have you been influenced by Freud and how do you regard him?*
5 *Do you take your stand with any political or politico-economic party or creed?*
6 *As a poet what distinguishes you, do you think, from an ordinary man?*

These questions were sent to forty poets, of whom twenty have replied.

1 See answer to number 5.
2 Of course – it only depends what story and by what poet.
3 Yes. Occasionally either verbal or visual impulses, but mostly cœnæsthetic, with specific sexual-physiological reference.
4 I am cognisant not only of Freud – and Adler and Jung – but of the workers of importance in my time in all the sciences – and these do of course influence me, but not essentially *qua* poet.
5 I am a member of the Communist Party; and – the British economic position being antithetical to that of Russia – see no reason why, especially in Britain, Communism should not incorporate the economic proposals of Major C.H. Douglas.
6 I regard poetry as the rarest and (not only therefore) most important of human faculties.

Hugh MacDiarmid, October 1934

The Bookman
1934

Scotland and the Arts

Scottish arts remain almost wholly derivative and constitute for the most part only very subordinate branches of their English counterparts. England not only has an overwhelming monopoly of influence in Scotland to the virtual exclusion of separate affiliations with Continental tendencies, but the centralisation of journalism and book-publishing in London makes Scotland culturally as provincial and dependent as Manchester or Liverpool. Whatever else it may have done, the Anglo-Scottish symbiosis has not proved stimulating to the Scottish spirit in the sphere of the arts. Our post-Union achievements are significantly poor in comparison with those of our pre-Union times. The further it has gone the more marked this disaster has been. The only way out would seem to be a complete reversal of the process. Certainly nothing is to be gained by hailing all our geese as swans, as is the tendency in many quarters today as a result of the general misconception of the aims of the Nationalist Movement, especially among most of the so-called Nationalists themselves.

Young Scottish artists of all kinds are drawn to London and become almost entirely subdued to the general art modes and material of the South. As in literature – where the entire Scottish contribution could be excised without impairing one iota the course of English literature, so in all the other arts the Scottish contributors have remained minor figures with little or no personal, and no really national effect of the slightest consequence on the course of development. The fact that Scottish traditions and psychology are radically different from the English, and that it cannot be maintained that the Scots are so intellectually and spiritually inferior to their Southern neighbours as this discrepancy in creative influence would suggest, means that the explanation lies elsewhere; in the general misdirection, handicapping and inappropriate relationships imposed on Scottish genius by the overriding factors involved in Scotland's connections with England. I do not propose to go into that far-reaching consideration here, nor into the distribution of money question, save to say that our poor people are the reliquary of our national spirit, and our wealthier classes devoid of it almost in proportion to their financial standing.

It is enough to cite a few of the more elementary facts. If the recent International P.E.N. Congress in Scotland marked Scotland's determination to re-emerge on the cultural map of Europe as a separate entity, it must also have shown up in a devastating way to the eyes of the foreign visitors the distance that has to be traversed before that commendable aspiration becomes a substantive achievement. With the exception of the quarterly *Modern Scot*, Scotland today – although it has two separate languages, Gaelic and Scots (which is a sister language to English and no mere dialect) – has no cultural organs. Scottish authors are mainly dependent on the English periodicals, publishers and public, and have to conform accordingly. But for this the work of many of our younger novelists and other writers would be far more veridically Scottish. James Bridie is not a dramatist comparable to Synge or O'Casey, and (perhaps this is the reason) he is proportionately less national. We are suffering from a time-lag too; thinking mainly in terms of rural Scotland and little in terms of our modern urban life. The Socialist movement produced nothing that was not culturally negligible. John Davidson came nearer to our modern life than any of our subsequent writers have done. Any so-called 'realism' we have developed is a mere belated naturalistic convention which nowhere approaches the realities of Scottish life. Scottish history, literature and Scottish affairs generally are not included in the curricula of our schools; despite the efforts of the Scottish Vernacular Movement, no attention is paid to the teaching of Scots; and even in the Gaelic-speaking areas Gaelic instruction suffers from being given through the hopelessly disabling medium of English. A like abandonment of the native tongue, and a like relegation or complete disregard of national subjects of all kinds, has never taken place in any other country in the world. The Scottish educational system used to be regarded as the finest in the world; it derived its character from the profound conviction that education was in itself a good thing apart from vocational uses, and the preparedness of Scottish parents to make enormous sacrifices to secure it for their children, irrespective of what their subsequent roles in life might be. That spirit has disappeared; the basis of the old system has been completely transformed – for the worse. Even our universities have practically ceased to be universities in any true sense of the term, and become mere technical schools and training colleges for certain occupations. The effort to raise funds for a Lectureship in Scottish Literature in Edinburgh University, made in connection with the Sir Walter Scott Centenary, evoked only a miserable and entirely inadequate response. (I would not have contributed a farthing to it myself, knowing with whom the appointment would have lain and what type of man would have got the job.) But if that Lectureship, had it been established, had done no more for Scottish Literature than the Chair in Glasgow University, its absence is small cause for any lament. Money is not lacking in other directions. The Edinburgh School of Art is a vastly wealthy body; but it seems incapable of devising any means of developing the creative spirit, and relapses on the production of slick commercial work of no particular value of any sort, let alone any distinctive national character. The activities of the Scottish National Academy of Music in Glasgow, and Professor Whittaker's Chair in Glasgow University, have been similarly unproductive. The one produces art-teachers, not artists; the other music-teachers, not composers. In the Edinburgh Chair of Music, with all his great qualities, Professor

Tovey has been a cuckoo in the nest, exerting anything but a Scottish influence. The Chair of Fine Arts in Edinburgh University has been dilettante and mainly antiquarian, except for a brief period under Professor Herbert Read, when it did set most of our self-esteemed *cognoscenti* by the ears. Our satirical faculty in the work of the late Dyke White and of Coia and others has produced merely local work and no graphic equivalent to Burns in satire. The Rev. Charles Warr, the Dean of the Thistle, recently declared that we were at the dawning of Scottish ecclesiastical art. It is perhaps more evident from his particular vantage point. The Scottish Episcopal Church alone seems to have paid much attention to the development of a distinctively national ecclesiastical art. The modern influence of the Roman Catholic Church has been all in a lamentably anti-æsthetic direction.

The Carnegie Trust has failed to encourage creative activities of any kind – although in America, for example, its counterpart subsidises poets. In architecture Charles Macfarlane had to leave Scotland to exercise a profound modernist influence on recent building all over the Continent (a change which has failed to have the slightest repercussions in his native country). The Scottish traditions themselves, admirably adapted to the character and coloration of the country, have given way to quite inappropriate English brick constructions and bungaloiditis generally. We have no distinctive tradition in furniture or furnishings or in any of the applied arts. The provisions in connection with the McCaig Memorial at Oban for the production *ad infinitum* of statues of the testator's family were set aside by the legal authorities; but so far as public money is spent on paintings in Scotland it is largely a like direction – on the portraits of the countless provosts and baillies which glut our public galleries. And even then the commissions are entrusted, not to the local artists, but to fashionable London painters. In other directions recent developments have been mostly of an arty-crafty kind. The immensely popular (if less in Scotland than outside it) Hebridean Songs of the late Mrs Kennedy-Fraser and her collaborator, the Rev. Kenneth MacLeod of Gigha, were simply the superimposition of an alien technique on the Gaelic originals. The Orpheus Choir and the Musical Festival Movement have both happily declined from the immense vogue they had a while back; they were too concerned with a bastard art and never with genuine creative developments. The evolution of Scottish music (save in the work of its one composer of genius, Francis George Scott) has neither addressed itself to its real problems (which are not the slick adaptation of foreign techniques but the evolution of authentic Scottish techniques – the refusal to leave the major initiative elsewhere – and the erection of art-song on old folk-song basis, or *ab ovo* on the *motifs* of our actual life today) nor acquired an adequate knowledge of what our people have done in the past – in for example the *Ceol Mor*, or 'big' pipe-music. Even those most concerned with piping have no thought of resuming this great tradition, but are content with tuney degenerate stuff. The cult of the clarsach is a mere waste of time, an irredeemable futility. The tapestry-weaving of the late Skeoch Cumming and his associates is another arty-crafty concern, with no relationship to creative art; the Gaelic ornamentalism and pseudo-mythological work of John Duncan and others falls into the same category. So does the revival of Scottish country dancing – or *contrée* dancing, to give it its proper name. It is only the gymnastic mimicry of old emotions of our people which embodied themselves in these forms; real creative work would be to find effective and æsthetically comparable dance-forms to embody contemporary feelings. A Scottish ballet comparable to the Russian (though the 'Highland Fling' propensity and general dramatic quality of native Scottish life suggest the right material) is inconceivable. Scottish dancing as a whole has been abominably occluded by jazz on the one hand, and on the other by the competitive spirit exemplified in the bemedalled exhibitors at so-called Highland gatherings.

The one sculptor of nation size – and more than nation size – we have ever produced, James Pittendreigh MacGillivray, has suffered from the lack of financial facilitation for the big classical works in public statuary for which is genius was best fitted, and has unfortunately had to confine himself for the most part to minor pieces. He is an isolated phenomenon, with no apparent disciple or successor. A striking feature in any consideration of modern Scottish arts is the absence of any emergence in this sphere of that scientific and constructional genius which has been one of Scotland's main contributions to the world, and which should surely have fitted us to excel in modernist art. We are a race of great engineers who are cutting no figure in the Machine Art era; we are a race of metaphysicians singularly inconspicuous in the development of abstract art; we are an eccentric and enterprising people inexplicably backward in artistic experimentation. This seems to be due to our unconsciousness of our national historical role and characteristics – or at least to our failure to bring these up to date and translate them effectively into the terms, not of their sterotyped bearings, but of the various arts, properly approached with a 'knowledge of our own time'. An almost incredible lack of knowledge of or interest in our own past accounts for this; we are almost wholly *deracinées*; our aggressive 'wha's-like-us-ism' denotes an inferiority complex of the worst description.

The great lag in Gaelic and Scots scholarship is only now beginning to be made up; but a vast amount of work, a veritable *kulturkampf*, remains to be accomplished before even an effective minority of our people can be put in possession of this dual spiritual birthright. The official Nationalist movement is a very superficial, unScottish and quite uncultural thing – a mere local variation of the current political staple, sedulously avoiding all fundamental considerations. The remarkable proliferation of new Scottish novelists has little bearing on my subject; the widespread Community Drama Movement calls for no mention in an article devoted to the arts; and there has been practically no radical revaluation or constructive criticism or philosophical implementation. The Scottish Players are on a much lower level than the Irish Players. The very tentative beginnings of Scottish Gaelic drama seem to have petered out with the untimely death of Donald Sinclair a couple of years ago. Although the past decade has produced a few able and active workers in most of the necessary spheres, their labours remain elementary, sectional and unsynthesised, while the overriding tendencies are all in the opposite direction. Despite the existence of several film guilds, national kinema art has scarcely made the merest beginnings in Scotland, though the excellent documentary work of John Grierson, Arthur Elton and others should be mentioned; but so far as the big public is concerned, this is swamped in atrocious Hollywood travesties of Bonnie Prince Charlie and the other great romantic stands-by. The Scottish BBC has a tiny margin of autonomy, but that is still for the most part adscripted to Harry-Lauder-Harry-Gordon funniosities – in other words, to what England and Anglicised Scotland regard as typically Scottish when it is actually the opposite. Distinctive Scottish arts of the slightest consequence must progressively found themselves on our real – as distinct from this music-hall – basis.

Hugh M'Diarmid, September 1934

New Scotland (Alba Nuadh)
incorporating *The Free Man*
1935–1936

Alleged Scots Scholarship

I had once occasion to write an article in which, *inter alia*, I quoted James Colville's amazing exposé of the pretended Scots scholarship of Mr George Eyre Todd; an exposé which listed some of the most egregious errors in the English glossing of Scots words which have yet been put on record. It would seem that the practice of such editors of Scots poetry, when they do not know the meaning of a word or phrase, is to try to guess it from the context, or to find an English word that approximates to it in sound. In either case they begin with English preconceptions, and it betrays them into the most ludicrous misinterpretations. It is commonly believed, however, that in recent years we have won to a higher level of Scots scholarship and possess researchers with the necessary linguistic and historical knowledge and literary gifts, who can be trusted to furnish adequate translations or explanations, and have recourse to these dangerous literalisms. One of the best of these is generally taken to be Dr William Mackay Mackenzie, and amongst his main services to Scots Letters was his Porpoise Press edition of *The Poems of William Dunbar* (1932). This was widely reviewed when it appeared and attracted a great deal of attention. Its appearance was also signalised by a special 'Dunbar' dinner given by the Scottish P.E.N. with Mr Cunninghame Graham in the chair, Mr Lewis Spence as the principal speaker of the evening, and Dr Mackay Mackenzie himself as another of the speakers. So far as I have been able to discover, however, Dr Mackay Mackenzie's qualifications and the thoroughness of his work were simply taken for granted on all hands, and nowhere subjected to informed critical attention.

Let me therefore begin that process now, by examining carefully Dr Mackay Mackenzie's treatment of Dunbar's 'Ballad of Kind Kittock', and his glossarial and explanatory notes thereto. The poem begins: –

> *My gudame wes a gay wif, bot scho wes ryght gend,*
> *Scho duelt furth fer in to France, apon Falkland Fell*

Dr Mackay Mackenzie rightly glosses gend as simple, but with regard to the reference to France he observes, *tout court*; 'France. No district so named is known near Falkland.' Apart from anything that follows, this shows that he completely and hopelessly misunderstands not only the point of the line in question, but the nature and method of the whole poem. What the two lines actually mean is that: 'My gudame aped the smart set though she was just a peasant woman, and lived as though she had been right in France itself, though actually she never got further than Falkland Fell.' 'Duelt furth fer in France' only means that she was always 'far ben in French fashions'. So immediately we have a recognisable and perennial type of femininity.

But the chief gaffe comes when Dr Mackay Mackenzie attempts to explain the second of the next two lines: –

They callit her Kynd Kittok, quhasa hir weill kend:
Scho wes like a caldrone cruke cler under kell.

He only glosses 'cler under kell', and this is how he does it: '"Clear" in the sense "beautiful" under her "headdress".' This is utter nonsense, as Dr Mackay Mackenzie must himself have found if he had for a moment tried to associate the phrase with the 'cauldron crook' to which it is applied. What the line really means is that she was as black as a cauldron or a cauldron crook, and clearly seen as such under her 'kell', which word applies both to her headdress and to the 'kell' (chain, rod, or swey) to which the cauldron was attached and which, in contradistinction to the cauldron itself, was usually kept polished. Dunbar is not handing out pretty compliments to the good dame by the mouth of her sardonic husband. Consider the preceding line, 'They callit her Kynd Kittock, quhasa hir weill kend'. They called her Kynd Kittock – whoso knew her well! In other words it is writ sarcastic, and the term too was applied sarcastic. But there is also a play upon words which further intensifies the sarcasm; the line can also be read: 'They called her Kynd Kittock – who saw her well knew why!'

It is not as if these lines alone were affected. Dr Mackay Mackenzie had the whole poem to guide him, and it proceeds throughout on the basis of such contrarieties. The husband means the very opposite of what he says, and phrases himself so that what he really means never fails to transpire through words that superficially have the opposite sense. The poem is a devastating satire on women. The key to the method lies in such a phrase as she 'rade ane inche behind the taill'. It should not take any portentous academic degrees to understand exactly what that means. The good dame was a hopeless drunkard – 'she ate no meat, and drank beyond measure and more'; 'she slept until the morn at noon, *and rose early*' (another delightful characteristic contradiction in terms, and, beyond that, a graphic realisation of drunken psychology in such circumstances). The whole thing is a mordant satire, all the more so as, despite all the lady's faults, the man's humanity breaks through and temporarily overcomes his contemptuously appreciative humour in the first three of the last four lines: –

Friends, I pray you heartfully,
If you be thirsty or dry,
Drink with my Good Dame as you go by.

– only to be clinched all the more tremendously by the inimitable last line:

Once for my sake.

I have not gone through Dr Mackay Mackenzie's book with a small tooth-comb, but I have no doubt it abounds in examples of the same kind of slip-shod interpretation. It is impossible that it should be otherwise. A flat-footed literalistic approach to imaginative work, especially work of this kind, which turns on deep psychological understanding and quirks of humour in expression in keeping with those in the conception must necessarily betray him constantly into bloomers of the sort I have instanced. His utter failure to understand 'Kynd Kittok' cannot be a solitary example of the dangers of letting essentially non-literary people pose as authorities on the interpretation of creative work.

C.M. Grieve, 12 October 1935

Scotland, France & Working-class Interests

Let the English do what they will.
We Scots to France must be steadfast still!

Dear Mr Editor,

Congratulations on the first issue of *New Scotland*, which has just reached me in my hyperborean home.

While agreeing with the tenor of most of the articles in it, may I express the hope that, it will, in subsequent issues, get into closer and closer grips with actual affairs and possibilities in Scotland itself and in particular concentrate the attention of its readers on the fact that any professedly Scottish Nationalism that is not radically proletarian and Republican is not worth a damn. In a recent article Professor Saunders Lewis, President of the Welsh Nationalist Party, wrote: 'The Welsh working people see now that the English Labour Party and Trade Union Congress are imperialists, pro-Capitalist organisations, prepared to go to war in defence of the English Empire. Welsh Nationalism is the Welsh working people's only defence against English militarism.' It is high time the Scottish working people came to a similar realisation with regard to Scottish Nationalism and *New Scotland* will be a sorry disappointment unless it drives that home.

The 'Auld Alliance' can still rouse the hearts and claim the allegiance of thousands of Scots and it is vitally necessary at this moment in the interests of Scotland and of France and of Europe as a whole that this old allegiance should be greatly intensified and effectively related to current issues and practical affairs. England is playing the opposite game and despite denial after denial our Foreign Office, and National Government generally, is working hand in hand with Hitlerite Germany.

SCOTS BORE THE BRUNT

The Auld Alliance of Scotland and France may seem at first glance to have little enough to do with proletarian interests today; but those who think this, need to think again.

It is not only vitally related to proletarian interests, alike in France and Scotland and everywhere else, but to the issues of the Douglasite propaganda to which *New Scotland* is specifically devoted. Let me illustrate this: but let me first quote a passage, which every true Scot should have off by heart, from a poem by a great Scottish poet (though he wrote in Latin) – to wit, George Buchanan. That poets frequently have a remarkable prophetic faculty is a fact amply attested in literary history; and the following passage might well enough have been revised as an apt reminder to us at the present time and a piece of the shrewdest practical counsel, viz. (I quote from a prose translation by Mr Geo. E. Davie): –

> Charlemagne, too, who to the French gave the Latin fasces and Quirinus' robe [i.e. the symbols of European hegemony], and the French by treaty joined the Scots; a treaty which neither the War-God with iron, nor unruly sedition, can undo, nor mad lust for power, nor the succession of years, nor any other force. Tell over the list of France's triumphs since that age and of the conspiracies of the world in all its airts for the destruction of the French name – without the help of Scottish soldiers never victory shone upon the French camp; never really cruel disaster crushed the French without the shedding of Scottish blood, too; Scotland – this one nation – has shared the brunt of all the vicissitudes of French fortune; and the swords that threatened the French it has often diverted against itself. The bellicose English know this, to this the Po's waters are witness, and Naples attacked again and again by unsuccessful invasion. This is the dowry your wife offers you [i.e. Mary, Queen of Scots, in marrying Francis of France, to whom the poem was addressed], a nation for so many centuries faithful to your subjects and conjoined with them by a treaty of alliance – a people unsubjugated by arms through so many dangerous crises.

This is the real meaning for Scotland of 'Soutra's' warning (in *New Scotland* No. 1) that 'the alignments in the coming war will thus probably be England, Germany, Italy, and Japan against France and America.' There is no question about that – and Scotland must stand by France then through thick and thin. The whole aim and object of Scottish National Party now should be to hamper England in effecting that new alignment – and when the crisis comes Scotland's part must be to divert and destroy England's power in this connection, by secession from her and the transformation of the impending war into a civil war in Great Britain itself.

HARD FACTS AND WISHFUL THINKERS

In considering the full bearings of these contentions it would be well if readers remembered that Buckle justly said of Buchanan that he was the first to define popular rights, and in his *De Jure Regni Apud Scotes* 'justified by anticipation all subsequent revolutions'.

If any reader should ask, 'But what about proletarian interests, and about Douglasism, in particular?' it would be well that he or she should remember what has been happening in France and realise the true inwardness of the following passage from a recent issue of *The Week* (which clearly reveals the relationship which makes the present author believe, not only that Communism and Nationalism can go hand in hand, but that Communism is the only safeguard of nationalism, and ultimately of human personality, in the world today), viz.: –

> Hard facts behind the more or less disingenuous interpretation placed upon the now famous Moscow–Paris communiqué issued after the Stalin–Laval talks in Moscow indicate a movement in the position of the Third International which is none the less sensational for the fact that it is a change very different from that suggested by the 'wishful thinking' of the big press. Subscribers – particularly those who read the *Daily Telegraph* and the *Daily Herald* – will recall that in the course of that communiqué Stalin 'approved the considerations' which have led the French to adopt defensive measures against the Hitler menace. 'Wishful thinkers' – not least those in the Second International who have developed politically disastrous self-deception into a habit – happily concluded that this, in fact, foreshadowed the co-operation of the French Communist Party – now the strongest single party in Paris – with the 'defence' armament schemes of the Comité des Forges and Marshal Petain. According to one of our Paris correspondents, this ludicrous suggestion was not only broadcast but actually believed by certain elements in France, who gleefully hailed the alignment of the Third International with the armaments policy. The real situation – which is of basic international importance – is as follows. The victories of the Communists in the French municipal elections have consolidated a position already extraordinarily powerful. The Moscow communiqué, without of itself altering the position of the Third International, in fact signalised a movement of major importance. *The movement is in the direction of the consolidation around the Third International of those who in each country are genuinely 'patriotic' – are genuinely in favour of the defence of 'la patrie' – as opposed, for example, to the Comité des Forges, the Bank of England, and the other 'patriotic' leaders who have 'patriotically' armed Hitler Germany in a manner comparable to the now notorious supply by the notably patriotic firm of Vickers of the guns which killed the Anzacs, etc., at Gallipoli.* The immediately interesting and important fact

is that the Third International is now stressing the fact that national defence is of course a necessity – *in the sense of the defence of the people and their country against Fascist attack from at home or abroad.* But (and here are alike disappointed the hopes of the big press and of the Scottish International, which demands 'co-operation with the capitalist governments for national defence'), the Third International and especially the French Communist Party are making clear that in their view *the first step towards effective defence of the workers of any country against Fascist aggression – internal and external – is the control of the Army by and for the workers.* The French Communist Party is putting forward the demand for the 'elimination of Fascist elements from the Army.' On this demand are implicit (a) the demand for workers' control and organisations of a genuinely anti-fascist workers' defence corps' – and it is now evident that the French Communists will be content to support nothing less; (b) the fact that the Third International in France is now advanced to the position where it can begin to put forward this demand effectively as a step on the road to its ultimate objective, namely, the upset of the whole Capitalist set-up and all that that implies and the establishment of a revolutionary regime for the protection of French civilisation from its enemies, external and domestic.

SCOTTISH FASCISM

The Communist Party is right in regarding the official National Party of Scotland as a Fascist organisation. That was the whole aim and object of the *Daily Record*'s manœuvre – its precious *Plan For Scotland* and the formation of the Scottish National Development Council – to which the old National Party succumbed, and, as a result, fused with the Duke of Montrose's Scottish Party and fell under the leadership of people like the Duke of Montrose, Sir Alexander McEwan, Professor Dewar Gibb, and 'Annie S. Swan'. The real nationalists left it en bloc, and have since occupied themselves in other directions.

I accurately described the *Daily Record*'s and Duke of Montrose's fascistic manœuvre at the time.

All these people – these pseudo-nationalists – are Anglo-Scots, with no real knowledge of Scottish language or literature – insulated from it by English, and by the fact that they are cut off from the Scottish proletariat, all their concrete connections being with the denationalised Anglicised bourgeoisie. From this point of view, what is wrong with them – as with our Scottish Socialist Movement – is a complete failure to appreciate the truth of Count Keyserling's realisation that 'until a vital nucleus of individuals stands for a programme which shall be only the external expression of a vitally existing inner state, it will remain powerless.' It cannot be fairly said that any reformers have as yet adopted this attitude. I know of no Socialist who really wills what he advocates; if he comes into power he very soon lives and acts in the spirit of the very life-philosophy he formerly opposed and for that matter may go on opposing outwardly. That is where the importance of realising that you cannot be a Socialist, let alone a Communist, without breaking not only with Capitalistic politics and economics, but Capitalist culture as a whole – that you cannot be a Scottish Nationalist without breaking with English culture, lock, stock and barrel – comes in. The French communists are not concerned with the preservation of French civilisation as it has been – but with getting down to French *Ur*-motives, under Communism.

The workers in Scotland must do likewise. It is the only way out. Continued association with England, either in the present relationship or any other, or even continued allegiance to the dangerously and anti-democratically conspiring clique of cosmopolitan careerists in Windsor Castle, cannot but commit us to Fascism, the antithesis of the Scottish genius and the negation of its natural destiny and world-function. We can only rightly direct our affairs at the present time and in the future by rigid adherence to the policy that inspired us in the past – unbreakable alliance with France and continual war with England.

Yours for Scotland,
Hugh MacDiarmid

[N.B. – Part of the above letter is an extract from MacDiarmid's forthcoming book, *Red Scotland*.][1]

26 October 1935

Songs of the Egregious

> Mrs Marjorie Kennedy-Fraser tapped an almost untried source in Gaelic folk-poetry (though Burns did use a few Gaelic airs) and made the nation her debtor with her edition of the *Songs of the Hebrides*. To deride work of this kind as a tampering with the genuine product of the folk-spirit is inept and ungracious, yet it is still occasionally done. Not only is it clear that the essentials of the originals are generally preserved and that the alterations and additions are improvements, it is even doubtful if, in many cases, anything would have survived the interested labours of these collectors.

So writes Dr George S. Pryde in his and Principal Sir Robert Rait's ghastly volume, *Scotland* (1934). Dr Pryde's ignorance of the subjects on which he dogmatises so heavily in his section of that volume is so egregious that it is not worth while correcting his errors, but the view he expresses of Mrs Kennedy-

1. 'Red Scotland' was never published. A typescript survives in the National Library of Scotland – *Eds*.

Fraser's (and her collaborator, Dr Kenneth Macleod's) work is so generally entertained and his attitude to criticism thereof so common that I feel impelled once again to denounce the collection in question. I shall give a few examples to show conclusively how absurdly untrue it is (despite Mrs Kennedy-Fraser's own assertion that she had not departed from the originals more than was absolutely necessary) that the essentials of the originals are preserved; and in regard to Dr Pryde's last sentence it is only necessary to point out how long the songs and airs in question were preserved before Mrs Kennedy-Fraser 'collected' them and to add that the amount so 'collected' and published up to date is still only a fraction of the amount available, and in quality poor in comparison to much that has still oral currency in the isles but has not yet been rendered available to a wider public (though, to a large extent, now taken down by real 'collectors', not 'improvers' – and ready for publication once funds and public interest – or the likelihood of the latter – justify the enterprise). Defenders of the *Songs of the Hebrides*, such as Dr Pryde and Mr Angus Robertson, have to explain away the very just sentiment (generally entertained by all Gaels who know the originals and the store of unpublished and far superior material) voiced (by an old woman) on the Island of Raasay who had a great repertoire of them and who asked to give a few of those she knew to Mrs Kennedy-Fraser, replied 'Dia cobhair do chorp, gun toirinn-se dhilh nah-orain aluinn air son am pronnadh!' (God help your body, that I should give her the beautiful songs to pound them!) (That – to pound them, to make a hash of them – is all that Mrs Kennedy-Fraser and her collaborator did with such of the material as came within their reach).

Proof? I wish I had space to deal with the matter thoroughly – to go through the whole of the *Songs of the Hebrides*, but the following few examples must suffice in the meantime. We find, for instance: –

> Mairead og, Mairead my girl,
> Thy sea-blue eyes with witchery
> Haunt me by night, out on the deep,
> I cannot sleep for love of thee.

What the Gaelic original actually says is: – 'O young Margaret, it is you who wounded me; you are the lovely graceful girl; Bluer your eye than in the calm morning the blaeberry behind the leaves.' Again, we are given 'Ailein duinn, thy winding sheet of white sea foam is loosely woven' for – God knows what! Perhaps for: – 'Wretched is the tale I hear tonight. It is not the cattle's loss in maytime, but the wetness of your shroud.' There are scores of

Similar and Grosser Falsifications

littered through the whole 'collection'; wholesale sacrifices of great beauty and the true Gaelic spirit to a wretched sloppiness and an entirely alien mysticism consorting as lamentably with the temper of the originals as unbridled and unscrupulous sexuality often does with certain kinds of intense religiosity.

It is one of those responsible for such egregious fraud and shoddy substitution – Dr Kenneth MacLeod – that Mr Angus Robertson can write: 'It would not be taxing the imagination too rigidly if we visualised Kenneth MacLeod symbolising the Coolins of Skye, the Scurr of Eigg, and the Bens of Jura as the Crom-Sleuchd of the bard's confessional – the beacon-heads from which the shades of

The Mysterious Druids

transmit the secrets of their Pherylt to those selected of the race who had inherited the gift of song.' Or, again the same

Incredibly Fatuous

writer can note 'the prolific versification of Donnachadh Ban MacIntyre and the majestic numbers of Alasdair Mac Mhaighstir Alasdair', and go on to say 'But the poetry of these masters of verse and assonance, compared to Kenneth MacLeod's, is like the crooning of a baby to the detonations of thunder.' The words in which such an utterance can be adequately characterised are all unprintable, alas; but Mr Robertson's ridiculous essays and the whole acceptance of the Kennedy-Fraser-Kenneth MacLeod product, amply under-score the clamant necessity for a Gaelic University (the project in which absurdly enough – unless he is to be credited with an incredible awareness of his own deficiences – Mr Robertson is so actively interested) and fully bear out what Mr William Power says in his *Literature and Oatmeal*, when he writes: –

> Most of the modern Scots-Gaelic poets seem merely to be emulating second-rate English poets. They had got out of touch with the real genius of the language. That is a reason or a symptom of the decline of Scots Gaelic from its old position as a tongue of bards and scholars to its lowly status as a kind of Taal whose ordinary possessors can hardly understand any Gaelic much earlier than 1800,

and claims that Alasdair MacMhaighstir Alasdair's great poem 'The Birlinn of Clanranald' 'is the supreme example, almost painful in its effect, of the complete indentification of the Celtic mind with all nature and life. But it is totally beyond the comprehension of the average Gael today.'

There is precious little that isn't.

Hugh MacDiarmid, 16 November 1935

The League and Little Me

Such Bunk

If it hadn't been for the *Daily Record* – 'Scotland's National Newspaper' – (with its wee red lion) – I'd never have known what a wonderful person I am. Now I know, thanks to Mr Sidney R. Campion *and* the *Daily Record*.

Sidney is evidently a most important person, high, high, up in the League of Nations. I never heard of him before, but that was when I was just me. Now I'll never forget him. Never!

Hark to the glad news, because you too, are a most important person.

Sidney speaks: –

> You, the individual voter, are a Member of the League of Nations. You do not attend the meetings of the League at Geneva. But you delegate your duties to the Foreign Minister, and to the Minister for League of Nations Affairs, whoever they may be.
>
> Through your vote you have expressed yourself as being in favour of collective security – the great principle which is enshrined in the heart of the Covenant of the League.
>
> Great Britain has joined with many nations in trying to make the League a success. She has signed the Kellogg Pact whereby she has solemnly pledged to renounce war as an instrument of national policy.
>
> You yourself did not sign that Kellogg Pact, but your elected representatives signed it for you. It was your wish, and that wish they fulfilled on your behalf.

Dear, dear, it leaves me speechless, but not quite. I can command breath enough to say I never read such bunk. Sidney R. Campion, and the people who publish such stuff must think Scotland has more nit-wits in it than it really has.

'The individual voter' has as much say in the appointments of the Foreign, or any other Ministers, as the man in the moon, while the suggestion that the electors were ever consulted about the Kellogg Pact, or given the requisite information upon which to base an opinion is too ridiculous to require refutation. The whole thing is ridiculous from the beginning, for there is no justification whatever for the opening statement, either constitutionally or otherwise, and what good this 'National Newspaper' expects to do to Scotland by propagating this sort of stuff is one of the mysteries of Hope Street.

H. McD., 23 November 1935

Communism and Nationalism: Mr Grieve Replies

We have received from Whalsay, Shetland Islands, a reply to the recent criticism by Mr P. Kerrigan of Hugh MacDiarmid. Mr Grieve writes: –

Dear Friend: –

It would have been wiser of Mr P. Kerrigan to read what is said in the *Soviet Encyclopaedia* concerning Hugh MacDiarmid before launching the attack upon me in *The Daily Worker* which you reproduced in your issue of 1st inst.

The whole question of how Scotland is to be won for Communism, and of the relation of Scottish Nationalism (as advocated by me and those associated with me – by, that is to say, the revolutionary section of Scottish Nationalists) to Communism requires to be thoroughly thrashed out, and, as a very small beginning to that urgently necessary and long overdue process I hope to have a public debate on the matter with Comrade Fred Douglas or some other Comrade at the very first available opportunity when I am next in the Edinburgh district.

As matters stand, Mr Kerrigan has butted in to an argument without any knowledge of the terms of debate whatever and as a consequence has shown nothing but presumptuous ignorance. My letter to you to which he took exception was, as stated, mainly composed of a few paragraphs from a book of mine entitled *Red Scotland* which is to be published in January – and would have been published ere this but for the fact that for several months I have been put out of the fighting line by a critical illness from which I am now convalescent. It was not, however, a *critical* illness in the same sense of the adjective as that from which Mr Kerrigan is suffering, in that blindness and an abject abandonment of the principles of dialects was not its character. Mr Kerrigan would have been

Well Advised to Wait

for the publication of that book instead of trying to pick me up on a few sentences torn out of their context in a work of over forty thousand words devoted to a whole series of vitally important and hitherto little-considered matters in relation to Scotland.

It is a pure assumption on his part that Scotland and England are an economic unit, and while he and his kind may consider the so-called Union indissoluble and any talk of separation fantastically impracticable a greater than he and they in the person of no less than Engels was of the same opinion in regard to the practicality of separating Ireland from the United Kingdom – *but had to change his view as Mr Kerrigan will soon have to change his.*

Scotland is in no other case than Ireland and Poland were, and the pronouncements of Communists in regard to Scottish Independence should not be otherwise than the quite unequivocal pronouncements of Marx, Engels, Quin and Stalin in the latter cases, nor the condition of Scotland from a Communist standpoint to be able unless it is given at least an autonomy equal to that of one of the smaller Russian republics and equal freedom and facilitation to develop its distinctive culture. That is what I and the Nationalists who think with me want. It does not conflict in the very slightest either with Communism or with the practice of the USSR in regard to minority languages and cultures. But it is the very antithesis of what prevails in Scotland today under the English Ascendancy.

The so-called 'Union' of Scotland and England is 'all my eye and Betty Martin'. It is

Simply An Illusion

created by pro-English propaganda to facilitate the subordination and exploitation of Scottish interests by English. To regard it as anything more or other than that requires a suspension of all examination and inquiry – an occlusion of

Scotland similar to that effected by pro-English propaganda in the great bulk of our population. Mr Kerrigan looks like a typical example of these. If, as he says, by calling the TUC and the Labour Party pro-Imperialist organisations I am libelling the hundreds of thousands of workers who create these bodies, I have no hesitation in replying that if he regards England and Scotland as united (in any other sense than its prey is lodged in the tiger's belly) or fails to recognise that, despite their proximity, there are no two peoples in Europe so different from each other as the English and the Scottish he is libelling the entire Scottish people and in doing so in the name of Communism he is libelling Communism too.

It is typical of such a poor controversialist as Mr Kerrigan that he cannot refrain from being personal and first insinuates that I am not really a proletarian and secondly that I do not understand Communism. With regard to the second I have certainly no need to covet Mr Kerrigan's 'understanding' of Communism or anything else. He has given no proofs of any intelligence worth a moment's notice and it is characteristic of his ill-conditioned stupidity that in the present state of affairs in Scotland he should attack me of all people. I may not be an ideal exponent of the Marxist cause but whether or not, the objective fact is that I am the only such exponent who has the ear of any considerable part of the Scottish reading public, or, in particular, of our student body (the importance of which, together with that of the teaching profession, to which I also have special access, was so rightly stressed from a Communist standpoint by D.S. Mirsky in his *The Intelligentsia of Great Britain*). I am also the only Scottish writer who is a professed Communist – a member of the CP – and engaged in a 'propaganda of ideas'. Communism in Scotland is not in so strong a position that it can afford to attack a man of my type instead of *getting on with the job* of disposing of its innumerable implacable enemies. For Mr Kerrigan is also wrong in his first insinuation – that I am not really a proletarian but only profess to be. I hope his own Socialist record is as clear and undeviating as mine has been since my early teens, and I hope that over a like period of nearly thirty years he has played as active a part as a Socialist in public affairs and by voice and by pen as I have done. I was born of working class parents and have never allowed myself to be divorced from the working class. The Capitalist system knows that well enough to keep me on its 'black list' and prevent my obtaining employment, so that, though I am nationally and internationally probably the best-known Scot of my age, I am debarred from pursuing my profession in the columns of all our Capitalist papers and compelled to subsist on no more than the equivalent of the dole.

The difference between Scotland's cause and the nationalist cause in countries like Ireland and Poland is simply that the case of these countries was effectively formulated and forced into the open. But shallow thinkers need not imagine that Scotland's cause is going to be allowed to go by default. The objective basis exists and will assert itself and progressively free itself from

All the Distortions

alike of Imperialism and Capitalist interests and of ignorance and lack of consideration. As Dimitrov says national proletarian movements do not conflict with proletarian internationalism. But Scotland is not going to be left out of account in that ultimate comity of nations but is going to have equal autonomy there with all the others. What are Communists doing in Scotland at all if not working to achieve a Communist Scotland? People like Mr Kerrigan simply cut the ground away from under their own feet if they deny the potential existence of a Scotland of sovereign independence.

There is nothing in what Mr Kerrigan quotes from Dimitrov with which I am not entirely in accord. But why does Mr Kerrigan quote Dimitrov? Dimitrov may be 'a great Communist', as Mr Kerrigan says, but he has no rank as a Communist thinker. I believe Mr Kerrigan quoted him for the same reason that he rushed to attack me in the *Daily Worker* – in other words, because Mr Kerrigan has read and understood exceedingly little but is so immersed in mere topicalities that he is entirely incapable of any objective viewpoint. Dimitrov has been 'in the news', by attacking me Mr Kerrigan gets into the news too for a brief moment, but long enough perhaps to give unaccustomed joy to his mean spirit. If his spirit is not too mean, it would pay him better to devote a little attention

To Objective Realities

in Scotland today; I will be glad to encounter him or anybody else on *that* basis at any time – but they will require to bring up heavier intellectual cannon than Dimitrov and a far more thorough knowledge of Communist ideology than Mr Kerrigan vouchsafes any glimpse of yet, and together with these a passionate concern with the knowledge of Scotland that can only be acquired as I have acquired them – by a lifetime's disinterested labour. If Mr Kerrigan had given – not a lifetime's – but only two minutes such attention to the matters upon which he writes, he would have written very differently, instead of rushing into a debate of which he has no understanding whatever.

Yours sincerely,
C.M. Grieve
('Hugh MacDiarmid')

14 December 1935

I Want No Empty Unity

As, perhaps, one of the 'hard-working and enthusiastic Nationalists' referred to in paragraph two of the quotation from the February issue of the *Scots Independent* with which the article entitled 'Is This The Time to Swither?' in *New Scotland* of 29 February opens, I crave space to make it clear:

1. That I am not prepared to let 'bygones be bygones' in regard to Scotland's enemies inside Scotland – inside professedly Scottish Nationalist movements even – any more than I am prepared to do so with regard to England itself.
2. I share to the full the anti-English sentiments of M. Béraud referred to in the same issue.
3. I do not consider a multiplicity of organisations a bad thing at this juncture, nor would I prefer to see a unity of Scottish Nationalists secured by postponing consideration of the whole range of fundamental issues upon which it is highly unlikely that any considerable number of Scotland's inhabitants can find themselves in INSTRUCTED agreement.
4. I stress the word INSTRUCTED – for I consider Scotland's worst enemies those who no matter for what reason have failed to come to right conclusions in the crucial problems of modern civilisation. These include the great majority of those who have up to now been prominently concerned in the promotion of our divers in Scotland Nationalist bodies. I am not going to waste time again in association with any of these gentry. My friend Guy Aldred, in one of his election addresses, asked only for thoroughly instructed supporters. He was right, and a popular movement, no matter how numerous its membership, which is open to the membership of the inadequately instructed is not worth a damn.
5. I, for one, am a Communist, and I would not lift a finger to secure any degree of Scottish Autonomy short of or other than a Scottish Workers' Republic.

In particular, since the article quoting the *Scots Independent* refers particularly to the 'unsuitability' of the Duke of Montrose (as to which I am, of course, in complete agreement), I wish to state that I am completely unconnected with any Protestant Church or Society, and hold no belief for these, but in view mainly of my attitude to the question of the so-called 'Irish Invasion' (the existence of which I deny) I must add that I am utterly opposed to Roman Catholicism, and refuse in any connection to associate myself with members of that Church which can have no place in Scotland I consider worth working to create and personally will have nothing to do with any movement which includes ANY of the office-bearers or Parliamentary candidates of the SNP or such ridiculous ignoramuses as the author of the article on 'This Obscurity Business' or as the F.M. who wrote the pitiably silly article on 'Conservative Critics and "Communist" Poets', (both of which articles appeared in *New Scotland* of 15 February).

In conclusion, let me say emphatically that despite the betrayal of the earlier and more promising movement by the SNP since the fusion, despite the stupidity and futility of the other petty little factions, and despite the number of vocal 'Scottish Nationalists' with whom it is an intolerable ignominy for any intelligent man to allow his name to be linked, however remotedly, the Scottish Movement as a whole is making splendid progress – much greater progress than the Irish Movement or the German Aufklarung, for example, made in a like interval of time – and will continue to do so, directed as it is to great ends which are beyond any possibility of popularising or even of 'giving any idea of' to the great bulk of our population, irretrievably sunk (as David Hume said of the English in 'Christianity and Ignorance').

Note: I write these few paragraphs because I find a widespread belief that my influence is behind the 'unity movement' to undo the disastrous action the National Party of Scotland took when it fused with the Scottish Party. I have nothing to do with these manoeuvres, and frankly regard the leaders of the SNP and its membership at large, as 'not worth bothering about' that is to say, not worth MY while, at any rate. Neither they, nor any of their kind, are necessary to the achievement of Scots Independence – nor can they do much to impede and delay the great movement which is, for the most part, moving completely over their heads.

Hugh McDiarmid, 28 March 1936

Constricting the Dynamic Spirit: we want life abundant

Owing to the bias given to human mentality by economic, political, religious, and other factors (including above all the *vis inertia*) what we call 'thought' but is generally only 'rationalism' of our preconceived or inherent prejudices, or limitations, conscious or unconscious, of our powers of thought to suit our interests or what we 'think' to be our interests, has got us into a rut – and we generally regard 'thought' as synonymous with particular habits of intellection which represent only a fraction of our latent powers of thought. A useful analogy is what is known as 'orthodox' economics – which has usually nothing whatever to do with economics but is a purely artificial and arbitrary substitution for economic thought. Bergson has a great deal to say of these misleading superficial 'crusts', which must be broken through to release the dynamic spirit which has no more to do with these incrustations than a running stream has to do with a layer of ice which forms on its surface.

The 'stream of consciousness' is still more independent of all the formulations of rationalism. The human spirit is not to be 'cribbed, cabbined and confined' in any creeds, conventions, or formulae whatever. It is no use asking the meaning of a poem; before one can profit by a poem one must get into line with it and let it flow through one. It is futile to ask what it 'means'. It is equally futile to ask what I mean – the question is what I am, what dynamic spirit I manifest. An apple and a pear may both be fruit and of a like size, but they have a very different flavour, and there exist no words in which to express this difference. It is nameless but obvious and complete to tasters. In the same way all people who try to pin writers down to 'consistency', to 'logic', are insisting on saying not an apple nor a pear, but 'fruit', I have no more use for 'consistency' of this kind than I have for any other shibboleth which tries to confine the infinite vitality and potentiality of humanity to any particular 'rut', and my objection to any such process is precisely the root of my nationalism. I do not believe in – or in the desirability of – any 'likemindness', any 'common purpose', any 'ultimate objective', but simply in 'life and all that more abundantly', in the lifting of all suppressions and thwarting or warping agencies. My communism in this sense is purely Platonic; as I have said in my 'First Hymn to Lenin' I do not believe that any one – and least of all the crowd – will willingly be deprived of the 'good', nor do I believe that my own, or anybody else's ideas of the latter are valid. I am as all poets and dynamic spirits must be – purely 'irrational'. (The emphasis is on the 'purely'.) Under the exigencies of the circumstances in which in Russia it evolved and triumphed Communism necessarily took a certain course and complexion which differentiates it from pure communism (without in any way detracting from its current political and practical consequences); and it is good Leninist-Marxian dialectic to take full account of its materialistic determination. Under existing circumstances I am an orthodox Communist, subscribing without any hesitation or qualification to Moscow direction – and, as such, am least liable to any correction from those otherwise minded politically who are, consciously or unconsciously, affected in their opinions by London or Threadneedle Street or Wall Street.

But I agree with A.R. Orage that the Soviet system is still unfortunately working within the limits of the existing financial system and has not faced up to the fact that Douglasism has knocked the bottom out of the whole economic problem. The character of its development, historically determined, has proceeded on other bases – psychological, racial, and so forth – and the force and significance of these remain, and call for their ultimate resolution, but on other than economic grounds. The complete solving of the economic problem – the ensuring of plenty for all – will not, to my mind, solve the essential issues bound up with the Communist question, but it will dispose of those purely economic issues generally regarded as the essence of the class war, but which to my mind obscure its real essentials. The warped mental processes which result in purely traditional or doctrinaire positions will, so far as Communism is concerned (to get rid of its 'NEP' adjustments and other compromises with circumambient 'Capitalism', and its terrible 'puritanical' circumscription to the theory of 'all must work' and the denial of that scientific trend towards the leisure state which tends to make it not Communism proper but simply a logical further development of Capitalism), be liquidated as soon as money is regarded not as something concrete but simply as a function, and Douglasism is seen to be not an idea at variance with Communism but as a technique equally available under

Capitalism or Communism just as physical functions such as breathing are.

We must oppose every attempt at finality – every system that seeks to constitute a closed order – every theory which threatens to put an end to the restless ever-changing spirit of mankind; and as Dostoievski pointed out long ago every human organisation sooner or later aims at that.

I remember Mr Johnston telling me years ago that the *Forward* wanted facts, not ideas. He ought to have borne in mind Macdonald's remark on the extreme complexity of that almost indefinable conception 'a fact', and realised that facts and figures are useless – what matters is the interpretation put upon them. There are too many of this kind in Scotland. That is why I have from the outset opposed all cut-and-dried programmes and held that the objective of the Scottish Nationalist Movement is simply and solely to rouse the dynamic spirit of our people, regardless of the course it subsequently takes. From this standpoint I appreciate the value of diverse incitements and all manner of apparently opposed and conflicting doctrines; and thoroughly detest all those who seek to reduce the variety of life to any particular mould.

C.M. Grieve, 2 May 1936

Outlook
1936

A Scottish-American Communist Poet

I have already expressed the opinion that Norman Macleod, the Scottish-American Communist poet, is one of the most important Scottish writers, or writers of Scottish extraction, now living. His latest book – *Thanksgiving before November* (The Parnassus Press, New York) greatly reinforces that view. It contains over sixty poems, grouped in three sections, respectively entitled 'Early Battle Cry', 'Footnote to These Days', and 'Communications from the Revolution', and illustrates impressively not only the great range of his work but, although there is only internal evidence to indicate the chronology of composition, the steady growth of his powers in keeping with the developing crisis of Capitalist society. All his work is vibrant with the tensions of the crucial problems of the proletariat and of revolutionary activity today, and his diction and figures have the freshness and power that comes from first-hand experience of the subjects of which he writes and every life-or-death involvement in them. There is no 'above the battle' attitude – no 'emotion recollected in tranquillity' – about these poems. But they have a steel-like strength that comes from their being informed throughout with the logic of dialectical materialism. Some time ago Macleod suggested to me that he might come back to Scotland. I wish he would. Scotland has probably nothing to give him, but he might give Scotland a great deal. How parochial we Scottish writers are in comparison! Our literary organization affords us, comparatively speaking, such a hole-and-corner opportunity, such an 'Ivory Tower' incarceration. Internationalism is no more than a phrase to most of us. But America affords – and ensures – a world platform. By dint of what indefatigable contriving power could any young Scottish poet put himself in the position of being able to say of his work, as Macleod says in his little author's note to this beautifully produced volume, 'most of these poems have appeared in English – or in French or in Russian or in German or in Italian or in Spanish or in Japanese translation', and find it necessary, as is done here, to make acknowledgements to periodicals published in Tokyo, Rome, Verona (Italy), Savona (Italy), Moscow, the Hague, Mexico, and St Andrews, Scotland? It happens naturally to a young American poet – or, at all events, to a young American poet in the full swim of the international Communist movement. It is not only in this sense that Macleod's range is great, however; his sympathies and interests extend in all directions, his 'local colour' is taken from a world palette; and he sings the immemorial things of life and love and death as passionately and convincingly as he sings of strikes, the physical environments of the working day in the Machine Age, the beauties of nature, or his personal memories and problems. His technical powers are fully equal to the great variety of his subject-matter – we have here long poems and short poems, *cris-de-cœur* and epigrams that have the snap of a man-trap. Achievements in any one of the dozen different kinds he brings off so conclusively here would equip a greater poet than any of the boy-scout communistic poets of the latest English school. It is not only because America is such a racial melting-pot, and still less simply because he is in the swim of the international revolutionary movement, that Macleod has been able to secure such a world platform, but because he carries conviction wherever he turns and is so identified with the aspirations of struggling humanity the world over – whether he is writing of 'Young Manhood in Idaho', 'Homestead in Alberta', 'Off Finland', 'Pueblo Transition', 'Flower of Spring in Southern Utah', 'Mill-Workers', 'Fishermen of San Pedro', or 'Cotton Pickers in Alabama' – that he can make himself the authentic spokesman of each, and secure the world-wide currency and recognition that he does. Consider this short poem, for example:

Design in Cotton Fabric

The children are born with a taste of cotton root
In the mouths of their mothers (desperate
With the thought of more to feed). And they grow up to see
Fathers slaving picking cotton
Until their heads are whiter than cotton,
And they grow with poverty,
To enter the mills (living by grace
Of a god who is absent and a hell of a distance
Away). They die and bury solemnity,
And the lint of cottonwoods
Covers their graves.

Everywhere in this remarkable volume he manifests a spirit identical with that which he indicates in a footnote to the second-last poem I mentioned, viz.:

> The secretary of the fishermen's union, the Progressive Fishermen of San Pedro, stood on the corner of Sixth and Palo Verde in the business district, and spread out the fingers of his hand fanwise and said, *Like that we are nothing*, and clenched his hand into brass knuckles of strength, and said, *Like that we are power*. These poems are clenched apprehensions of actuality at the end of a sensitivity and dauntless human sympathy and determination coterminous with the whole Earth.

There is no indication of the price of this book on the copy that Macleod has sent me; it is certainly worth infinitely more than any price that is likely to be asked for it. Bravo, Macleod! More power to your elbow! The hour is at hand.

Hugh MacDiarmid, July 1936

Students' Front
1936

The Students' Front Agains the Students' Affront
Principle Against the Principal
A Culture With A Lie In Its Right Hand

TRADITION, AND –

We read, in the biography of the celebrated Dr William Cullen, once Professor of Medicine in the University of Edinburgh, that in 1766 when certain vacancies were under consideration

> the students came forward, and presented an address to the Lord Provost, Magistrates, and Town Council, wherein they boldly stated 'we are humbly of the opinion that the reputation of the University and magistrates, the good of the city, and our improvement will all, in an eminent manner, be consulted by engaging Dr Gregory to relinquish the professorship of the practice for that of the theory of medicine, by appointing Dr Cullen, present professor of chemistry, to the practical chair, and by electing Dr Black professor of chemistry.'

The students' proposals were adopted.

TRUTH

Imagine any such representations being entertained from the student body today – let alone adopted! The trend is all in the opposite direction; and at no point has that change operated to the advantage of the students, the relative reputation of the University of Edinburgh, the higher calibre of its alumni, or the strengthening of our national culture.

HARVARD FIRST

'To the surprise of almost no one,' says a recent writer,

> the ambitious plan of Harvard University on its three-hundredth birthday to synthesize the specialised branches of modern scholarship into a unified and coherent system of thought and belief progressed no further than the titles of the symposia. Even the most remarkable assemblage of scholars ever to gather in the United States, including eleven Nobel Prize winners, and representing institutions which span the entire genealogy of the University tradition from Abelard to Antioch, could not produce from all their academic

mortarboards the white rabbit of spiritual and intellectual unity.

EDINBURGH NOWHERE

I believe that our Universities should give a lead to our national life. They conspicuously fail to do anything of the sort. Harvard at least tried. Edinburgh has made no such effort and if, as presently constituted, it did, its failure would be still more utterly ignominious. The authorities are committed to shameful courses which they dare not openly avow but covertly pursue. The University is handed over to an abject service of the 'status quo'. The besetting problems of our time are officially eschewed instead of being brought to the imagination of the student body, and to prevent a healthy realisation of these problems and a response to them in keeping with the best traditions of Scottish national life, while, at the same time, encouraging the employment of the students as scabs in labour troubles and prostituting them to the foul purposes of the war-makers of English Finance, Capitalism and Imperialism is a tragic breach of public responsibility. The whole attitude of our University authorities is time-serving and treacherous and callous and cowardly in the extreme. Their base betrayal of the spirit of our people in the face of the crucial problems of the age follows naturally upon their whole tradition of trickery and treachery in lesser things. The gravamen of my case against the present attitude of the University Authorities lies in the facts: –

1. That in a country in which the majority of the entire electorate vote for the Left (a vote stultified by the English connection) the University is a centre of obstinate and unscrupulous reaction.
2. That the University has an insolent English Ascendancy contempt and disregard for our Scottish national culture, which does nothing whatever to preserve and promote and everything it possibly can do to belittle, ignore, or subvert.

BACKSTAIRS INTRIGUES

In regard to the shameful treatment of our Scottish Universities *vis-à-vis* the English Universities in respect of Government grants, our University authorities have signally failed to bring this gross injustice to the due notice of the Scottish people, but on the contrary have indulged in disgraceful backstairs intrigues of which the open support of the authorities of Mr Ramsay Macdonald was the most striking, with a view to wheedling out of the English Government some portion of these unjustly-withheld monies in order to apply these in various surreptitious ways for hostelisation schemes and other fascising purposes at complete variance alike with the traditions of the Scottish Universities and with the repeatedly expressed desires of the majority of the Scottish people.

DEMAND – DON'T INTRIGUE

It is time to put an end once and for all these base intrigues and the best way to ensure that this is done seems to me by means of a working Lord Rector, truly representative of and responsible to the student body.

It is high time, too, to protest against the misrepresentations of Lord Macmillan and other agents of Capitalism and tools of Imperialism that this, that, and the other limitation of our University facilities is due to poverty or to any cause whatever except the rationalisation of education in the interests of decadent Capitalism and anti-Scottish Imperialism, and the gross financial injustice of the English Government to the Scottish Universities, an injustice in keeping with the injustice of the English Ascendancy to every aspect of Scottish arts and affairs.

I need only recapitulate here the main points of the programme in regard to purely academic politics on which my present campaign is based:

1. Sir Thomas Holland's unconstitutional fostering of Dr Pollock on the unwilling SRC as their assessor in the autumn of 1935.
2. His public declaration (in an interview printed in the *Edinburgh Evening Dispatch* and *Edinburgh Evening News*) in June 1936, about the necessity for destroying the office of Lord Rector.
3. His statement about the advisability of giving the SRC semi-proctorial powers of fining students etc. for offences against discipline.
4. The fact that the quinquennial report of the Grants-in-Aid Committee published in June 1936, outlining Government policy towards the Scots Universities makes no mention of their claim for financial equality with the English Universities and urges bringing them into conformity with the English Universities by means of hostelisation, tutorial systems, better discipline, etc. – all of which, however apparently harmless, represent a deep-laid scheme for the final subversion of Scottish culture, the transformation of students into Boy Scouts-on-Promotion, and the complete assimilation of our Universities (*except in liberality of Government grants*) to English technical colleges.

BUNDLES OF BLOODY RAGS

I wish to see the big arrears of Government grants and the greatly increased annual grants hereafter if the Scottish Universities are at least treated on the basis to which they are entitled and which the English Universities now enjoy, not devoted to erecting fascising barracks of hostels (from which in the interests of culture? – *The New Statesman and Nation* can be quietly excluded in favour of *The Bystander*) as a breeding place for the officer class and for strike-breakers, sycophants, and snobs who believe that the chief end of man is, as D.H. Lawrence said, 'to be trained like beasts to make movements when they hear a shout' – in short, a better purpose than as an ante-room to the so-called Scottish National War Memorial and manufactory for better-educated 'bundles of bloody rags', but to the provision of additional cultural facilities in the Scottish Universities (e.g. Chairs in Scottish Literature and Scots and Gaelic, and in Russian, Scandinavian, and other modern languages and literatures), and the endowment of all kinds of research other than for the purposes of Imperialist War. I wish to see a big improvement in the personnel of our professionate and a profound change in their sense of human and national responsibility. I wish to see the Scottish Universities regain their lost international prestige, and I believe that the way to these objectives lies through the remedying of the scandalous injustice of the Government to our Universities financially; in a proper relation of our Universities to our distinctive national culture and will of the majority of our people; and in the extirpation of the prostitution of our Universities to the foul ends of Imperialism, snobbery and vicious futility, and in the undoing of the disastrous assimilation to English standards, and a *wholesale, and wholesome, reversion to a free student democracy in keeping with the noblest traditions of the Scottish Educational System.*

C.M. Grieve ('Hugh MacDiarmid'), 1936

Commentary

SCOTTISH HOME RULE (1927)

'Sir Walter Scott and Scottish National Finance'

p.9 *international Jew-controlled* Anti-Semitism went along with faith in Social Credit, in Ezra Pound as in Major Douglas himself. It is highly significant, then, that MacDiarmid only very rarely, as here, breathes the faintest hint of anti-Semitism, of which a casual and callow form was then commonplace even in liberal literary circles.

THE NEW AGE (1927–8)

'Scotland and the Banking System'

p.10 *new Government of Scotland Bill* 'Talked out' in the Commons.

Scottish National Convention Sponsored by the Scottish Home Rule Association, with more nominal than actual support from MPs, the Convention first met in Glasgow in November 1924. It drafted a Bill presented in the Commons in 1926 which provided for the end of Scottish representation at Westminster and 'Dominion' status for Scotland within the Empire.

p.11 *Harry Lauderism* MacDiarmid detested popular acclaim for Harry Lauder (1870–1950, knighted in 1919) who represented on the music hall stage a stereotype of the sentimental kilted Scot.

p.16 *New Economics* Social Credit.

p.19 *Irish leader, John Wheatley* Wheatley (1869–1930) was indeed born in Co. Waterford, Ireland. His family migrated to Lanarkshire when he was 9 and his father became a coalminer. Wheatley himself went down the pit at the age of 11, but attended evening classes and eventually became a successful businessman. He joined the ILP in 1908, and was soon an influential local councillor. He did more than anyone to woo the West of Scotland Catholic vote over to the Labour Party, a key factor in the electoral successes of the 1920s. He held Glasgow Shettleston as MP from 1922 till his death. After his distinguished service as Minister responsible for housing in the first Labour Government of 1923–4, he moved to the Left.

'The Truth About Scotland'

p.28 *Scottish National Convention* See above.

'The Poetry of Robert Graves'

p.29 *Hindemith the composer* A remarkably early reference to the work of Paul Hindemith (1895–1963), the important Modernist German composer.

THE PICTISH REVIEW (1927–8)

'The National Idea and the Company It Keeps'

p.46 *Mrs Kennedy-Fraser* Marjorie Kennedy (1857–1930) was a well-trained musician whose husband, A.J. Fraser, soon left her a widow. She became interested in folksong, and visited the Outer Hebrides in 1905. Her collecting and (genteel) setting of folksongs in Gaelic led people to compare her to Cecil Sharp of the English Folksong Revival.

'Backward *Forward*'

p.49 *James Maxton MP* MP for Glasgow Bridgeton from 1922, Maxton was a member of the Independent Labour Party which was affiliated to the Labour Party, from which he led it out in 1932. Only four ILP members, all representing Glasgow constituencies, were successful in the 1935 General Election. Maxton, a much loved, chain-smoking man and a witty orator, held Bridgeton until his death in 1945.

'Clyde Rebels' After Labour swept to dominance in Glasgow, and several areas adjacent, in the 1922 General Election, some truculent left-wingers among the new Scots MPs became known as habitual 'rebels' in the House of Commons. The press saw Maxton as their leader.

p.50 *John S. Clarke* (1885–1959) – an Englishman who served as a Labour member of Glasgow Corporation for thirty years (1926–56), Clarke was briefly MP for Glasgow Maryhill (1929–31). He was a popular lecturer and journalist, a man of sprightly mind and many talents, who published poetry, took an interest in art – and practised as a circus-animal trainer and occasional public lion-tamer. He kept a couple of live snakes in his locker at the House of Commons, from time to time dropping them into colleagues' pockets.

THE SCOTS INDEPENDENT (1927–9)

from 'Neo-Gaelic Economics'

p.64 *Jix* Nickname of Sir William Joynson Hicks, Conservative Home Secretary, 1924–9, a devout Low Churchman who earned the ridicule of posterity by his persecution of D.H. Lawrence. Beside the police prosecution of *Lady Chatterley's Lover*, the original ms of Lawrence's poems, *Pansies*, was confiscated, and his exhibition of paintings in London was censored.

'Four Candidates'

p.68 *R.B. Cunninghame Graham* 'Don Roberto' (1856–1936) is described by DNB as 'traveller, poet, horseman, scholar, Scottish nationalist, laird and socialist.' This leaves out his gifts as a prose writer. He spent much time in South America, where a town in Argentina was named after him. From 1886, he sat briefly as Liberal MP for North Lanarkshire. When the National Party of Scotland was founded in 1928, he was elected its first President. With his picturesque appearance and multifarious talents, he was one of MacDiarmid's cardinal heroes. He lost the 1928 Glasgow University Rectorial Elections to the Prime Minister Stanley Baldwin by only 66 votes, leaving Liberal and Labour opponents behind him.

'Nationalism and Socialism'

p.70 *John S. Clarke* See above.
p.73 *Joe Corrie* (1894–1978), a miner who wrote plays and became a full-time writer in 1923. His very popular plays about working class life, with their humour and sentiment, were staple fare for the Community Drama movement, which MacDiarmid despised.

'Scottish Nationalism versus Socialism'

p.75 *supersession of Westminster as our Imperial Parliament* This is strange, ignorant nonsense. Though talk of an Imperial Parliament had gone on for decades, there had never been any real hope of getting one, and if there had been, there was no plausible alternative to Westminster as a location. Any system allotting seats proportionately to population would have left England comfortably in the ascendancy.
this Welsh MP MacDonald was MP for Aberavon in South Wales from 1924 to 1929.

THE STEWARTRY OBSERVER (1927–30)

'Scotland as a Colony'

p.110 *Colonies* MacDiarmid, either through ignorance or wilfully, blurs the distinction between the self-governing Dominions – Canada, Australia, New Zealand, South Africa and the Irish Free State – which by 1928 were effectually free to act, if they so wished, as independent countries; colonies of recent white settlement – Rhodesia and Kenya – where immigrant whites wanted self-government at the expense of local native majorities; and the Crown Colonies in which Britons ruled non-white populations. In these last, calls for freedom had barely begun. MacDiarmid combines confusion over this matter with the very strange notion that non-English elements could dominate the Empire. Where from? With whose Navy?

p.111 *so-called Imperial Parliament* The periodic meetings of Empire, or 'Commonwealth', Prime Ministers could be so called, journalistically.
the youngest colonies If 'colonies of white settlement' are intended by this phrase, it must refer to Rhodesia and Kenya. These colonies did not have self-governing Dominion status and were not represented at conferences of Commonwealth leaders.

'Scottish People and "Scotch Comedians"'

p.113 *Lauder… Fyffe* For Lauder, see above. Will Fyffe (1885–1947) was another music-hall singer, but would move on to become a much-loved character actor in British and Hollywood films.
p.115 *John Davidson* (1857–1909) A prime hero for MacDiarmid – a major Scottish poet who committed suicide by drowning himself in the sea off Cornwall.

'Scottish Nationalism and the Churches'

p.116 *imminent consummation of the Union between the Established and UF Churches* Prior to 1843, the monolith of Scottish Presbyterianism had splintered and flaked off a number of small sects, but the 'Disruption' of that year created a powerful Free Church of Scotland. As this moved in the late nineteenth century towards fusion with the United Presbyterian Church (itself a compound of former sects), a fundamentalist minority broke to form the Free Presbyterian Church. In 1900 the Free and UP churches did come together, as the United Free Church, whereupon a diehard minority elected to carry on as the Free Church (still powerful in parts of the Highlands and Islands). In 1929, the long-pending reunion of the Established Church of Scotland with the UF did take place.

'The Farce of the Scottish Debate'

p.117 *Local Government Bill* The Local Government (Scotland) Act of 1929 abolished Parish Councils and similar bodies and vested control in larger units – county or burgh councils. The concentration of power which this entailed was not, at the time, popular.

'The Importance of Arbroath'

p.126 *National Memorial* That is, the War Memorial, inside Edinburgh Castle.
smokies Arbroath smokies are a subtle version of smoked haddock, delicious, and latterly rather expensive.

'Major Elliot and Scottish Nationalism'

p.127 *Major Walter Elliot* (1888–1958) Under-Secretary of State for

Scotland. Became Secretary of State, 1936–8. What would now be called a 'wet' Tory, popular with his opponents.

Act for the Reorganisation of Offices The 'devolutionary' shift, from the 1920s, of executive responsibility for Scottish affairs from Whitehall to Scotland was consummated in 1939 when St Andrew's House, a new building, brought all the Scottish Departments together in Edinburgh.

'Politics - A Meditation'

p.143 *Fletcher of Saltoun* Andrew Fletcher (1655–1716) was the most resolute and eloquent opponent in the Scottish Parliament of Union with England in the debates down to 1707.

VOX (1929–30)

'More About the Regional Scheme'

p.172 *Captain P.P. Eckersley... Regional Scheme* Peter Eckersley shared the conviction of Sir John Reith, the Scot who was Director General of the BBC, that listeners must be offered an alternative to what became known as the National Programme (2LO). He developed the 'Regional Scheme' from 1926 onwards. It involved building new transmitting stations. Rather predictably the first regional programmes were available in the Midlands and (March 1930) London. North followed in 1931, Scottish 'Regional' in 1932, West and Wales in 1933.

'Programmes and Problems'

p.188 *restriction placed on the broadcasting of news* Newspaper interests were not finally overridden until during the Second World War.

'Mrs Grundy at Savoy Hill'

p.190 *Mrs Grundy* Why the phrase 'What will Mrs Grundy say?' from a relatively obscure play – Thomas Morton's *Speed the Plough* (1798) – should have made the lady an archetype of primness and prudery, it is impossible to ascertain.

p.191 *Mencken* H. L. Mencken (1880–1956) – journalist, literary editor, and expert on the 'American', as distinct from 'British' language – was a witty, iconoclastic voice attacking prudery and pomposity.

THE SCOTS OBSERVER (1928–34)

'What Is the Book of the Year?'

p.201 *C.M. Grieve* was one of a number of well-known Scots to whom this question was put.

'Not Merely Philosophical Piety'

p.205 *Fascist Pantheon* The break seems clean. MacDiarmid now equates Fascism with 'oppression'. But see John Manson's letter in *Cencrastus* 57 (1997) for evidence of MacDiarmid's flirtation with Fascist (Hitlerite) ideas as late as 1932.

'Behind the Scaffolding'

p.212 *'Granite City'* The third volume of Grassic Gibbon's great trilogy was eventually published as *Grey Granite*.

THE SCOTTISH EDUCATIONAL JOURNAL (1928–34)

'Paul Valéry'

p.217 *H.A.L. Fisher* (1865–1940) Oxford historian, author of a very influential *History of Europe* (1935), and Liberal statesman. As President of the Board of Education under Lloyd George's premiership (1916–22), introduced the important reforming Education Act of 1918.

p.219 *Dr J.S. Haldane* (1860–1936) – the father of the distinguished scientist J.B.S. Haldane and the writer Naomi Mitchison – was a distinguished Scottish physiologist, educated in Edinburgh, though later a teacher at Oxford University. It must be ignorance which lets MacDiarmid accuse Fisher of an *English* partiality.

'An Irish Poet: Oliver St John Gogarty'

p.221 *'The Hidden Ireland'* MacDiarmid often refers to the influential book with this title by Daniel Corkery (Dublin, 1925) about the maintenance of Gaelic culture under the eighteenth-century Protestant Ascendancy.

'Literature and the Occult'

p.240 *Professor Denis Saurat* In 'Is the Scottish Renaissance a Reality?', *Scots Observer*, 4 February 1933, MacDiarmid states: 'The phrase "Scottish Renaissance Group" was applied first of all by Professor Denis Saurat in an article he wrote in a French review, to the group associated with me in "Northern Numbers" and "The Scottish Chapbook".' Saurat's writings were a frequent reference point for MacDiarmid's literary journalism in the 1920s. It is salutory to be reminded by this review that Saurat's primary interests were in English and French literature. Born in 1890, he taught briefly in Glasgow (1918–19), then for several years at the University of Bordeaux, before coming to London to direct the Institut Français. From 1933, he was Professor of French Language and Literature at London University.

'Scottish Music'

p.242 *Orpheus Choir* Hugh Roberton (no 's', 1874–1952) founded this choir in 1906. Until he disbanded it just before he died, it was a potent force in Scottish musical life and acquired world-wide fame. Though he accepted a knighthood in 1931, Roberton was a pacifist and socialist, not an Establishment ninny.

p.244 *Sorabji… Opus Clavicembalisticum* Kaikhosru Sorabji (1892–1988) had come to MacDiarmid's attention when he was music critic of the *New Age*. English-born son of a Parsee father, he had his own eccentric version of compositional modernism. The *Opus Clavicembalisticum*, dedicated to C.M. Grieve, and first performed in Glasgow in December 1930 was, at nearly three hours, the longest work ever written for piano.

'Whither Scotland?'

p.259 *Mr Grieve's 'Clann Albain'* 'Children of Scotland', a secret society first discussed between MacDiarmid and Compton Mackenzie after the NPS had done very badly in the 1929 General Election. MacDiarmid embarrassed Mackenzie by telling the *Daily Record* in May 1930 that Clann Albain had been in existence for two years, that it was a Scottish equivalent of Sinn Fein, and that it was militaristic and thus resembled the Fascist movement. There seems to be no evidence that the Clann ever had corporeal substance.

p.262 *the continuance of white supremacy* We are afraid that there is no way to decode this, set though it is in a badly-written passage, except as implying approval for colonial rule in the tropical world, and connivance in racism.

PEN: 'Poets, Playwrights, Editors, Essayists and Novelists' – an international organisation founded by Mrs Dawson Scott in 1921. MacDiarmid helped set up the Scottish Branch in 1928.

p.264 *Patrick Geddes* Sir Patrick (1854–1932) was a pioneering urban ecologist whose ideas had international influence.

p.271 *Sir Harry Lauder* See above.

p.282 *the regimentation of Young Italy* As late as September 1931, MacDiarmid is still not automatically hostile to Fascism.

'Scotland and the World of Today'

p.293 *Tooley Street Taylors* Three tailors of Tooley Street, Southwark, London, were said to have addressed a petition of grievances to the House of Commons beginning, 'We, the people of England…' Hence the phrase applies to any little clique claiming to represent a nation.

p.297 *Dr Lauchlan Maclean Watt* Minister of Glasgow Cathedral, 1923–34, and Moderator of the Church of Scotland in 1933, also a prolific littérateur with a special interest in poetry.

p.299 *Roy Campbell* No volume on Burns by the brilliant young South African poet did in fact appear from Faber and Faber.

'The Course of Scottish Poetry'

p.330 *another Scot, Hermann Melville* MacDiarmid habitually adds an extra 'n' to Melville's given name. His calling the great novelist (1819–91) a 'Scot' is an example of his tendency, noted several times in Volume I, to privilege Scots heredity over nurture furth of Scotland. Melville's Scottish ancestry can indeed be traced back to the 13th century, but his family had lived in North America for generations, while his mother's people, initially Dutch, had been in the area which became New York State since the seventeenth century. By MacDiarmidian standards, Robert Bruce and Edmund Burke, of originally Norman stock, would have been Norsemen.

'Fish in Scottish Poetry'

p.346 *Melville, an American writer of Scottish descent* Precisely.

'English in the Melting Pot'

p.350 *The verse of Mr MacDiarmid's I had in mind* Far from commencing a 'very simple and straightforward description of one of the Shetland Islands', the lines quoted here are found (*Complete Poems, Vol. I*, Carcanet, pp.416–19) in the middle of an elaborate poem *Vestigia Nulla Retrorsum: In Memoriam Rainer Maria Rilke 1875–1926*, from *Stony Limits* (1934).

'Scotland and Europe'

p.370 *Poe* The American writer Edgar Allan Poe (1809–49) was of 'Scotch-Irish' descent, from people originally from Scotland who had settled in Ulster. Orphaned in 1811, he was brought up by a Scottish merchant, John Allan, sent to a dame school kept by an old Scotswoman, and when Allan took his family to Britain, 1815–20, briefly schooled in Irvine, Ayrshire.

p.371 *Melville, an American Scot* See above. This is *not* so precise.

PURPOSE (1930)

'Allen Upward and the Facilitation of Genius'

p.373 *Allen Upward* (1863–1926) had a varied career, including spells as a barrister in Ireland, England and Wales, volunteer soldier for the Greeks against the Turks, British Resident in Northern Nigeria and Headmaster of Inverness College.

THE MODERN SCOT (1931–2)

'Domhnull Mac-na-Ceardaich'

p.384 *Dear Brutus* A play by J.M. Barrie, first performed in 1917.

THE FREE MAN (1932–4)

'C.M. Grieve Speaks Out'

p.391 *Coueism* Emile Coué (1857–1926) was a Frenchman who developed a form of psychotherapy by auto-suggestion. His key phrase was: 'Every day, and in every way, I am getting better and better.' He suggested this should be said between 15 and 20 times daily.

p.392 *Rosslyn Mitchell* Labour politician. *Hugh Roberton*: Founder of the Orpheus Choir – see above.

'Mr Eyre Todd and Scots Poetry'

p395 *rigwoodie… crummock* The Scottish National Dictionary glosses 'rigwoodie' (or '-widdie' or '-wudy') as 'Of a person, esp. an old hag: wizened and gnarled, tough and rugged-looking, ill-shaped.' SND believes that Burns meant by 'crummock' a stick with a crooked head.

'Lenin and Us'

p.399 *Dundee riots and… Kilbirnie sentences* These obscure incidents have made no impact on history books.

'Mr Pooh Bah'

p.399 *Mr Cleghorn Thomson* David Cleghorn Thomson, Regional Director of the BBC in Scotland since 1928.

'The Future of Scotland'

p.404 *the Stirling Castle incident* Nationalists tried to run up a Scottish flag over the castle.

p405 *Sir Hugh Roberton*: See above. *Mr Rosslyn Mitchell*: Ditto.

'Scotland, Hitler and Wyndham Lewis'

p.406 *Gasworth* Really, 'John Gawsworth' (1912–70), the pseudonym of Terence Ian Fytton Armstrong, poet, editor and bibliographer. MacDiarmid worked with him, and wrote an essay in honour of his 50th birthday, privately printed (40 copies) in London in 1962; reprinted in *Albyn* (Carcanet, 1996).

'Gasset versus Gas'

p.408 *the Lausanne farce* The Germans in 1932 were still expected to pay reparations to their victorious opponents in the 1914–18 war. In the Great Depression, American finance to support these payments ceased to be forthcoming. The Allies and Germany conferred at Lausanne, in Switzerland, in 1932 and agreed a convention whereby one last payment would be made. But this was never ratified, and payments simply ceased.

p.410 *Lossiemouth* Prime Minister MacDonald's birthplace; he was a 'Lossie Loon'.

p.411 *Fouché* Joseph Fouché (1763–1829) was the revolutionary Chief of Police who helped Napoleon to power in France in 1799 and stayed in post, dealing with the regime's opponents, till 1815.

'D.H. Lawrence and the Essential Fact'

p.417 *certain things (I can think right off of twenty)* This opaque passage seems to hint at the continuing existence of 'Clann Albain' (see note to p.259 above).

'On Standing One's Ground'

p.418 *Hugh Walpole* A very popular English novelist.

'Dunbar and Burns'

p.428 *Burns… gave no new impetus to Scots poetry* Here, as elsewhere, MacDiarmid neglects to consider the 'impetus' which Burns, through Walter Scott, gave to the rendering of Scots in prose fiction.

p.429 *Harry Lauderism* See note to p.11 above.

'Professor Berriedale Keith and Imperial Constitution'

p.434 *Westminster Statutes* Making *de jure* what *de facto* had already happened, the 1931 Statute of Westminster clarified that Dominions were in effect independent, though owing allegiance to the Crown, and associated freely in what was now officially called the 'Commonwealth of Nations'.

'Goodbye to the National Party'

p.447 *John MacCormick* (1904–61) – would be chairman of the National Party from its founding until 1942. Moderate in his aims and 'ecumenical' in his approach to other parties.

'The MacCrimmon Memorials'

p.459 *Sorabji* See note to p.244 above.

'Edinburgh University and Scots Literature'

p.464 *Strindberg* An uncharacteristic howler. Strindberg, of course, wrote in Swedish.

THE NEW ENGLISH WEEKLY (1933–4)

'"AE" and Poetry'

p.490 *The Road to Xanadu* J.L. Lowes's immensely influential study of that name, published in 1927, then in a revised version in 1930, investigated the sources and composition of Coleridge's 'Ancient Mariner' and 'Kubla Khan'.

p.492 *Francis Thompson* (1859–1907), poet, author of 'The Hound of Heaven', quoted in MacDiarmid's earlier *NEW* piece on 'Problems of Poetry Today'.

'Poets, Consider!'

p.497 *Francis Adams* (1862–93) Anti-imperialist poet, still neglected.

'The Poetry of Ruth Pitter'

p.504 *Don Marquis' Archy and Mehitabel* American: Archy the cockroach types the poems; his friend is Mehitabel the cat. Marquis (1878–1937) receives their news.

'Denis Saurat: Supernatural Rationalist'

p.507 *Eliot… 'freethinking Jews'* Eliot himself came to regret this remark, published in a set of lectures, *After Strange Gods* (1933), which he never reprinted, unlike his other prose books. Quoting it here is perhaps MacDiarmid's largest concession to the anti-Semitism which infested the Social Credit 'movement'.

p.508 *Sir James Frazer* (1854–1941) was an immensely influential Scottish anthropologist whose chief work, *The Golden Bough: A Study in Comparative Religion* had appeared in 12 volumes from 1890 to 1915. It is odd that MacDiarmid should thus dismiss a Glasgow-born and -educated fellow countryman.

THE BOOKMAN (1934)

'Scotland and the Arts'

p.532 *or* contrée *dancing, to give it its proper name* MacDiarmid's point is obscure to us. *Contrée* , in French, denotes 'region, province, country'. Does MacDiarmid mean that this dancing belongs to urban as well as, or rather than, rural Scotland?

p.533 *Harry Lauder* See above. *Harry Gordon*: (1893–1957) Aberdonian comedian, a popular radio star.

NEW SCOTLAND (1935–6)

'Scotland, France & Working-class Interests'

p.538 *The Week* a gadfly periodical edited by Claud Cockburn, then a Communist.

Third International That is, the Communist International, controlled from Moscow.

p.539 *Annie S. Swan* (1859–1943) – a prolific light romantic novelist.

'Songs of the Egregious'

p.540 *Marjorie Kennedy Fraser* See note to p.46 above.

'Communism and Nationalism'

p.543 *Mr P. Kerrigan* Peter Kerrigan was one of the CPGB's most significant organisers in the 1930s, often remembered in connection with the Hunger Marches and the Spanish Civil War.

p.544 *Red Scotland* Not in fact published; rejected by the intended publishers, Routledge, on the grounds that more than half of it consisted of quotations, that MacDiarmid libelled the Royal Family, and that it wouldn't sell.

Russian republics Should be 'Soviet republics' – a curious slip.

p.546 *Dimitrov* Bulgarian Communist, much admired elsewhere in Europe for his bold and successful defiance of the Nazi court where he was tried for alleged complicity in the 1933 Reichstag Fire.

'Constructing the Dynamic Spirit'

p.550 *Johnston*… Forward Tom Johnston (1881–1965), Labour MP for Stirling on-and-off between the wars, and eventually Secretary of State for Scotland in Churchill's wartime Coalition Government. He had founded *Forward* as Glasgow's Socialist weekly in 1906, and edited it for many years.

Index